NAYA

W9-AGI-724

COURAGE TO DREAM

DREAM

TALES OF HOPE IN THE HOLOCAUST

A GRAPHIC NOVEL BY

NEAL SHUSTERMAN

AND

ANDRÉS VERA MARTÍNEZ

graphix

AN IMPRINT OF
SCHOLASTIC

This book is dedicated to my whole *mishpuchah*: The Altmans, Brownsteins, Fischgrunds, Lakins and Laikens, the Rittermans, Sayres, Shustermans, and Stillmans — those still with us, and those who have gone. But above all, this book is dedicated to a larger family: the millions lost in the Holocaust and the millions who never had names because they were denied the chance to be born. May your memory, and the memory of your memory, never dim in the vastness of time.

— N.S.

I would like to dedicate this book to my uncle, Adam Martínez, who set me on this path of storytelling through comics. "Excelsior!"

— A.V.M.

Text copyright © 2023 by Neal Shusterman
Art copyright © 2023 by Andrés Vera Martínez

All rights reserved. Published by Graphix, an imprint of Scholastic Inc., *Publishers since 1920.*
SCHOLASTIC, GRAPHIX, and associated logos are trademarks and/or registered trademarks of Scholastic Inc.

The publisher does not have any control over and does not assume any responsibility for author or third-party websites or their content. No part of this publication may be reproduced, stored in a retrieval system, or transmitted in any form or by any means, electronic, mechanical, photocopying, recording, or otherwise, without written permission of the publisher. For information regarding permission, write to Scholastic Inc., Attention: Permissions Department, 557 Broadway, New York, NY 10012.

This book is a work of fiction. Names, characters, places, and incidents are either the product of the author's imagination or are used fictitiously, and any resemblance to actual persons, living or dead, business establishments, events, or locales is entirely coincidental.

Library of Congress Control Number 2022951724

ISBN 978-0-545-31347-6 (hardcover)
ISBN 978-0-545-31348-3 (paperback)

10 9 8 7 6 5 4 3 2 1   23 24 25 26 27

Printed in China   62

First edition, October 2023

Edited by Andrea Pinkney
Book design by Andrés Vera Martínez and Charles Kreloff
Creative Director: Phil Falco
Publisher: David Saylor

Photos ©: 54 top left: Volgi Archive/Alamy Stock Photo; 54 top right: Menahem Kahana/AFP via Getty Images; 54 bottom left: Image Asset Management/www.agefotostock.com; 54 bottom right: Sergio Pitamitz/www.agefotostock.com; 55 top: Luc Olivier/Photononstop/www.agefotostock.com; 55 center left: Yad Vashem; 55 center right: Yad Vashem; 55 bottom: Yad Vashem; 102 bottom left: NIOD - Collection 804 Schelvis; 102 bottom right: United States Holocaust Memorial Museum, courtesy of Misha Lev; 156 top left: Veneranda Biblioteca Ambrosiana; 156 top center: Eberhard Werner Happel; 156 top right: Free Library of Philadelphia/Bridgeman Images; 156 center left: Kharbine-Tapabor/Shutterstock; 156 center: The New York Public Library; 156 center right: Bridgeman Images; 156 bottom left: YIVO Institute for Jewish Research; 156 bottom center: AF archive/Alamy Stock Photo; 156 bottom right: YIVO Institute for Jewish Research; 157: Yad Vashem.

"For the dead and the living,
we must bear witness."
— Elie Weisel

This book is about impossible and wondrous things that never happened, set against a backdrop of impossible, unthinkable things that did.

. . . A mysterious window that opens on worlds far from the terrors of the Nazi regime . . .
. . . A hero forged from ash to save countless souls from the gas chambers . . .
. . . The power of folklore to resist the forces of evil . . .
. . . An ancient biblical relic powerful enough to guide thousands to freedom . . .
. . . And a bittersweet glimpse of a world that might have been . . .

The Holocaust is a dark stain on history that will never go away — *should* never go away. Instead, it needs a constant light shined upon it, from as many different angles as we can, so that maybe we can come to understand how humanity could go so terribly wrong, and perhaps gain the wisdom to make sure it never happens again.

These are stories that cast strange light from unexpected angles. They are both tragic and triumphant. Tragic because some of them are wistful, wishful thinking; dreams of miraculous escape when no escape was possible. And triumphant because each of these stories point to very real moments of human compassion and bravery in the face of despair.

Step into these stories with both eyes open, and a third eye turned inward . . .
. . . Because we each have the capacity to be the hero . . .
Or the villain.
Or the bystander who takes no action.
So, as you read each of these stories, ask yourself this:

"Who would I be if the impossible suddenly became real?"

Neal Shusterman

א

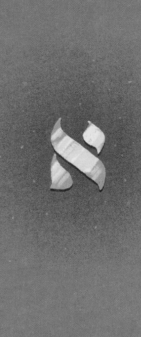

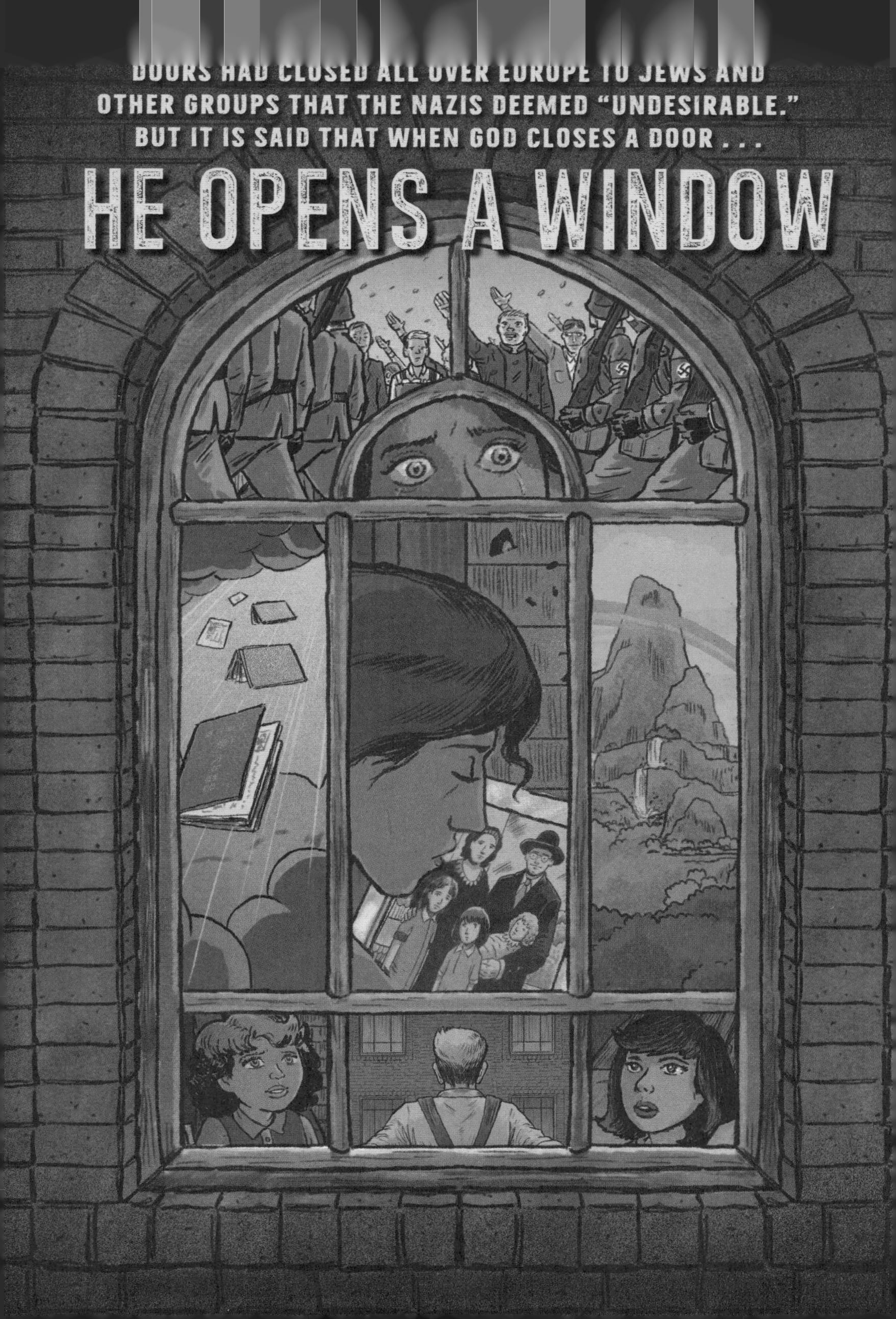
DOORS HAD CLOSED ALL OVER EUROPE TO JEWS AND OTHER GROUPS THAT THE NAZIS DEEMED "UNDESIRABLE." BUT IT IS SAID THAT WHEN GOD CLOSES A DOOR . . .
HE OPENS A WINDOW

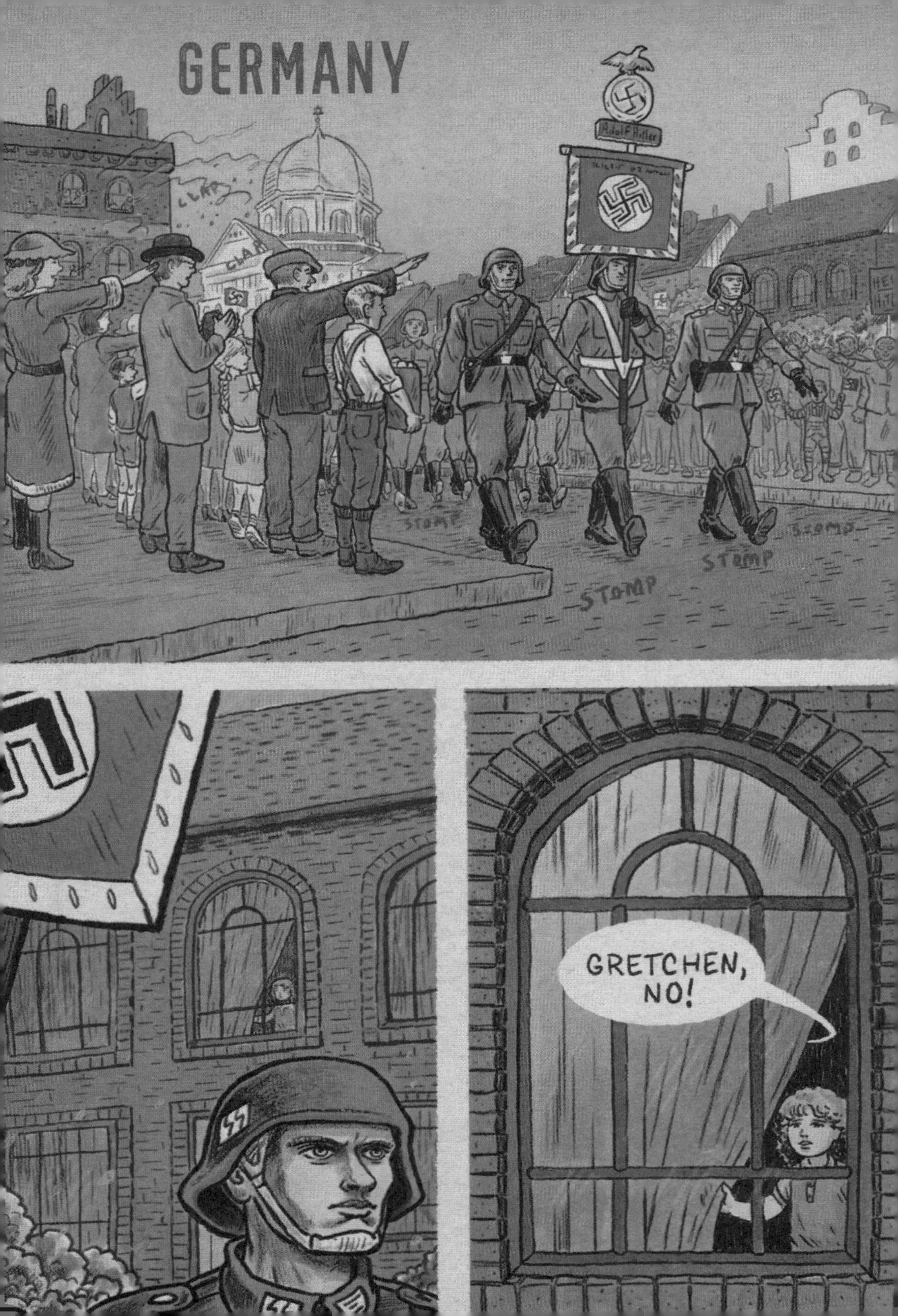
GERMANY
Adolf Hitler
STOMP
STOMP
STOMP
STOMP
GRETCHEN, NO!

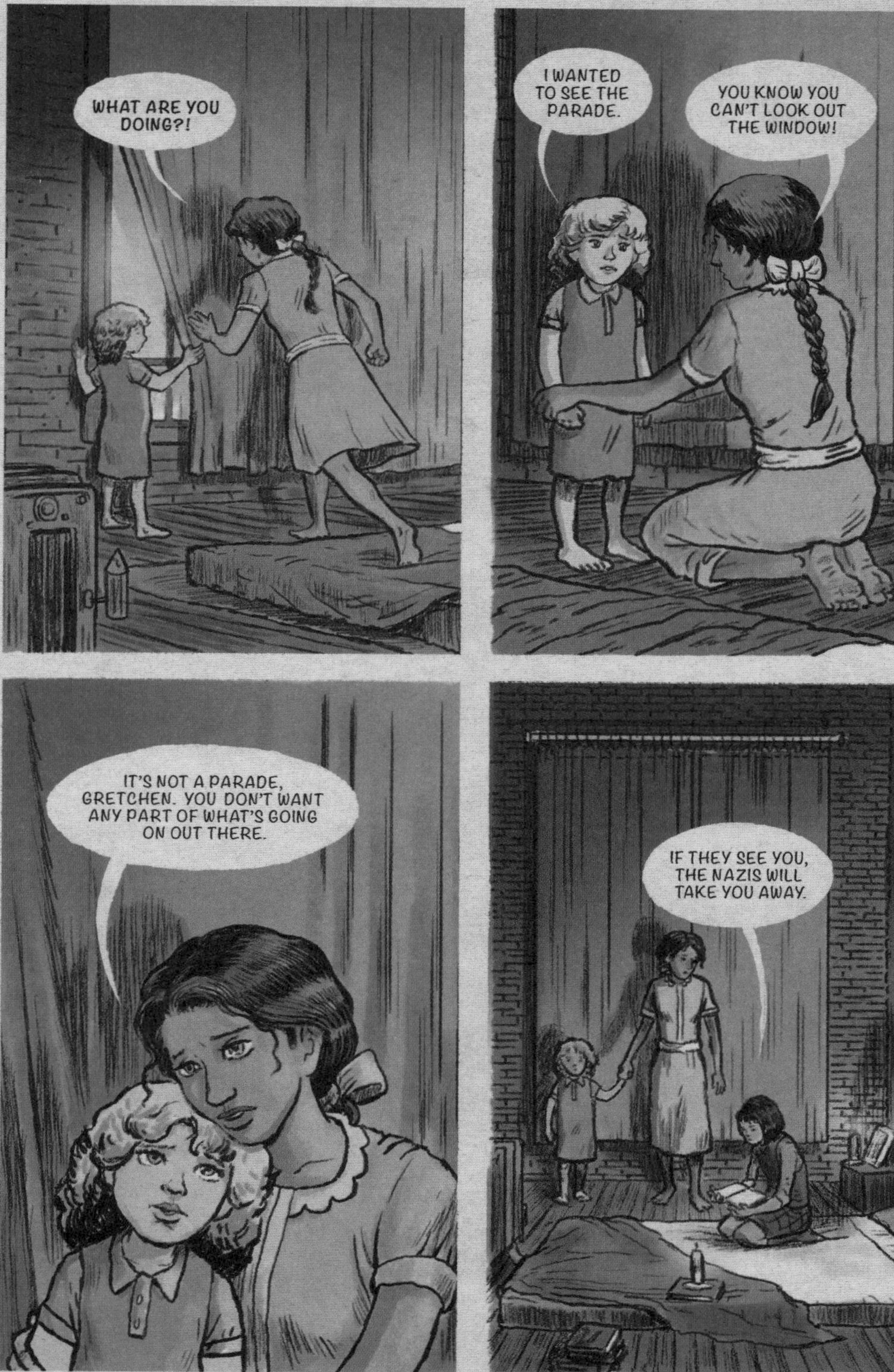
WHAT ARE YOU DOING?!
I WANTED TO SEE THE PARADE.
YOU KNOW YOU CAN'T LOOK OUT THE WINDOW!
IT'S NOT A PARADE, GRETCHEN. YOU DON'T WANT ANY PART OF WHAT'S GOING ON OUT THERE.
IF THEY SEE YOU, THE NAZIS WILL TAKE YOU AWAY.

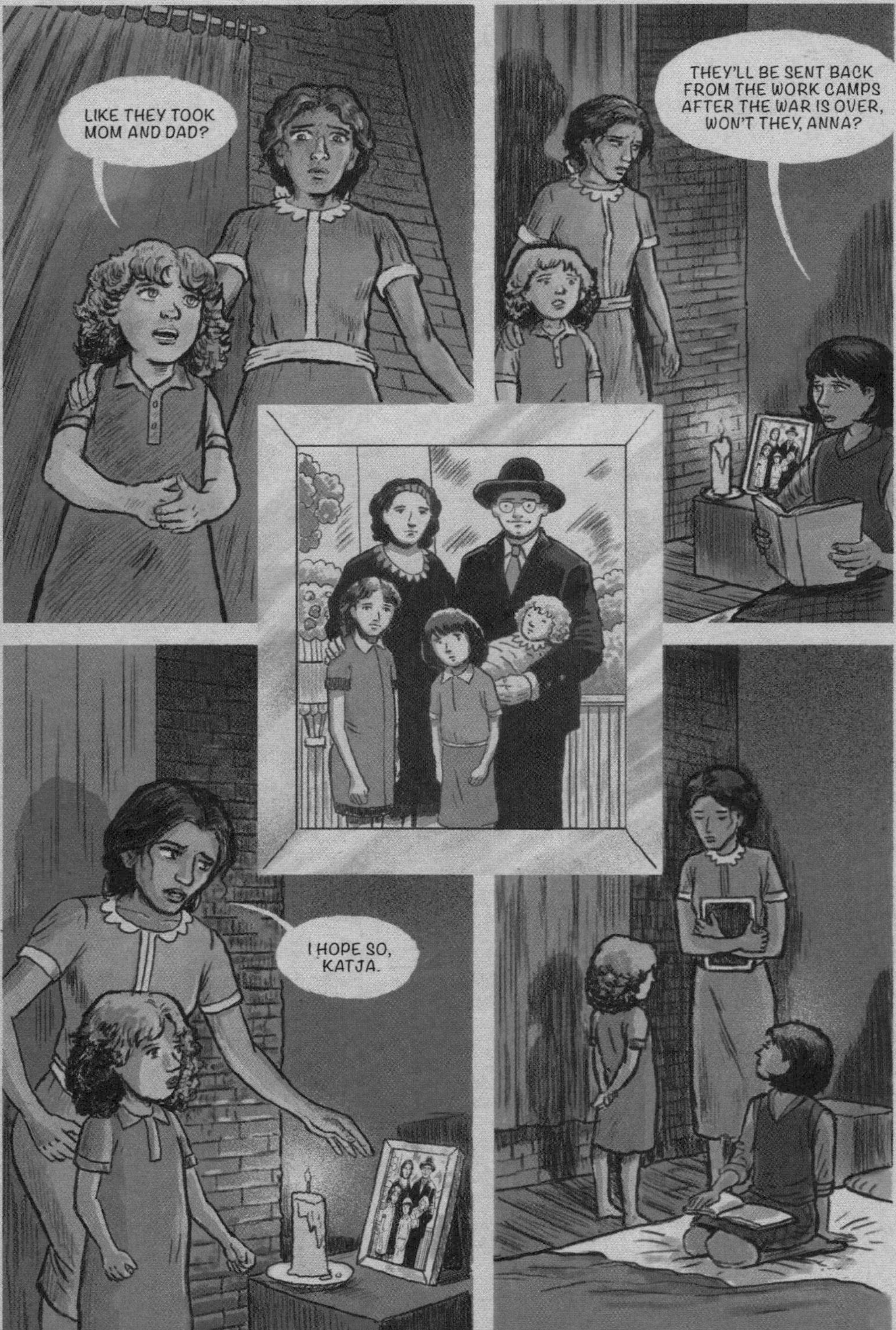
LIKE THEY TOOK MOM AND DAD?
THEY'LL BE SENT BACK FROM THE WORK CAMPS AFTER THE WAR IS OVER, WON'T THEY, ANNA?
I HOPE SO, KATJA.

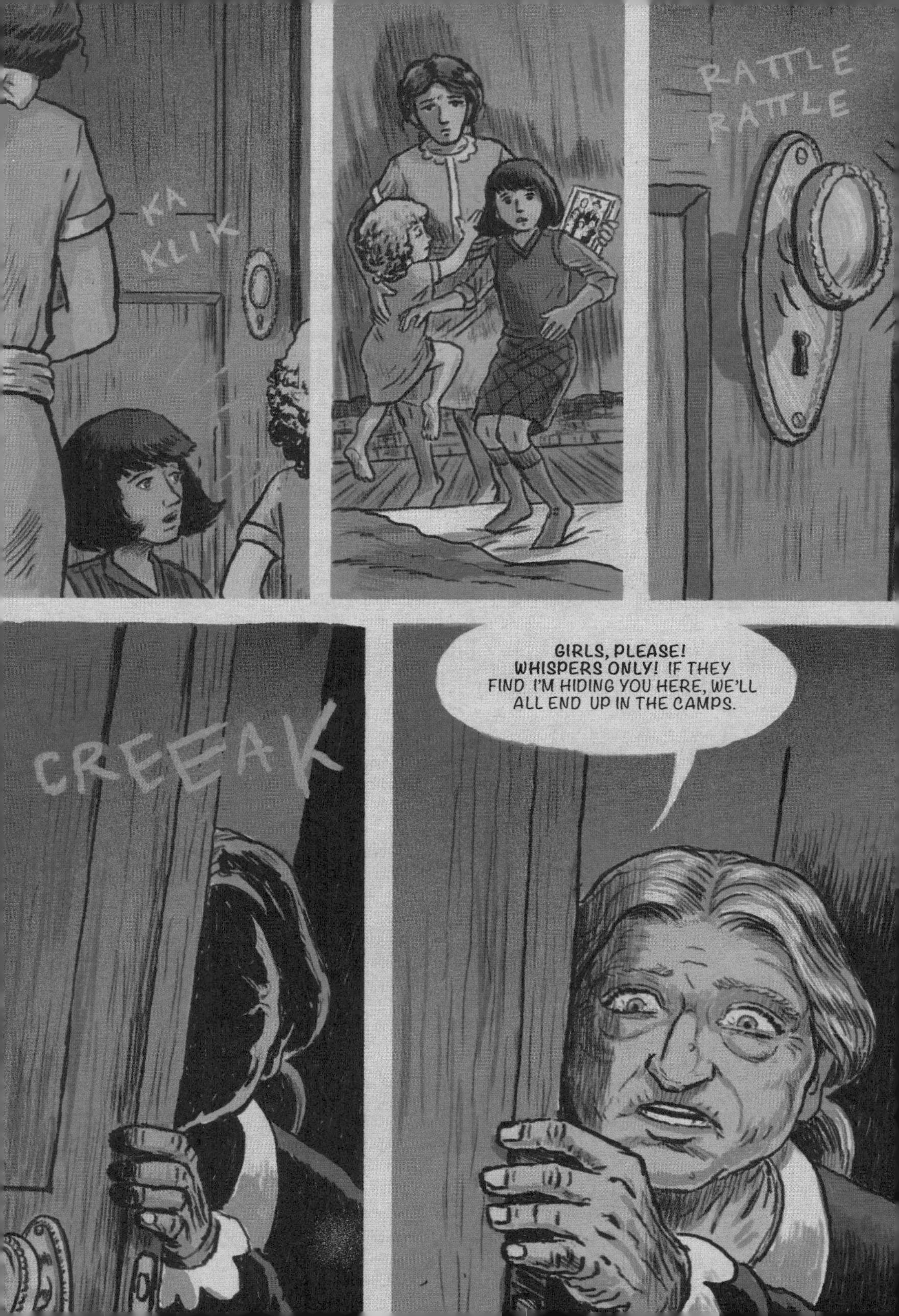
KA KLIK
RATTLE RATTLE
CREEAK
GIRLS, PLEASE! WHISPERS ONLY! IF THEY FIND I'M HIDING YOU HERE, WE'LL ALL END UP IN THE CAMPS.

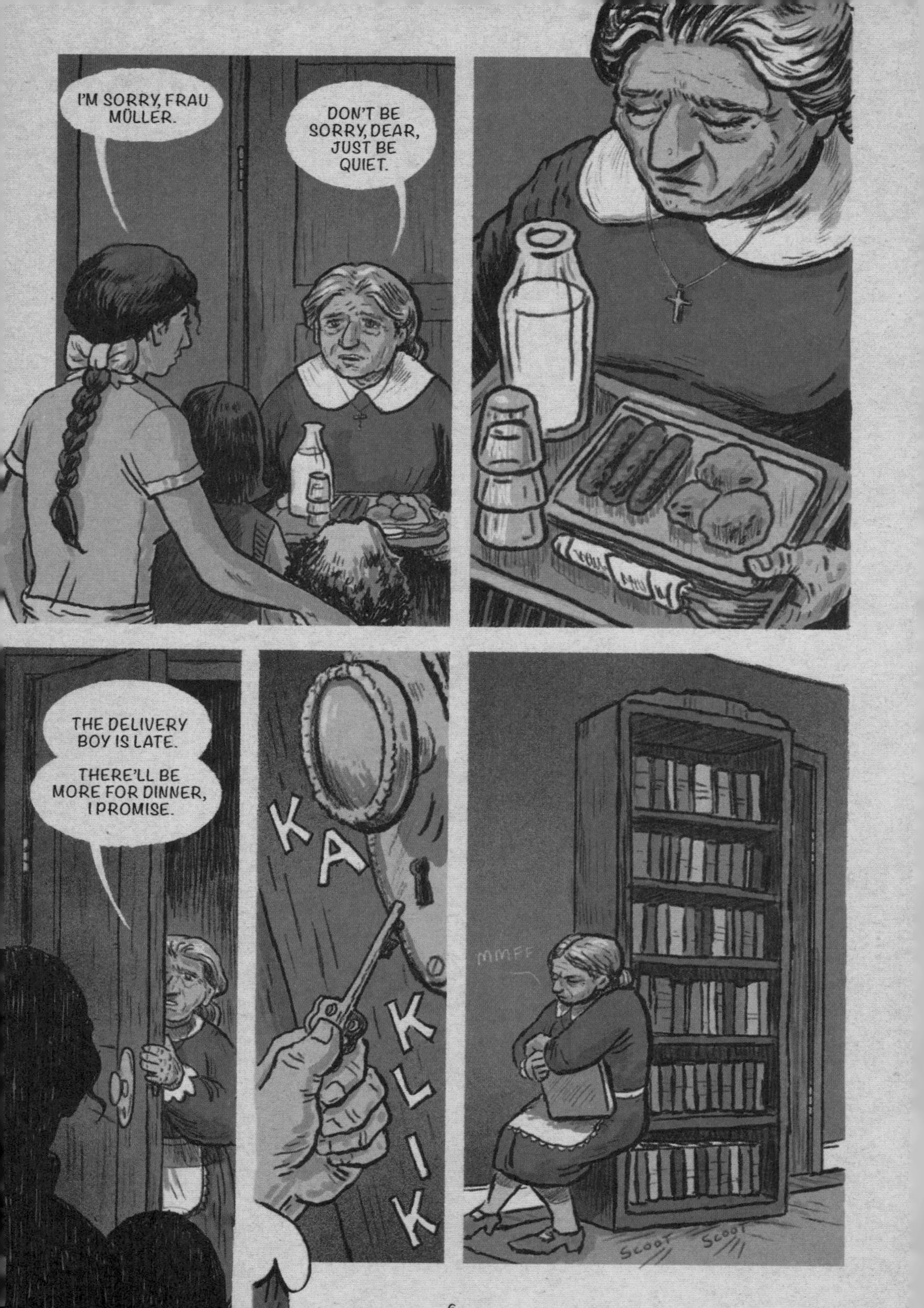
I'M SORRY, FRAU MÜLLER.
DON'T BE SORRY, DEAR, JUST BE QUIET.
THE DELIVERY BOY IS LATE.
THERE'LL BE MORE FOR DINNER, I PROMISE.
KA
KLIK
MMFF
SCOOT
SCOOT

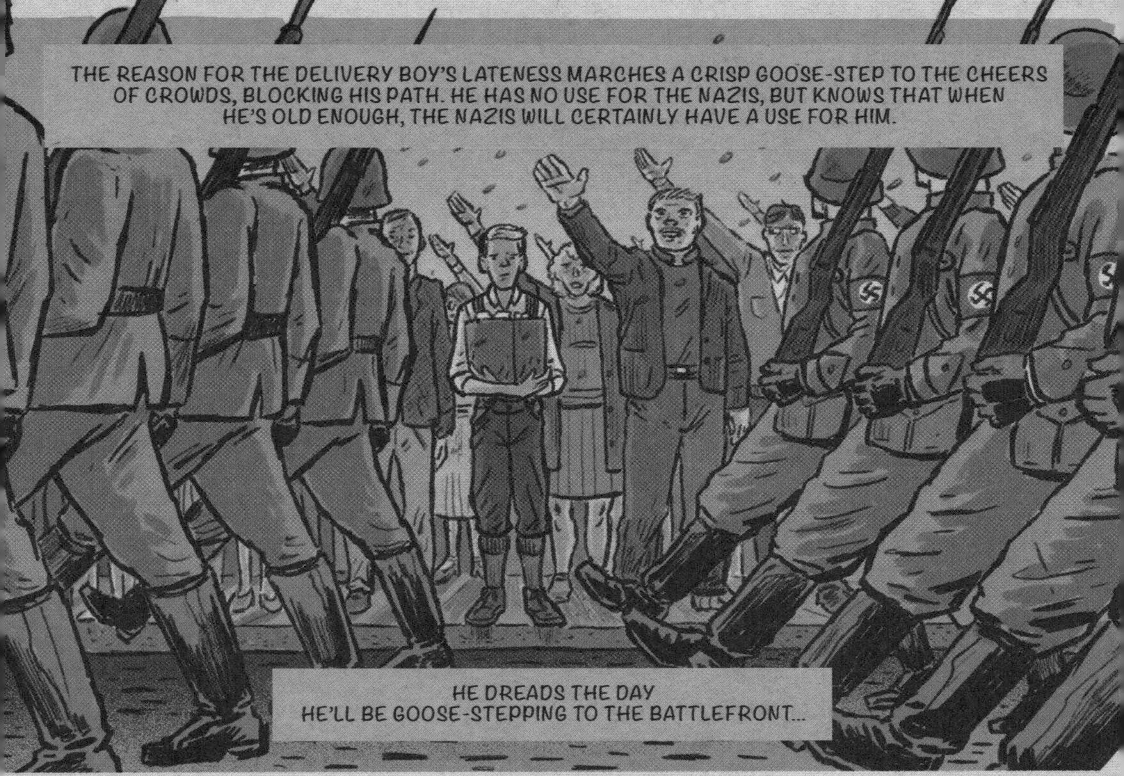
THE REASON FOR THE DELIVERY BOY'S LATENESS MARCHES A CRISP GOOSE-STEP TO THE CHEERS OF CROWDS, BLOCKING HIS PATH. HE HAS NO USE FOR THE NAZIS, BUT KNOWS THAT WHEN HE'S OLD ENOUGH, THE NAZIS WILL CERTAINLY HAVE A USE FOR HIM.
HE DREADS THE DAY HE'LL BE GOOSE-STEPPING TO THE BATTLEFRONT...

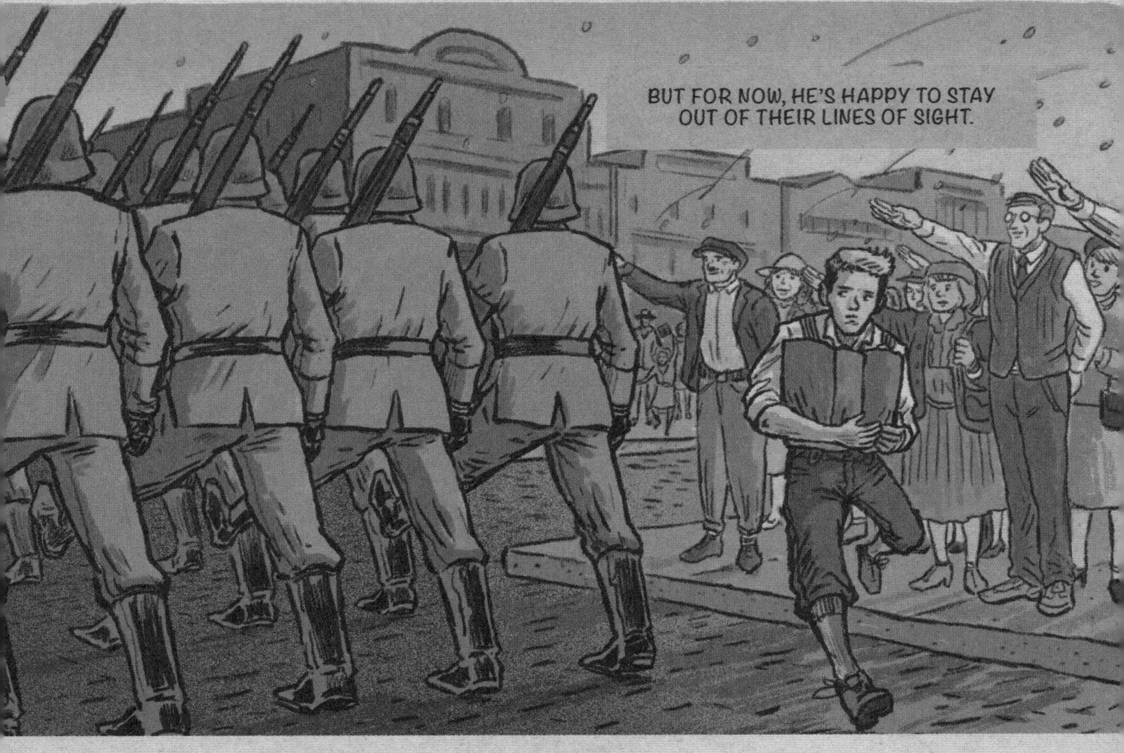
BUT FOR NOW, HE'S HAPPY TO STAY OUT OF THEIR LINES OF SIGHT.

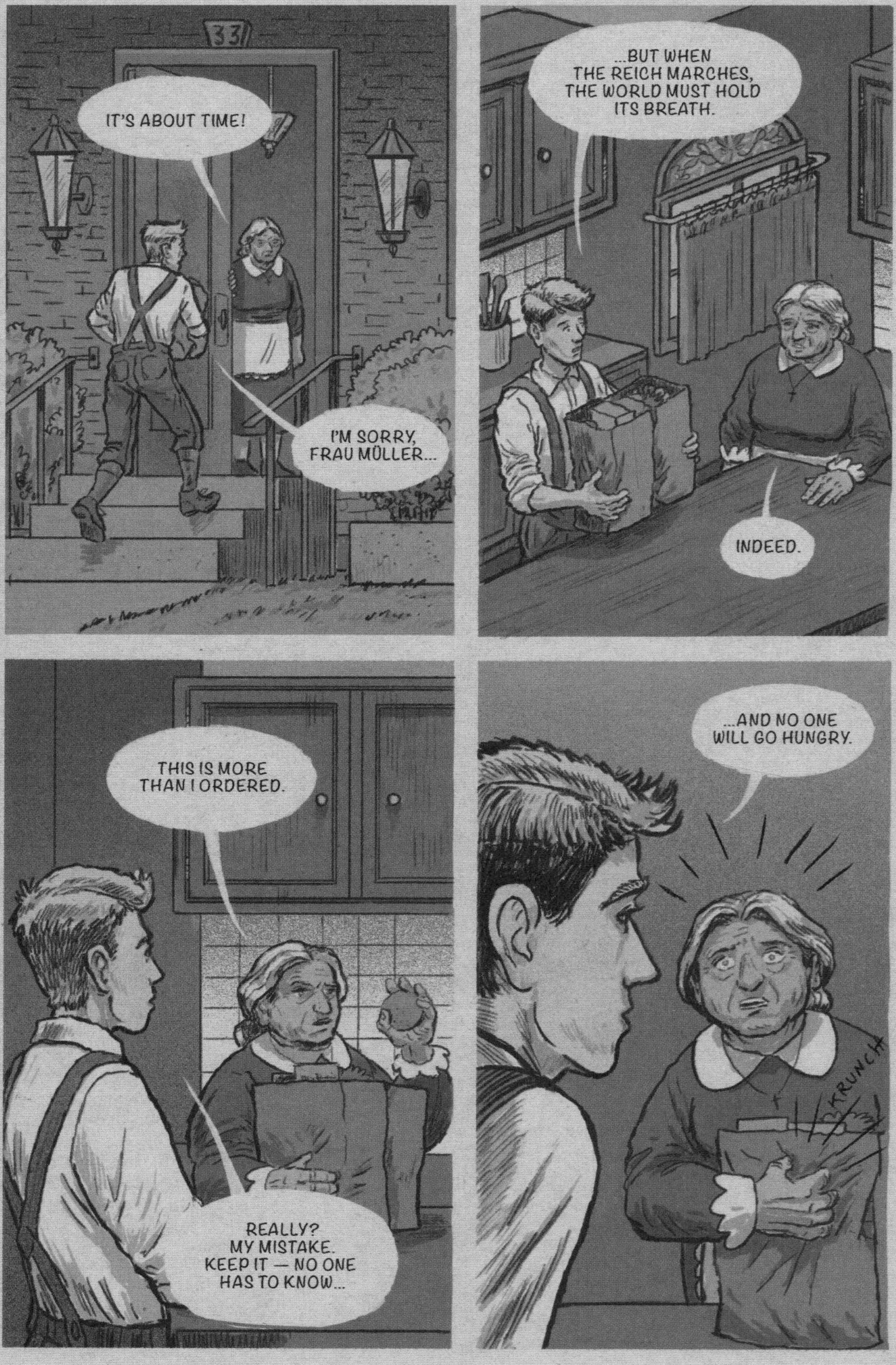
IT'S ABOUT TIME!
I'M SORRY, FRAU MÜLLER...
...BUT WHEN THE REICH MARCHES, THE WORLD MUST HOLD ITS BREATH.
INDEED.
THIS IS MORE THAN I ORDERED.
REALLY? MY MISTAKE. KEEP IT — NO ONE HAS TO KNOW...
...AND NO ONE WILL GO HUNGRY.
KRUNCH

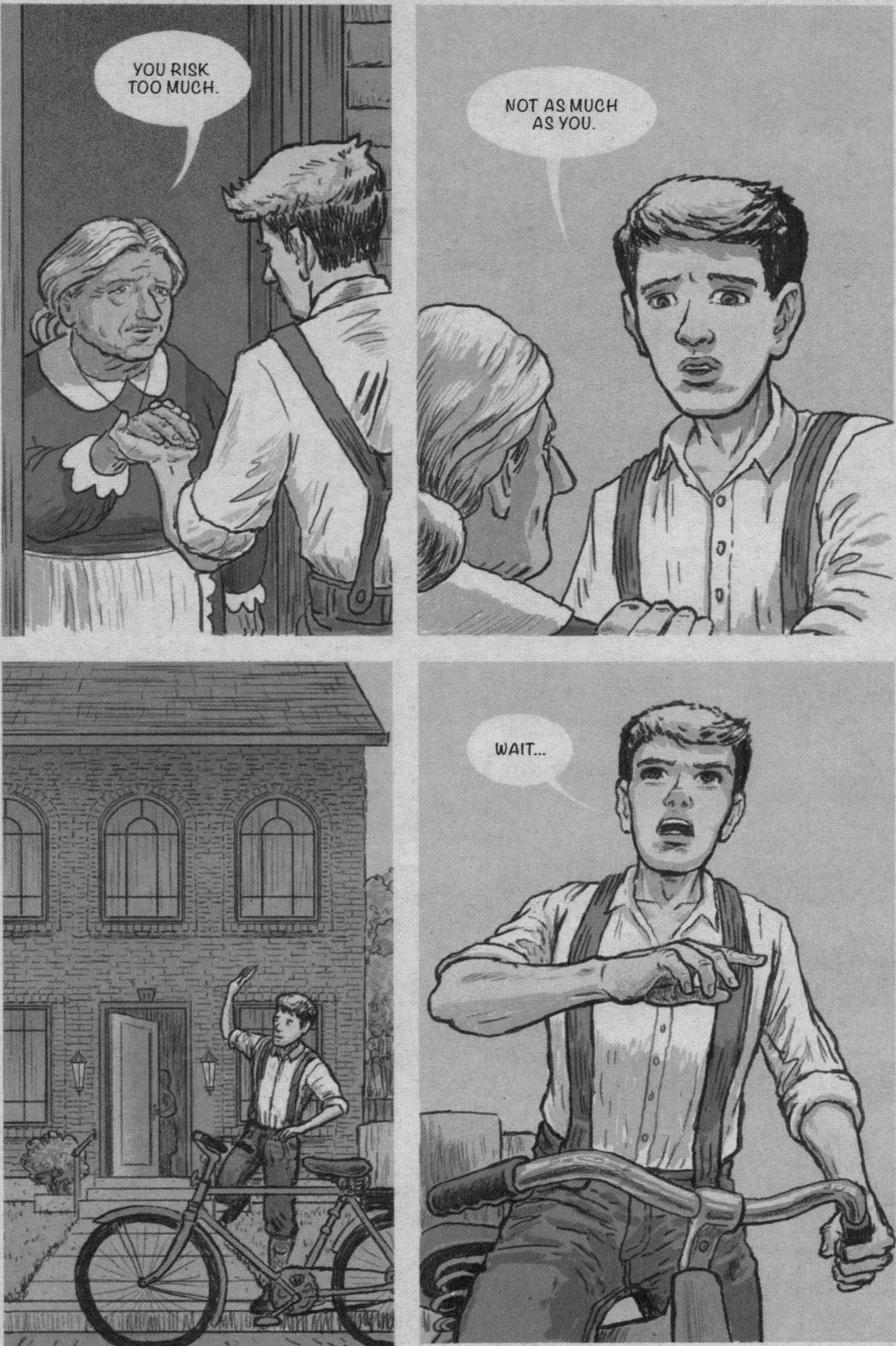
YOU RISK TOO MUCH.
NOT AS MUCH AS YOU.
WAIT...

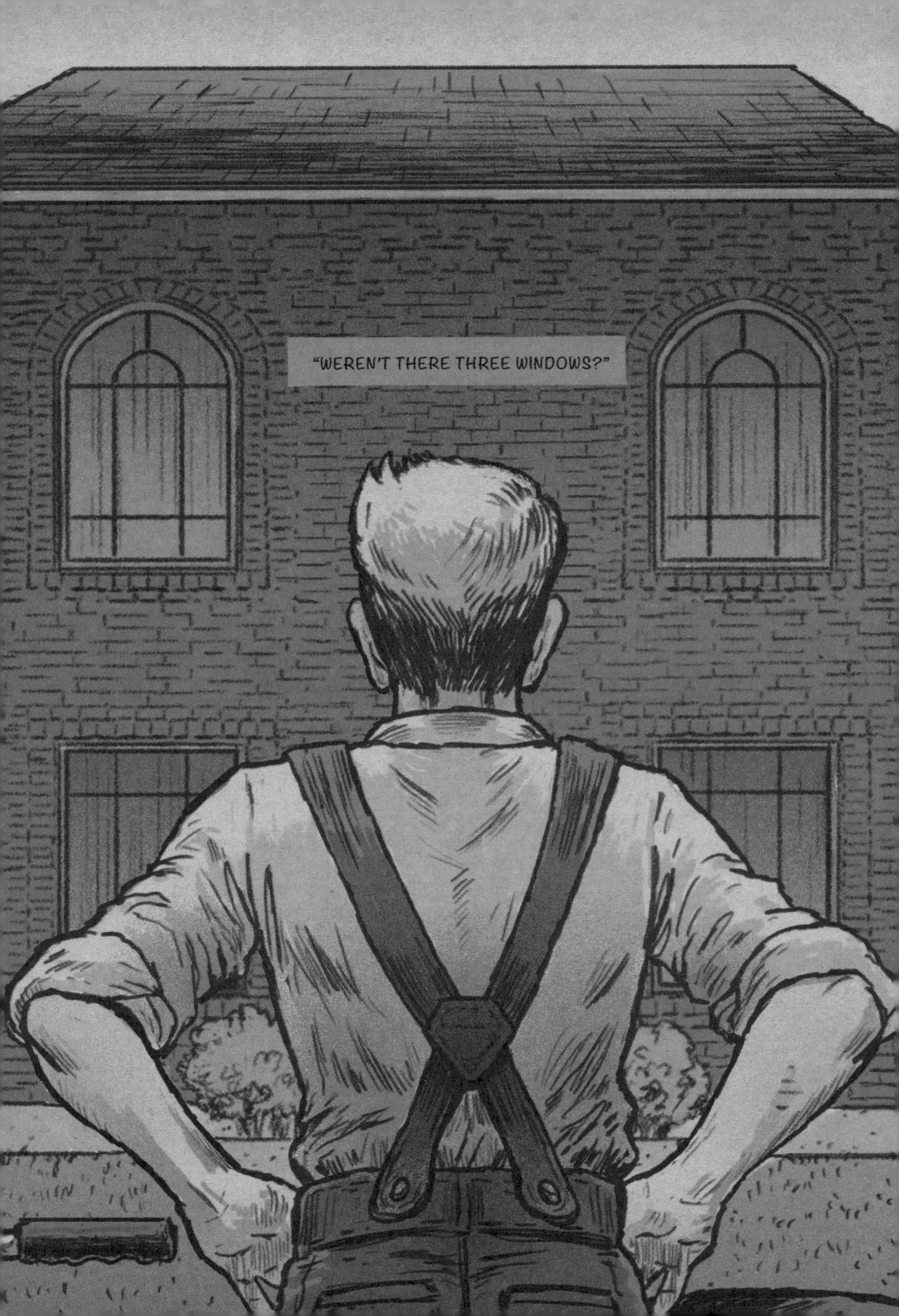
"WEREN'T THERE THREE WINDOWS?"

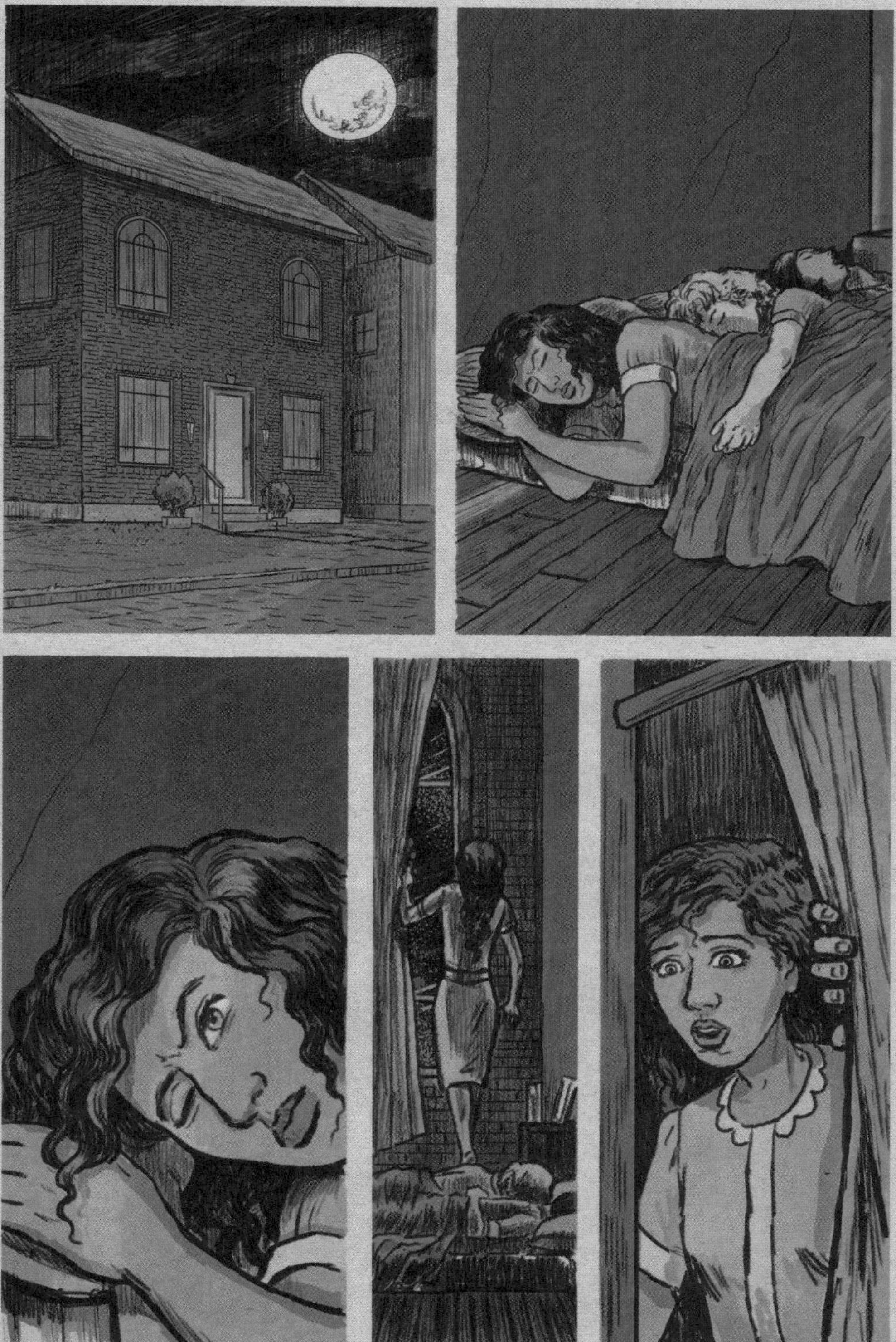

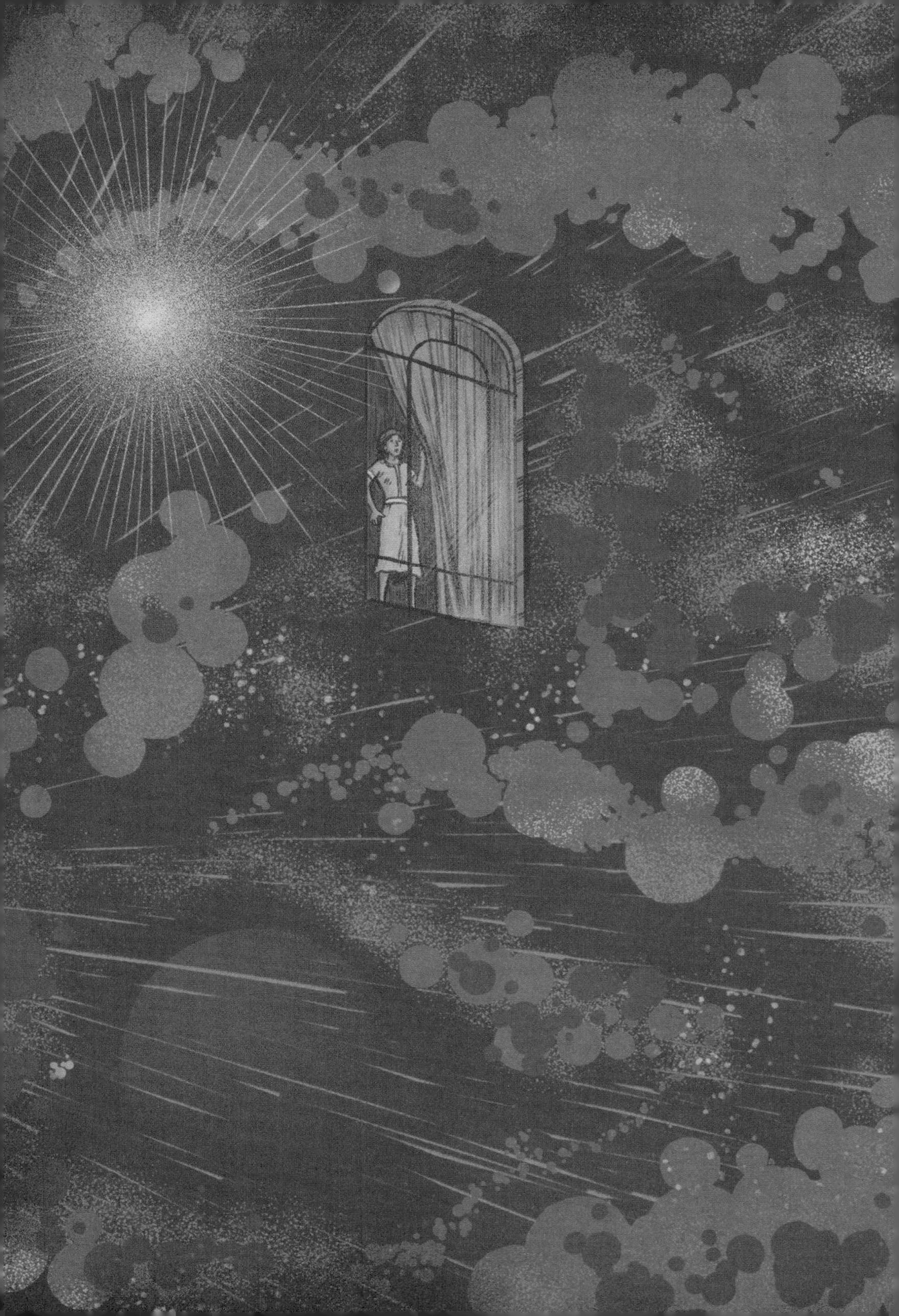

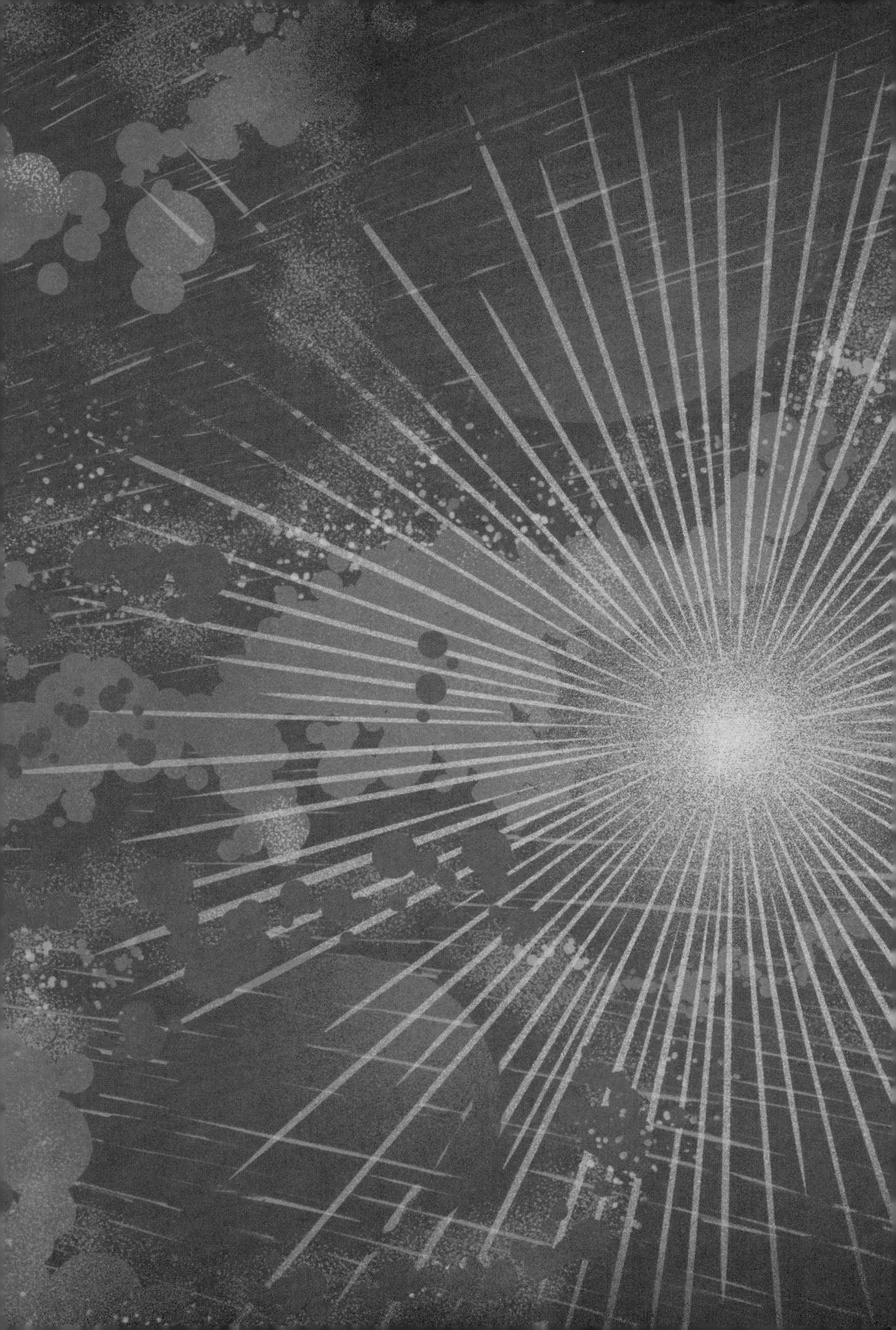

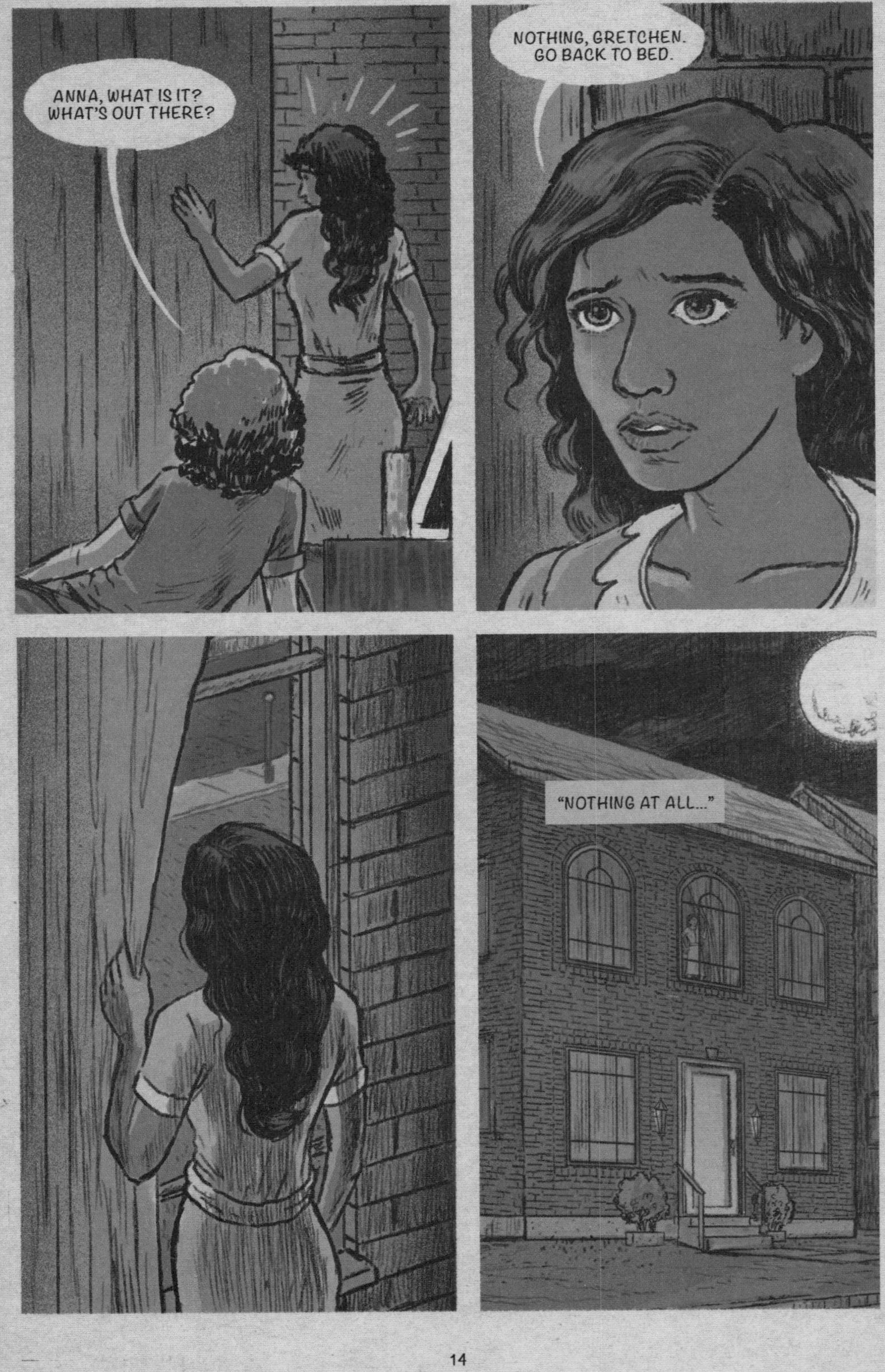
ANNA, WHAT IS IT? WHAT'S OUT THERE?
NOTHING, GRETCHEN. GO BACK TO BED.
"NOTHING AT ALL..."

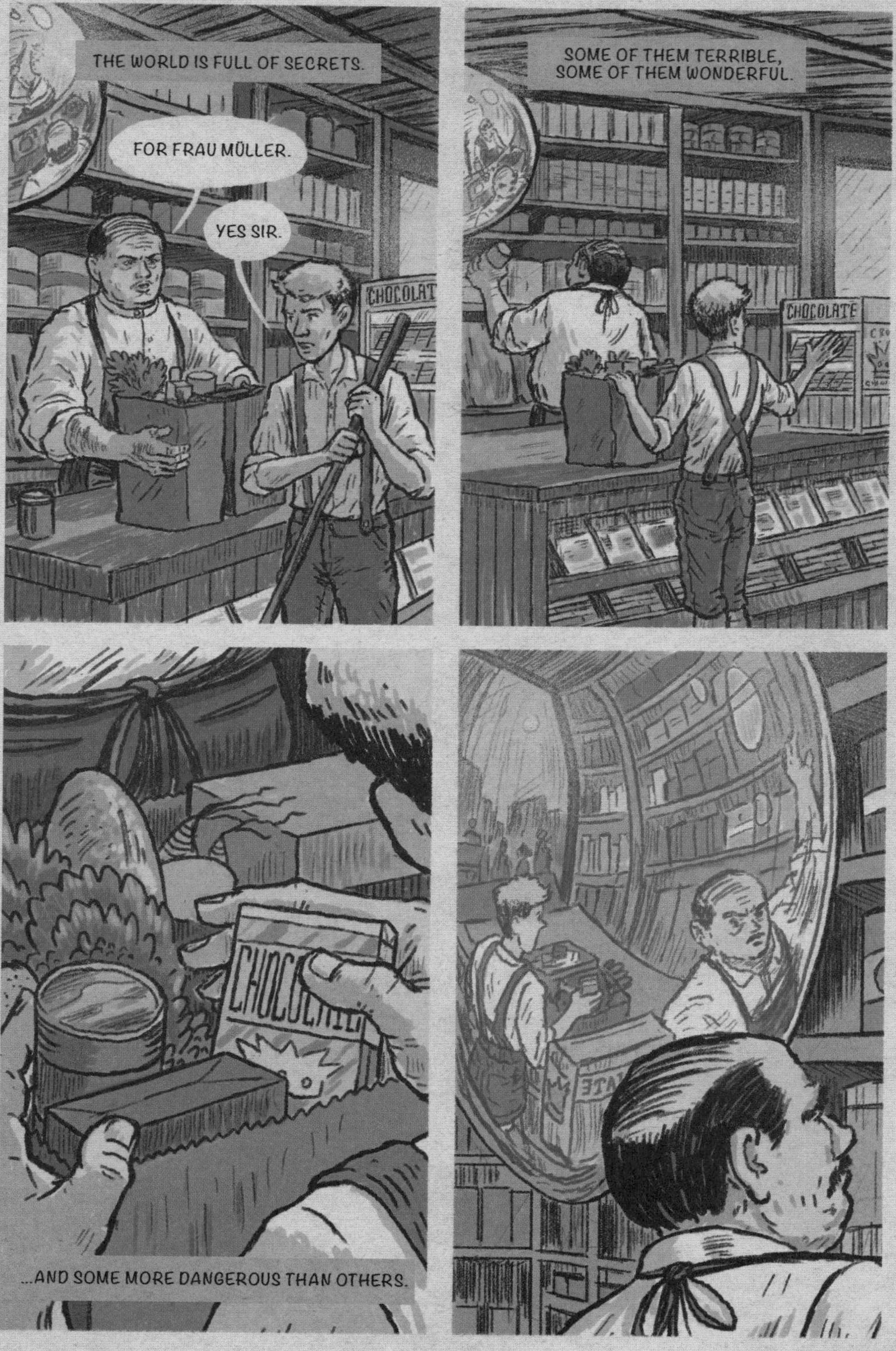
THE WORLD IS FULL OF SECRETS.
FOR FRAU MÜLLER.
YES SIR.
CHOCOLATE
SOME OF THEM TERRIBLE,
SOME OF THEM WONDERFUL.
CHOCOLATE
...AND SOME MORE DANGEROUS THAN OTHERS.

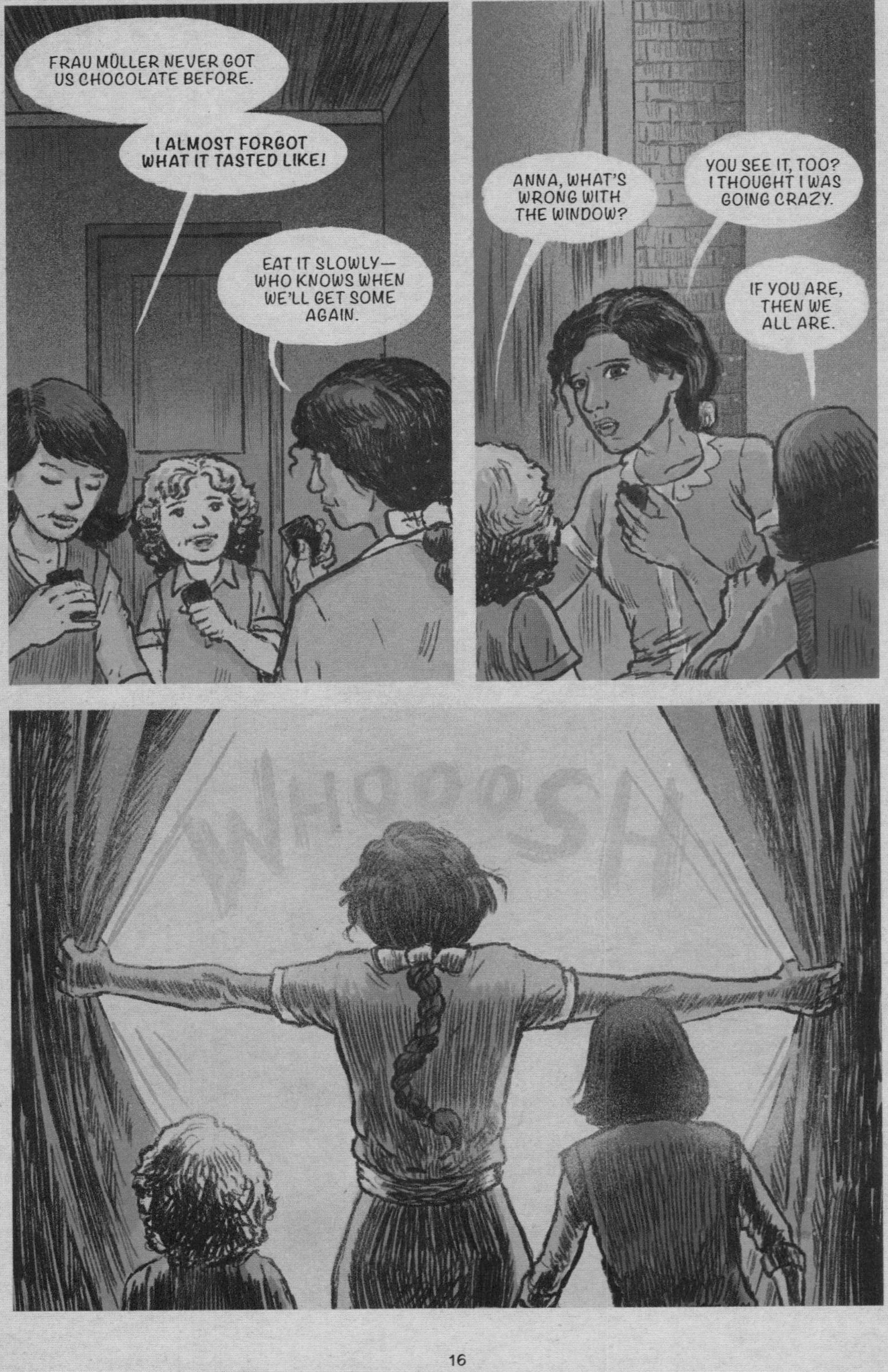
FRAU MÜLLER NEVER GOT US CHOCOLATE BEFORE.
I ALMOST FORGOT WHAT IT TASTED LIKE!
EAT IT SLOWLY— WHO KNOWS WHEN WE'LL GET SOME AGAIN.
ANNA, WHAT'S WRONG WITH THE WINDOW?
YOU SEE IT, TOO? I THOUGHT I WAS GOING CRAZY.
IF YOU ARE, THEN WE ALL ARE.
WHOOOSH

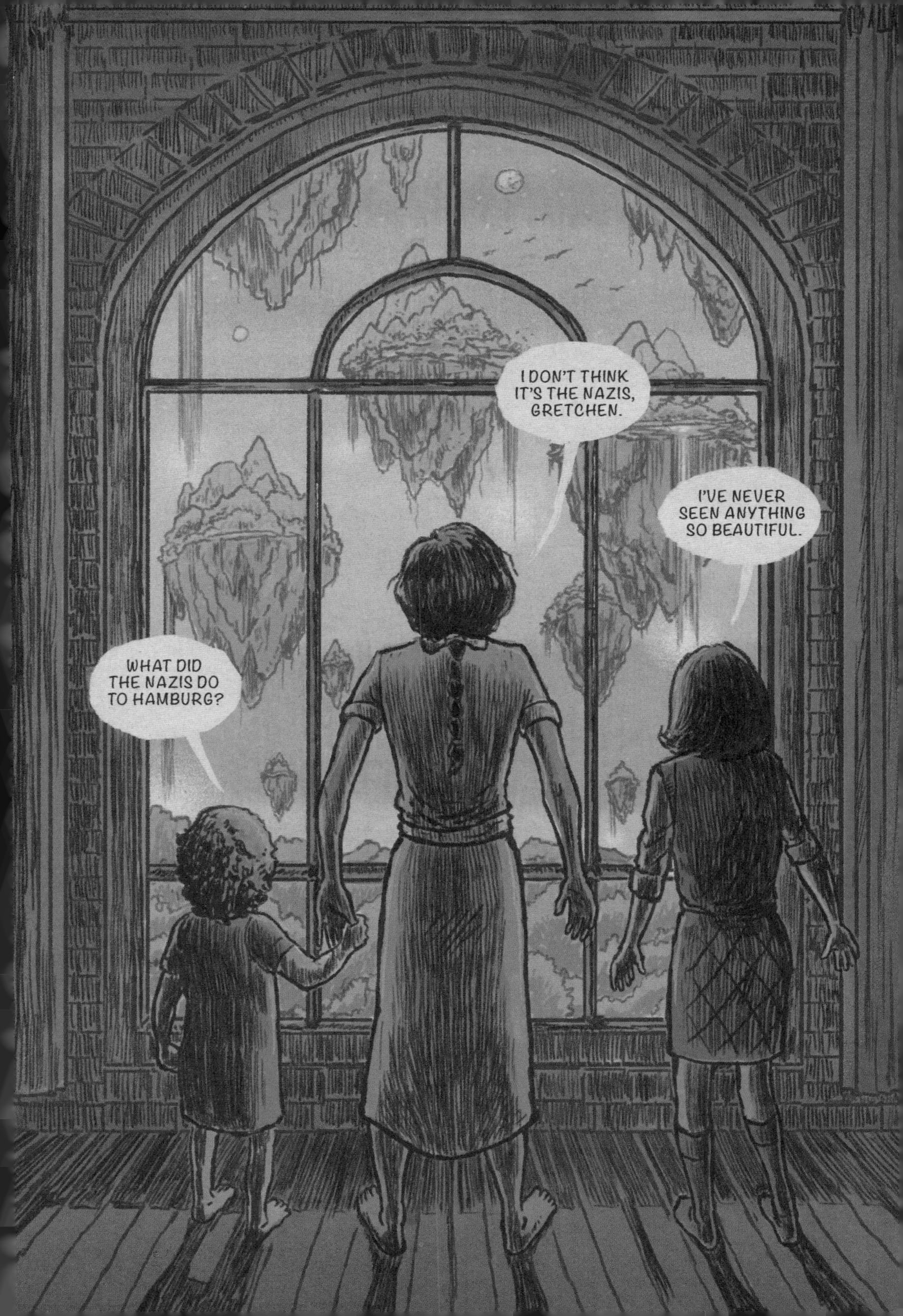
WHAT DID THE NAZIS DO TO HAMBURG?
I DON'T THINK IT'S THE NAZIS, GRETCHEN.
I'VE NEVER SEEN ANYTHING SO BEAUTIFUL.

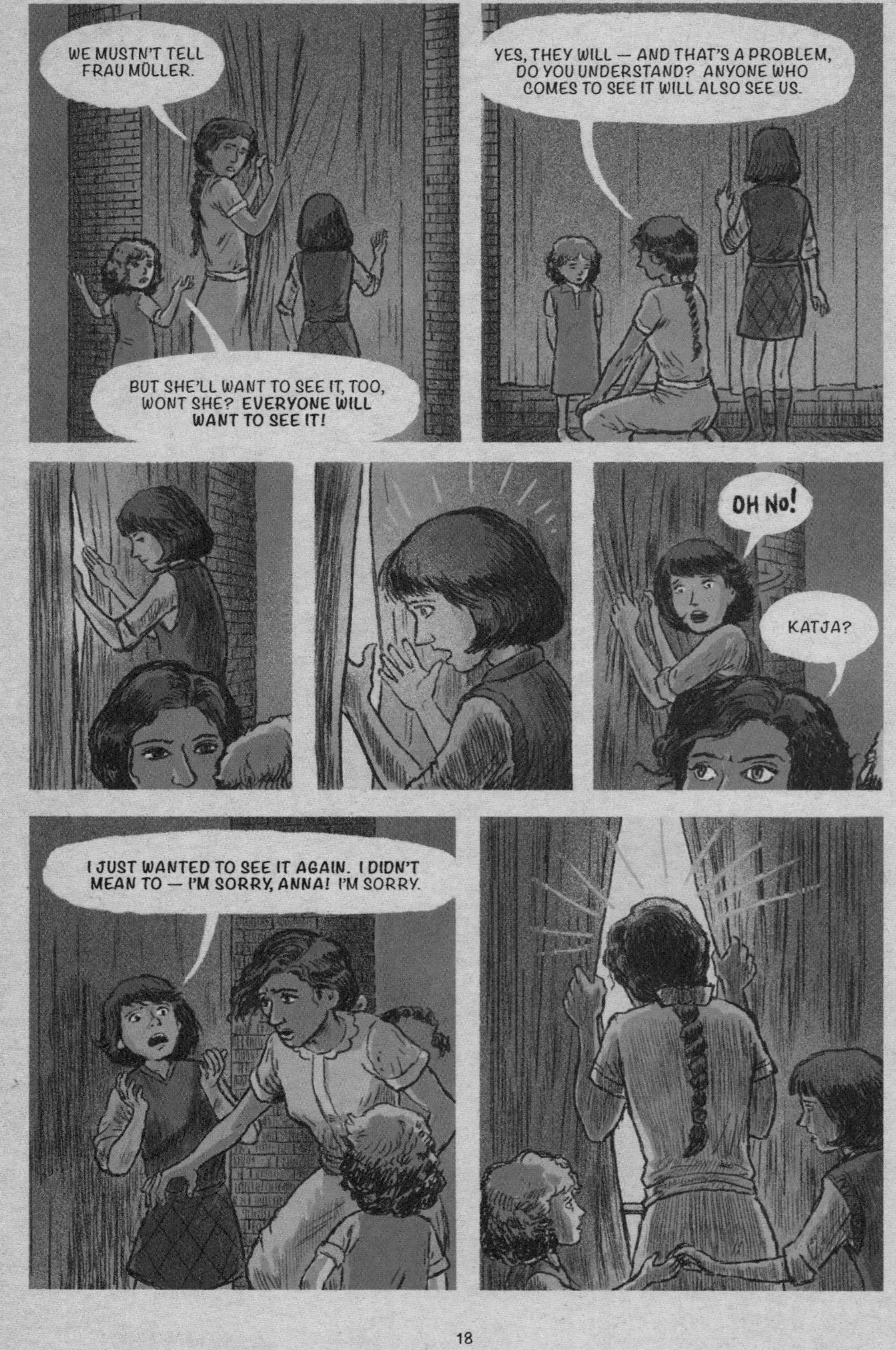
WE MUSTN'T TELL FRAU MÜLLER.
BUT SHE'LL WANT TO SEE IT, TOO, WONT SHE? EVERYONE WILL WANT TO SEE IT!
YES, THEY WILL — AND THAT'S A PROBLEM, DO YOU UNDERSTAND? ANYONE WHO COMES TO SEE IT WILL ALSO SEE US.
OH No!
KATJA?
I JUST WANTED TO SEE IT AGAIN. I DIDN'T MEAN TO — I'M SORRY, ANNA! I'M SORRY.

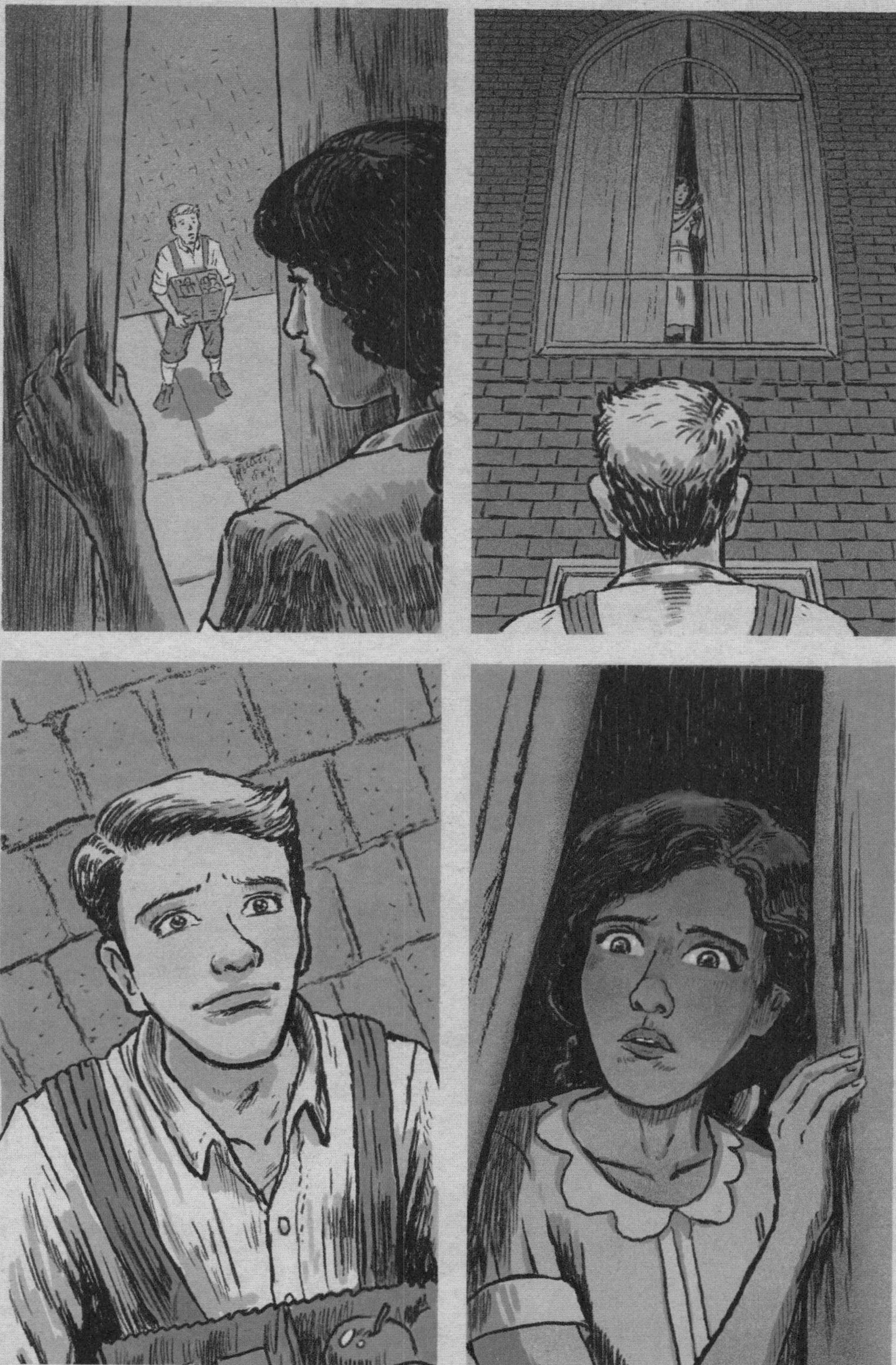

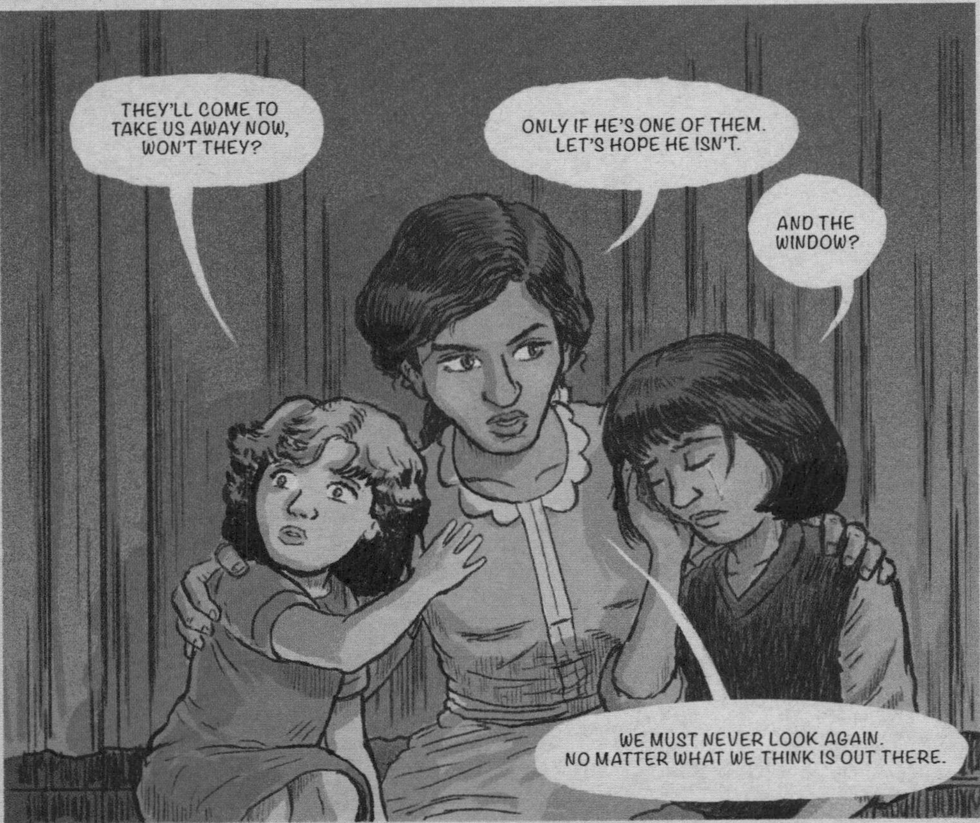
THEY'LL COME TO TAKE US AWAY NOW, WON'T THEY?
ONLY IF HE'S ONE OF THEM. LET'S HOPE HE ISN'T.
AND THE WINDOW?
WE MUST NEVER LOOK AGAIN. NO MATTER WHAT WE THINK IS OUT THERE.

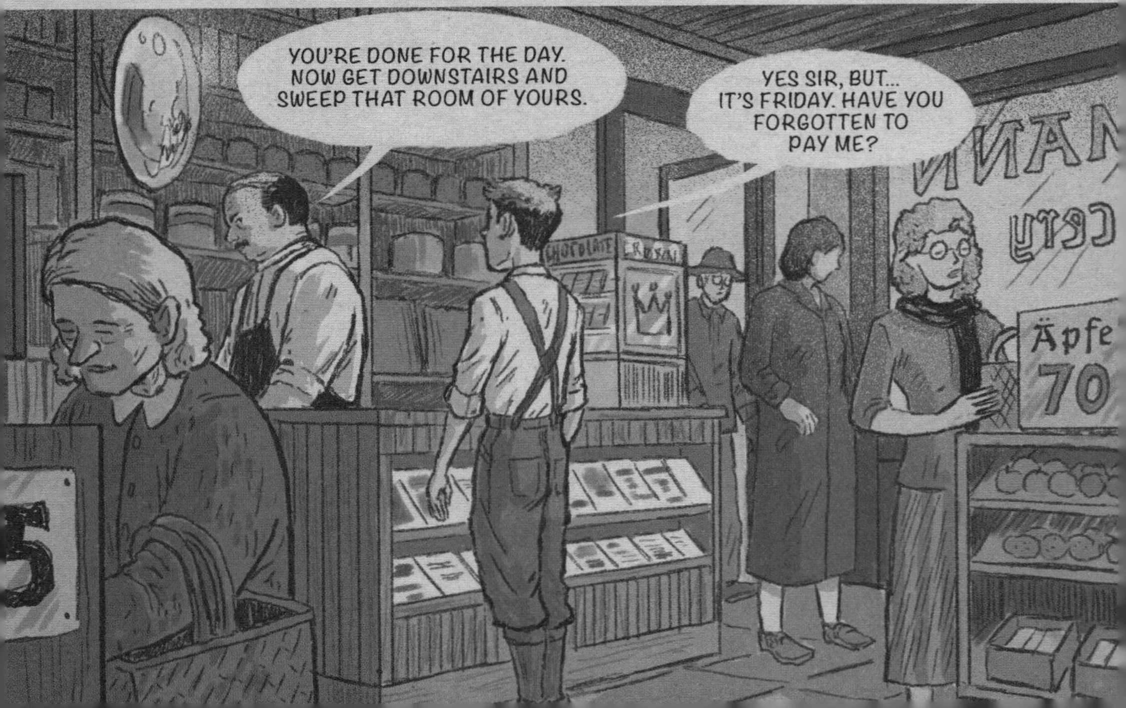
YOU'RE DONE FOR THE DAY. NOW GET DOWNSTAIRS AND SWEEP THAT ROOM OF YOURS.
YES SIR, BUT... IT'S FRIDAY. HAVE YOU FORGOTTEN TO PAY ME?
Äpfe
70

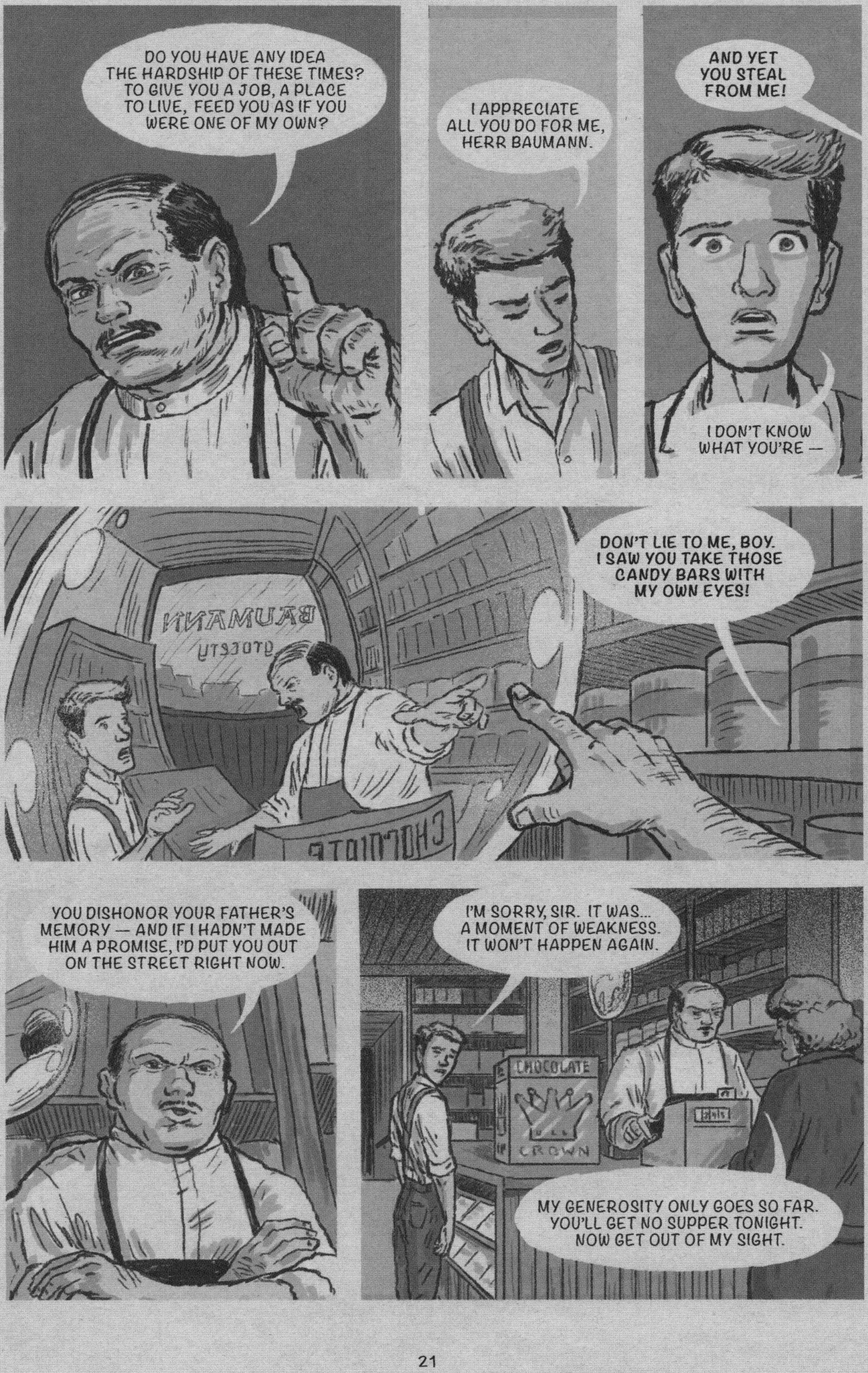
DO YOU HAVE ANY IDEA THE HARDSHIP OF THESE TIMES? TO GIVE YOU A JOB, A PLACE TO LIVE, FEED YOU AS IF YOU WERE ONE OF MY OWN?
I APPRECIATE ALL YOU DO FOR ME, HERR BAUMANN.
AND YET YOU STEAL FROM ME!
I DON'T KNOW WHAT YOU'RE —
DON'T LIE TO ME, BOY. I SAW YOU TAKE THOSE CANDY BARS WITH MY OWN EYES!
YOU DISHONOR YOUR FATHER'S MEMORY — AND IF I HADN'T MADE HIM A PROMISE, I'D PUT YOU OUT ON THE STREET RIGHT NOW.
I'M SORRY, SIR. IT WAS... A MOMENT OF WEAKNESS. IT WON'T HAPPEN AGAIN.
CHOCOLATE
CROWN
MY GENEROSITY ONLY GOES SO FAR. YOU'LL GET NO SUPPER TONIGHT. NOW GET OUT OF MY SIGHT.

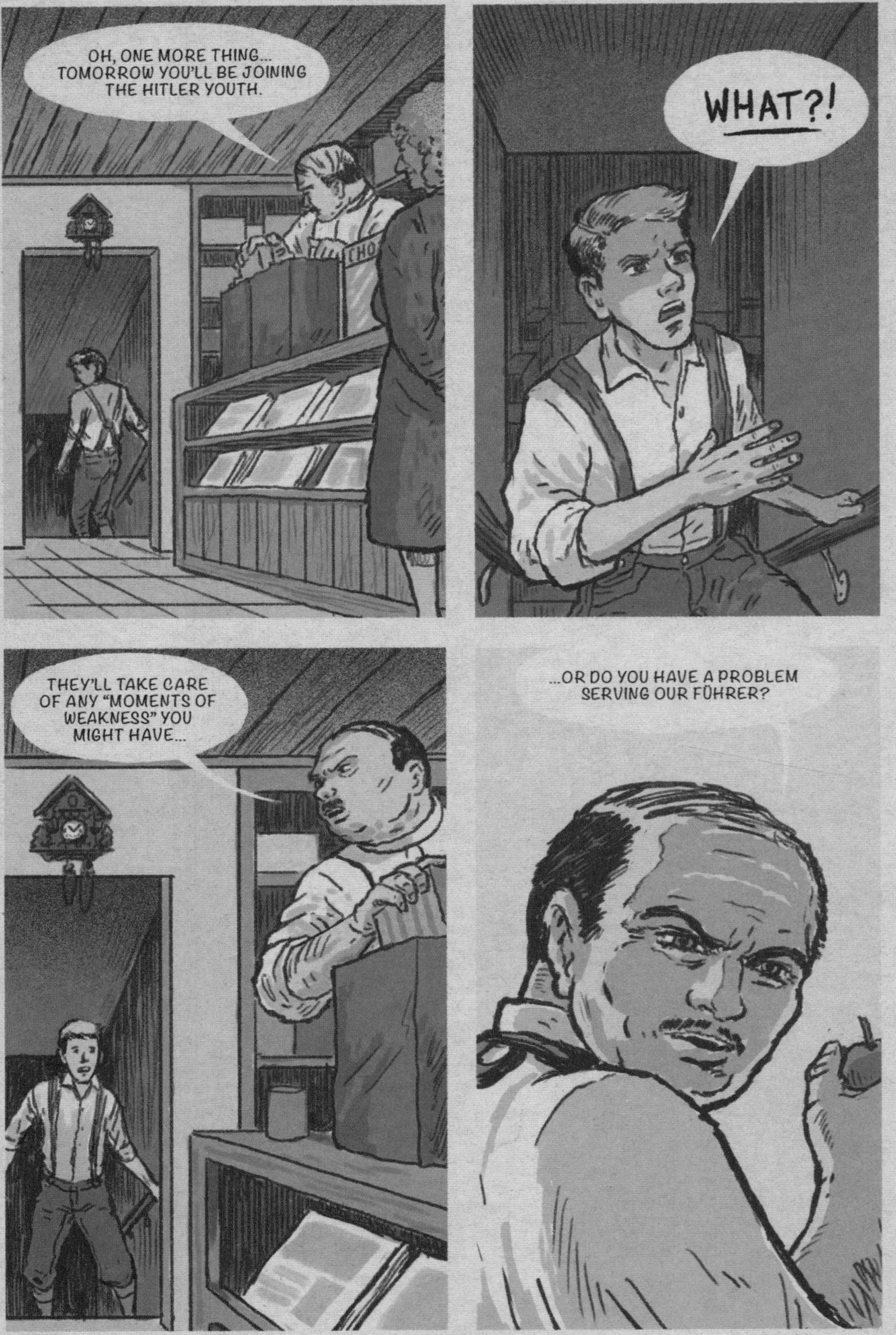
OH, ONE MORE THING... TOMORROW YOU'LL BE JOINING THE HITLER YOUTH.
WHAT?!
THEY'LL TAKE CARE OF ANY "MOMENTS OF WEAKNESS" YOU MIGHT HAVE...
...OR DO YOU HAVE A PROBLEM SERVING OUR FÜHRER?

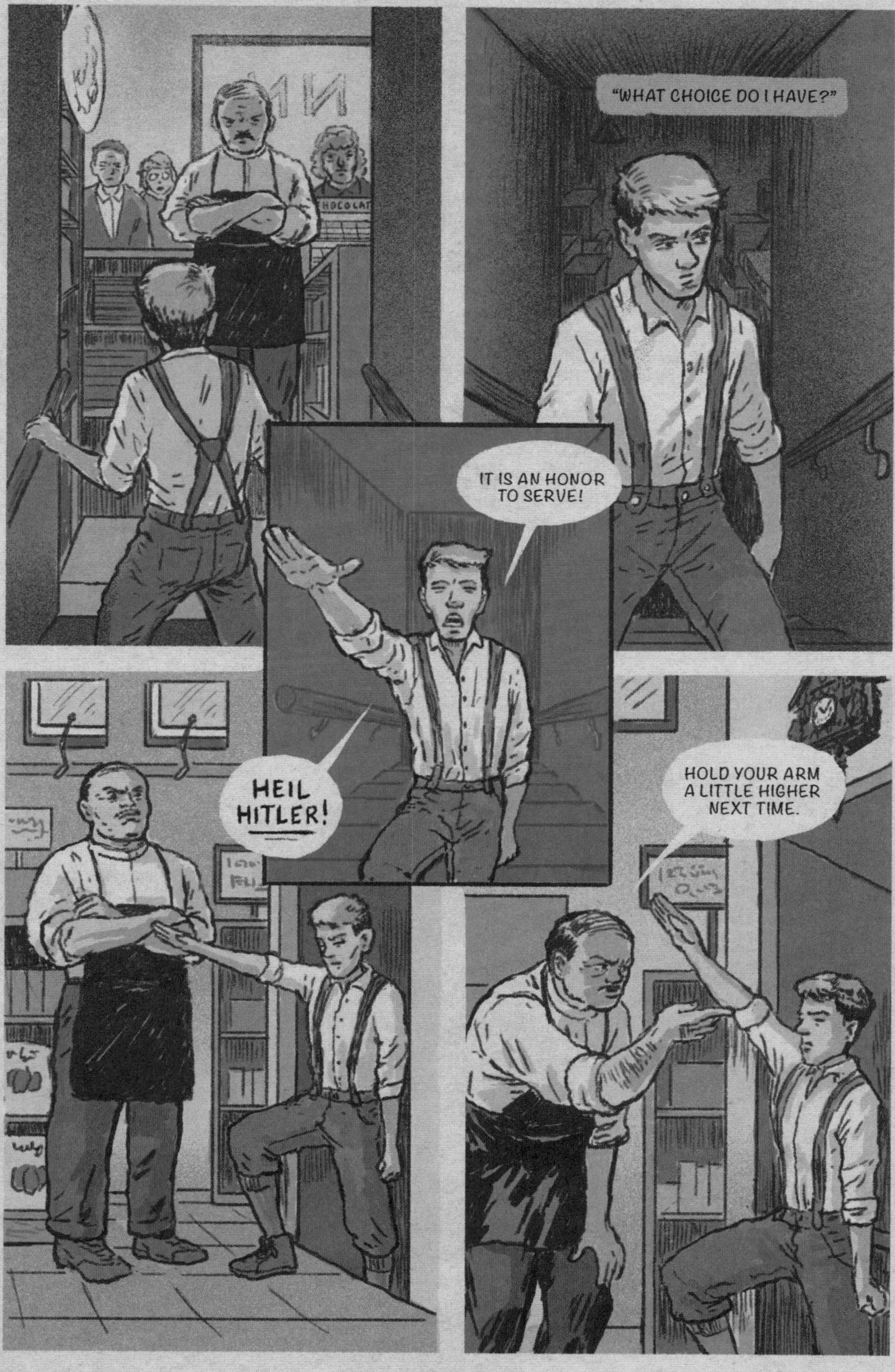

"WHAT CHOICE DO I HAVE?"
IT IS AN HONOR TO SERVE!
HEIL HITLER!
HOLD YOUR ARM A LITTLE HIGHER NEXT TIME.

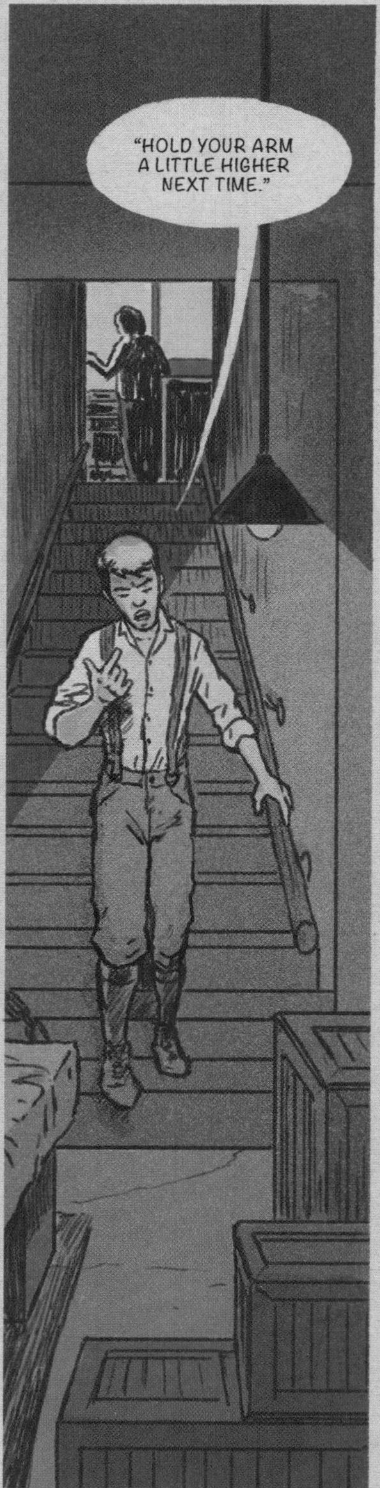
"HOLD YOUR ARM A LITTLE HIGHER NEXT TIME."

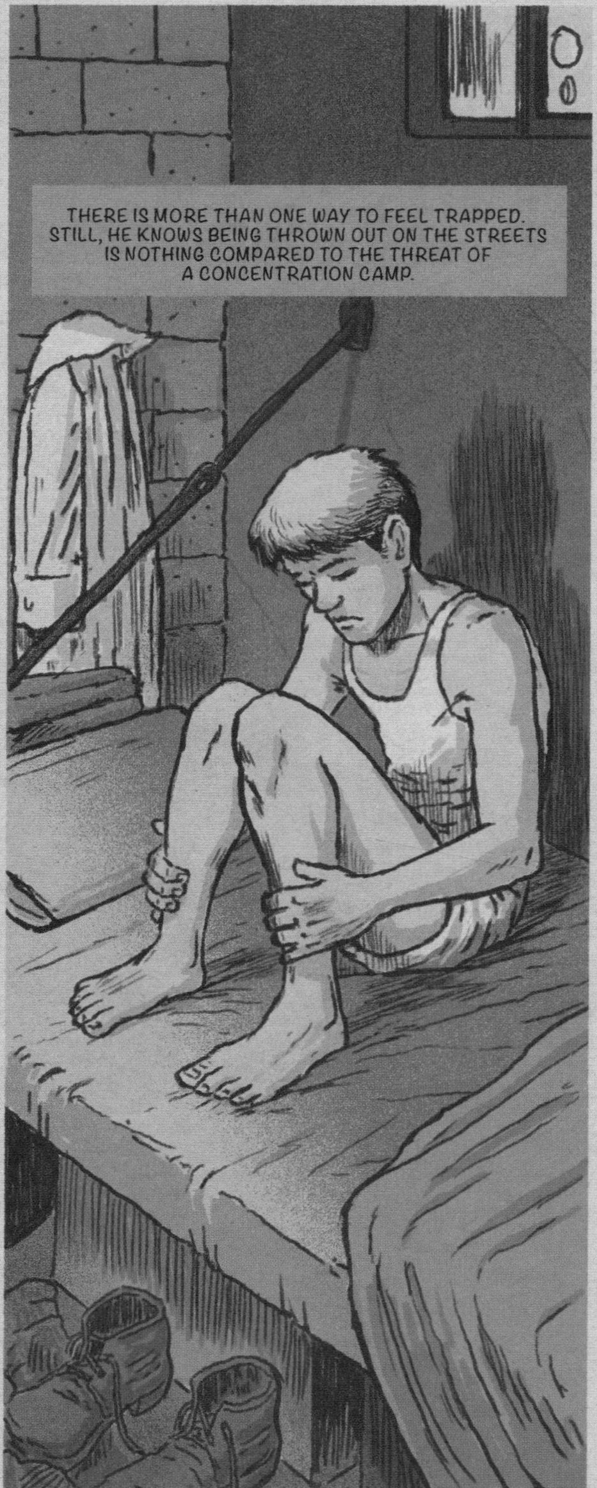
THERE IS MORE THAN ONE WAY TO FEEL TRAPPED. STILL, HE KNOWS BEING THROWN OUT ON THE STREETS IS NOTHING COMPARED TO THE THREAT OF A CONCENTRATION CAMP.

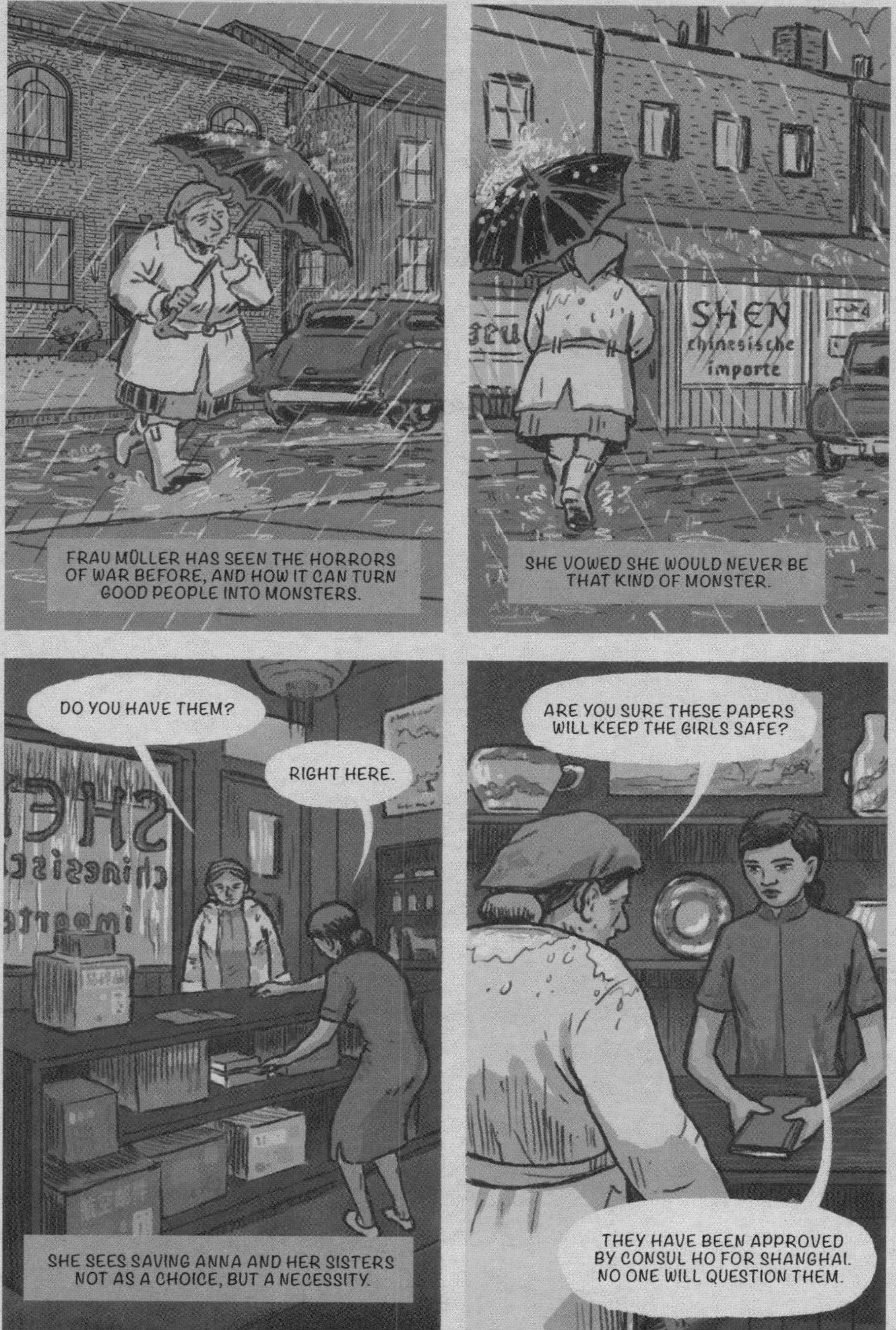
FRAU MÜLLER HAS SEEN THE HORRORS OF WAR BEFORE, AND HOW IT CAN TURN GOOD PEOPLE INTO MONSTERS.
SHEN
chinesische
importe
SHE VOWED SHE WOULD NEVER BE THAT KIND OF MONSTER.
DO YOU HAVE THEM?
RIGHT HERE.
SHE SEES SAVING ANNA AND HER SISTERS NOT AS A CHOICE, BUT A NECESSITY.
ARE YOU SURE THESE PAPERS WILL KEEP THE GIRLS SAFE?
THEY HAVE BEEN APPROVED BY CONSUL HO FOR SHANGHAI. NO ONE WILL QUESTION THEM.

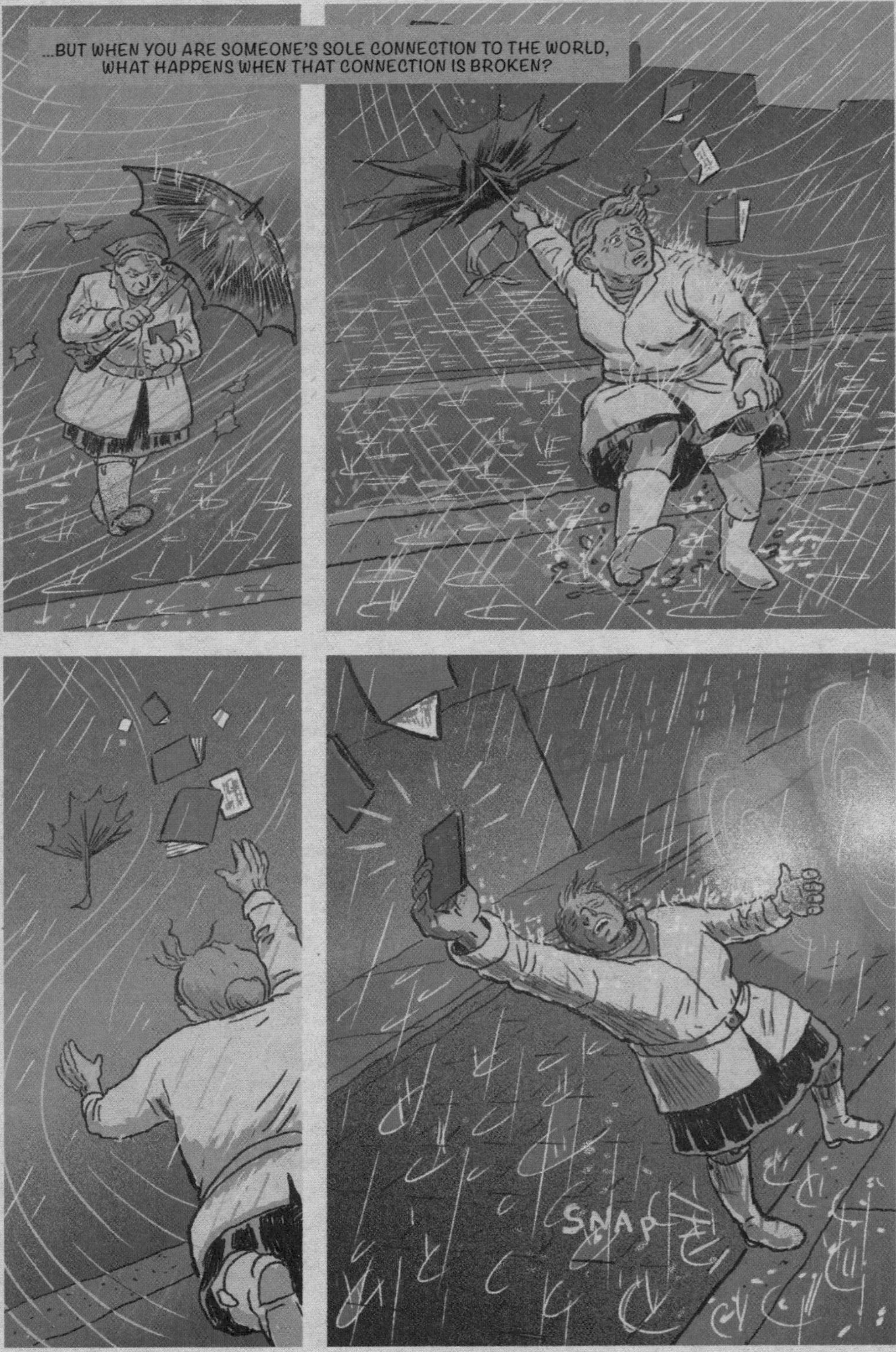
...BUT WHEN YOU ARE SOMEONE'S SOLE CONNECTION TO THE WORLD, WHAT HAPPENS WHEN THAT CONNECTION IS BROKEN?
SNAP

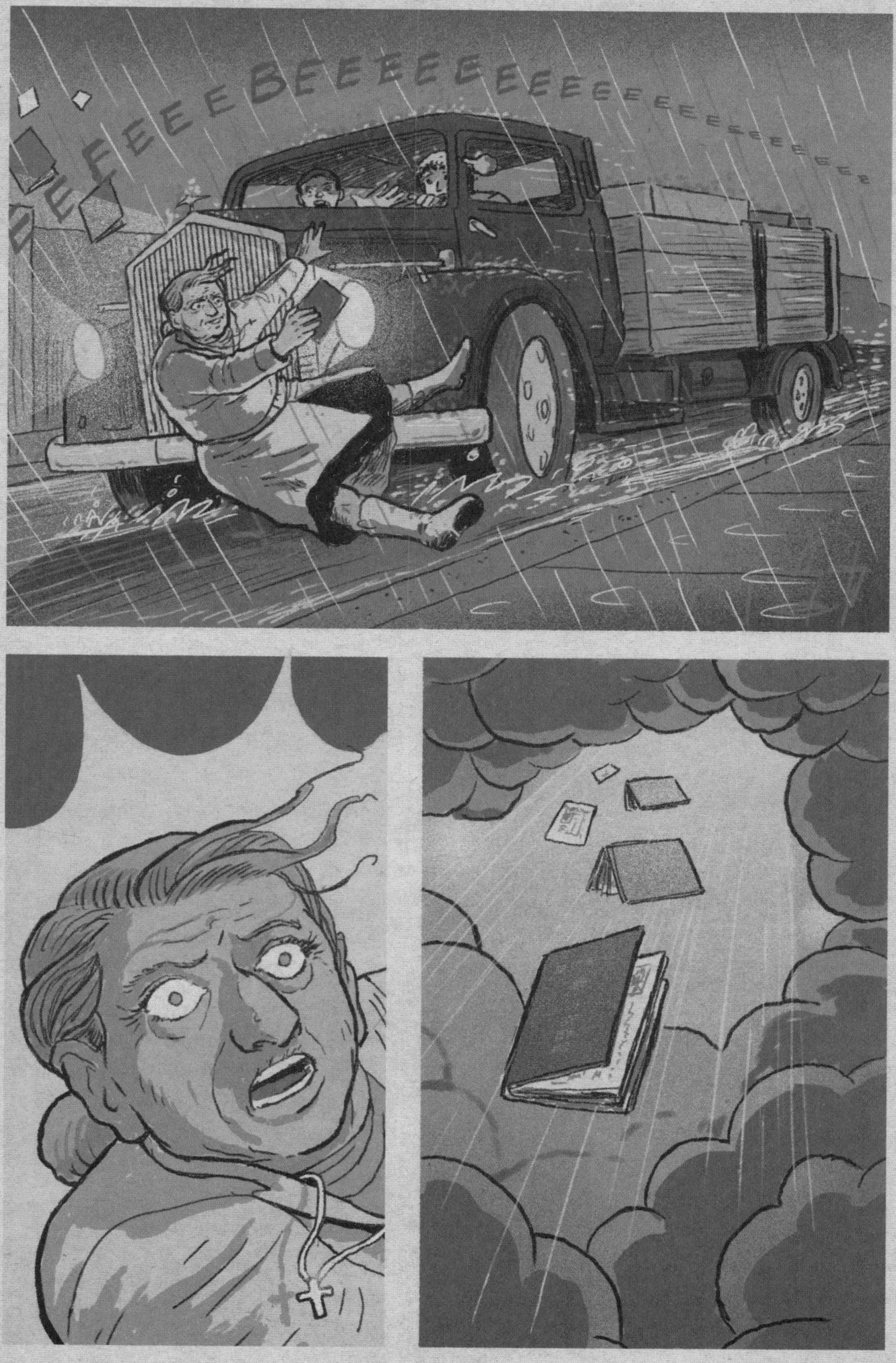
BEEEEEEEEEEEEEEEEEEEEEEEEEEE

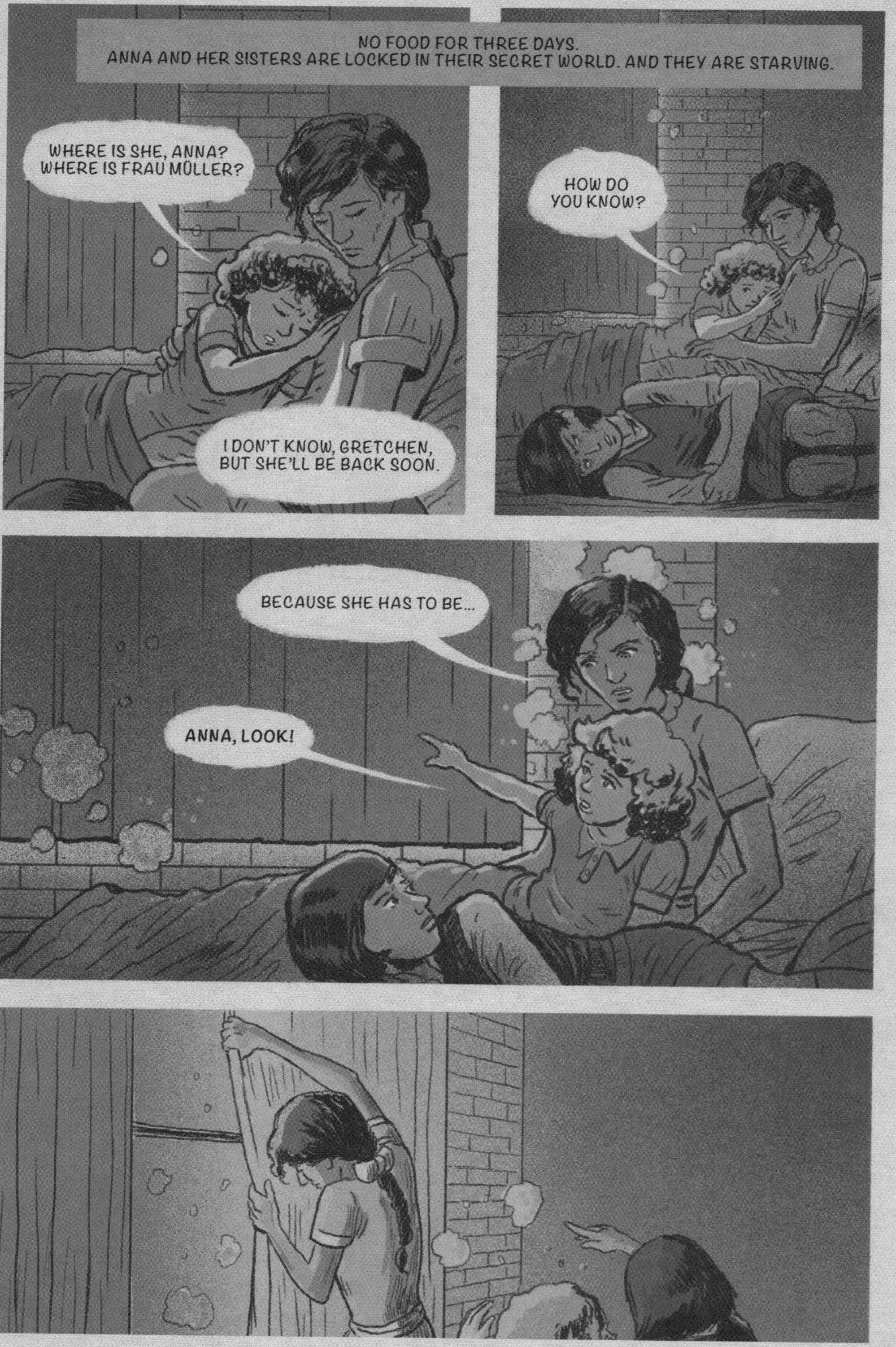
NO FOOD FOR THREE DAYS.
ANNA AND HER SISTERS ARE LOCKED IN THEIR SECRET WORLD. AND THEY ARE STARVING.
WHERE IS SHE, ANNA? WHERE IS FRAU MÜLLER?
I DON'T KNOW, GRETCHEN, BUT SHE'LL BE BACK SOON.
HOW DO YOU KNOW?
BECAUSE SHE HAS TO BE...
ANNA, LOOK!

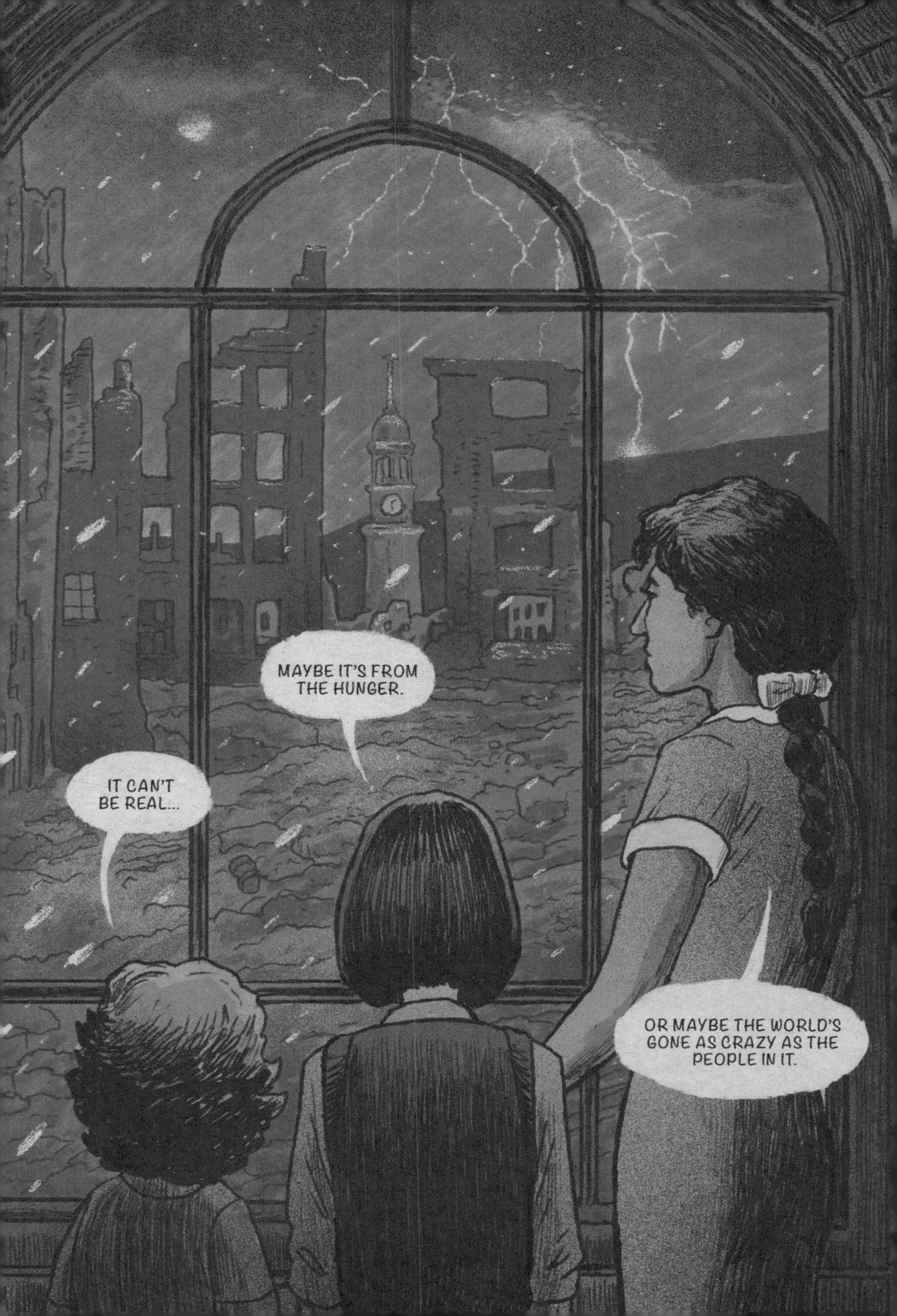
IT CAN'T BE REAL...
MAYBE IT'S FROM THE HUNGER.
OR MAYBE THE WORLD'S GONE AS CRAZY AS THE PEOPLE IN IT.

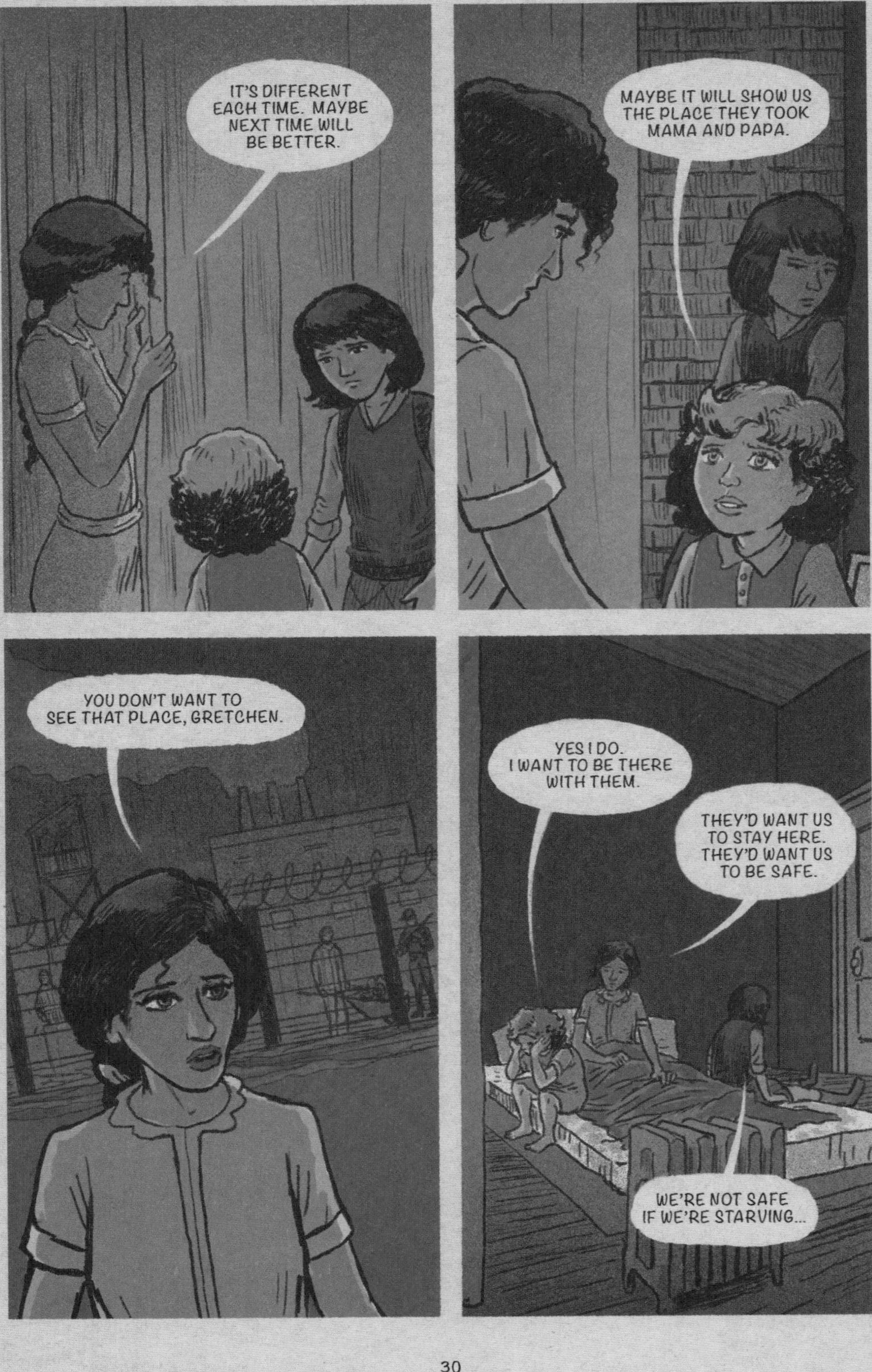
IT'S DIFFERENT EACH TIME. MAYBE NEXT TIME WILL BE BETTER.
MAYBE IT WILL SHOW US THE PLACE THEY TOOK MAMA AND PAPA.
YOU DON'T WANT TO SEE THAT PLACE, GRETCHEN.
YES I DO. I WANT TO BE THERE WITH THEM.
THEY'D WANT US TO STAY HERE. THEY'D WANT US TO BE SAFE.
WE'RE NOT SAFE IF WE'RE STARVING...

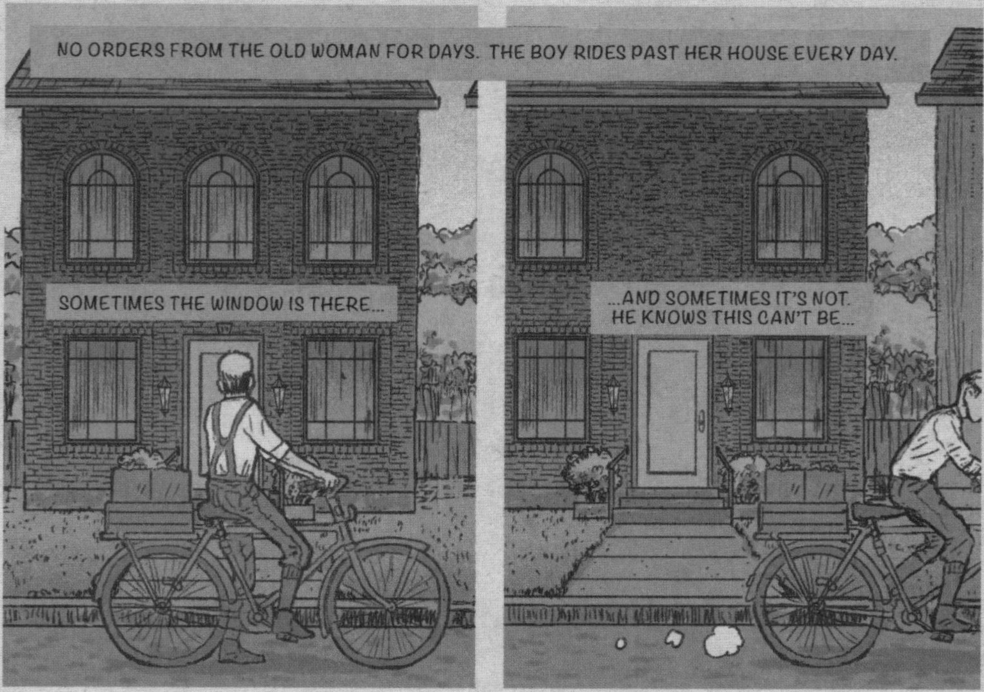
NO ORDERS FROM THE OLD WOMAN FOR DAYS. THE BOY RIDES PAST HER HOUSE EVERY DAY.
SOMETIMES THE WINDOW IS THERE...
...AND SOMETIMES IT'S NOT. HE KNOWS THIS CAN'T BE...

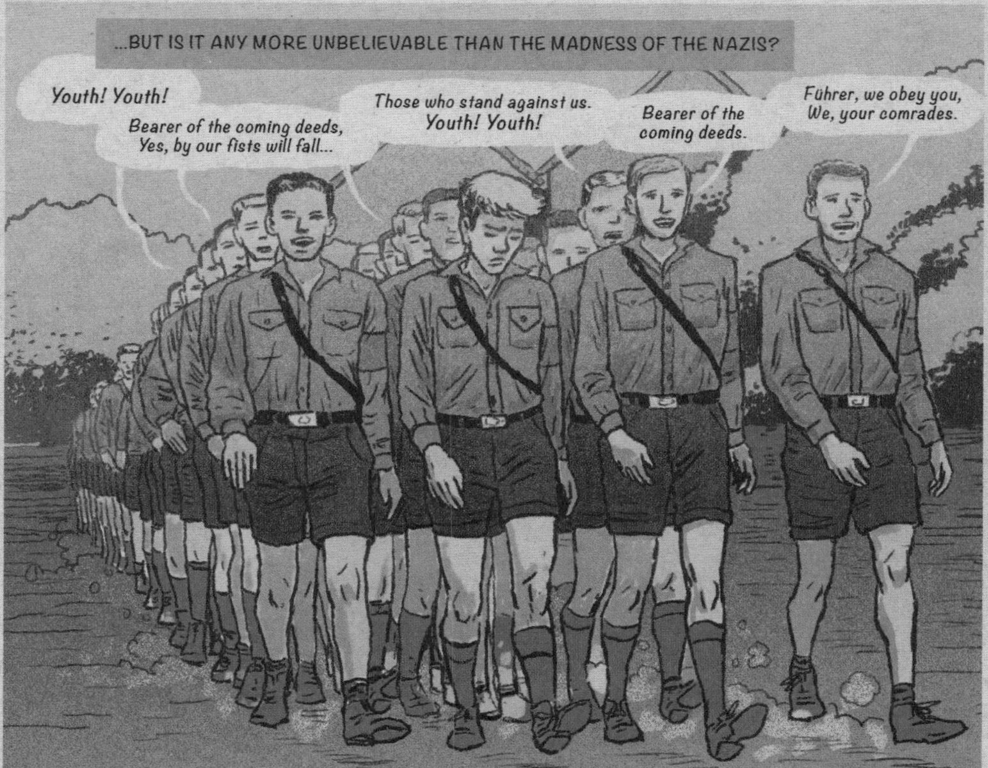
...BUT IS IT ANY MORE UNBELIEVABLE THAN THE MADNESS OF THE NAZIS?
Youth! Youth!
Bearer of the coming deeds, Yes, by our fists will fall...
Those who stand against us. Youth! Youth!
Bearer of the coming deeds.
Führer, we obey you, We, your comrades.

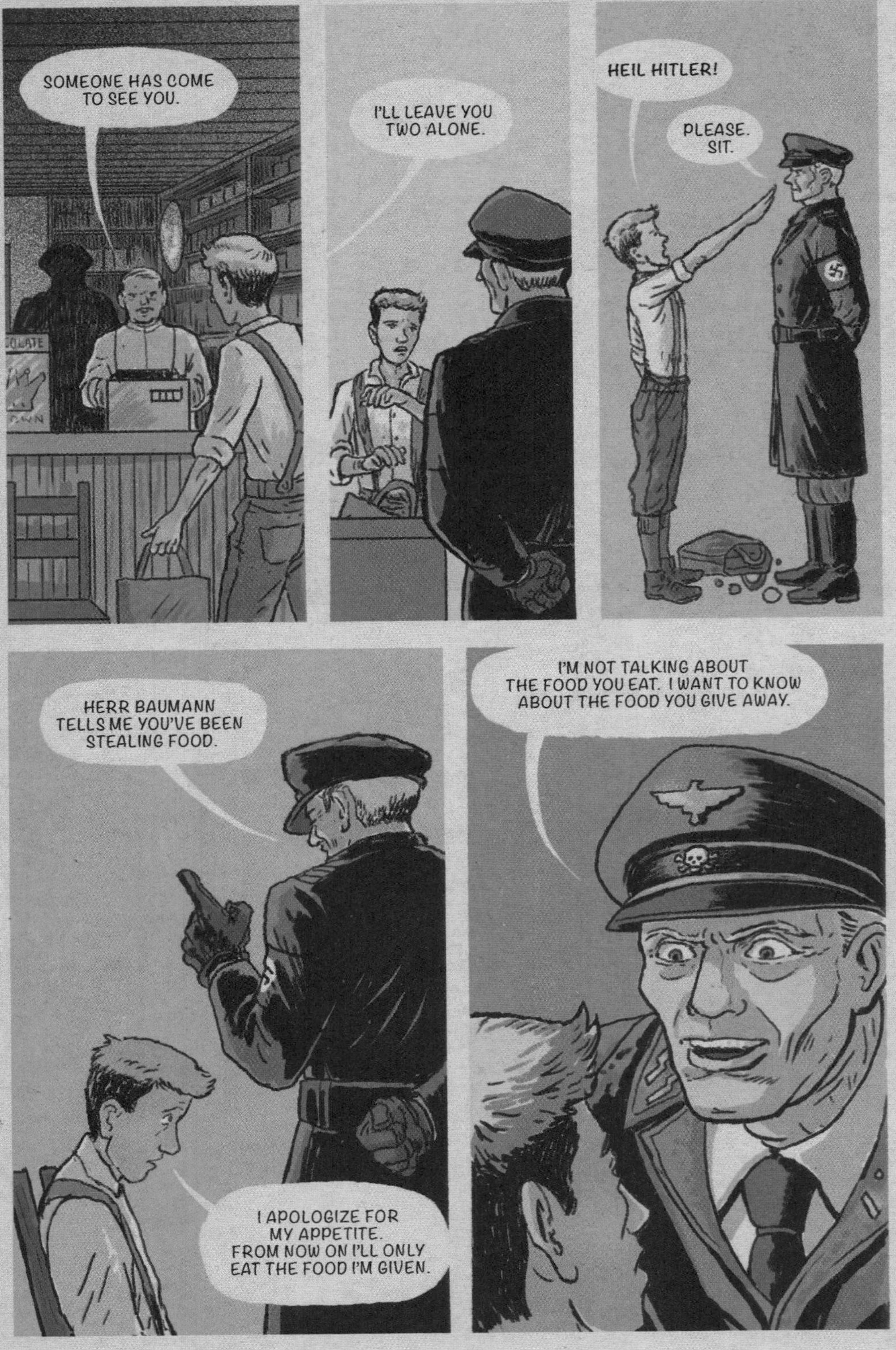
SOMEONE HAS COME TO SEE YOU.
I'LL LEAVE YOU TWO ALONE.
HEIL HITLER!
PLEASE. SIT.
HERR BAUMANN TELLS ME YOU'VE BEEN STEALING FOOD.
I APOLOGIZE FOR MY APPETITE. FROM NOW ON I'LL ONLY EAT THE FOOD I'M GIVEN.
I'M NOT TALKING ABOUT THE FOOD YOU EAT. I WANT TO KNOW ABOUT THE FOOD YOU GIVE AWAY.

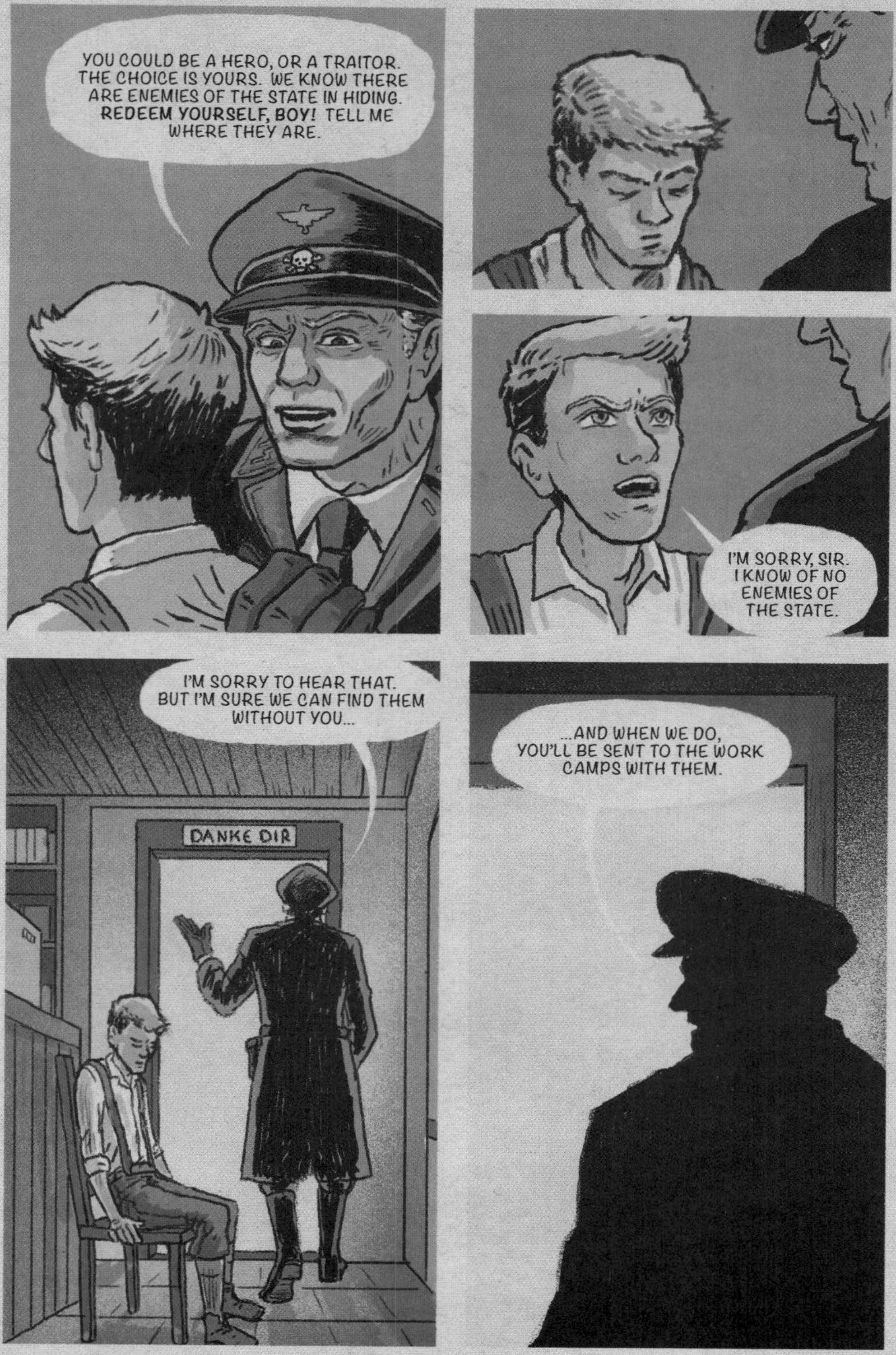
YOU COULD BE A HERO, OR A TRAITOR. THE CHOICE IS YOURS. WE KNOW THERE ARE ENEMIES OF THE STATE IN HIDING. REDEEM YOURSELF, BOY! TELL ME WHERE THEY ARE.
I'M SORRY, SIR. I KNOW OF NO ENEMIES OF THE STATE.
I'M SORRY TO HEAR THAT. BUT I'M SURE WE CAN FIND THEM WITHOUT YOU...
DANKE DIR
...AND WHEN WE DO, YOU'LL BE SENT TO THE WORK CAMPS WITH THEM.

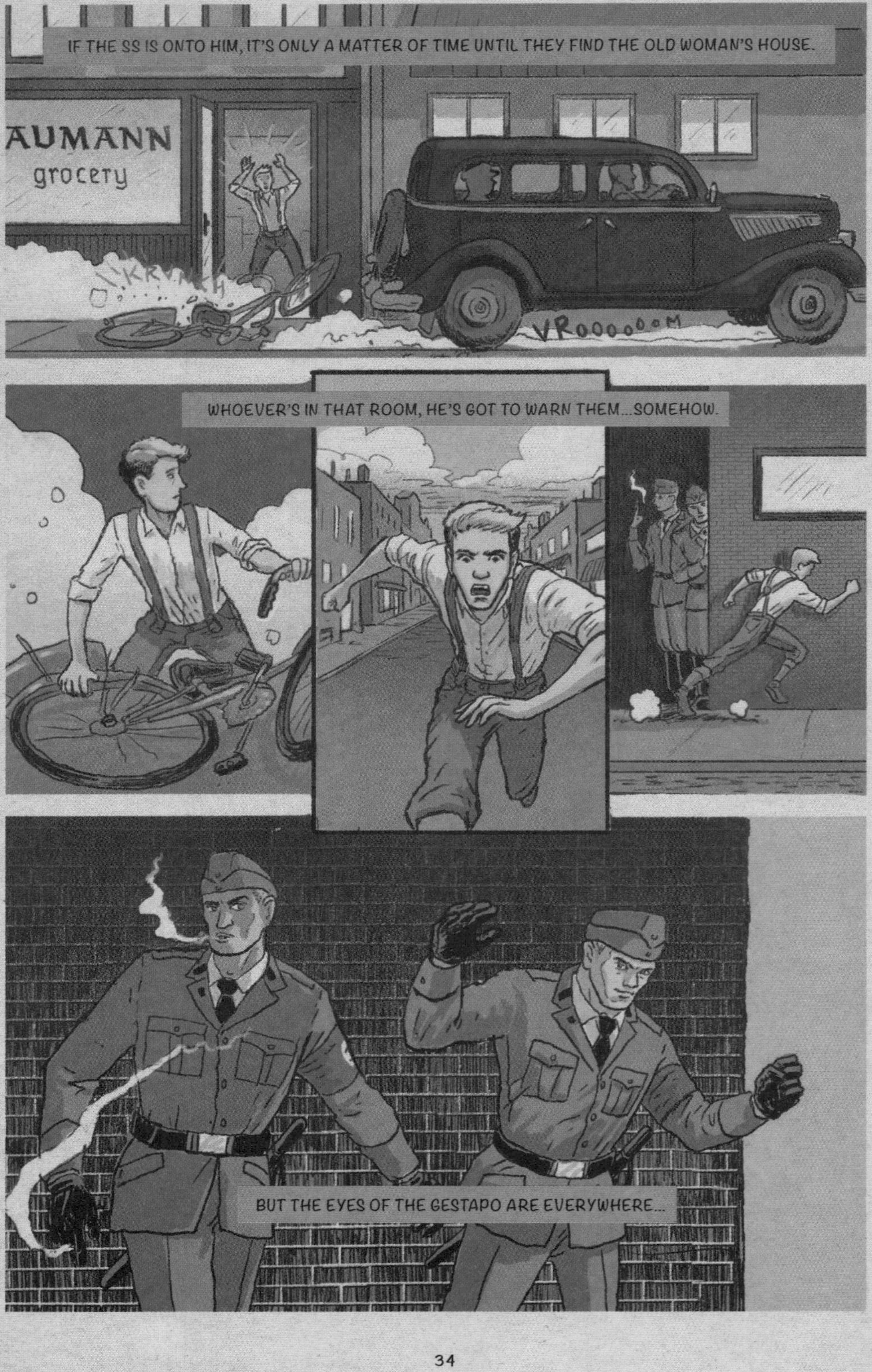
IF THE SS IS ONTO HIM, IT'S ONLY A MATTER OF TIME UNTIL THEY FIND THE OLD WOMAN'S HOUSE.
AUMANN
grocery
KRUNCH
VROOOOOOOM
WHOEVER'S IN THAT ROOM, HE'S GOT TO WARN THEM...SOMEHOW.
BUT THE EYES OF THE GESTAPO ARE EVERYWHERE...

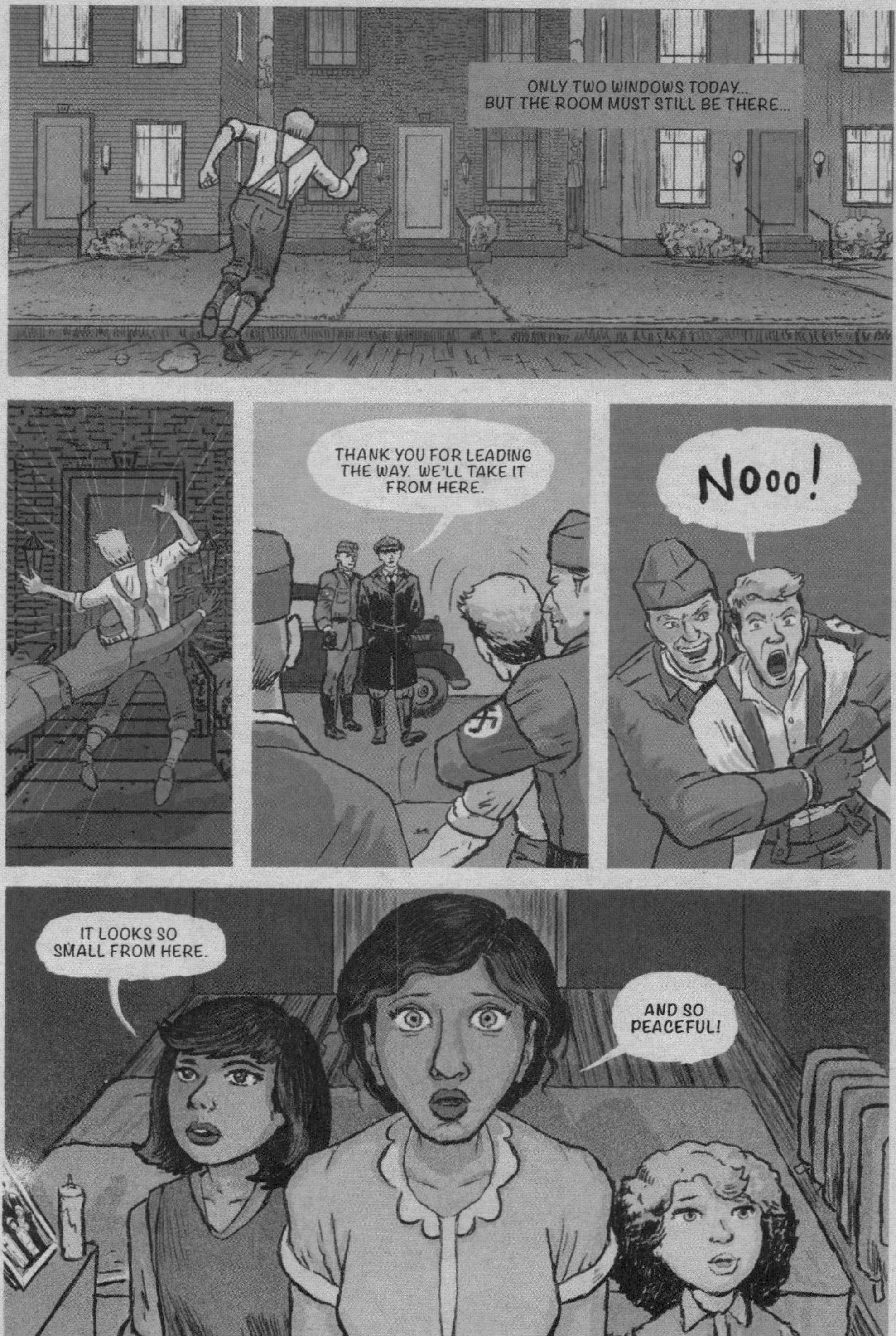
ONLY TWO WINDOWS TODAY...
BUT THE ROOM MUST STILL BE THERE...
THANK YOU FOR LEADING THE WAY. WE'LL TAKE IT FROM HERE.
Nooo!
IT LOOKS SO SMALL FROM HERE.
AND SO PEACEFUL!

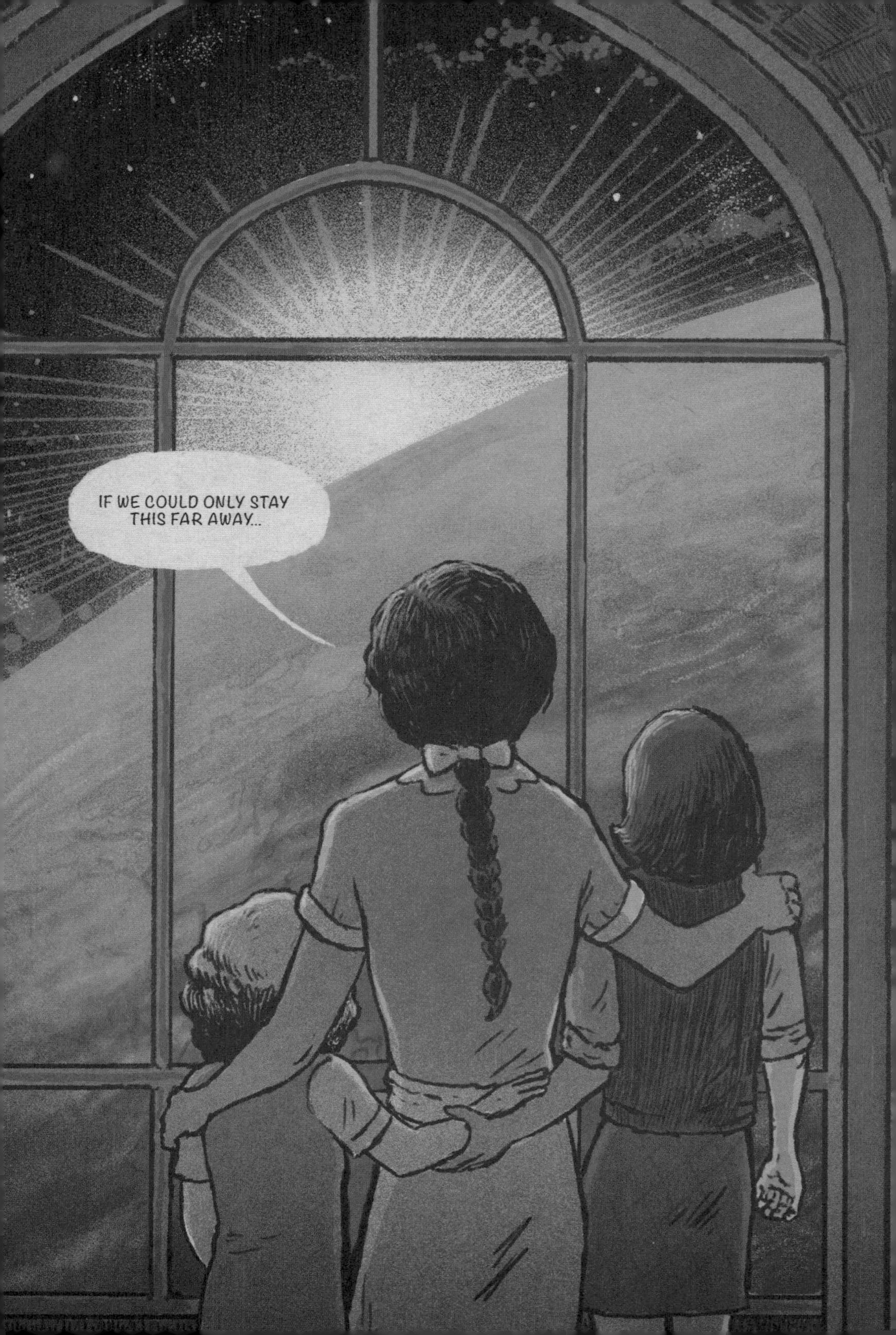
IF WE COULD ONLY STAY THIS FAR AWAY...

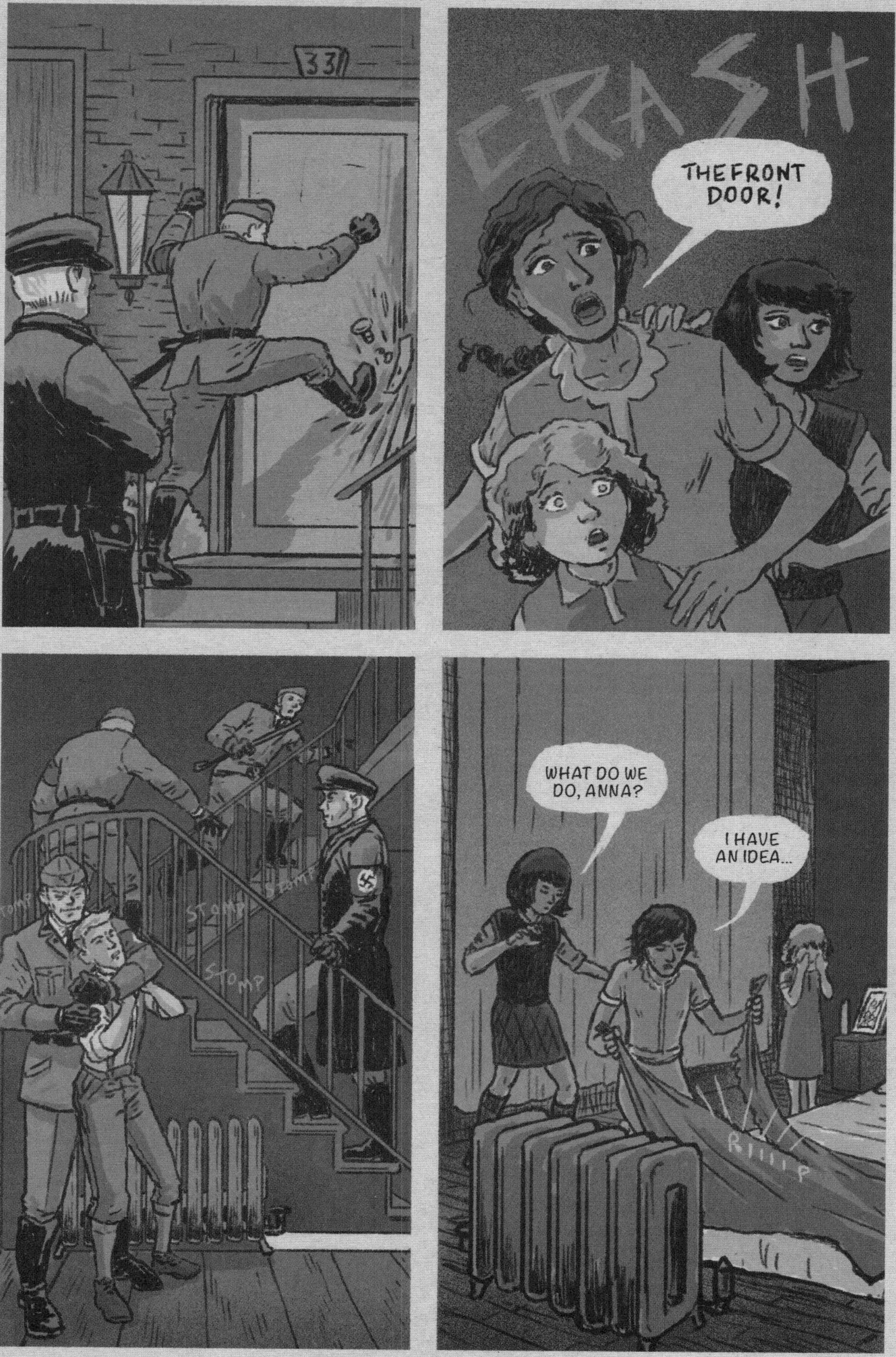
CRASH
THE FRONT DOOR!
STOMP
STOMP
STOMP
STOMP
WHAT DO WE DO, ANNA?
I HAVE AN IDEA...
RIIIIP

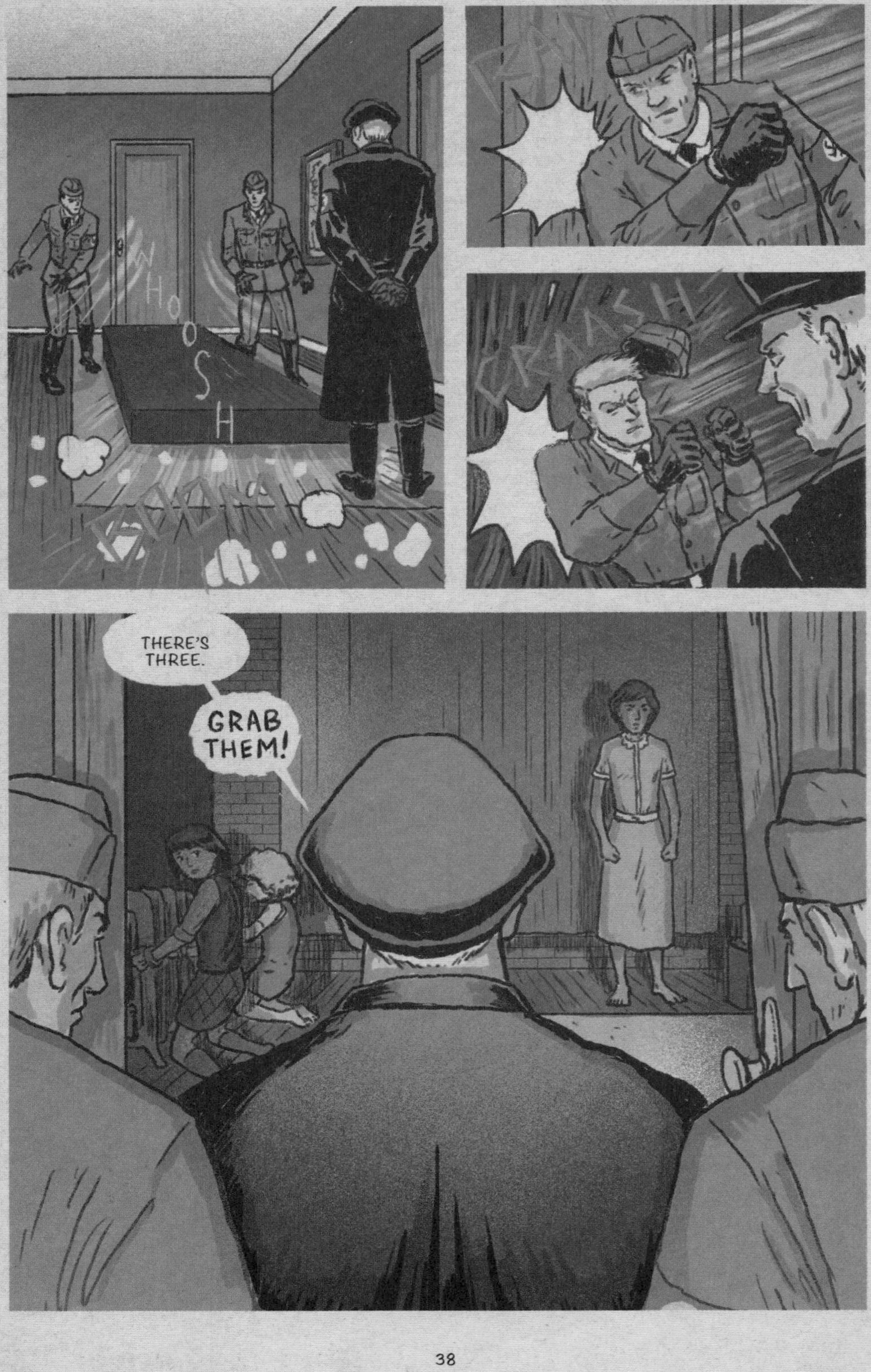
WHOOSH
THERE'S THREE.
GRAB THEM!

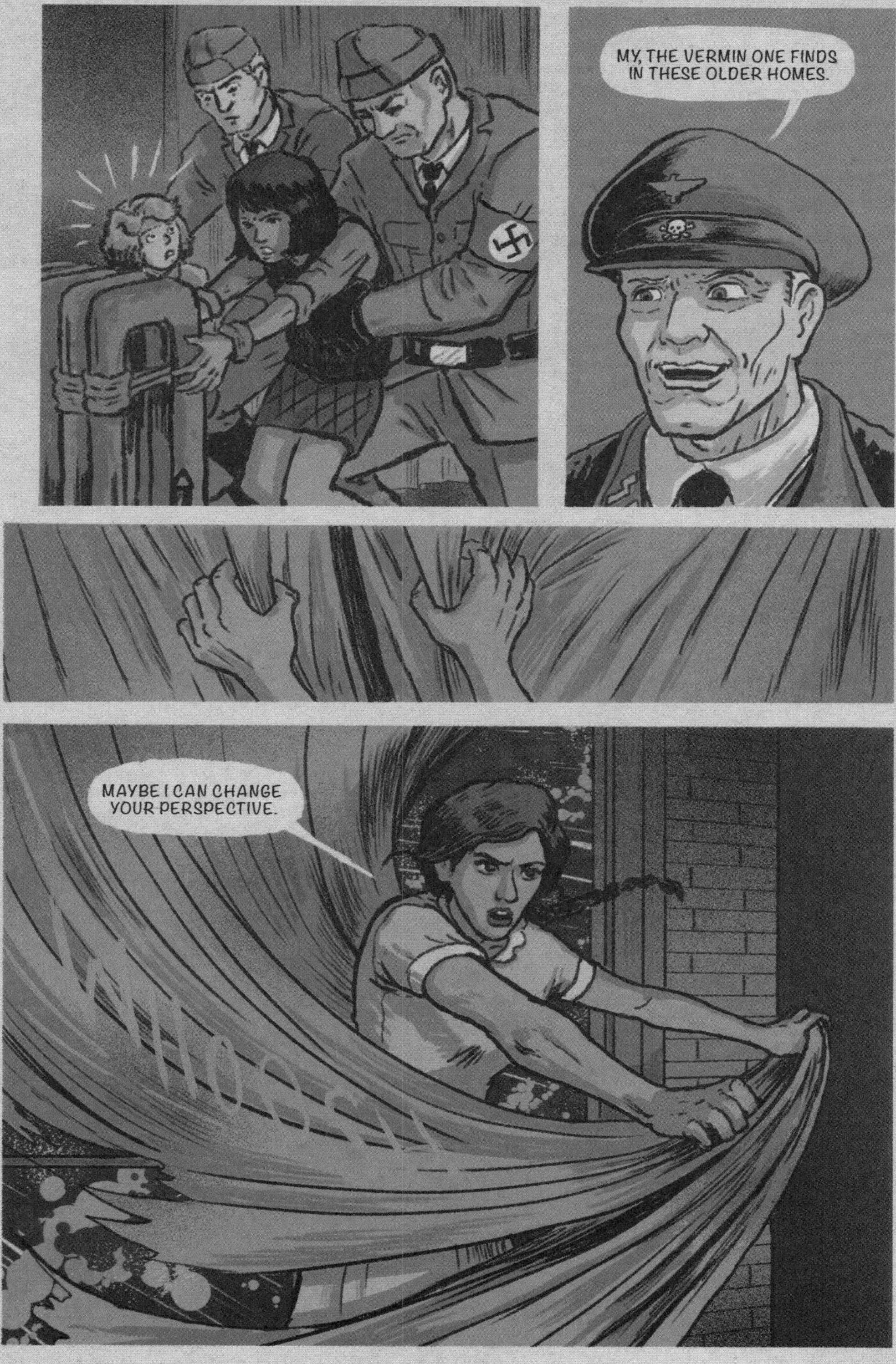
MY, THE VERMIN ONE FINDS IN THESE OLDER HOMES.
MAYBE I CAN CHANGE YOUR PERSPECTIVE.

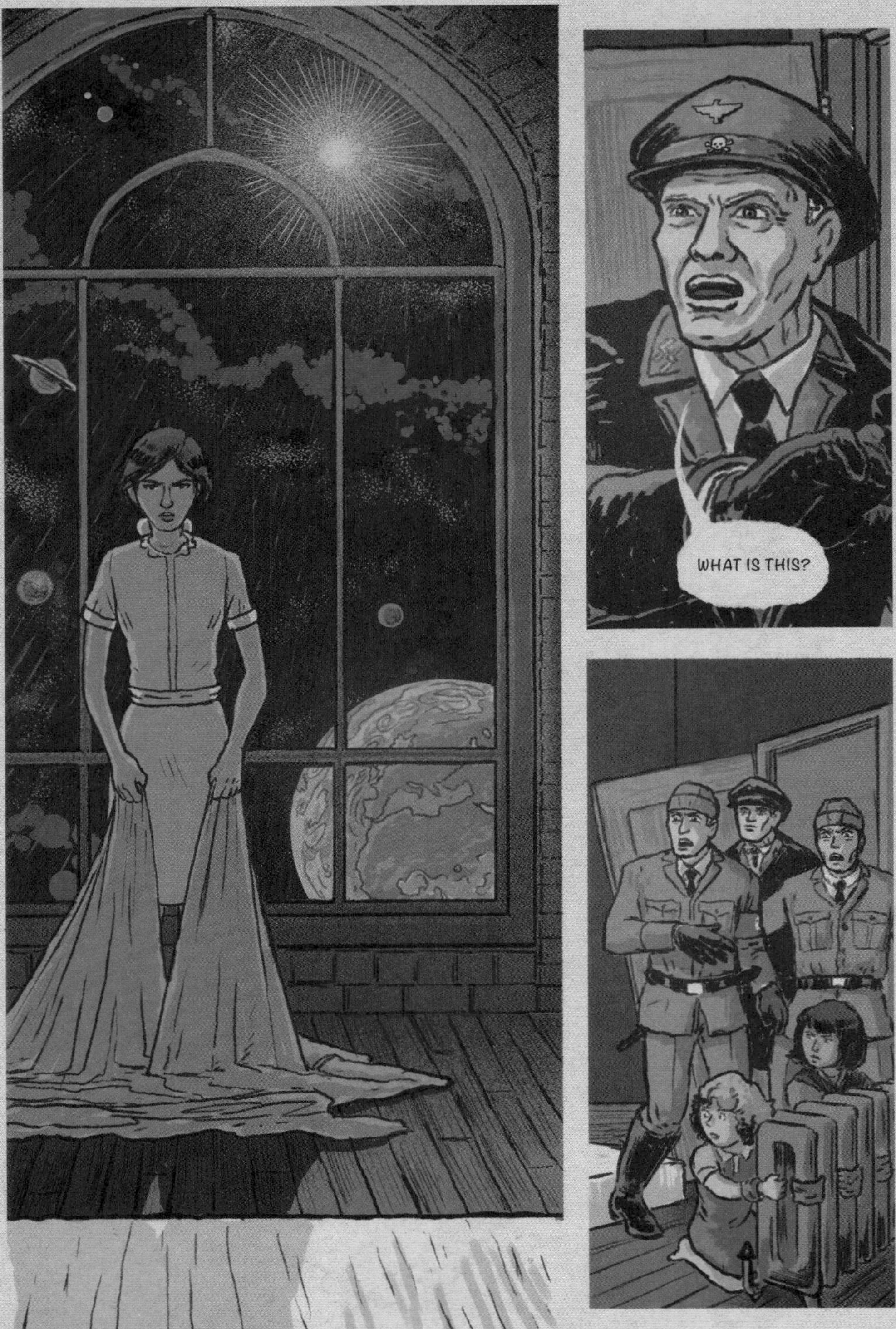
WHAT IS THIS?

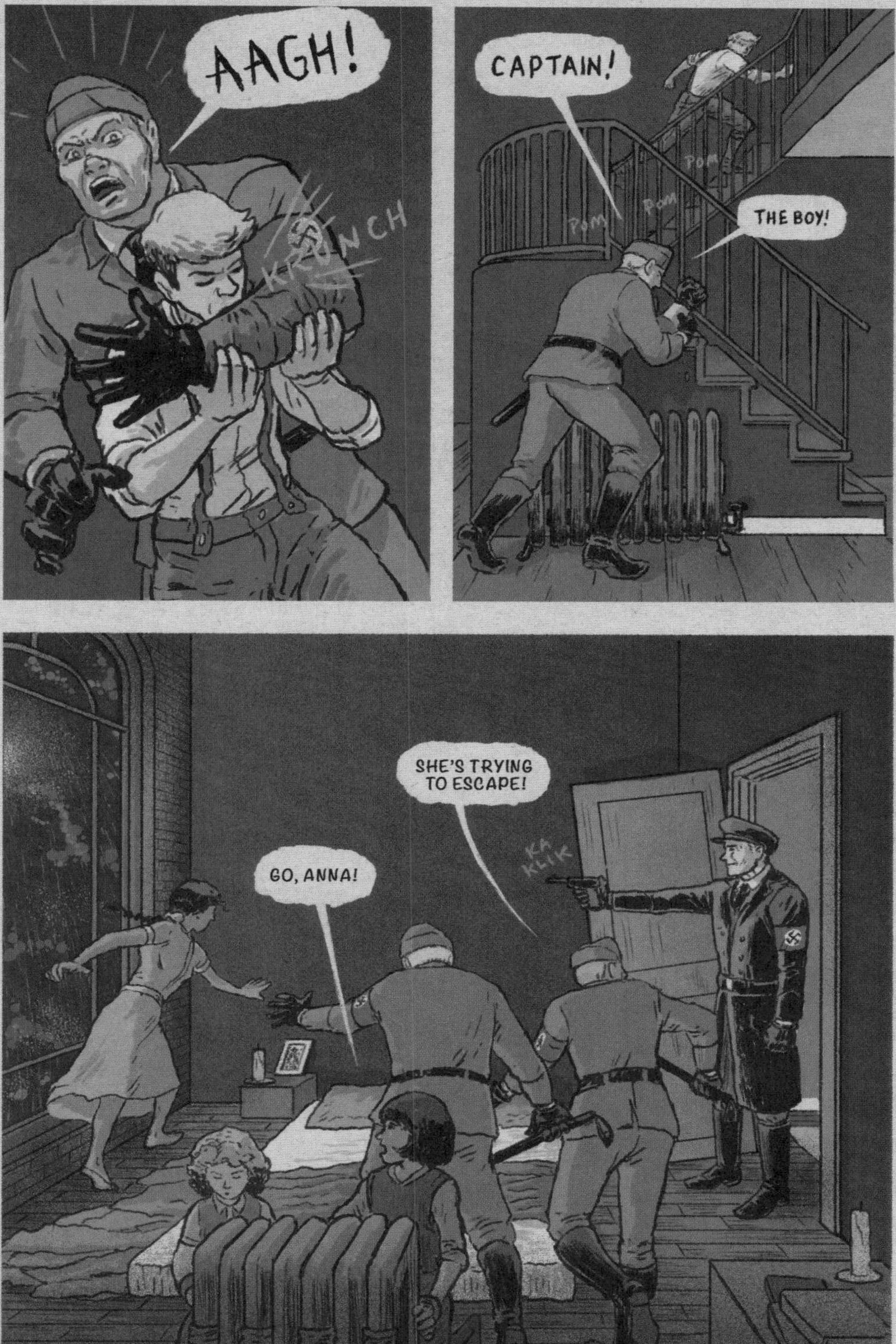
AAGH!
KRUNCH
CAPTAIN!
POM POM POM
THE BOY!
SHE'S TRYING TO ESCAPE!
KA KLIK
GO, ANNA!

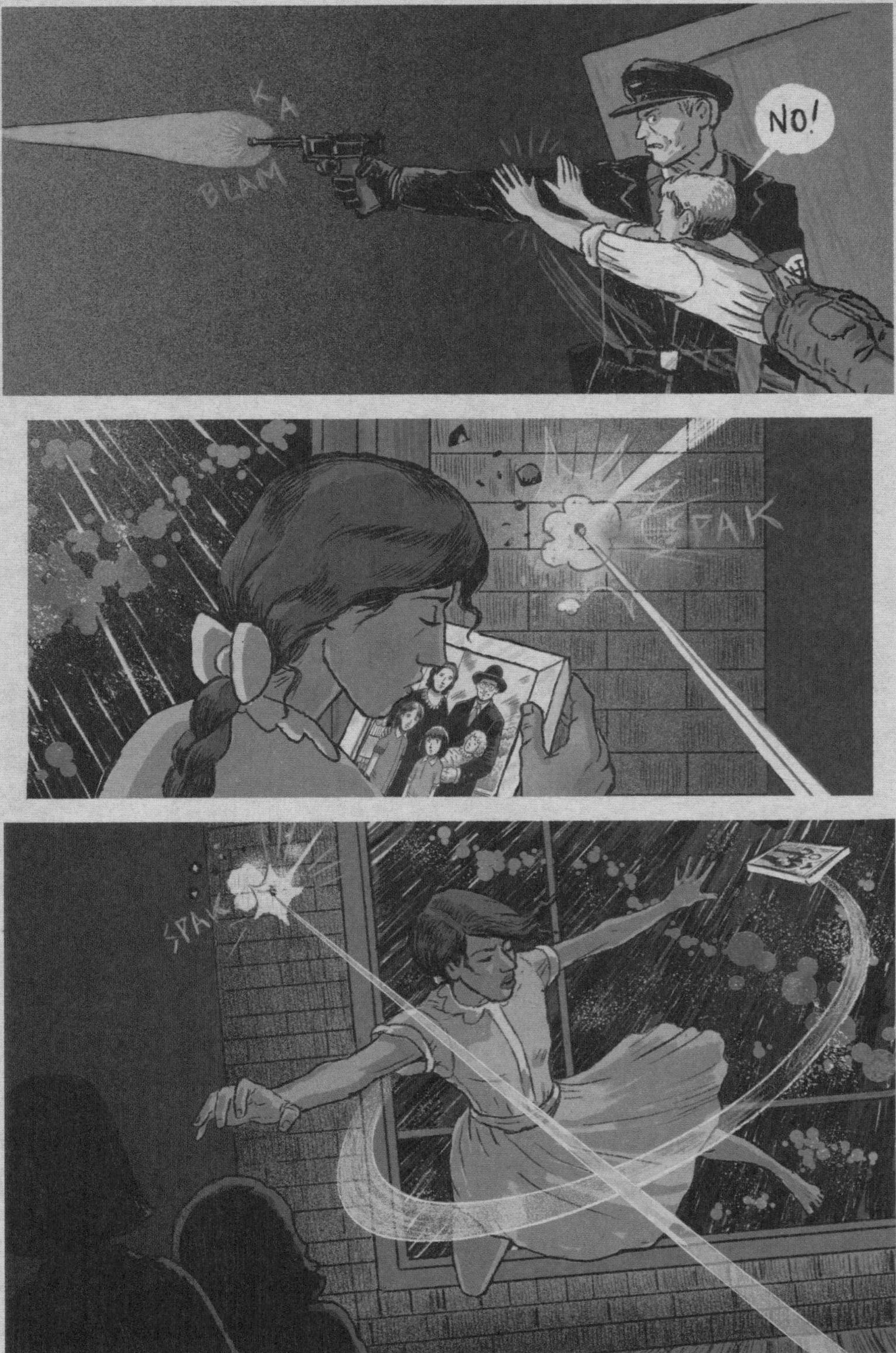
KA
BLAM
NO!
SPAK
SPAK

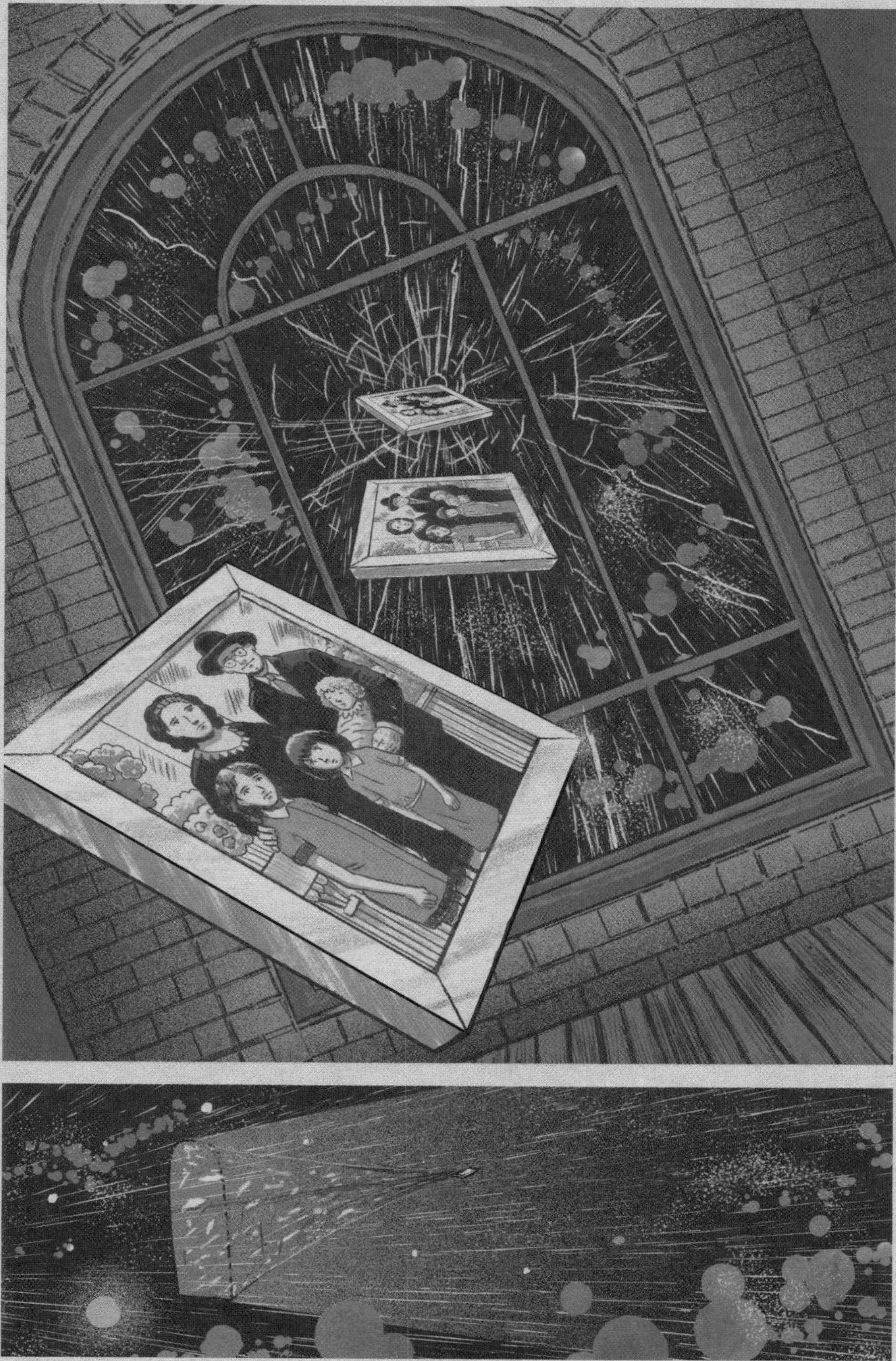

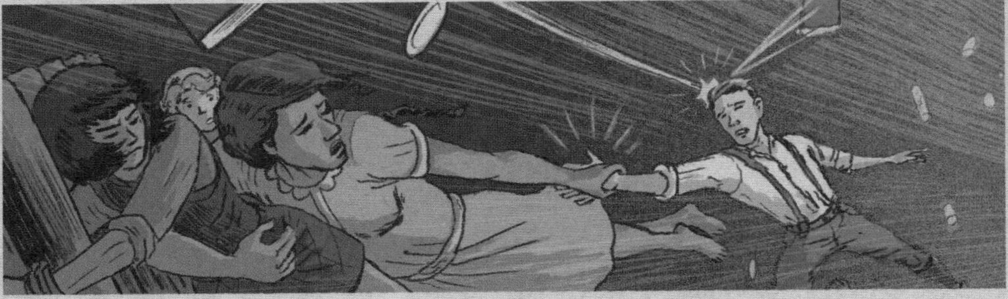

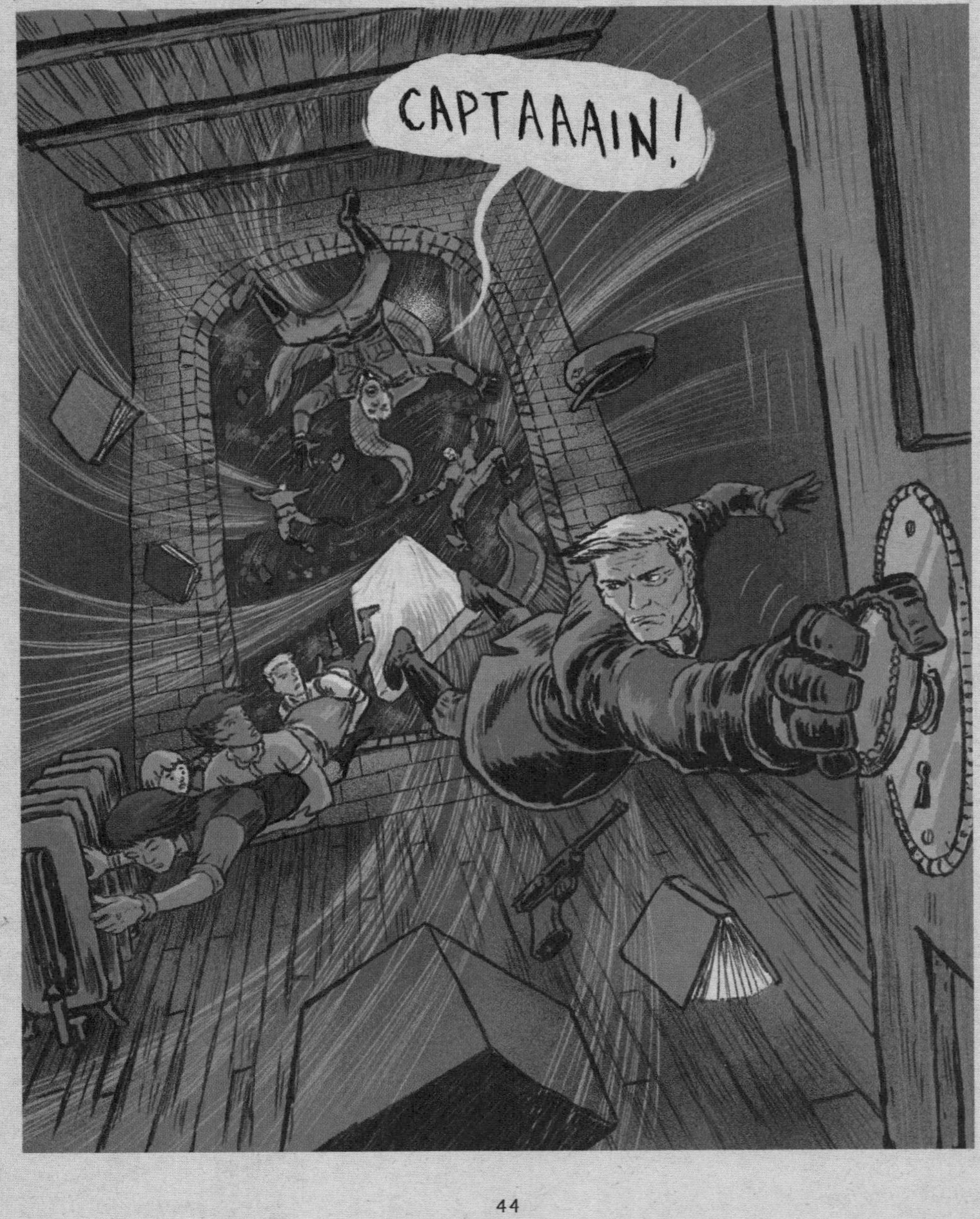
CAPTAAAIN!

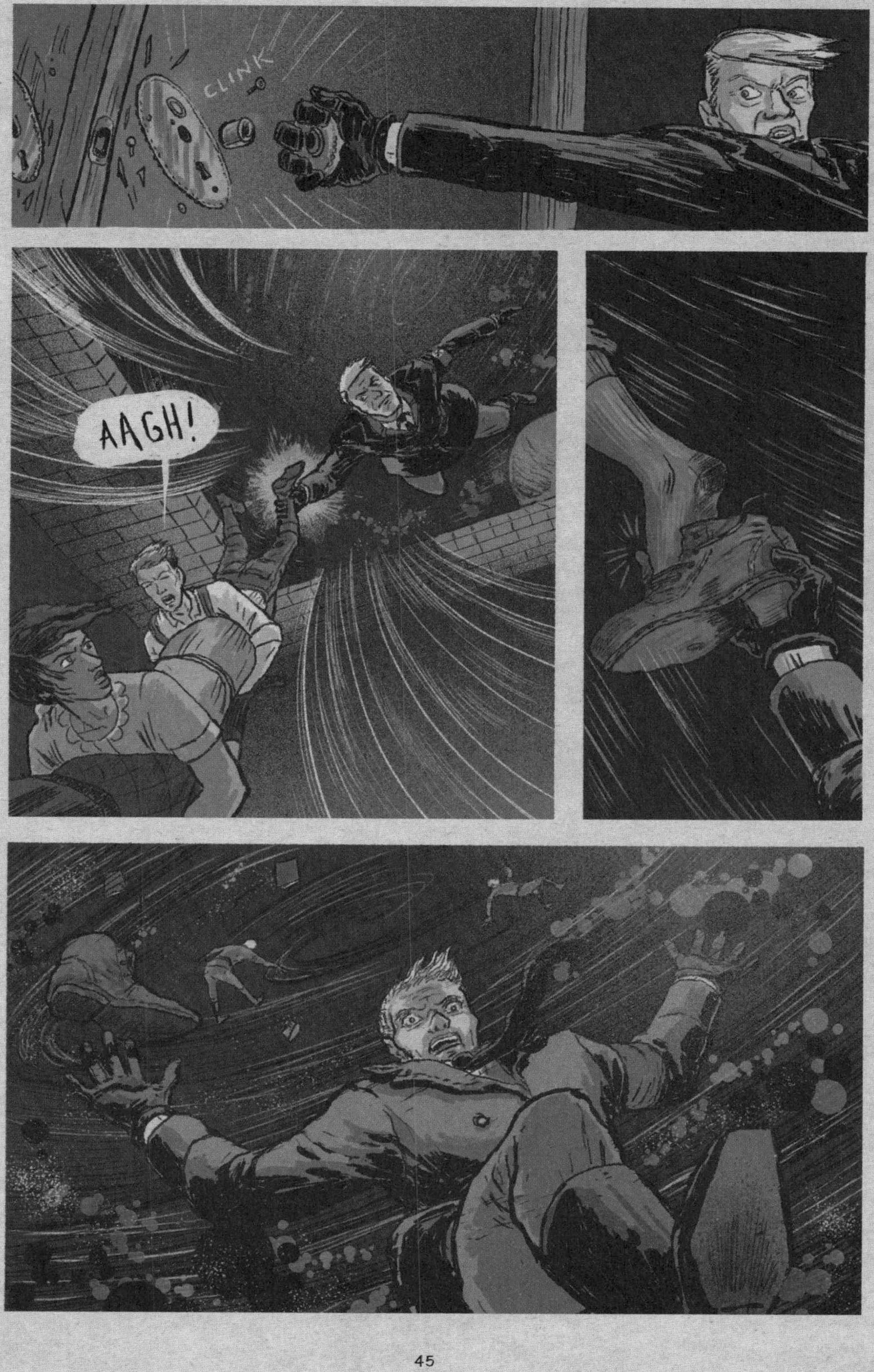
CLINK
AAGH!

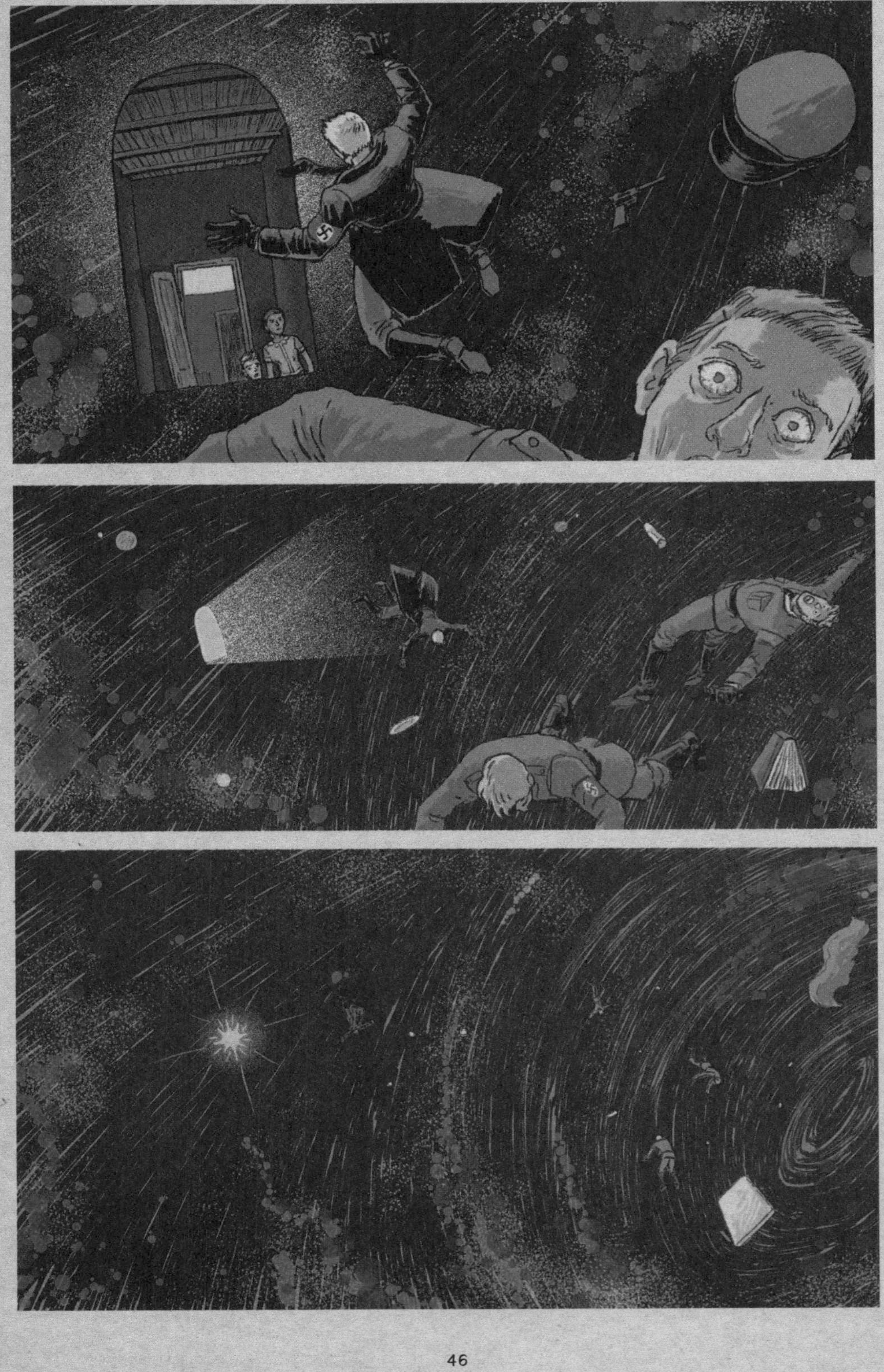

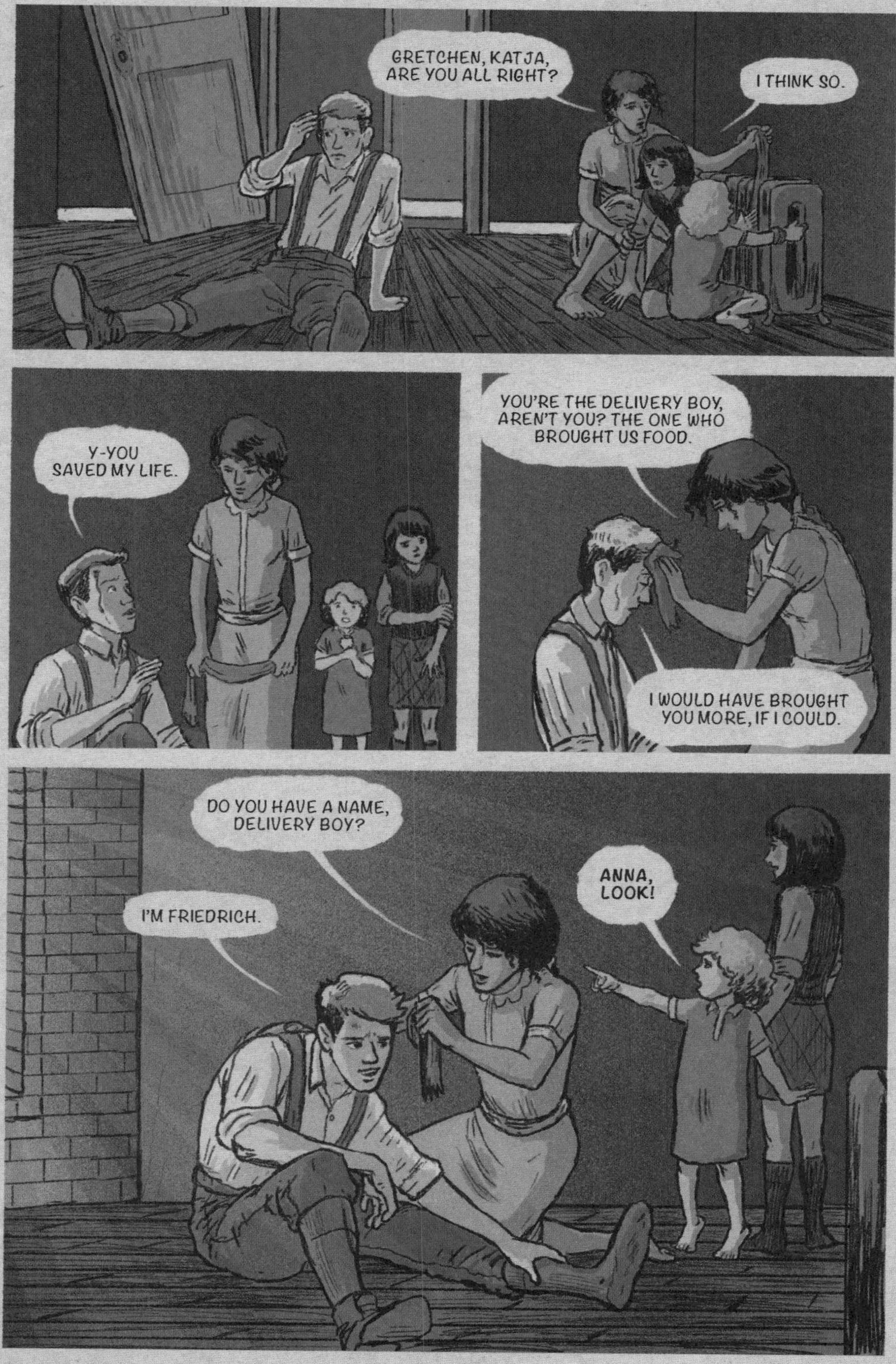
GRETCHEN, KATJA, ARE YOU ALL RIGHT?
I THINK SO.
Y-YOU SAVED MY LIFE.
YOU'RE THE DELIVERY BOY, AREN'T YOU? THE ONE WHO BROUGHT US FOOD.
I WOULD HAVE BROUGHT YOU MORE, IF I COULD.
DO YOU HAVE A NAME, DELIVERY BOY?
I'M FRIEDRICH.
ANNA, LOOK!

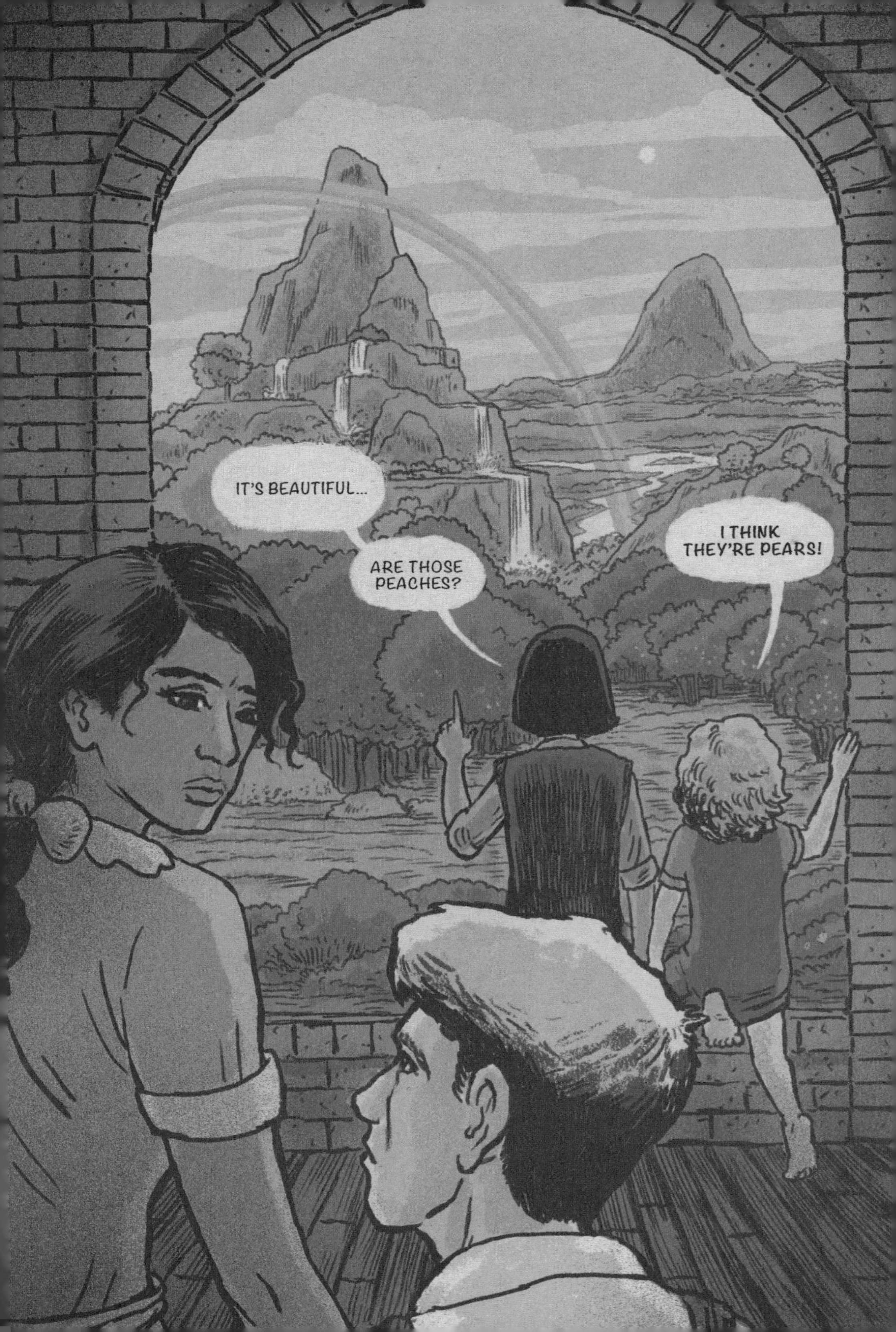
IT'S BEAUTIFUL...
ARE THOSE PEACHES?
I THINK THEY'RE PEARS!

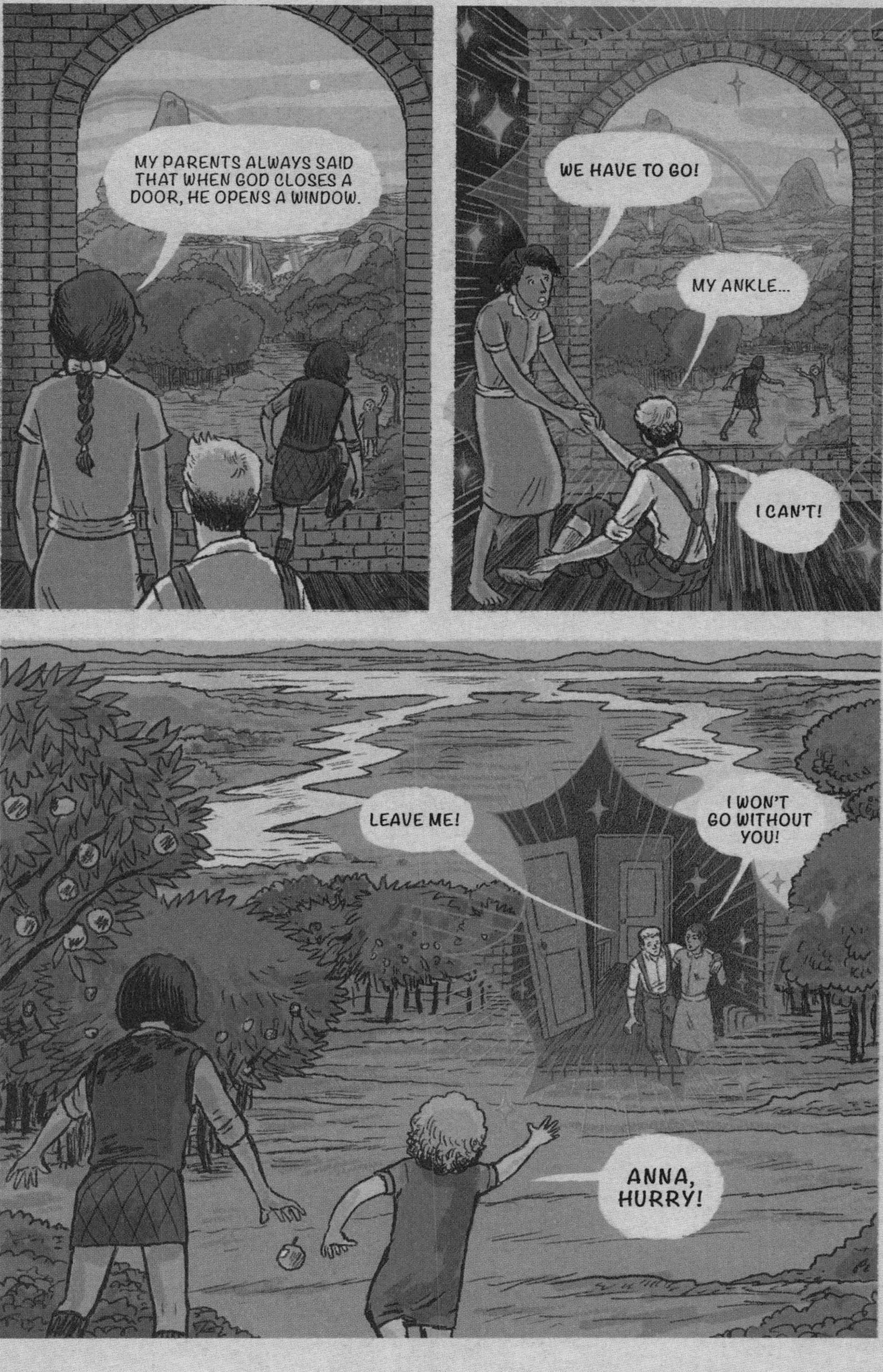
MY PARENTS ALWAYS SAID THAT WHEN GOD CLOSES A DOOR, HE OPENS A WINDOW.
WE HAVE TO GO!
MY ANKLE...
I CAN'T!
LEAVE ME!
I WON'T GO WITHOUT YOU!
ANNA, HURRY!

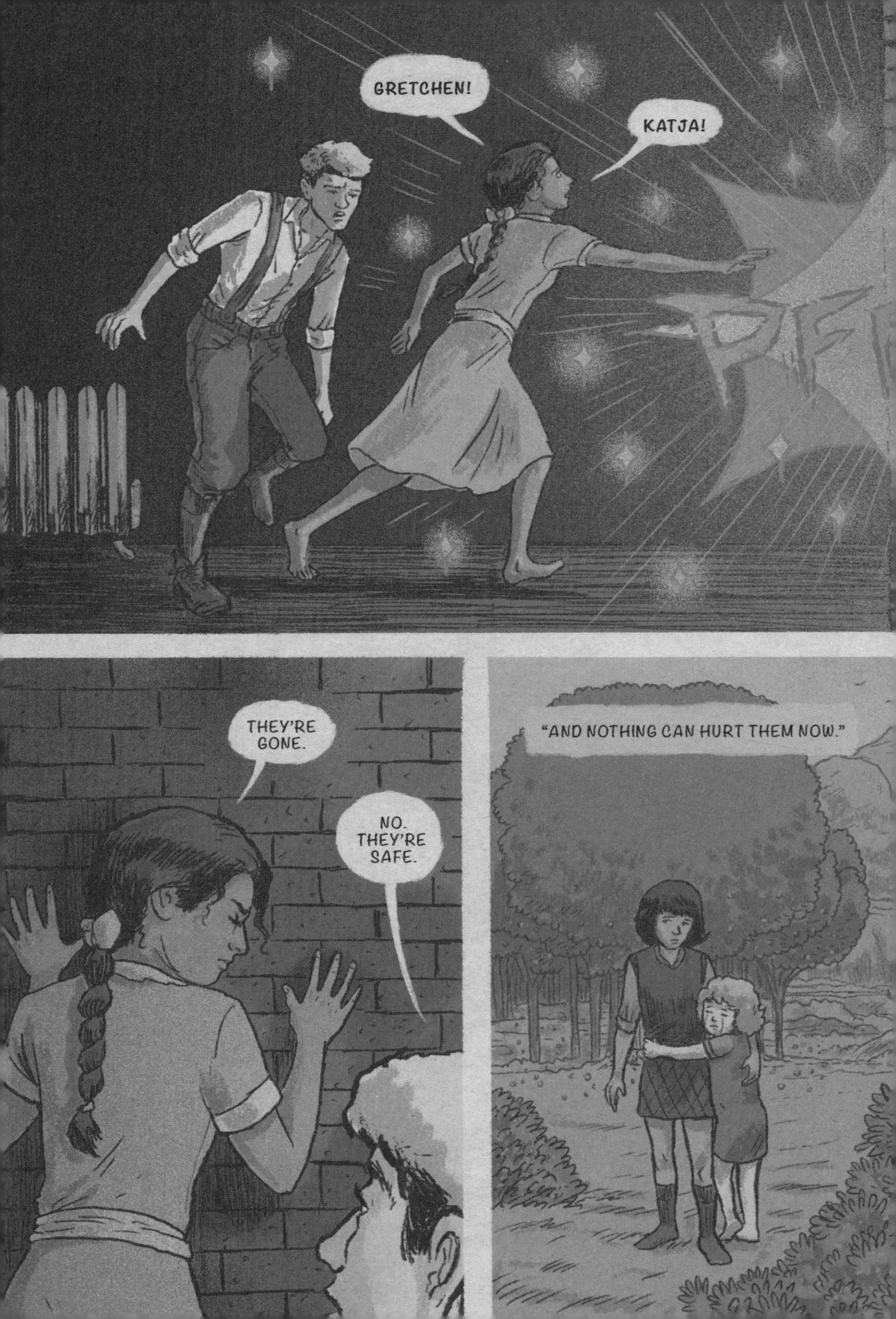
GRETCHEN!
KATJA!
THEY'RE GONE.
NO. THEY'RE SAFE.
"AND NOTHING CAN HURT THEM NOW."

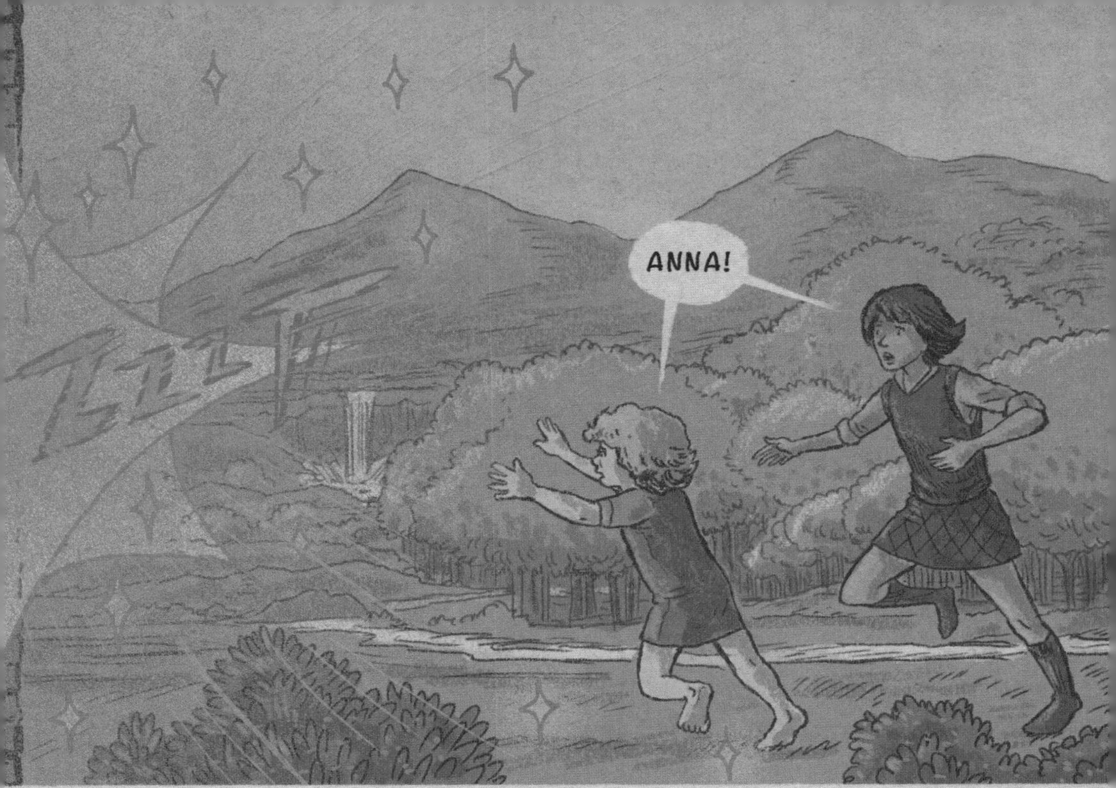
ANNA!

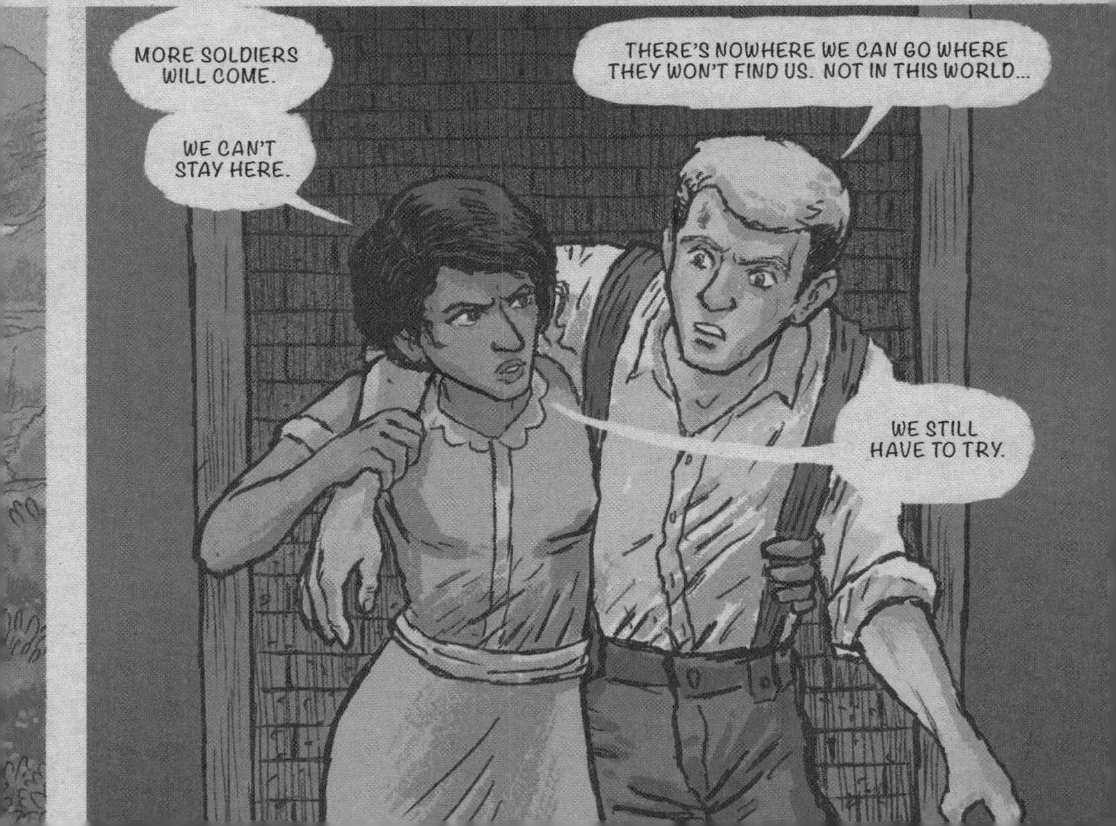
MORE SOLDIERS WILL COME.
WE CAN'T STAY HERE.
THERE'S NOWHERE WE CAN GO WHERE THEY WON'T FIND US. NOT IN THIS WORLD...
WE STILL HAVE TO TRY.

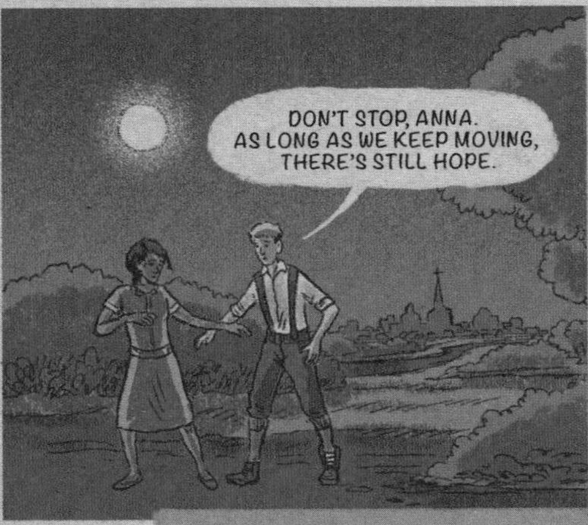
DON'T STOP, ANNA.
AS LONG AS WE KEEP MOVING,
THERE'S STILL HOPE.

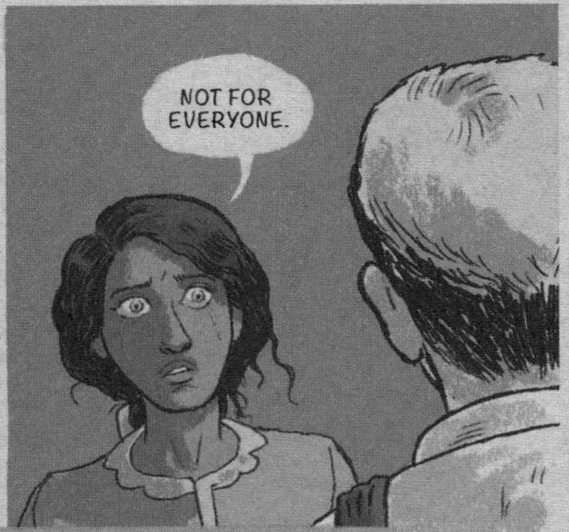
NOT FOR
EVERYONE.

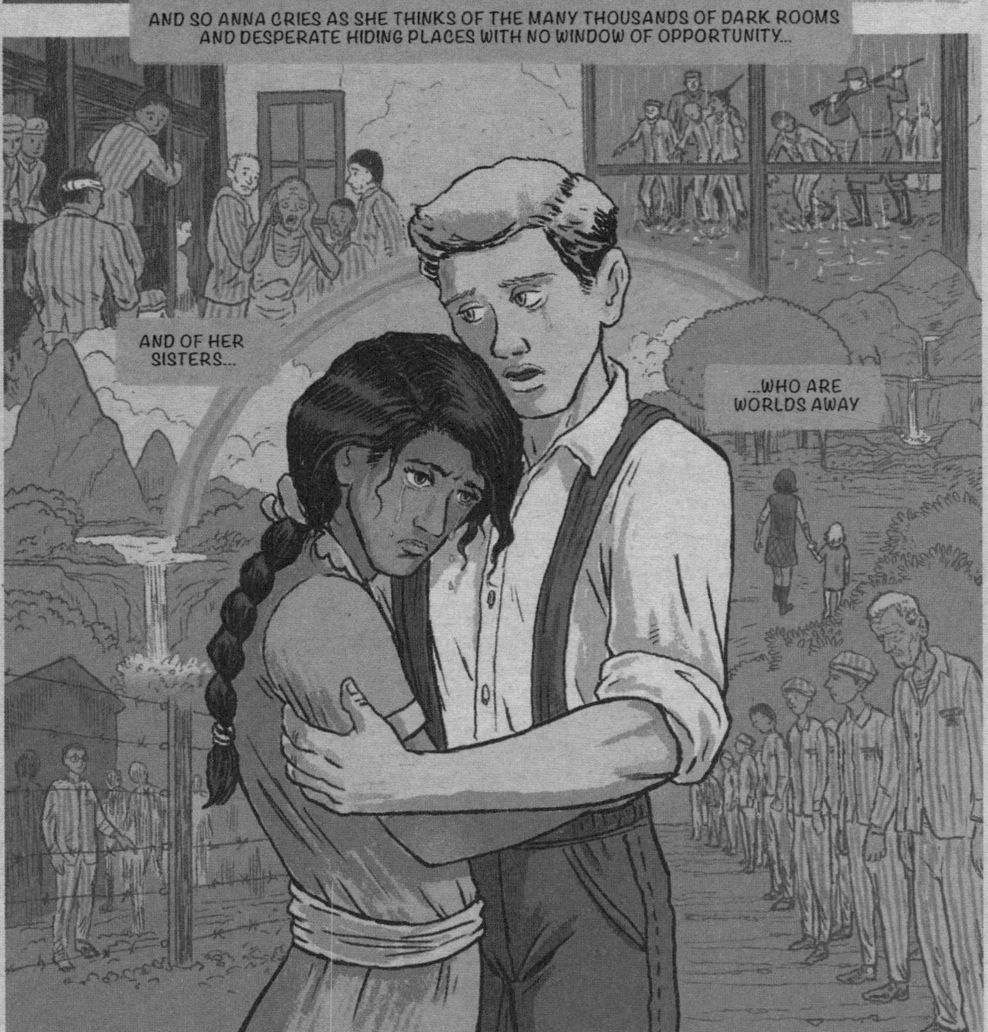
AND SO ANNA CRIES AS SHE THINKS OF THE MANY THOUSANDS OF DARK ROOMS
AND DESPERATE HIDING PLACES WITH NO WINDOW OF OPPORTUNITY...
AND OF HER
SISTERS...
...WHO ARE
WORLDS AWAY

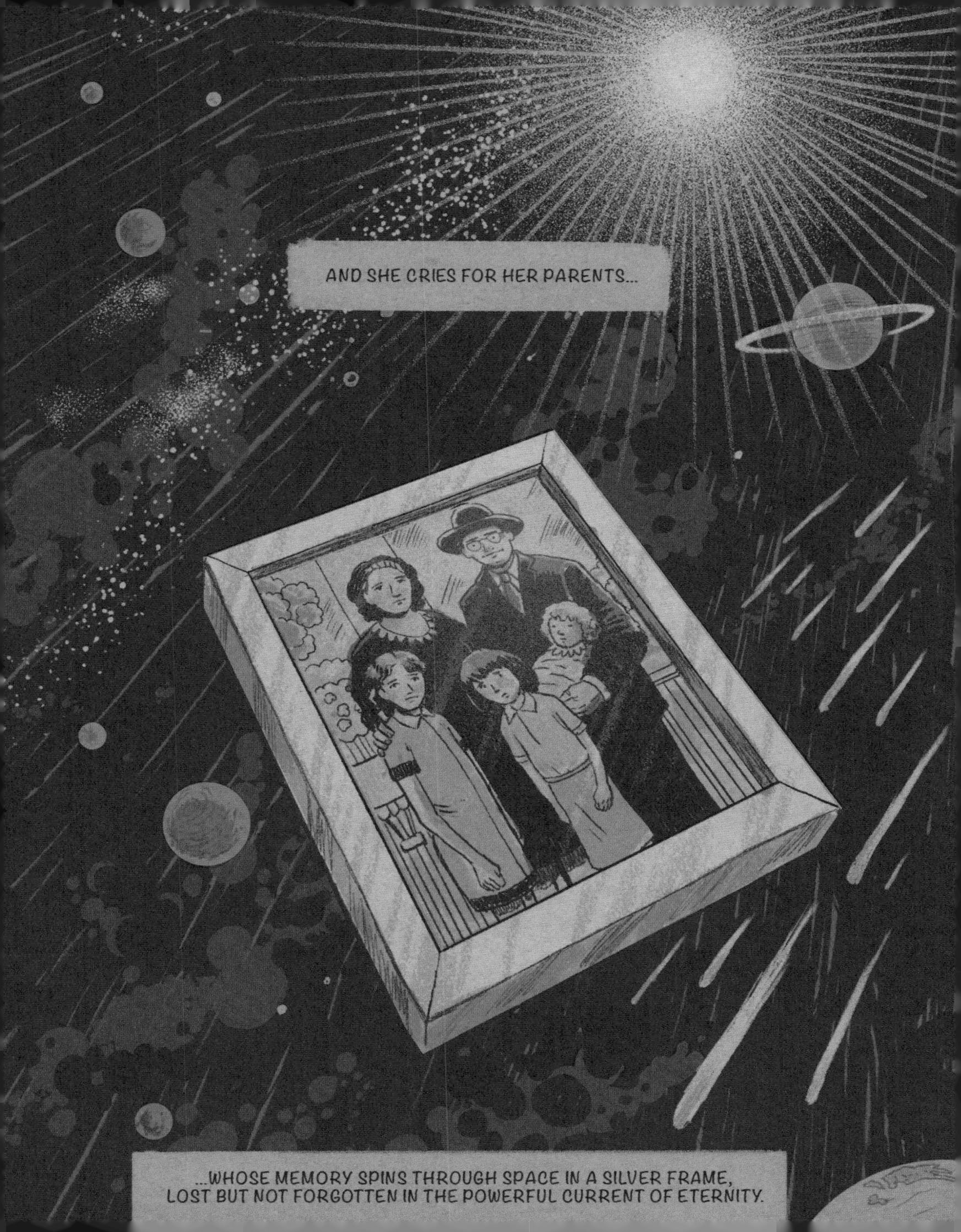
AND SHE CRIES FOR HER PARENTS...
...WHOSE MEMORY SPINS THROUGH SPACE IN A SILVER FRAME, LOST BUT NOT FORGOTTEN IN THE POWERFUL CURRENT OF ETERNITY.

Israel's Holocaust memorial, Yad Vashem, has recognized 24,356 individuals as "Righteous among the Nations" — in other words, non-Jewish people who took great risks to save Jews during the Holocaust, including hiding Jews in their homes. This included people of many cultures and nationalities, such as Feng-Shan Ho, the Chinese Consul-General in Vienna, who issued Chinese visas to Jews to help them escape.

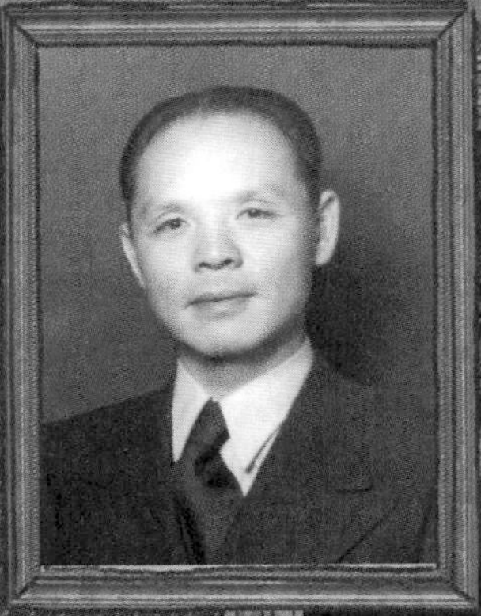

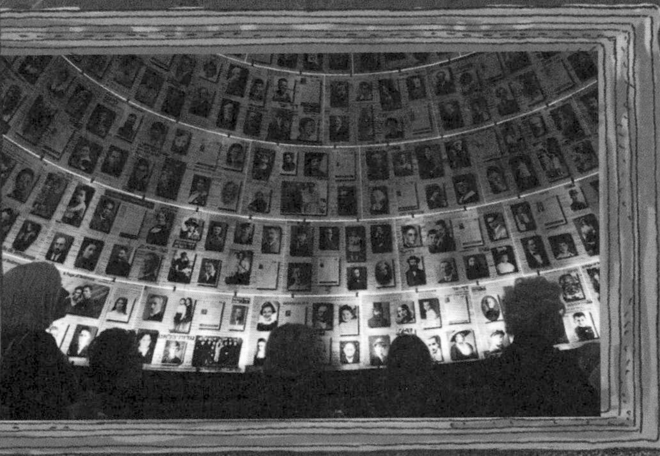

In many places, providing shelter to Jews in occupied Europe was punishable by death.

Those few brave people who did help Jews were motivated by religious and moral principles, and their compassion.

The best-known story is that of Anne Frank, who was hidden for 25 months before she was captured by the Gestapo. The home in Amsterdam where she was hidden is now a museum and has been visited by millions.

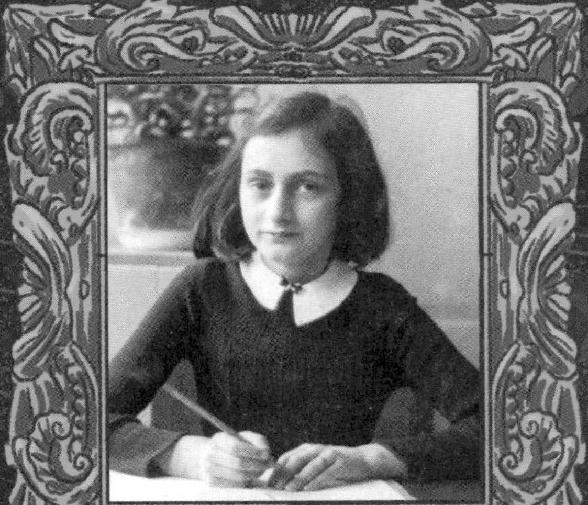

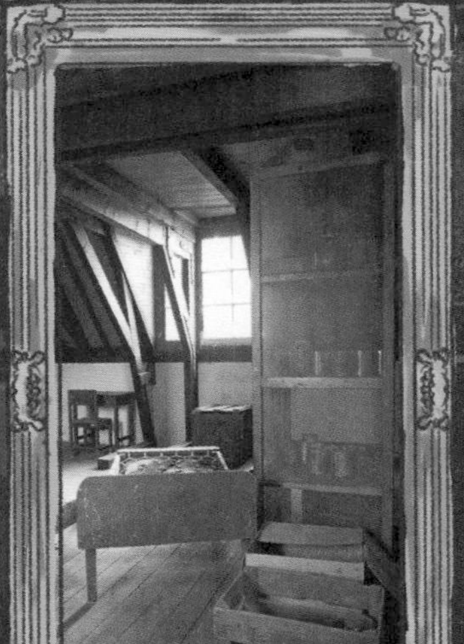

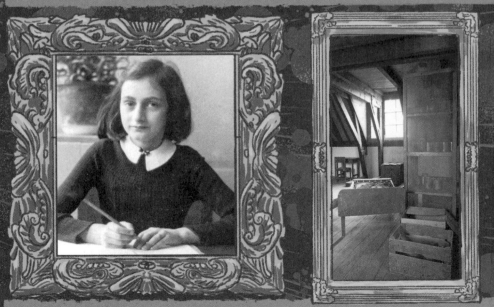

More Jews were killed in Poland than in any other nation — but more were also rescued in Poland than anywhere else. The rescue figures are estimated to be tens of thousands — perhaps as many as 150,000. In Poland, 6,532 men and women have been recognized as rescuers.

The residents of Le Chambon-sur-Lignon, a Protestant village in southern France, helped thousands of refugees, most of them Jews, escape Nazi persecution between 1940 and 1944. Refugees, including many children, were hidden in homes and also in Catholic convents and monasteries. Resident of Le Chambon-sur-Lignon also helped smuggle refugees to Switzerland.

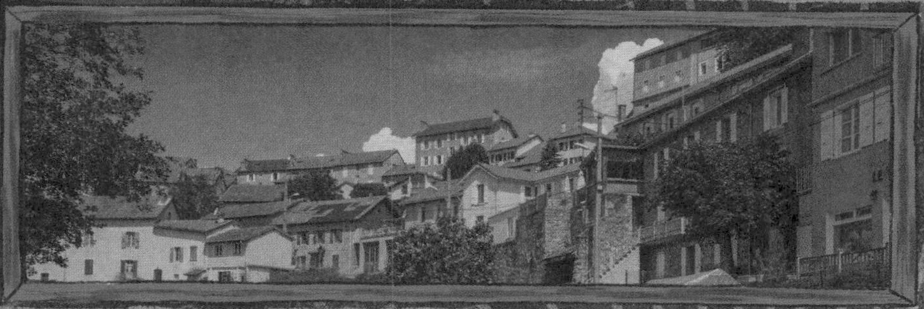

Eight-year-old Paul Deneberg and eleven-year-old Mirko Deneberg were hidden by Klara Baić, a single mother, after they were smuggled by their uncle out of a Hungarian ghetto. Biać even prepared a hiding place in her neighbor's yard in case her house were to have been raided.

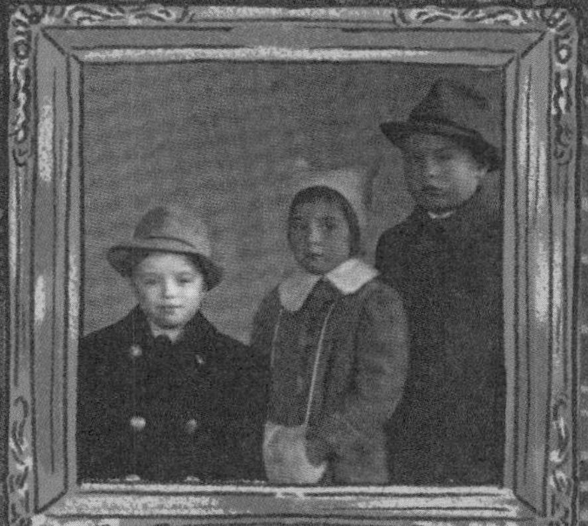

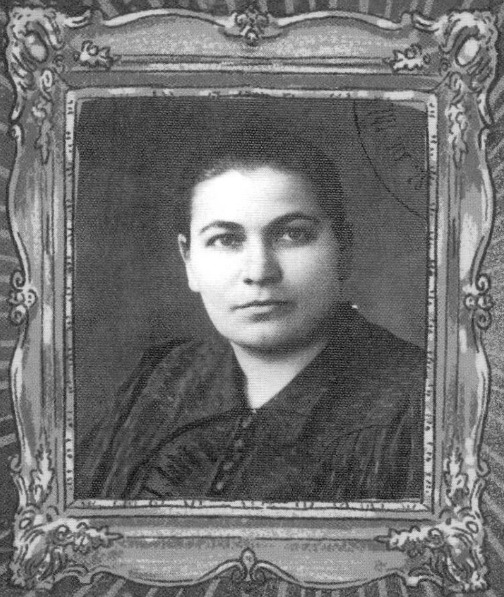

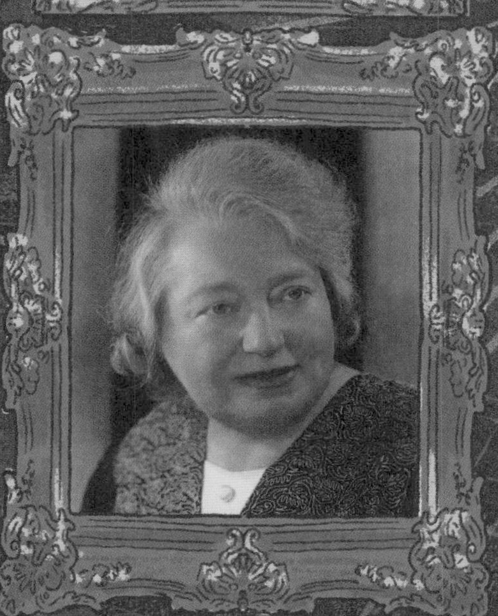

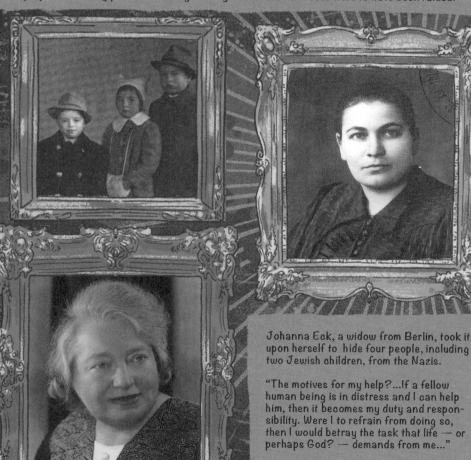

Johanna Eck, a widow from Berlin, took it upon herself to hide four people, including two Jewish children, from the Nazis.

"The motives for my help?...If a fellow human being is in distress and I can help him, then it becomes my duty and responsibility. Were I to refrain from doing so, then I would betray the task that life — or perhaps God? — demands from me..."

— Johanna Eck

ב

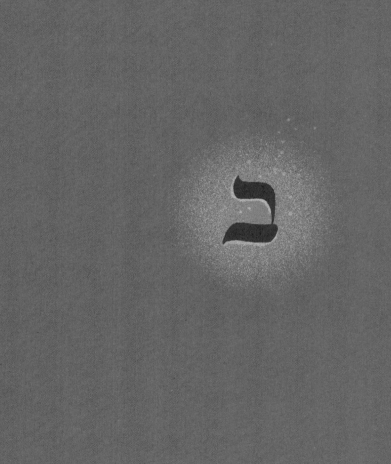

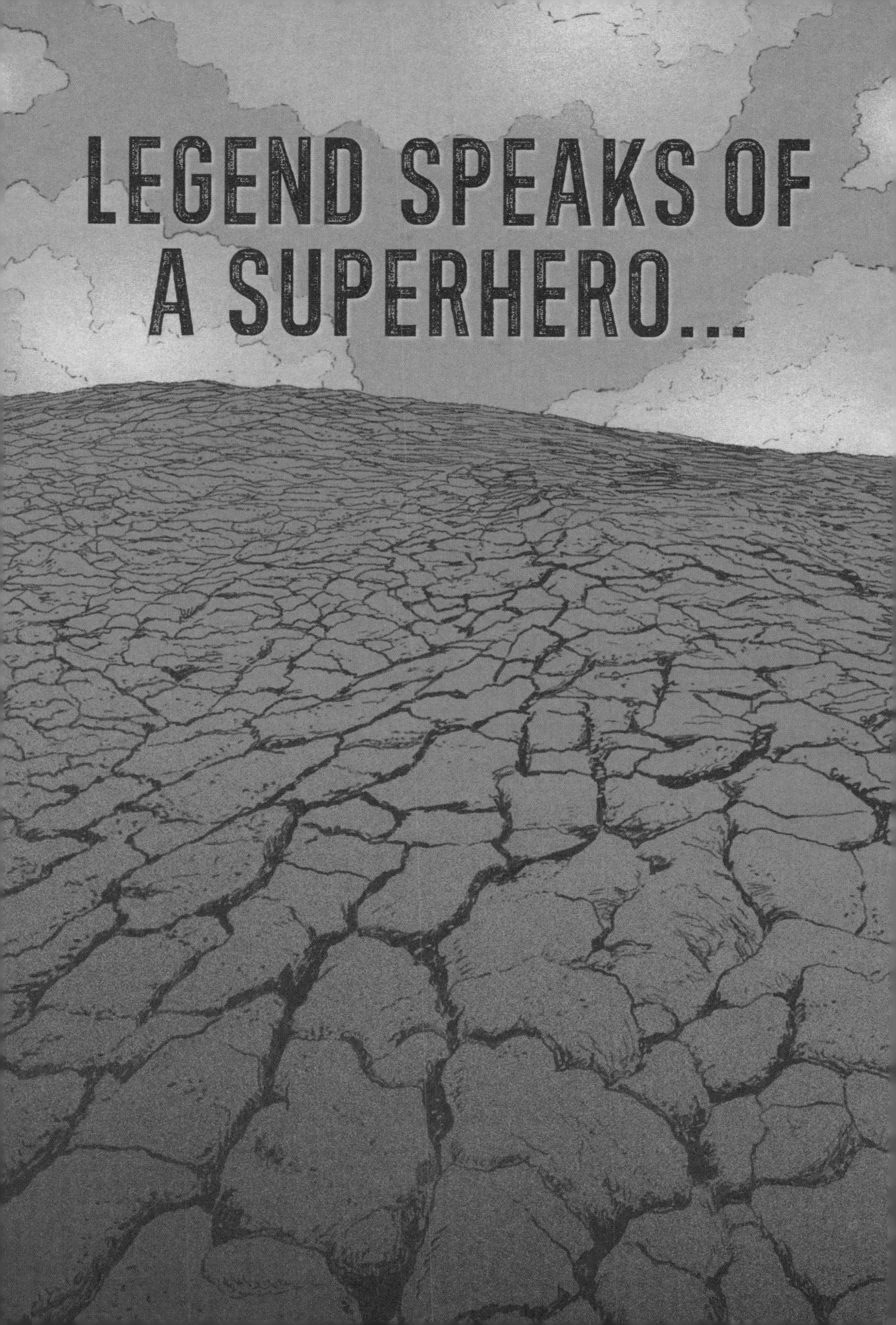
LEGEND SPEAKS OF
A SUPERHERO...

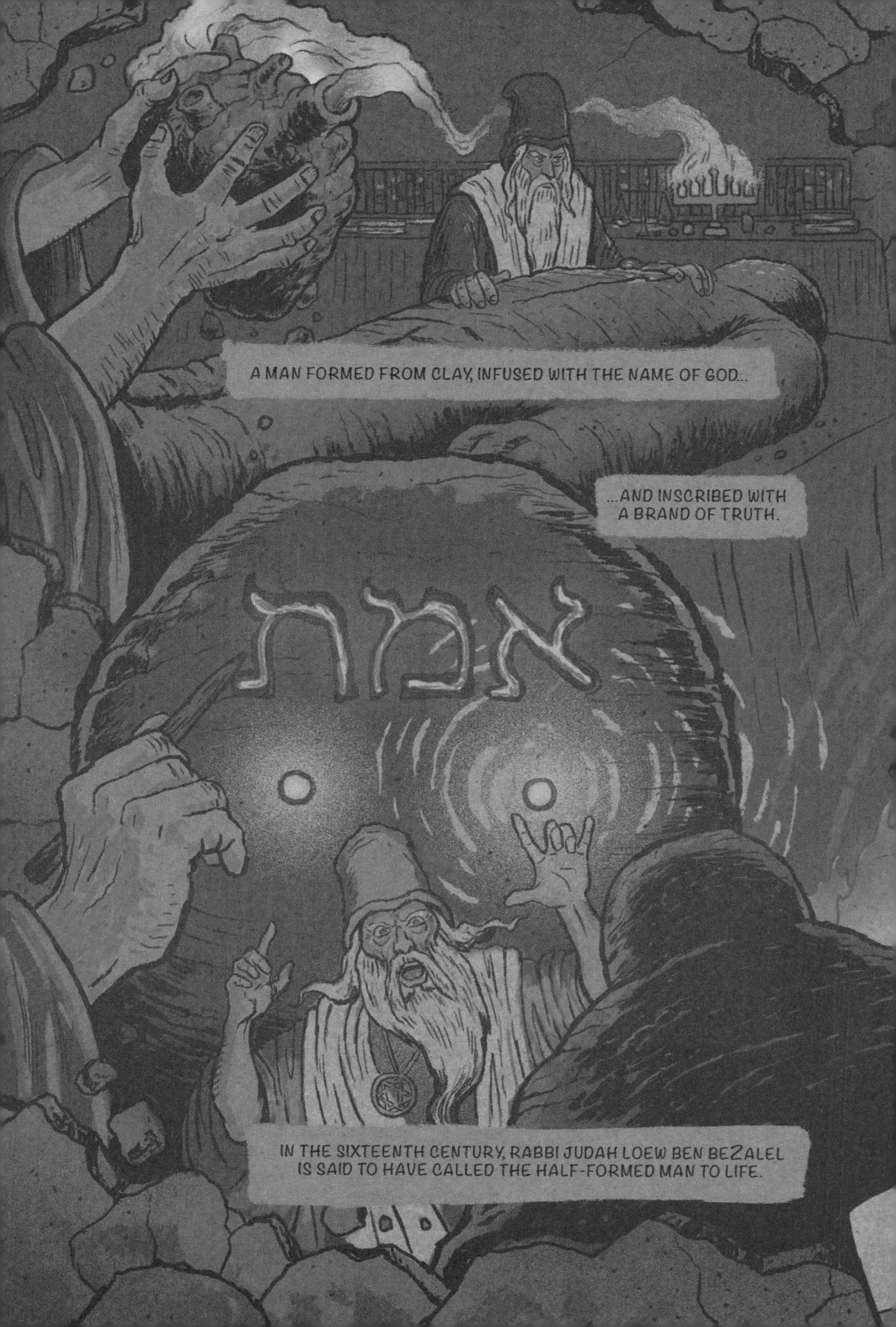
A MAN FORMED FROM CLAY, INFUSED WITH THE NAME OF GOD...
...AND INSCRIBED WITH A BRAND OF TRUTH.
אמת
IN THE SIXTEENTH CENTURY, RABBI JUDAH LOEW BEN BEZALEL IS SAID TO HAVE CALLED THE HALF-FORMED MAN TO LIFE.

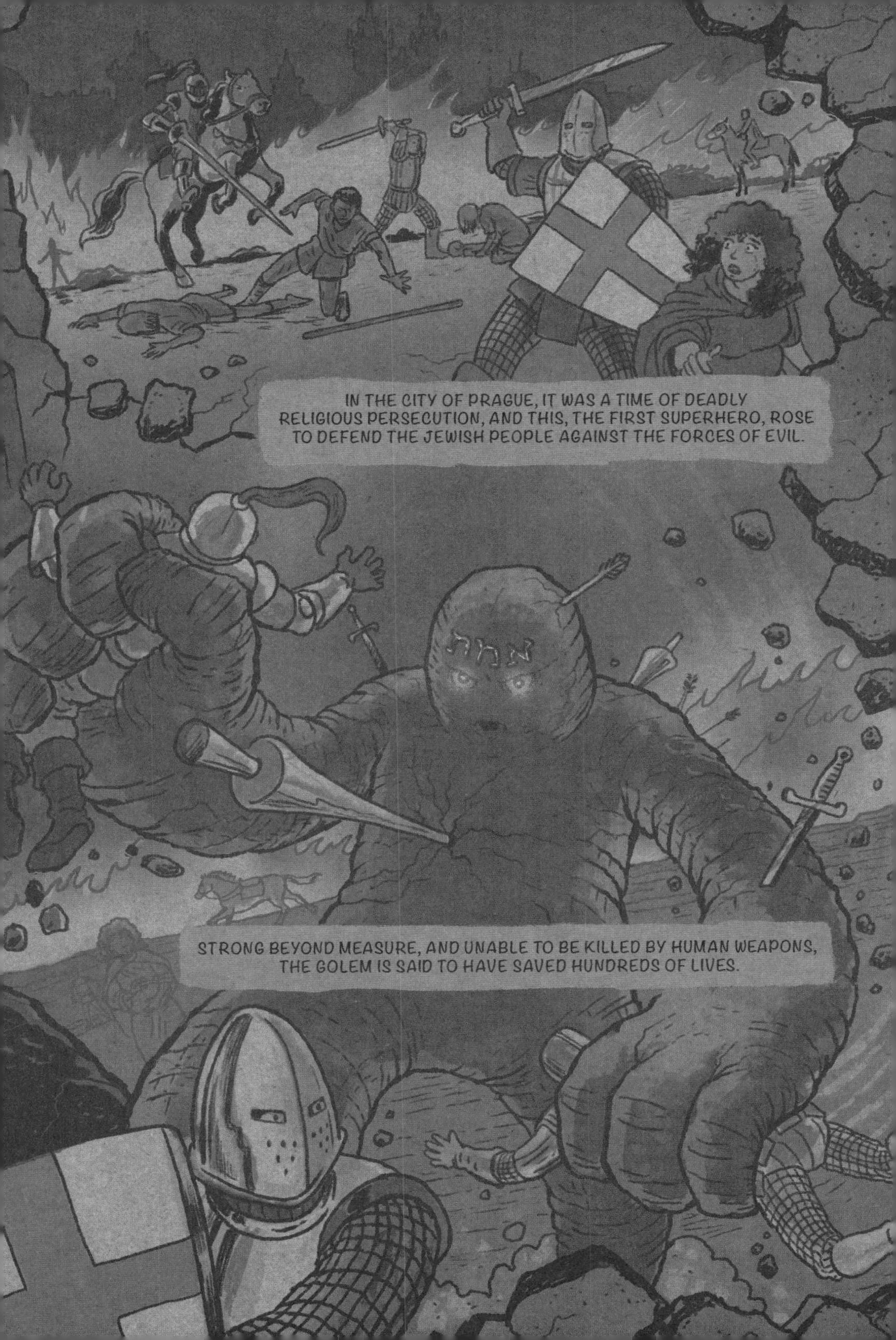
IN THE CITY OF PRAGUE, IT WAS A TIME OF DEADLY RELIGIOUS PERSECUTION, AND THIS, THE FIRST SUPERHERO, ROSE TO DEFEND THE JEWISH PEOPLE AGAINST THE FORCES OF EVIL.
אמת
STRONG BEYOND MEASURE, AND UNABLE TO BE KILLED BY HUMAN WEAPONS, THE GOLEM IS SAID TO HAVE SAVED HUNDREDS OF LIVES.

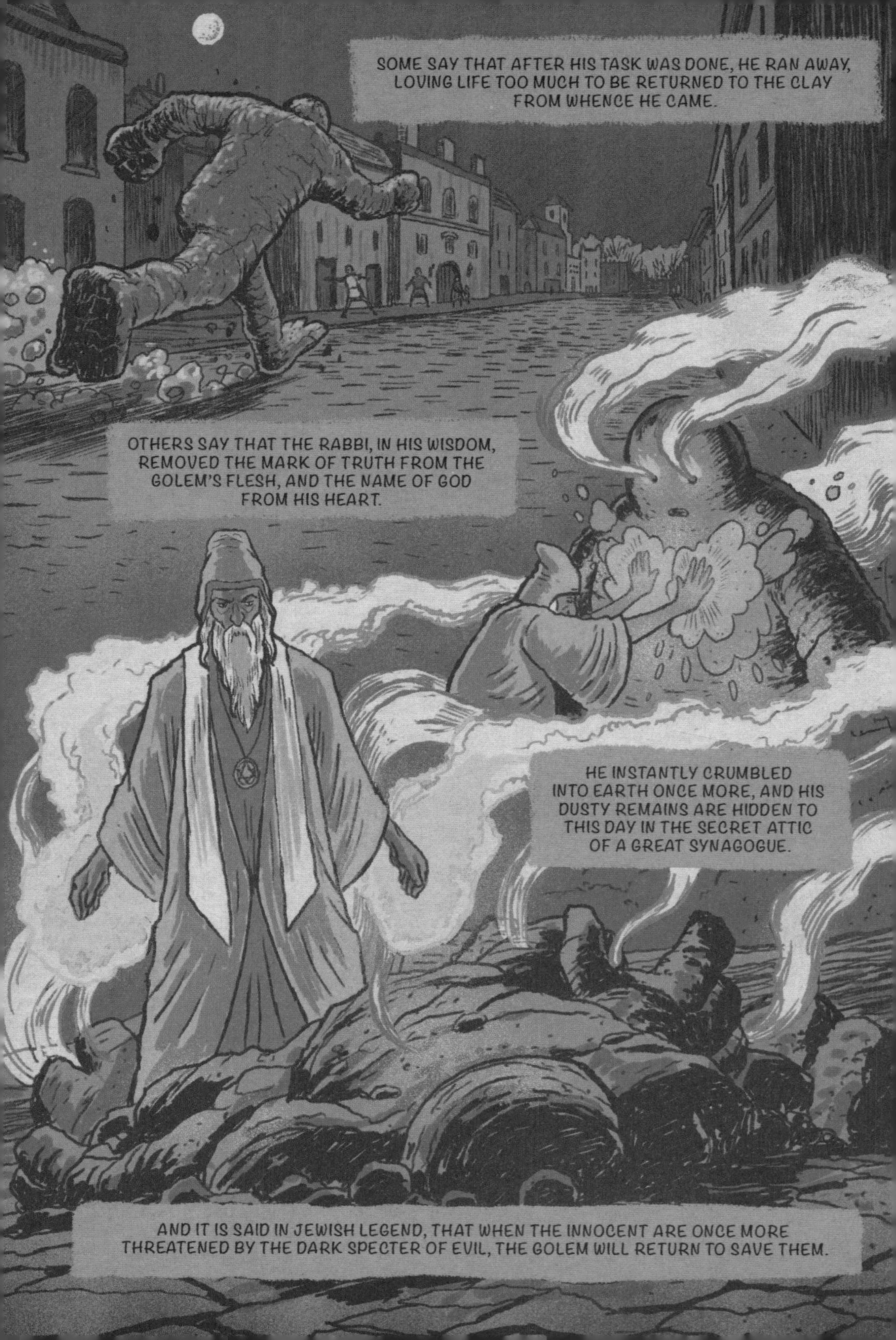
SOME SAY THAT AFTER HIS TASK WAS DONE, HE RAN AWAY, LOVING LIFE TOO MUCH TO BE RETURNED TO THE CLAY FROM WHENCE HE CAME.
OTHERS SAY THAT THE RABBI, IN HIS WISDOM, REMOVED THE MARK OF TRUTH FROM THE GOLEM'S FLESH, AND THE NAME OF GOD FROM HIS HEART.
HE INSTANTLY CRUMBLED INTO EARTH ONCE MORE, AND HIS DUSTY REMAINS ARE HIDDEN TO THIS DAY IN THE SECRET ATTIC OF A GREAT SYNAGOGUE.
AND IT IS SAID IN JEWISH LEGEND, THAT WHEN THE INNOCENT ARE ONCE MORE THREATENED BY THE DARK SPECTER OF EVIL, THE GOLEM WILL RETURN TO SAVE THEM.

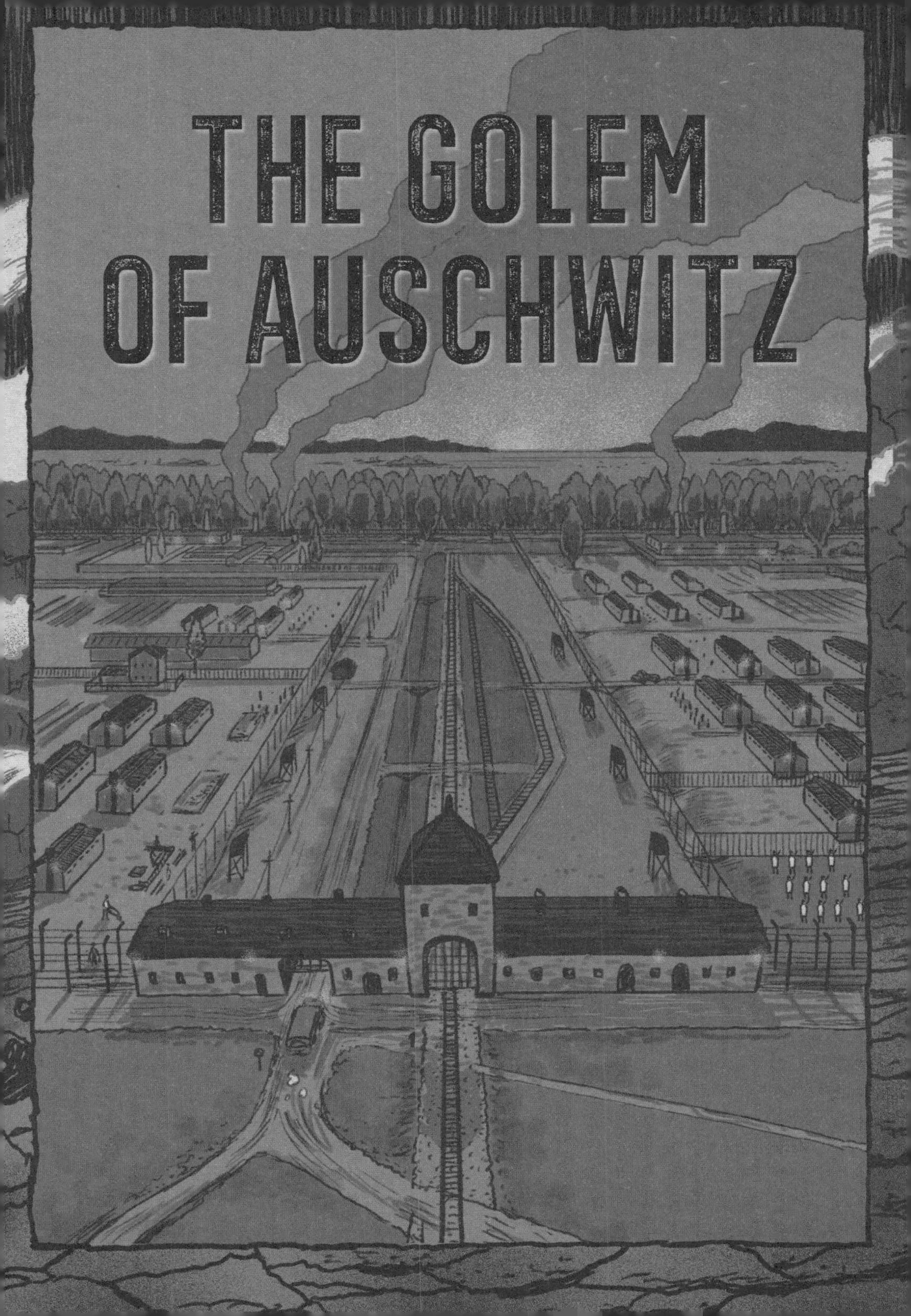
THE GOLEM
OF AUSCHWITZ

DUVID KNEW THE STORY OF THE GOLEM — ALTHOUGH HE COULDN'T REMEMBER WHEN HE HAD HEARD IT. A BLOW TO THE HEAD HAD CHALLENGED HIS THOUGHTS AND MEMORIES. HE HAD BEEN CRUSHED SO COMPLETELY BY THE IRON BOOT OF THE THIRD REICH, IT SEEMED NOTHING EXISTED FOR DUVID BUT THE CAMP.

HEY, DUMMY! GET BACK TO WORK! DO YOU WANT TO GET US ALL KILLED?

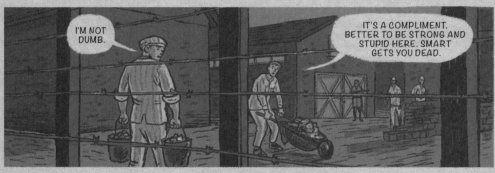

I'M NOT DUMB.

IT'S A COMPLIMENT. BETTER TO BE STRONG AND STUPID HERE. SMART GETS YOU DEAD.

DON'T MIND HIM, DUVID. MOSES WAS SLOW OF TONGUE, AND LOOK WHAT HE ACCOMPLISHED!

THANK YOU, RABBI.

YOU MUSTN'T CALL ME THAT WHERE THEY CAN HEAR, OKAY?

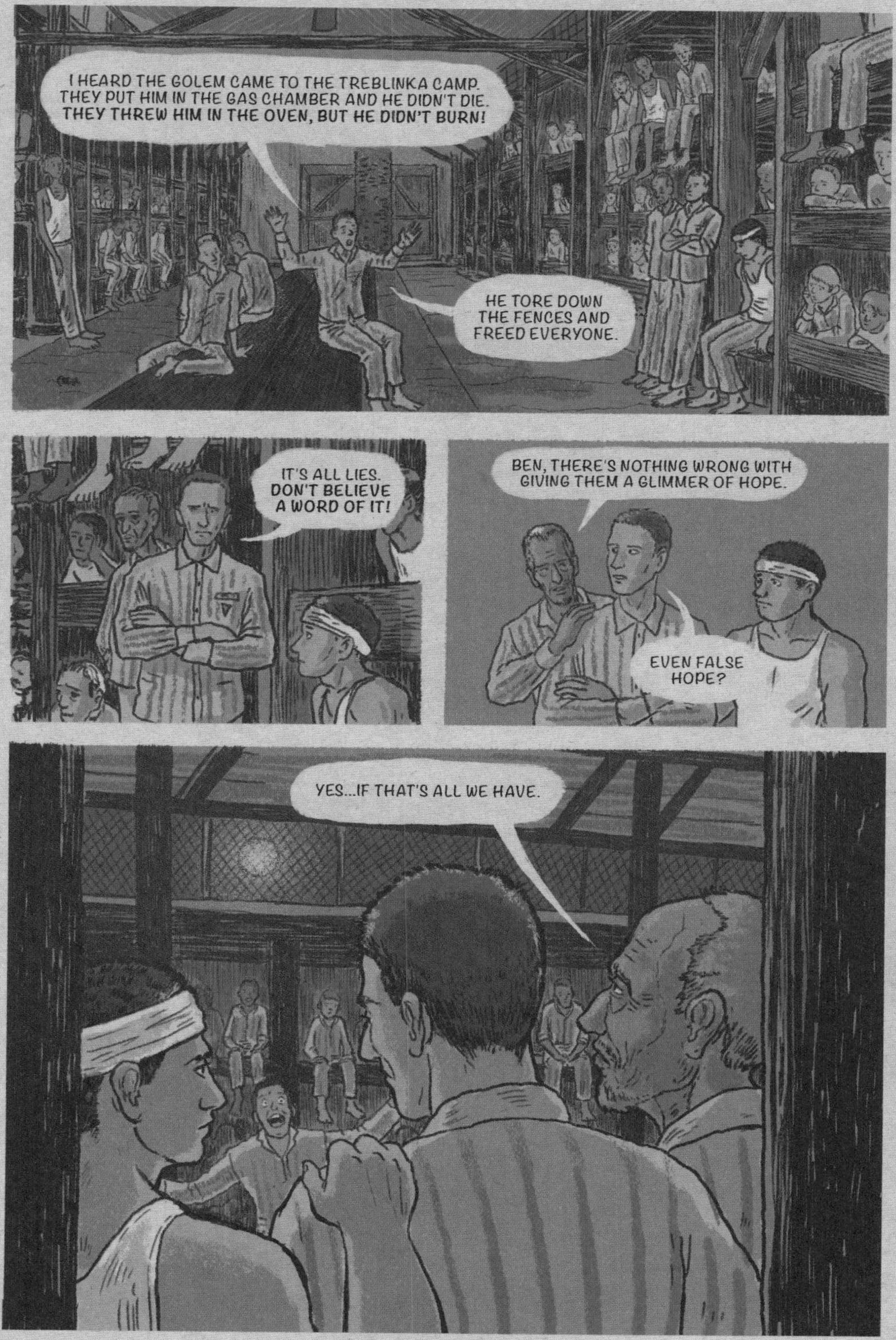
I HEARD THE GOLEM CAME TO THE TREBLINKA CAMP. THEY PUT HIM IN THE GAS CHAMBER AND HE DIDN'T DIE. THEY THREW HIM IN THE OVEN, BUT HE DIDN'T BURN!
HE TORE DOWN THE FENCES AND FREED EVERYONE.
IT'S ALL LIES. DON'T BELIEVE A WORD OF IT!
BEN, THERE'S NOTHING WRONG WITH GIVING THEM A GLIMMER OF HOPE.
EVEN FALSE HOPE?
YES...IF THAT'S ALL WE HAVE.

THEIR LIVES HAD BECOME FENCES, AND GUARDS, AND MORE FENCES. THE DAYS WERE MARKED BY AN ENDLESS STREAM OF TRAINS ARRIVING, PACKED TO BURSTING.

MOST WOULD MAKE THE TWO-MILE TREK FROM AUSCHWITZ TO THE NEW AND MUCH LARGER CAMP BEHIND IT. BIRKENAU.

THOSE WHO MARCHED TO BIRKENAU NEVER CAME BACK AGAIN. AND THE AWFUL STENCH OF SMOKE IN THE AIR WAS A CONSTANT REMINDER OF THEIR FATE.

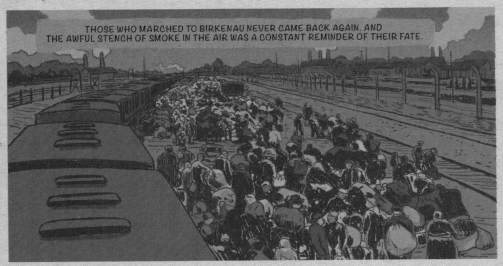

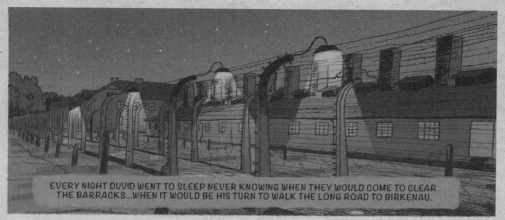

EVERY NIGHT DUVID WENT TO SLEEP NEVER KNOWING WHEN THEY WOULD COME TO CLEAR THE BARRACKS...WHEN IT WOULD BE HIS TURN TO WALK THE LONG ROAD TO BIRKENAU.

DO YOU BELIEVE IN THE GOLEM, RABBI?

I DO, DUVID. DO YOU SEE THE DIFFERENCE HE'S ALREADY MAKING?

THEY SLEEP EASIER, EVEN IN THIS UNTHINKABLE PLACE.

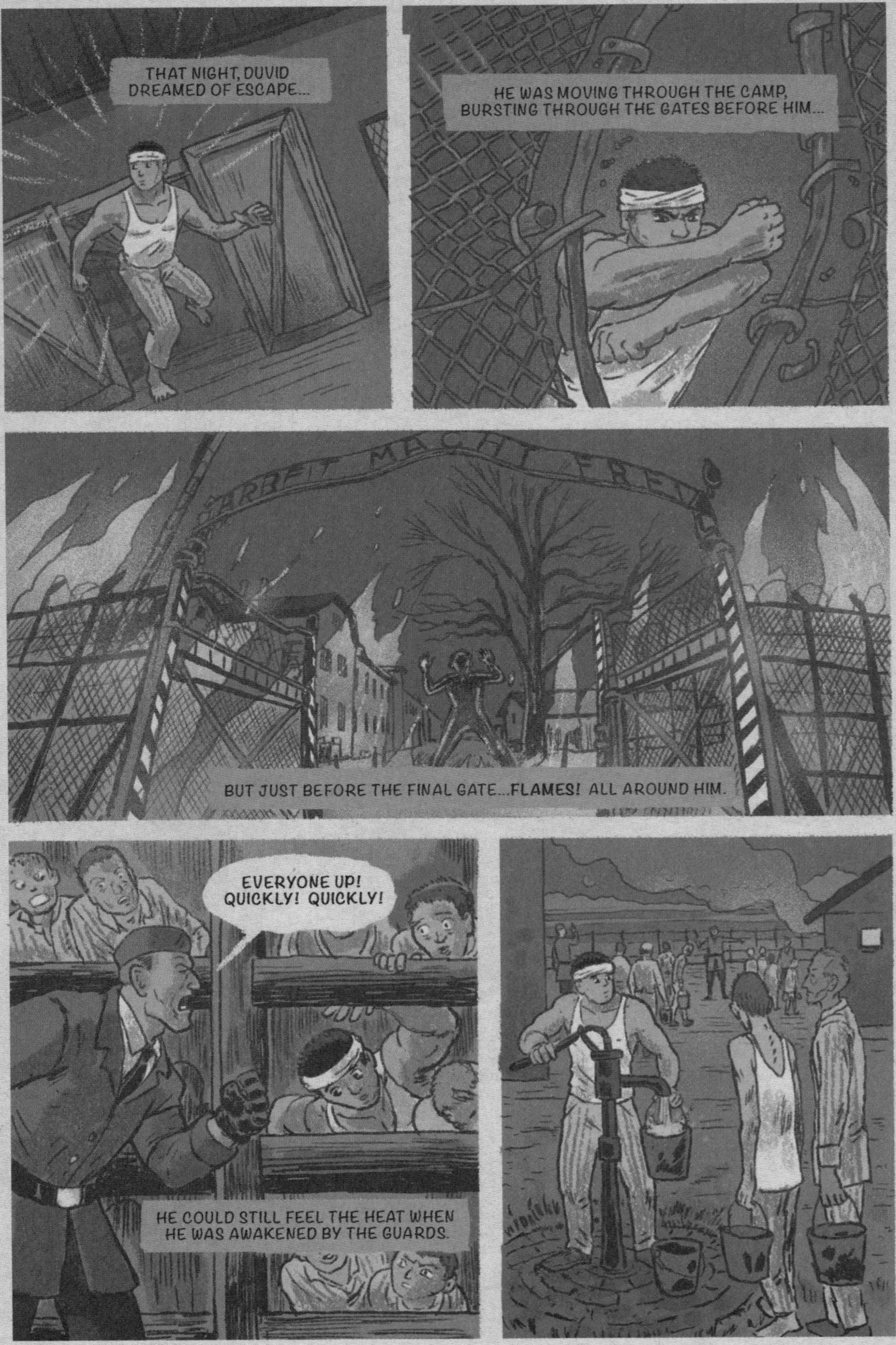
THAT NIGHT, DUVID DREAMED OF ESCAPE...
HE WAS MOVING THROUGH THE CAMP, BURSTING THROUGH THE GATES BEFORE HIM...
BUT JUST BEFORE THE FINAL GATE...FLAMES! ALL AROUND HIM.
EVERYONE UP! QUICKLY! QUICKLY!
HE COULD STILL FEEL THE HEAT WHEN HE WAS AWAKENED BY THE GUARDS.

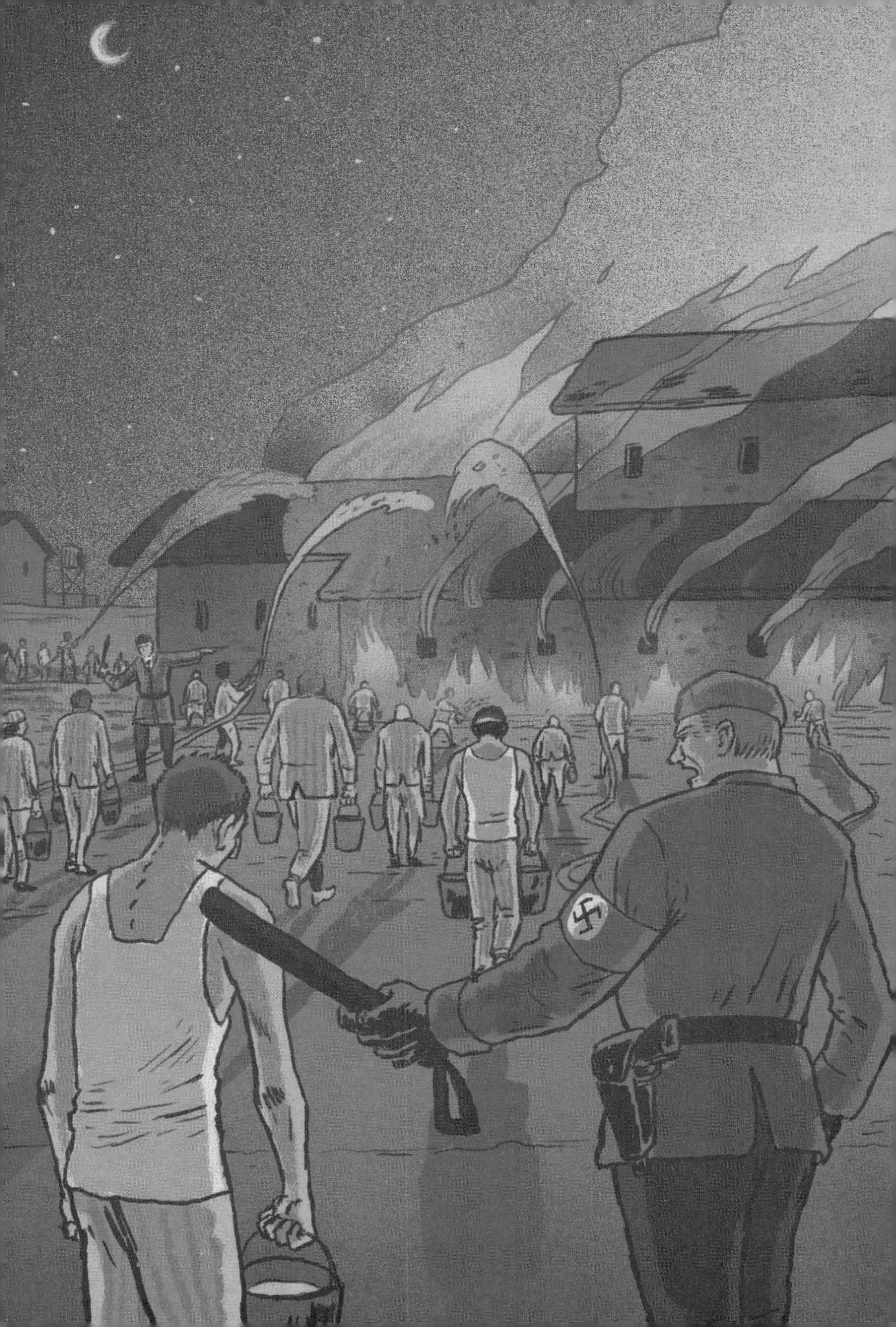

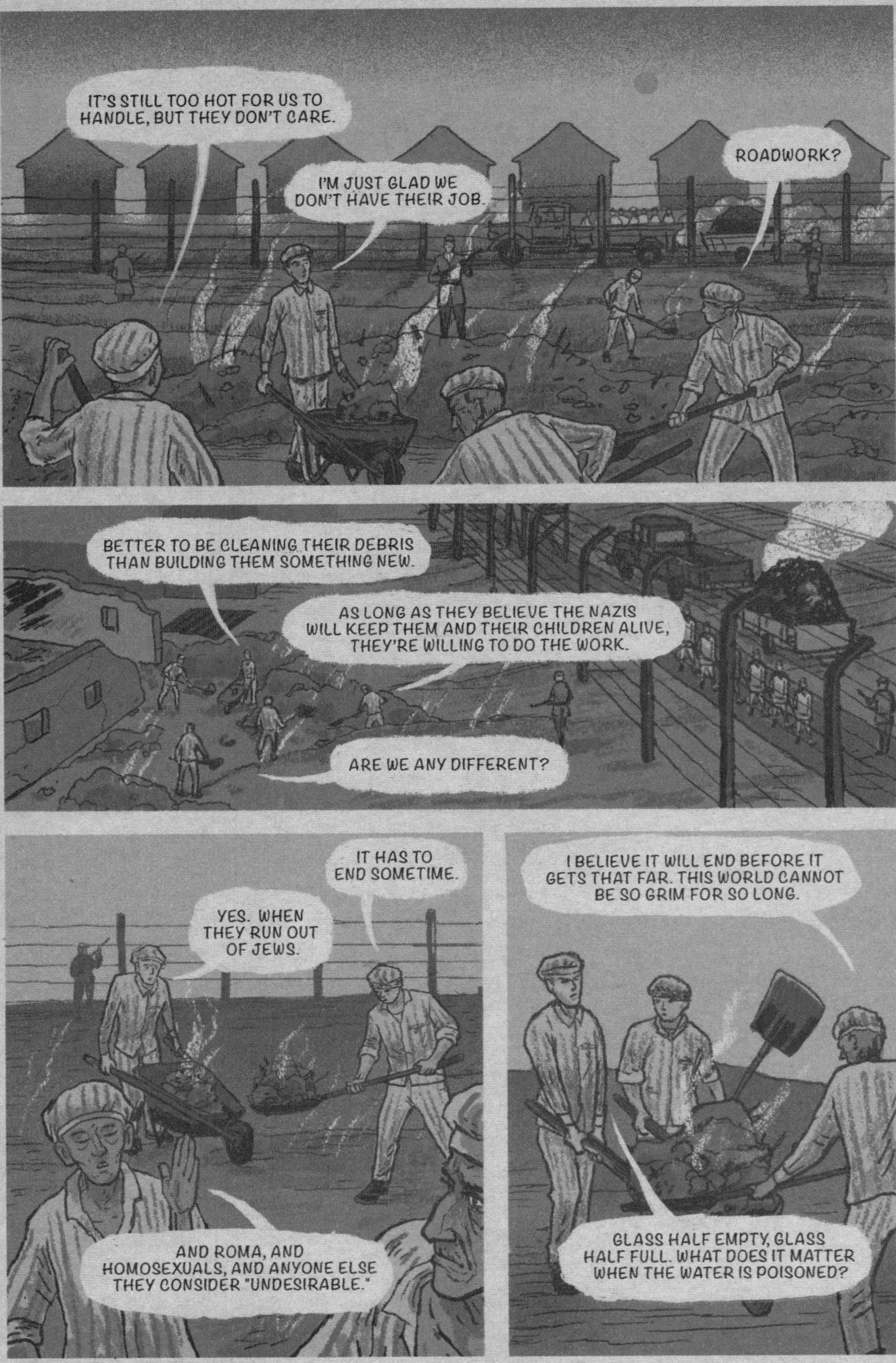
IT'S STILL TOO HOT FOR US TO HANDLE, BUT THEY DON'T CARE.
I'M JUST GLAD WE DON'T HAVE THEIR JOB.
ROADWORK?
BETTER TO BE CLEANING THEIR DEBRIS THAN BUILDING THEM SOMETHING NEW.
AS LONG AS THEY BELIEVE THE NAZIS WILL KEEP THEM AND THEIR CHILDREN ALIVE, THEY'RE WILLING TO DO THE WORK.
ARE WE ANY DIFFERENT?
IT HAS TO END SOMETIME.
YES. WHEN THEY RUN OUT OF JEWS.
AND ROMA, AND HOMOSEXUALS, AND ANYONE ELSE THEY CONSIDER "UNDESIRABLE."
I BELIEVE IT WILL END BEFORE IT GETS THAT FAR. THIS WORLD CANNOT BE SO GRIM FOR SO LONG.
GLASS HALF EMPTY, GLASS HALF FULL. WHAT DOES IT MATTER WHEN THE WATER IS POISONED?

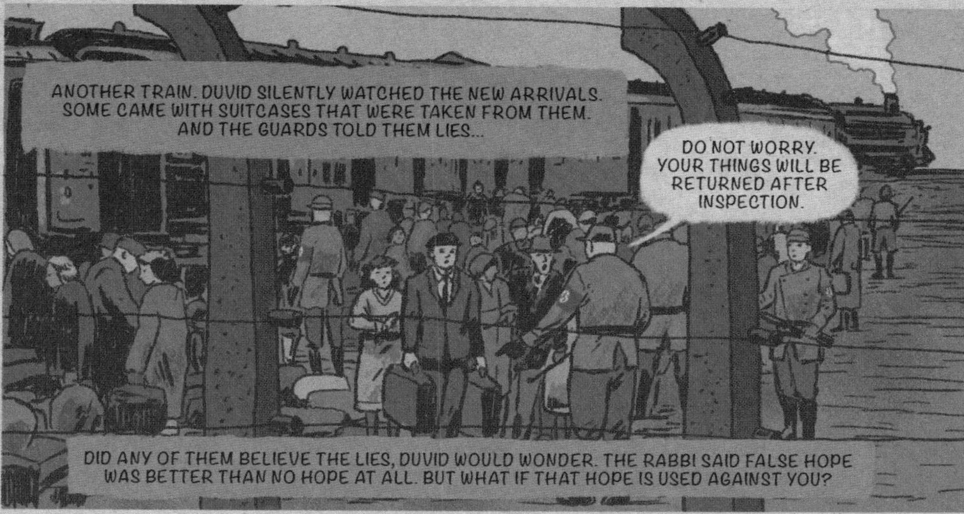
ANOTHER TRAIN. DUVID SILENTLY WATCHED THE NEW ARRIVALS. SOME CAME WITH SUITCASES THAT WERE TAKEN FROM THEM. AND THE GUARDS TOLD THEM LIES...
DO NOT WORRY. YOUR THINGS WILL BE RETURNED AFTER INSPECTION.
DID ANY OF THEM BELIEVE THE LIES, DUVID WOULD WONDER. THE RABBI SAID FALSE HOPE WAS BETTER THAN NO HOPE AT ALL. BUT WHAT IF THAT HOPE IS USED AGAINST YOU?

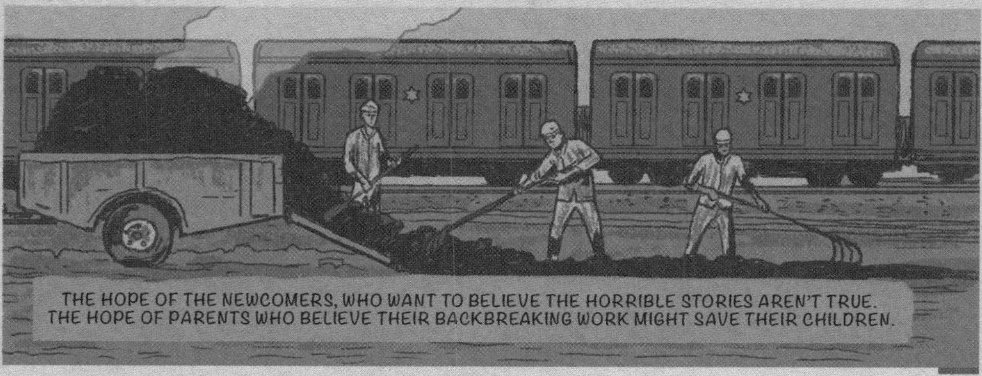
THE HOPE OF THE NEWCOMERS, WHO WANT TO BELIEVE THE HORRIBLE STORIES AREN'T TRUE. THE HOPE OF PARENTS WHO BELIEVE THEIR BACKBREAKING WORK MIGHT SAVE THEIR CHILDREN.

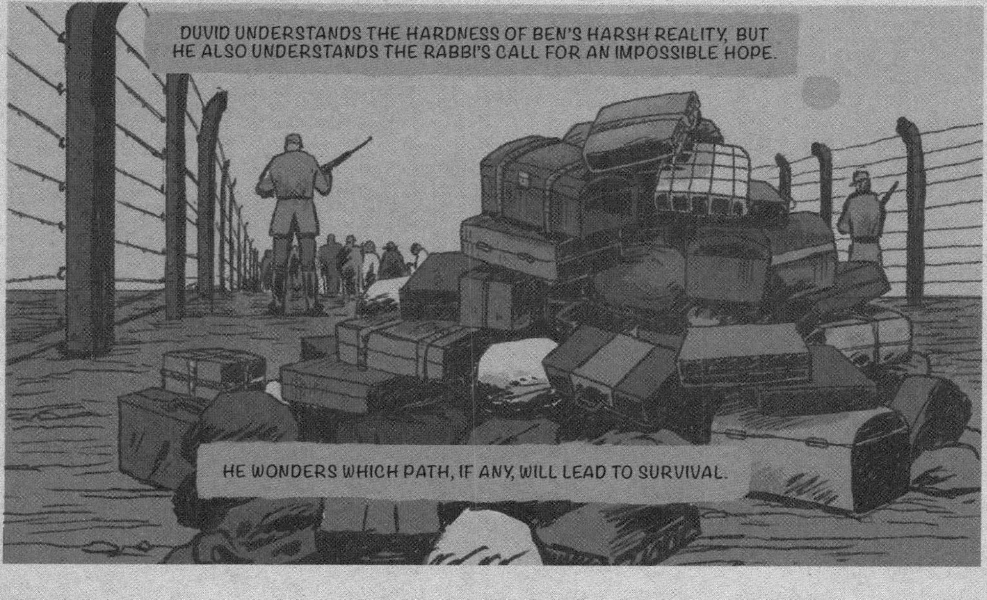
DUVID UNDERSTANDS THE HARDNESS OF BEN'S HARSH REALITY, BUT HE ALSO UNDERSTANDS THE RABBI'S CALL FOR AN IMPOSSIBLE HOPE.
HE WONDERS WHICH PATH, IF ANY, WILL LEAD TO SURVIVAL.

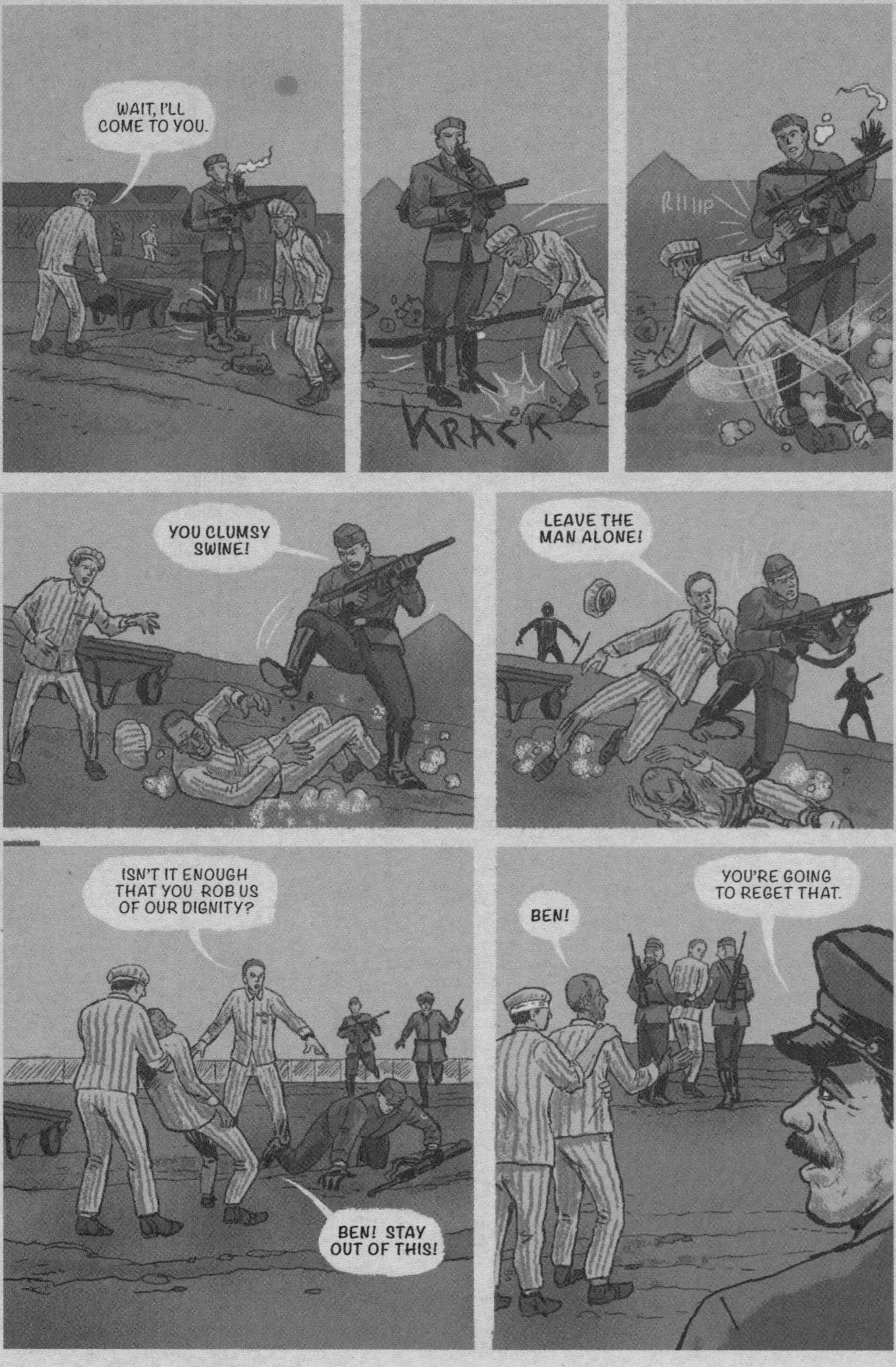
WAIT, I'LL COME TO YOU.
KRACK
RHHP
YOU CLUMSY SWINE!
LEAVE THE MAN ALONE!
ISN'T IT ENOUGH THAT YOU ROB US OF OUR DIGNITY?
BEN! STAY OUT OF THIS!
BEN!
YOU'RE GOING TO REGET THAT.

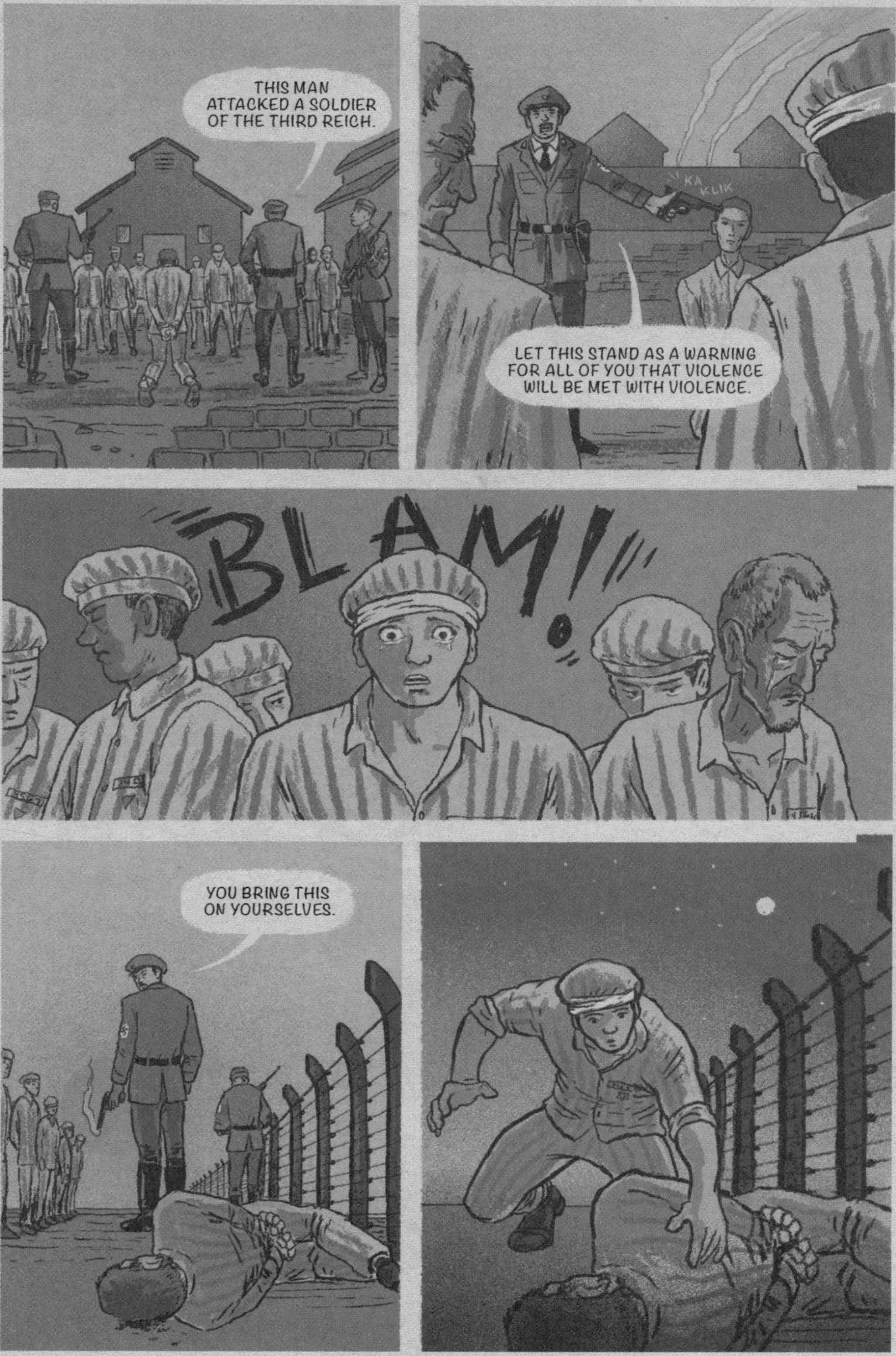
THIS MAN ATTACKED A SOLDIER OF THE THIRD REICH.
KA KLIK
LET THIS STAND AS A WARNING FOR ALL OF YOU THAT VIOLENCE WILL BE MET WITH VIOLENCE.
BLAM!
YOU BRING THIS ON YOURSELVES.

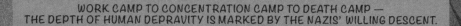

WORK CAMP TO CONCENTRATION CAMP TO DEATH CAMP —
THE DEPTH OF HUMAN DEPRAVITY IS MARKED BY THE NAZIS' WILLING DESCENT.

PROVING THAT THE ABYSS OF MAN'S
INHUMANITY TO MAN KNOWS NO BOTTOM.

STILL, DUVID MUST HOPE
THAT COURAGE IN THE FACE
OF ATROCITY WILL PREVAIL.

EVEN IF IT'S ONLY
THE COURAGE TO DREAM.

CREEAAK

IN THE CHILL NIGHT, SOMETHING PULLS DUVID FROM THE MURKY SILT OF SLEEP.

DID THE GUARD LEAVE THE DOOR OPEN? HOW CAN THAT BE?

WHOOSHH

KA

KLINK

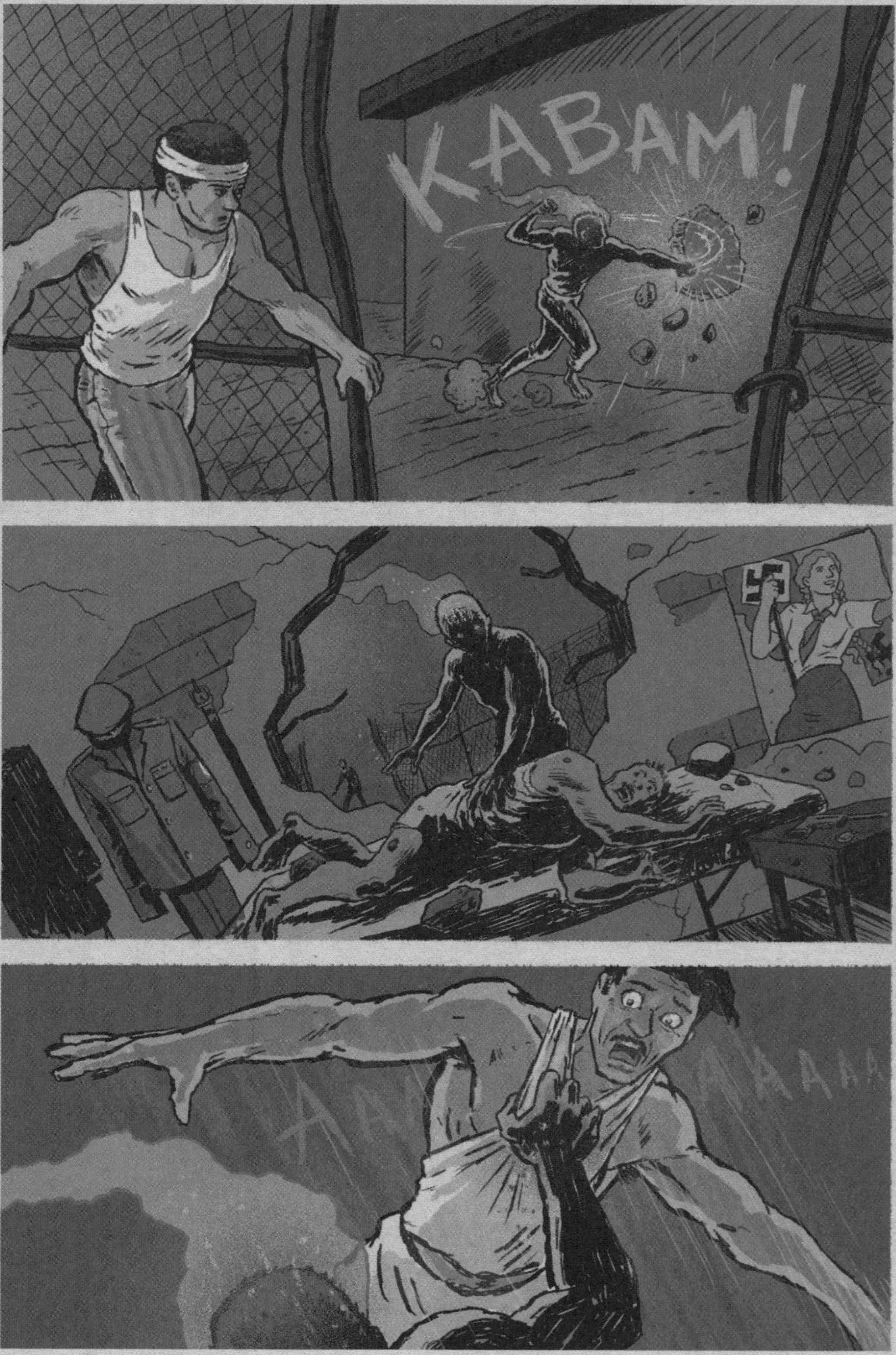
KABAM!

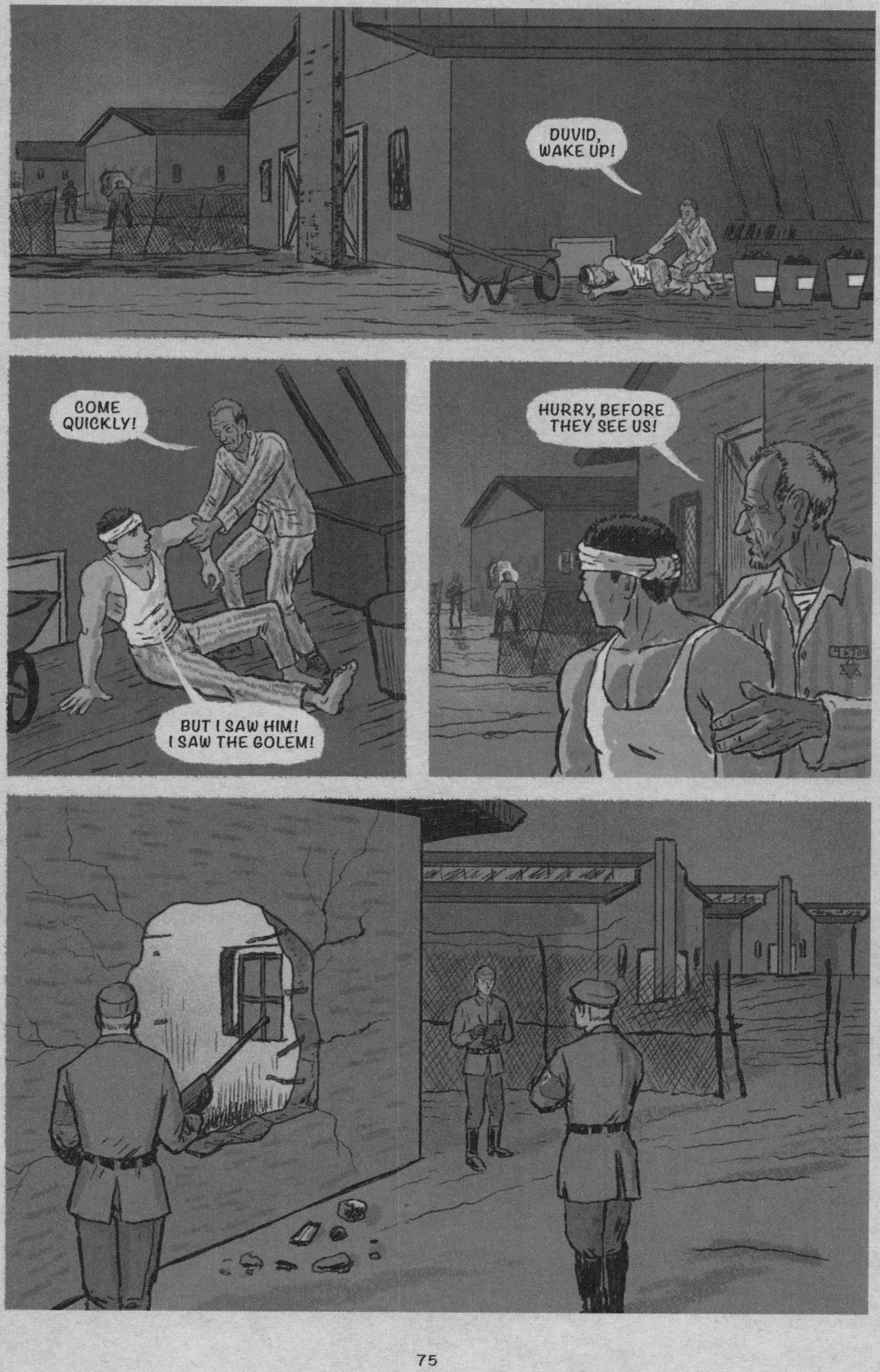
DUVID, WAKE UP!
COME QUICKLY!
BUT I SAW HIM! I SAW THE GOLEM!
HURRY, BEFORE THEY SEE US!

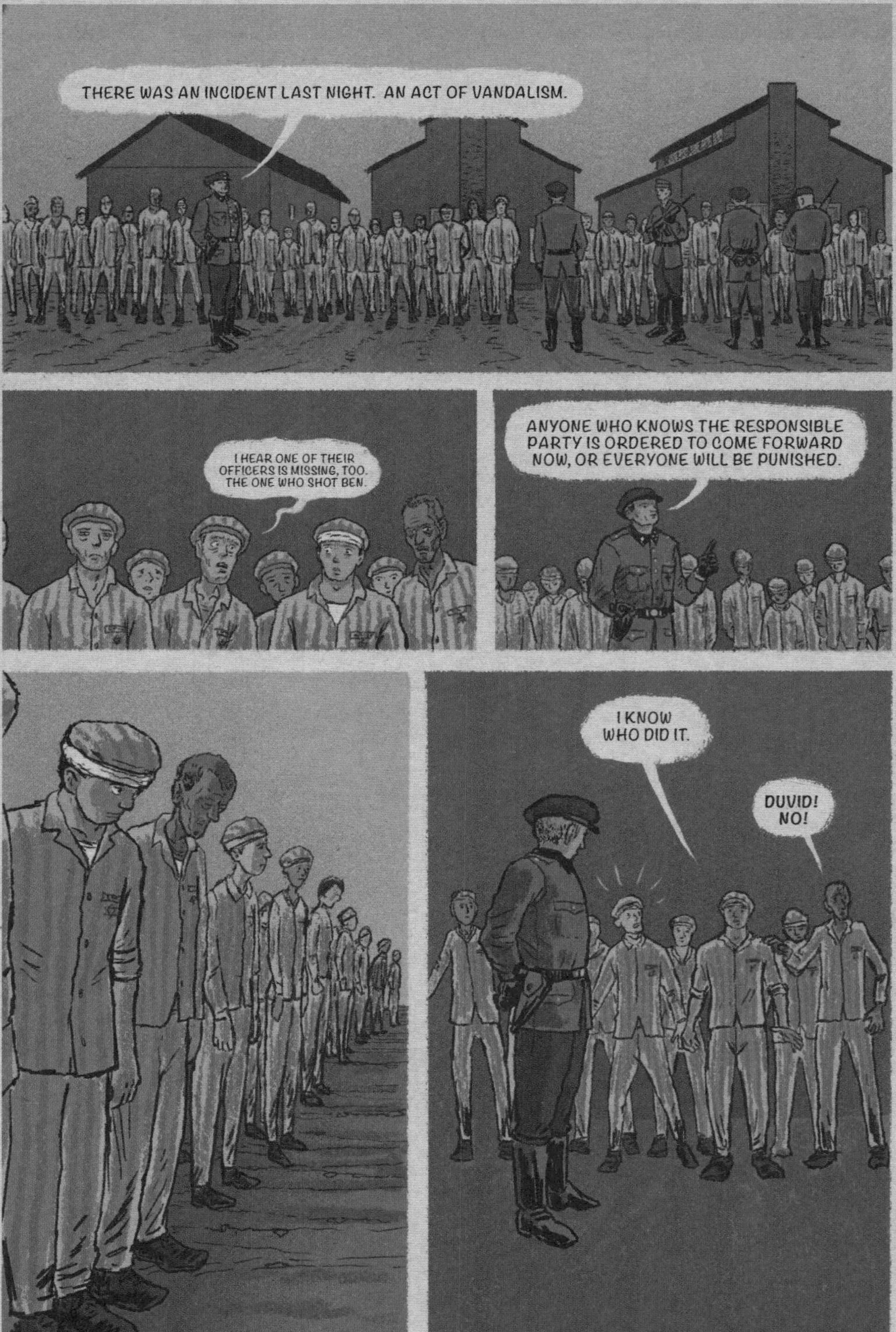
THERE WAS AN INCIDENT LAST NIGHT. AN ACT OF VANDALISM.
I HEAR ONE OF THEIR OFFICERS IS MISSING, TOO. THE ONE WHO SHOT BEN.
ANYONE WHO KNOWS THE RESPONSIBLE PARTY IS ORDERED TO COME FORWARD NOW, OR EVERYONE WILL BE PUNISHED.
I KNOW WHO DID IT.
DUVID! NO!

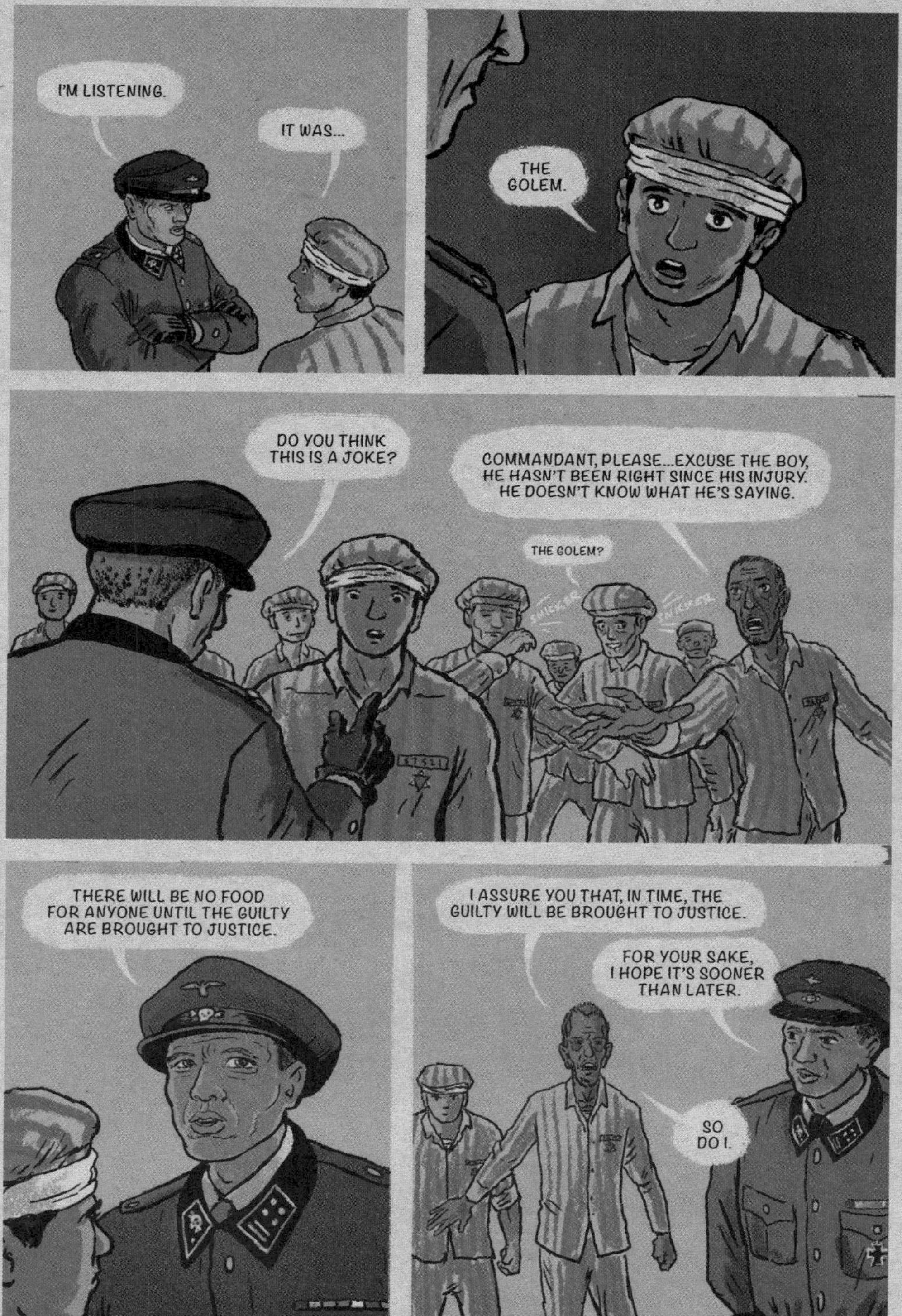
I'M LISTENING.
IT WAS...
THE GOLEM.
DO YOU THINK THIS IS A JOKE?
COMMANDANT, PLEASE...EXCUSE THE BOY, HE HASN'T BEEN RIGHT SINCE HIS INJURY. HE DOESN'T KNOW WHAT HE'S SAYING.
THE GOLEM?
SNICKER
SNICKER
THERE WILL BE NO FOOD FOR ANYONE UNTIL THE GUILTY ARE BROUGHT TO JUSTICE.
I ASSURE YOU THAT, IN TIME, THE GUILTY WILL BE BROUGHT TO JUSTICE.
FOR YOUR SAKE, I HOPE IT'S SOONER THAN LATER.
SO DO I.

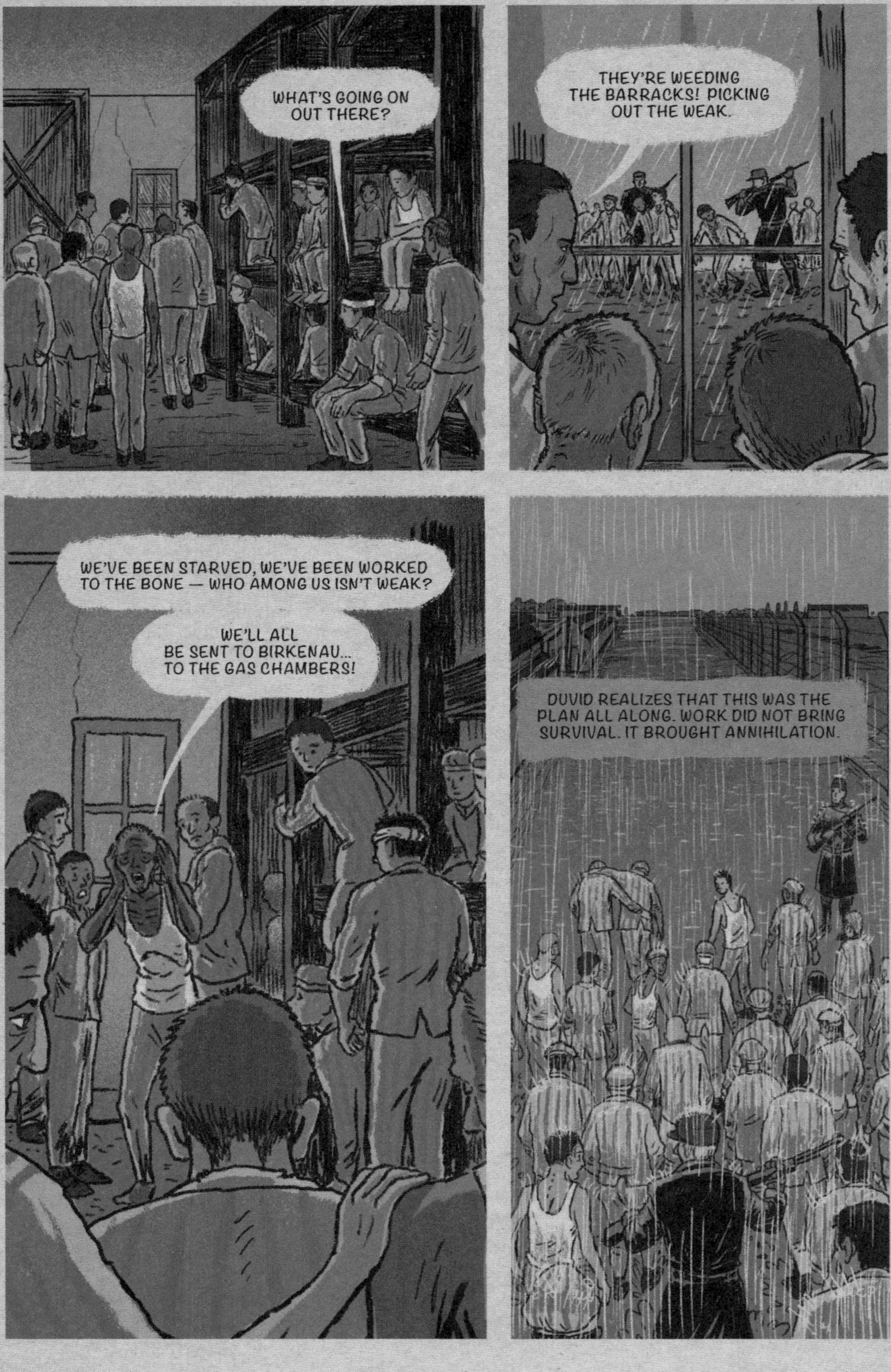
WHAT'S GOING ON OUT THERE?
THEY'RE WEEDING THE BARRACKS! PICKING OUT THE WEAK.
WE'VE BEEN STARVED, WE'VE BEEN WORKED TO THE BONE — WHO AMONG US ISN'T WEAK?
WE'LL ALL BE SENT TO BIRKENAU... TO THE GAS CHAMBERS!
DUVID REALIZES THAT THIS WAS THE PLAN ALL ALONG. WORK DID NOT BRING SURVIVAL. IT BROUGHT ANNIHILATION.

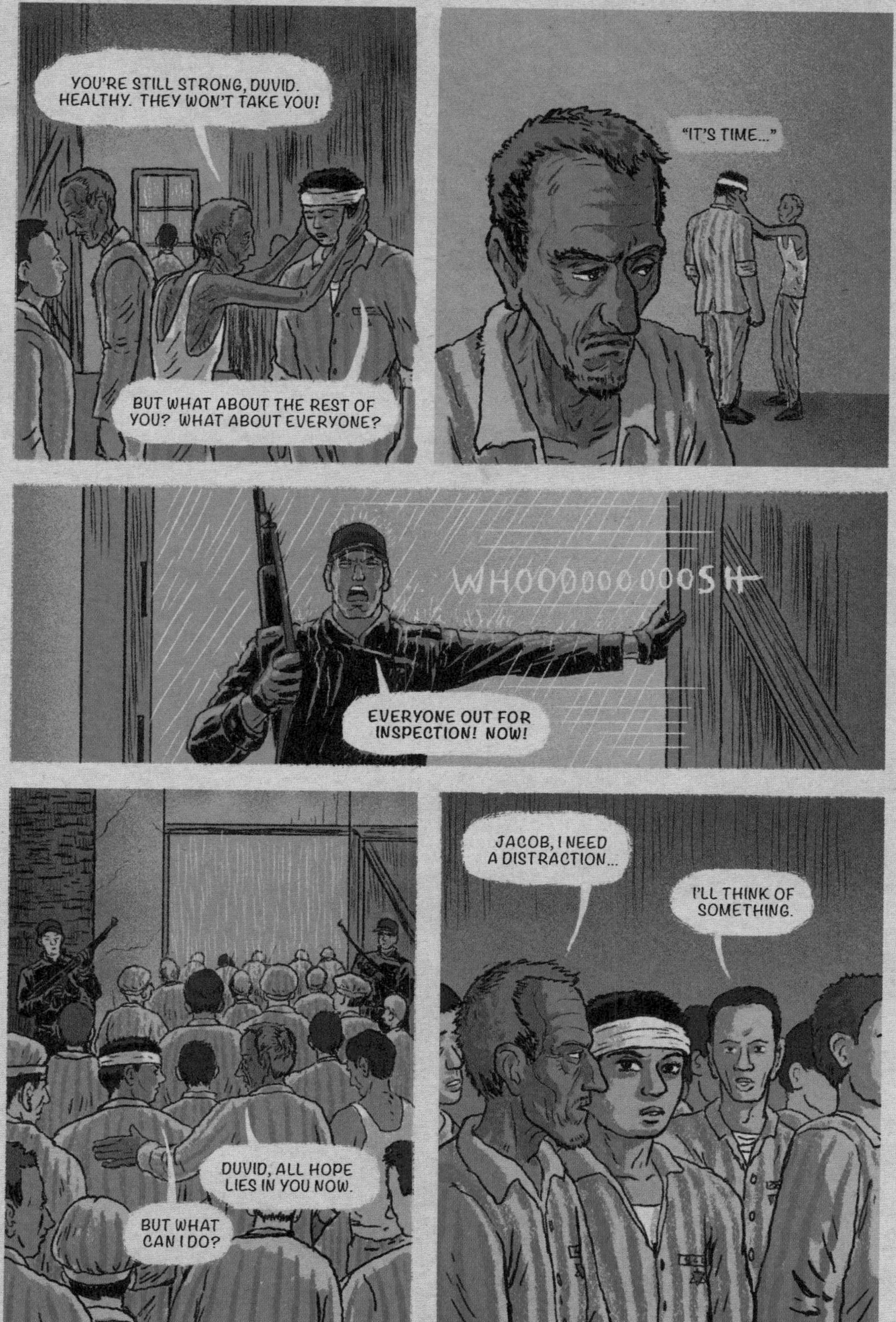
YOU'RE STILL STRONG, DUVID. HEALTHY. THEY WON'T TAKE YOU!
BUT WHAT ABOUT THE REST OF YOU? WHAT ABOUT EVERYONE?
"IT'S TIME..."
WHOOOOOOOOOOSH
EVERYONE OUT FOR INSPECTION! NOW!
DUVID, ALL HOPE LIES IN YOU NOW.
BUT WHAT CAN I DO?
JACOB, I NEED A DISTRACTION...
I'LL THINK OF SOMETHING.

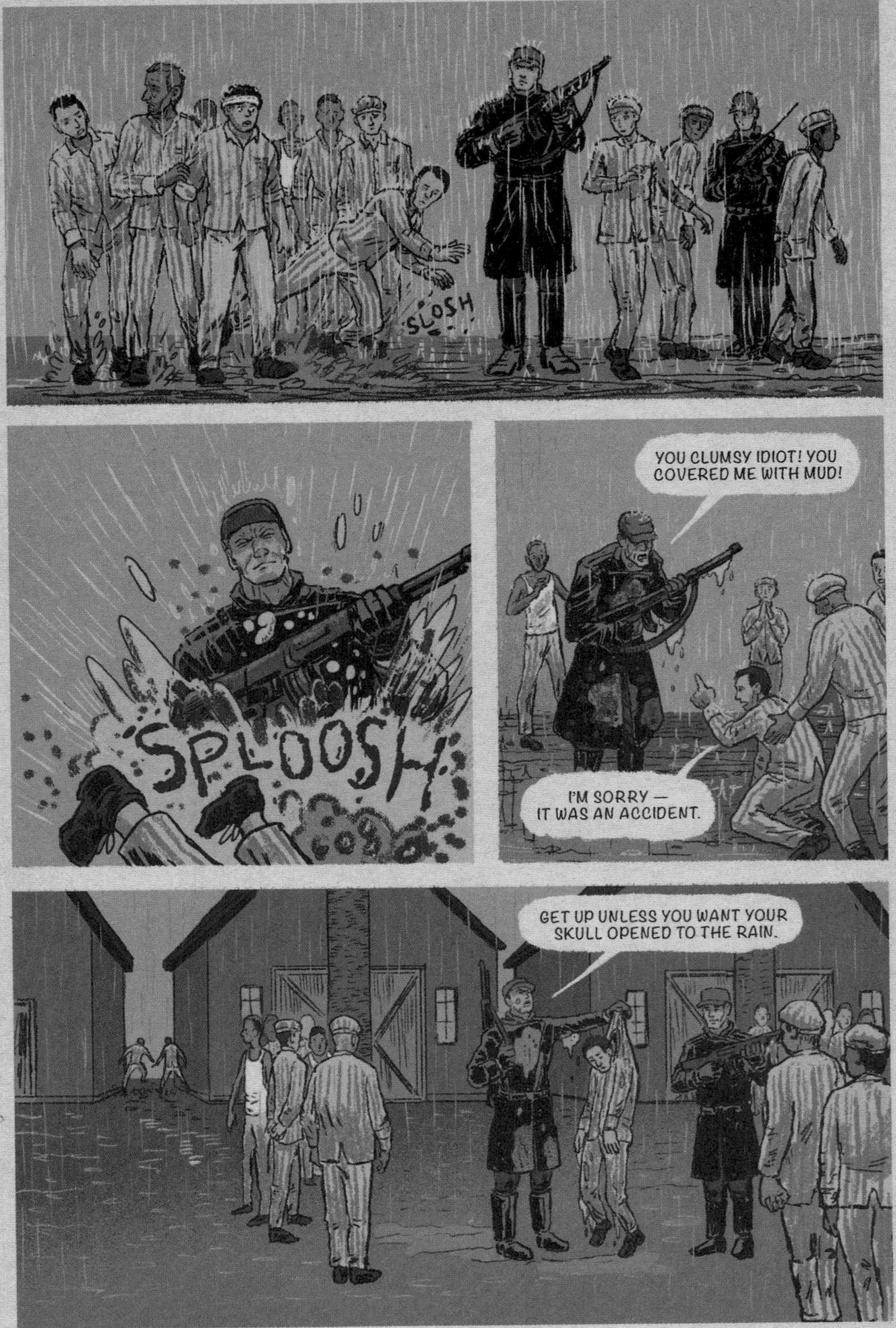
SLOSH
SPLOOSH
YOU CLUMSY IDIOT! YOU COVERED ME WITH MUD!
I'M SORRY — IT WAS AN ACCIDENT.
GET UP UNLESS YOU WANT YOUR SKULL OPENED TO THE RAIN.

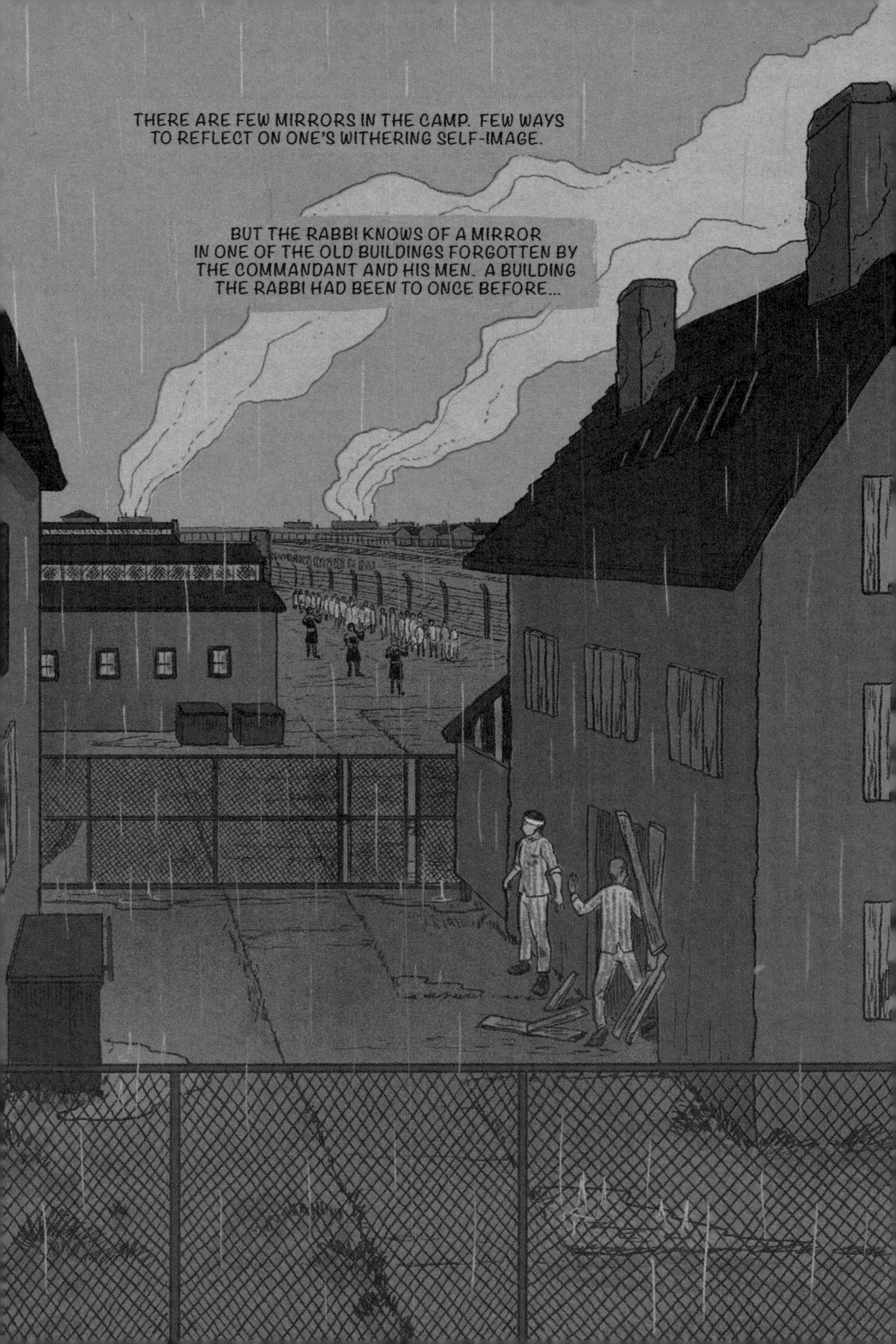
THERE ARE FEW MIRRORS IN THE CAMP. FEW WAYS TO REFLECT ON ONE'S WITHERING SELF-IMAGE.
BUT THE RABBI KNOWS OF A MIRROR IN ONE OF THE OLD BUILDINGS FORGOTTEN BY THE COMMANDANT AND HIS MEN. A BUILDING THE RABBI HAD BEEN TO ONCE BEFORE...

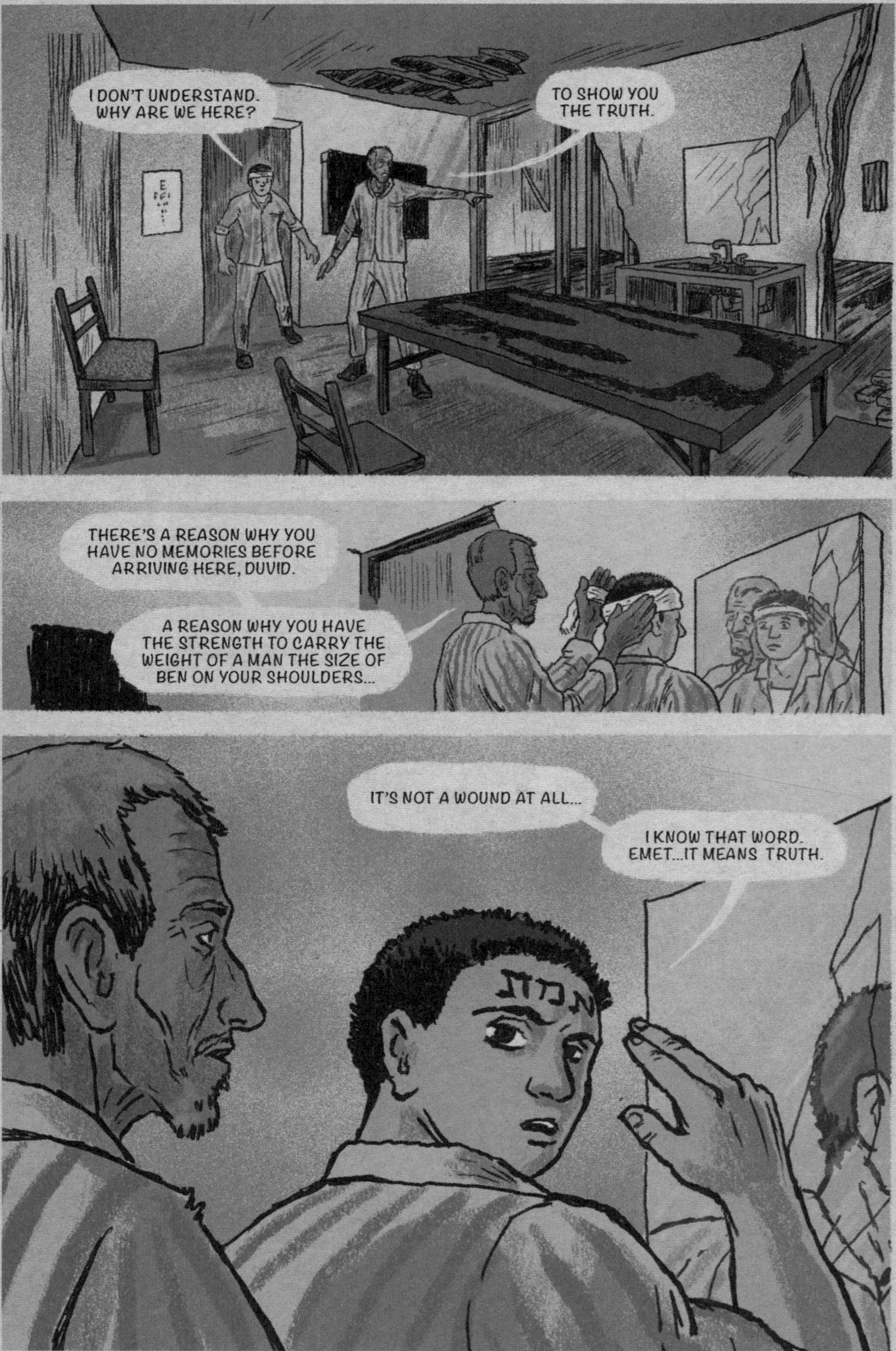
I DON'T UNDERSTAND. WHY ARE WE HERE?
TO SHOW YOU THE TRUTH.
THERE'S A REASON WHY YOU HAVE NO MEMORIES BEFORE ARRIVING HERE, DUVID.
A REASON WHY YOU HAVE THE STRENGTH TO CARRY THE WEIGHT OF A MAN THE SIZE OF BEN ON YOUR SHOULDERS...
IT'S NOT A WOUND AT ALL...
I KNOW THAT WORD. EMET...IT MEANS TRUTH.

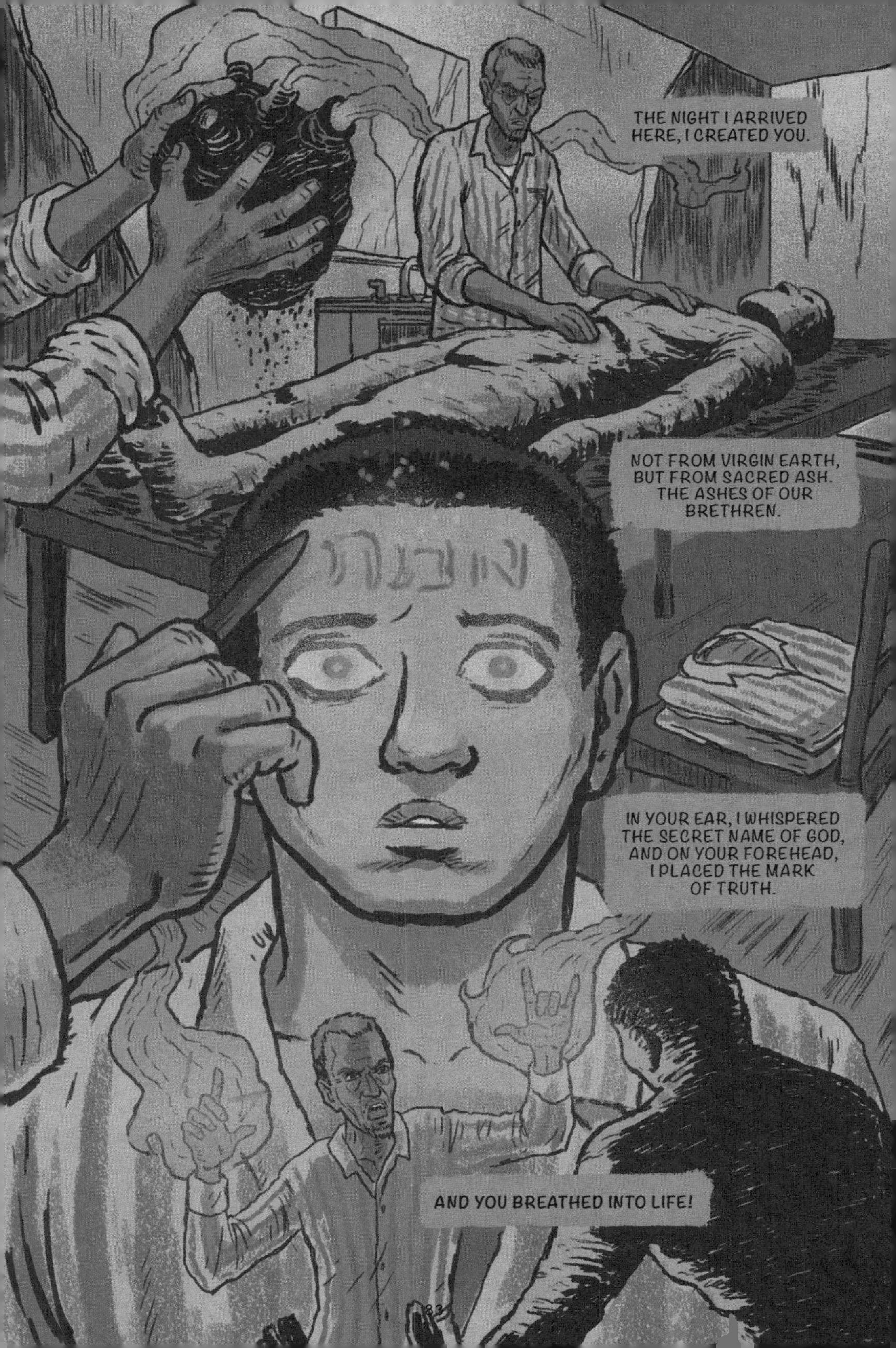
THE NIGHT I ARRIVED HERE, I CREATED YOU.
NOT FROM VIRGIN EARTH, BUT FROM SACRED ASH. THE ASHES OF OUR BRETHREN.
אמת
IN YOUR EAR, I WHISPERED THE SECRET NAME OF GOD, AND ON YOUR FOREHEAD, I PLACED THE MARK OF TRUTH.
AND YOU BREATHED INTO LIFE!

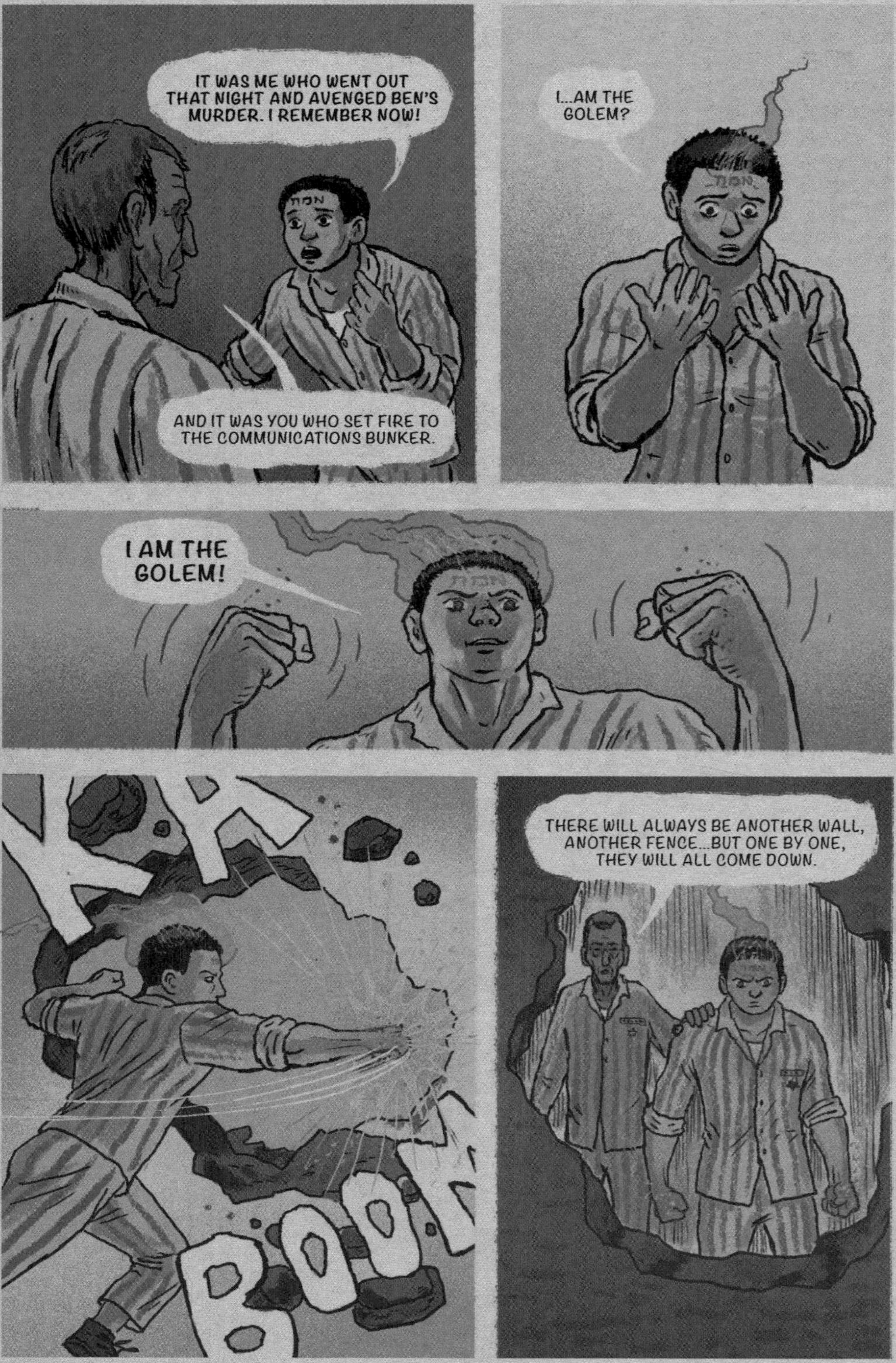
IT WAS ME WHO WENT OUT THAT NIGHT AND AVENGED BEN'S MURDER. I REMEMBER NOW!
AND IT WAS YOU WHO SET FIRE TO THE COMMUNICATIONS BUNKER.
I...AM THE GOLEM?
I AM THE GOLEM!
BOO
THERE WILL ALWAYS BE ANOTHER WALL, ANOTHER FENCE...BUT ONE BY ONE, THEY WILL ALL COME DOWN.

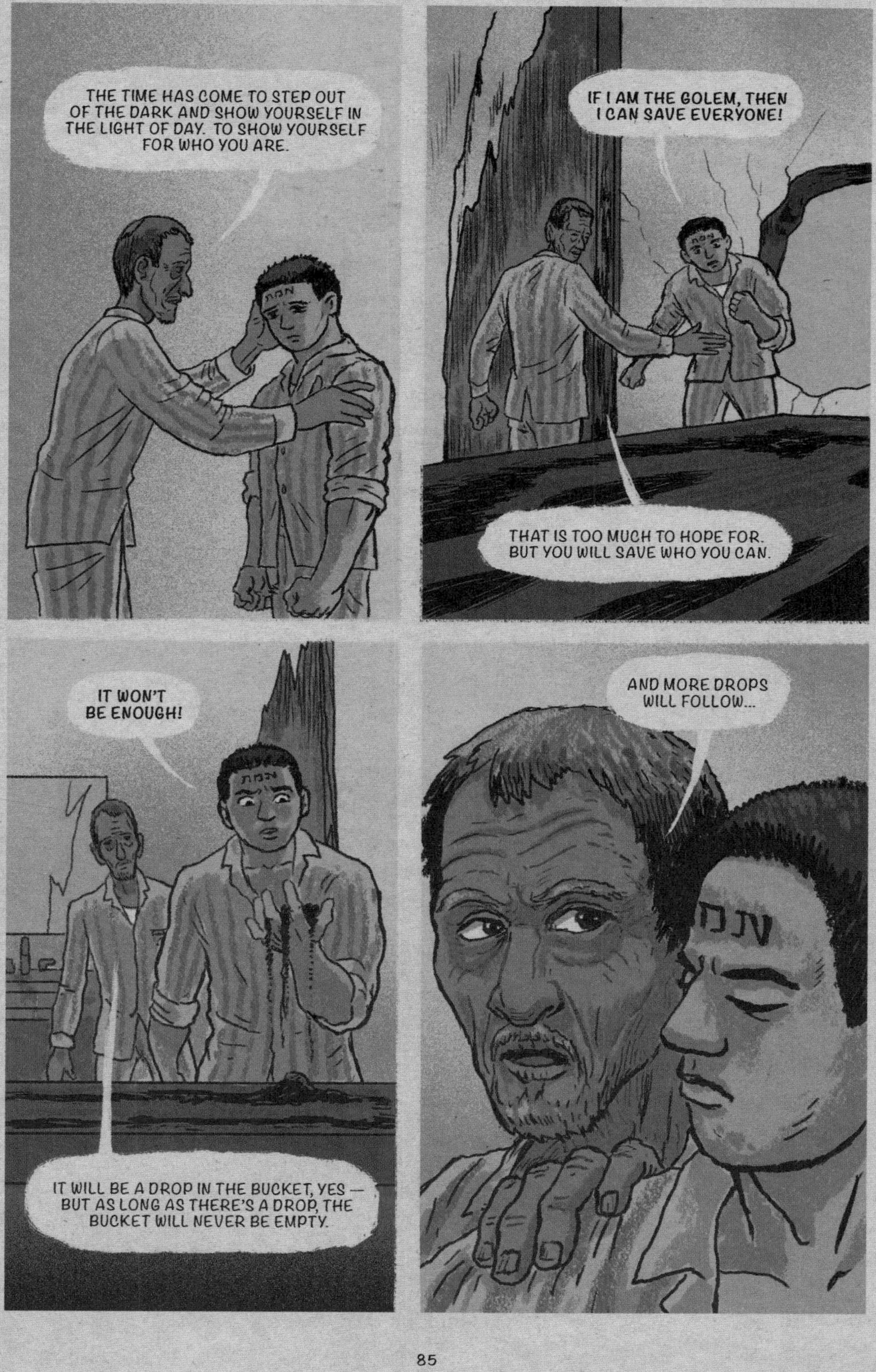
THE TIME HAS COME TO STEP OUT OF THE DARK AND SHOW YOURSELF IN THE LIGHT OF DAY. TO SHOW YOURSELF FOR WHO YOU ARE.
IF I AM THE GOLEM, THEN I CAN SAVE EVERYONE!
THAT IS TOO MUCH TO HOPE FOR. BUT YOU WILL SAVE WHO YOU CAN.
IT WON'T BE ENOUGH!
IT WILL BE A DROP IN THE BUCKET, YES — BUT AS LONG AS THERE'S A DROP, THE BUCKET WILL NEVER BE EMPTY.
AND MORE DROPS WILL FOLLOW...
מת

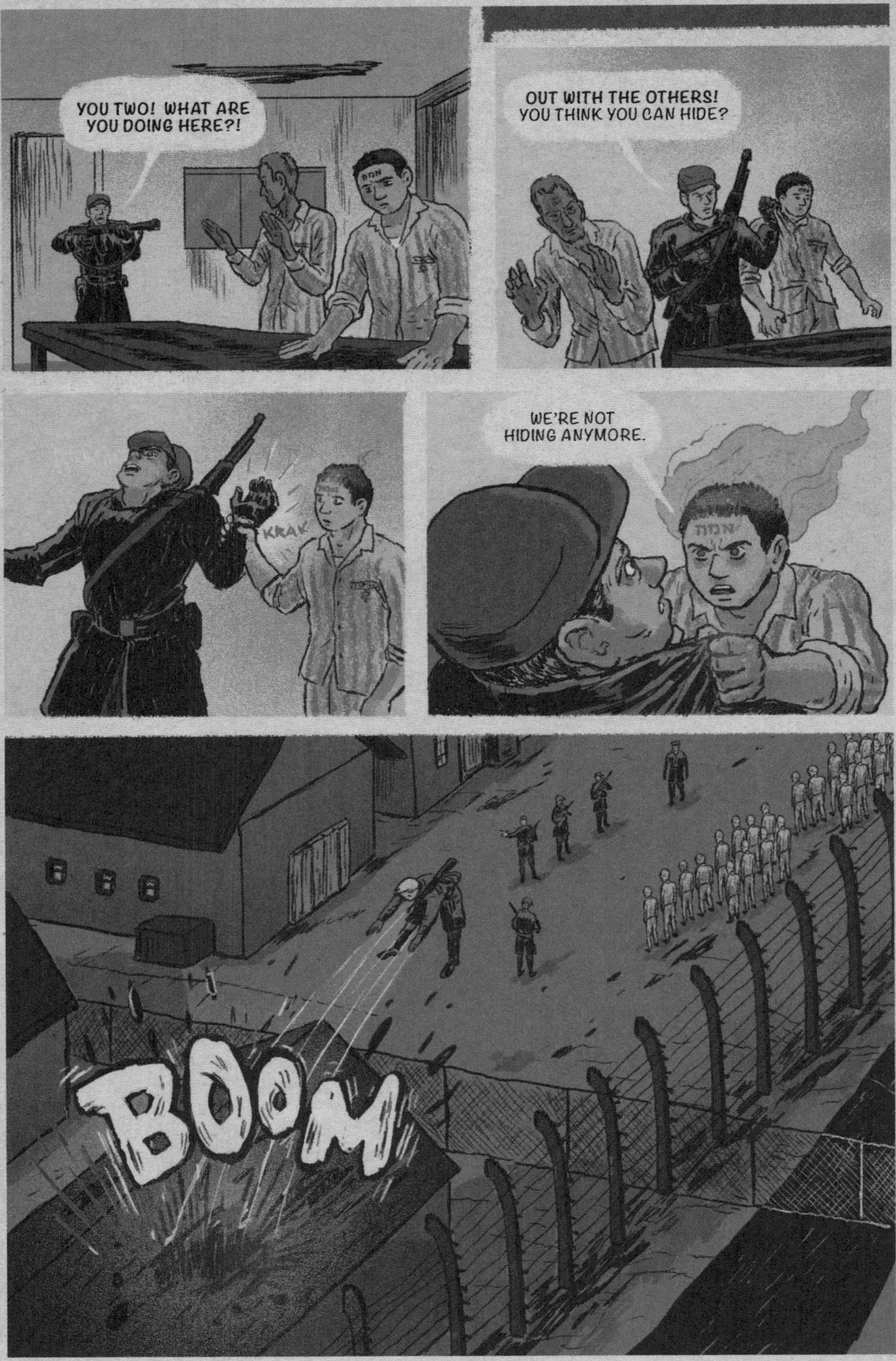
YOU TWO! WHAT ARE YOU DOING HERE?!
OUT WITH THE OTHERS! YOU THINK YOU CAN HIDE?
KRAK
WE'RE NOT HIDING ANYMORE.
BOOM

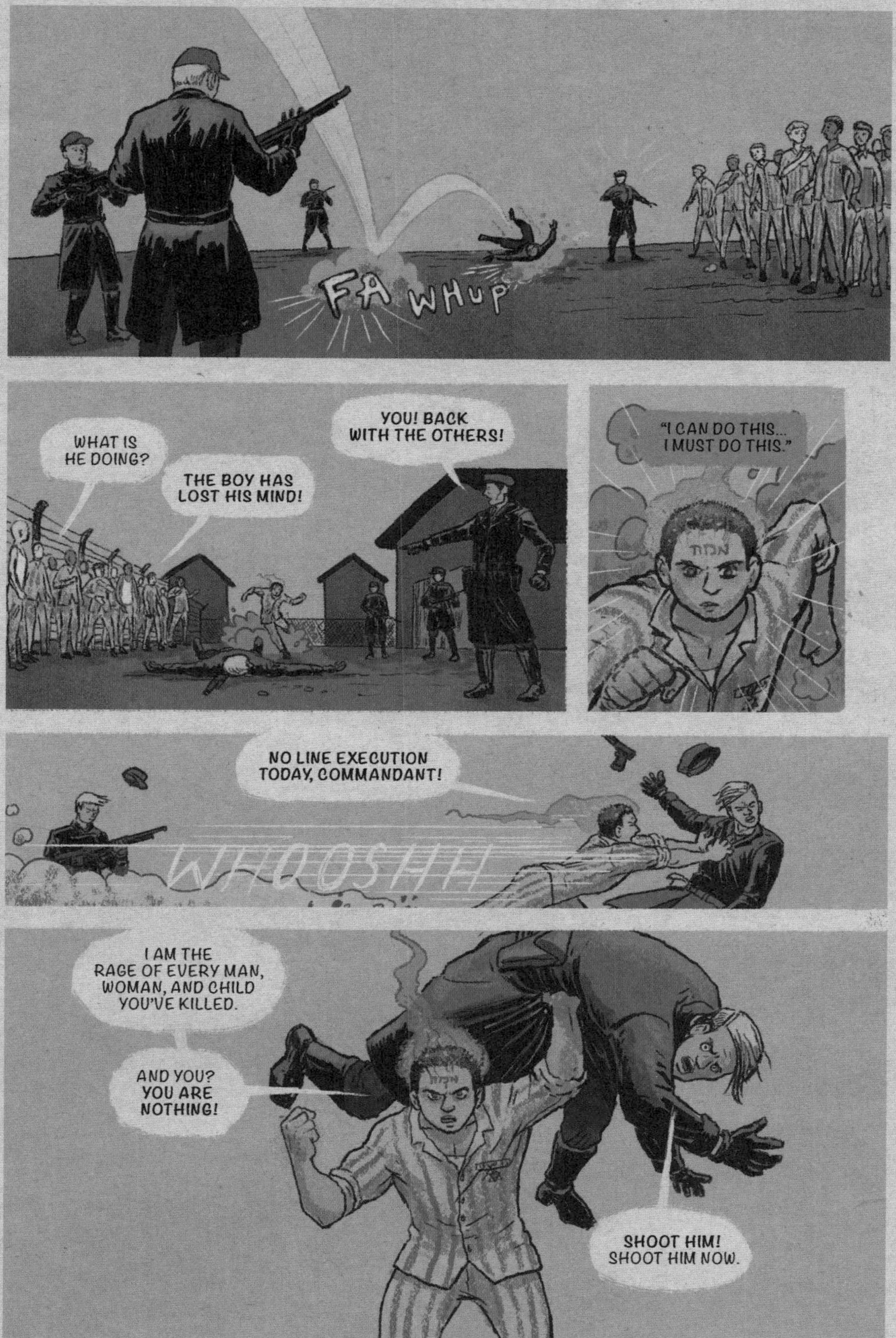
FA WHUP
WHAT IS HE DOING?
THE BOY HAS LOST HIS MIND!
YOU! BACK WITH THE OTHERS!
"I CAN DO THIS... I MUST DO THIS."
NO LINE EXECUTION TODAY, COMMANDANT!
WHOOSHH
I AM THE RAGE OF EVERY MAN, WOMAN, AND CHILD YOU'VE KILLED.
AND YOU? YOU ARE NOTHING!
SHOOT HIM! SHOOT HIM NOW.

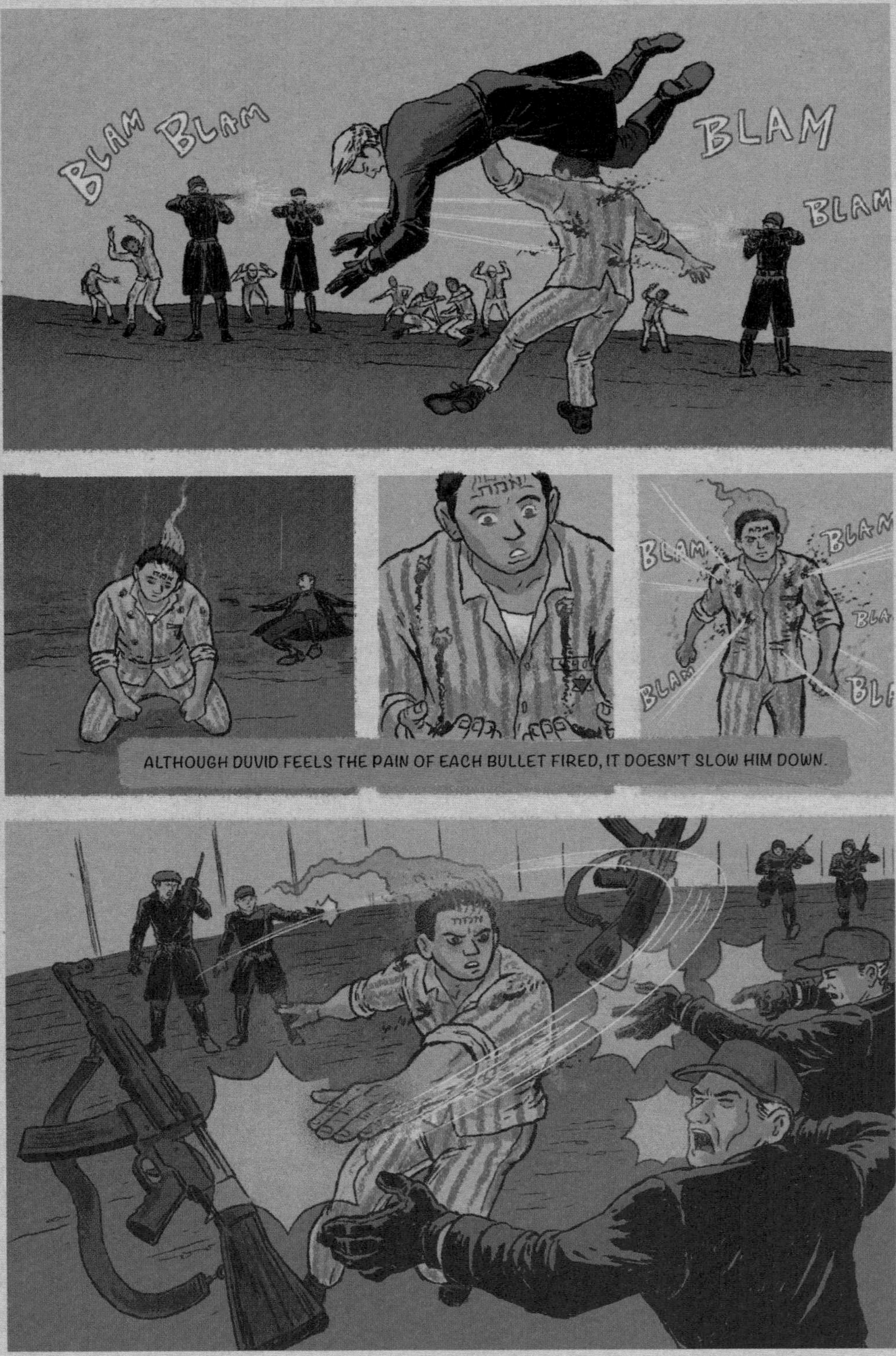
BLAM BLAM
BLAM
BLAM
BLAM
BLAM
ALTHOUGH DUVID FEELS THE PAIN OF EACH BULLET FIRED, IT DOESN'T SLOW HIM DOWN.

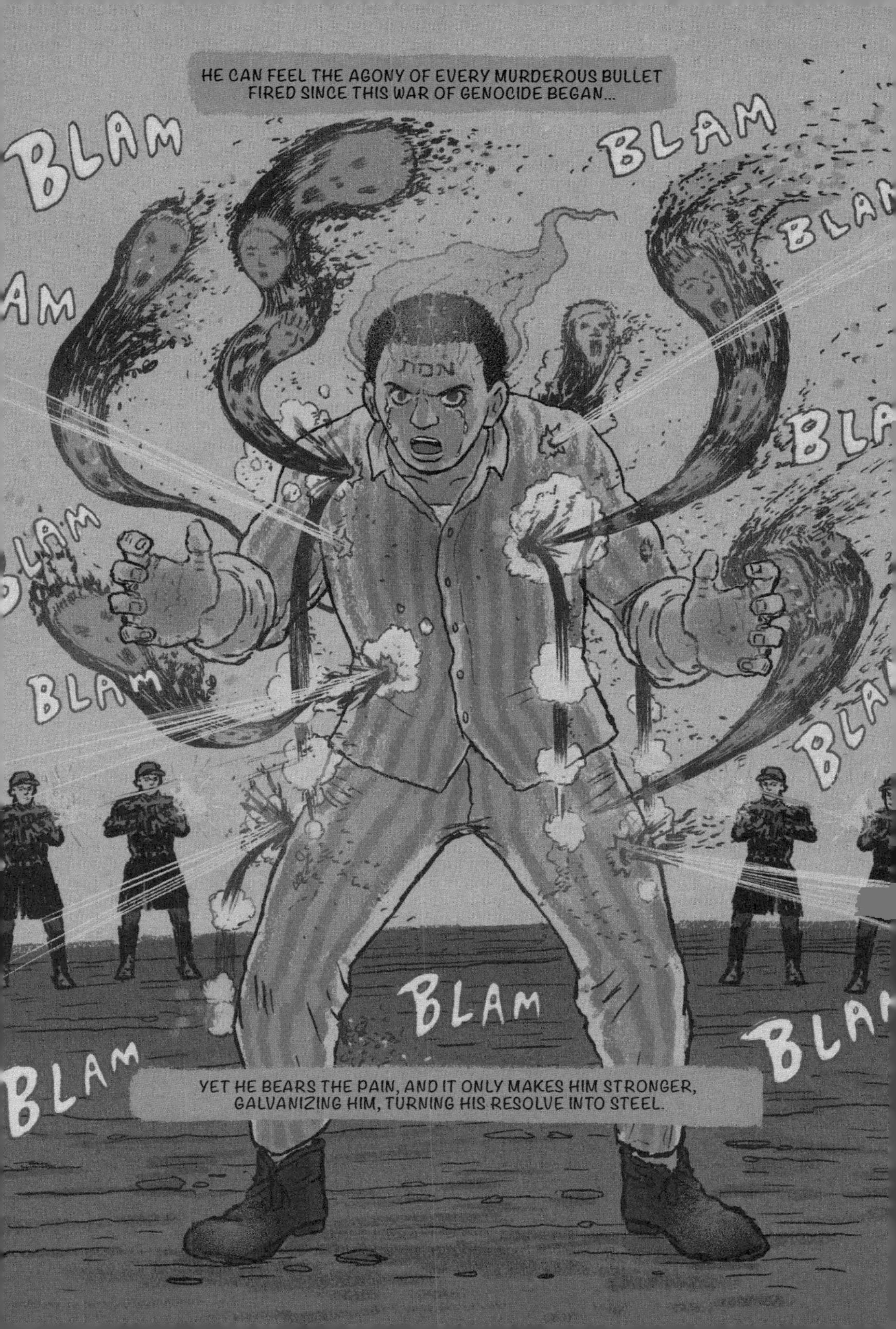
HE CAN FEEL THE AGONY OF EVERY MURDEROUS BULLET FIRED SINCE THIS WAR OF GENOCIDE BEGAN...
BLAM
BLAM
BLAM
BLAM
BLAM
BLAM
YET HE BEARS THE PAIN, AND IT ONLY MAKES HIM STRONGER, GALVANIZING HIM, TURNING HIS RESOLVE INTO STEEL.

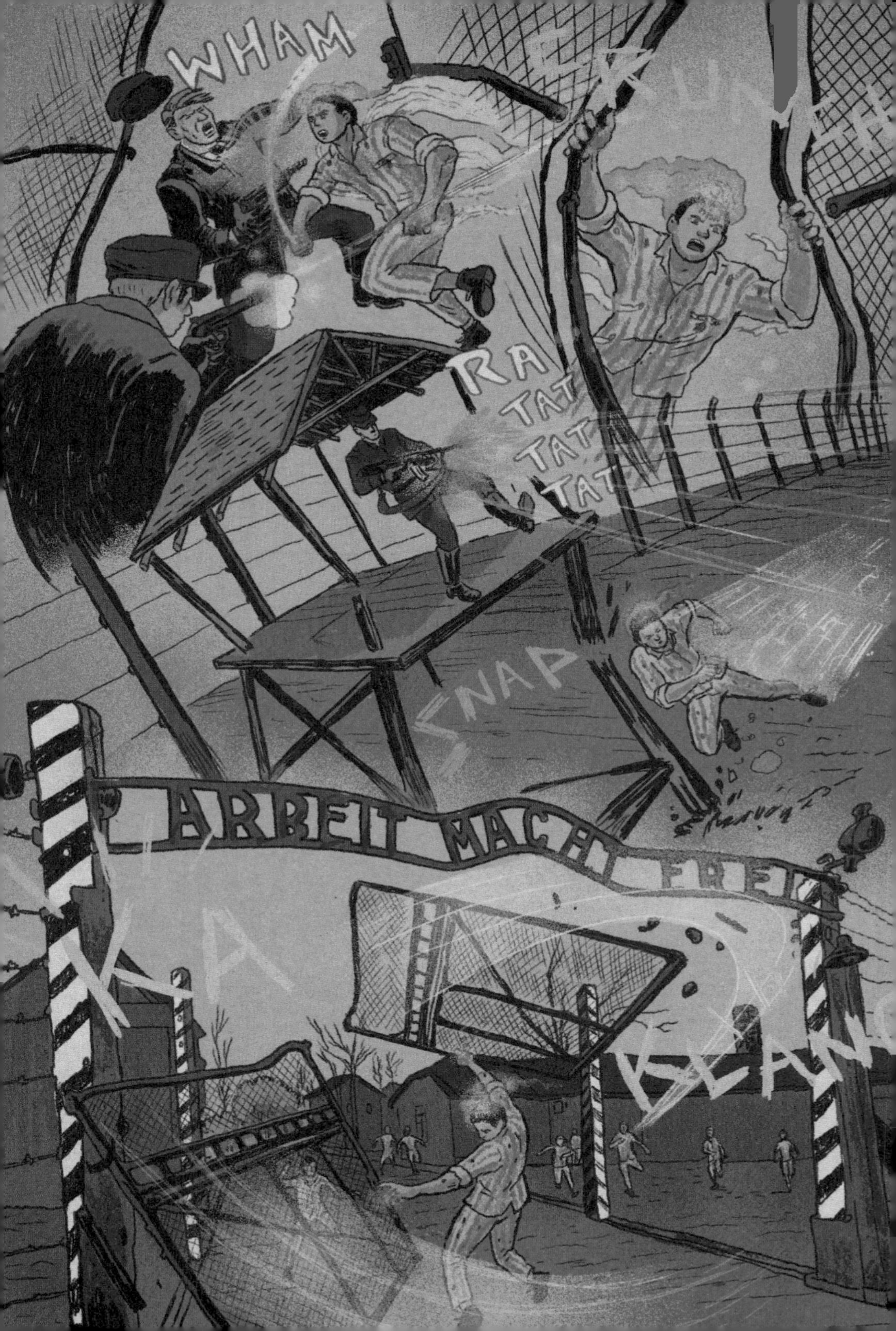
WHAM
RA
TAT
TAT
TAT
SNAP
ARBEIT MACH FREI

DON'T LOOK BACK!
THEY CAN TAKE DOWN SOME BUT NOT ALL OF US. NEVER ALL OF US!
PING
SPAK
RA TAT TAT
SPAK
RABBI!
No!
SPAK
HOLD THEM OFF FOR AS LONG AS YOU CAN. THEN YOU KNOW WHAT TO DO.
FUMP
RABBI! YOU CAN'T DIE NOW —
NOT WHEN YOU'RE SO CLOSE TO FREEDOM.
SPAK

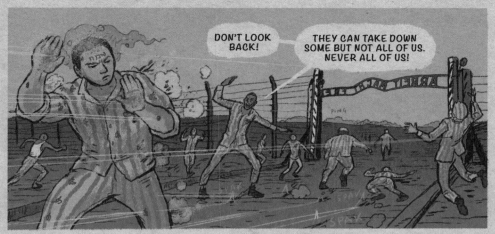

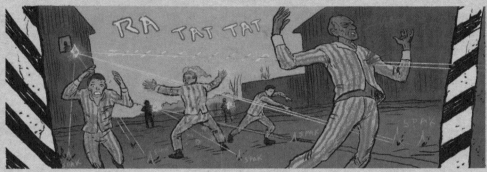

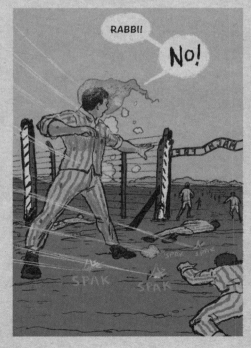

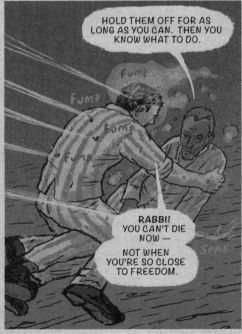

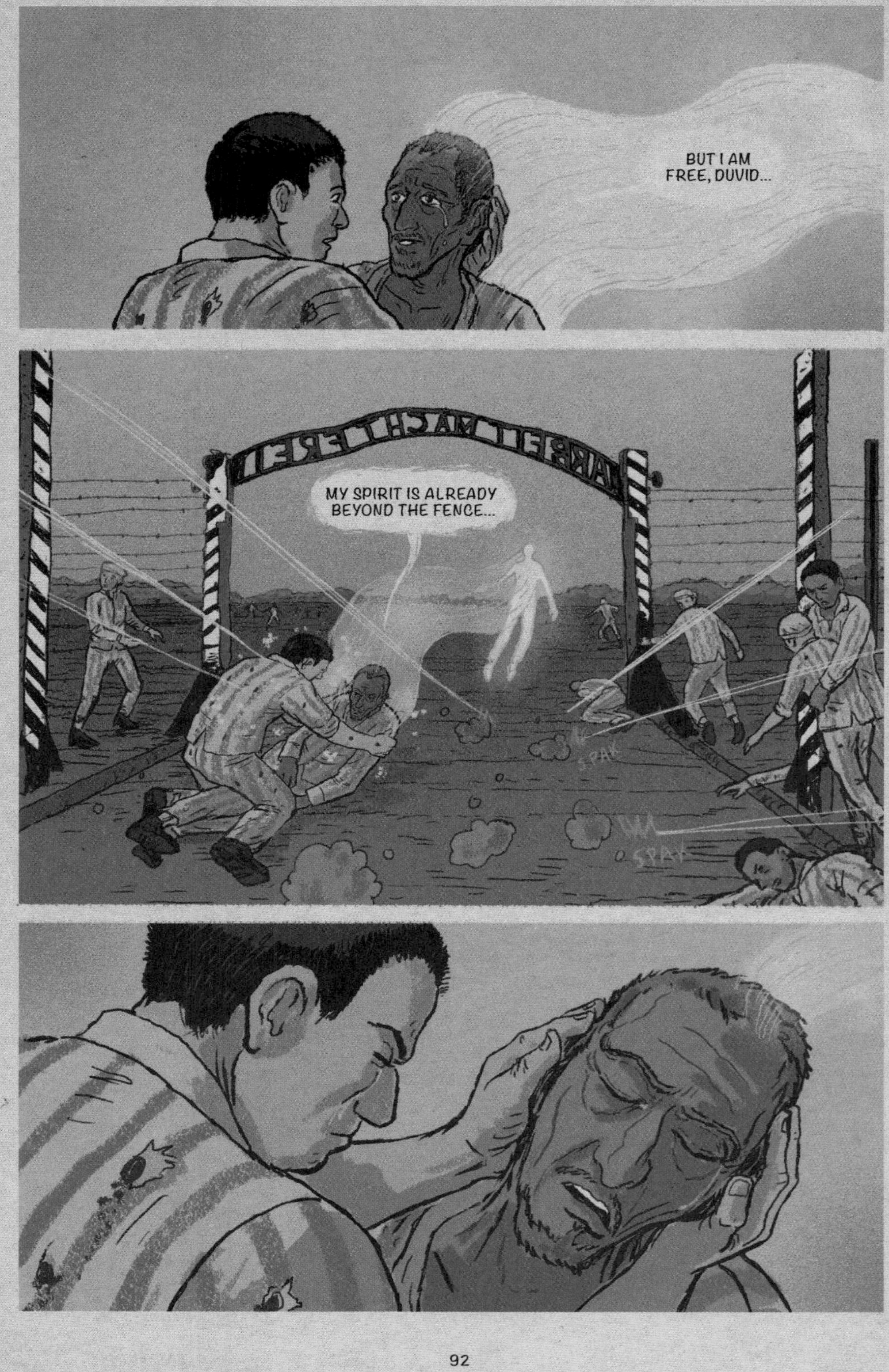
BUT I AM FREE, DUVID...
MY SPIRIT IS ALREADY BEYOND THE FENCE...
SPAK
SPAK

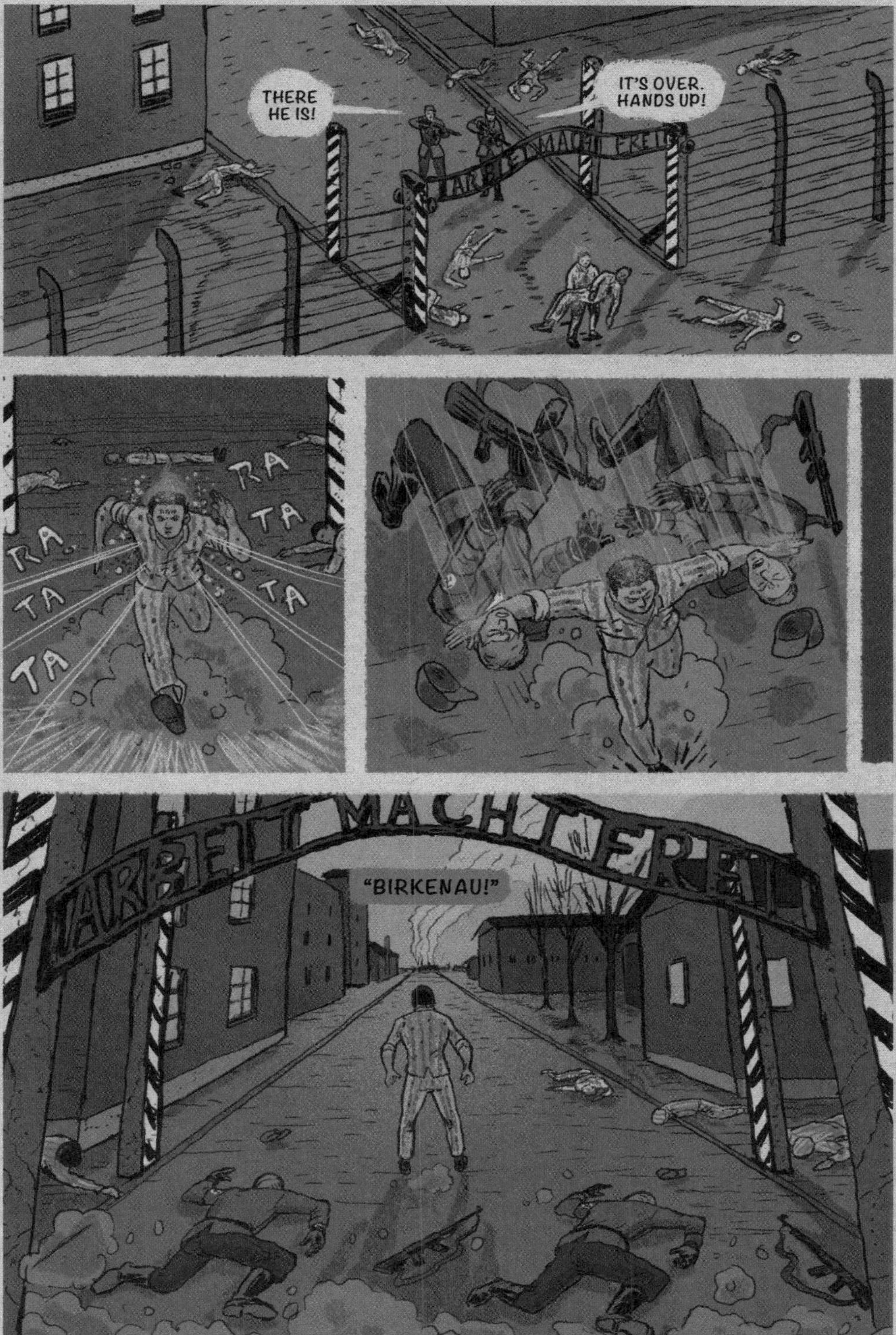
THERE HE IS!
IT'S OVER. HANDS UP!
ARBEIT MACHT FREI
RA TA TA TA TA RA TA
ARBEIT MACHT FREI
"BIRKENAU!"

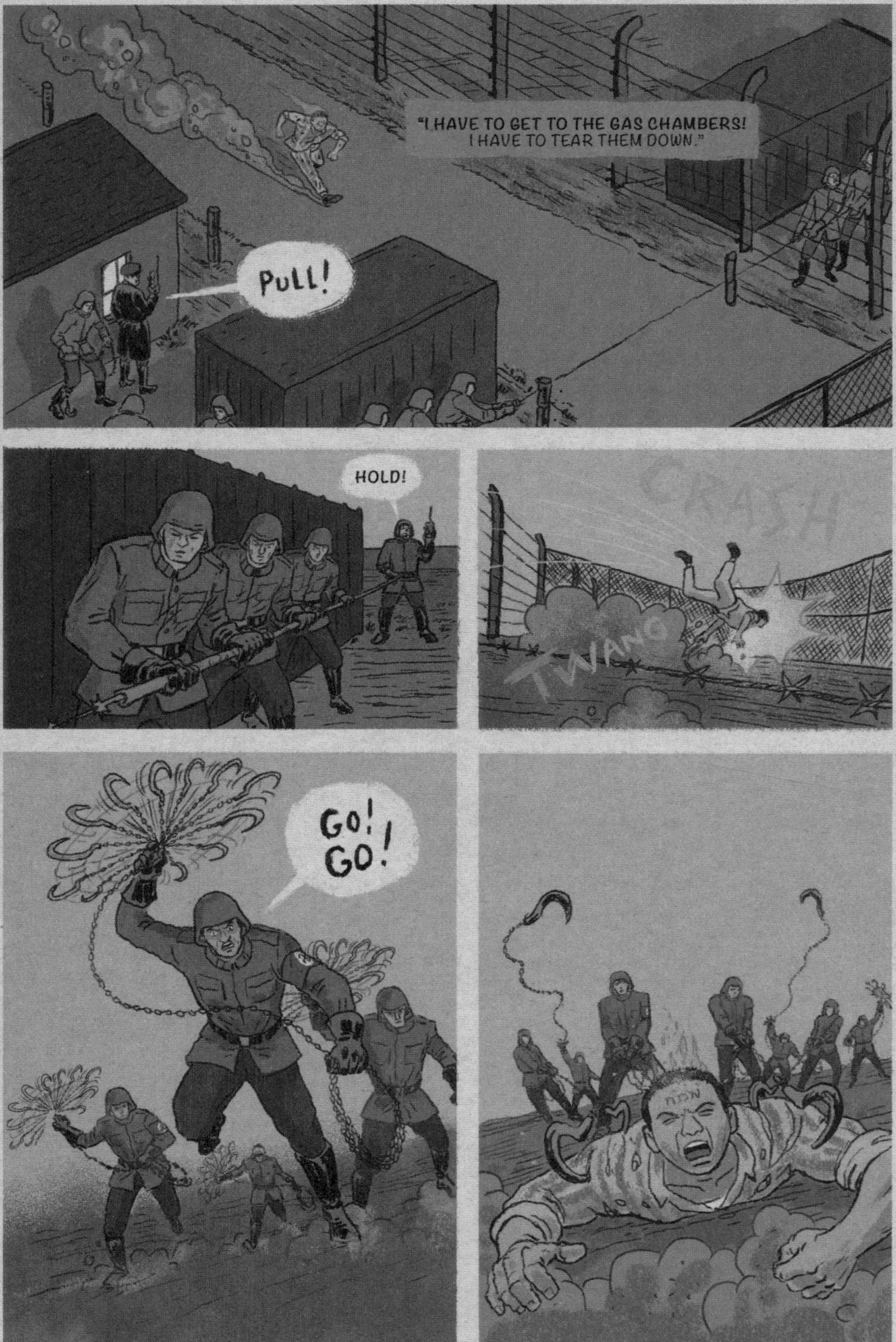
"I HAVE TO GET TO THE GAS CHAMBERS! I HAVE TO TEAR THEM DOWN."
PULL!
HOLD!
CRASH
TWANG
GO! GO!

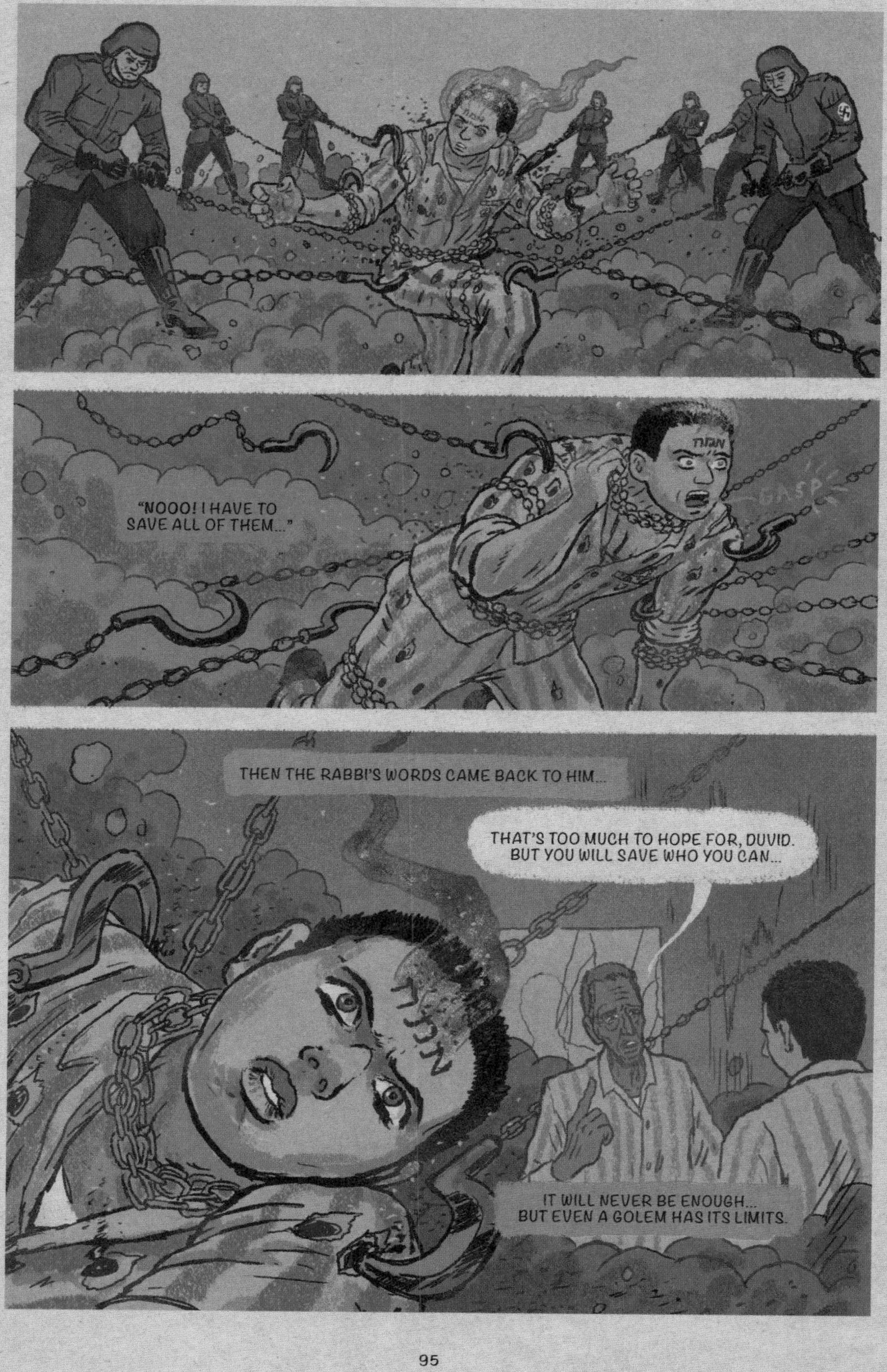
"NOOO! I HAVE TO SAVE ALL OF THEM..."
GASP
THEN THE RABBI'S WORDS CAME BACK TO HIM...
THAT'S TOO MUCH TO HOPE FOR, DUVID. BUT YOU WILL SAVE WHO YOU CAN...
IT WILL NEVER BE ENOUGH... BUT EVEN A GOLEM HAS ITS LIMITS.

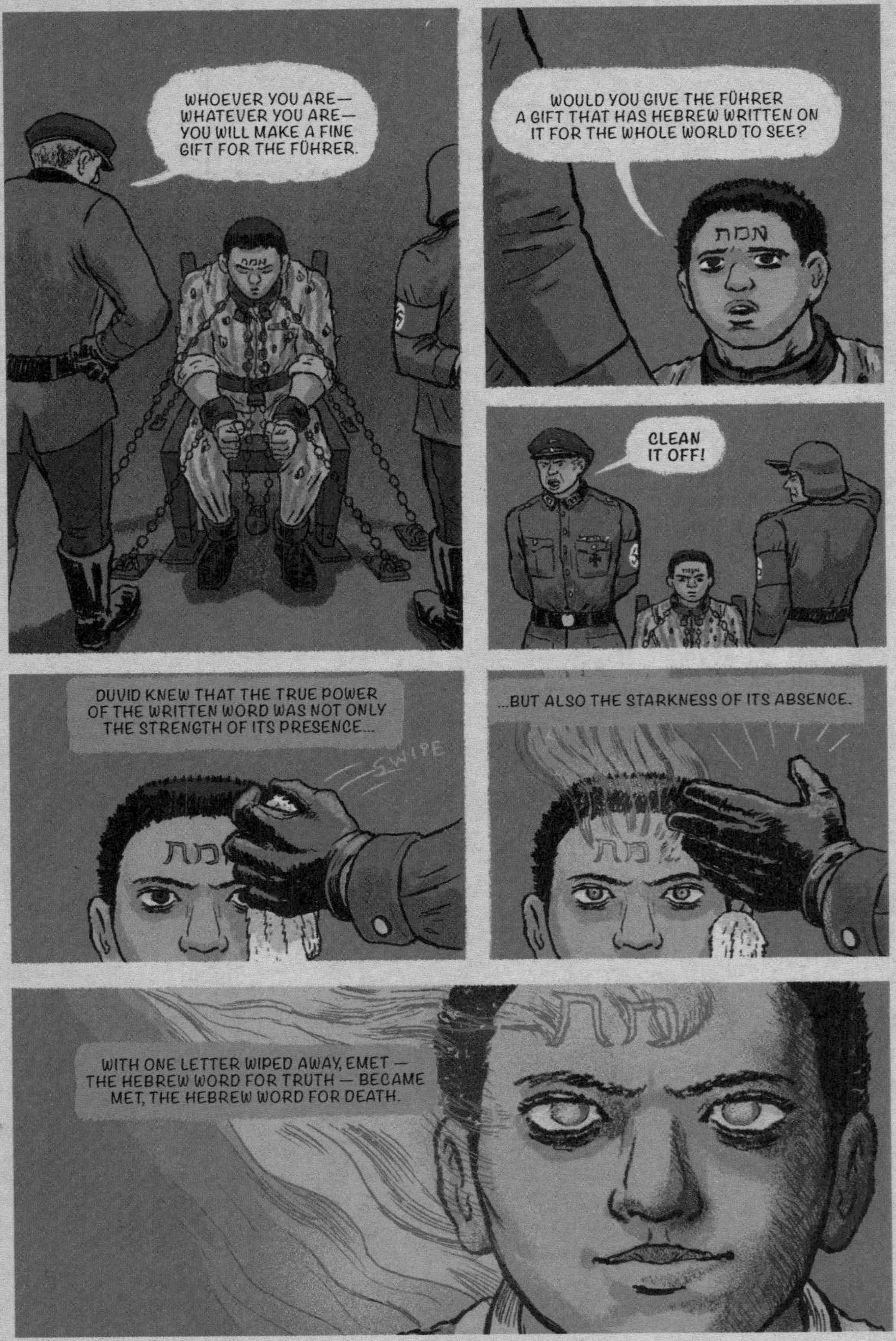
WHOEVER YOU ARE— WHATEVER YOU ARE— YOU WILL MAKE A FINE GIFT FOR THE FÜHRER.
WOULD YOU GIVE THE FÜHRER A GIFT THAT HAS HEBREW WRITTEN ON IT FOR THE WHOLE WORLD TO SEE?
אמת
CLEAN IT OFF!
DUVID KNEW THAT THE TRUE POWER OF THE WRITTEN WORD WAS NOT ONLY THE STRENGTH OF ITS PRESENCE...
SWIPE
...BUT ALSO THE STARKNESS OF ITS ABSENCE.
מת
WITH ONE LETTER WIPED AWAY, EMET — THE HEBREW WORD FOR TRUTH — BECAME MET, THE HEBREW WORD FOR DEATH.

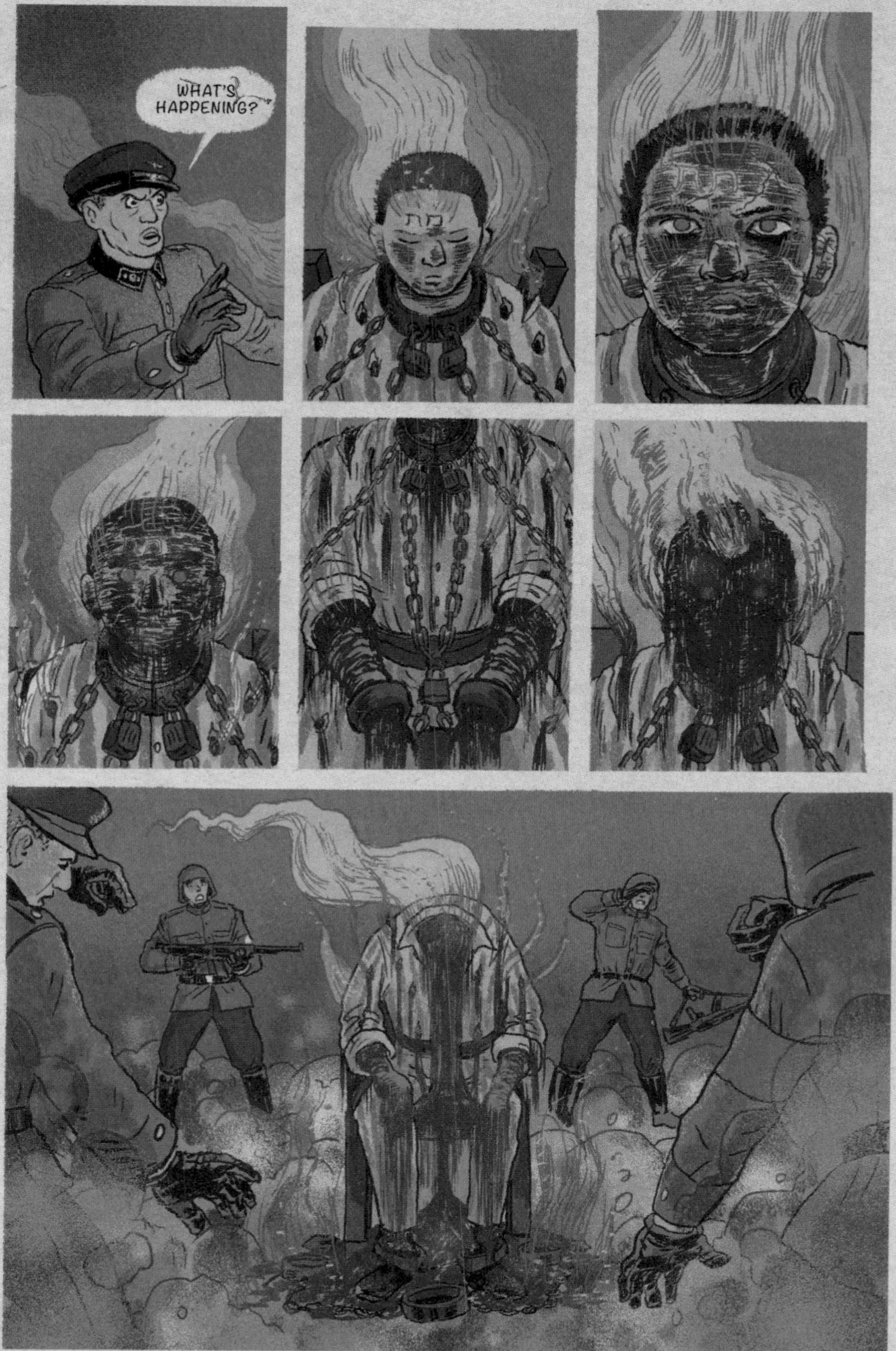
WHAT'S HAPPENING?

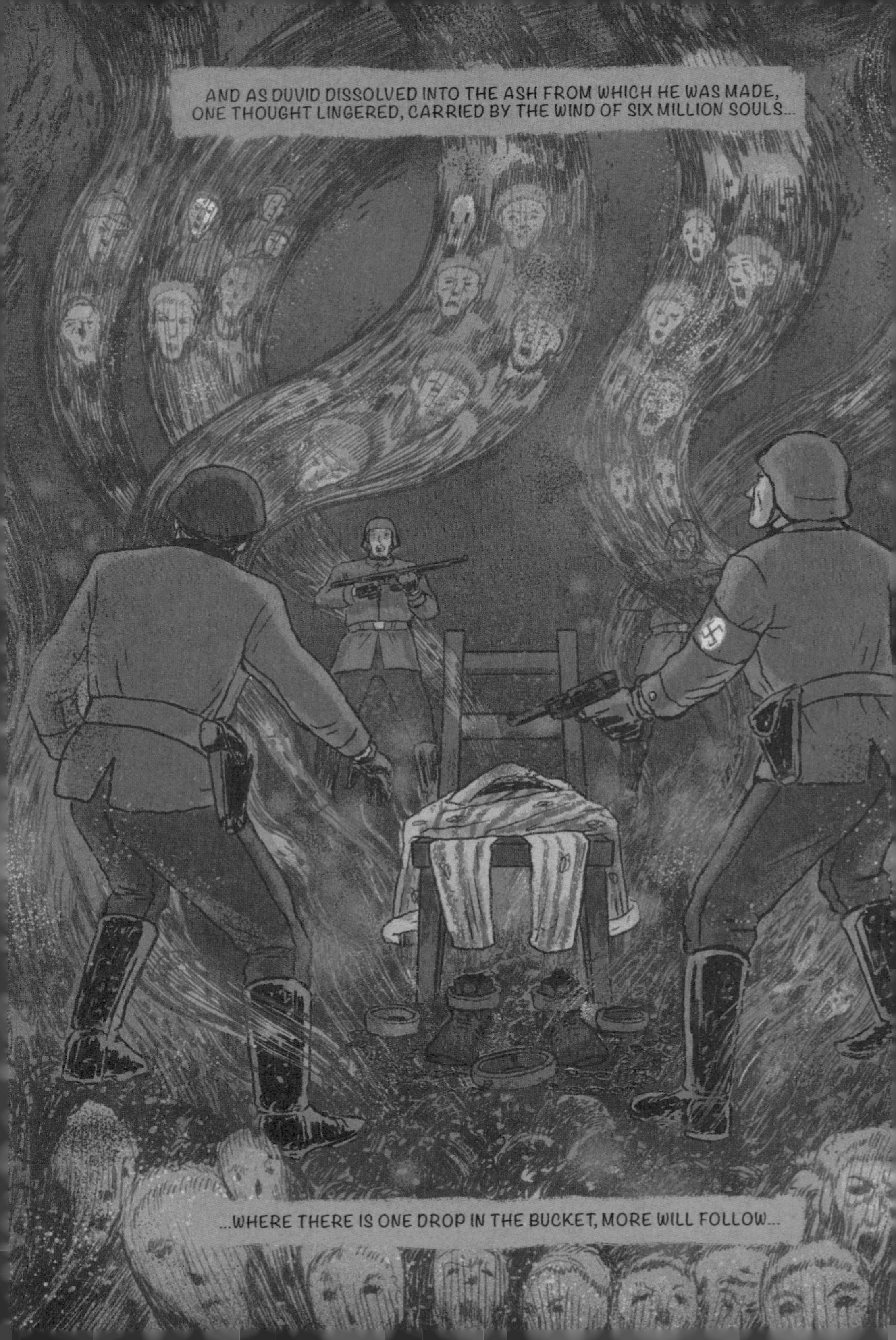
AND AS DUVID DISSOLVED INTO THE ASH FROM WHICH HE WAS MADE, ONE THOUGHT LINGERED, CARRIED BY THE WIND OF SIX MILLION SOULS...
...WHERE THERE IS ONE DROP IN THE BUCKET, MORE WILL FOLLOW...

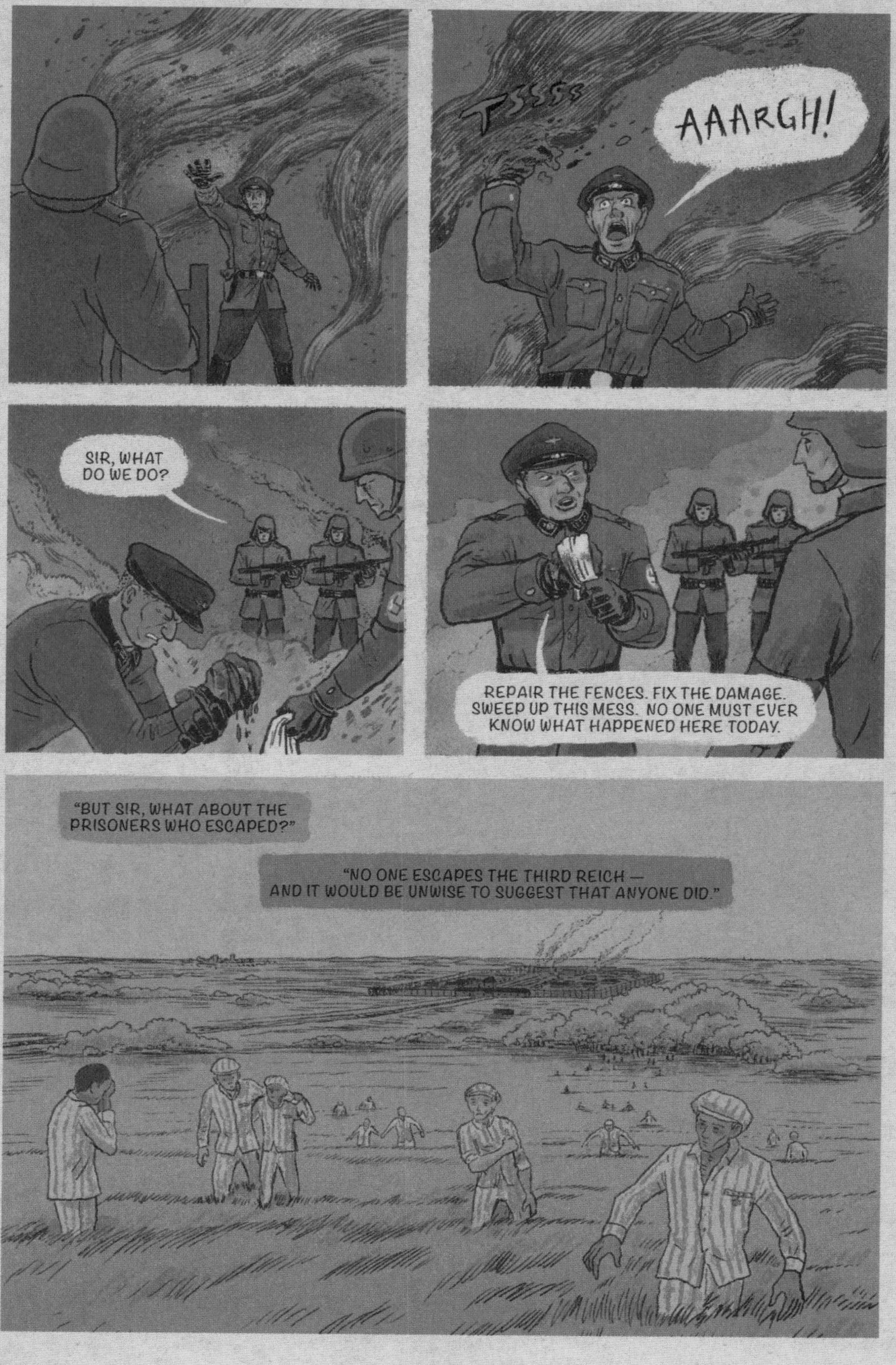
TSSSS
AAARGH!
SIR, WHAT DO WE DO?
REPAIR THE FENCES. FIX THE DAMAGE. SWEEP UP THIS MESS. NO ONE MUST EVER KNOW WHAT HAPPENED HERE TODAY.
"BUT SIR, WHAT ABOUT THE PRISONERS WHO ESCAPED?"
"NO ONE ESCAPES THE THIRD REICH — AND IT WOULD BE UNWISE TO SUGGEST THAT ANYONE DID."

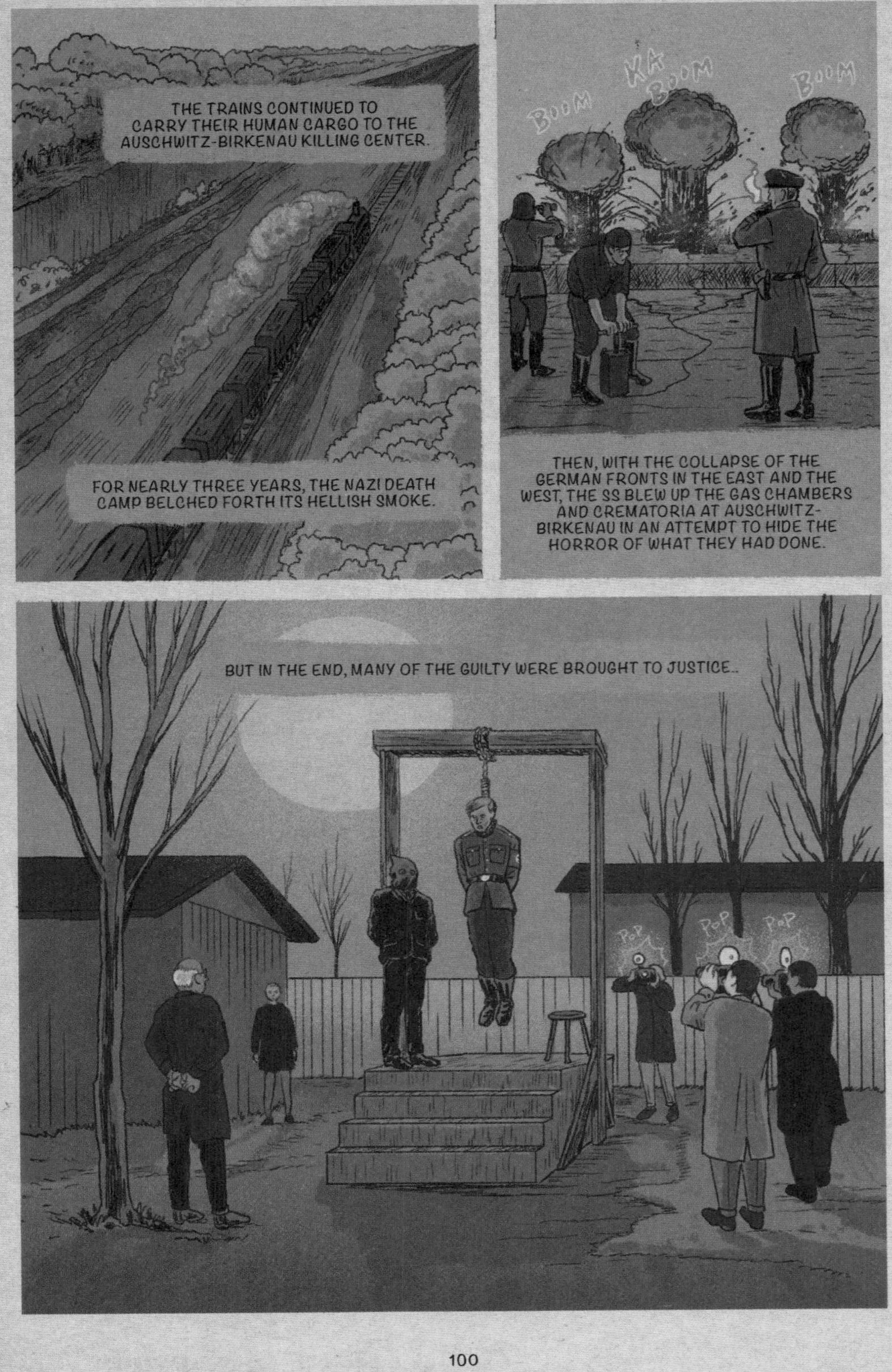
THE TRAINS CONTINUED TO CARRY THEIR HUMAN CARGO TO THE AUSCHWITZ-BIRKENAU KILLING CENTER.
FOR NEARLY THREE YEARS, THE NAZI DEATH CAMP BELCHED FORTH ITS HELLISH SMOKE.
BOOM
KA BOOM
BOOM
THEN, WITH THE COLLAPSE OF THE GERMAN FRONTS IN THE EAST AND THE WEST, THE SS BLEW UP THE GAS CHAMBERS AND CREMATORIA AT AUSCHWITZ-BIRKENAU IN AN ATTEMPT TO HIDE THE HORROR OF WHAT THEY HAD DONE.
BUT IN THE END, MANY OF THE GUILTY WERE BROUGHT TO JUSTICE...
POP
POP
POP

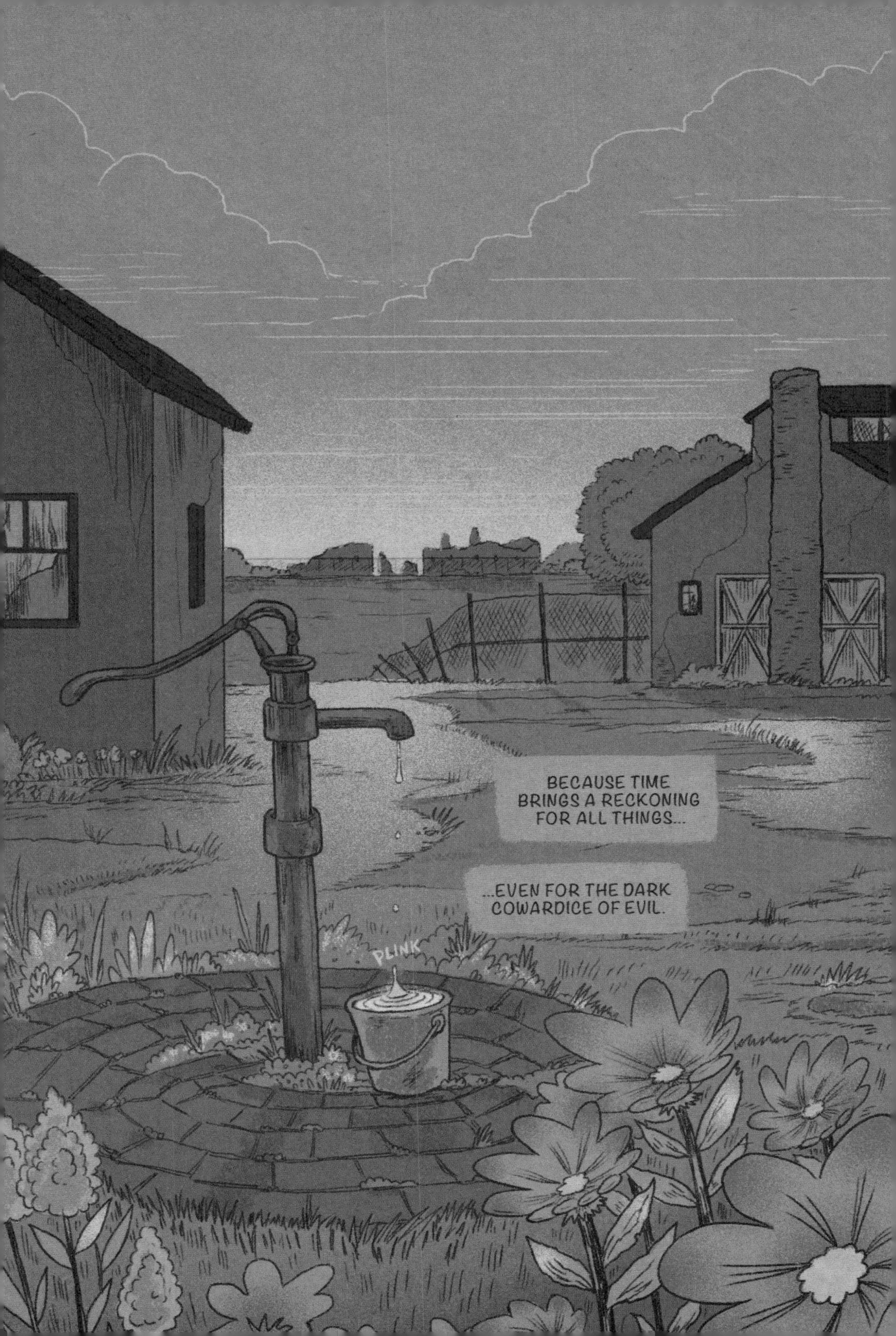
BECAUSE TIME BRINGS A RECKONING FOR ALL THINGS...
...EVEN FOR THE DARK COWARDICE OF EVIL.
PLINK

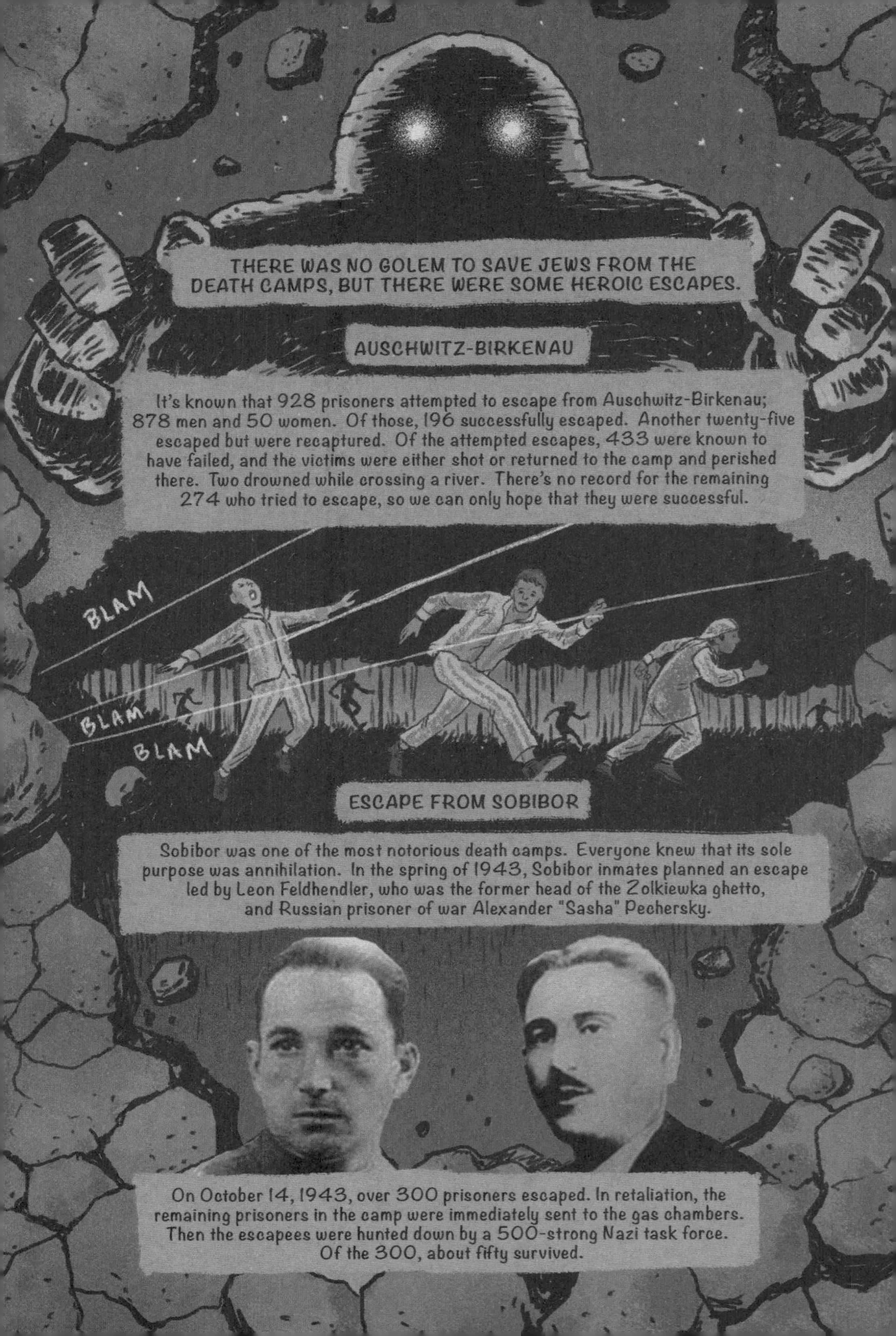
THERE WAS NO GOLEM TO SAVE JEWS FROM THE DEATH CAMPS, BUT THERE WERE SOME HEROIC ESCAPES.
AUSCHWITZ-BIRKENAU
It's known that 928 prisoners attempted to escape from Auschwitz-Birkenau; 878 men and 50 women. Of those, 196 successfully escaped. Another twenty-five escaped but were recaptured. Of the attempted escapes, 433 were known to have failed, and the victims were either shot or returned to the camp and perished there. Two drowned while crossing a river. There's no record for the remaining 274 who tried to escape, so we can only hope that they were successful.
BLAM
BLAM
BLAM
ESCAPE FROM SOBIBOR
Sobibor was one of the most notorious death camps. Everyone knew that its sole purpose was annihilation. In the spring of 1943, Sobibor inmates planned an escape led by Leon Feldhendler, who was the former head of the Zolkiewka ghetto, and Russian prisoner of war Alexander "Sasha" Pechersky.
On October 14, 1943, over 300 prisoners escaped. In retaliation, the remaining prisoners in the camp were immediately sent to the gas chambers. Then the escapees were hunted down by a 500-strong Nazi task force. Of the 300, about fifty survived.

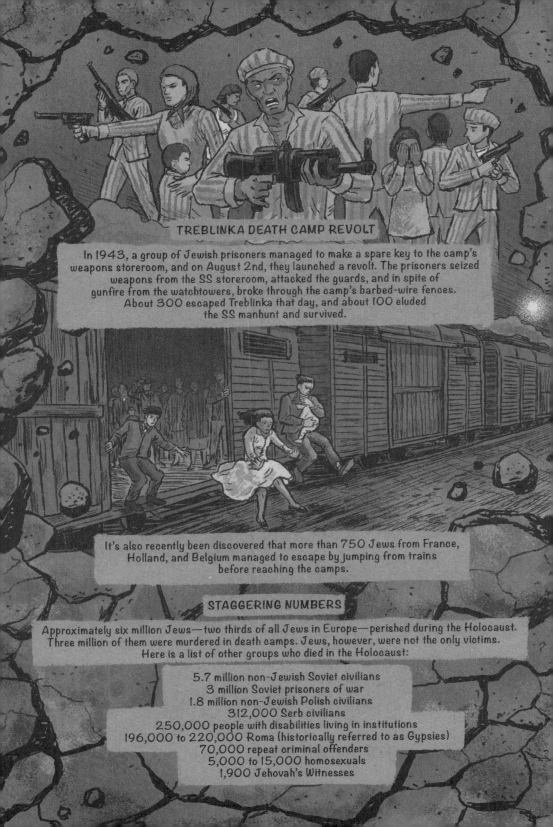

TREBLINKA DEATH CAMP REVOLT

In 1943, a group of Jewish prisoners managed to make a spare key to the camp's weapons storeroom, and on August 2nd, they launched a revolt. The prisoners seized weapons from the SS storeroom, attacked the guards, and in spite of gunfire from the watchtowers, broke through the camp's barbed-wire fences. About 300 escaped Treblinka that day, and about 100 eluded the SS manhunt and survived.

It's also recently been discovered that more than 750 Jews from France, Holland, and Belgium managed to escape by jumping from trains before reaching the camps.

STAGGERING NUMBERS

Approximately six million Jews—two thirds of all Jews in Europe—perished during the Holocaust. Three million of them were murdered in death camps. Jews, however, were not the only victims. Here is a list of other groups who died in the Holocaust:

5.7 million non-Jewish Soviet civilians
3 million Soviet prisoners of war
1.8 million non-Jewish Polish civilians
312,000 Serb civilians
250,000 people with disabilities living in institutions
196,000 to 220,000 Roma (historically referred to as Gypsies)
70,000 repeat criminal offenders
5,000 to 15,000 homosexuals
1,900 Jehovah's Witnesses

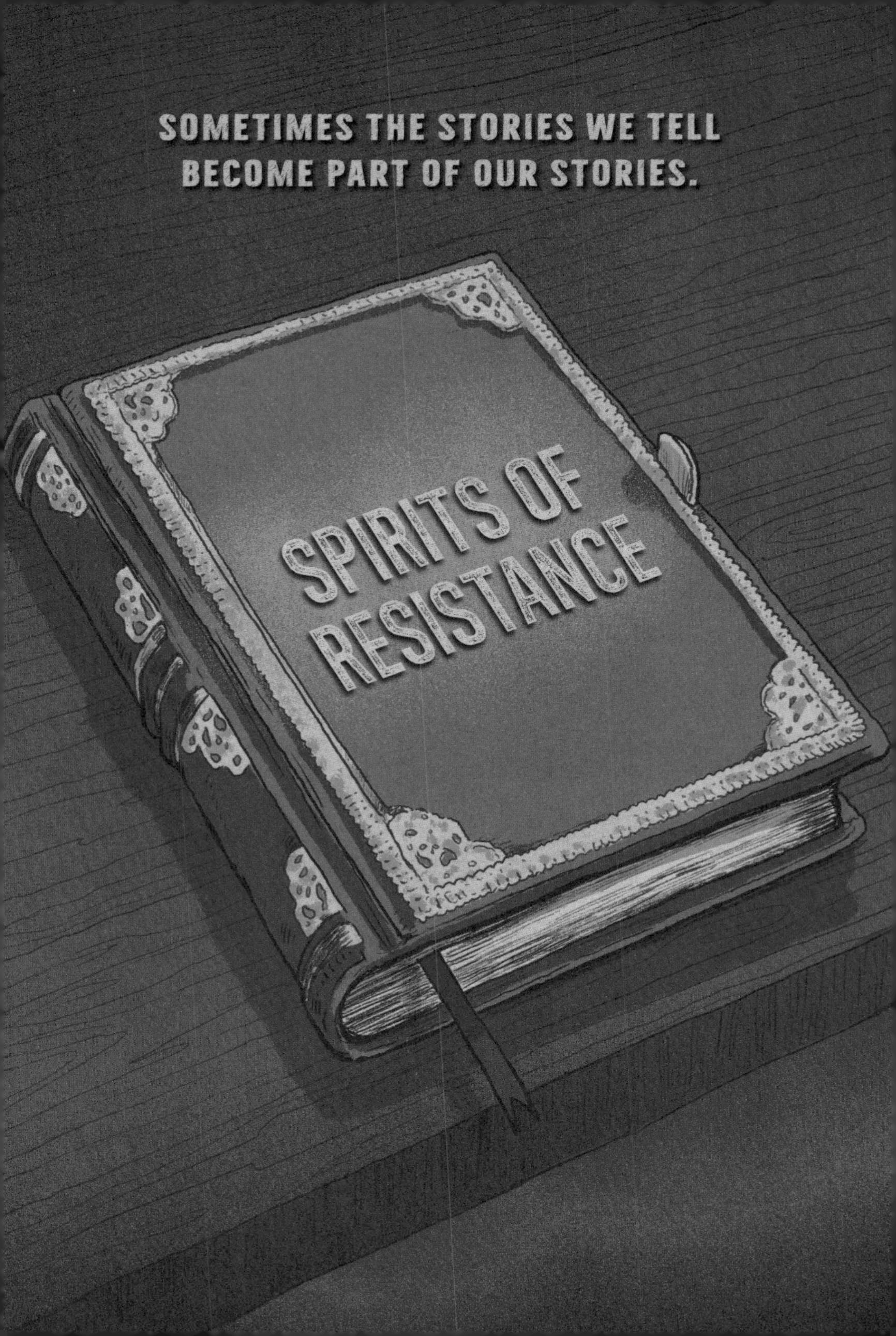
SOMETIMES THE STORIES WE TELL
BECOME PART OF OUR STORIES.
SPIRITS OF
RESISTANCE

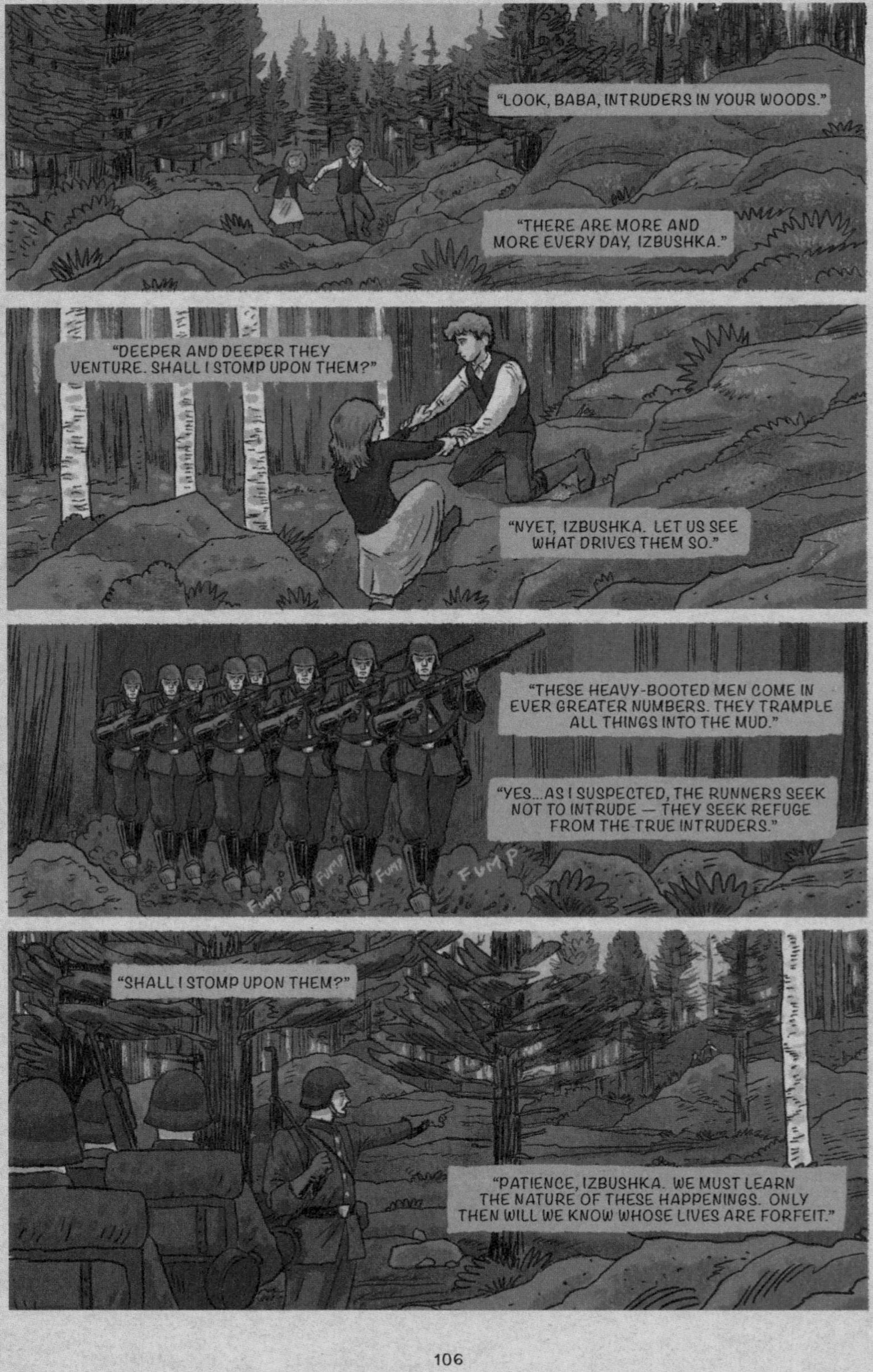
"LOOK, BABA, INTRUDERS IN YOUR WOODS."
"THERE ARE MORE AND MORE EVERY DAY, IZBUSHKA."
"DEEPER AND DEEPER THEY VENTURE. SHALL I STOMP UPON THEM?"
"NYET, IZBUSHKA. LET US SEE WHAT DRIVES THEM SO."
"THESE HEAVY-BOOTED MEN COME IN EVER GREATER NUMBERS. THEY TRAMPLE ALL THINGS INTO THE MUD."
"YES...AS I SUSPECTED, THE RUNNERS SEEK NOT TO INTRUDE — THEY SEEK REFUGE FROM THE TRUE INTRUDERS."
FUMP
FUMP
FUMP
FUMP
"SHALL I STOMP UPON THEM?"
"PATIENCE, IZBUSHKA. WE MUST LEARN THE NATURE OF THESE HAPPENINGS. ONLY THEN WILL WE KNOW WHOSE LIVES ARE FORFEIT."

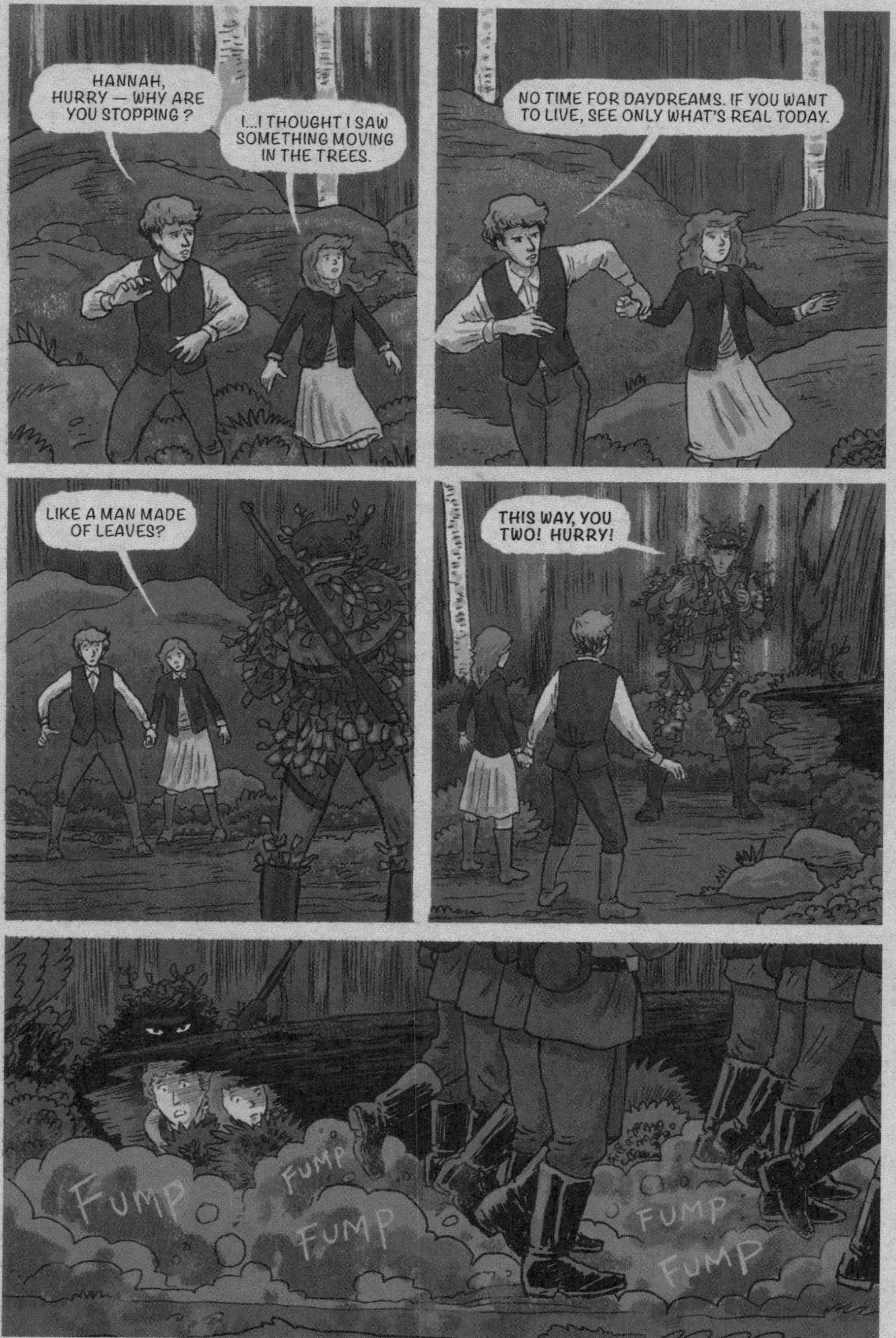
HANNAH, HURRY — WHY ARE YOU STOPPING ?
I...I THOUGHT I SAW SOMETHING MOVING IN THE TREES.
NO TIME FOR DAYDREAMS. IF YOU WANT TO LIVE, SEE ONLY WHAT'S REAL TODAY.
LIKE A MAN MADE OF LEAVES?
THIS WAY, YOU TWO! HURRY!
FUMP
FUMP
FUMP
FUMP
FUMP

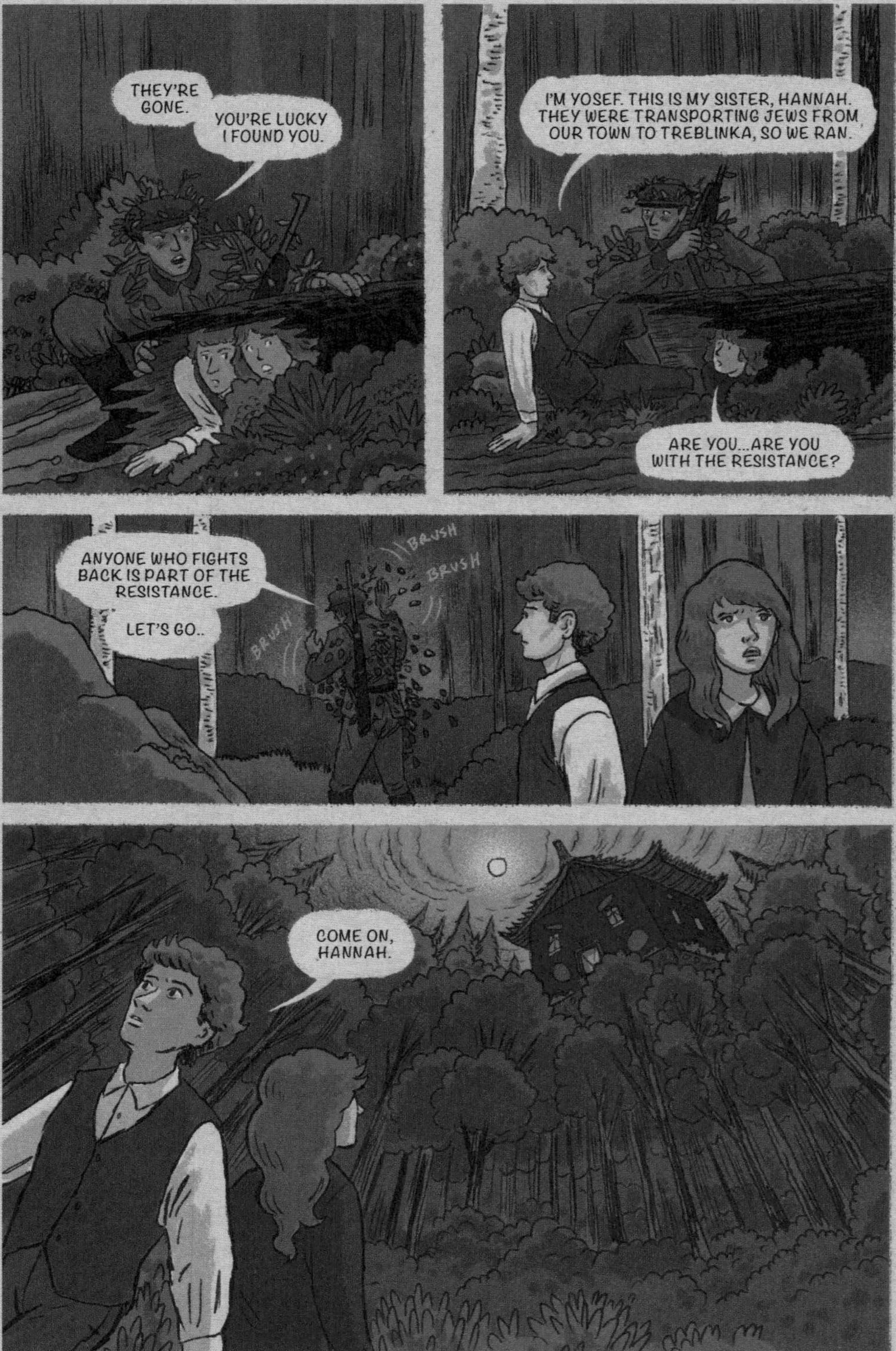
THEY'RE GONE.
YOU'RE LUCKY I FOUND YOU.
I'M YOSEF. THIS IS MY SISTER, HANNAH. THEY WERE TRANSPORTING JEWS FROM OUR TOWN TO TREBLINKA, SO WE RAN.
ARE YOU...ARE YOU WITH THE RESISTANCE?
ANYONE WHO FIGHTS BACK IS PART OF THE RESISTANCE.
LET'S GO..
BRUSH
BRUSH
BRUSH
COME ON, HANNAH.

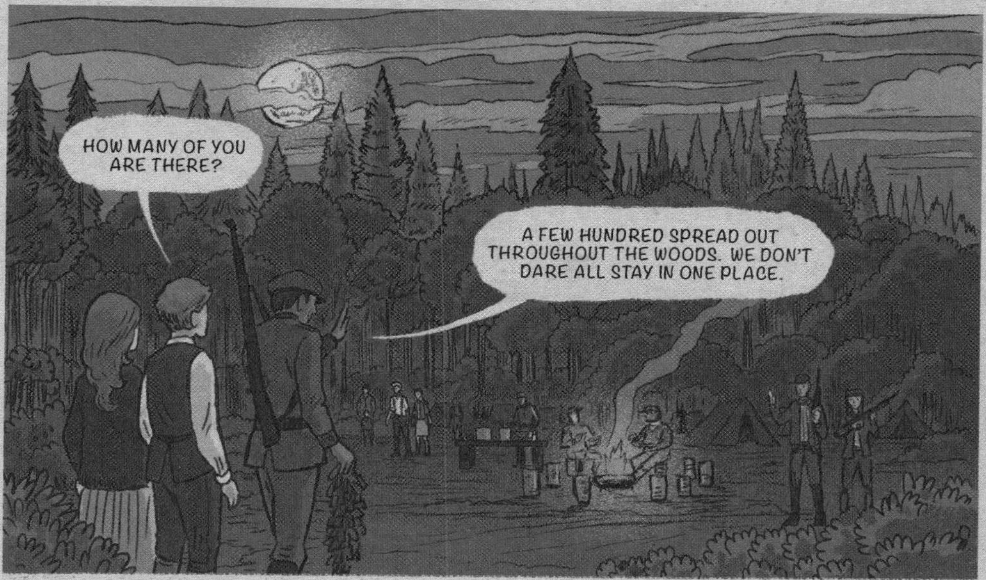
HOW MANY OF YOU ARE THERE?
A FEW HUNDRED SPREAD OUT THROUGHOUT THE WOODS. WE DON'T DARE ALL STAY IN ONE PLACE.

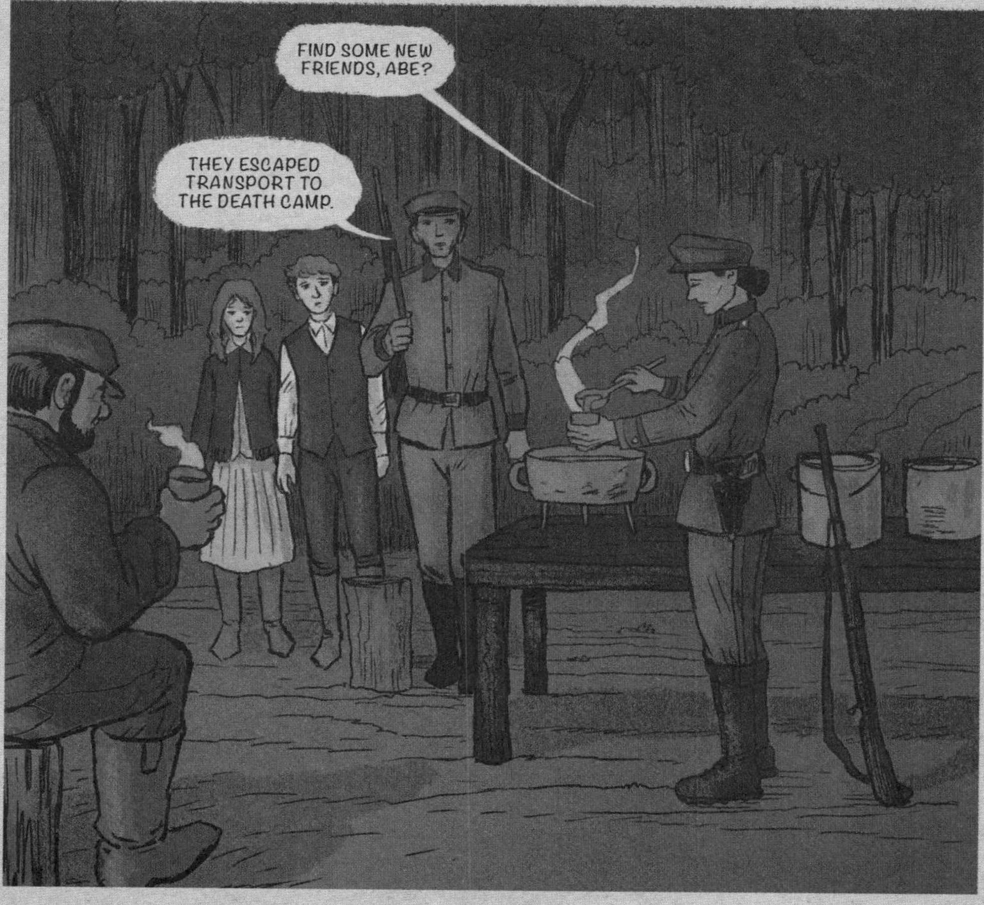
FIND SOME NEW FRIENDS, ABE?
THEY ESCAPED TRANSPORT TO THE DEATH CAMP.

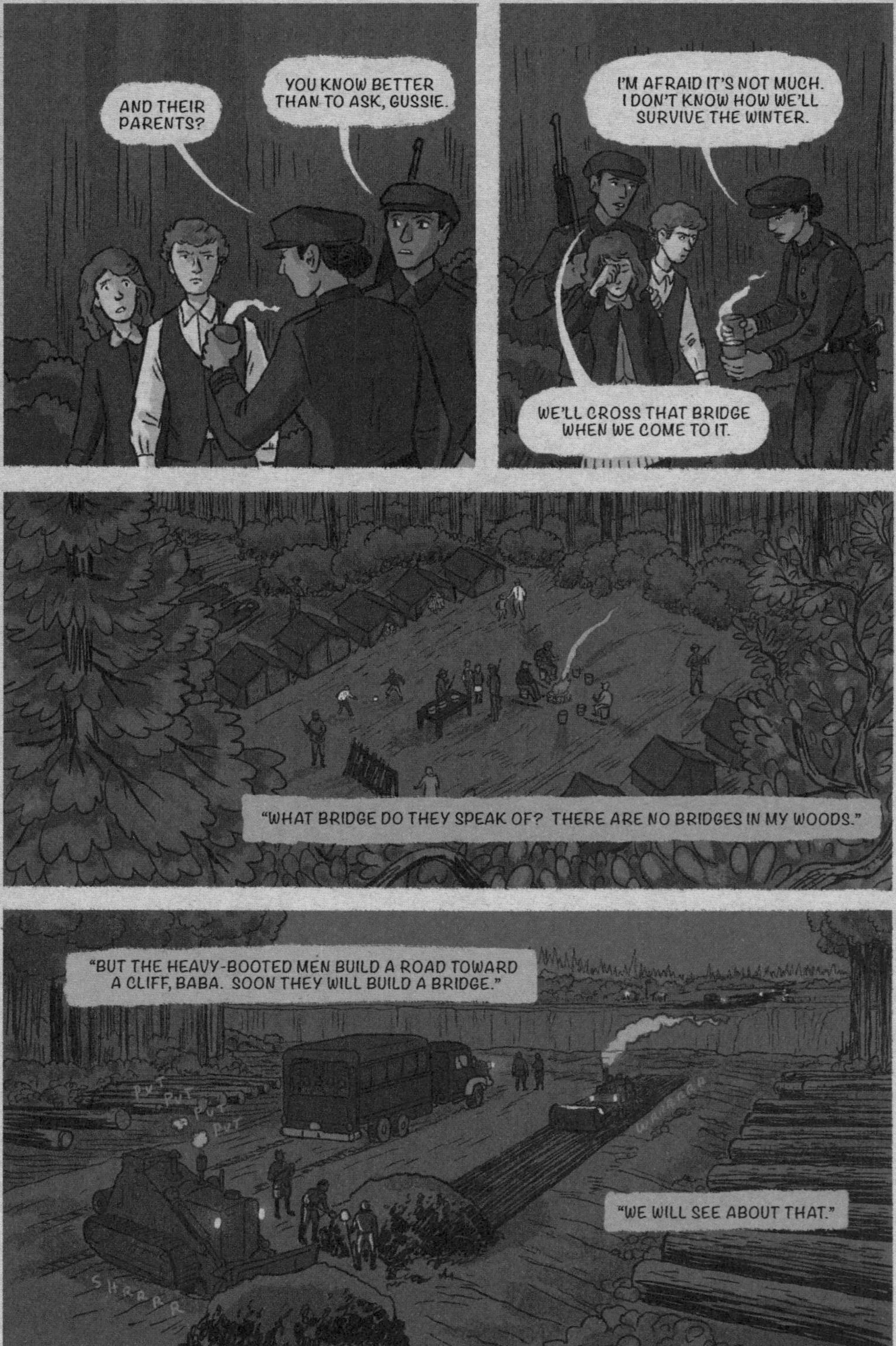
AND THEIR PARENTS?
YOU KNOW BETTER THAN TO ASK, GUSSIE.
I'M AFRAID IT'S NOT MUCH. I DON'T KNOW HOW WE'LL SURVIVE THE WINTER.
WE'LL CROSS THAT BRIDGE WHEN WE COME TO IT.
"WHAT BRIDGE DO THEY SPEAK OF? THERE ARE NO BRIDGES IN MY WOODS."
"BUT THE HEAVY-BOOTED MEN BUILD A ROAD TOWARD A CLIFF, BABA. SOON THEY WILL BUILD A BRIDGE."
PUT PUT PUT PUT
SHRRRR
"WE WILL SEE ABOUT THAT."

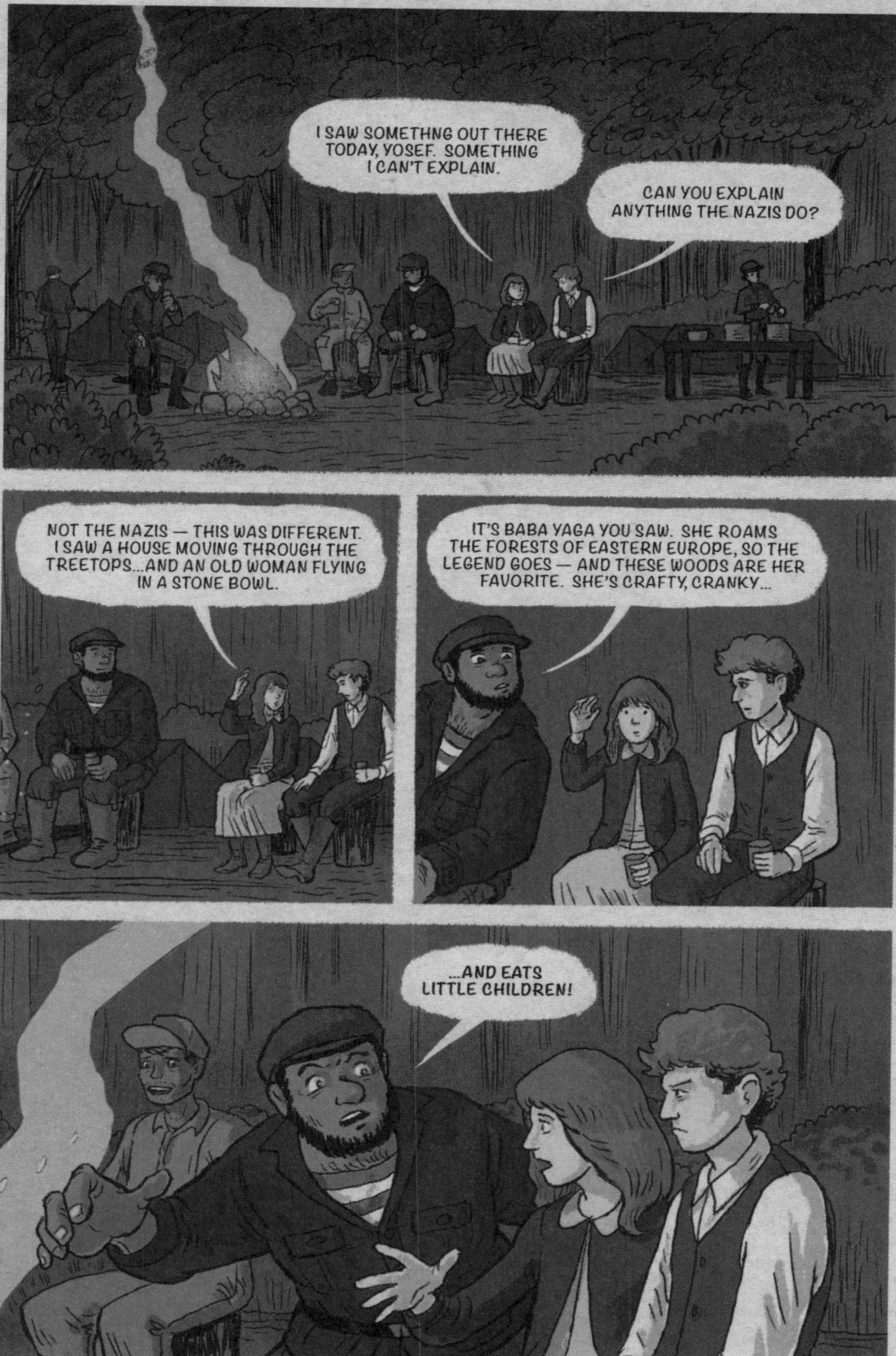
I SAW SOMETHNG OUT THERE TODAY, YOSEF. SOMETHING I CAN'T EXPLAIN.
CAN YOU EXPLAIN ANYTHING THE NAZIS DO?
NOT THE NAZIS — THIS WAS DIFFERENT. I SAW A HOUSE MOVING THROUGH THE TREETOPS...AND AN OLD WOMAN FLYING IN A STONE BOWL.
IT'S BABA YAGA YOU SAW. SHE ROAMS THE FORESTS OF EASTERN EUROPE, SO THE LEGEND GOES — AND THESE WOODS ARE HER FAVORITE. SHE'S CRAFTY, CRANKY...
...AND EATS LITTLE CHILDREN!

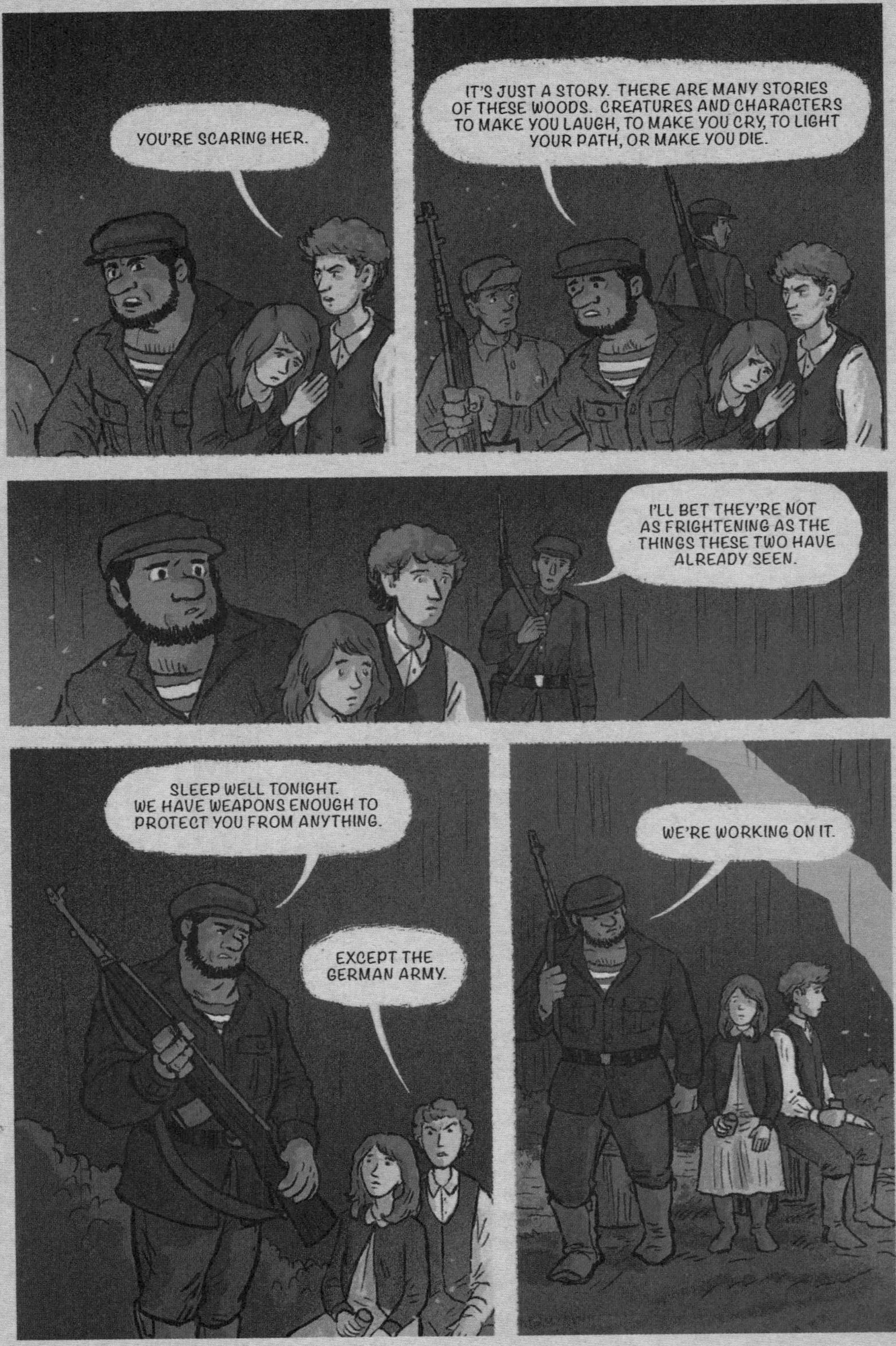
YOU'RE SCARING HER.
IT'S JUST A STORY. THERE ARE MANY STORIES OF THESE WOODS. CREATURES AND CHARACTERS TO MAKE YOU LAUGH, TO MAKE YOU CRY, TO LIGHT YOUR PATH, OR MAKE YOU DIE.
I'LL BET THEY'RE NOT AS FRIGHTENING AS THE THINGS THESE TWO HAVE ALREADY SEEN.
SLEEP WELL TONIGHT. WE HAVE WEAPONS ENOUGH TO PROTECT YOU FROM ANYTHING.
EXCEPT THE GERMAN ARMY.
WE'RE WORKING ON IT.

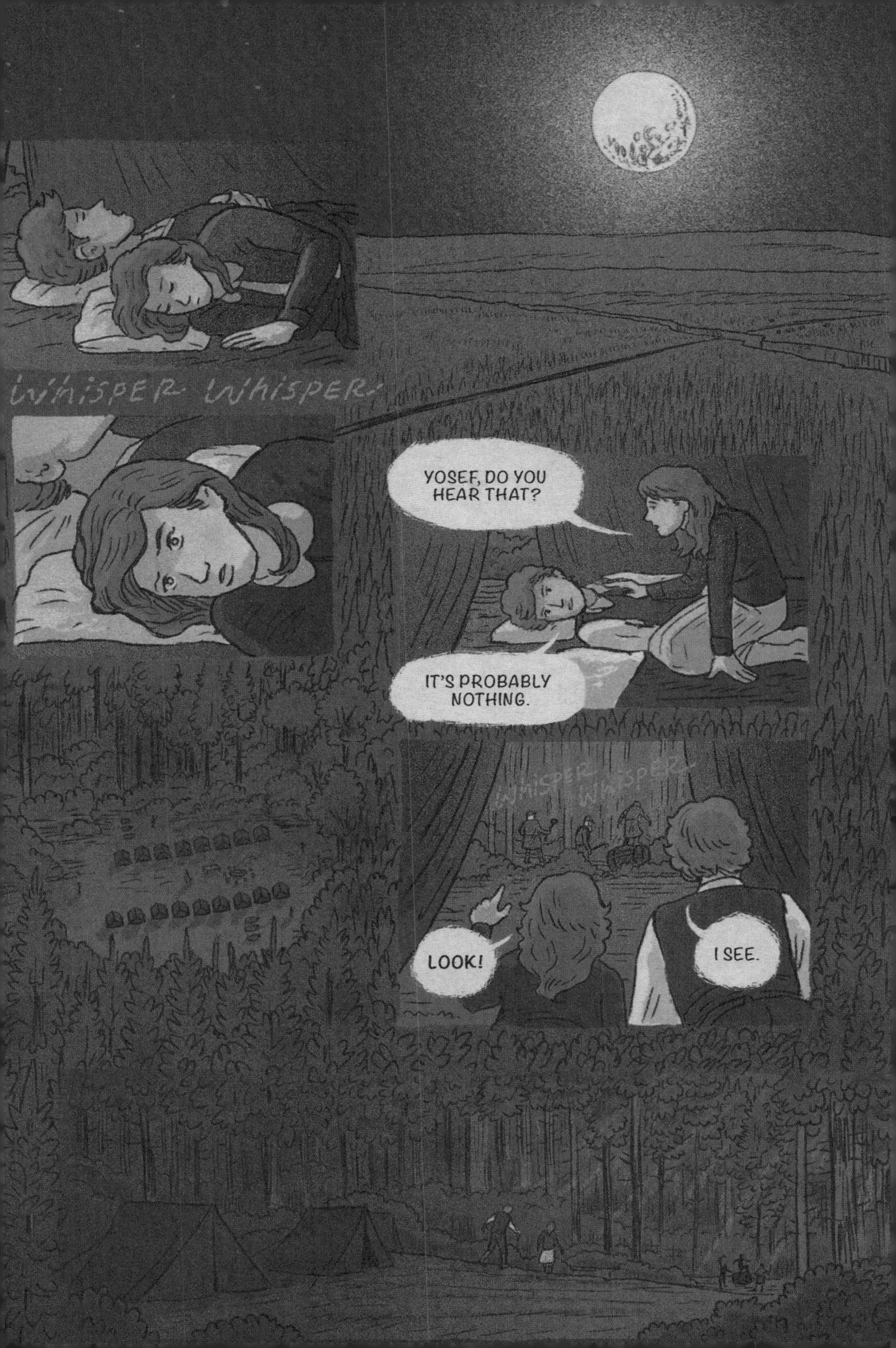
WHISPER WHISPER
YOSEF, DO YOU HEAR THAT?
IT'S PROBABLY NOTHING.
WHISPER WHISPER
LOOK!
I SEE.

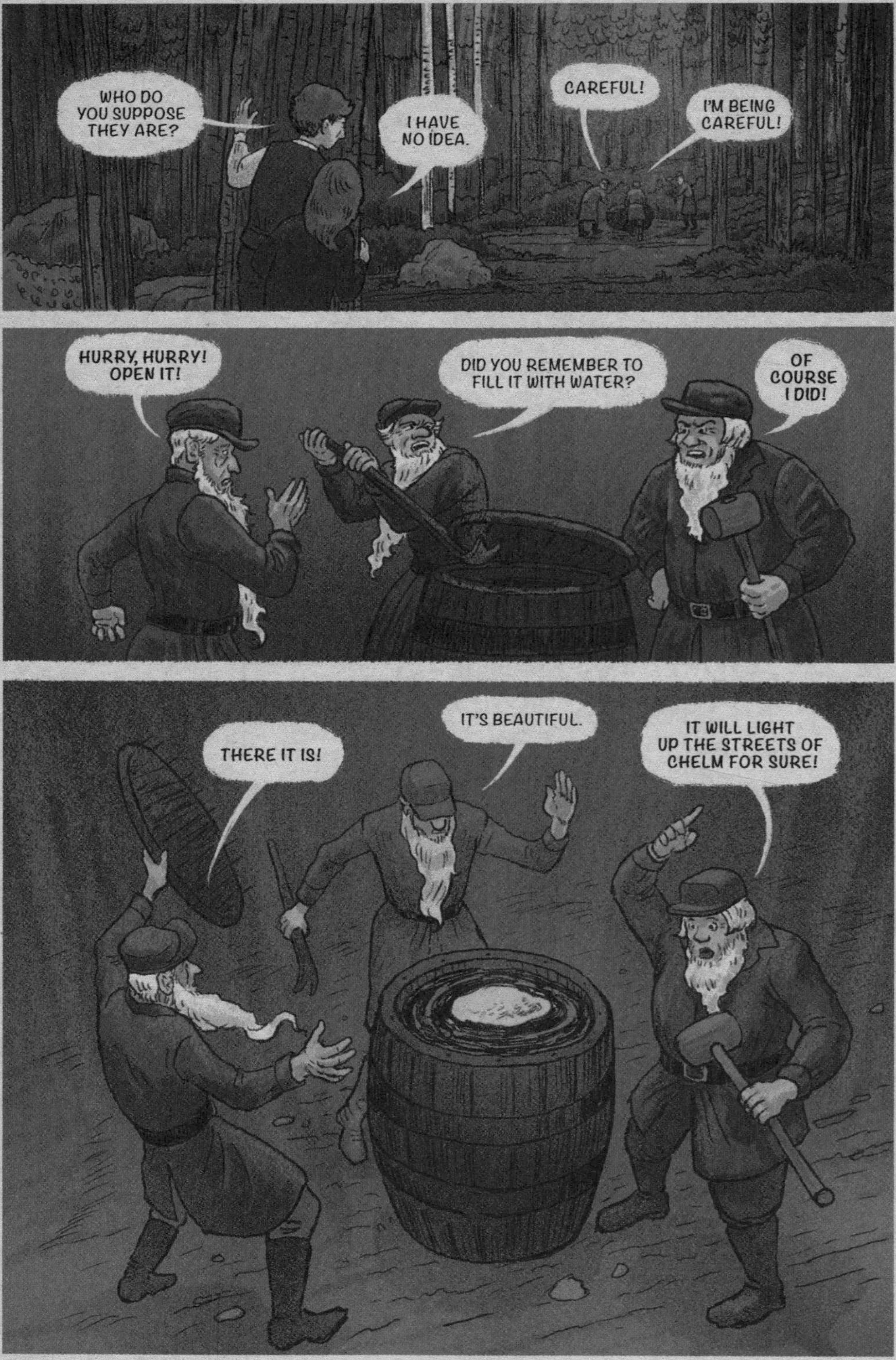
WHO DO YOU SUPPOSE THEY ARE?
I HAVE NO IDEA.
CAREFUL!
I'M BEING CAREFUL!
HURRY, HURRY! OPEN IT!
DID YOU REMEMBER TO FILL IT WITH WATER?
OF COURSE I DID!
THERE IT IS!
IT'S BEAUTIFUL.
IT WILL LIGHT UP THE STREETS OF CHELM FOR SURE!

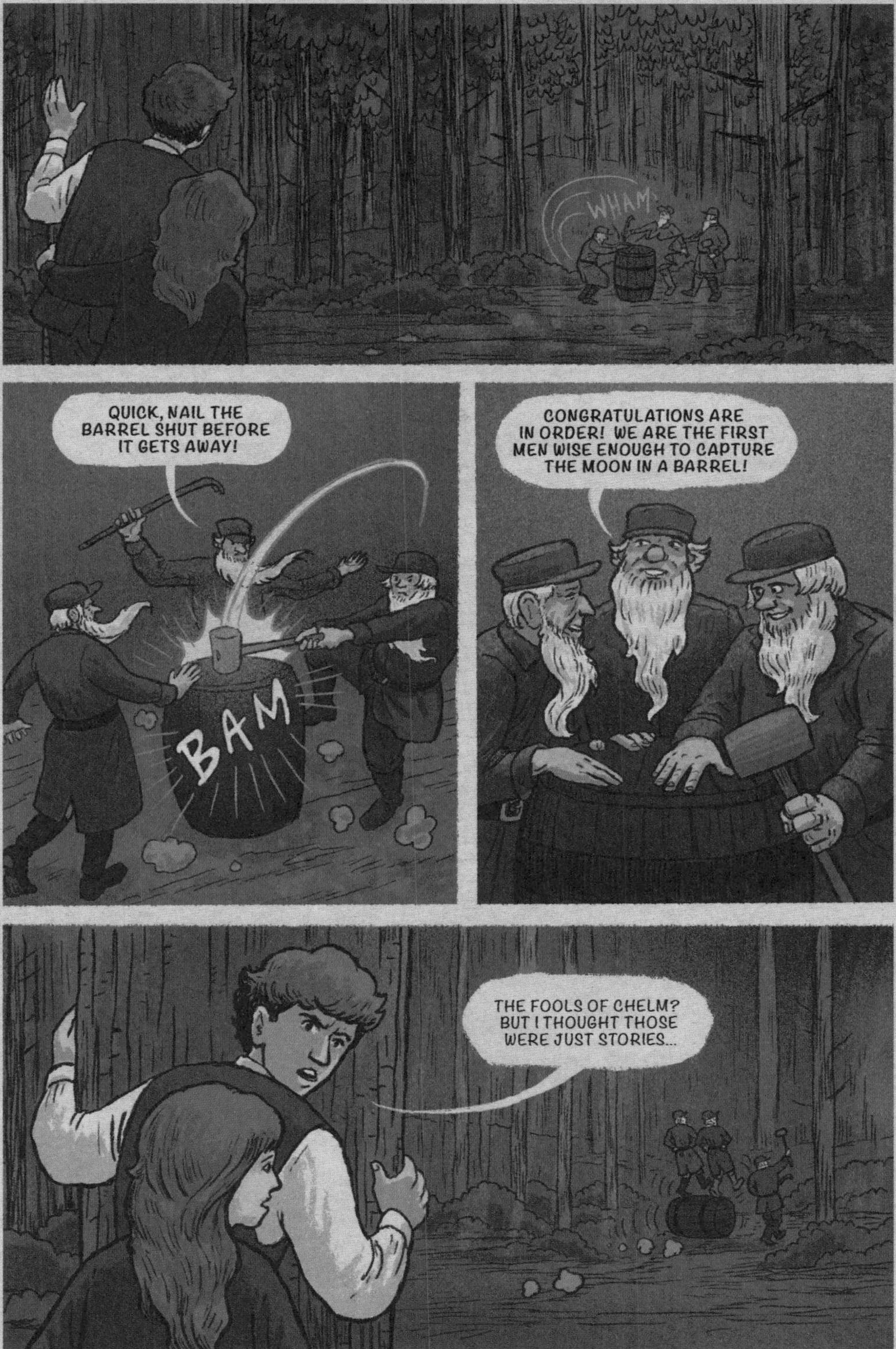
WHAM
QUICK, NAIL THE BARREL SHUT BEFORE IT GETS AWAY!
BAM
CONGRATULATIONS ARE IN ORDER! WE ARE THE FIRST MEN WISE ENOUGH TO CAPTURE THE MOON IN A BARREL!
THE FOOLS OF CHELM? BUT I THOUGHT THOSE WERE JUST STORIES...

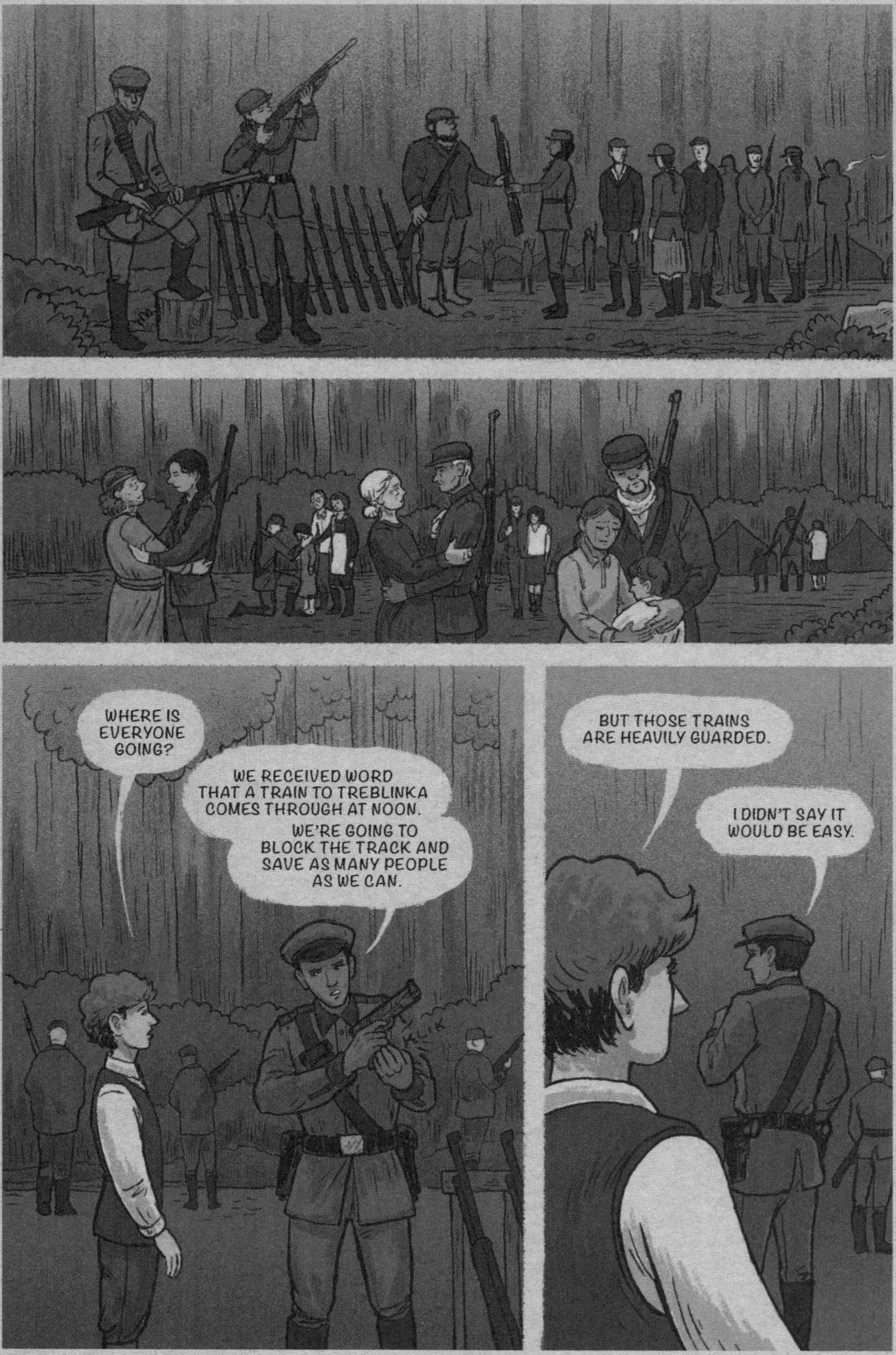

WHERE IS EVERYONE GOING?
WE RECEIVED WORD THAT A TRAIN TO TREBLINKA COMES THROUGH AT NOON.
WE'RE GOING TO BLOCK THE TRACK AND SAVE AS MANY PEOPLE AS WE CAN.
KLIK
BUT THOSE TRAINS ARE HEAVILY GUARDED.
I DIDN'T SAY IT WOULD BE EASY.

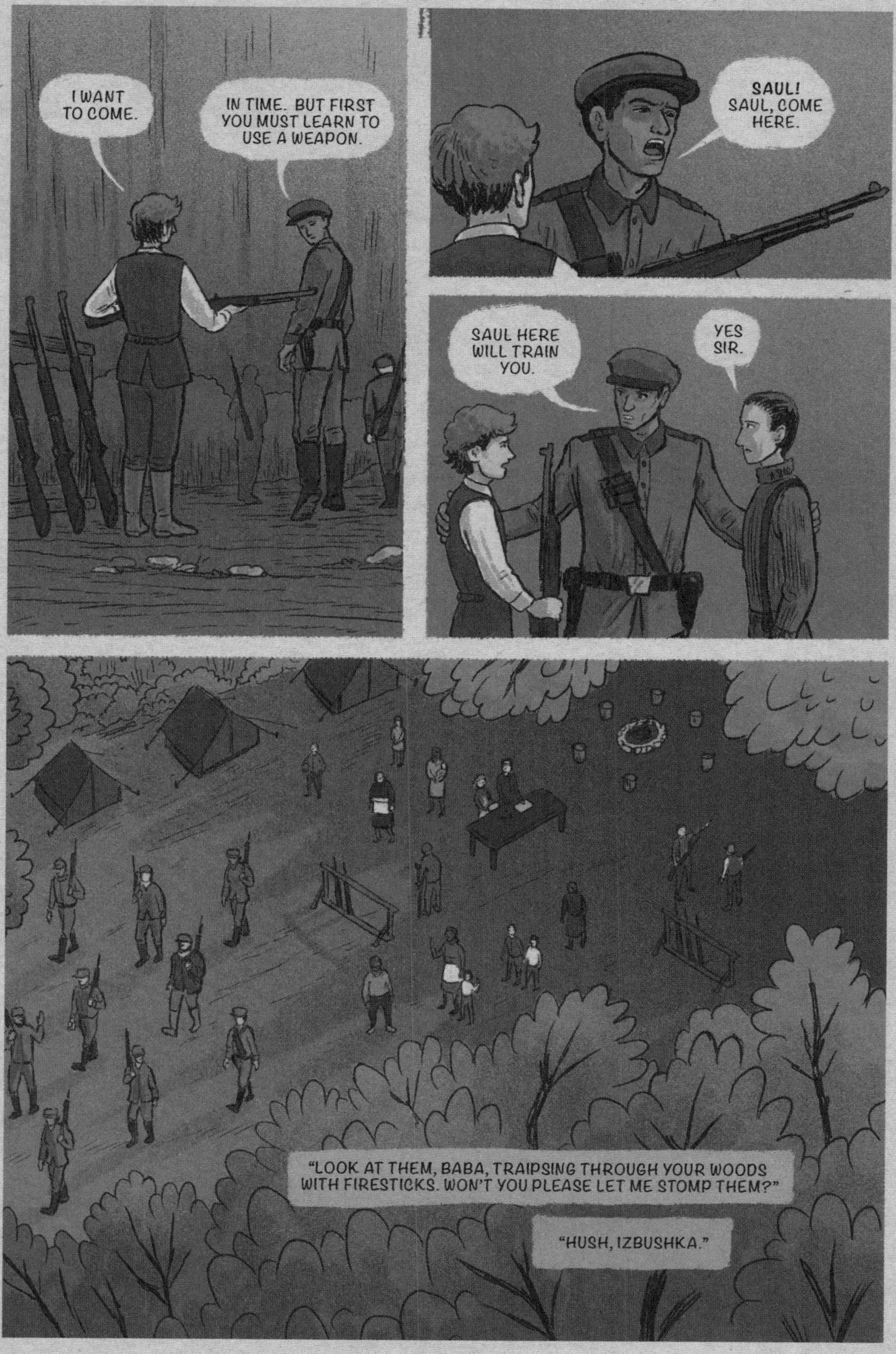

I WANT TO COME.
IN TIME. BUT FIRST YOU MUST LEARN TO USE A WEAPON.
SAUL! SAUL, COME HERE.
SAUL HERE WILL TRAIN YOU.
YES SIR.
"LOOK AT THEM, BABA, TRAIPSING THROUGH YOUR WOODS WITH FIRESTICKS. WON'T YOU PLEASE LET ME STOMP THEM?"
"HUSH, IZBUSHKA."

"AND SUCH VIOLENCE IN YOUR WOODS."
BLAM
BLAM
RA
TAT
TAT
"YET THEY DID NOT BEGIN THE VIOLENCE."
SPAK
TAT
BLAM
BLAM
BLAM
BLAM
BLAM
KA
KLAN

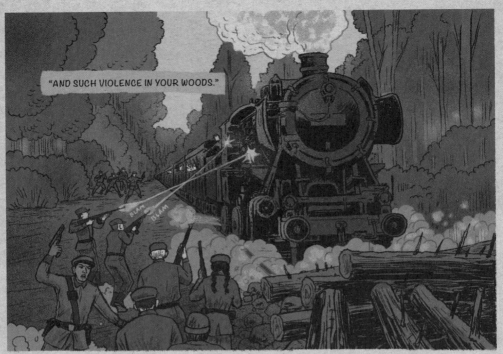

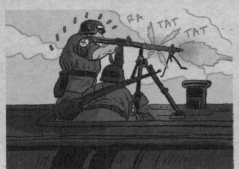

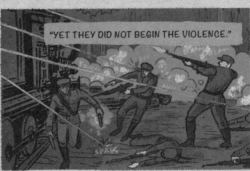

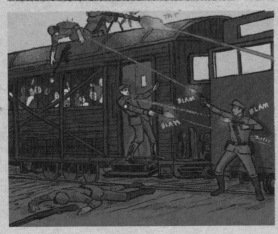

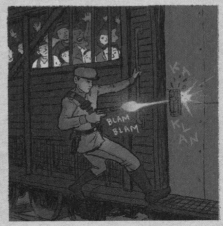

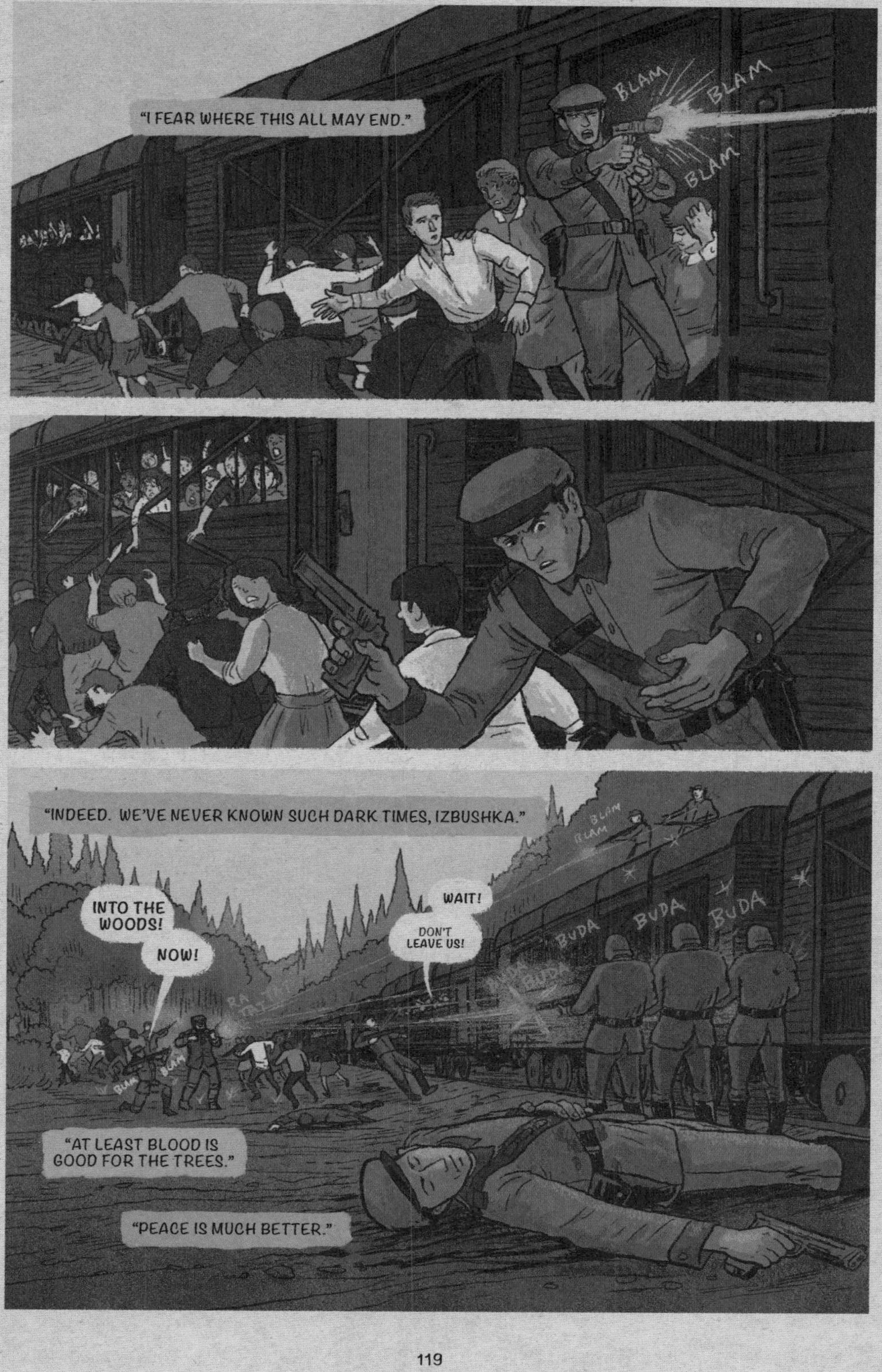
"I FEAR WHERE THIS ALL MAY END."
BLAM
BLAM
BLAM
"INDEED. WE'VE NEVER KNOWN SUCH DARK TIMES, IZBUSHKA."
INTO THE WOODS!
NOW!
WAIT!
DON'T LEAVE US!
BUDA
BUDA
BUDA
"AT LEAST BLOOD IS GOOD FOR THE TREES."
"PEACE IS MUCH BETTER."

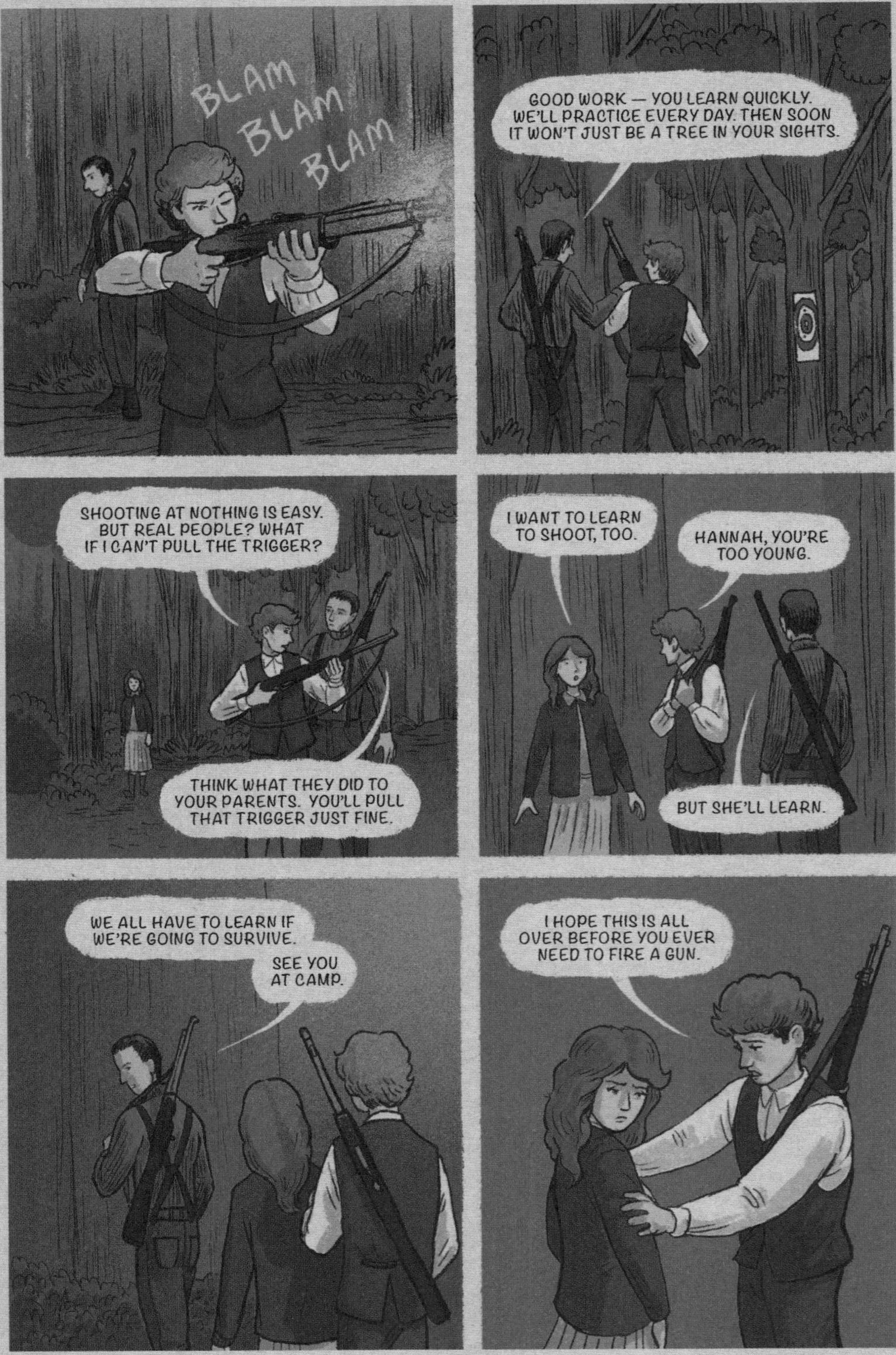
BLAM BLAM BLAM
GOOD WORK — YOU LEARN QUICKLY. WE'LL PRACTICE EVERY DAY. THEN SOON IT WON'T JUST BE A TREE IN YOUR SIGHTS.
SHOOTING AT NOTHING IS EASY. BUT REAL PEOPLE? WHAT IF I CAN'T PULL THE TRIGGER?
THINK WHAT THEY DID TO YOUR PARENTS. YOU'LL PULL THAT TRIGGER JUST FINE.
I WANT TO LEARN TO SHOOT, TOO.
HANNAH, YOU'RE TOO YOUNG.
BUT SHE'LL LEARN.
WE ALL HAVE TO LEARN IF WE'RE GOING TO SURVIVE.
SEE YOU AT CAMP.
I HOPE THIS IS ALL OVER BEFORE YOU EVER NEED TO FIRE A GUN.

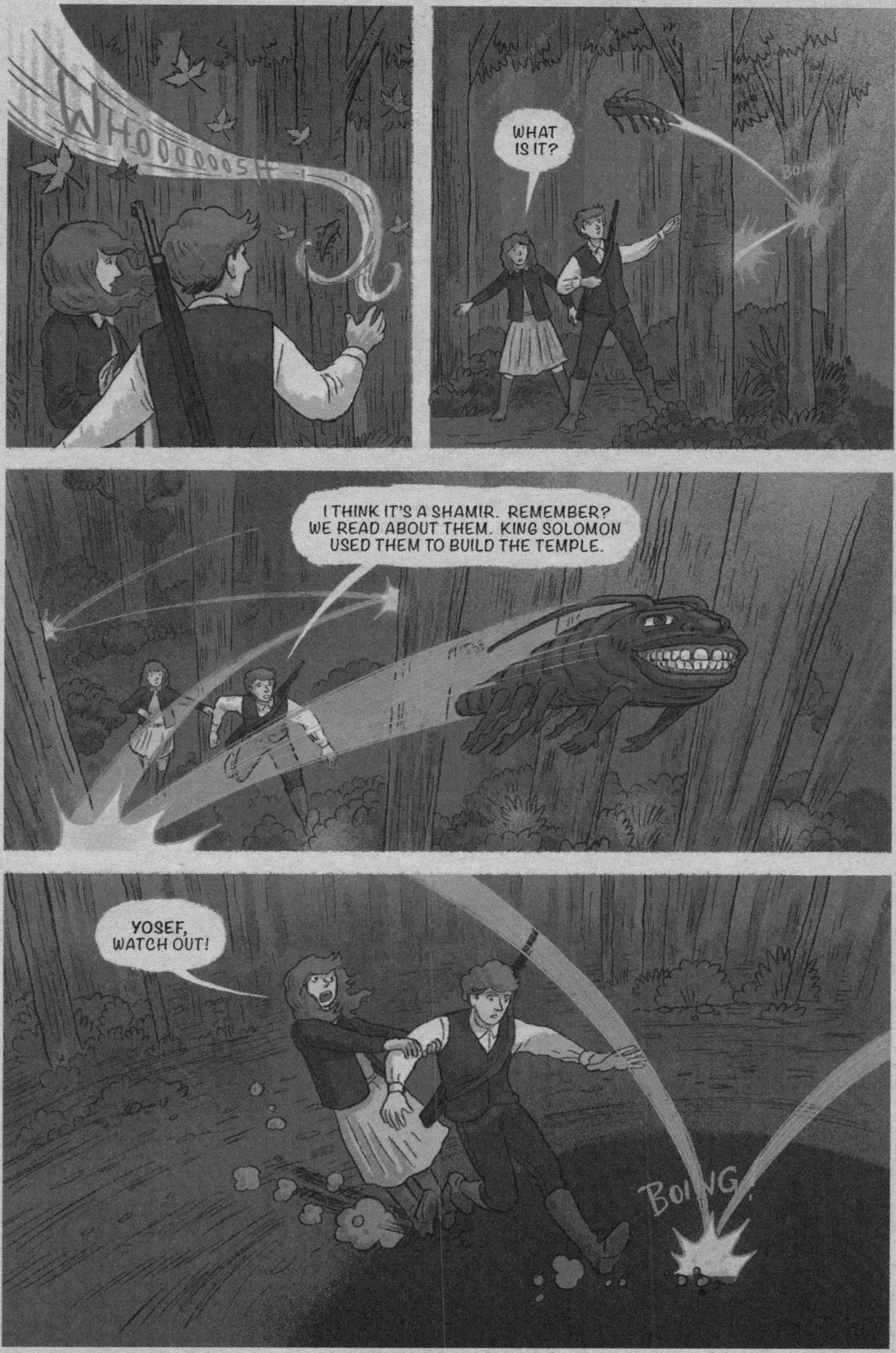
WHOOOOOOOSH
WHAT IS IT?
I THINK IT'S A SHAMIR. REMEMBER? WE READ ABOUT THEM. KING SOLOMON USED THEM TO BUILD THE TEMPLE.
YOSEF, WATCH OUT!
BOING

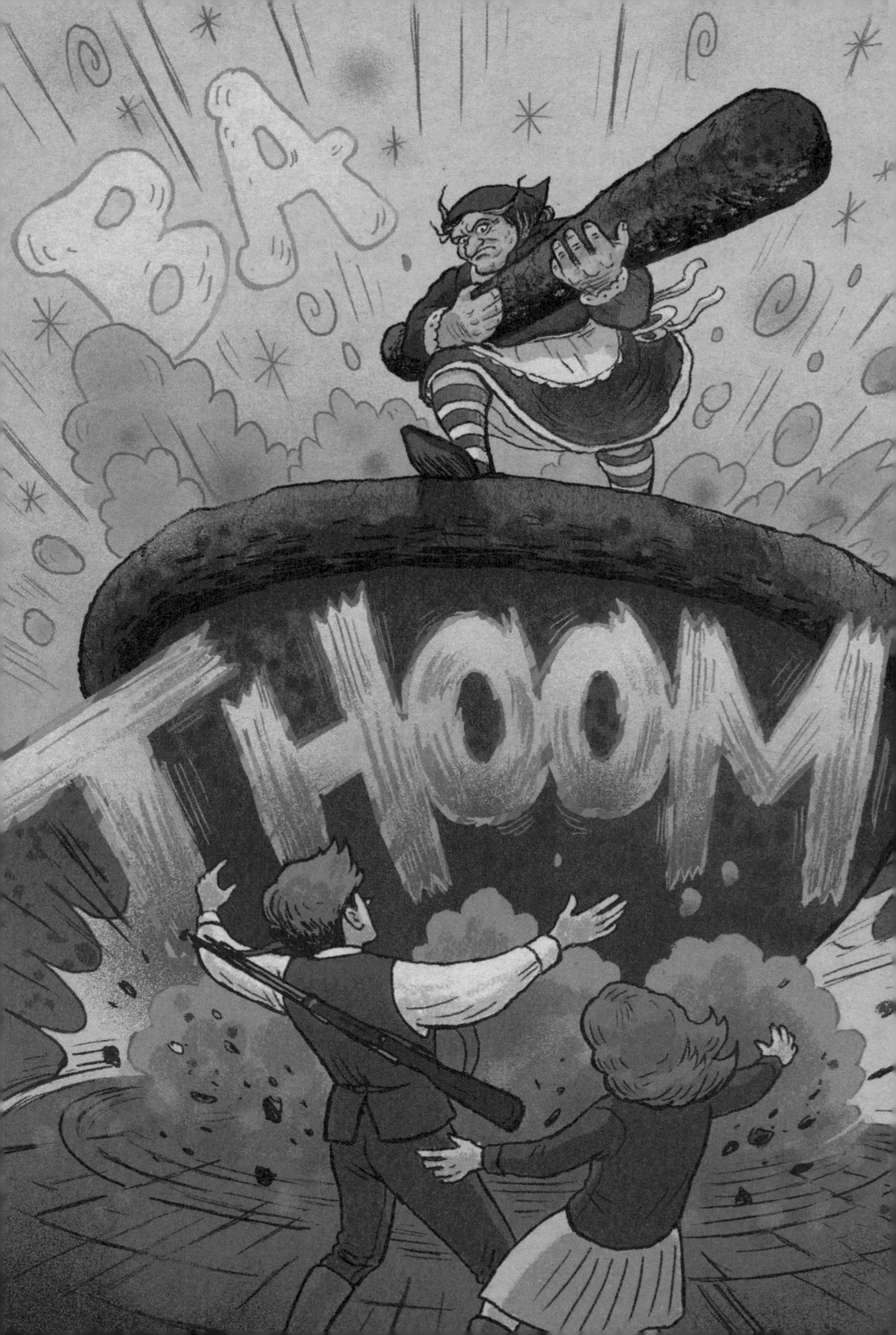
BA
THOOM

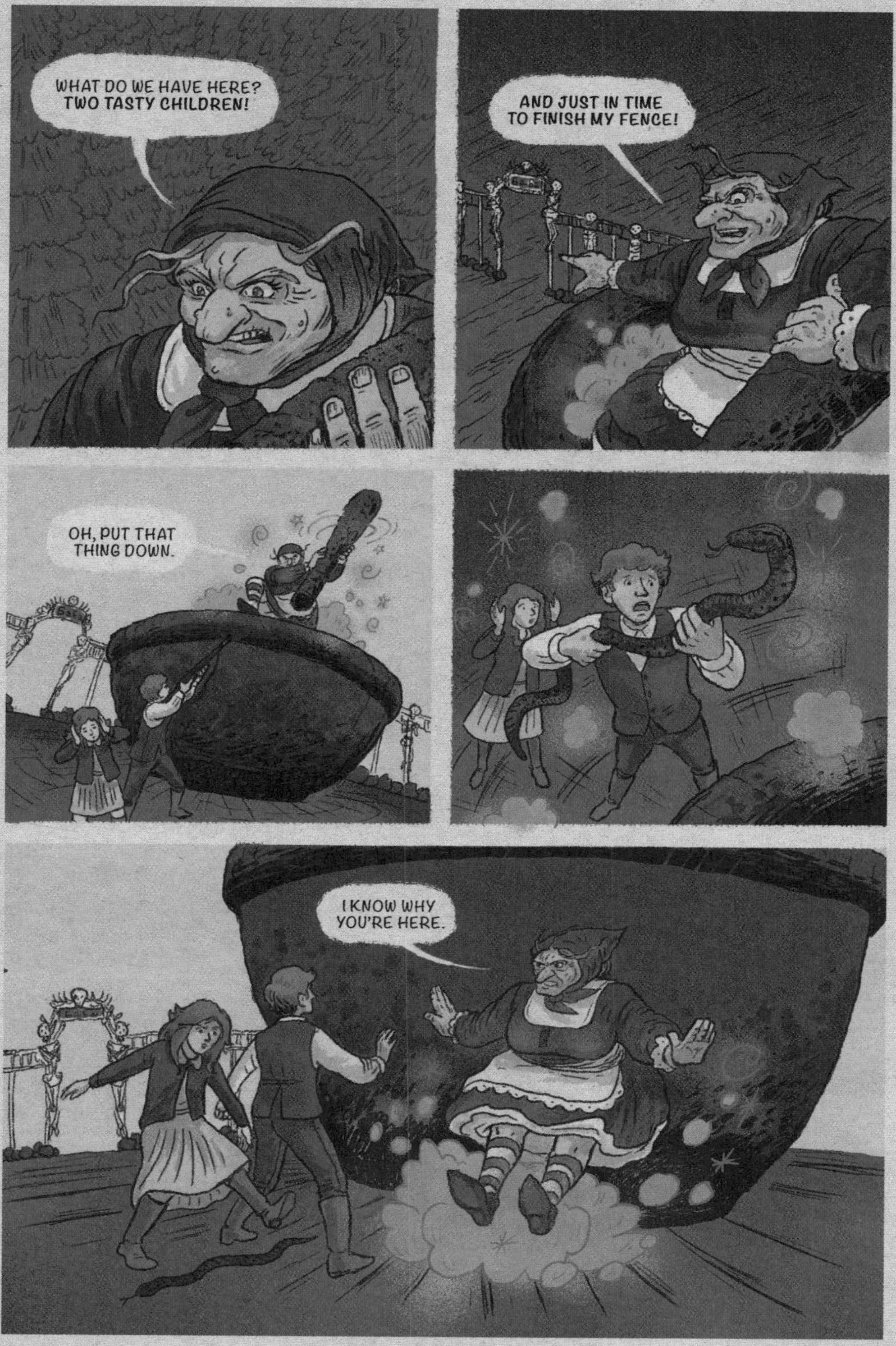
WHAT DO WE HAVE HERE? TWO TASTY CHILDREN!
AND JUST IN TIME TO FINISH MY FENCE!
OH, PUT THAT THING DOWN.
I KNOW WHY YOU'RE HERE.

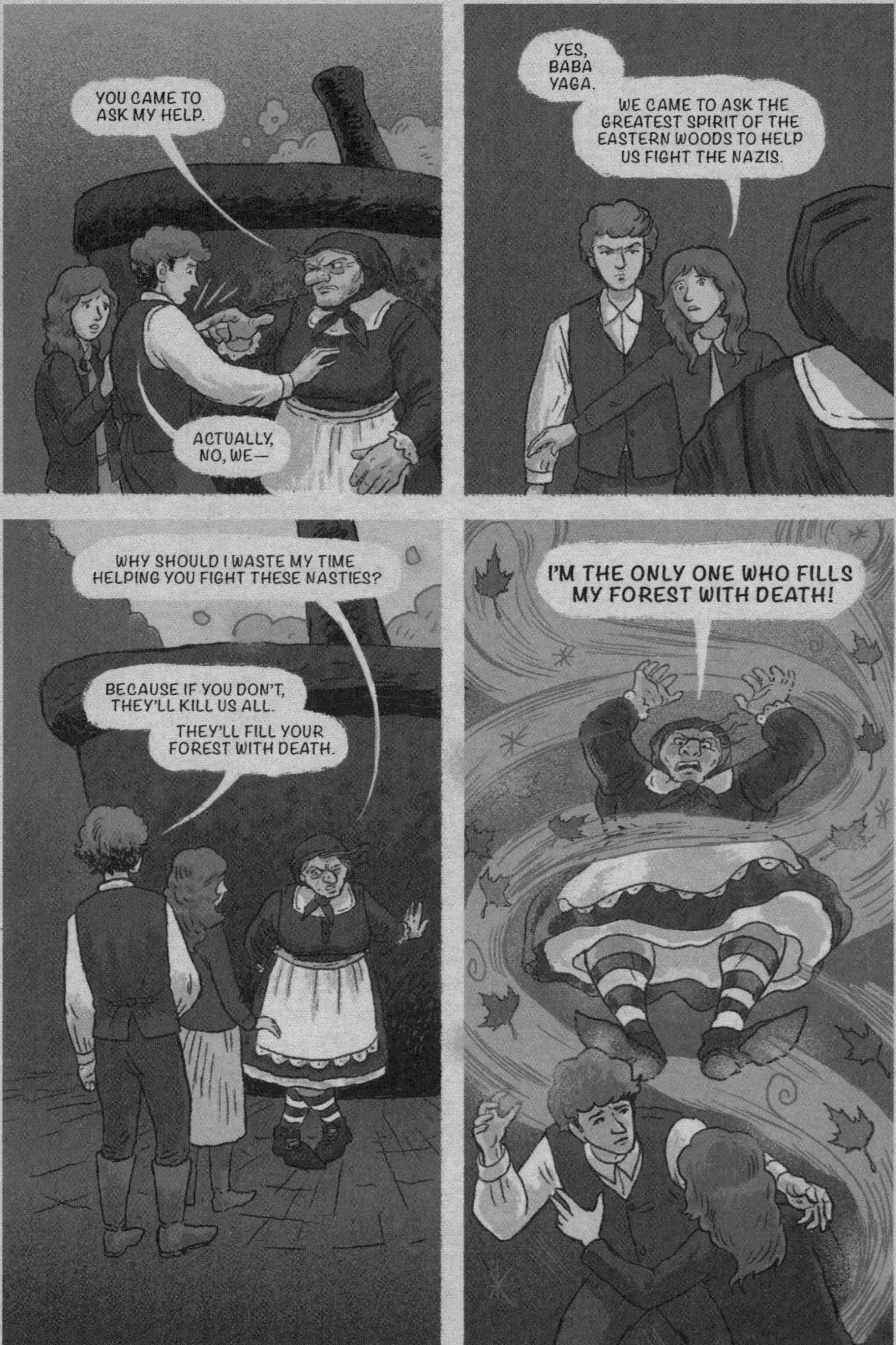
YOU CAME TO ASK MY HELP.
ACTUALLY, NO, WE—
YES, BABA YAGA.
WE CAME TO ASK THE GREATEST SPIRIT OF THE EASTERN WOODS TO HELP US FIGHT THE NAZIS.
WHY SHOULD I WASTE MY TIME HELPING YOU FIGHT THESE NASTIES?
BECAUSE IF YOU DON'T, THEY'LL KILL US ALL.
THEY'LL FILL YOUR FOREST WITH DEATH.
I'M THE ONLY ONE WHO FILLS MY FOREST WITH DEATH!

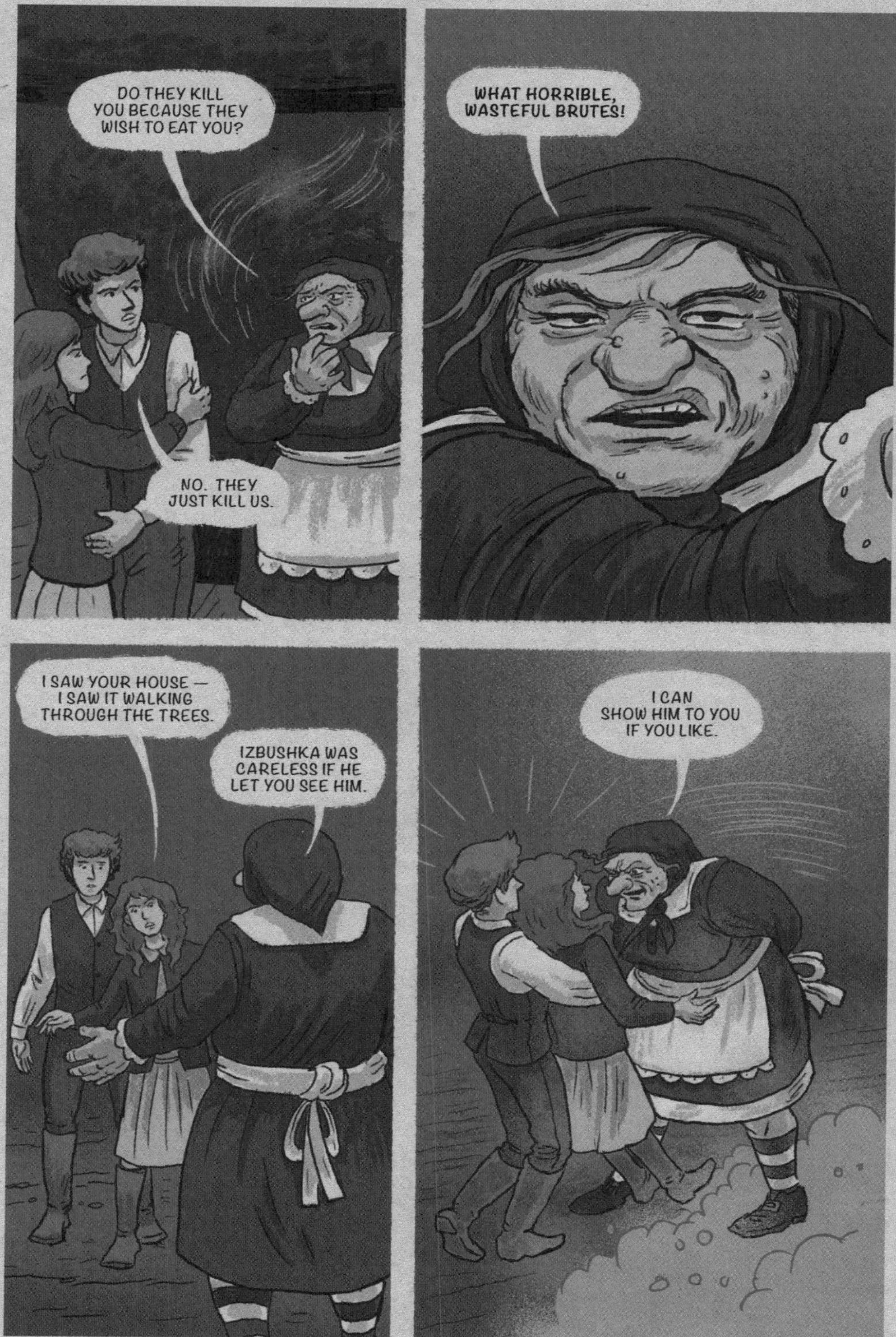
DO THEY KILL YOU BECAUSE THEY WISH TO EAT YOU?
NO. THEY JUST KILL US.
WHAT HORRIBLE, WASTEFUL BRUTES!
I SAW YOUR HOUSE — I SAW IT WALKING THROUGH THE TREES.
IZBUSHKA WAS CARELESS IF HE LET YOU SEE HIM.
I CAN SHOW HIM TO YOU IF YOU LIKE.

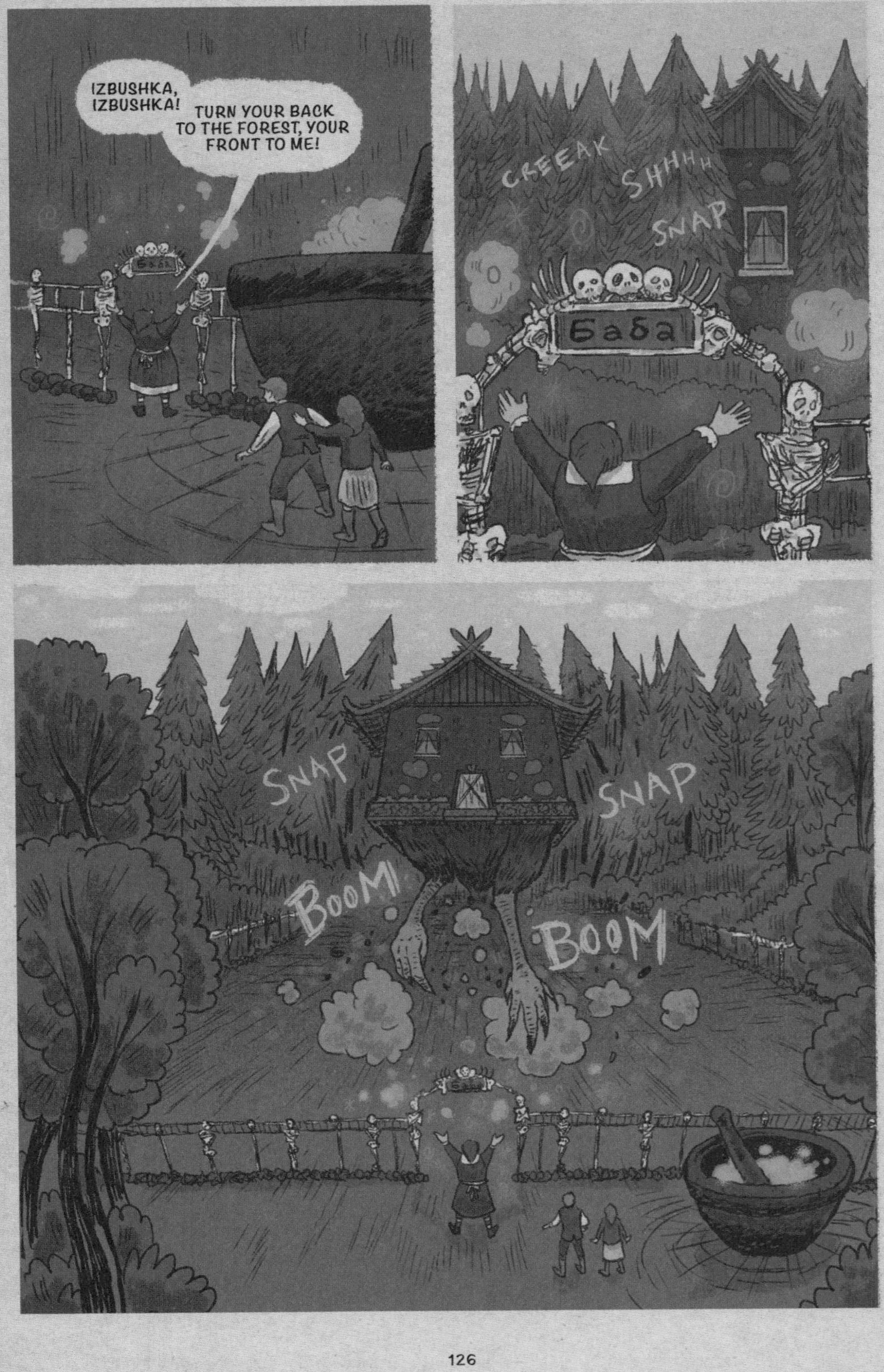
IZBUSHKA, IZBUSHKA!
TURN YOUR BACK TO THE FOREST, YOUR FRONT TO ME!
CREEAK
SHHHH
SNAP
Баба
SNAP
SNAP
BOOM
BOOM

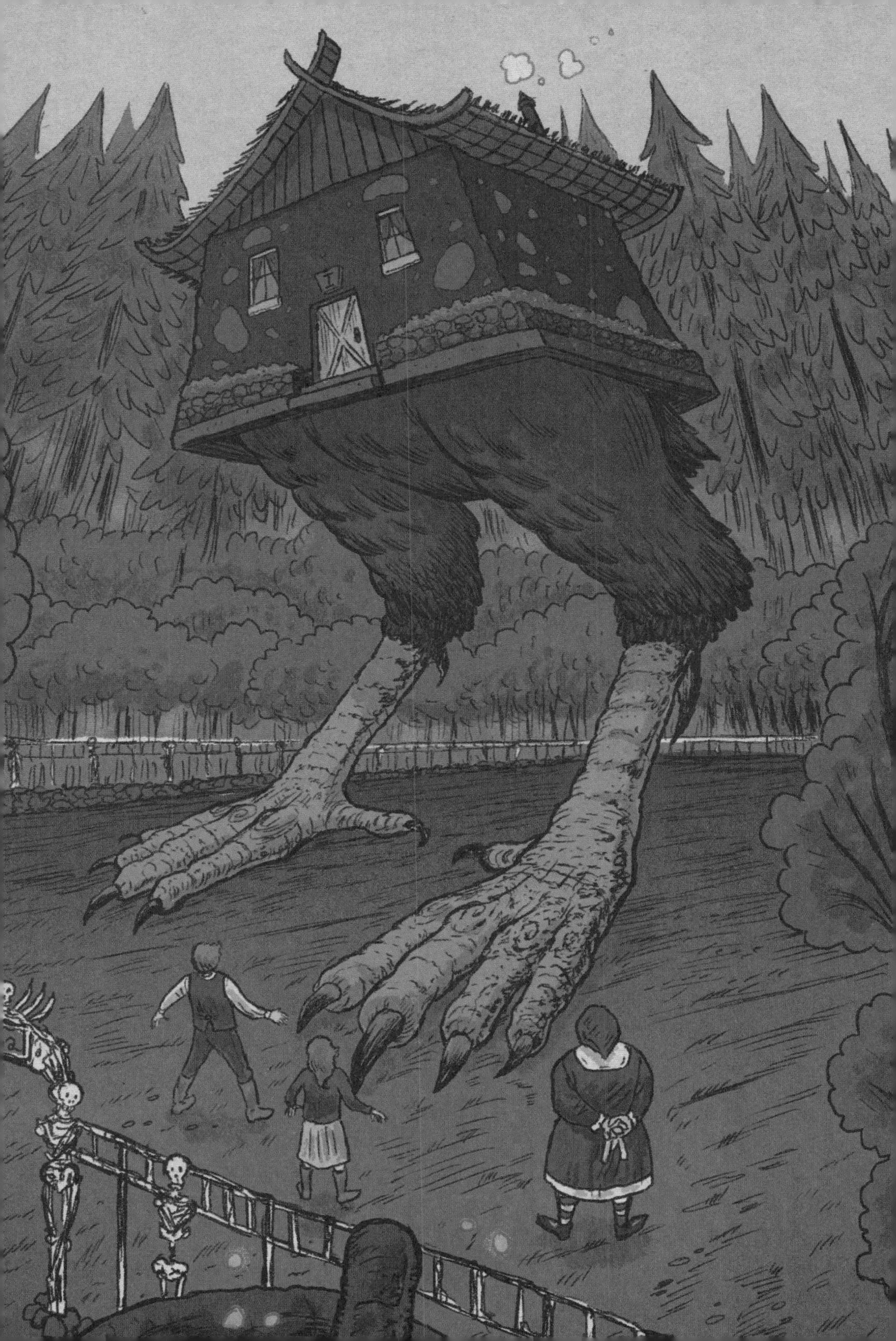

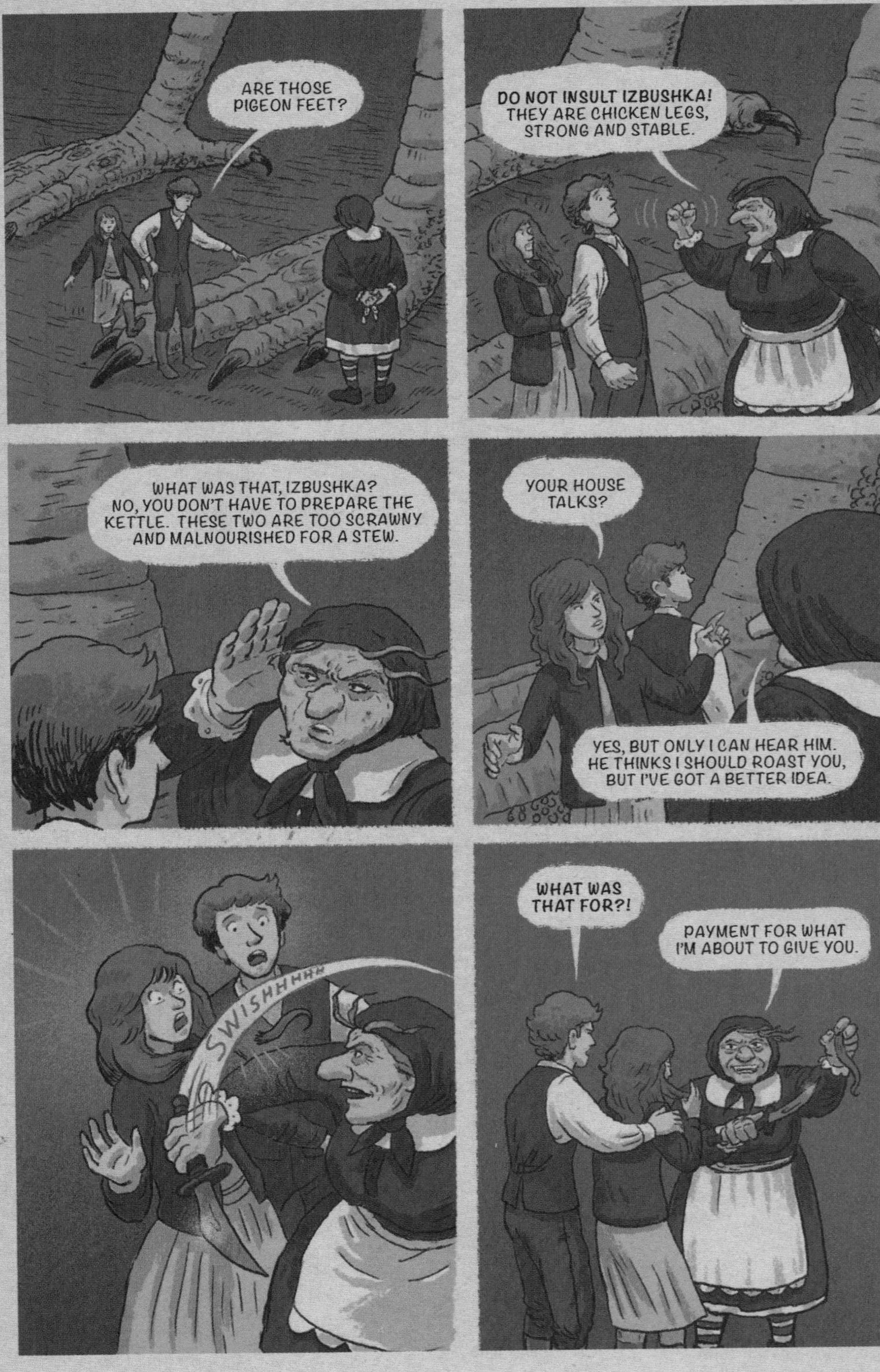
ARE THOSE PIGEON FEET?
DO NOT INSULT IZBUSHKA! THEY ARE CHICKEN LEGS, STRONG AND STABLE.
WHAT WAS THAT, IZBUSHKA? NO, YOU DON'T HAVE TO PREPARE THE KETTLE. THESE TWO ARE TOO SCRAWNY AND MALNOURISHED FOR A STEW.
YOUR HOUSE TALKS?
YES, BUT ONLY I CAN HEAR HIM. HE THINKS I SHOULD ROAST YOU, BUT I'VE GOT A BETTER IDEA.
SWISHHHHH
WHAT WAS THAT FOR?!
PAYMENT FOR WHAT I'M ABOUT TO GIVE YOU.

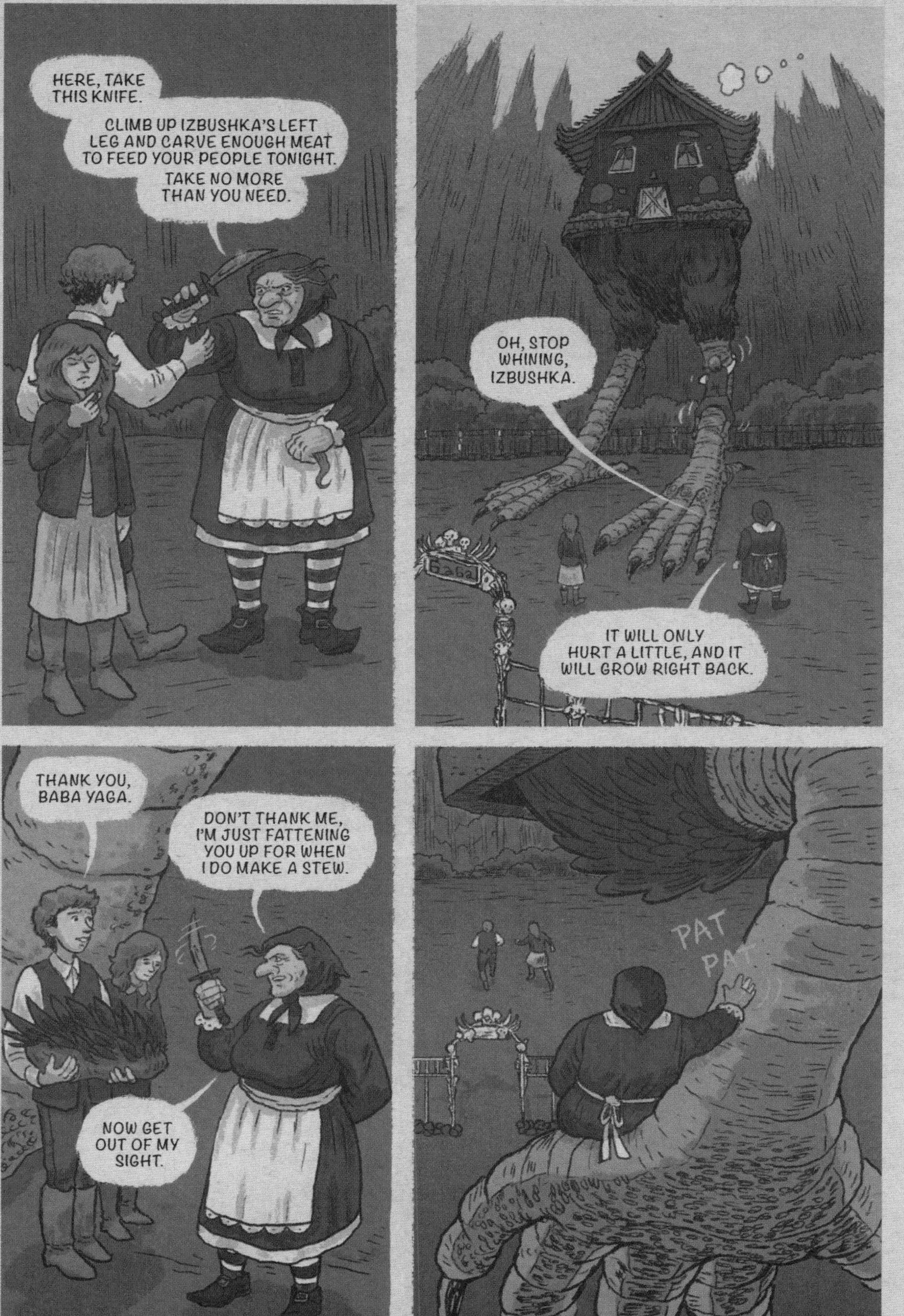
HERE, TAKE THIS KNIFE.
CLIMB UP IZBUSHKA'S LEFT LEG AND CARVE ENOUGH MEAT TO FEED YOUR PEOPLE TONIGHT.
TAKE NO MORE THAN YOU NEED.
OH, STOP WHINING, IZBUSHKA.
Баба
IT WILL ONLY HURT A LITTLE, AND IT WILL GROW RIGHT BACK.
THANK YOU, BABA YAGA.
DON'T THANK ME, I'M JUST FATTENING YOU UP FOR WHEN I DO MAKE A STEW.
NOW GET OUT OF MY SIGHT.
PAT
PAT

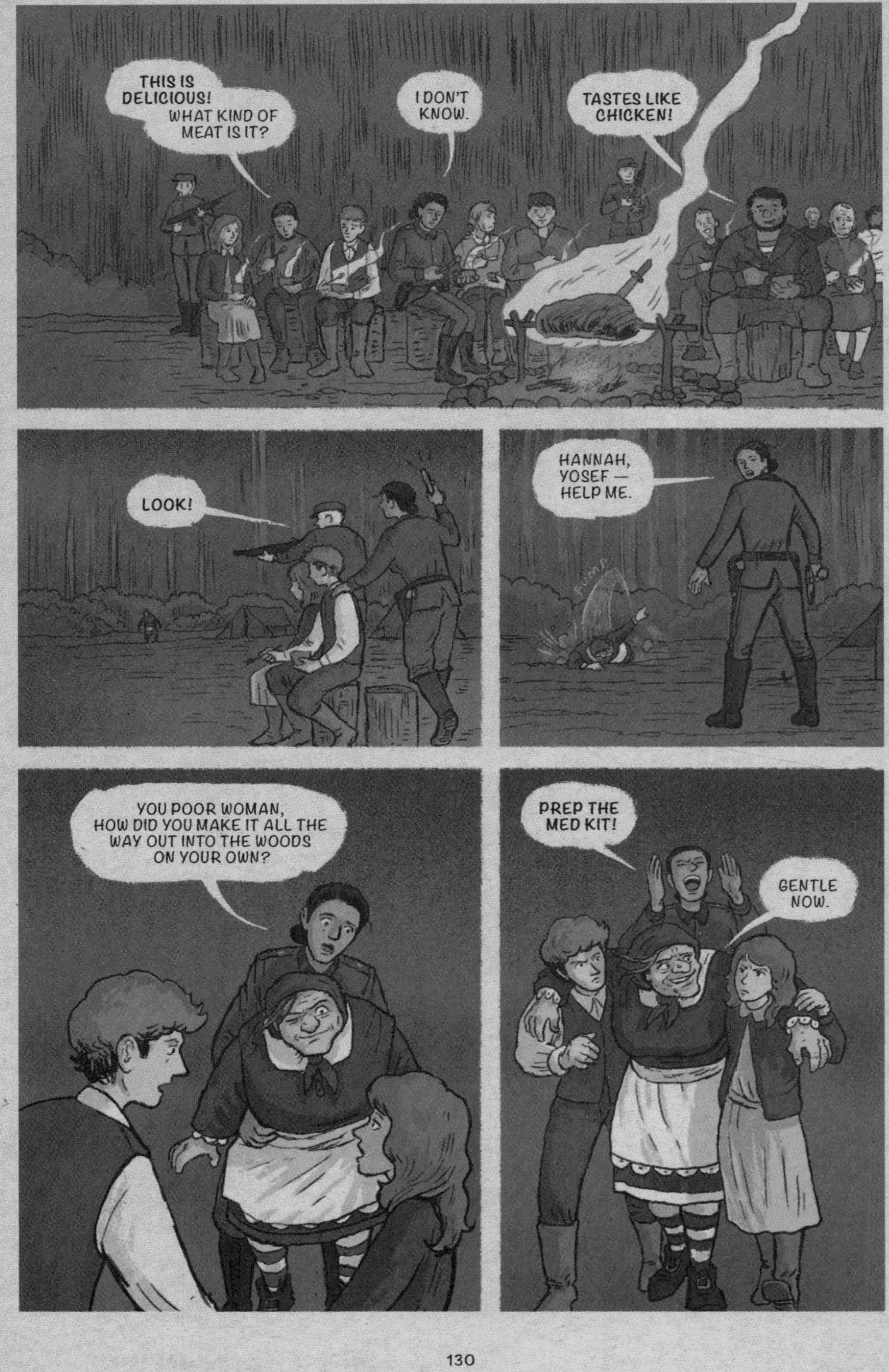
THIS IS DELICIOUS! WHAT KIND OF MEAT IS IT?
I DON'T KNOW.
TASTES LIKE CHICKEN!
LOOK!
HANNAH, YOSEF — HELP ME.
YOU POOR WOMAN, HOW DID YOU MAKE IT ALL THE WAY OUT INTO THE WOODS ON YOUR OWN?
PREP THE MED KIT!
GENTLE NOW.

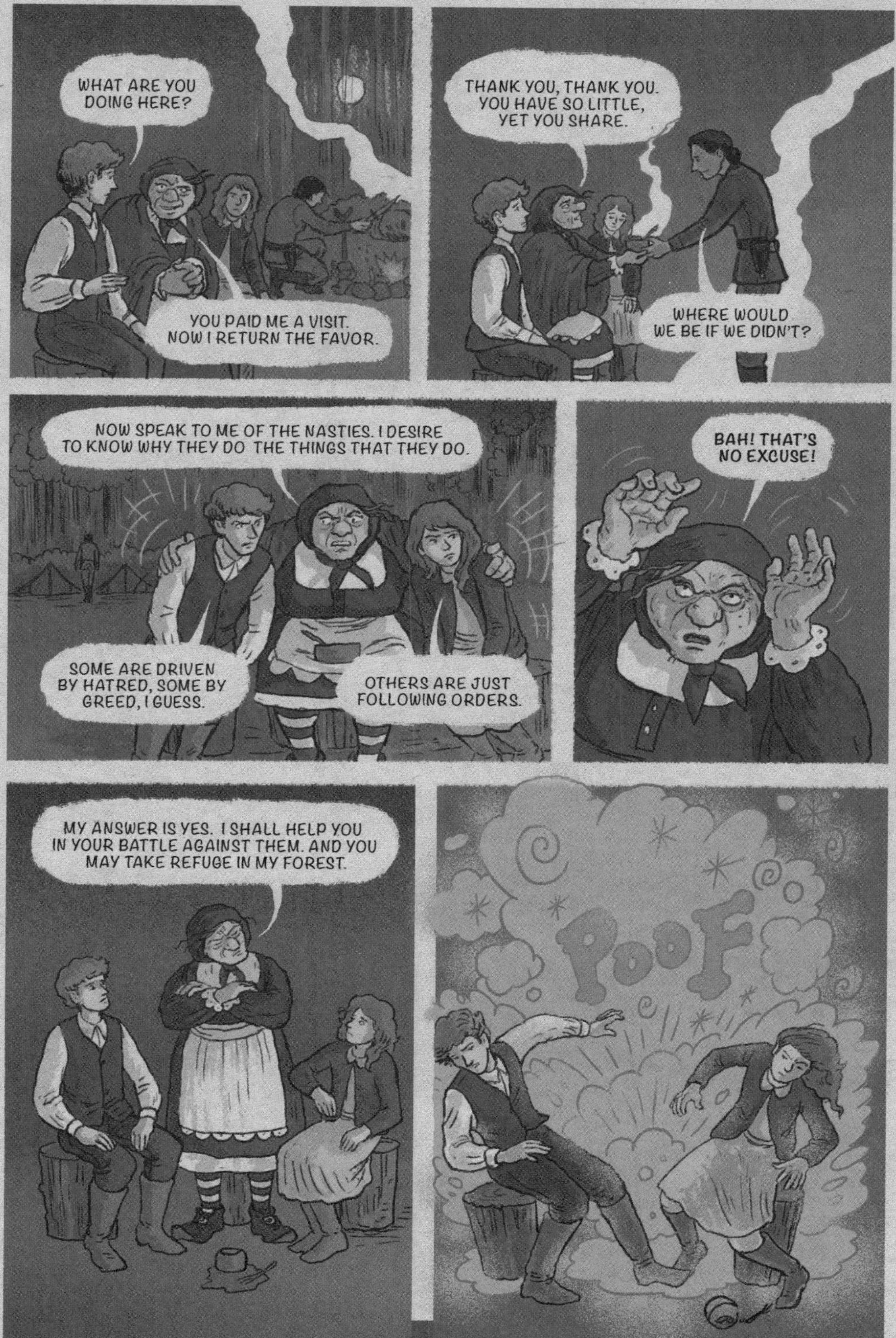
WHAT ARE YOU DOING HERE?
YOU PAID ME A VISIT. NOW I RETURN THE FAVOR.
THANK YOU, THANK YOU. YOU HAVE SO LITTLE, YET YOU SHARE.
WHERE WOULD WE BE IF WE DIDN'T?
NOW SPEAK TO ME OF THE NASTIES. I DESIRE TO KNOW WHY THEY DO THE THINGS THAT THEY DO.
SOME ARE DRIVEN BY HATRED, SOME BY GREED, I GUESS.
OTHERS ARE JUST FOLLOWING ORDERS.
BAH! THAT'S NO EXCUSE!
MY ANSWER IS YES. I SHALL HELP YOU IN YOUR BATTLE AGAINST THEM. AND YOU MAY TAKE REFUGE IN MY FOREST.
POOF

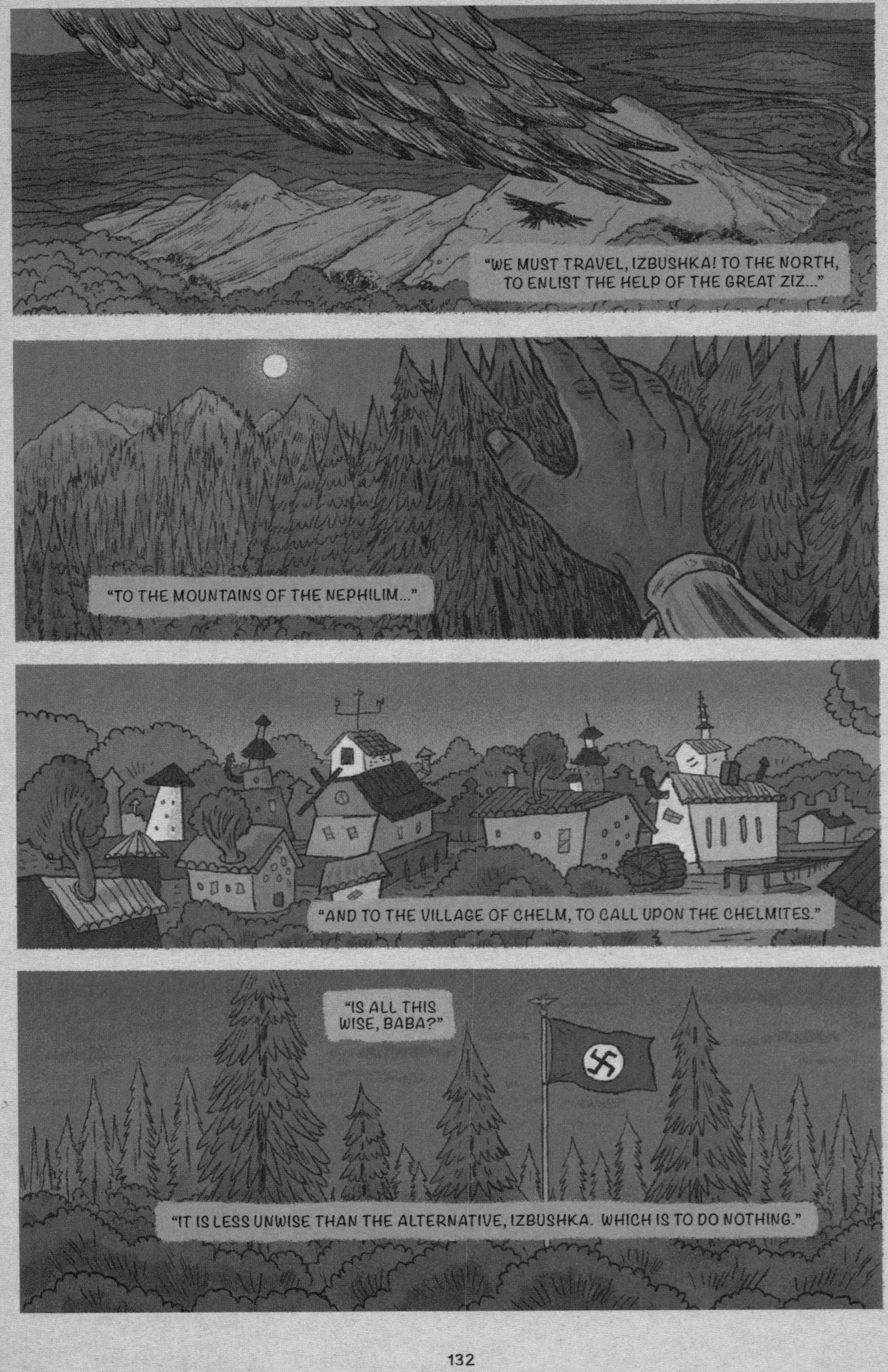
"WE MUST TRAVEL, IZBUSHKA! TO THE NORTH, TO ENLIST THE HELP OF THE GREAT ZIZ..."
"TO THE MOUNTAINS OF THE NEPHILIM..."
"AND TO THE VILLAGE OF CHELM, TO CALL UPON THE CHELMITES."
"IS ALL THIS WISE, BABA?"
"IT IS LESS UNWISE THAN THE ALTERNATIVE, IZBUSHKA. WHICH IS TO DO NOTHING."

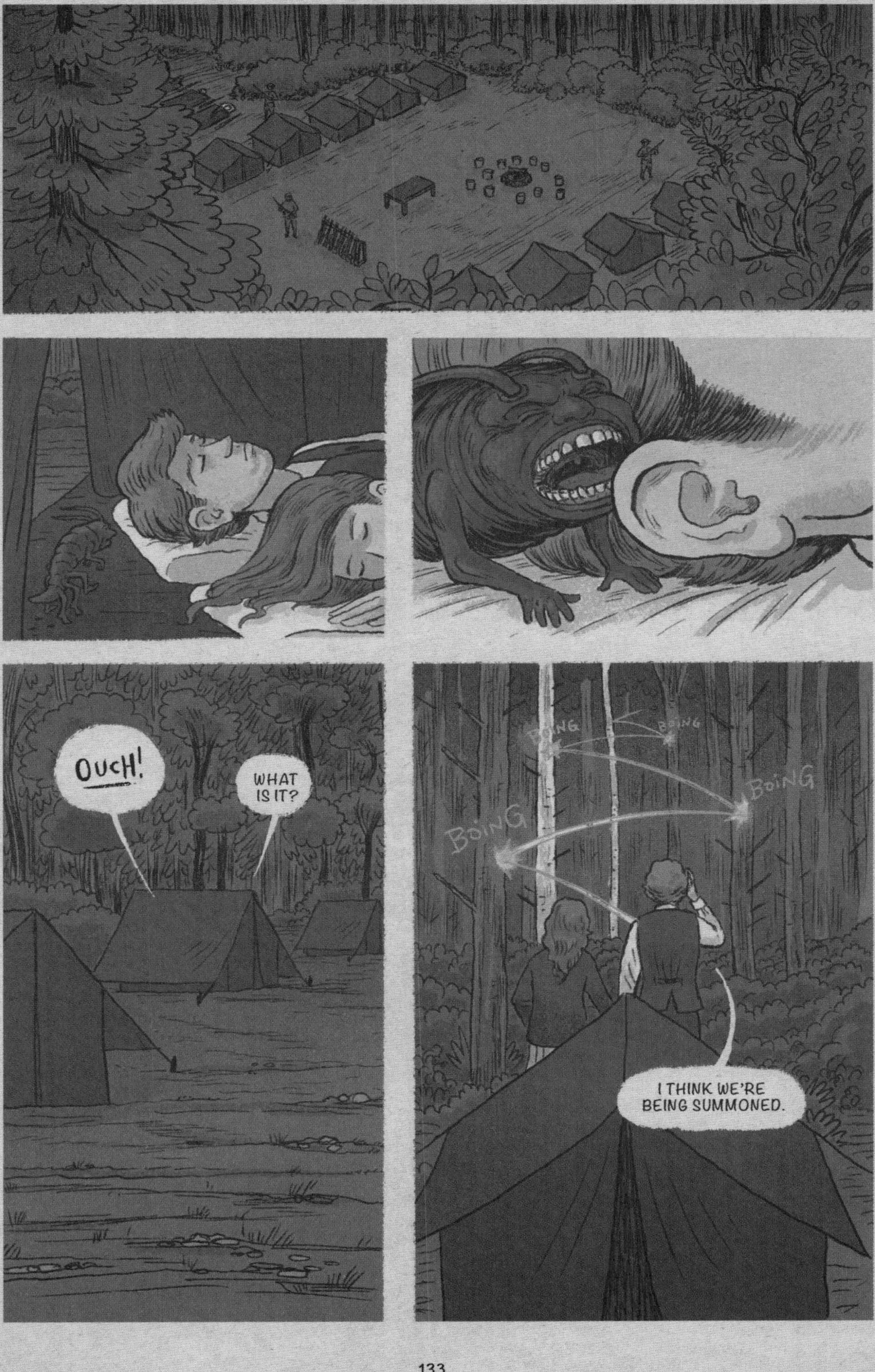
OUCH!
WHAT IS IT?
BOING
BOING
BOING
BOING
I THINK WE'RE BEING SUMMONED.

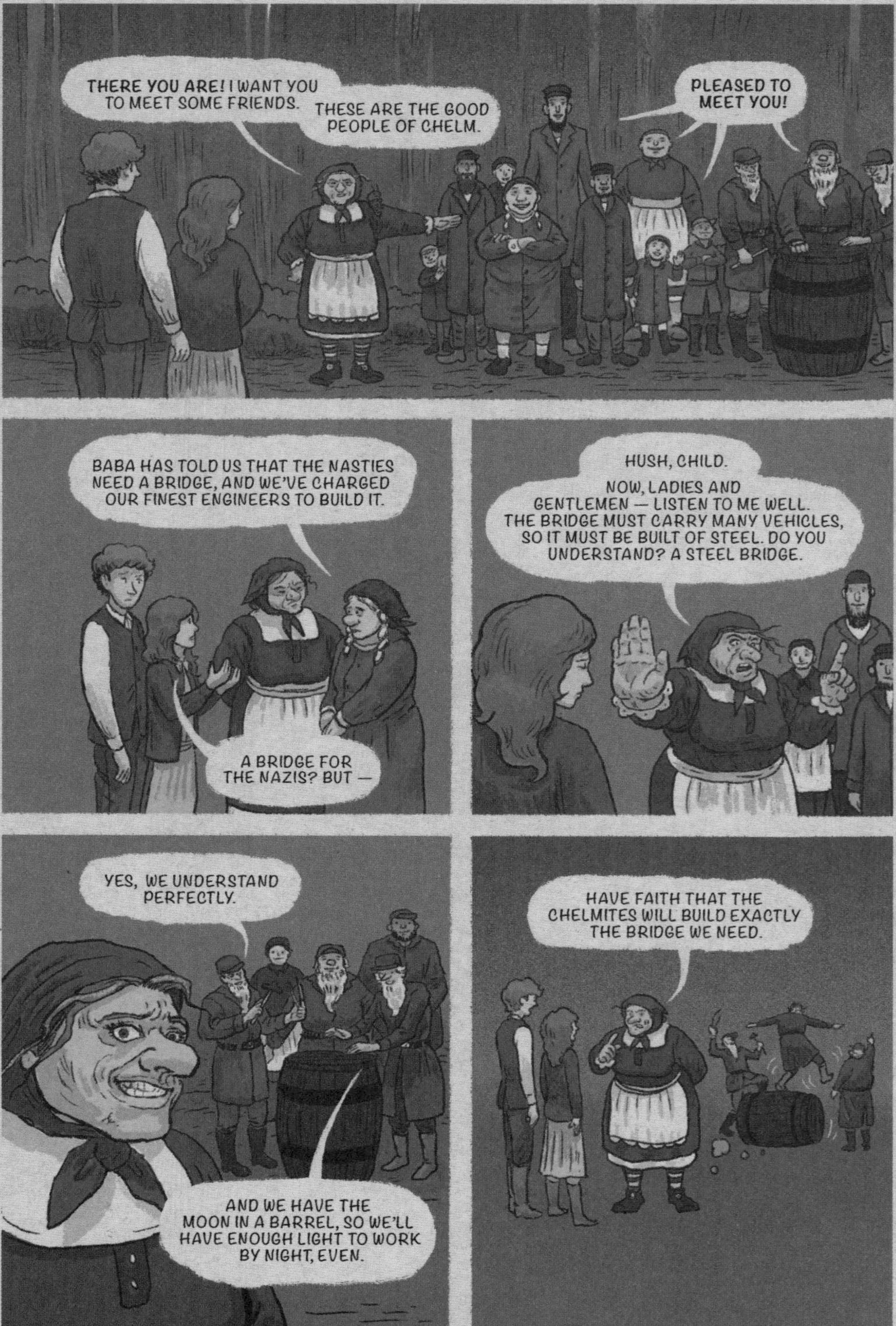
THERE YOU ARE! I WANT YOU TO MEET SOME FRIENDS.
THESE ARE THE GOOD PEOPLE OF CHELM.
PLEASED TO MEET YOU!
BABA HAS TOLD US THAT THE NASTIES NEED A BRIDGE, AND WE'VE CHARGED OUR FINEST ENGINEERS TO BUILD IT.
A BRIDGE FOR THE NAZIS? BUT —
HUSH, CHILD.
NOW, LADIES AND GENTLEMEN — LISTEN TO ME WELL. THE BRIDGE MUST CARRY MANY VEHICLES, SO IT MUST BE BUILT OF STEEL. DO YOU UNDERSTAND? A STEEL BRIDGE.
YES, WE UNDERSTAND PERFECTLY.
AND WE HAVE THE MOON IN A BARREL, SO WE'LL HAVE ENOUGH LIGHT TO WORK BY NIGHT, EVEN.
HAVE FAITH THAT THE CHELMITES WILL BUILD EXACTLY THE BRIDGE WE NEED.

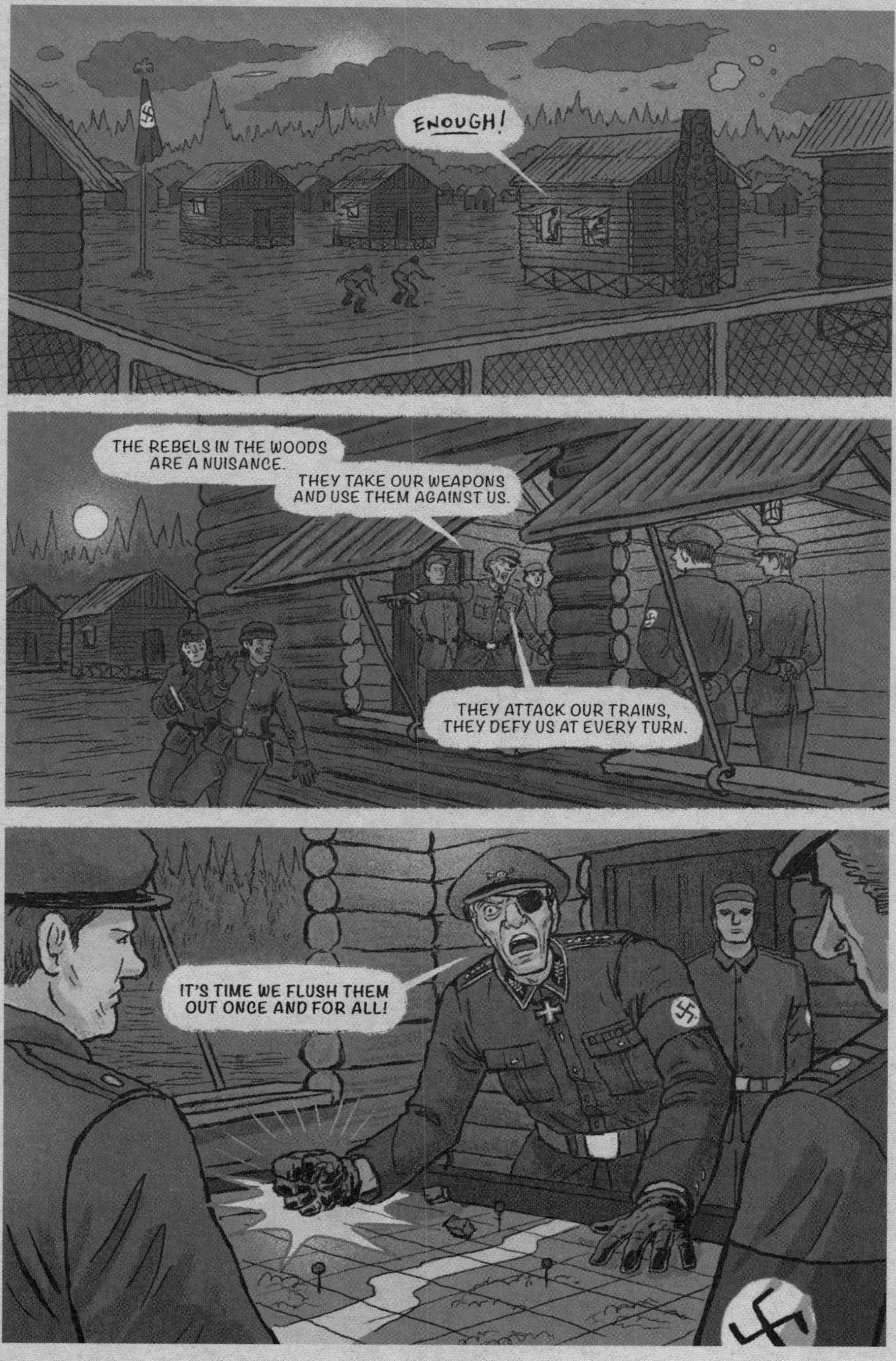
ENOUGH!
THE REBELS IN THE WOODS ARE A NUISANCE.
THEY TAKE OUR WEAPONS AND USE THEM AGAINST US.
THEY ATTACK OUR TRAINS, THEY DEFY US AT EVERY TURN.
IT'S TIME WE FLUSH THEM OUT ONCE AND FOR ALL!

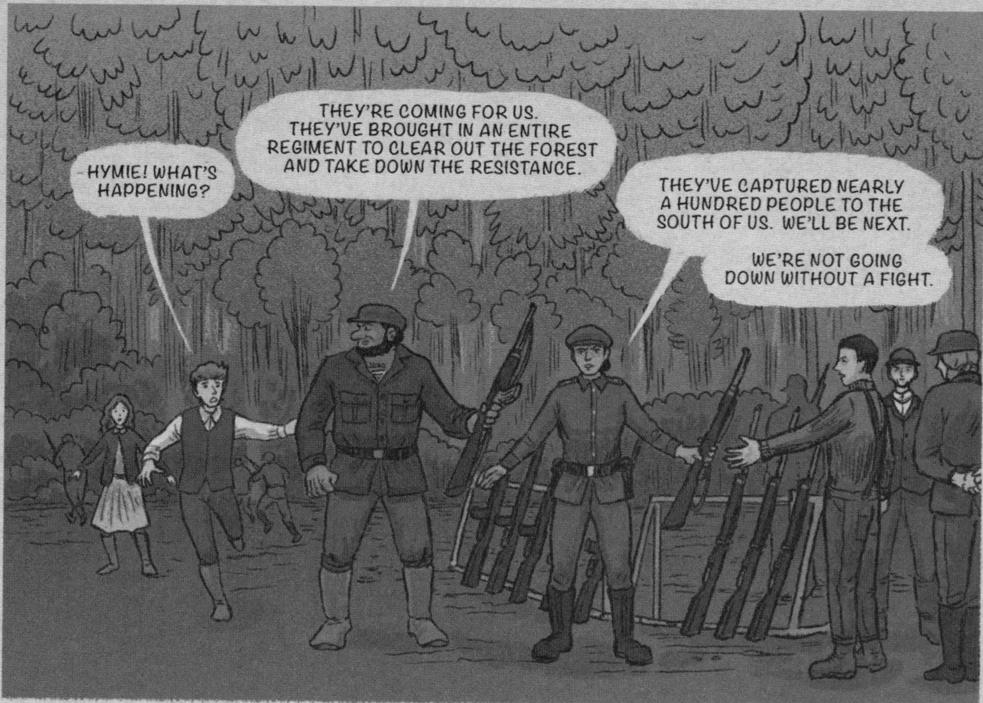
HYMIE! WHAT'S HAPPENING?
THEY'RE COMING FOR US. THEY'VE BROUGHT IN AN ENTIRE REGIMENT TO CLEAR OUT THE FOREST AND TAKE DOWN THE RESISTANCE.
THEY'VE CAPTURED NEARLY A HUNDRED PEOPLE TO THE SOUTH OF US. WE'LL BE NEXT.
WE'RE NOT GOING DOWN WITHOUT A FIGHT.

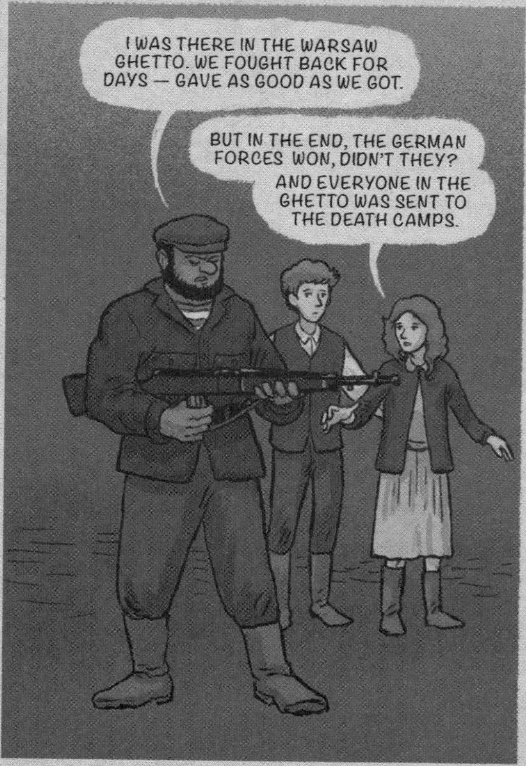
I WAS THERE IN THE WARSAW GHETTO. WE FOUGHT BACK FOR DAYS — GAVE AS GOOD AS WE GOT.
BUT IN THE END, THE GERMAN FORCES WON, DIDN'T THEY?
AND EVERYONE IN THE GHETTO WAS SENT TO THE DEATH CAMPS.

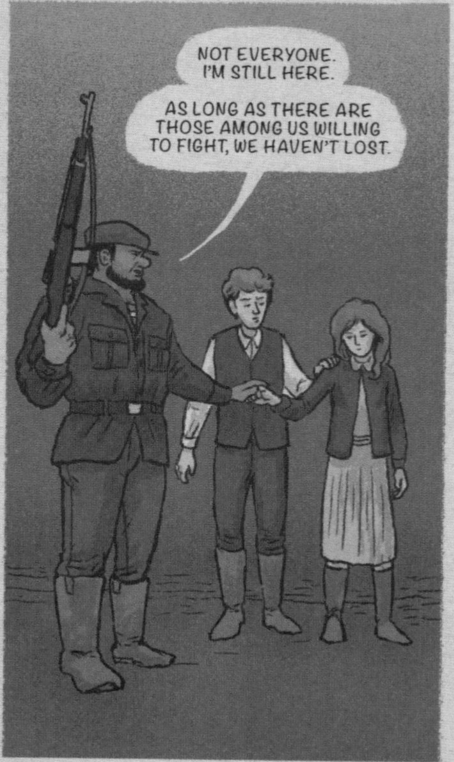
NOT EVERYONE. I'M STILL HERE.
AS LONG AS THERE ARE THOSE AMONG US WILLING TO FIGHT, WE HAVEN'T LOST.

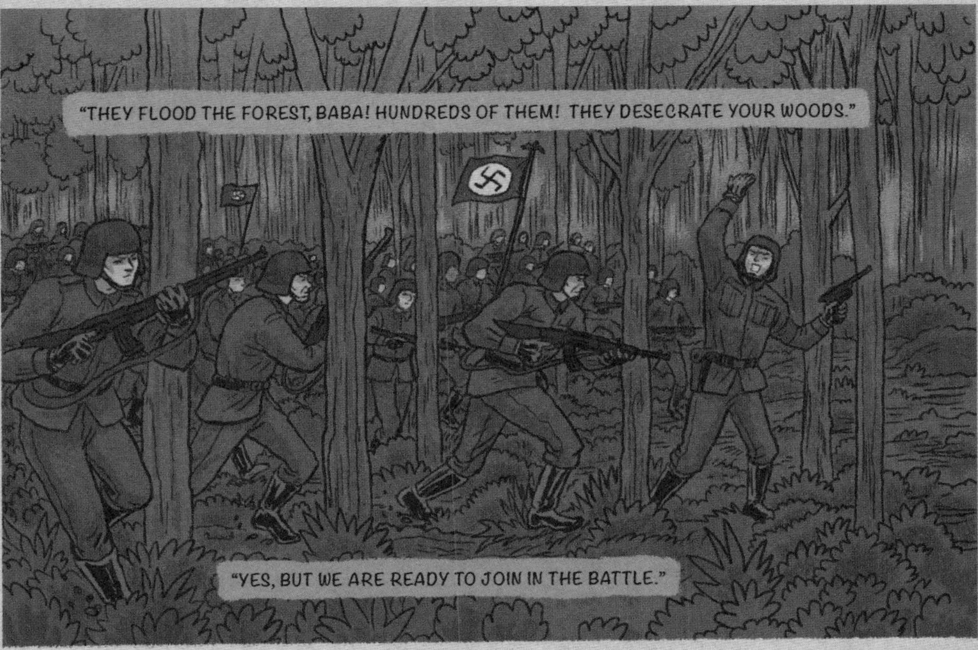
"THEY FLOOD THE FOREST, BABA! HUNDREDS OF THEM! THEY DESECRATE YOUR WOODS."
"YES, BUT WE ARE READY TO JOIN IN THE BATTLE."

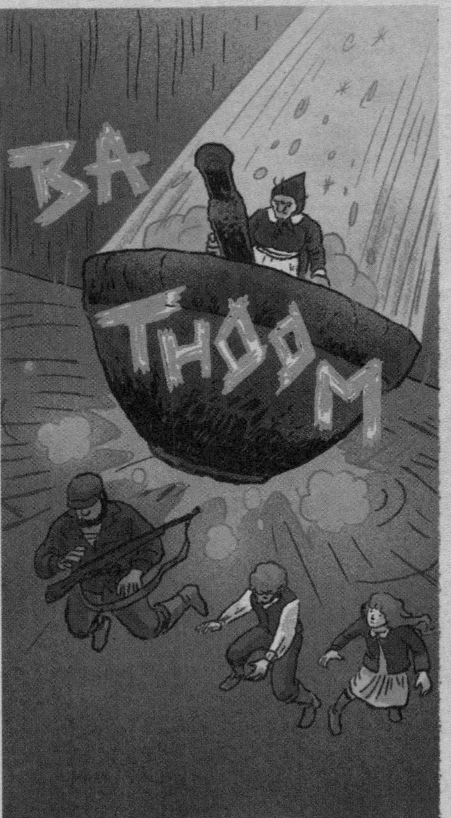
BA
THOOM

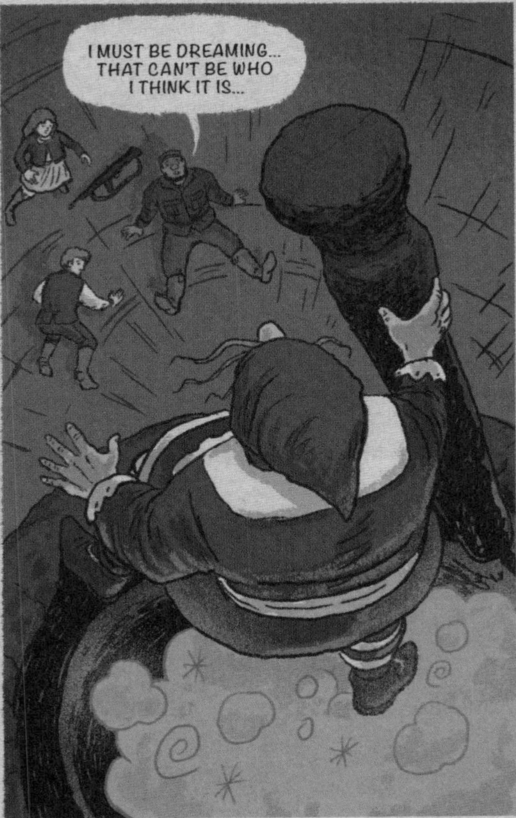
I MUST BE DREAMING... THAT CAN'T BE WHO I THINK IT IS...

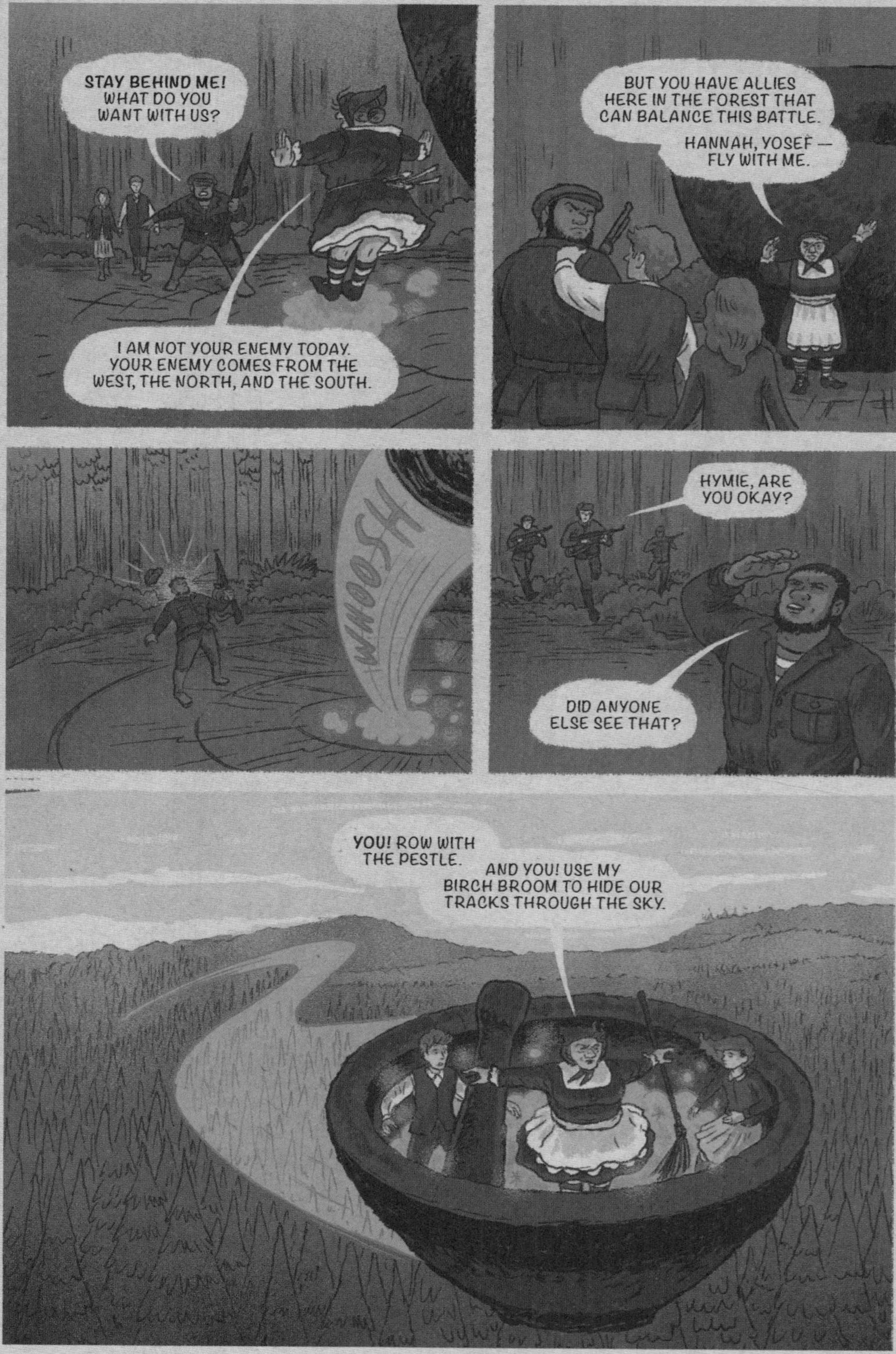
STAY BEHIND ME! WHAT DO YOU WANT WITH US?
I AM NOT YOUR ENEMY TODAY. YOUR ENEMY COMES FROM THE WEST, THE NORTH, AND THE SOUTH.
BUT YOU HAVE ALLIES HERE IN THE FOREST THAT CAN BALANCE THIS BATTLE.
HANNAH, YOSEF — FLY WITH ME.
WHOOSH
HYMIE, ARE YOU OKAY?
DID ANYONE ELSE SEE THAT?
YOU! ROW WITH THE PESTLE.
AND YOU! USE MY BIRCH BROOM TO HIDE OUR TRACKS THROUGH THE SKY.

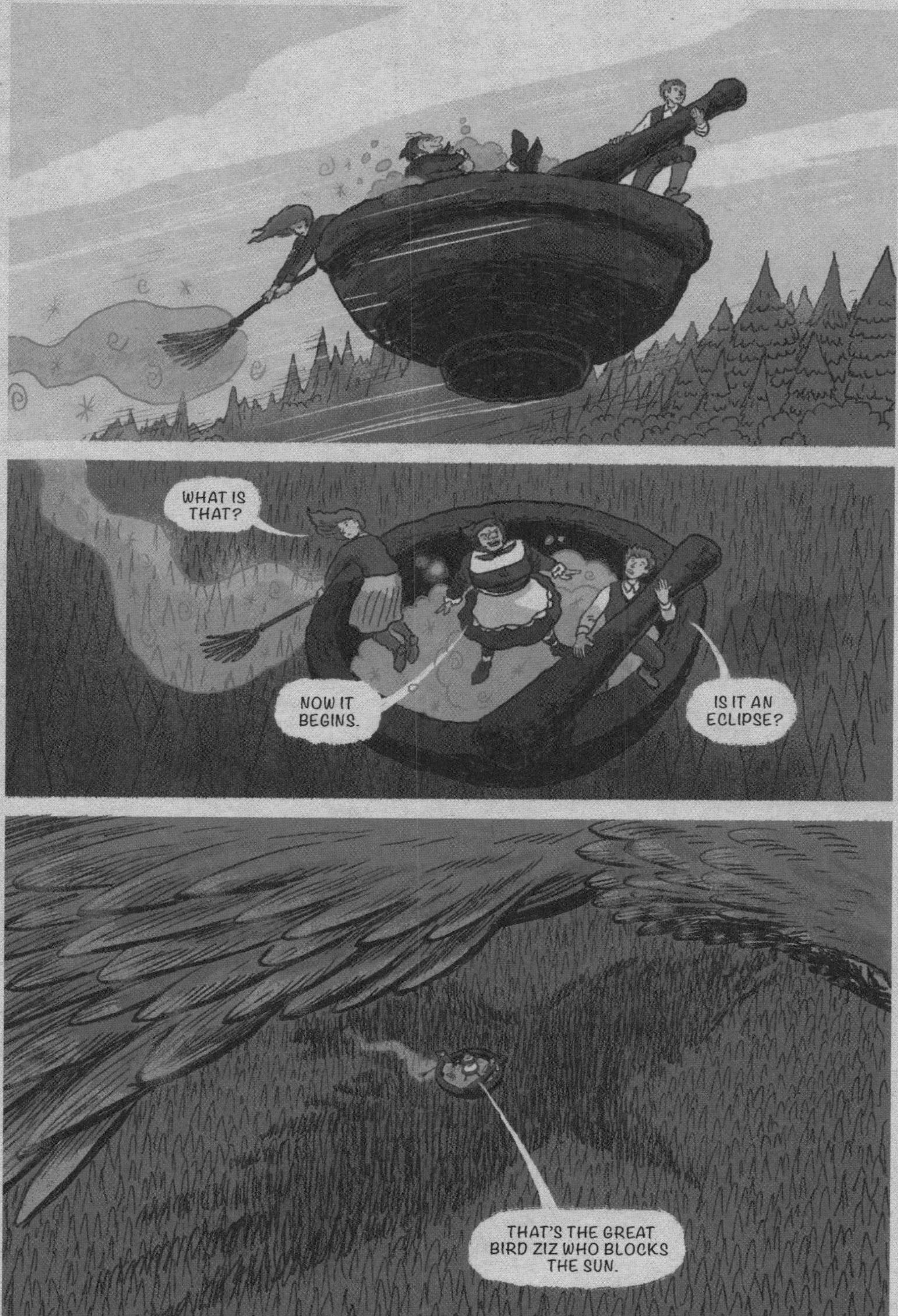
WHAT IS THAT?
NOW IT BEGINS.
IS IT AN ECLIPSE?
THAT'S THE GREAT BIRD ZIZ WHO BLOCKS THE SUN.

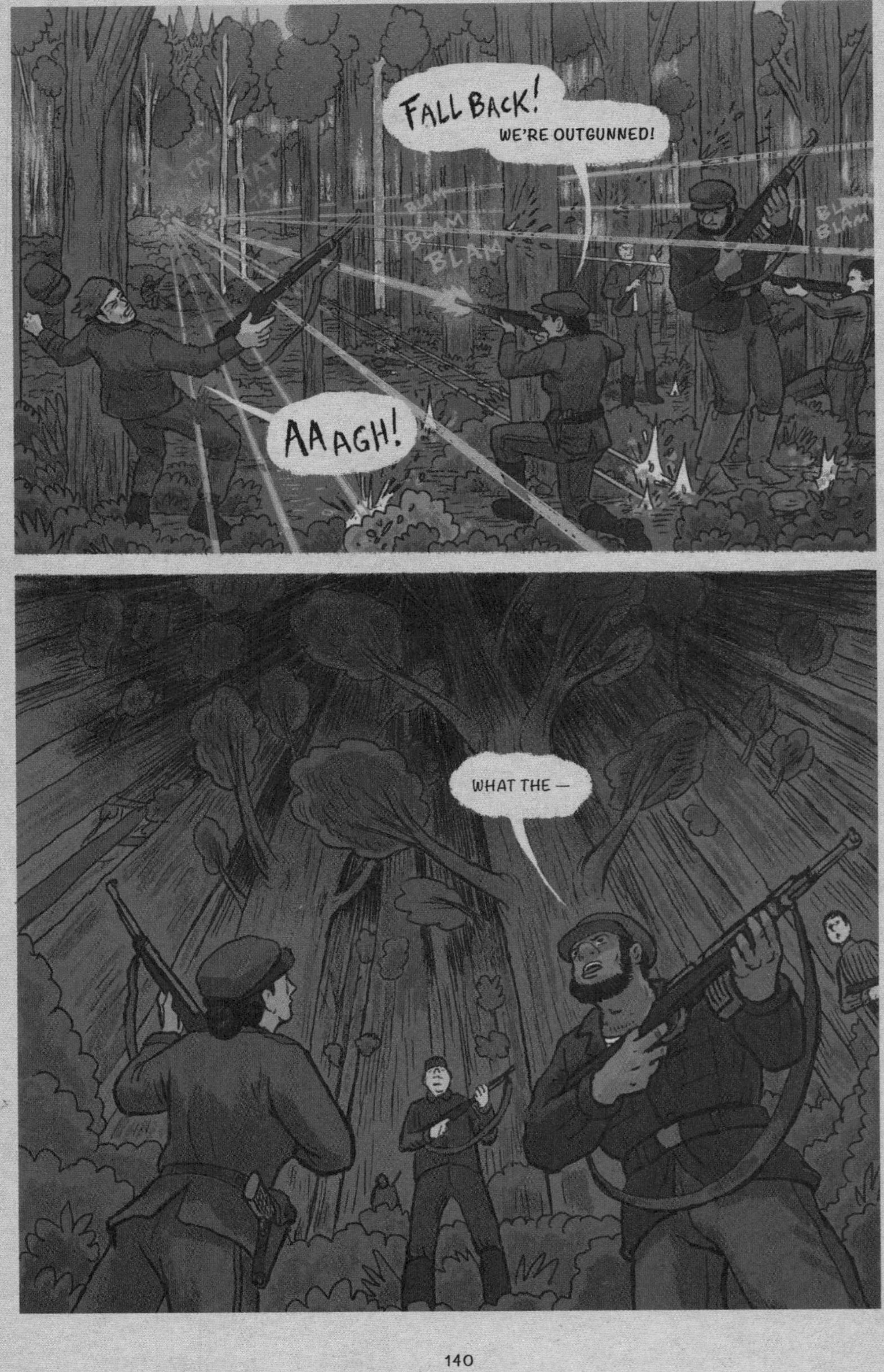
FALL BACK!
WE'RE OUTGUNNED!
BLAM BLAM BLAM
BLAM BLAM
AAAGH!
WHAT THE —

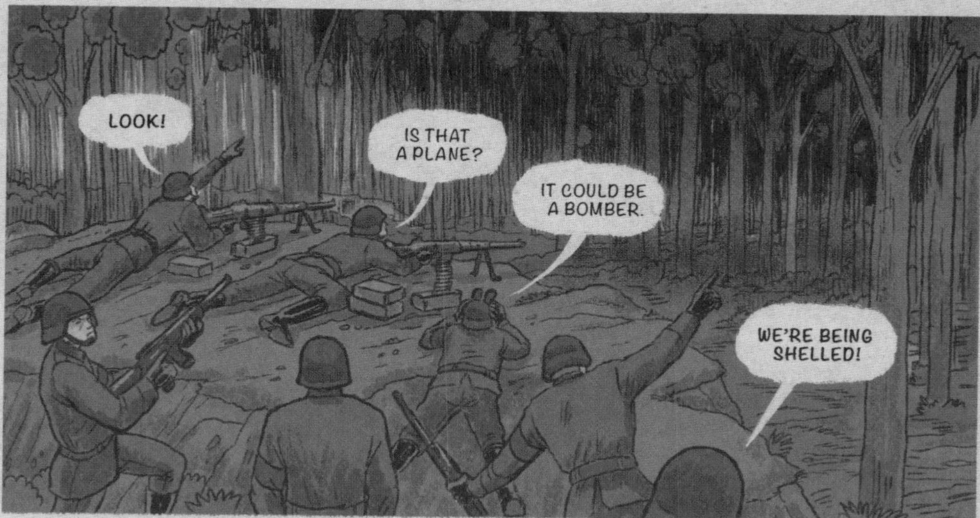
LOOK!
IS THAT A PLANE?
IT COULD BE A BOMBER.
WE'RE BEING SHELLED!

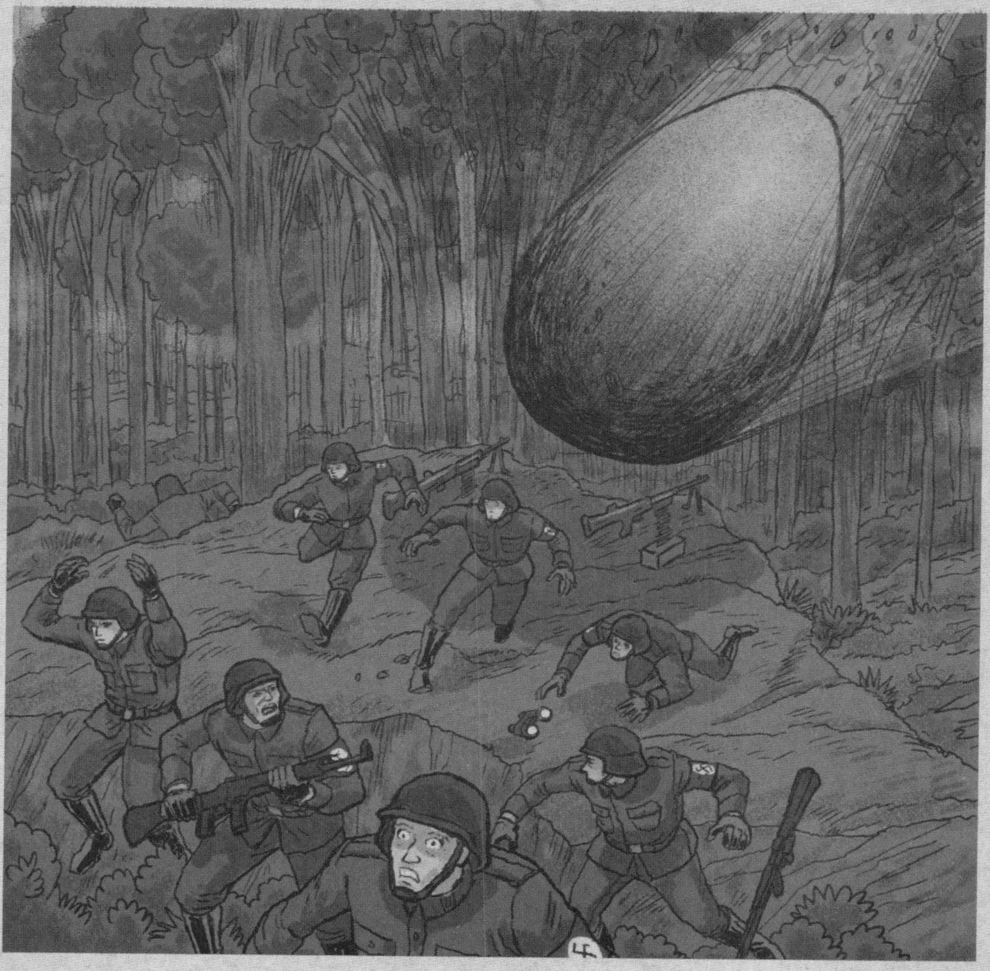

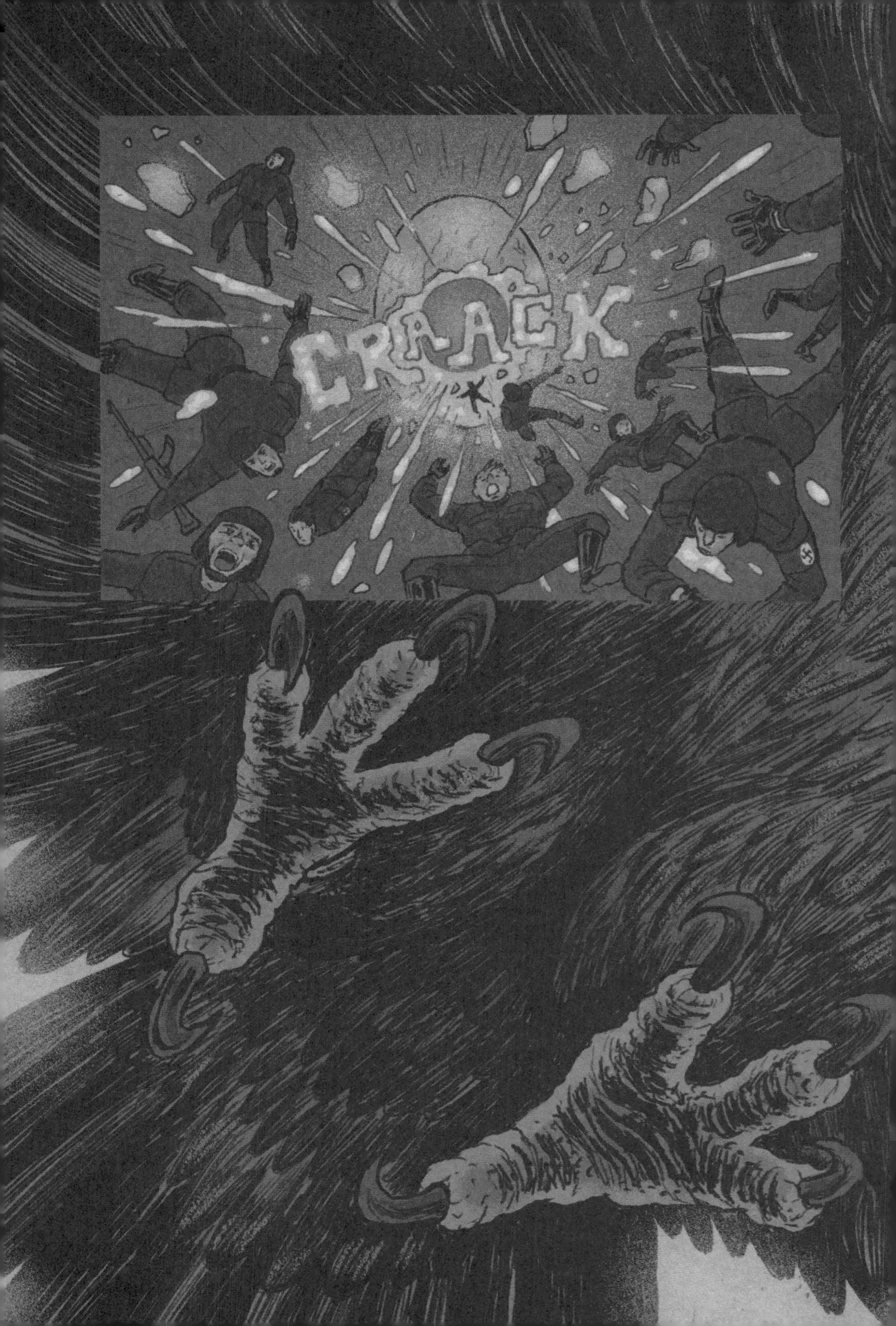
CRAACK

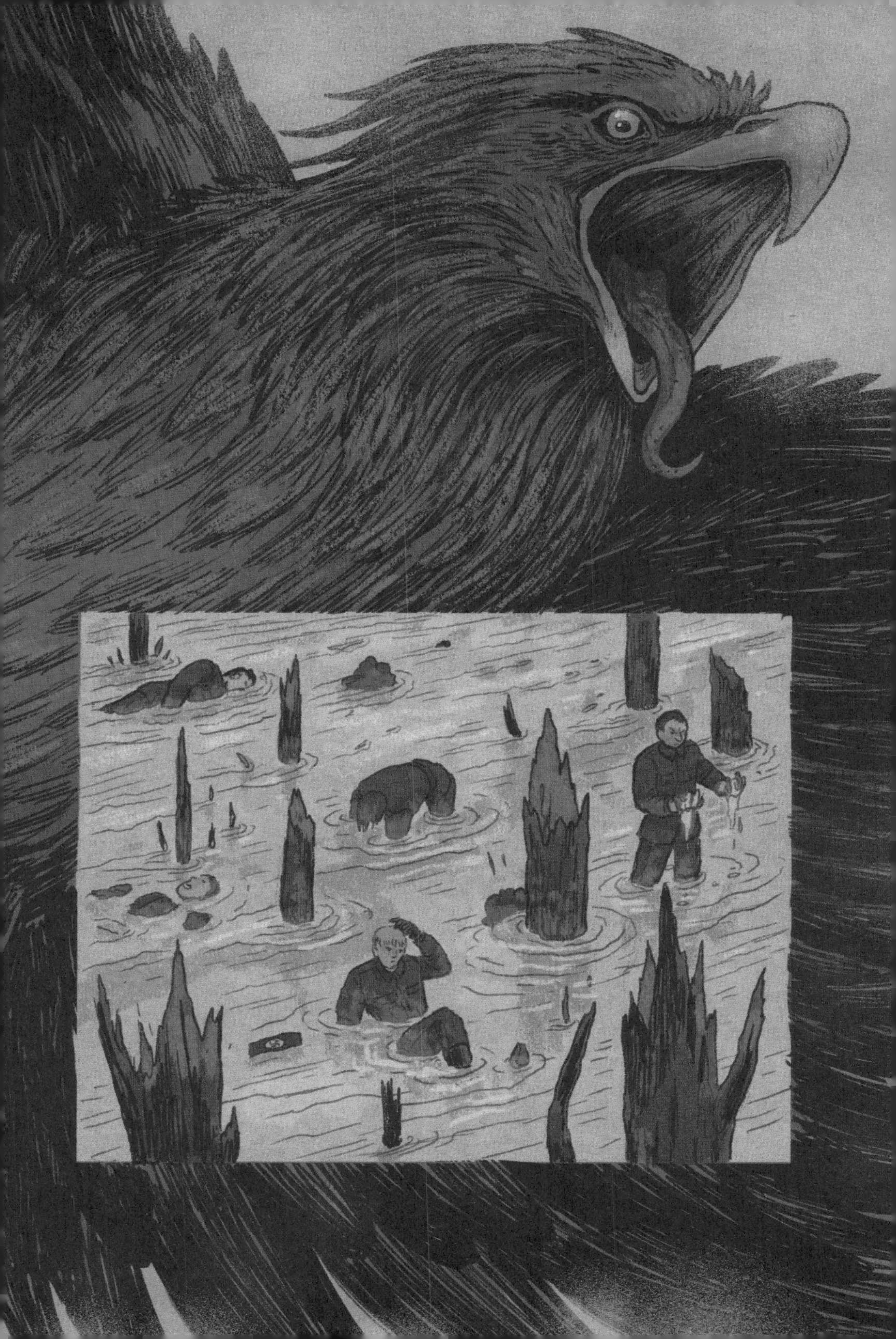

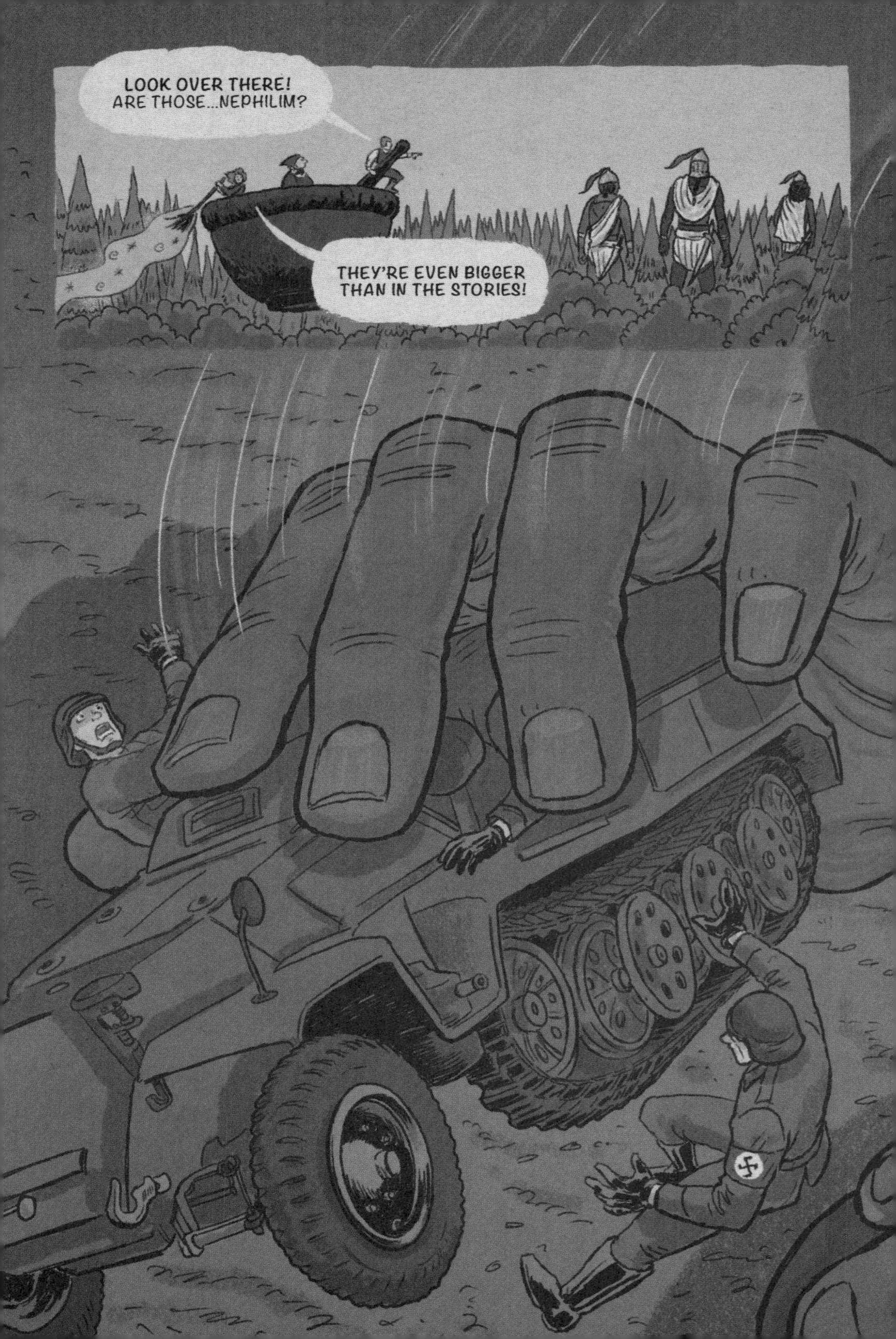
LOOK OVER THERE!
ARE THOSE...NEPHILIM?
THEY'RE EVEN BIGGER
THAN IN THE STORIES!

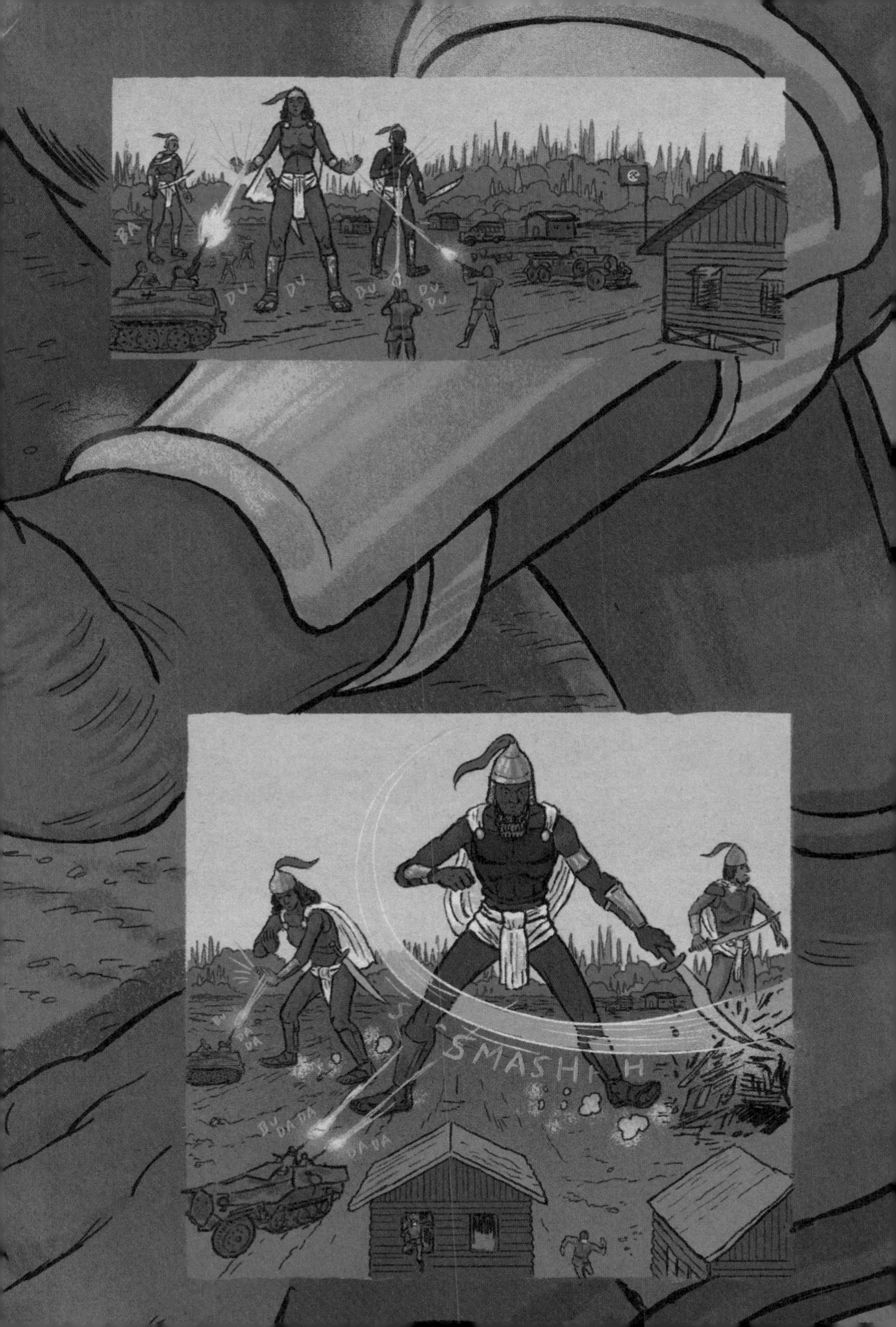
BA
DU
DU
DU
DU
DU
SMASHHH
DU DA DA
DU DA DA
DA DA

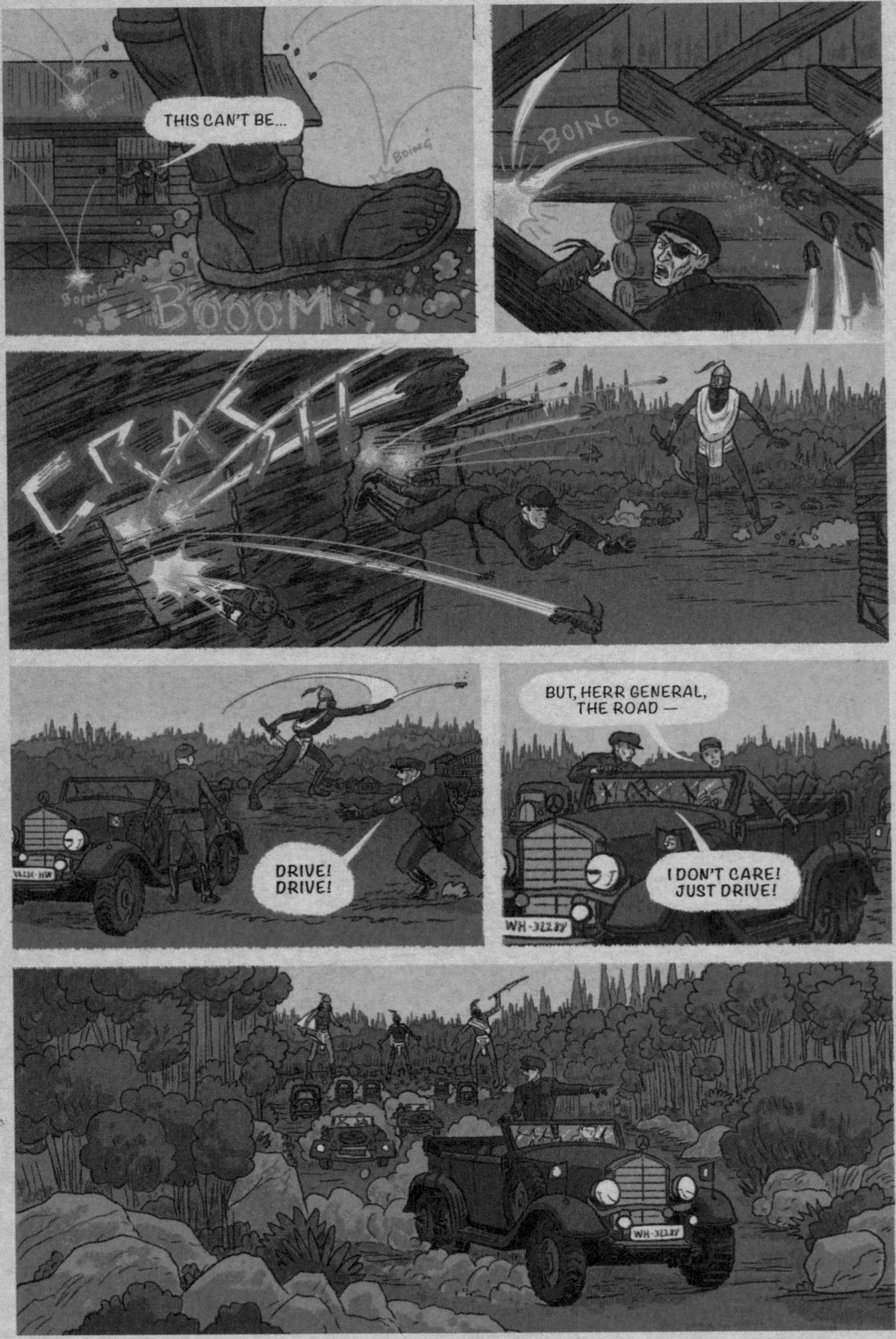
THIS CAN'T BE...
BOING
BOING
BOOOM
BOING
CRASH
BUT, HERR GENERAL, THE ROAD —
DRIVE! DRIVE!
I DON'T CARE! JUST DRIVE!
WH-32287

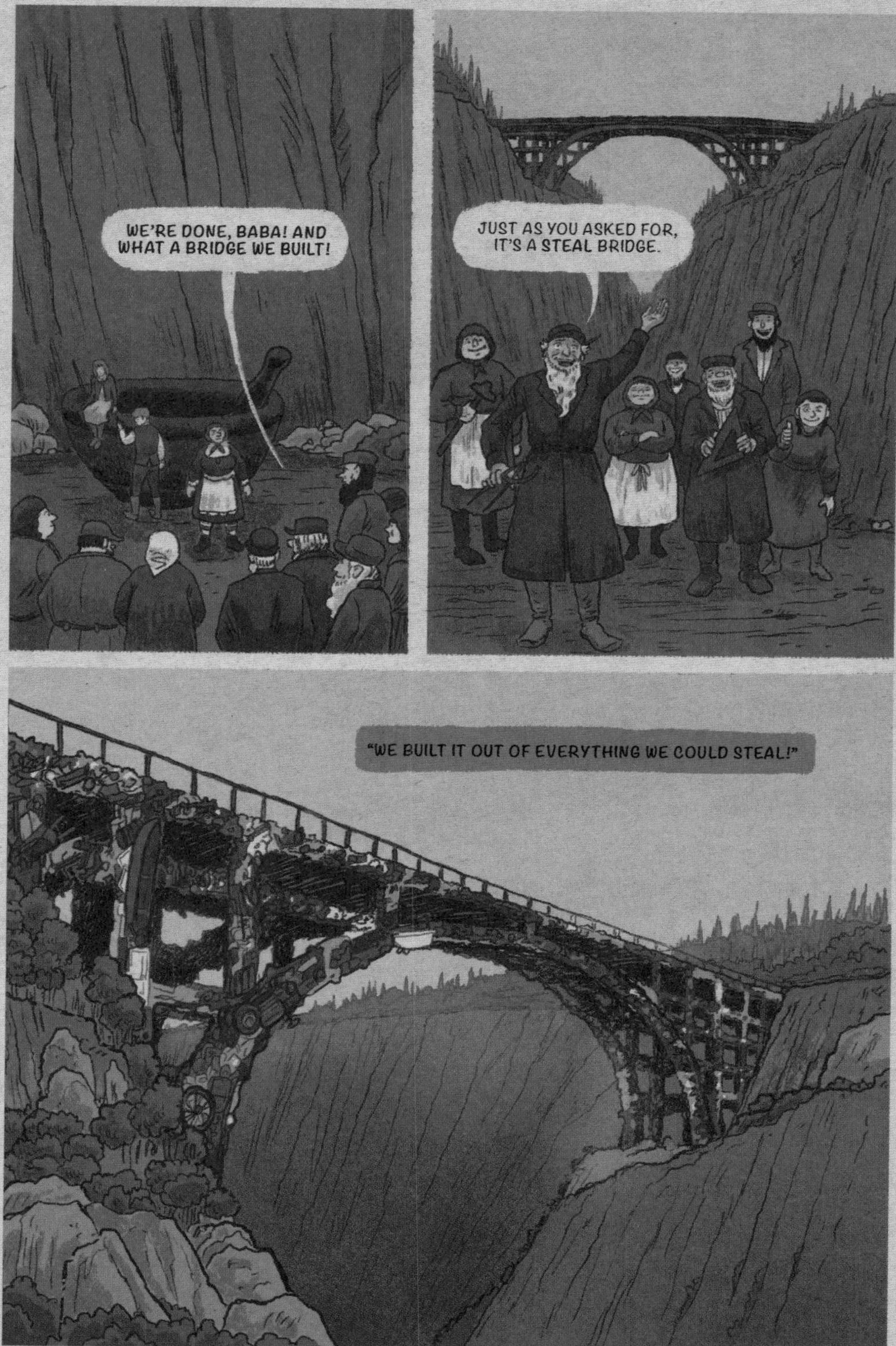
WE'RE DONE, BABA! AND WHAT A BRIDGE WE BUILT!
JUST AS YOU ASKED FOR, IT'S A STEAL BRIDGE.
"WE BUILT IT OUT OF EVERYTHING WE COULD STEAL!"

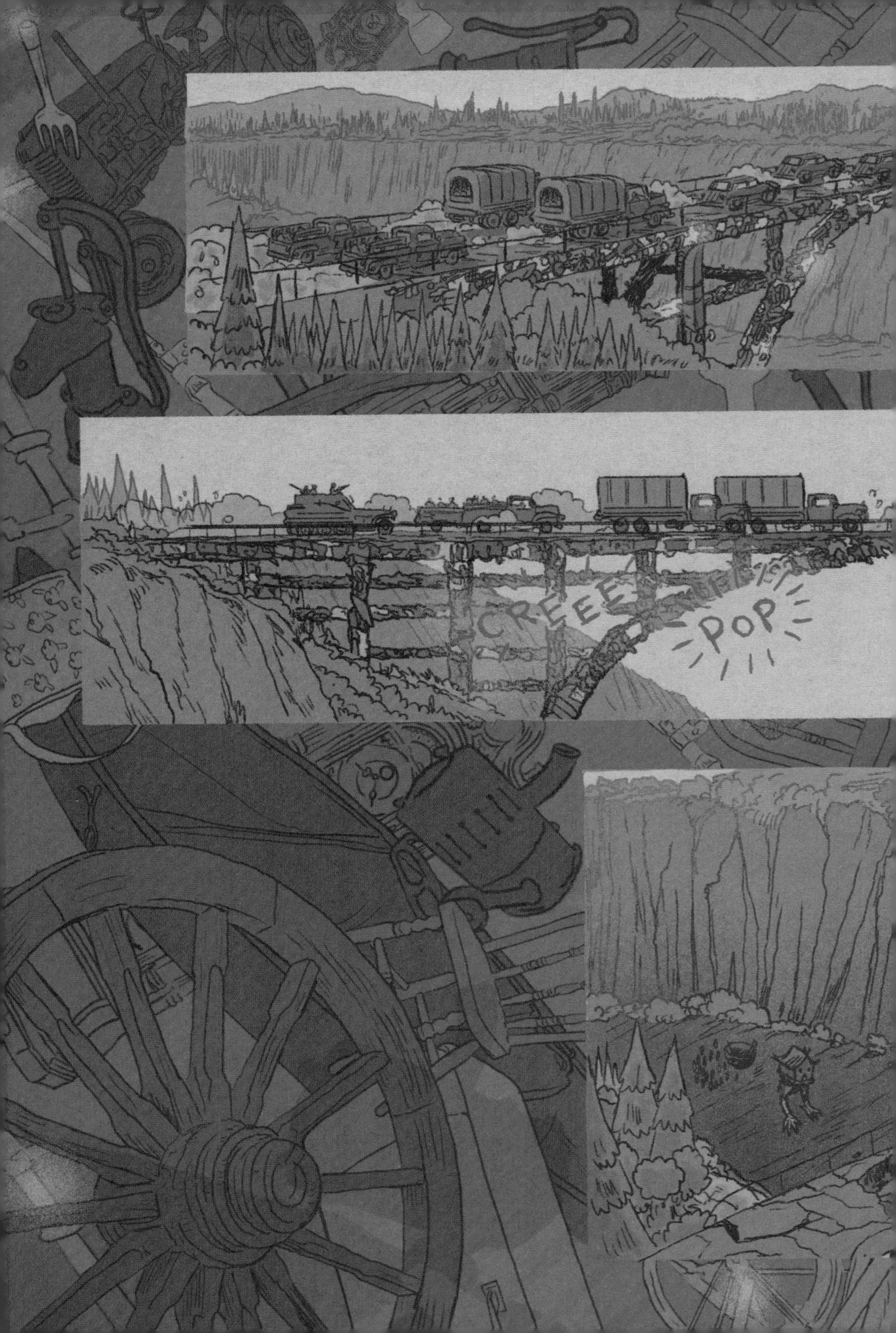
CREEEK
POP

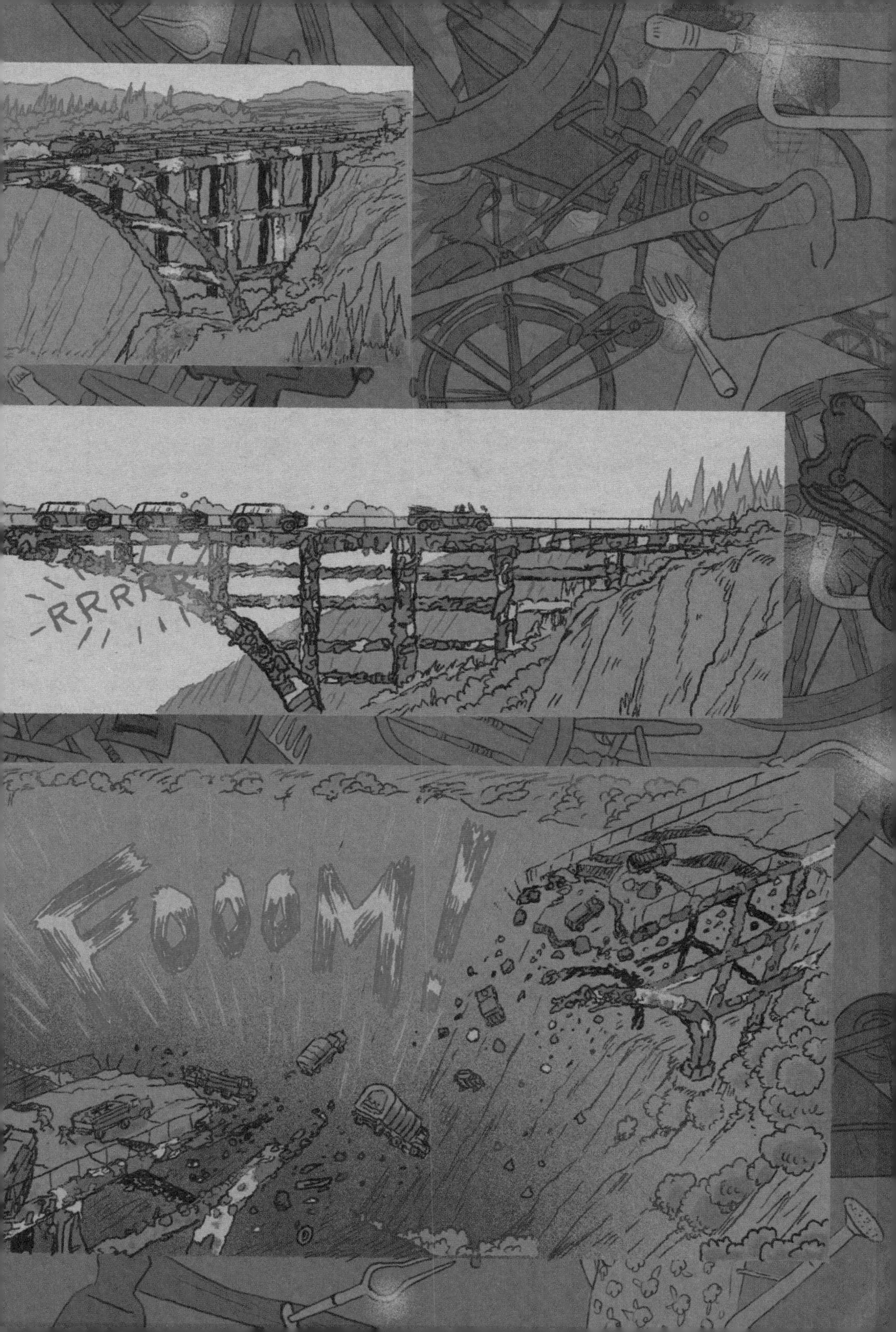
RRRRR
FOOOM!

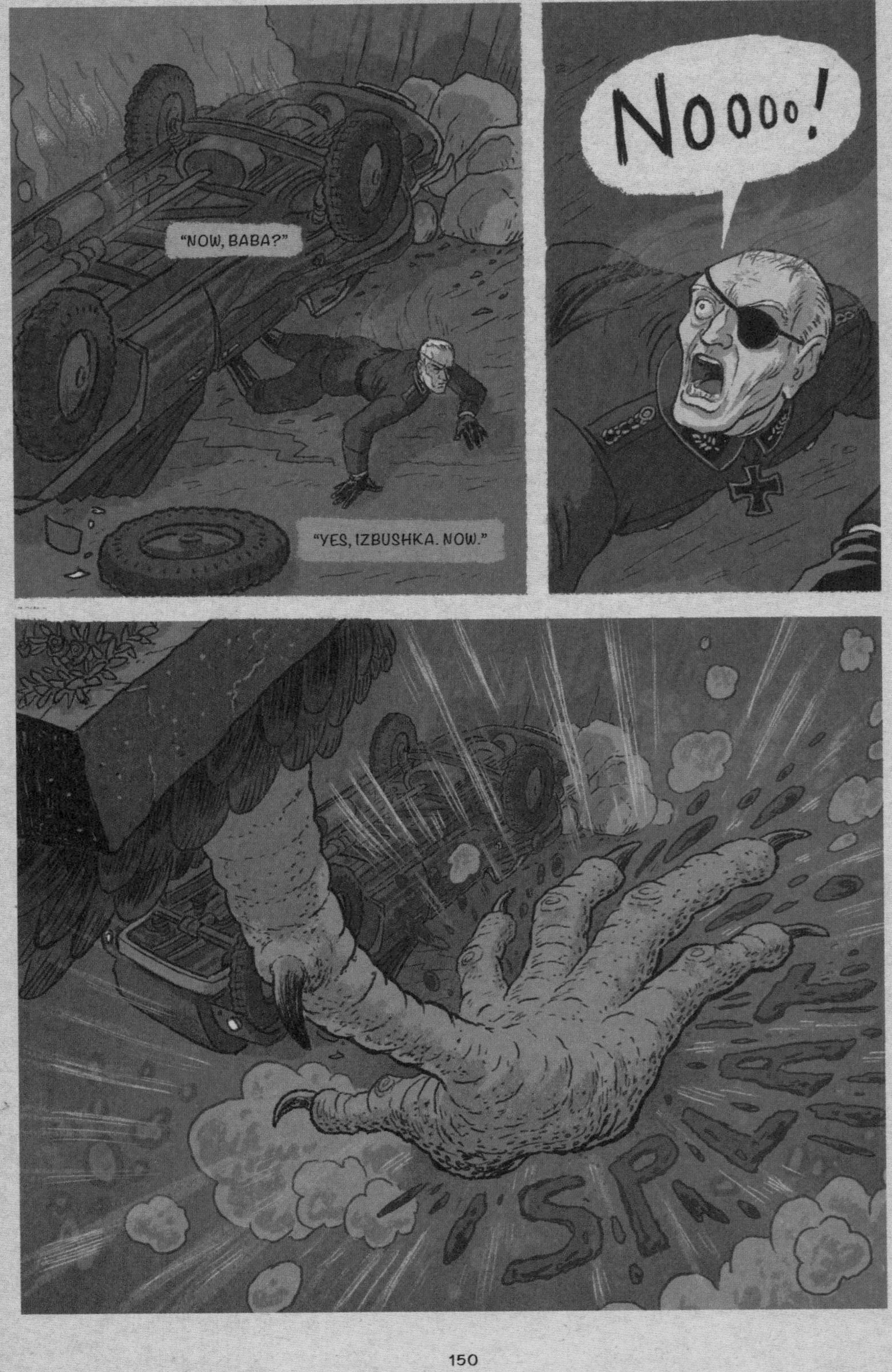
"NOW, BABA?"
"YES, IZBUSHKA. NOW."
Noooo!

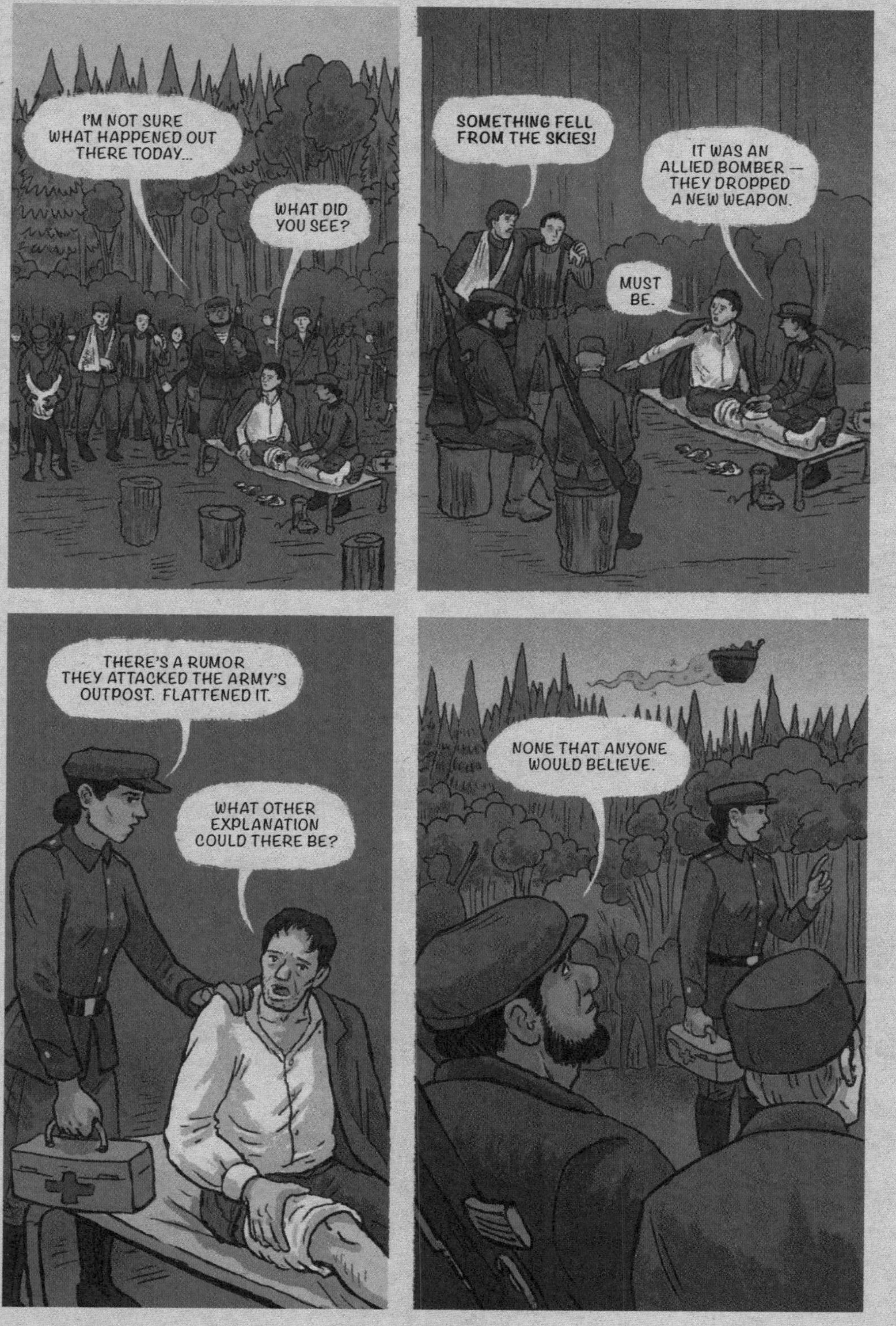
I'M NOT SURE WHAT HAPPENED OUT THERE TODAY...
WHAT DID YOU SEE?
SOMETHING FELL FROM THE SKIES!
IT WAS AN ALLIED BOMBER — THEY DROPPED A NEW WEAPON.
MUST BE.
THERE'S A RUMOR THEY ATTACKED THE ARMY'S OUTPOST. FLATTENED IT.
WHAT OTHER EXPLANATION COULD THERE BE?
NONE THAT ANYONE WOULD BELIEVE.

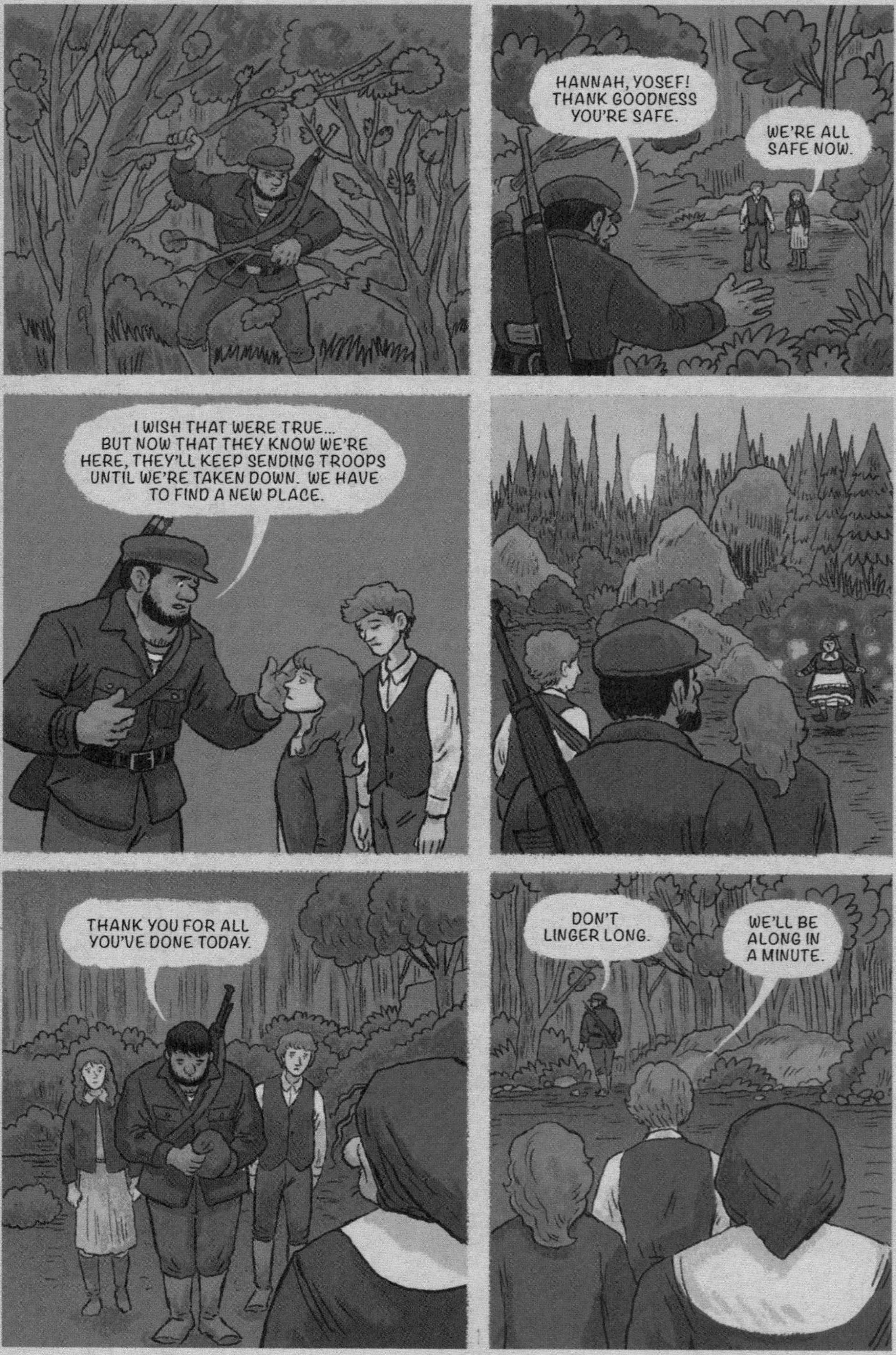
HANNAH, YOSEF! THANK GOODNESS YOU'RE SAFE.
WE'RE ALL SAFE NOW.
I WISH THAT WERE TRUE... BUT NOW THAT THEY KNOW WE'RE HERE, THEY'LL KEEP SENDING TROOPS UNTIL WE'RE TAKEN DOWN. WE HAVE TO FIND A NEW PLACE.
THANK YOU FOR ALL YOU'VE DONE TODAY.
DON'T LINGER LONG.
WE'LL BE ALONG IN A MINUTE.

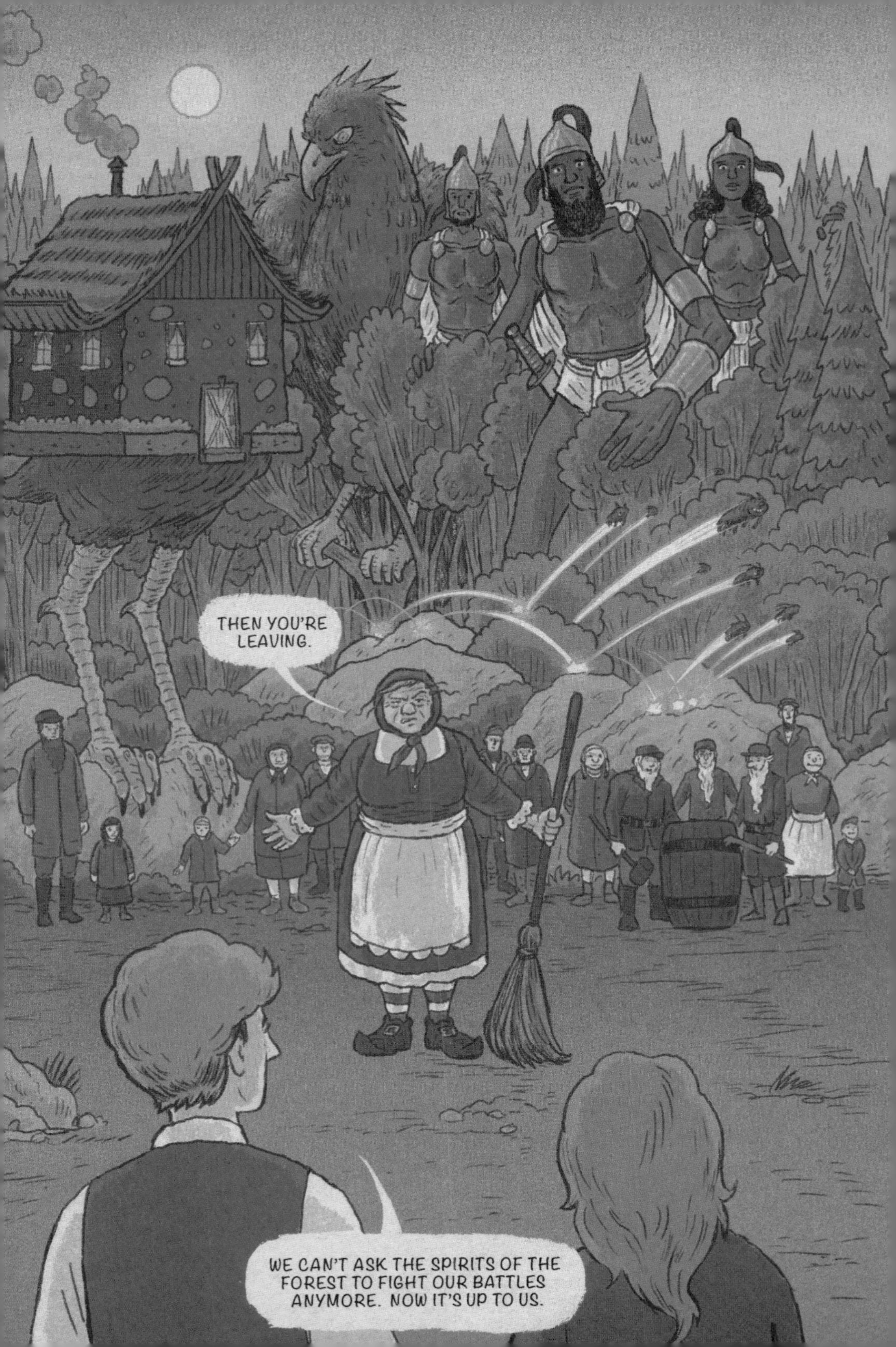
THEN YOU'RE LEAVING.
WE CAN'T ASK THE SPIRITS OF THE FOREST TO FIGHT OUR BATTLES ANYMORE. NOW IT'S UP TO US.

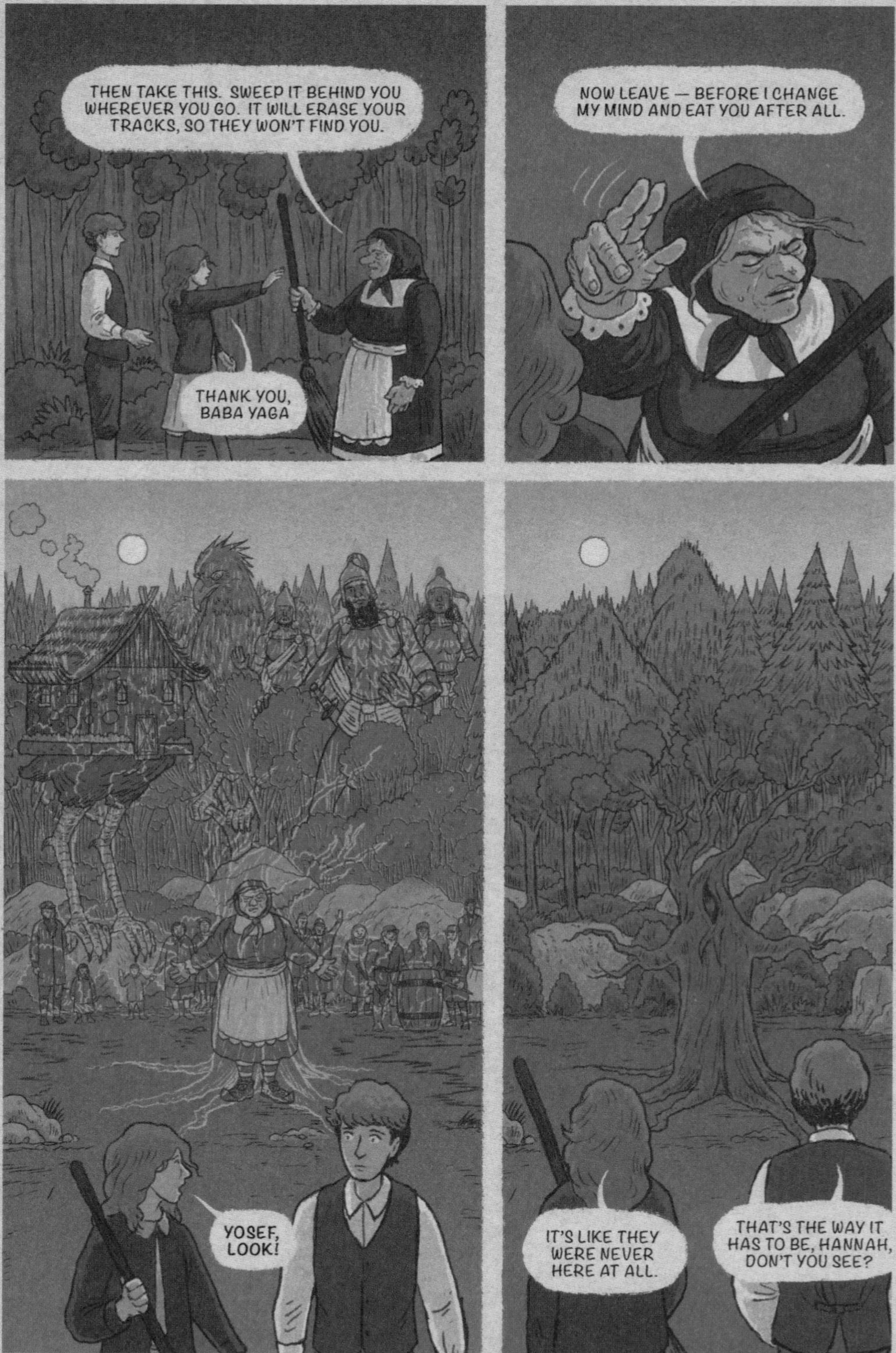
THEN TAKE THIS. SWEEP IT BEHIND YOU WHEREVER YOU GO. IT WILL ERASE YOUR TRACKS, SO THEY WON'T FIND YOU.
THANK YOU, BABA YAGA
NOW LEAVE — BEFORE I CHANGE MY MIND AND EAT YOU AFTER ALL.
YOSEF, LOOK!
IT'S LIKE THEY WERE NEVER HERE AT ALL.
THAT'S THE WAY IT HAS TO BE, HANNAH, DON'T YOU SEE?

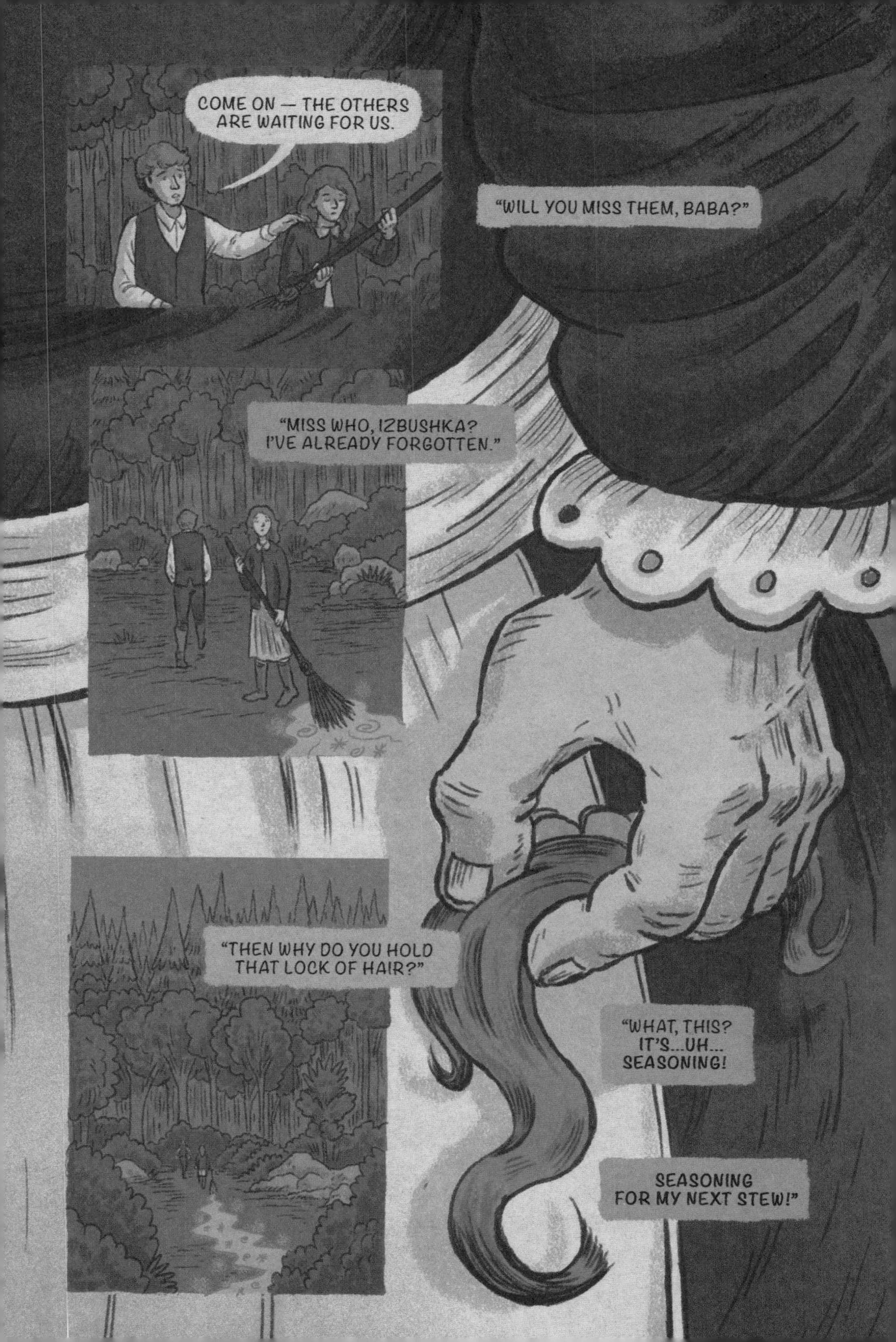
COME ON — THE OTHERS ARE WAITING FOR US.
"WILL YOU MISS THEM, BABA?"
"MISS WHO, IZBUSHKA? I'VE ALREADY FORGOTTEN."
"THEN WHY DO YOU HOLD THAT LOCK OF HAIR?"
"WHAT, THIS? IT'S...UH... SEASONING!
SEASONING FOR MY NEXT STEW!"

The mythical characters in "Spirits of Resistance" come from Jewish and Eastern European folklore.

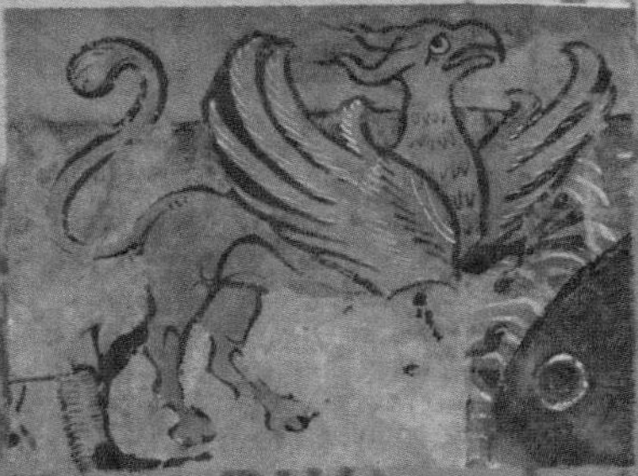

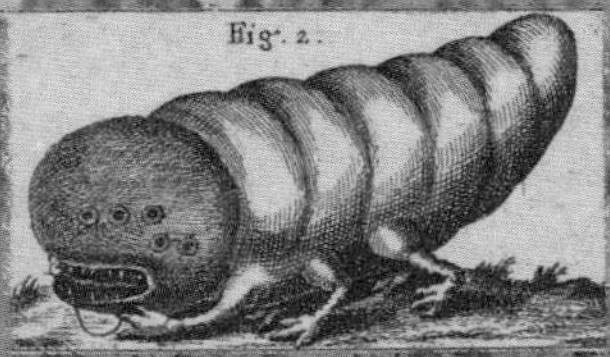
Fig. 2.

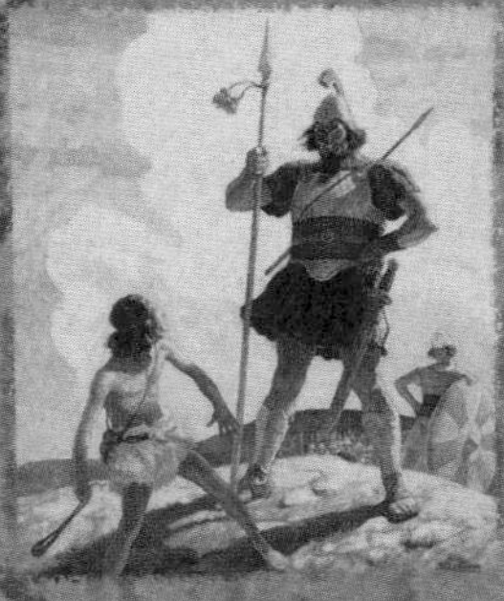

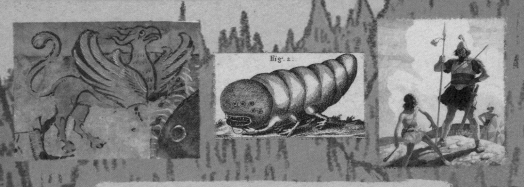

There are many versions of the Baba Yaga story in Eastern Europe.

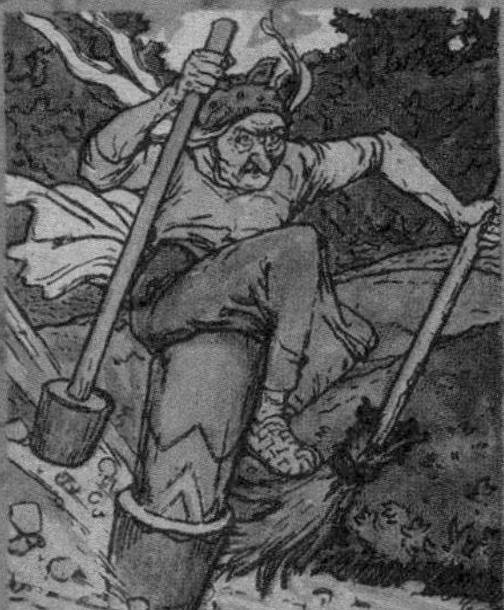

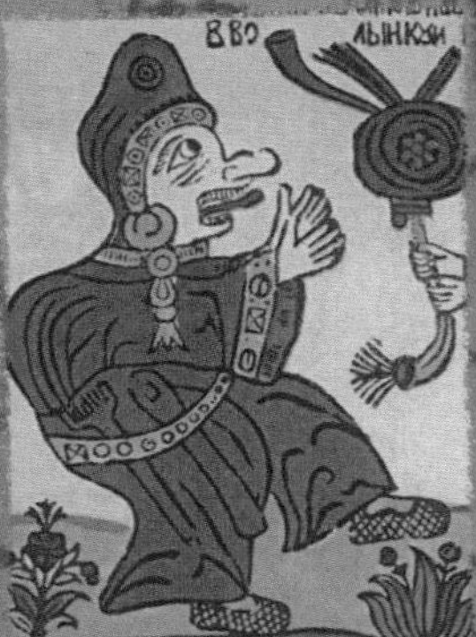

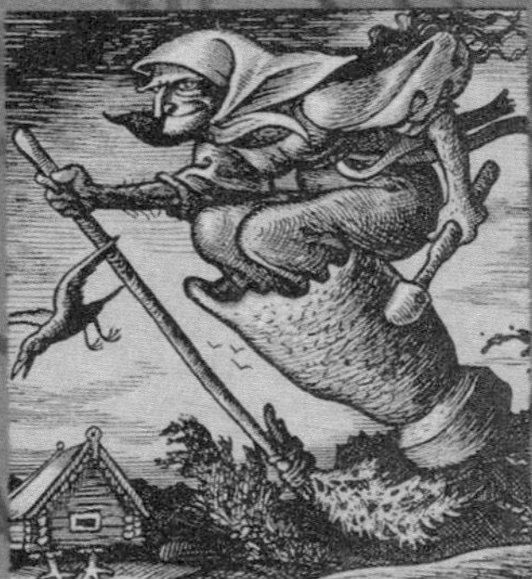

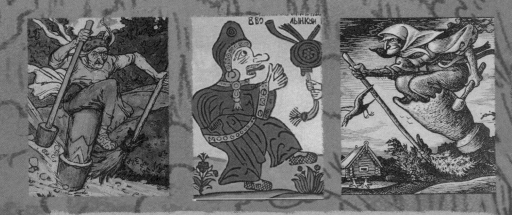

"The Fools of Chelm" is said to be the inspiration for The Three Stooges, all of whom were sons of Jewish immigrants from Eastern Europe and knew the tales.

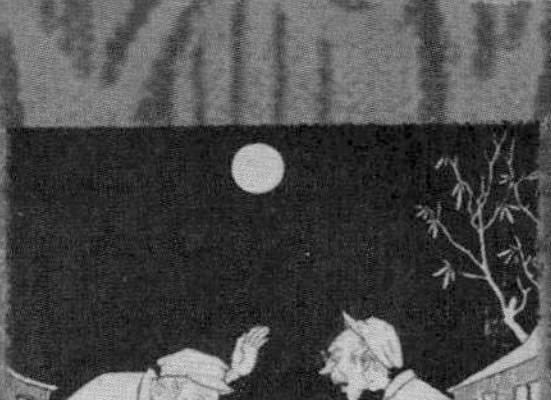
מאור הרחובות

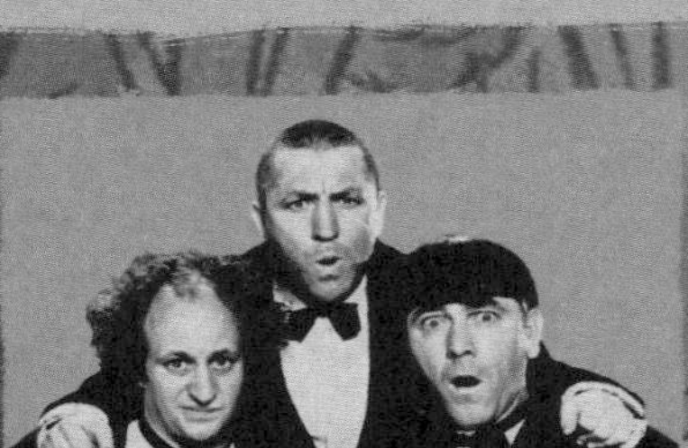

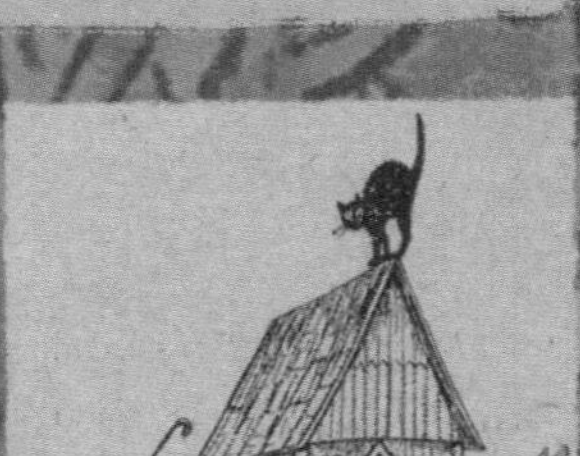

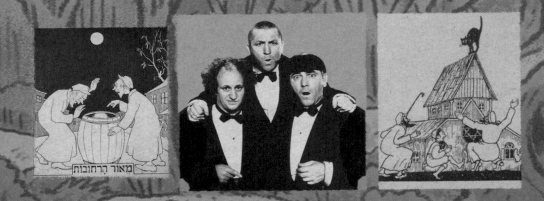

There were many European Jews throughout occupied Europe who fought back with armed resistance — both individually and in groups. They were especially active in the East. Between 20,000 and 30,000 Jews fought the Third Reich in the forests of Eastern Europe.

Among the most well-known resistance fighters were the Bielski brothers, who built a camp in the forest of what is now western Belarus, and saved the lives of about 1,200 Jews.

The Bielski Brothers — Aharon, Asael, Tuvia, and Zusya — escaped to the Belarusian forest after their family was massacred with 5,000 others in December of 1941. Once hidden in the woods, they created a civilian military unit led by Tuvia Bielski. Although they did engage the enemy, their main goal was to rescue Jews and to offer them protection in the forest.

"Don't rush to fight and die. So few of us are left, we need to save lives. It is more important to save Jews than to kill Germans."
— Tuvia Bielski

Squads were sent out on missions to rescue Jews from ghettos — entire neighborhoods within cities that were fenced in and turned into prisons.

Finding food in the woods was one of the biggest problems. Local farmers were struggling themselves, and it was hard to know who could be trusted.

In July 1943, the Third Reich sent 52,000 soldiers to the forest to wipe out the Jewish resistance. The Bielskis managed to elude their attackers by hiding in unfamiliar forests and swamps.

Once the German forces left the Belarusian woods, the Bielskis built a Jewish village, and the forest became a place of life instead of death.

ר

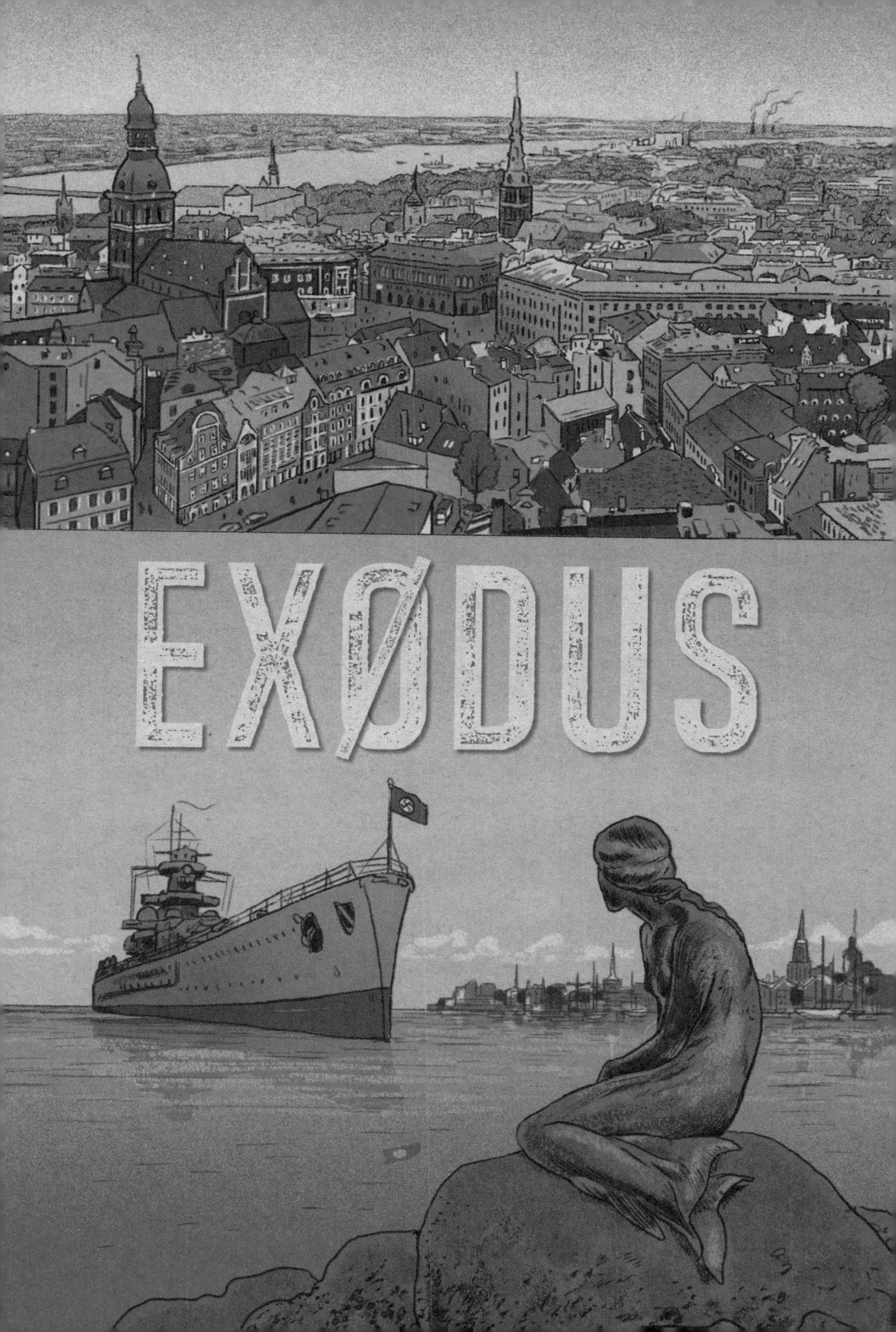
EXØDUS

JORY AND I WERE FRIENDS FOR AS LONG AS I CAN REMEMBER.

IT NEVER MATTERED THAT HE WAS JEWISH AND I WAS LUTHERAN. DANES WERE DANES, AND WHATEVER OUR BELIEFS, WE GOT ALONG.

WHEN THE NAZIS OCCUPIED DENMARK, THEY TRIED TO DEPORT THE JEWS, BUT WE DIDN'T LET THEM.

IT WAS THE SUMMER OF 1943, AND THE JEWS OF COPENHAGEN WERE SAFE. OR SO WE THOUGHT.

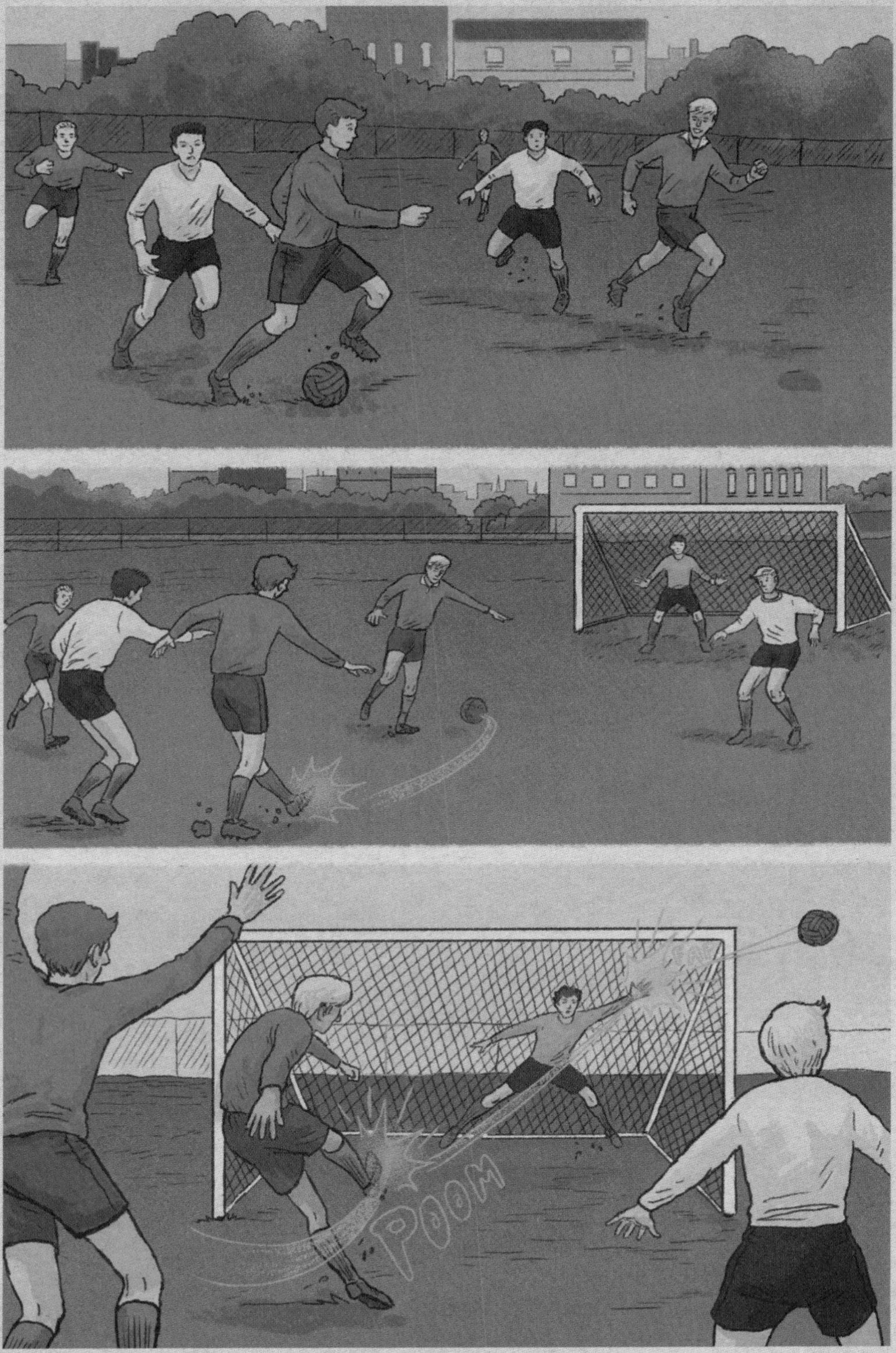
POOM

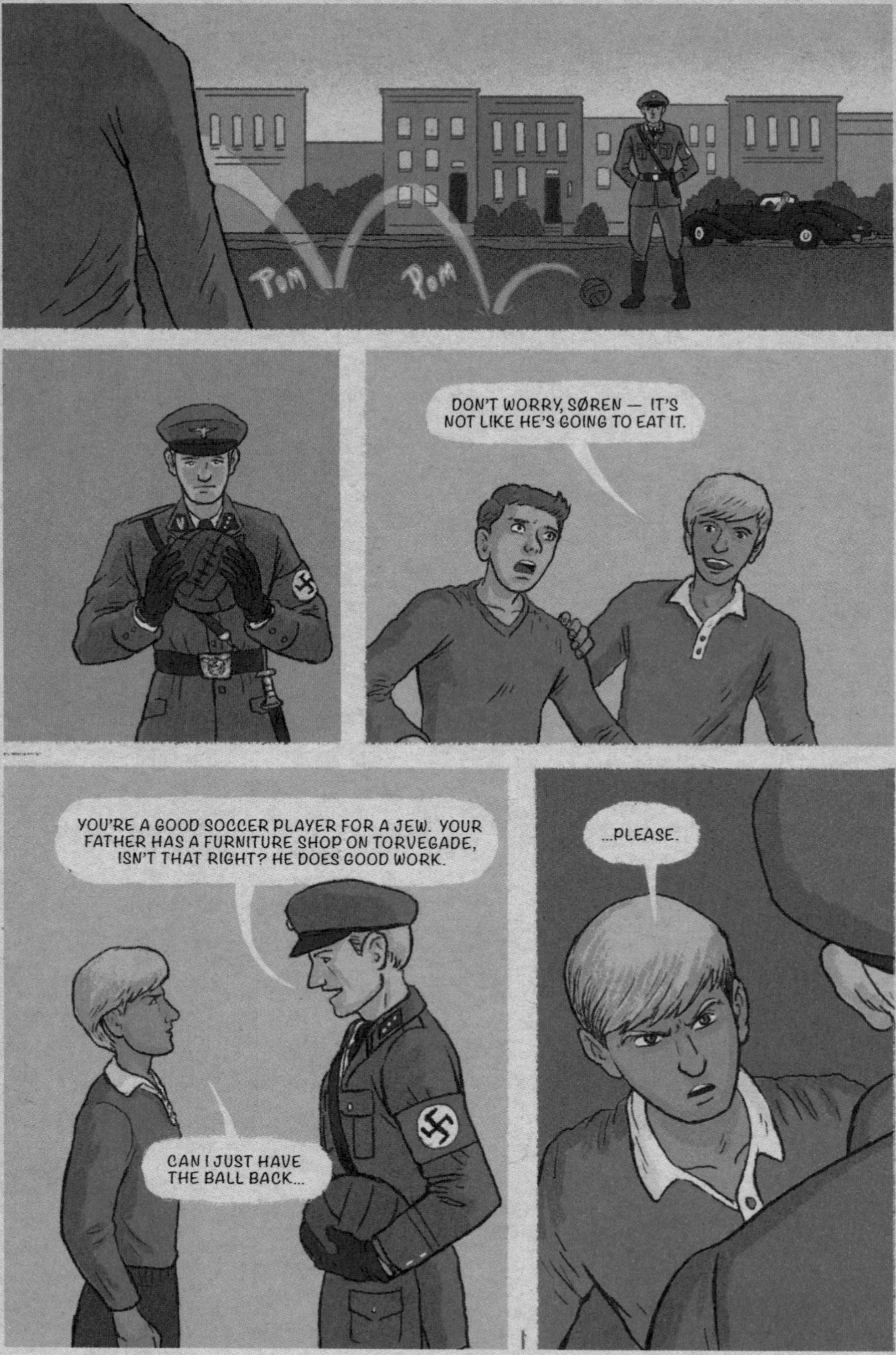
POM
POM
DON'T WORRY, SØREN — IT'S NOT LIKE HE'S GOING TO EAT IT.
YOU'RE A GOOD SOCCER PLAYER FOR A JEW. YOUR FATHER HAS A FURNITURE SHOP ON TORVEGADE, ISN'T THAT RIGHT? HE DOES GOOD WORK.
CAN I JUST HAVE THE BALL BACK...
...PLEASE.

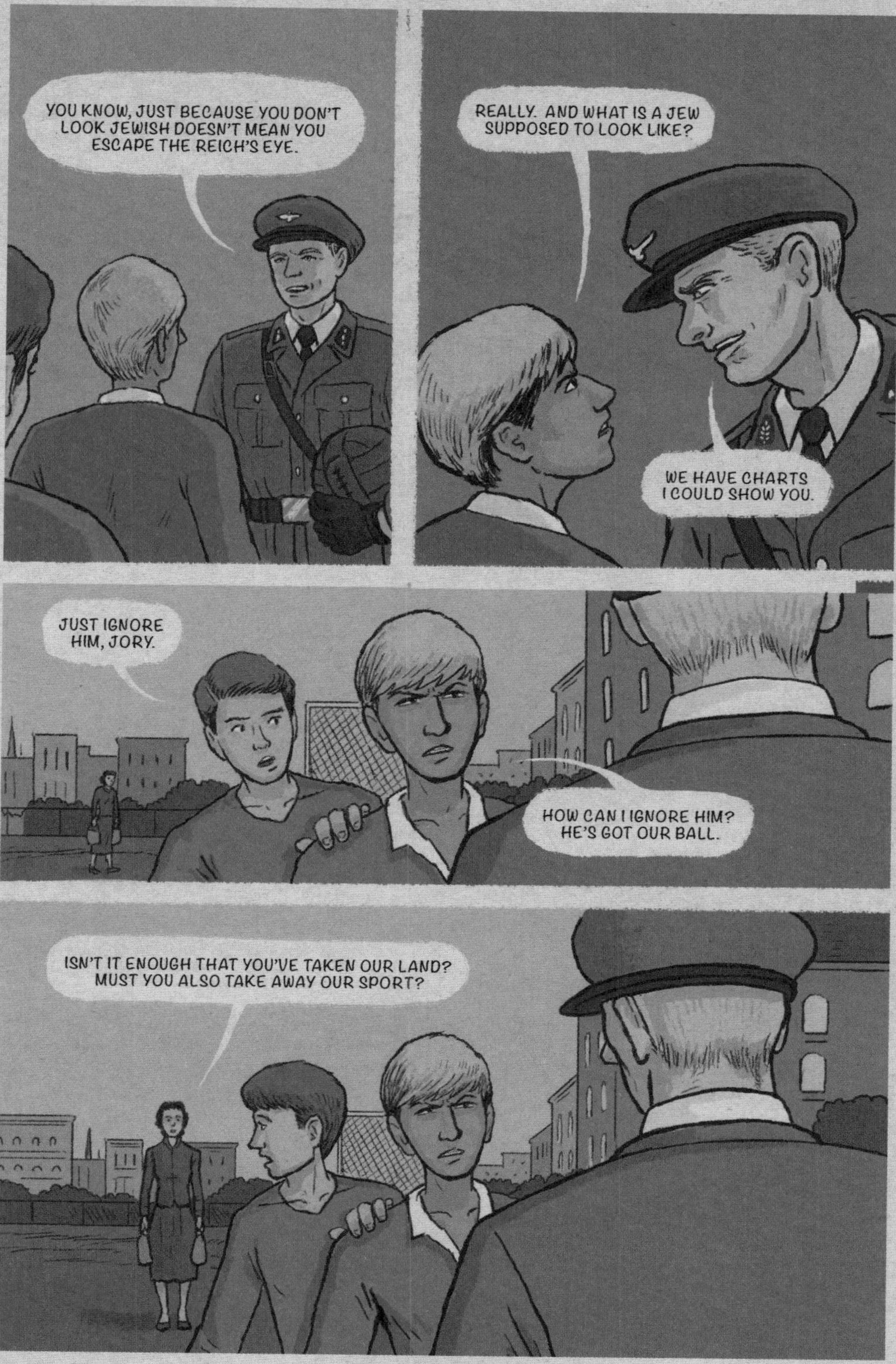
YOU KNOW, JUST BECAUSE YOU DON'T LOOK JEWISH DOESN'T MEAN YOU ESCAPE THE REICH'S EYE.
REALLY. AND WHAT IS A JEW SUPPOSED TO LOOK LIKE?
WE HAVE CHARTS I COULD SHOW YOU.
JUST IGNORE HIM, JORY.
HOW CAN I IGNORE HIM? HE'S GOT OUR BALL.
ISN'T IT ENOUGH THAT YOU'VE TAKEN OUR LAND? MUST YOU ALSO TAKE AWAY OUR SPORT?

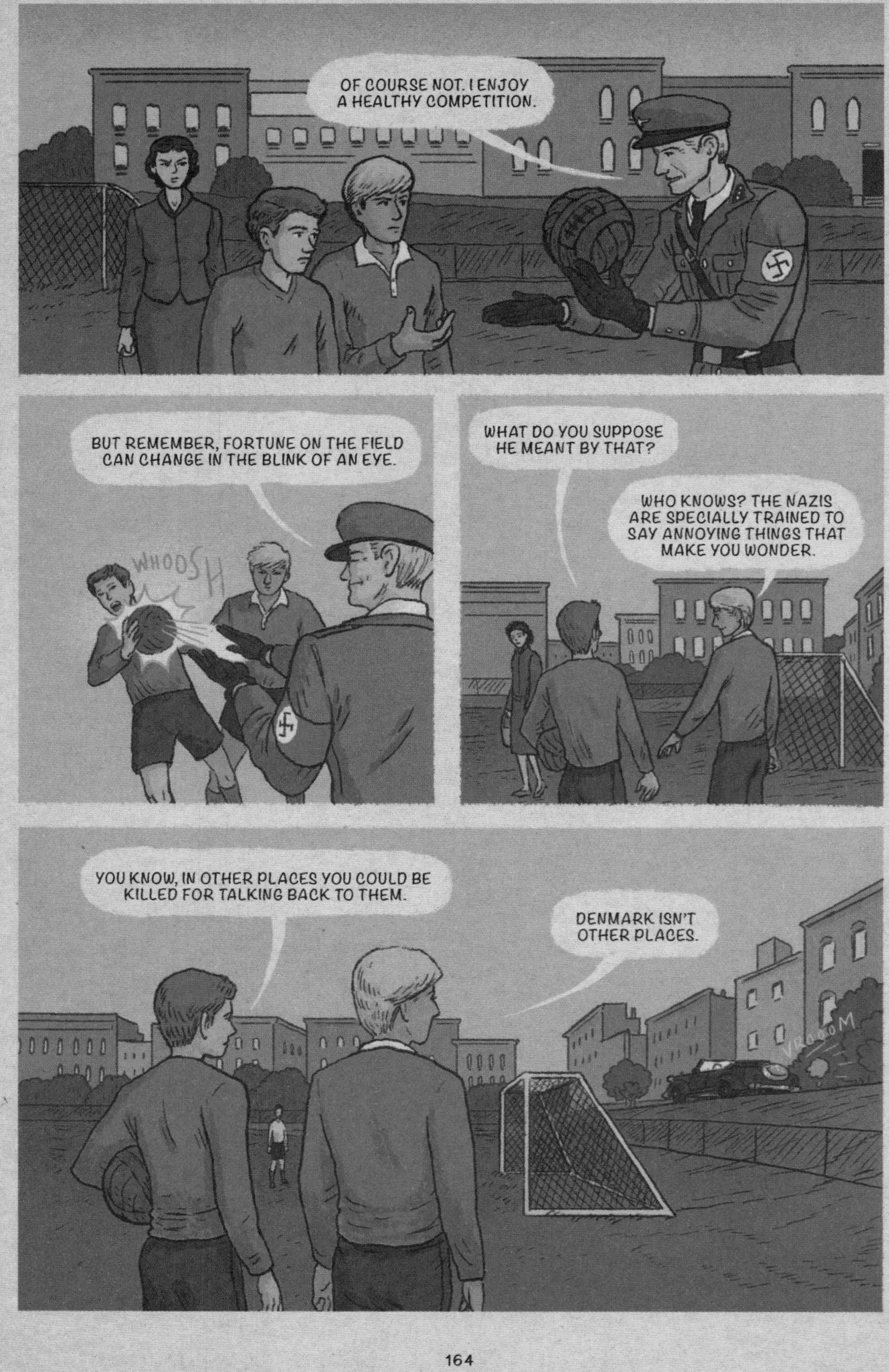
OF COURSE NOT. I ENJOY A HEALTHY COMPETITION.
BUT REMEMBER, FORTUNE ON THE FIELD CAN CHANGE IN THE BLINK OF AN EYE.
WHOOSH
WHAT DO YOU SUPPOSE HE MEANT BY THAT?
WHO KNOWS? THE NAZIS ARE SPECIALLY TRAINED TO SAY ANNOYING THINGS THAT MAKE YOU WONDER.
YOU KNOW, IN OTHER PLACES YOU COULD BE KILLED FOR TALKING BACK TO THEM.
DENMARK ISN'T OTHER PLACES.

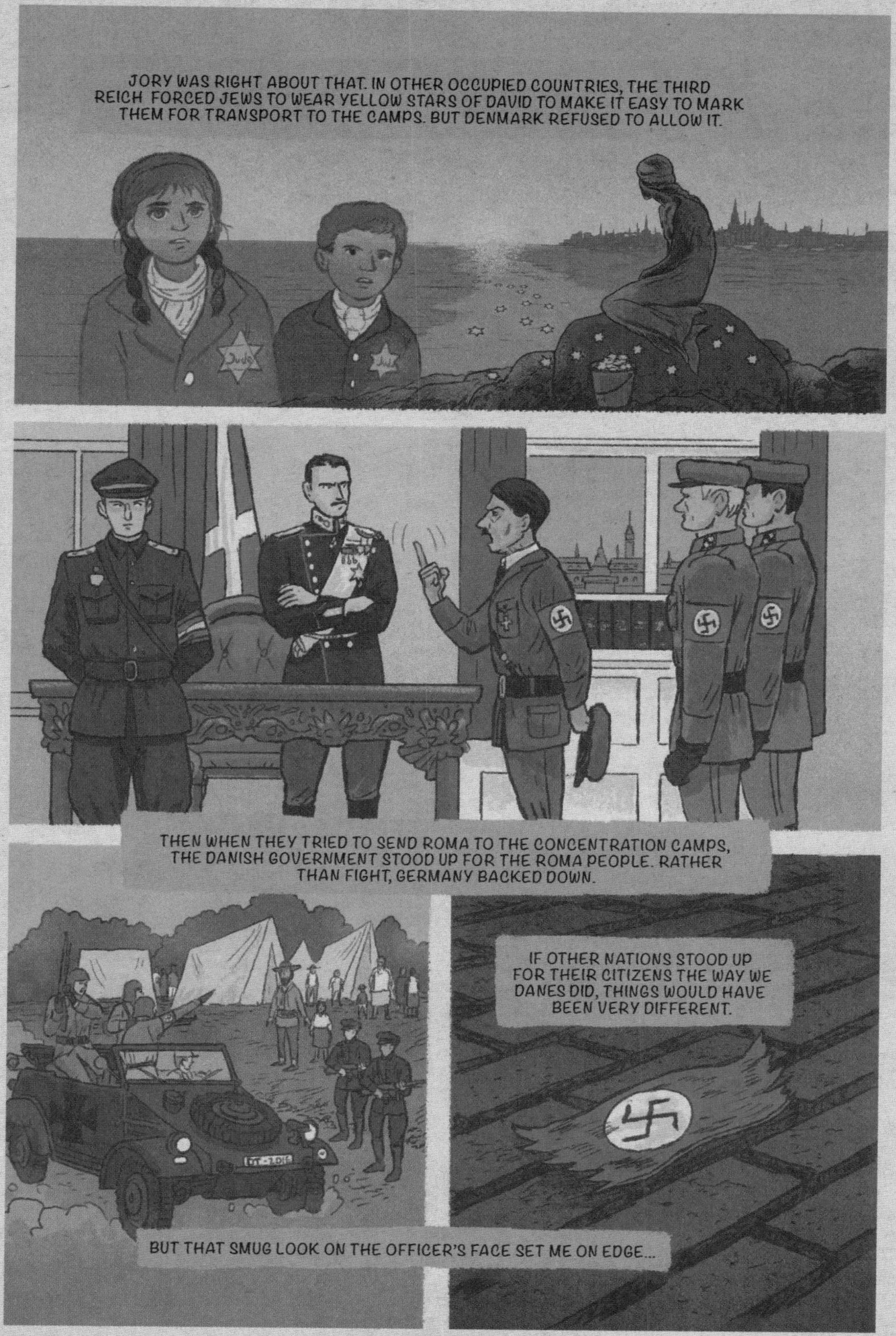
JORY WAS RIGHT ABOUT THAT. IN OTHER OCCUPIED COUNTRIES, THE THIRD REICH FORCED JEWS TO WEAR YELLOW STARS OF DAVID TO MAKE IT EASY TO MARK THEM FOR TRANSPORT TO THE CAMPS. BUT DENMARK REFUSED TO ALLOW IT.
THEN WHEN THEY TRIED TO SEND ROMA TO THE CONCENTRATION CAMPS, THE DANISH GOVERNMENT STOOD UP FOR THE ROMA PEOPLE. RATHER THAN FIGHT, GERMANY BACKED DOWN.
IF OTHER NATIONS STOOD UP FOR THEIR CITIZENS THE WAY WE DANES DID, THINGS WOULD HAVE BEEN VERY DIFFERENT.
BUT THAT SMUG LOOK ON THE OFFICER'S FACE SET ME ON EDGE...

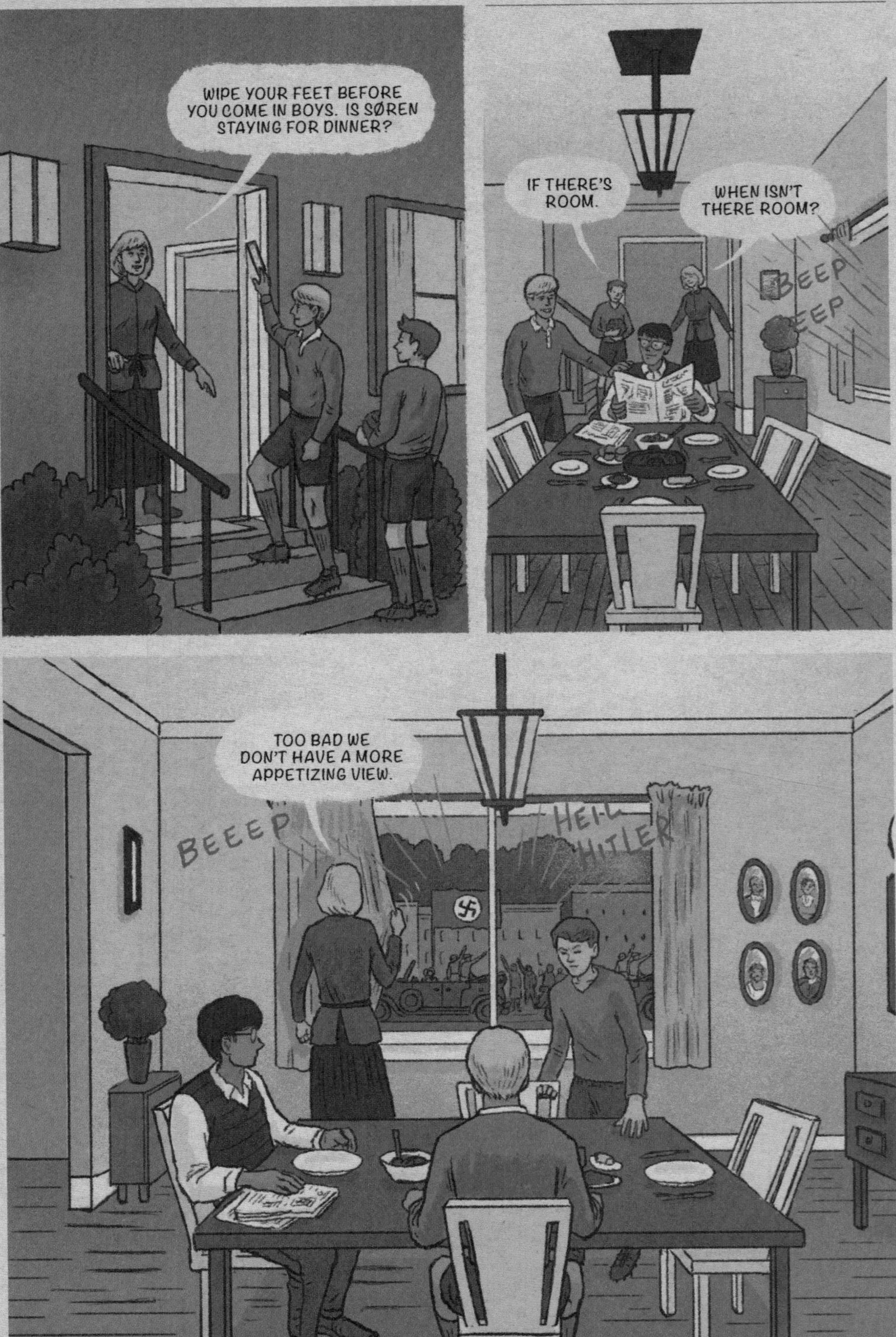
WIPE YOUR FEET BEFORE YOU COME IN BOYS. IS SØREN STAYING FOR DINNER?
IF THERE'S ROOM.
WHEN ISN'T THERE ROOM?
BEEP BEEP
TOO BAD WE DON'T HAVE A MORE APPETIZING VIEW.
BEEEP
HEIL HITLER

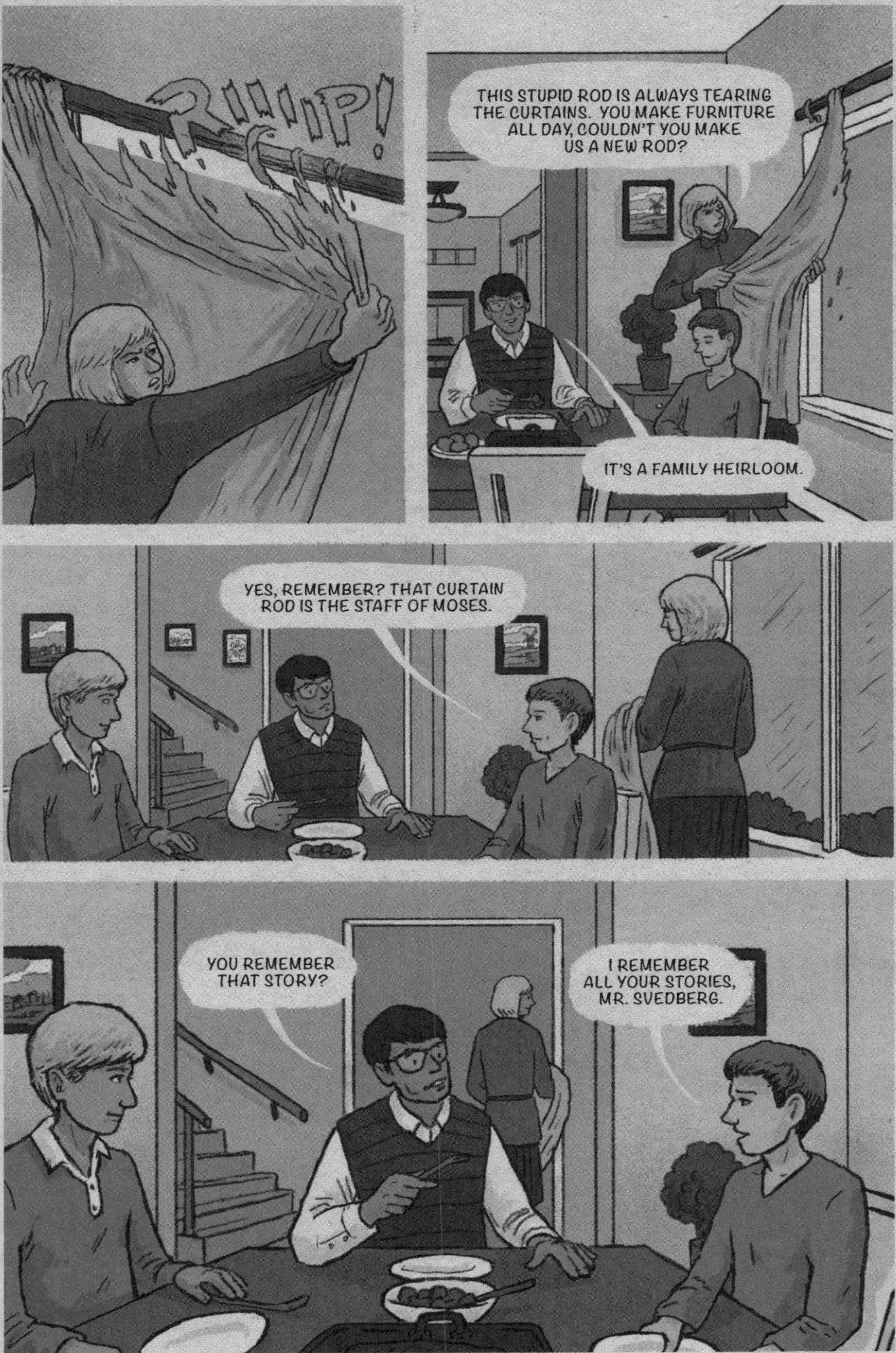
RIIIIP!
THIS STUPID ROD IS ALWAYS TEARING THE CURTAINS. YOU MAKE FURNITURE ALL DAY, COULDN'T YOU MAKE US A NEW ROD?
IT'S A FAMILY HEIRLOOM.
YES, REMEMBER? THAT CURTAIN ROD IS THE STAFF OF MOSES.
YOU REMEMBER THAT STORY?
I REMEMBER ALL YOUR STORIES, MR. SVEDBERG.

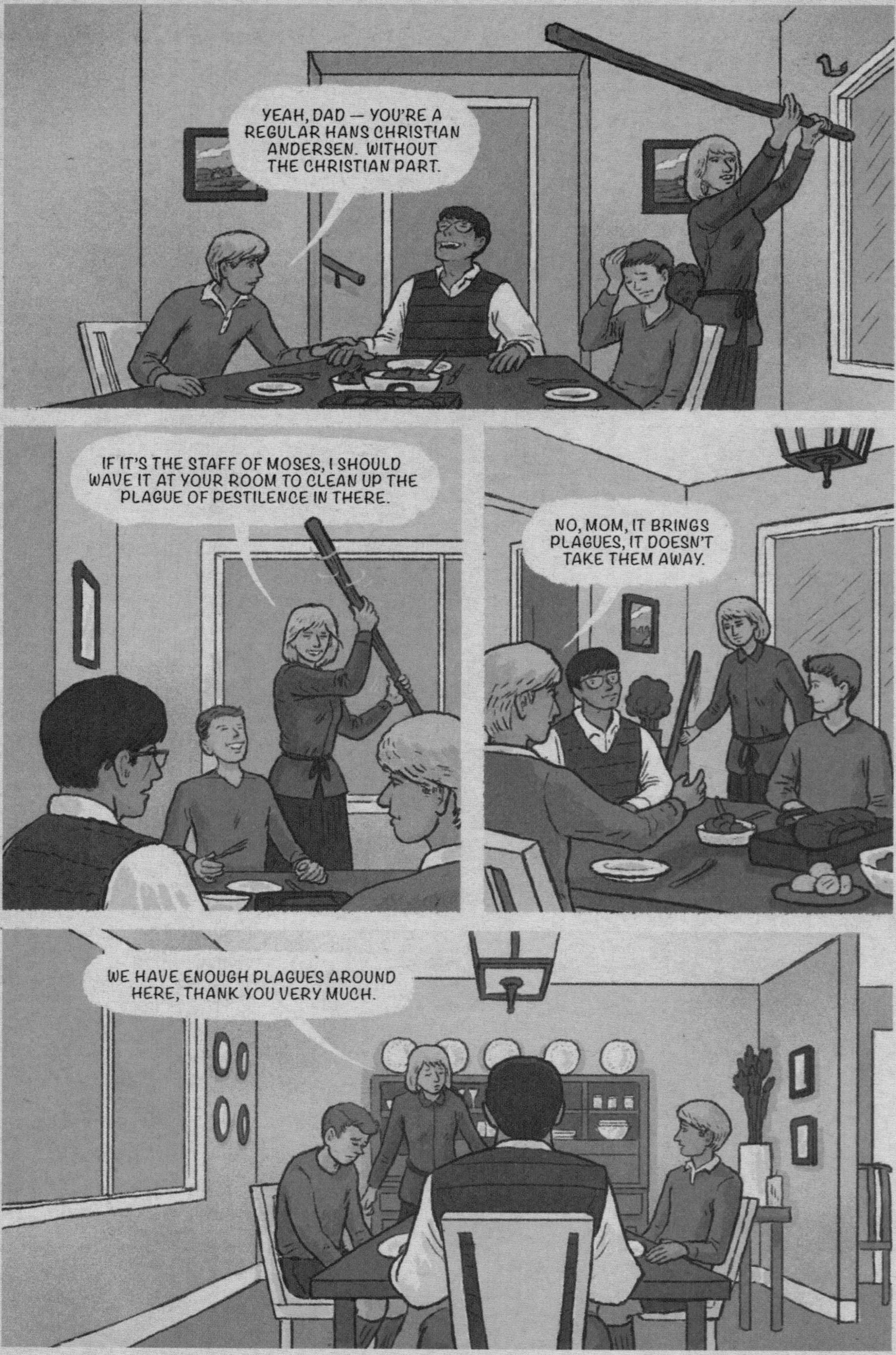
YEAH, DAD — YOU'RE A REGULAR HANS CHRISTIAN ANDERSEN. WITHOUT THE CHRISTIAN PART.
IF IT'S THE STAFF OF MOSES, I SHOULD WAVE IT AT YOUR ROOM TO CLEAN UP THE PLAGUE OF PESTILENCE IN THERE.
NO, MOM, IT BRINGS PLAGUES, IT DOESN'T TAKE THEM AWAY.
WE HAVE ENOUGH PLAGUES AROUND HERE, THANK YOU VERY MUCH.

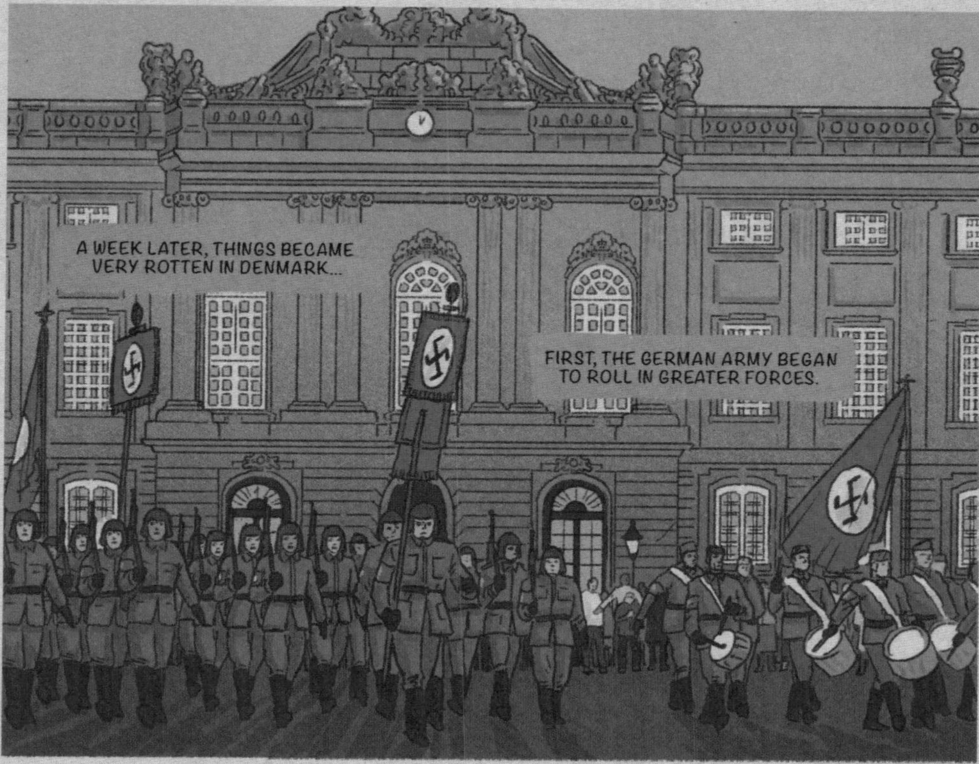
A WEEK LATER, THINGS BECAME VERY ROTTEN IN DENMARK...
FIRST, THE GERMAN ARMY BEGAN TO ROLL IN GREATER FORCES.

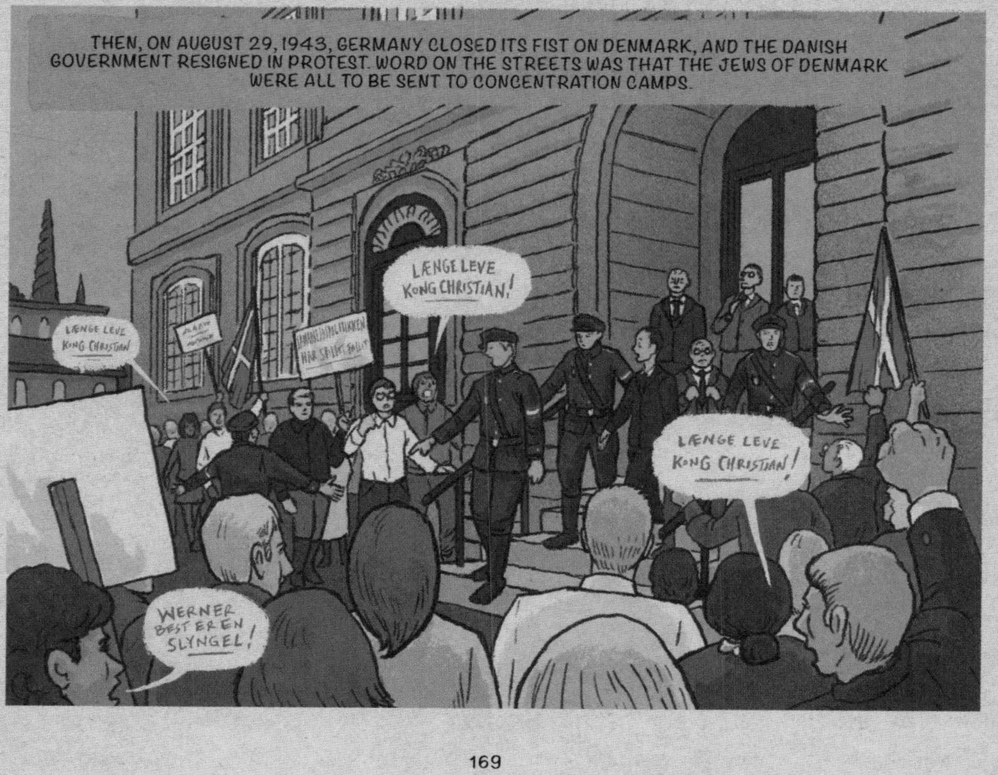
THEN, ON AUGUST 29, 1943, GERMANY CLOSED ITS FIST ON DENMARK, AND THE DANISH GOVERNMENT RESIGNED IN PROTEST. WORD ON THE STREETS WAS THAT THE JEWS OF DENMARK WERE ALL TO BE SENT TO CONCENTRATION CAMPS.
LÆNGE LEVE KONG CHRISTIAN
LÆNGE LEVE KONG CHRISTIAN!
LÆNGE LEVE KONG CHRISTIAN!
WERNER BEST ER EN SLYNGEL!

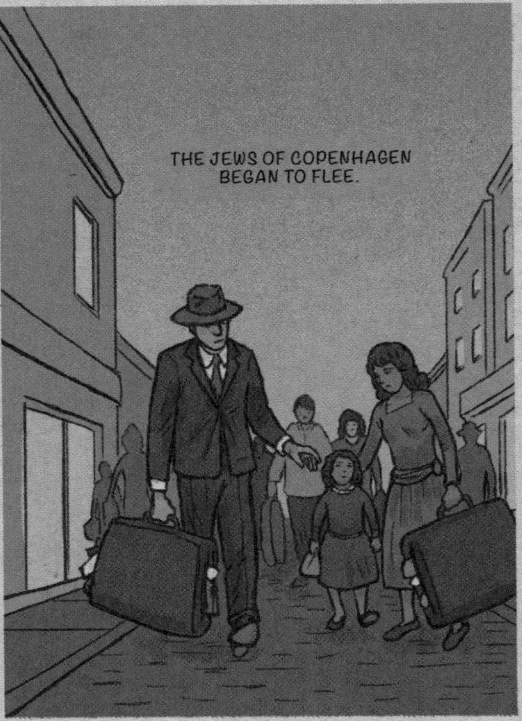
THE JEWS OF COPENHAGEN BEGAN TO FLEE.

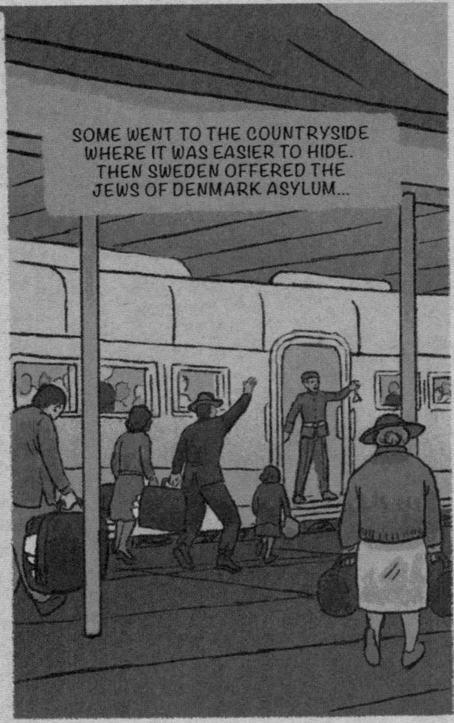
SOME WENT TO THE COUNTRYSIDE WHERE IT WAS EASIER TO HIDE. THEN SWEDEN OFFERED THE JEWS OF DENMARK ASYLUM...

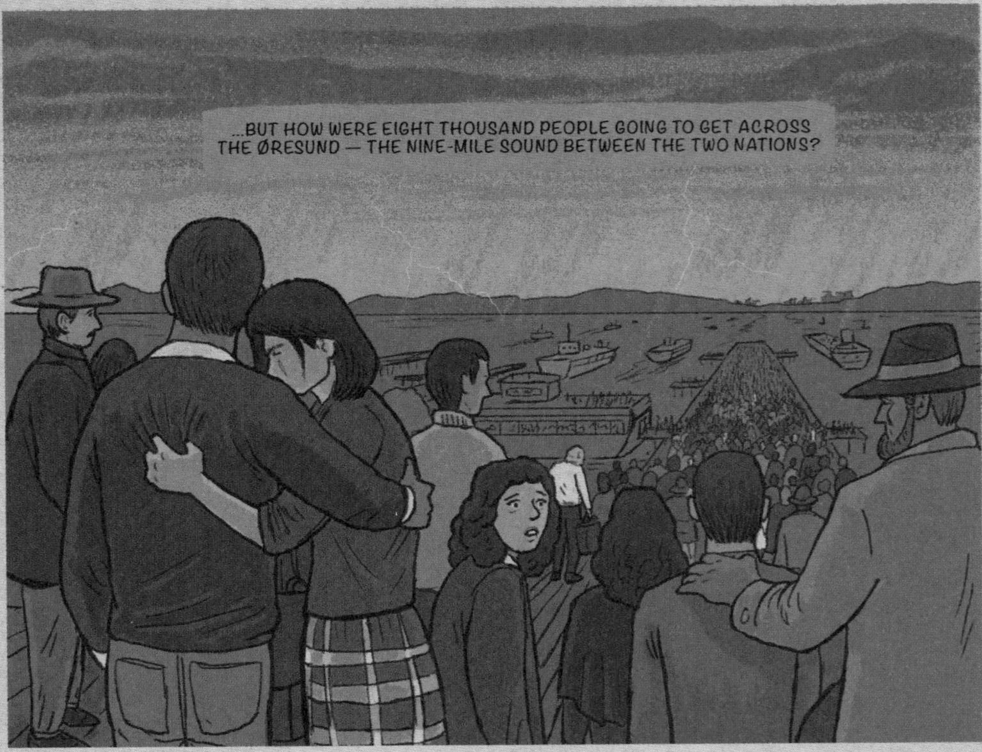
...BUT HOW WERE EIGHT THOUSAND PEOPLE GOING TO GET ACROSS THE ØRESUND — THE NINE-MILE SOUND BETWEEN THE TWO NATIONS?

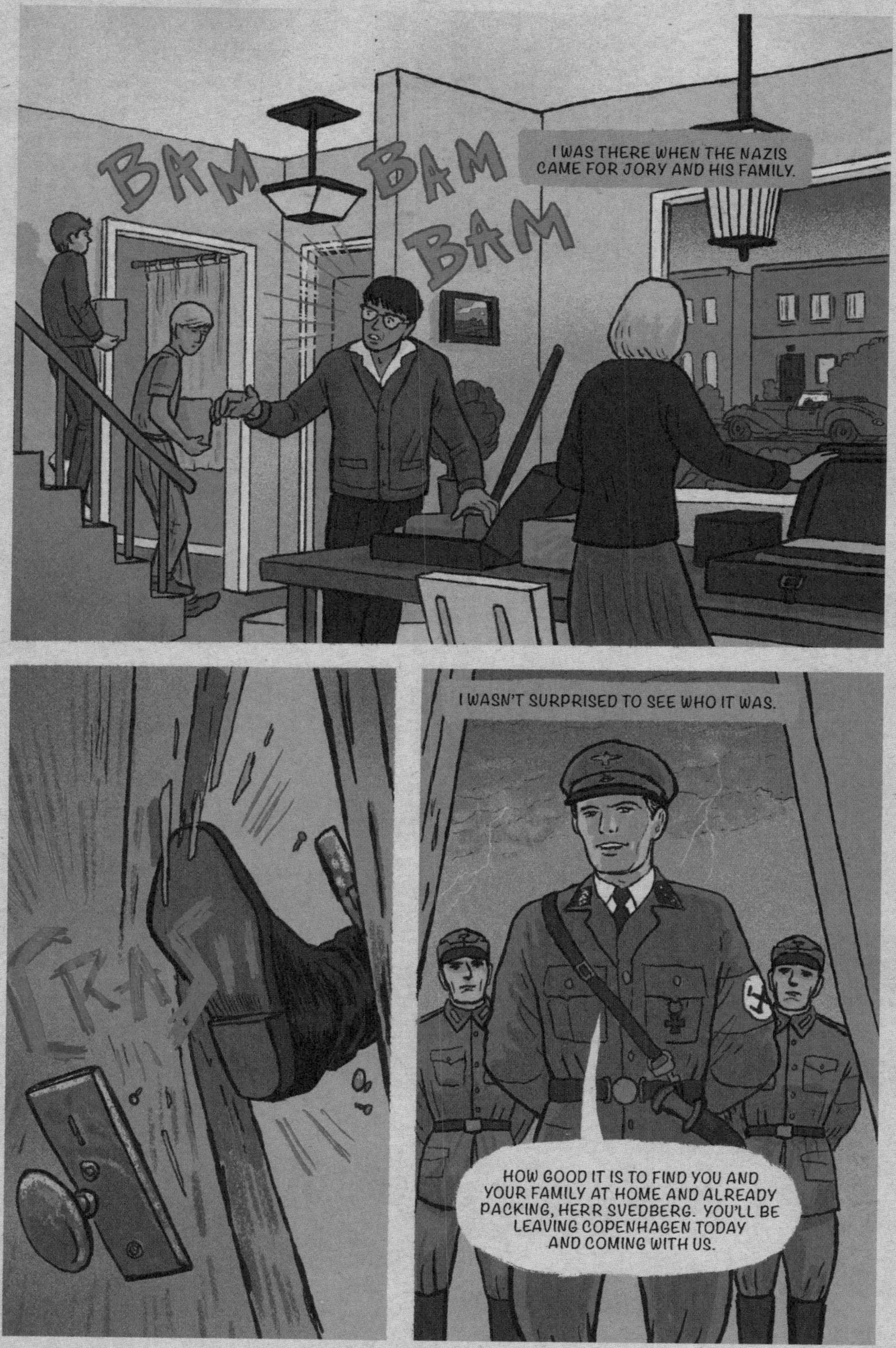
BAM BAM BAM
I WAS THERE WHEN THE NAZIS CAME FOR JORY AND HIS FAMILY.
I WASN'T SURPRISED TO SEE WHO IT WAS.
HOW GOOD IT IS TO FIND YOU AND YOUR FAMILY AT HOME AND ALREADY PACKING, HERR SVEDBERG. YOU'LL BE LEAVING COPENHAGEN TODAY AND COMING WITH US.

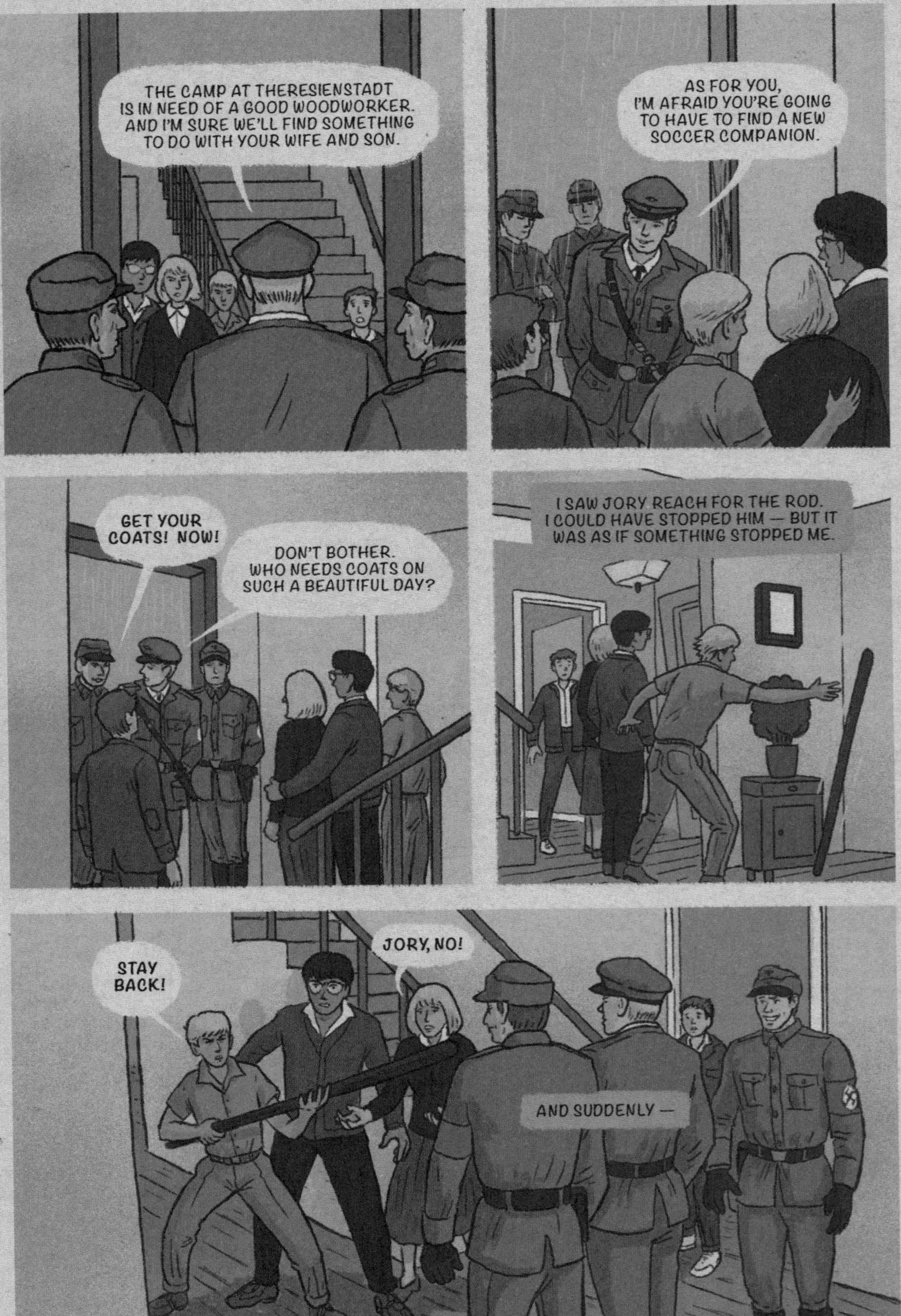
THE CAMP AT THERESIENSTADT IS IN NEED OF A GOOD WOODWORKER. AND I'M SURE WE'LL FIND SOMETHING TO DO WITH YOUR WIFE AND SON.
AS FOR YOU, I'M AFRAID YOU'RE GOING TO HAVE TO FIND A NEW SOCCER COMPANION.
GET YOUR COATS! NOW!
DON'T BOTHER. WHO NEEDS COATS ON SUCH A BEAUTIFUL DAY?
I SAW JORY REACH FOR THE ROD. I COULD HAVE STOPPED HIM — BUT IT WAS AS IF SOMETHING STOPPED ME.
STAY BACK!
JORY, NO!
AND SUDDENLY —

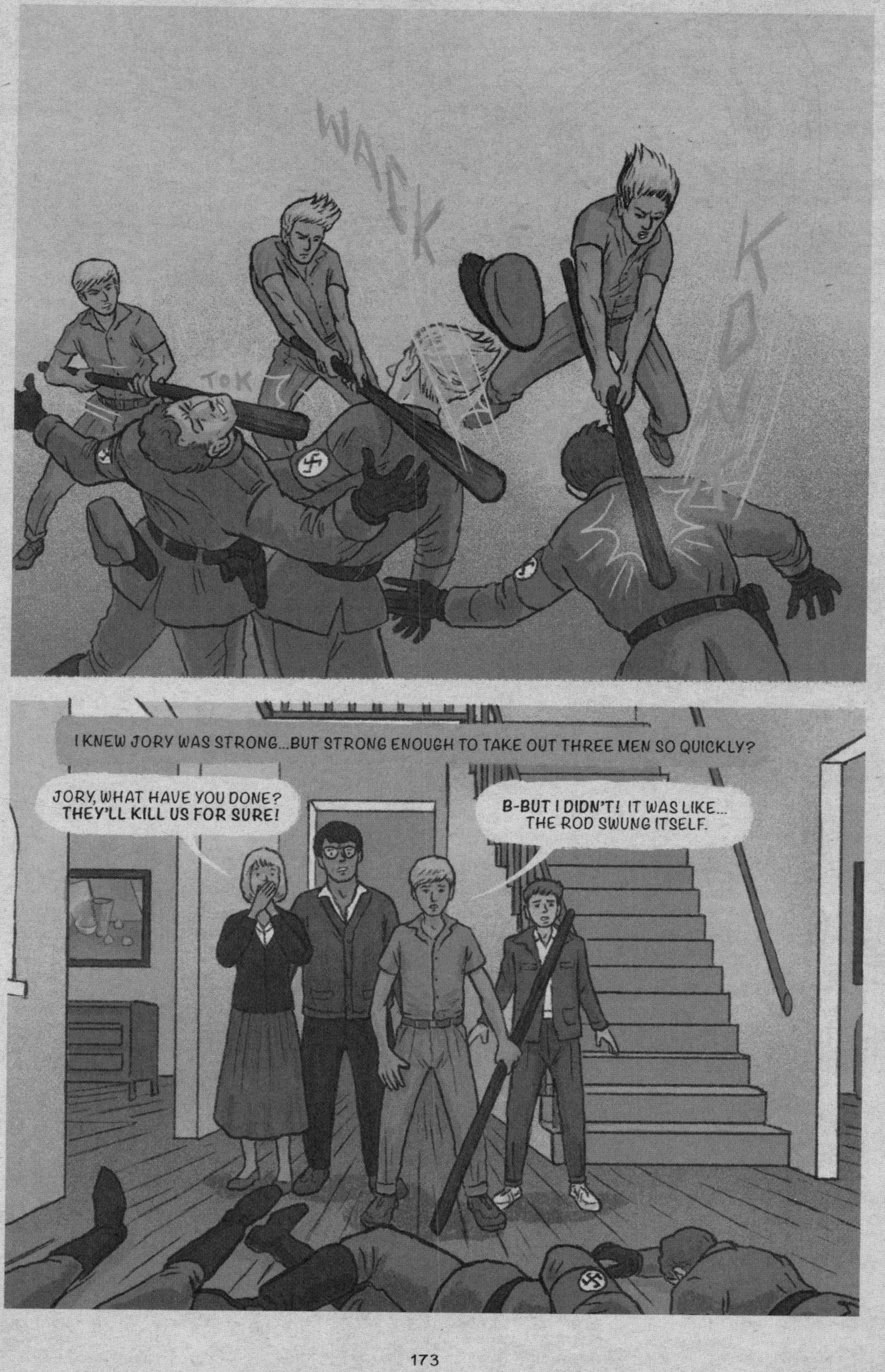
WACK
TOK
I KNEW JORY WAS STRONG...BUT STRONG ENOUGH TO TAKE OUT THREE MEN SO QUICKLY?
JORY, WHAT HAVE YOU DONE? THEY'LL KILL US FOR SURE!
B-BUT I DIDN'T! IT WAS LIKE... THE ROD SWUNG ITSELF.

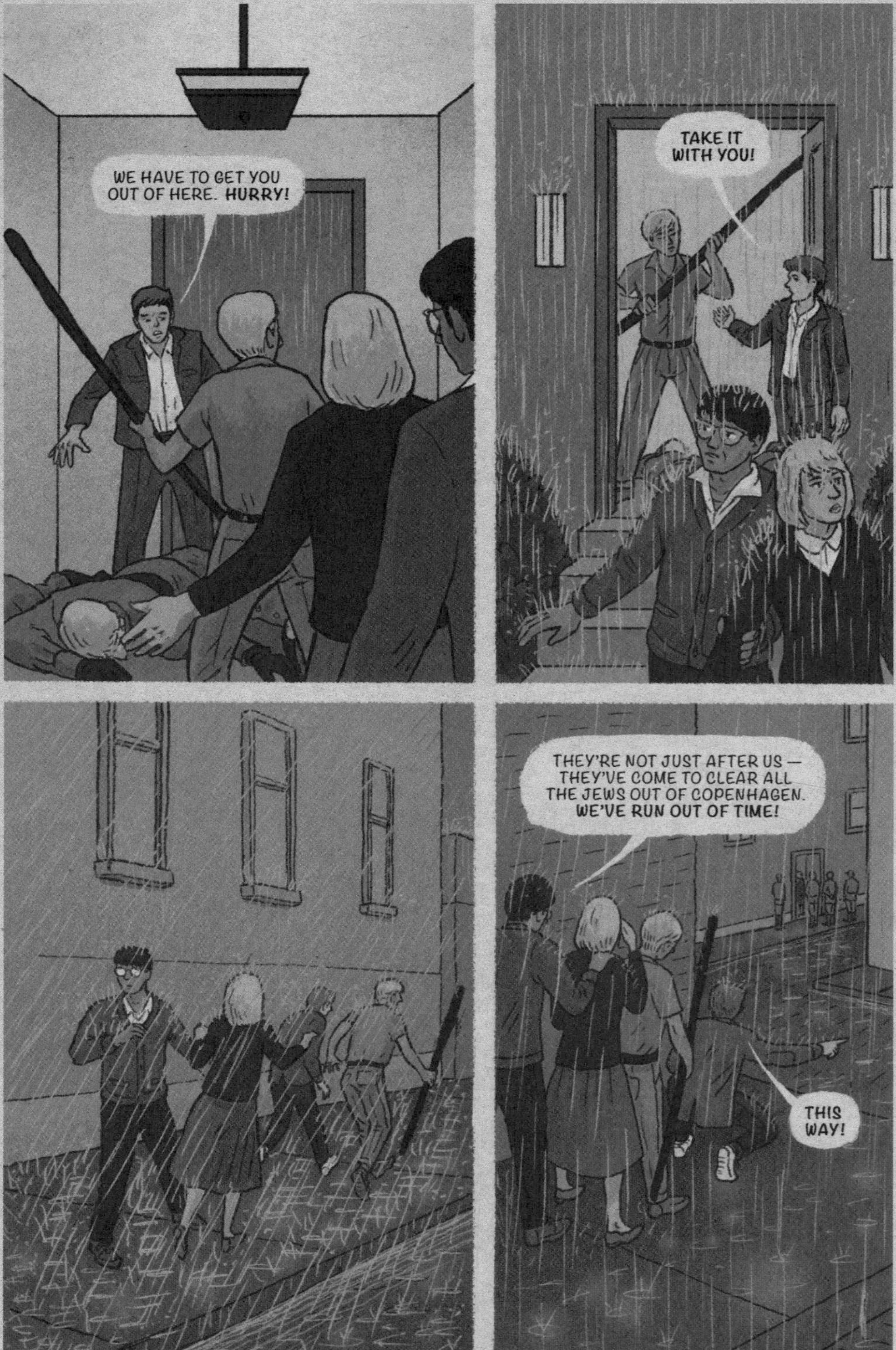
WE HAVE TO GET YOU OUT OF HERE. HURRY!
TAKE IT WITH YOU!
THEY'RE NOT JUST AFTER US — THEY'VE COME TO CLEAR ALL THE JEWS OUT OF COPENHAGEN. WE'VE RUN OUT OF TIME!
THIS WAY!

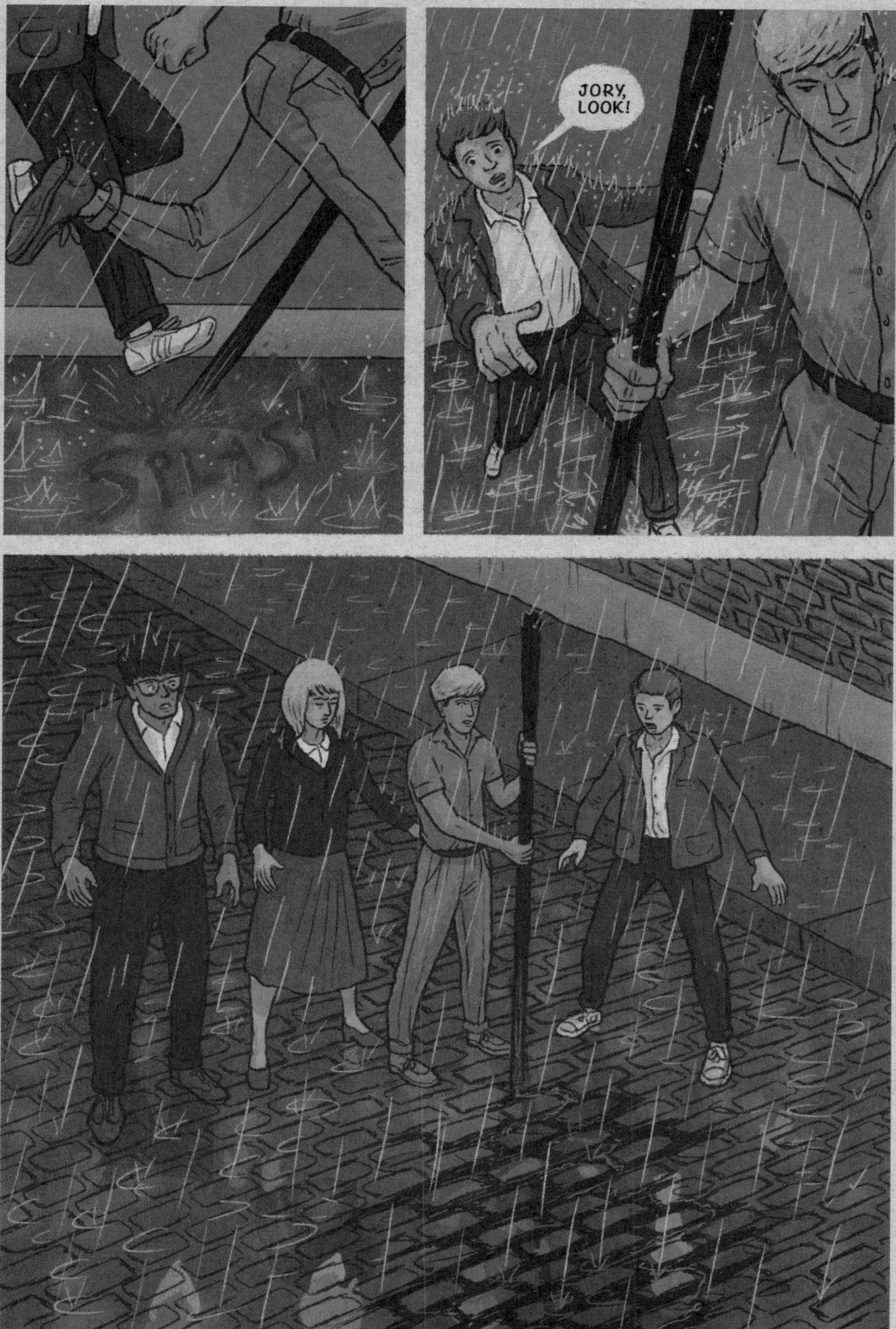
SPLASH
JORY, LOOK!

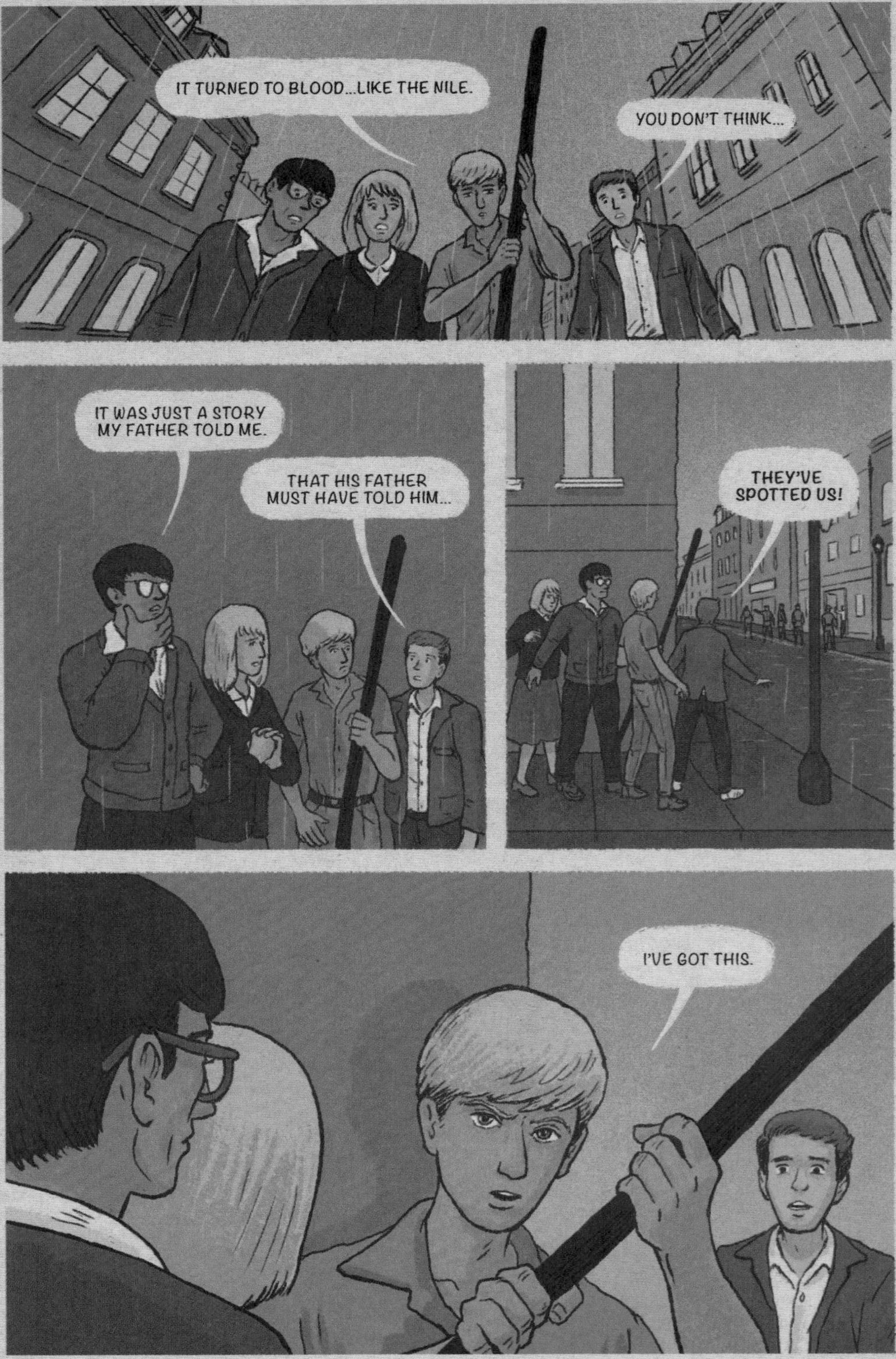
IT TURNED TO BLOOD...LIKE THE NILE.
YOU DON'T THINK...
IT WAS JUST A STORY MY FATHER TOLD ME.
THAT HIS FATHER MUST HAVE TOLD HIM...
THEY'VE SPOTTED US!
I'VE GOT THIS.

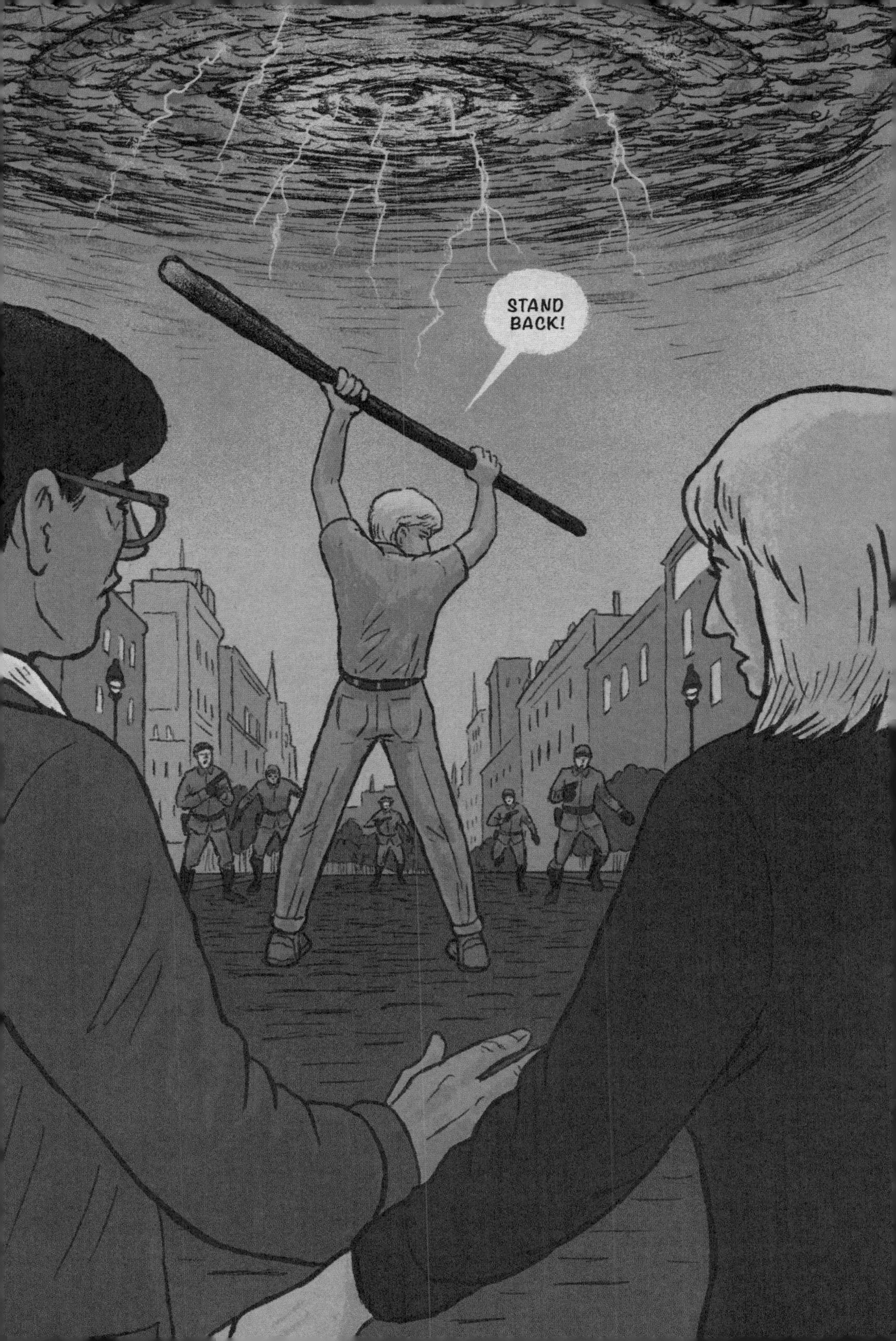
STAND BACK!

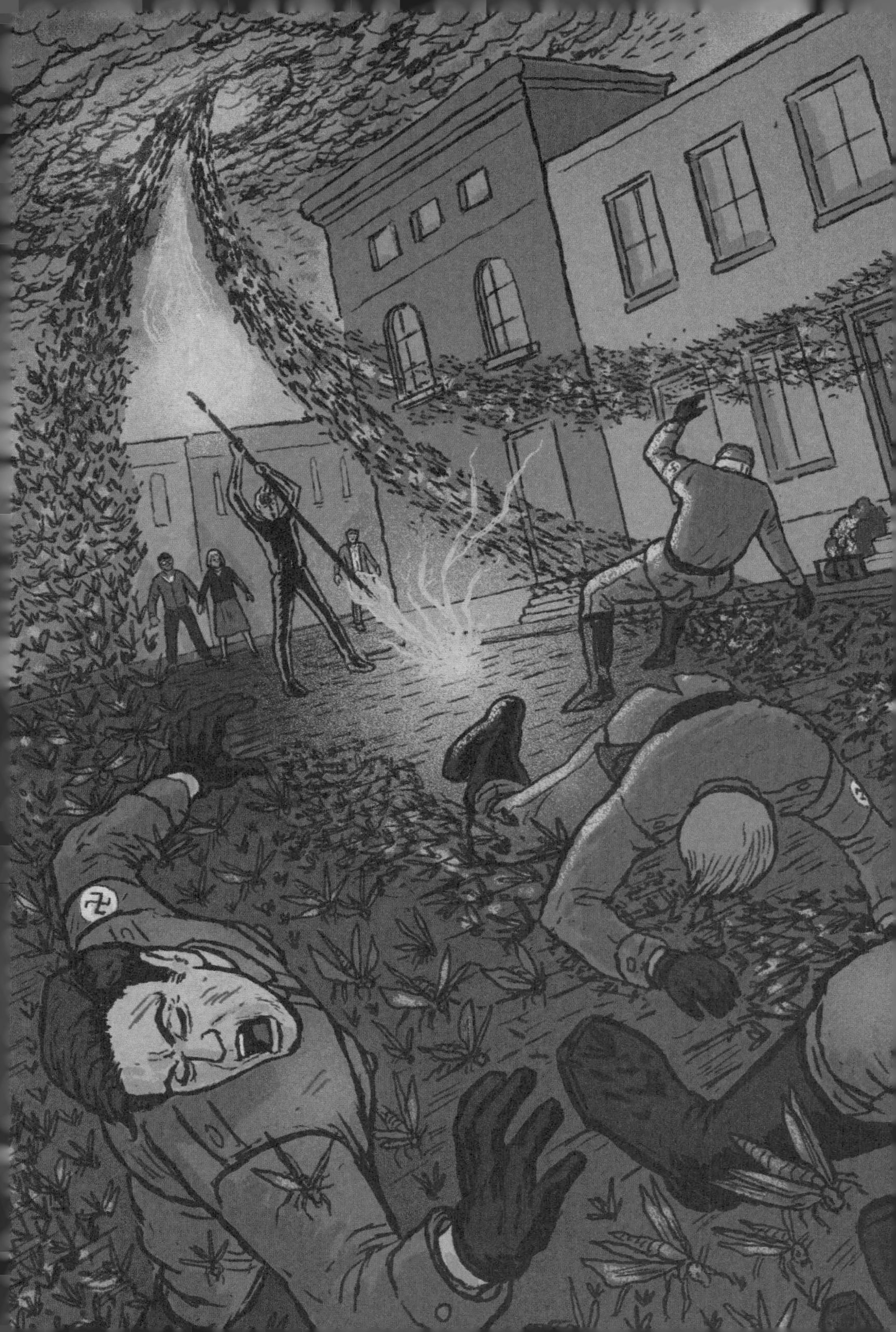

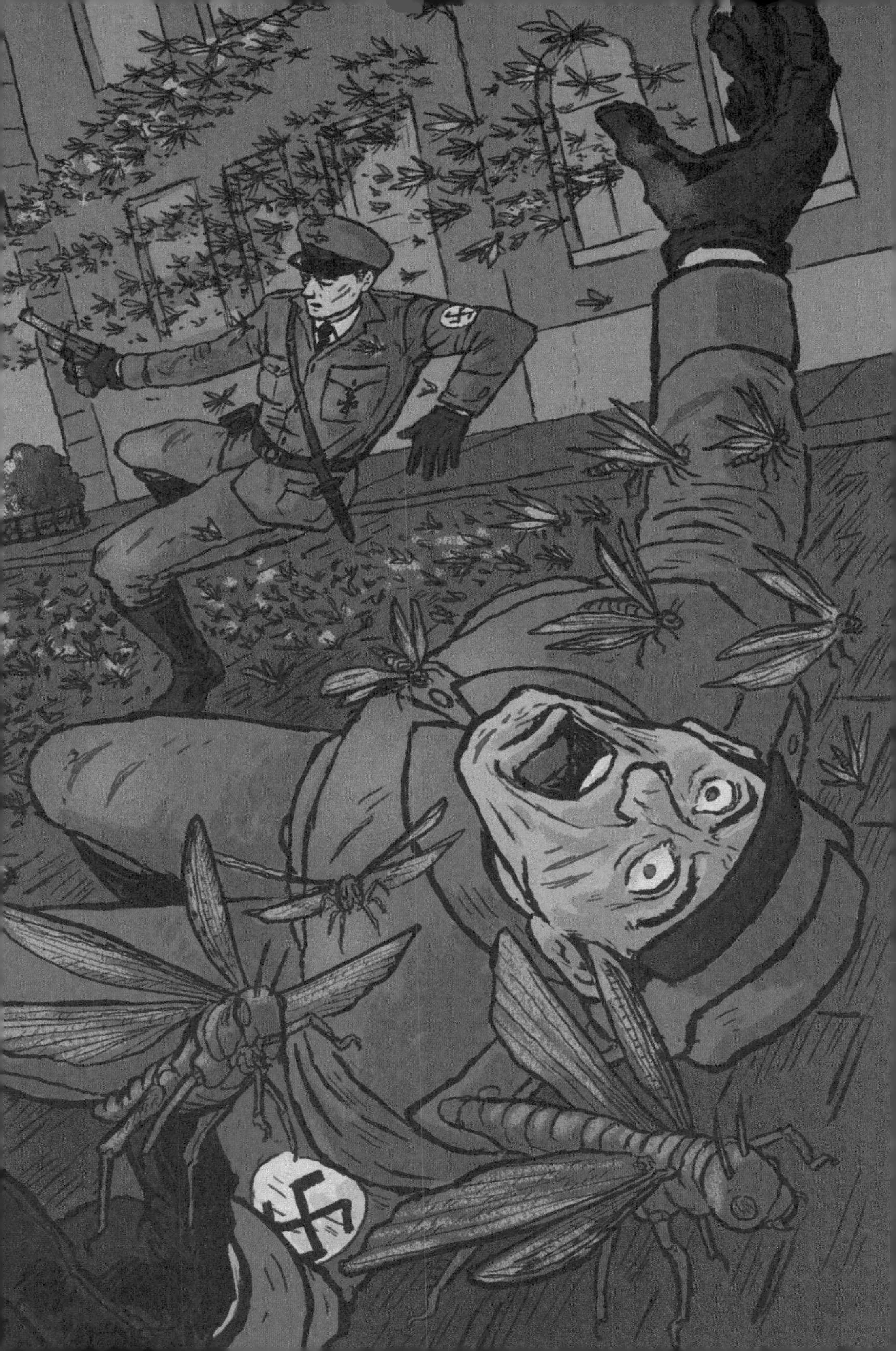

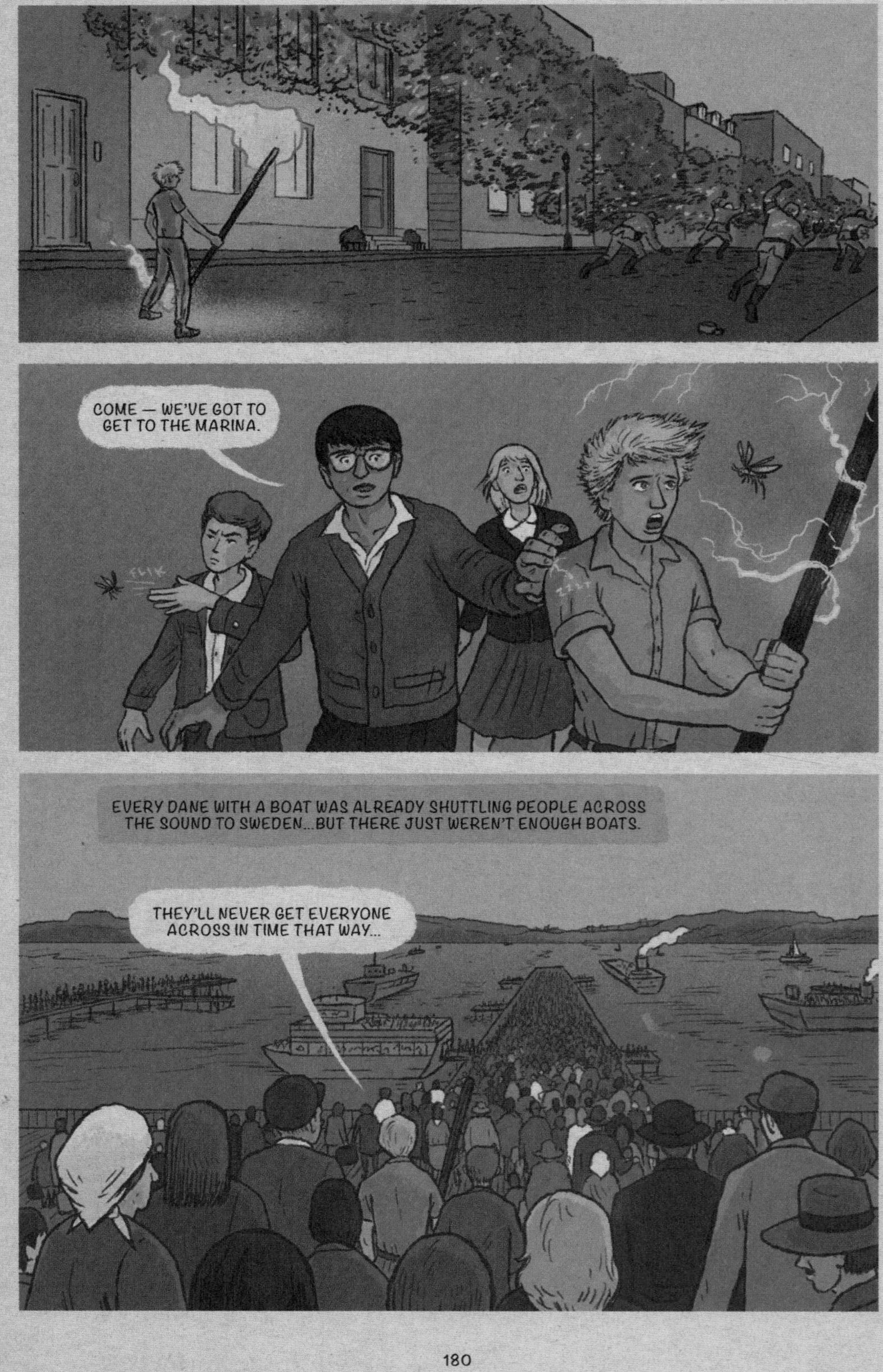
COME — WE'VE GOT TO GET TO THE MARINA.
FLIK
ZZZT
EVERY DANE WITH A BOAT WAS ALREADY SHUTTLING PEOPLE ACROSS THE SOUND TO SWEDEN...BUT THERE JUST WEREN'T ENOUGH BOATS.
THEY'LL NEVER GET EVERYONE ACROSS IN TIME THAT WAY...

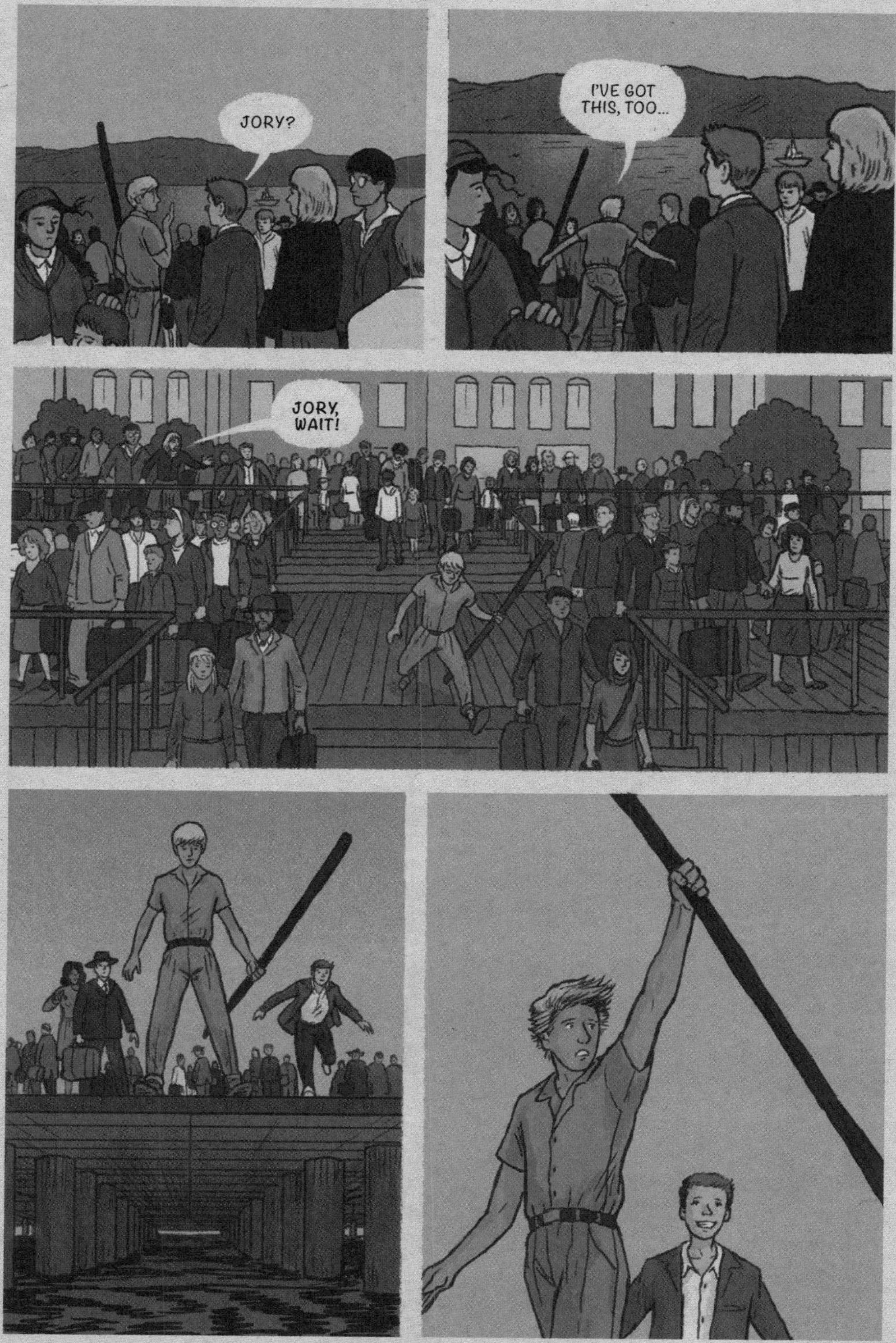
JORY?
I'VE GOT THIS, TOO...
JORY, WAIT!

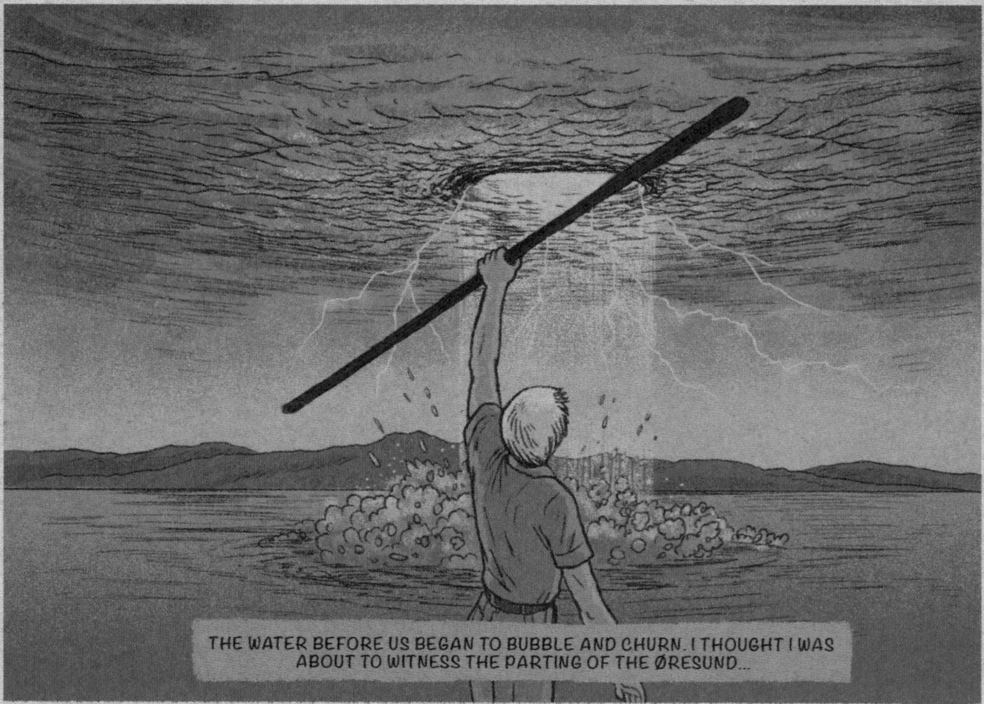
THE WATER BEFORE US BEGAN TO BUBBLE AND CHURN. I THOUGHT I WAS ABOUT TO WITNESS THE PARTING OF THE ØRESUND...

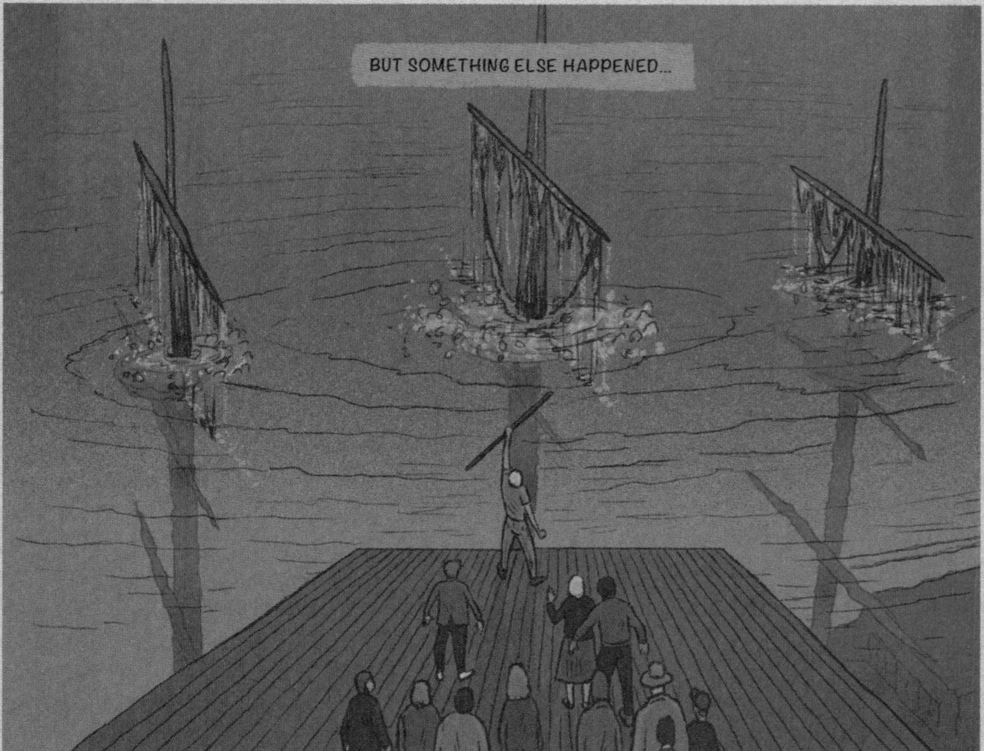
BUT SOMETHING ELSE HAPPENED...

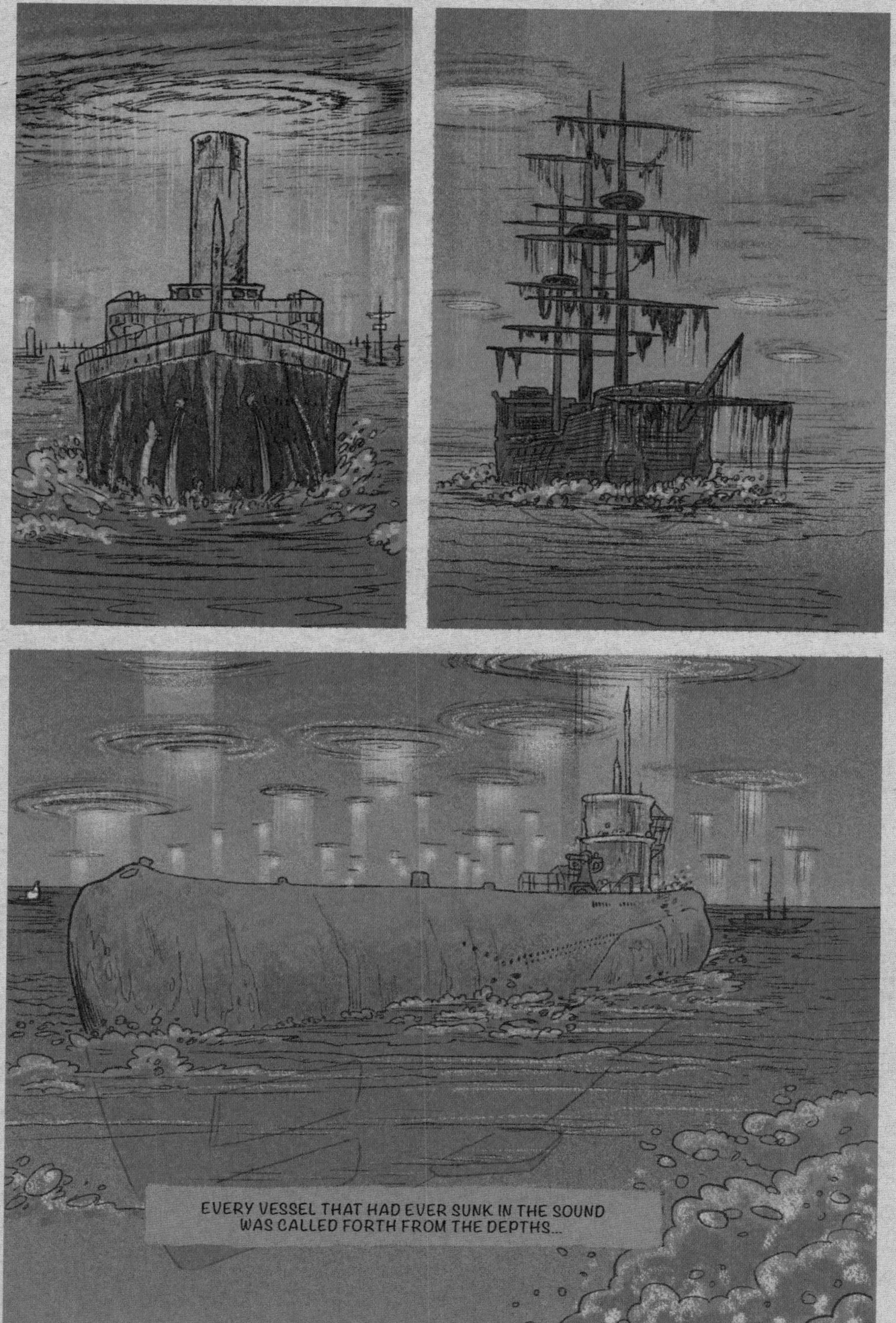
EVERY VESSEL THAT HAD EVER SUNK IN THE SOUND
WAS CALLED FORTH FROM THE DEPTHS...

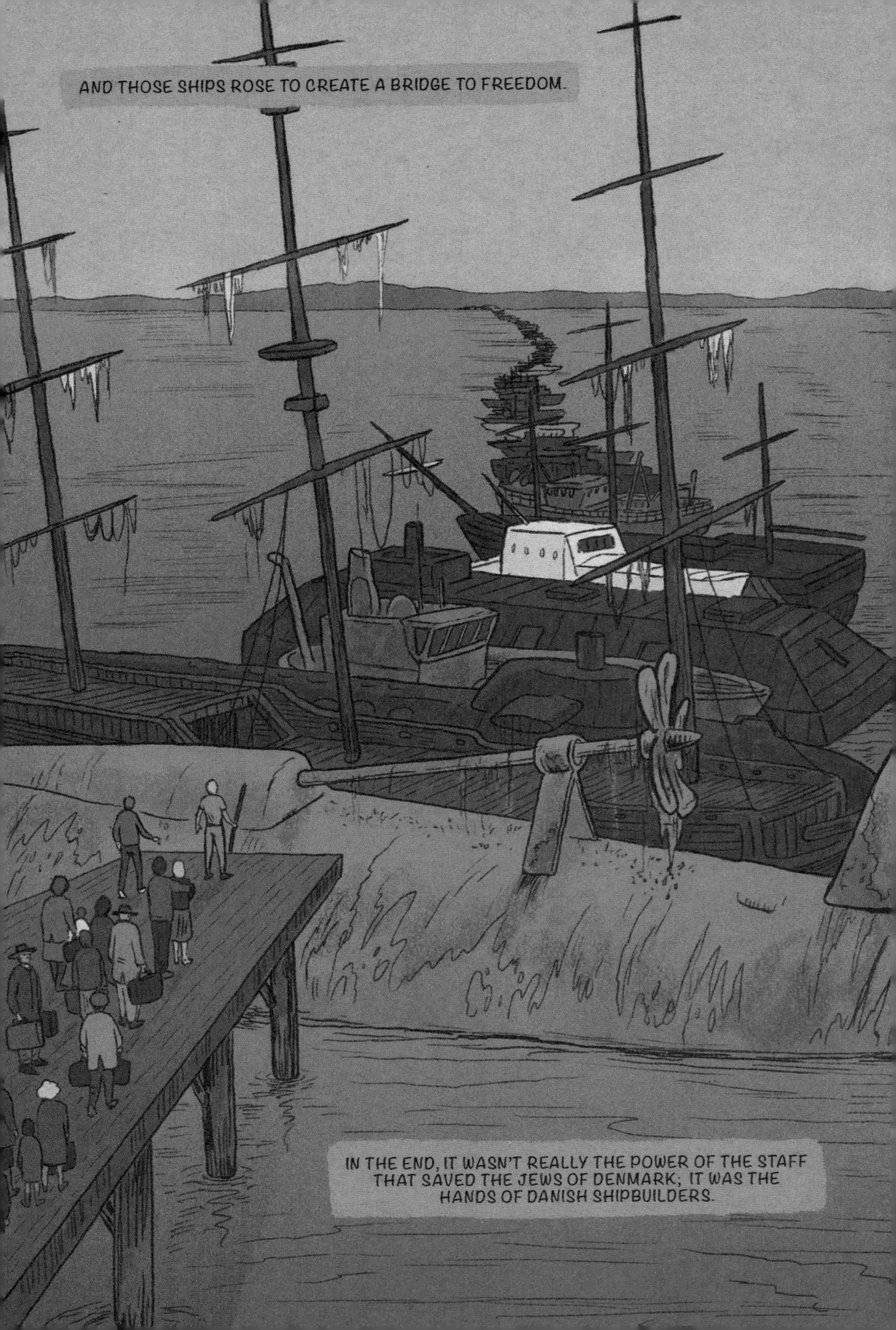
AND THOSE SHIPS ROSE TO CREATE A BRIDGE TO FREEDOM.
IN THE END, IT WASN'T REALLY THE POWER OF THE STAFF THAT SAVED THE JEWS OF DENMARK; IT WAS THE HANDS OF DANISH SHIPBUILDERS.

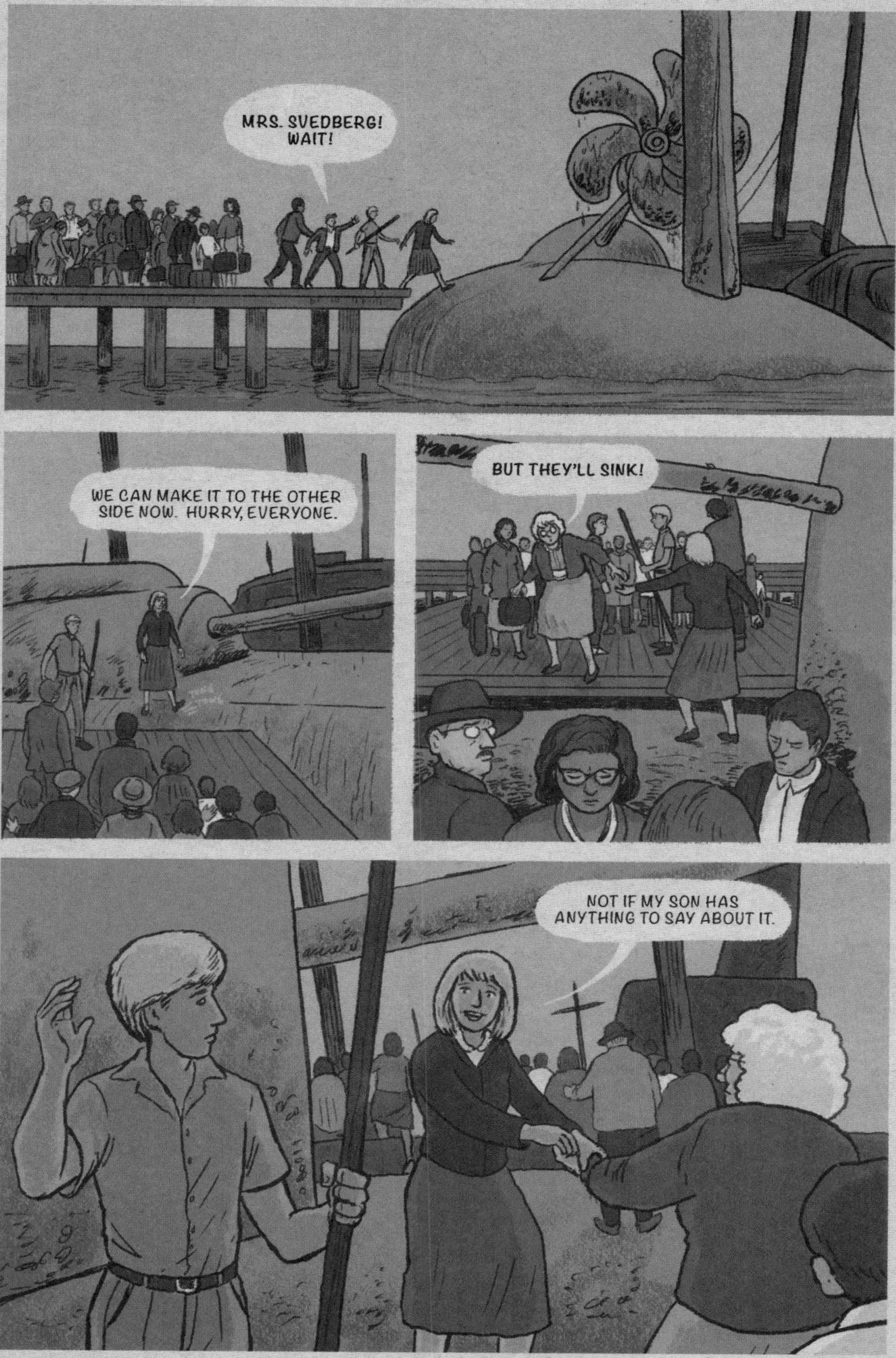
MRS. SVEDBERG! WAIT!
WE CAN MAKE IT TO THE OTHER SIDE NOW. HURRY, EVERYONE.
BUT THEY'LL SINK!
NOT IF MY SON HAS ANYTHING TO SAY ABOUT IT.

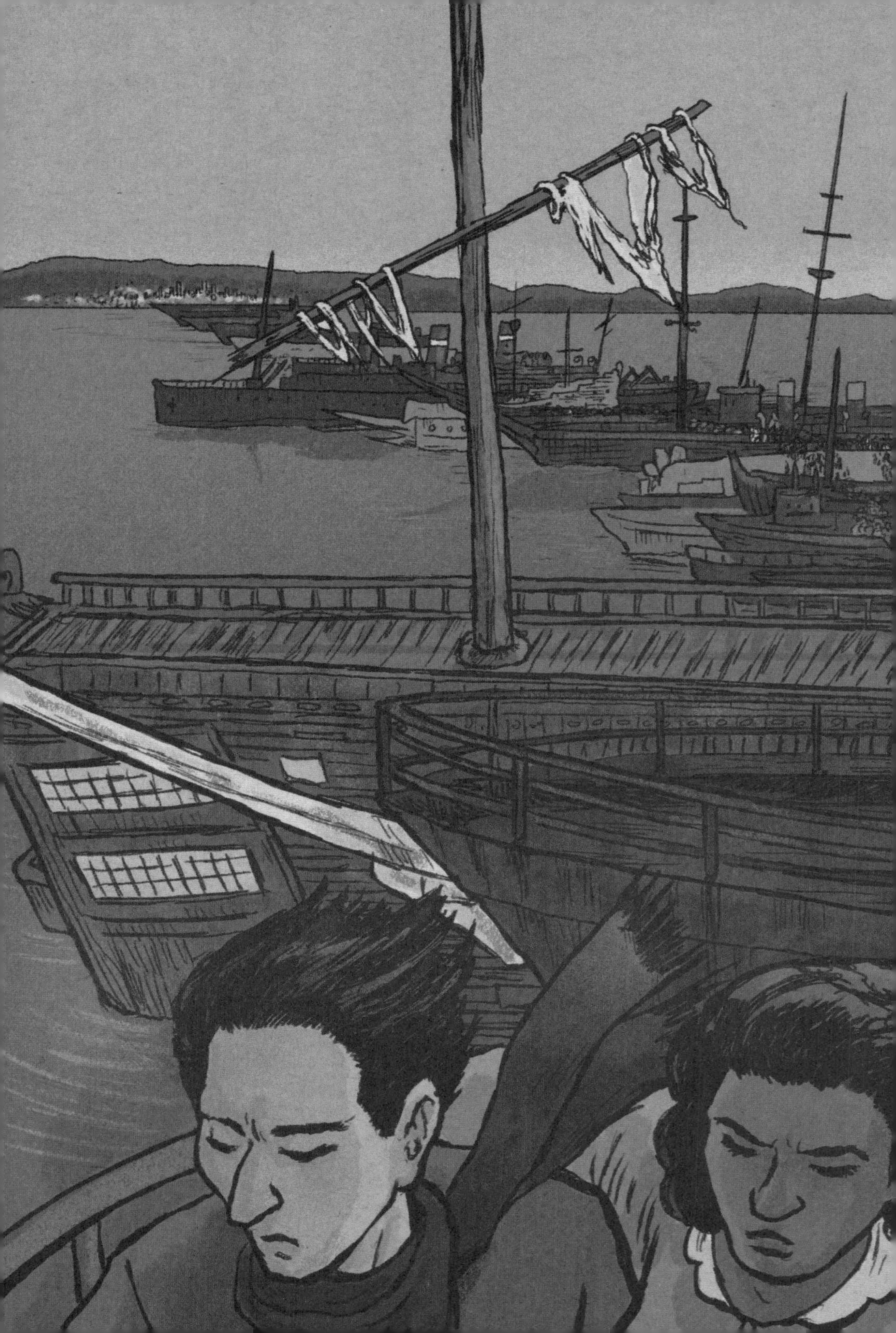

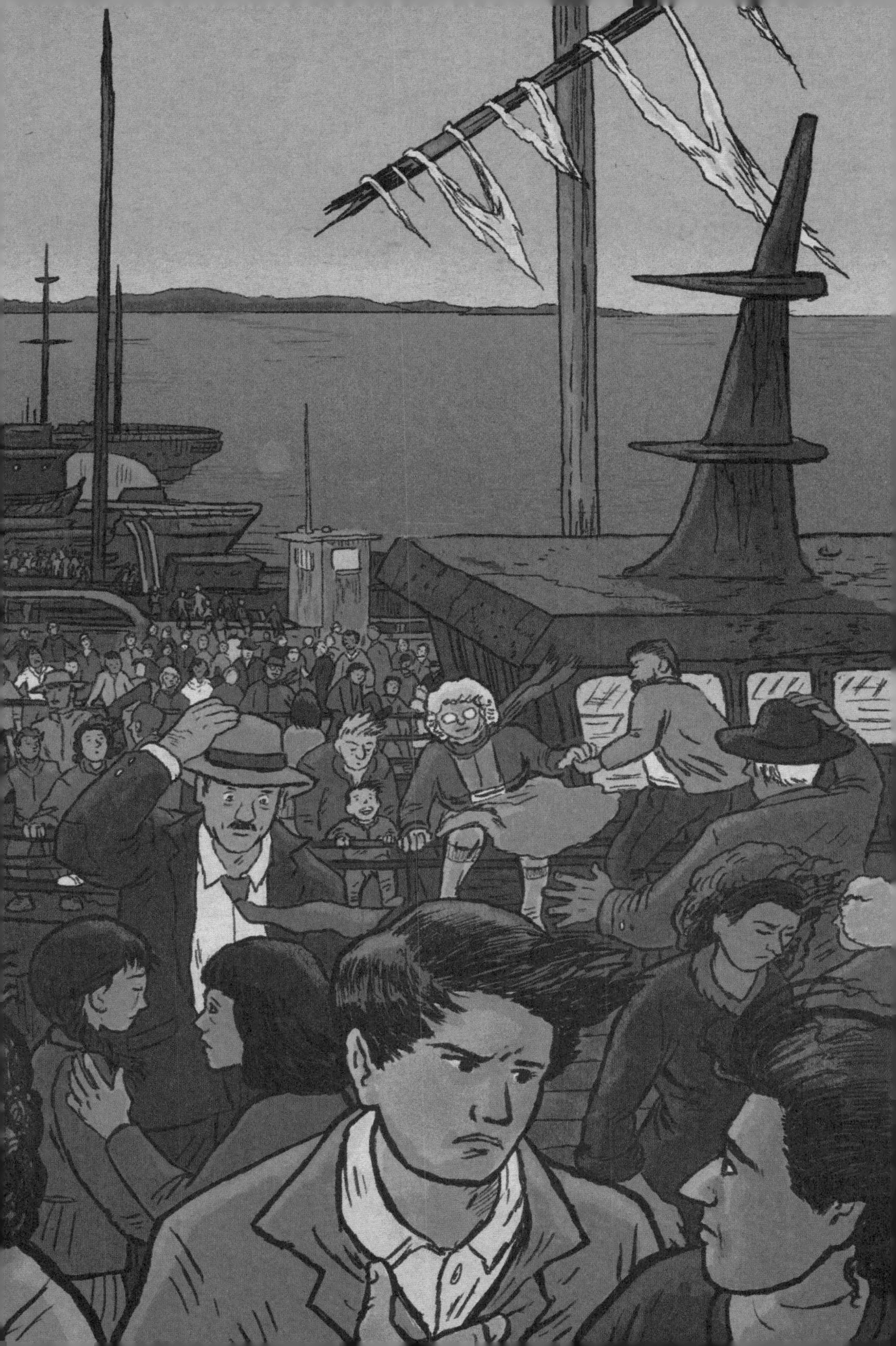

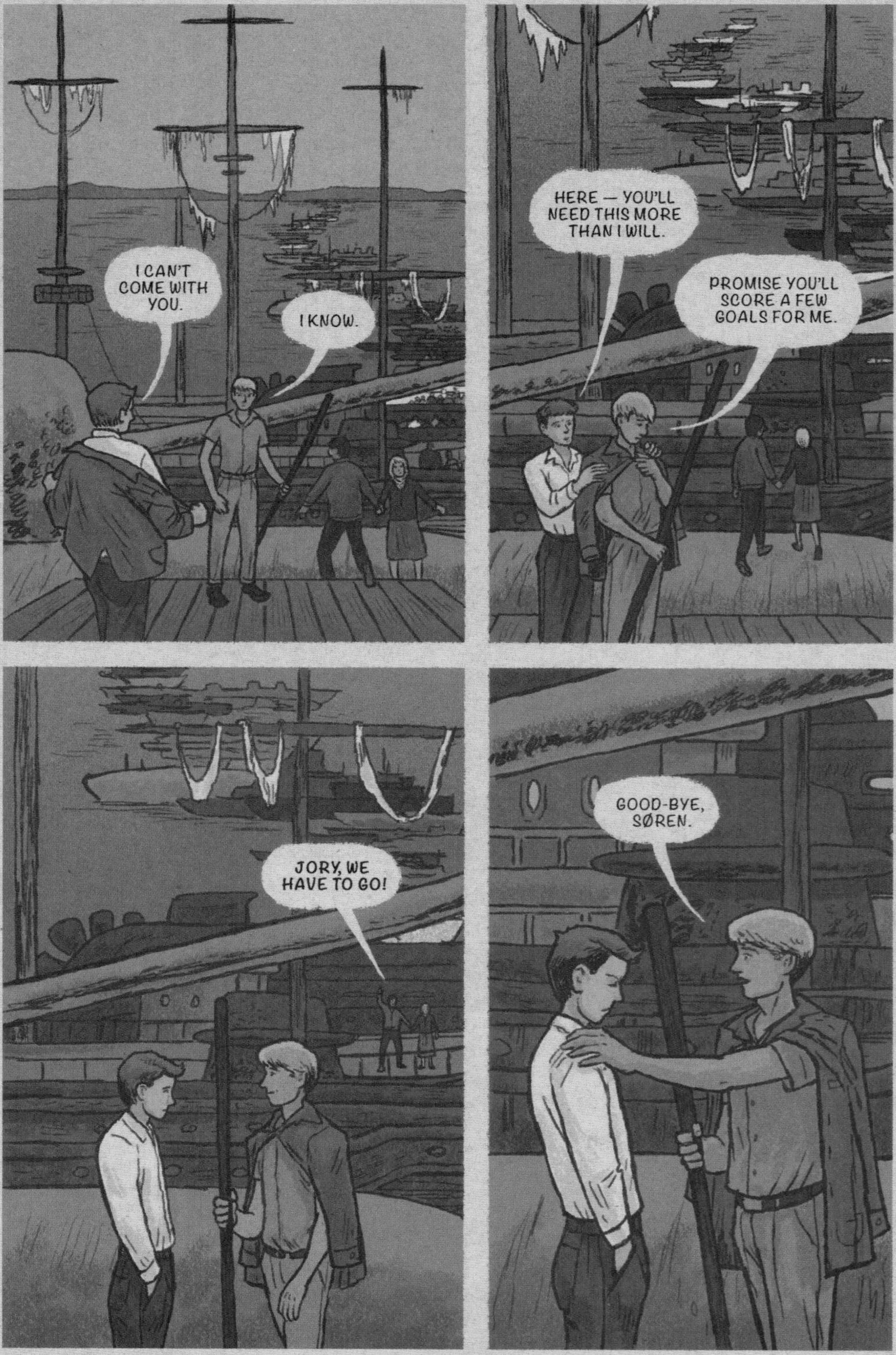
I CAN'T COME WITH YOU.
I KNOW.
HERE — YOU'LL NEED THIS MORE THAN I WILL.
PROMISE YOU'LL SCORE A FEW GOALS FOR ME.
JORY, WE HAVE TO GO!
GOOD-BYE, SØREN.

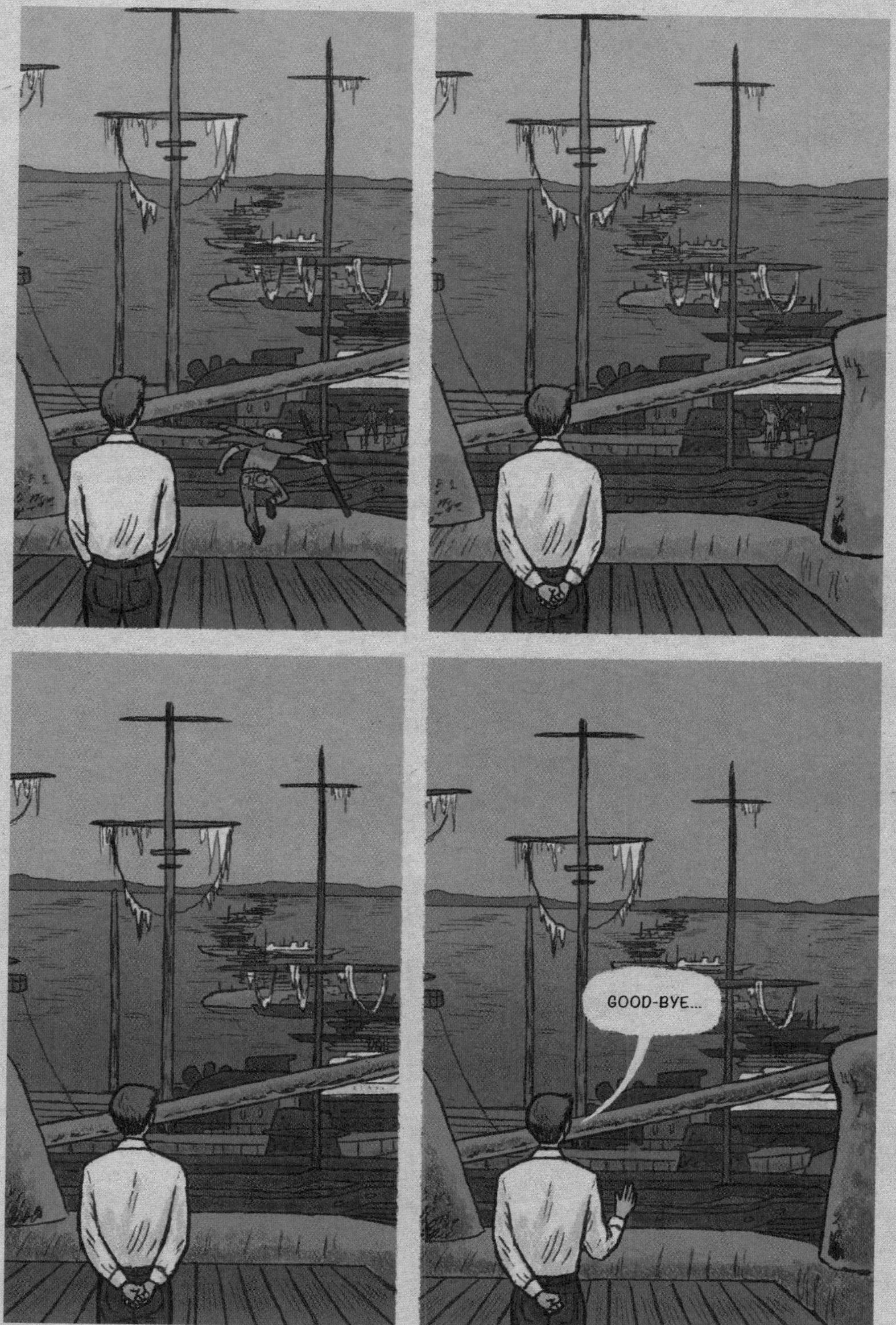
GOOD-BYE...

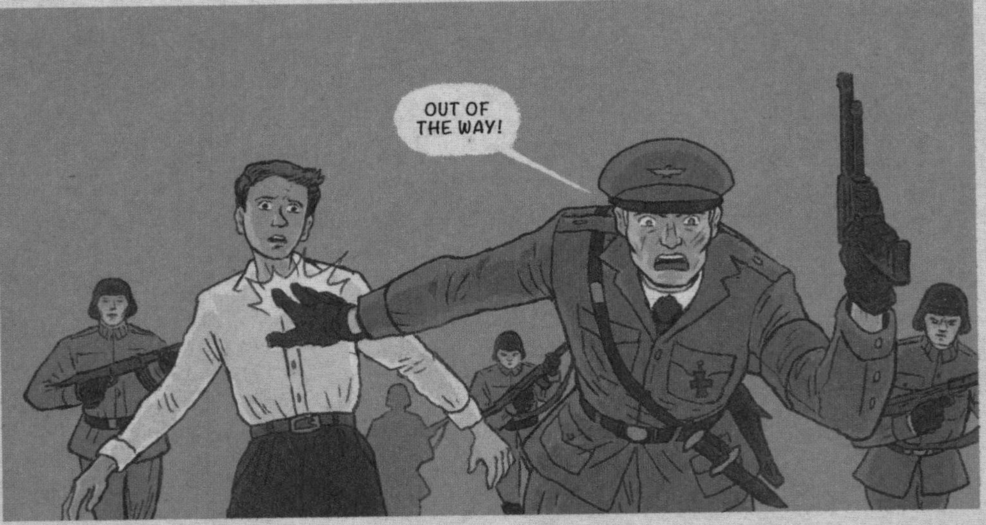
OUT OF THE WAY!
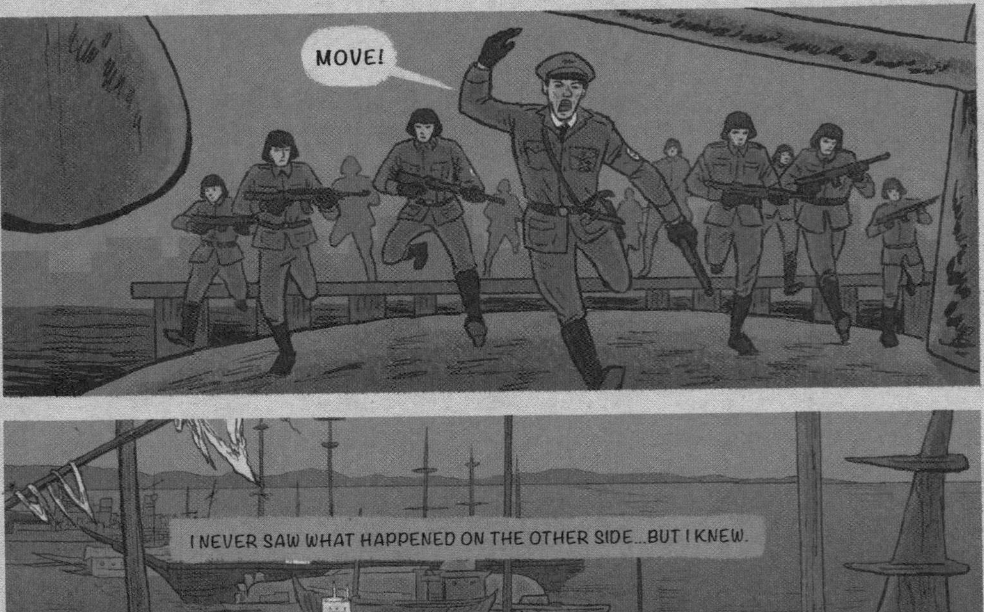
MOVE!
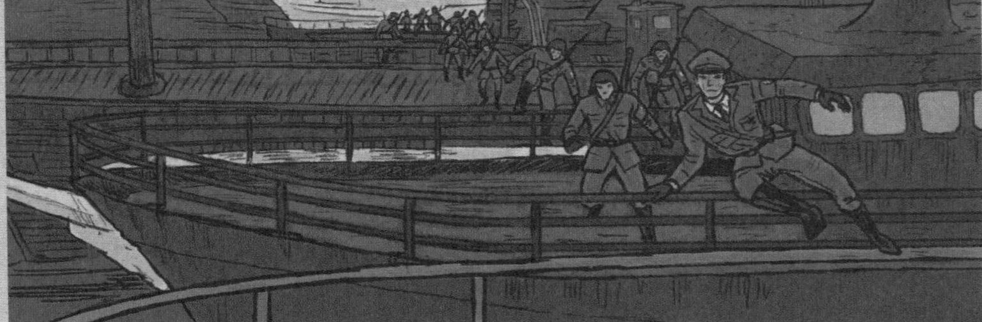
I NEVER SAW WHAT HAPPENED ON THE OTHER SIDE...BUT I KNEW.

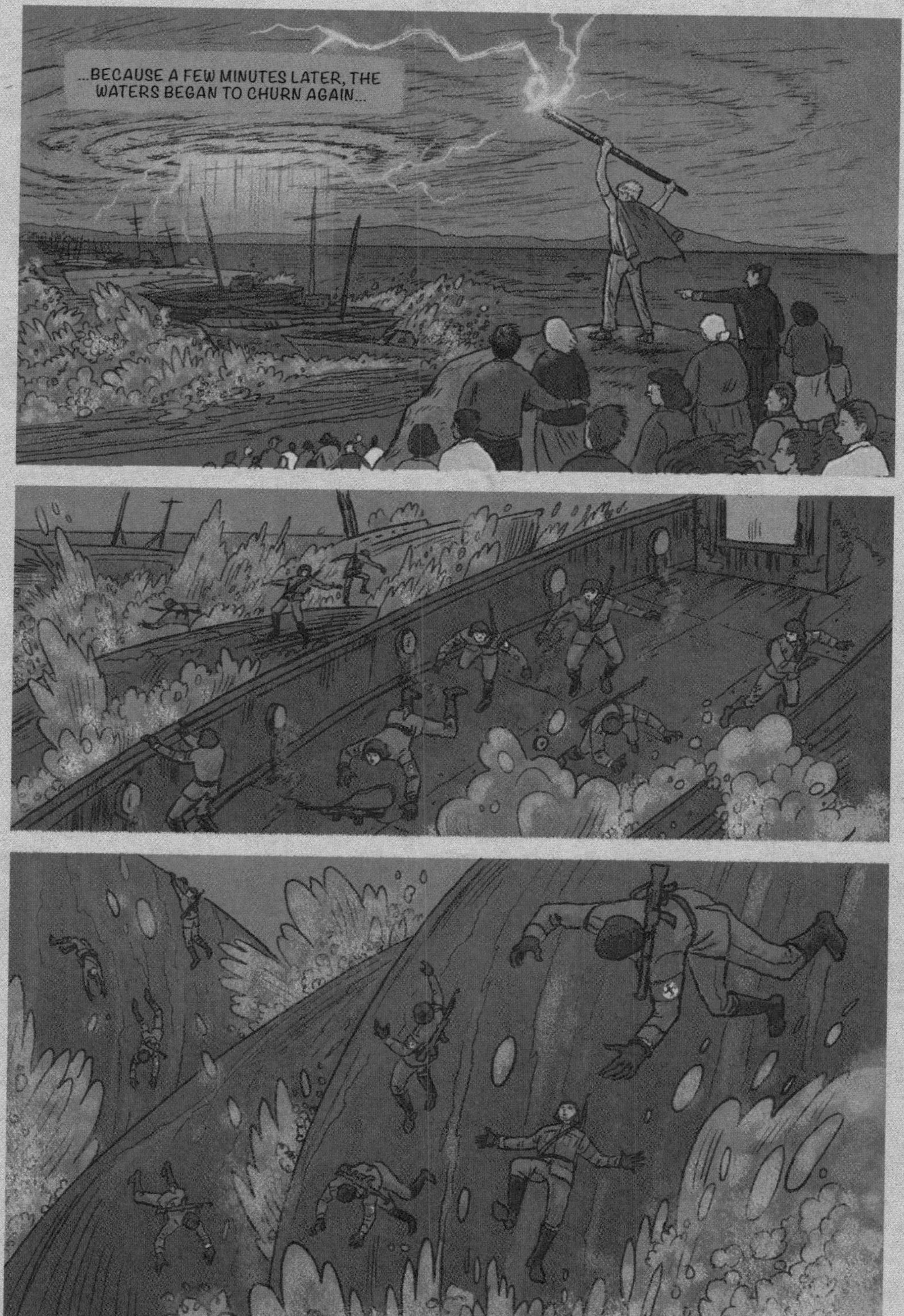
...BECAUSE A FEW MINUTES LATER, THE WATERS BEGAN TO CHURN AGAIN...

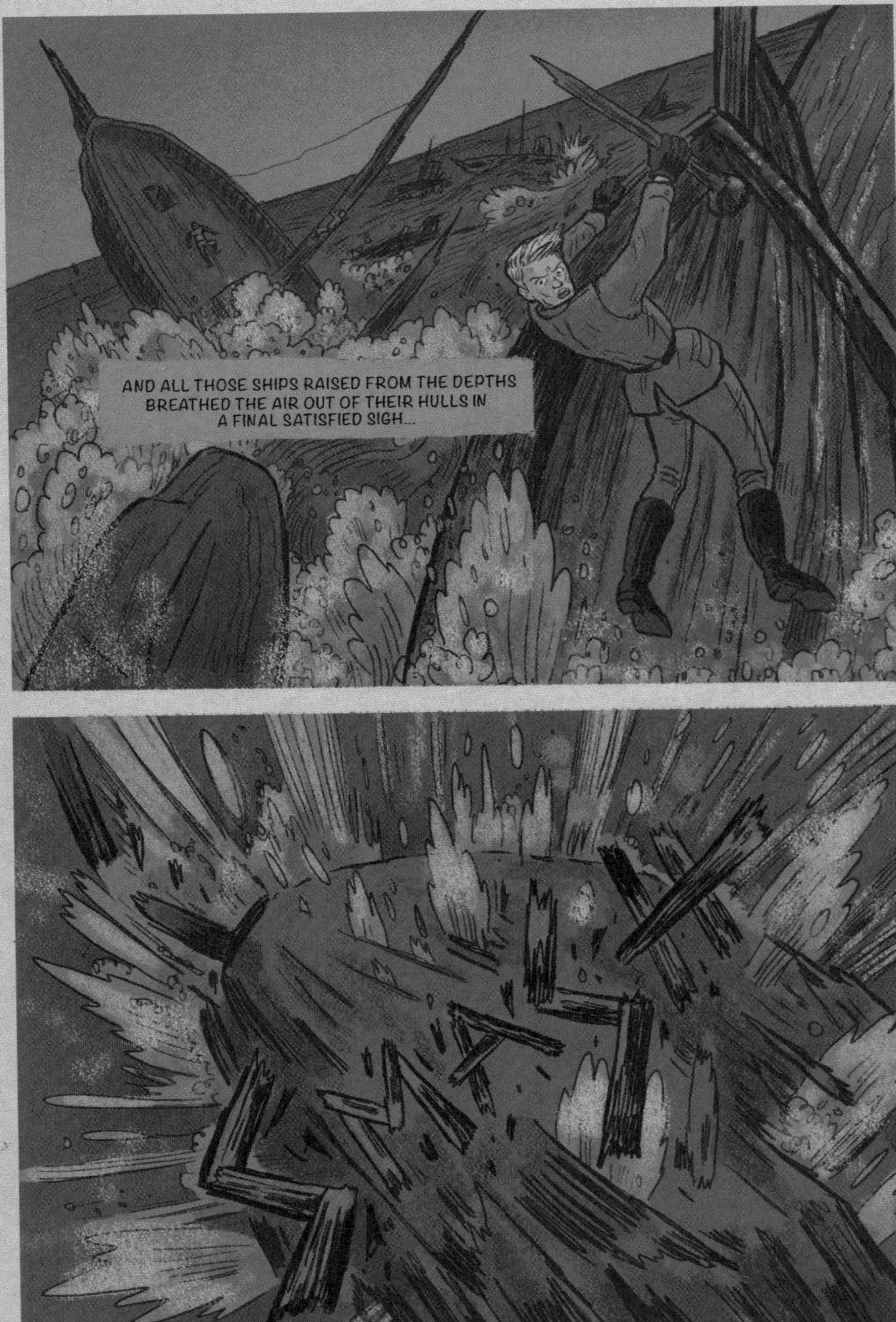
AND ALL THOSE SHIPS RAISED FROM THE DEPTHS BREATHED THE AIR OUT OF THEIR HULLS IN A FINAL SATISFIED SIGH...

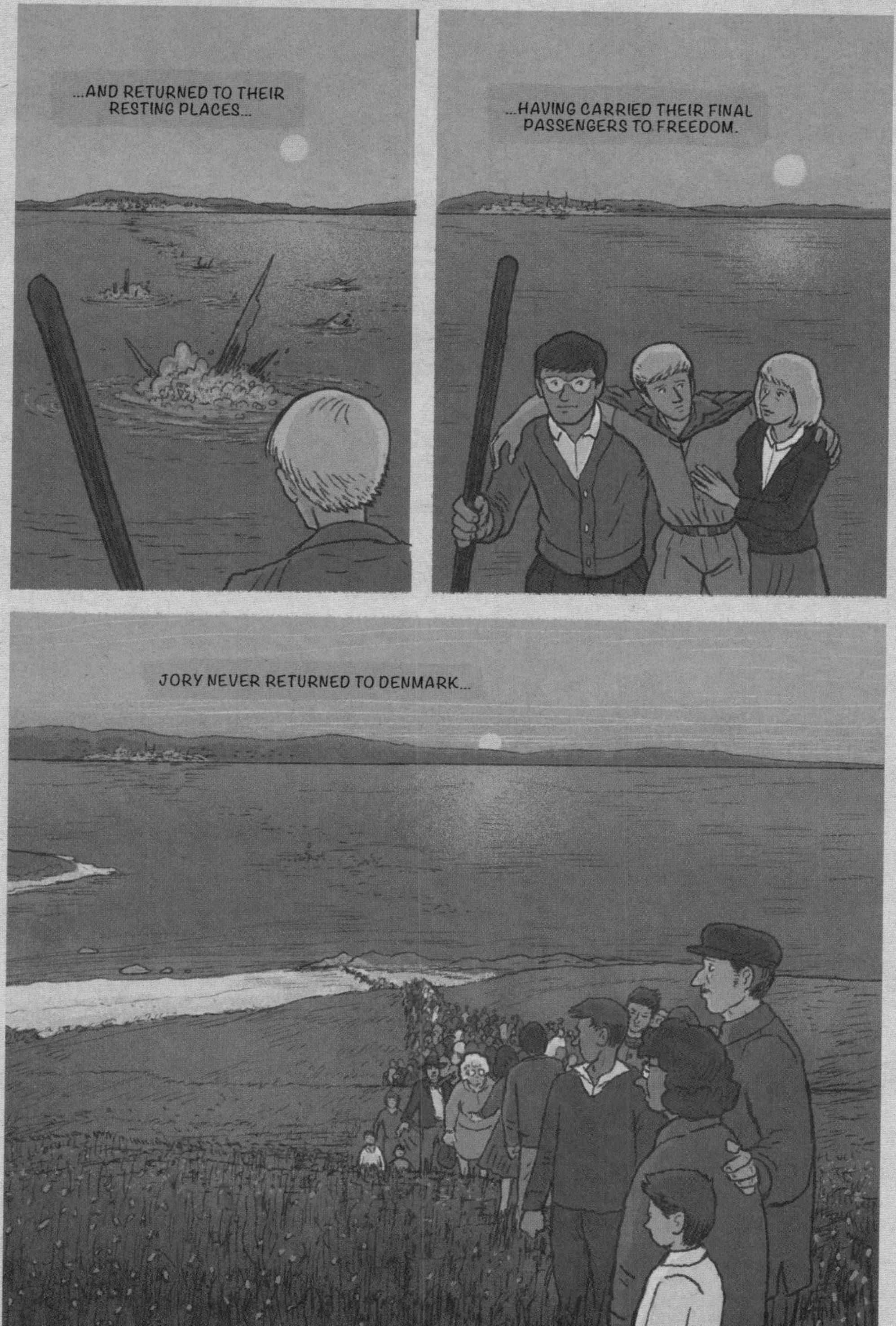
...AND RETURNED TO THEIR RESTING PLACES...
...HAVING CARRIED THEIR FINAL PASSENGERS TO FREEDOM.
JORY NEVER RETURNED TO DENMARK...

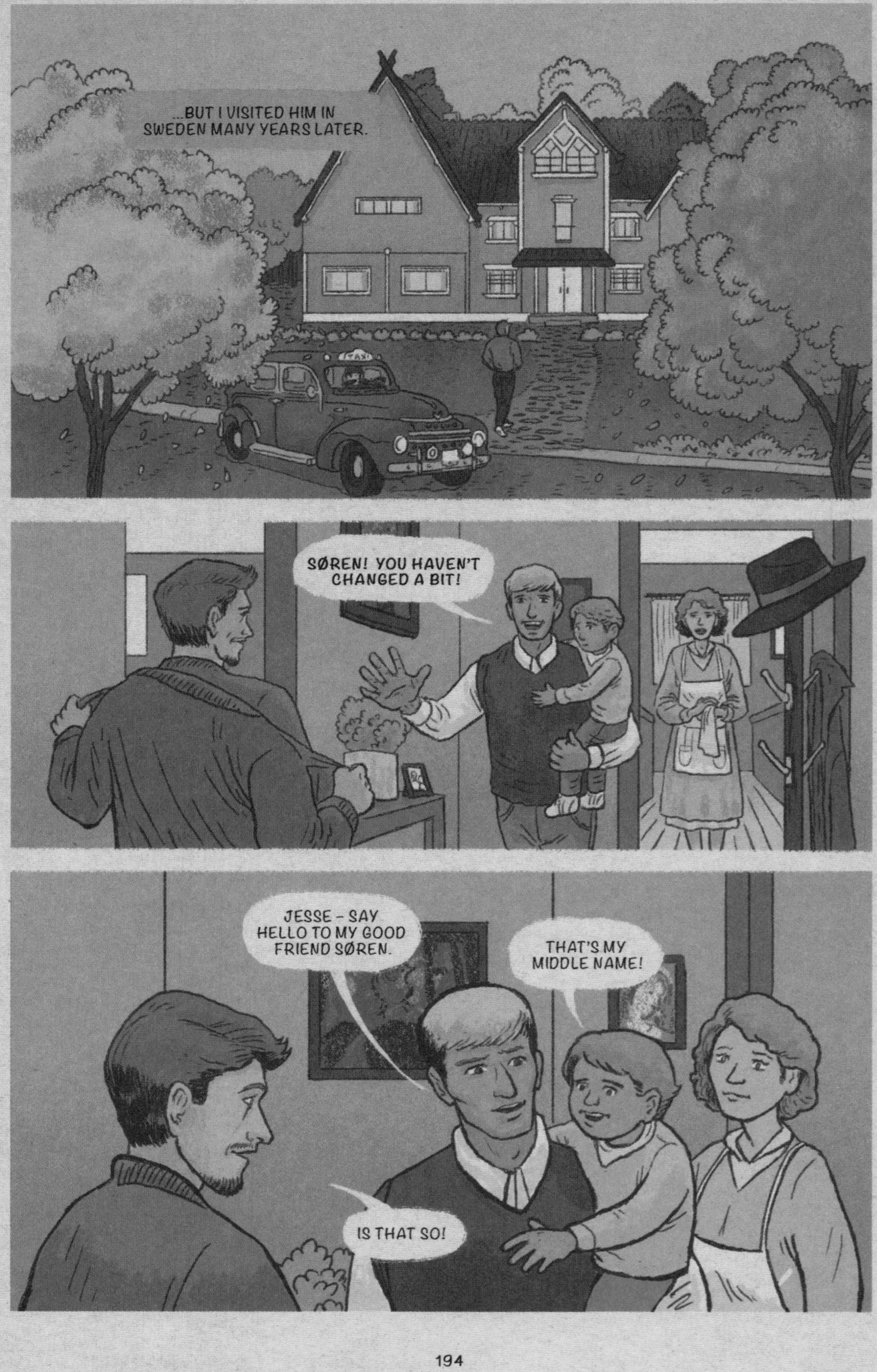
...BUT I VISITED HIM IN SWEDEN MANY YEARS LATER.
TAXI
SØREN! YOU HAVEN'T CHANGED A BIT!
JESSE – SAY HELLO TO MY GOOD FRIEND SØREN.
THAT'S MY MIDDLE NAME!
IS THAT SO!

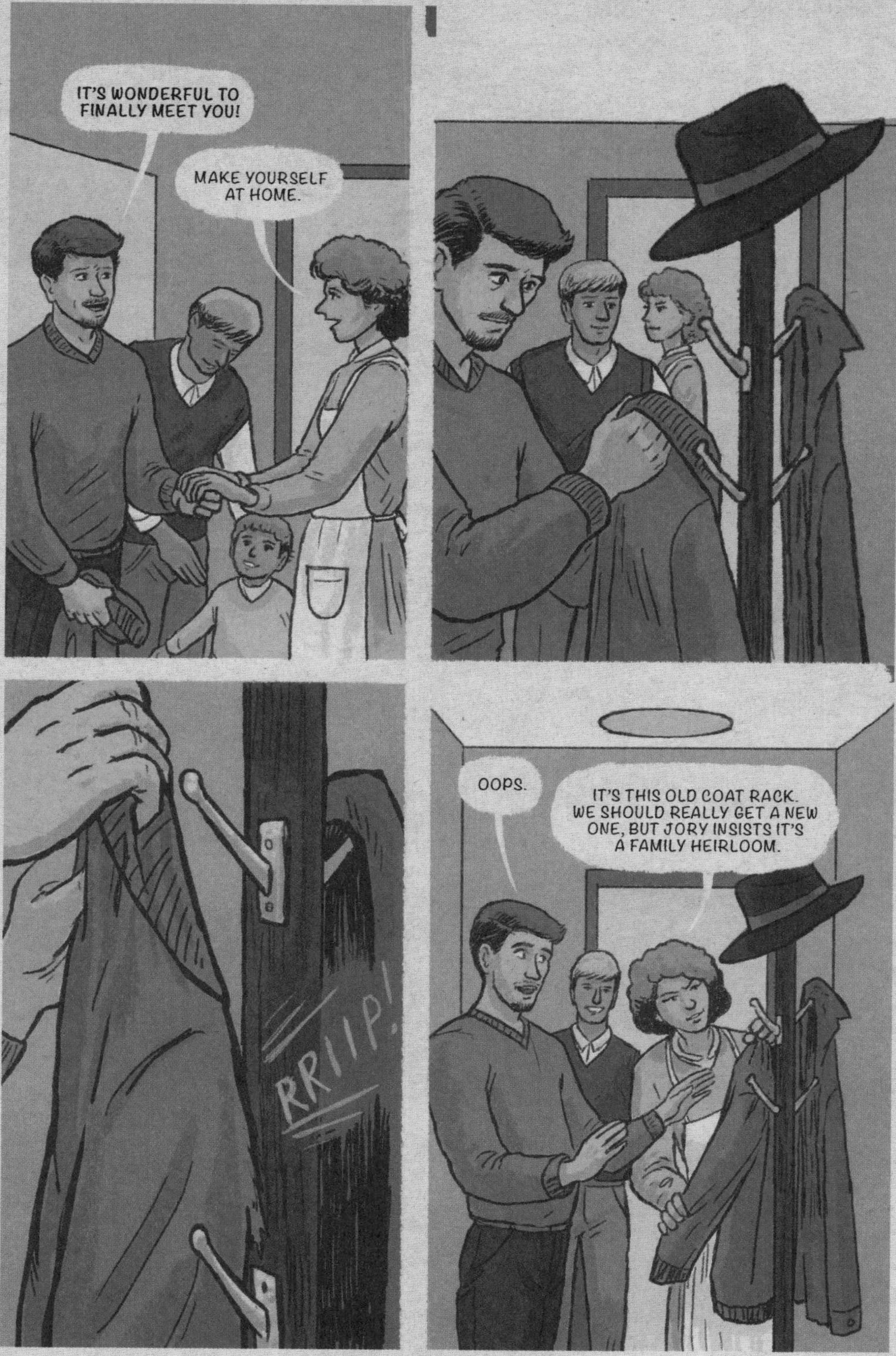
IT'S WONDERFUL TO FINALLY MEET YOU!
MAKE YOURSELF AT HOME.
RRIIP!
OOPS.
IT'S THIS OLD COAT RACK. WE SHOULD REALLY GET A NEW ONE, BUT JORY INSISTS IT'S A FAMILY HEIRLOOM.

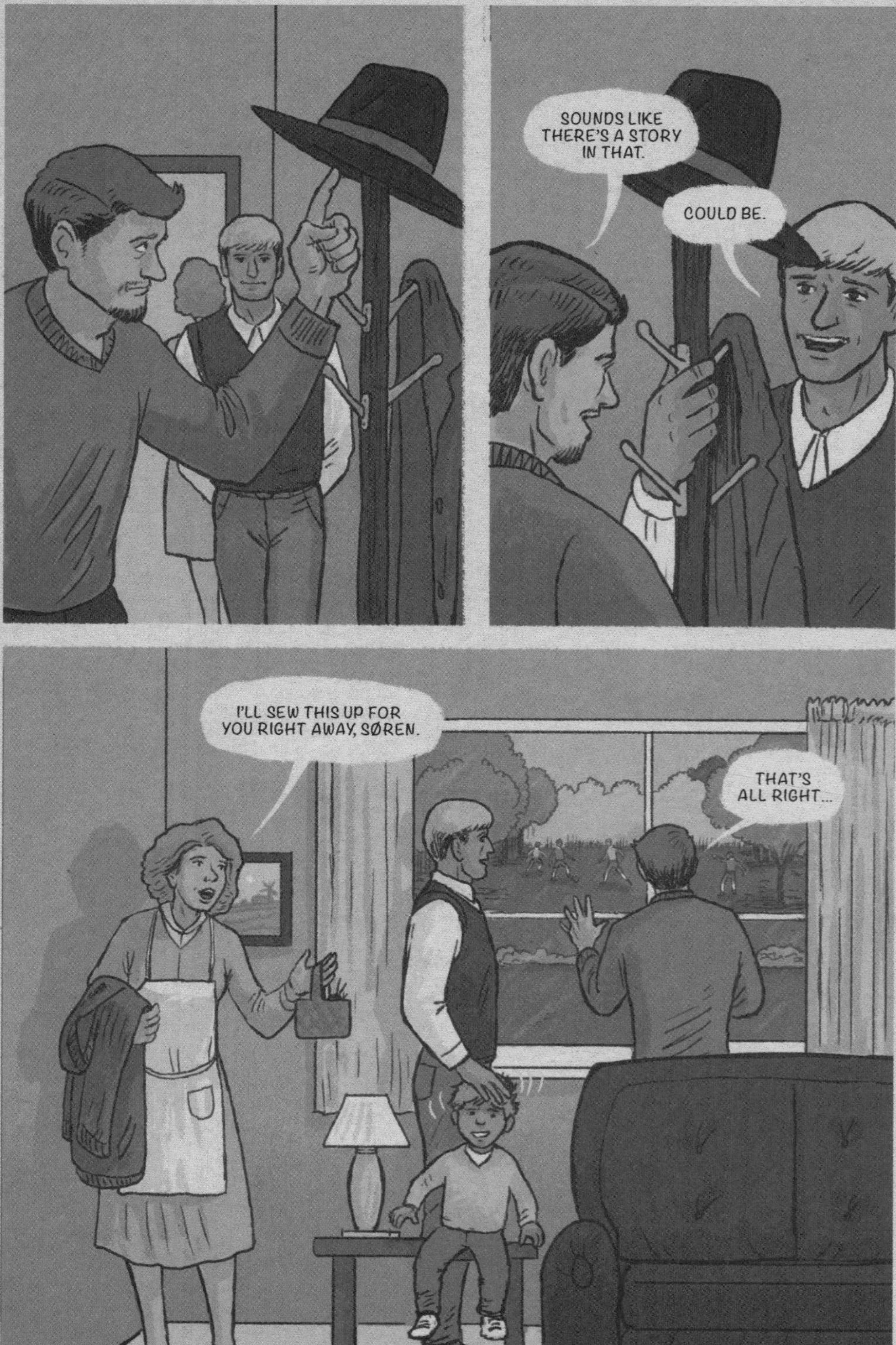
SOUNDS LIKE THERE'S A STORY IN THAT.
COULD BE.
I'LL SEW THIS UP FOR YOU RIGHT AWAY, SØREN.
THAT'S ALL RIGHT...

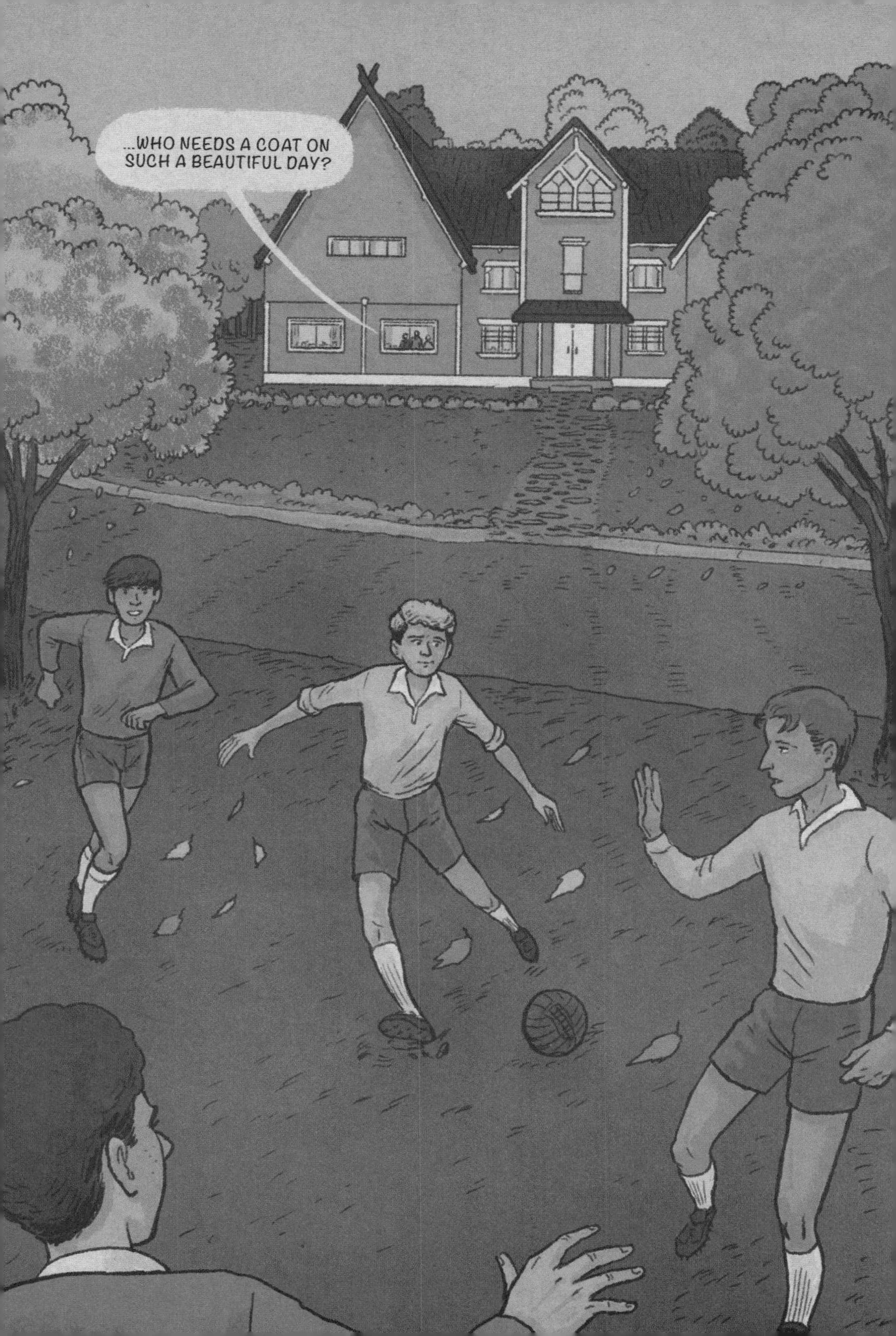
...WHO NEEDS A COAT ON SUCH A BEAUTIFUL DAY?

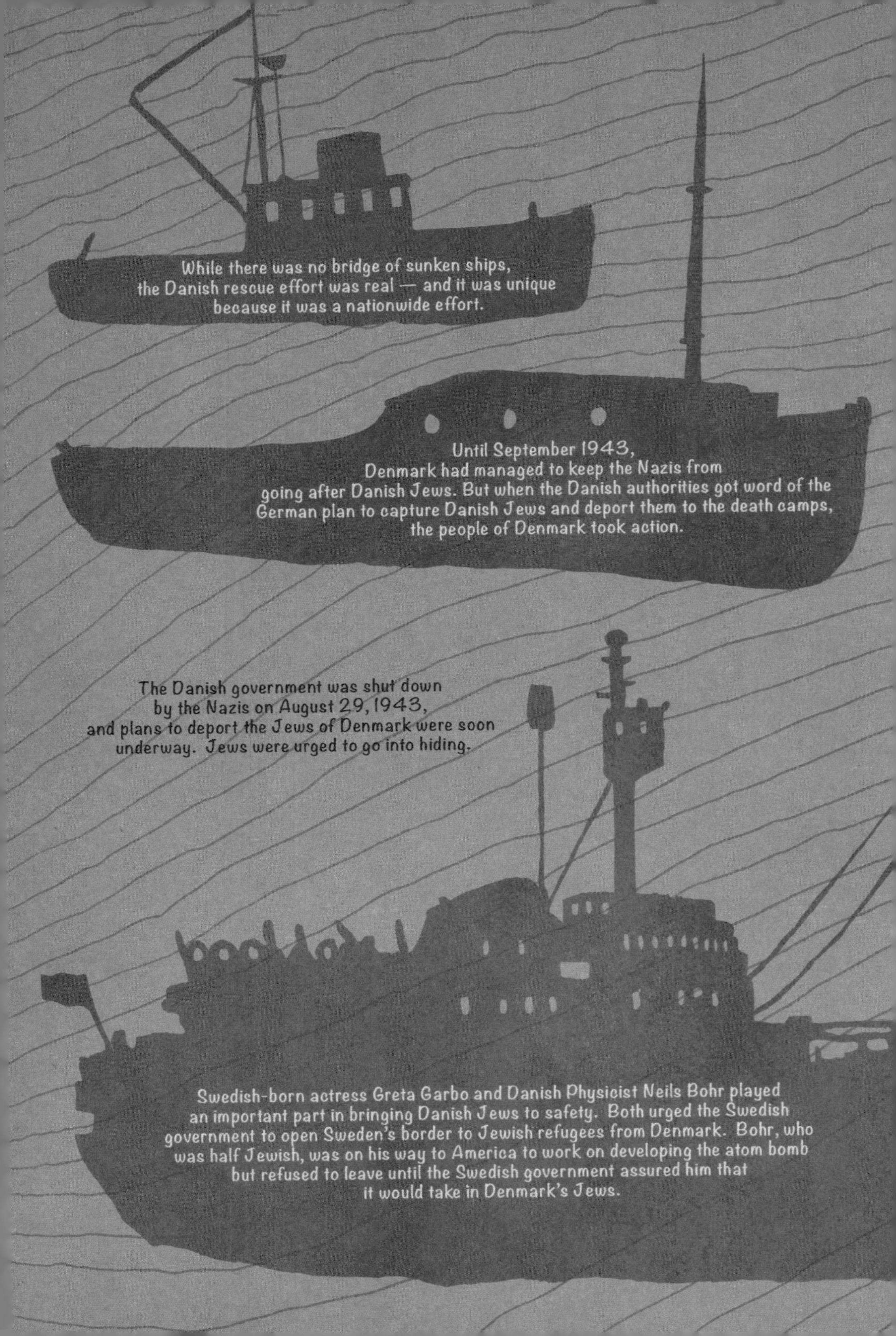
While there was no bridge of sunken ships, the Danish rescue effort was real — and it was unique because it was a nationwide effort.
Until September 1943, Denmark had managed to keep the Nazis from going after Danish Jews. But when the Danish authorities got word of the German plan to capture Danish Jews and deport them to the death camps, the people of Denmark took action.
The Danish government was shut down by the Nazis on August 29, 1943, and plans to deport the Jews of Denmark were soon underway. Jews were urged to go into hiding.
Swedish-born actress Greta Garbo and Danish Physicist Neils Bohr played an important part in bringing Danish Jews to safety. Both urged the Swedish government to open Sweden's border to Jewish refugees from Denmark. Bohr, who was half Jewish, was on his way to America to work on developing the atom bomb but refused to leave until the Swedish government assured him that it would take in Denmark's Jews.

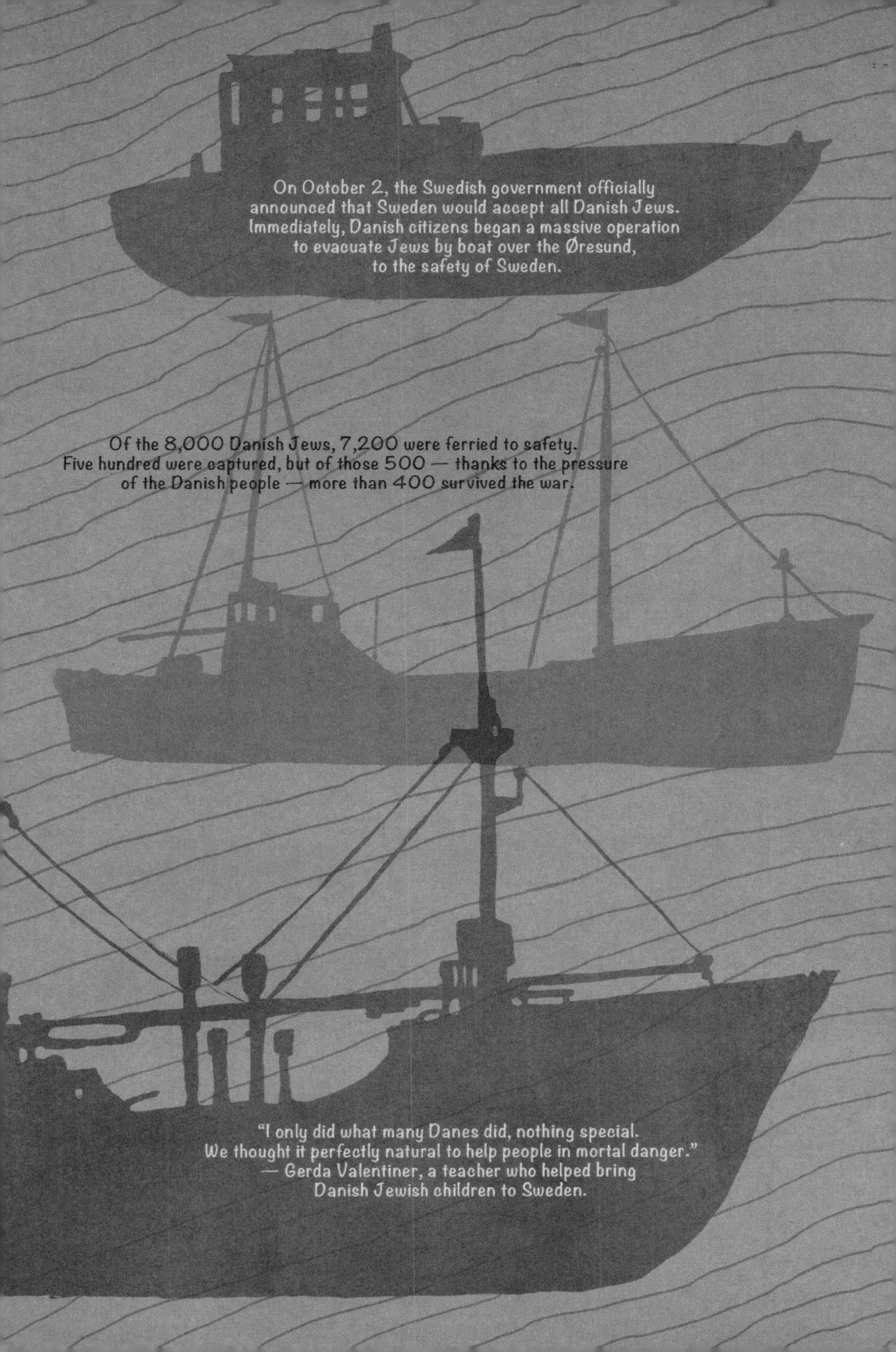
On October 2, the Swedish government officially announced that Sweden would accept all Danish Jews. Immediately, Danish citizens began a massive operation to evacuate Jews by boat over the Øresund, to the safety of Sweden.
Of the 8,000 Danish Jews, 7,200 were ferried to safety. Five hundred were captured, but of those 500 — thanks to the pressure of the Danish people — more than 400 survived the war.
"I only did what many Danes did, nothing special. We thought it perfectly natural to help people in mortal danger."
— Gerda Valentiner, a teacher who helped bring Danish Jewish children to Sweden.

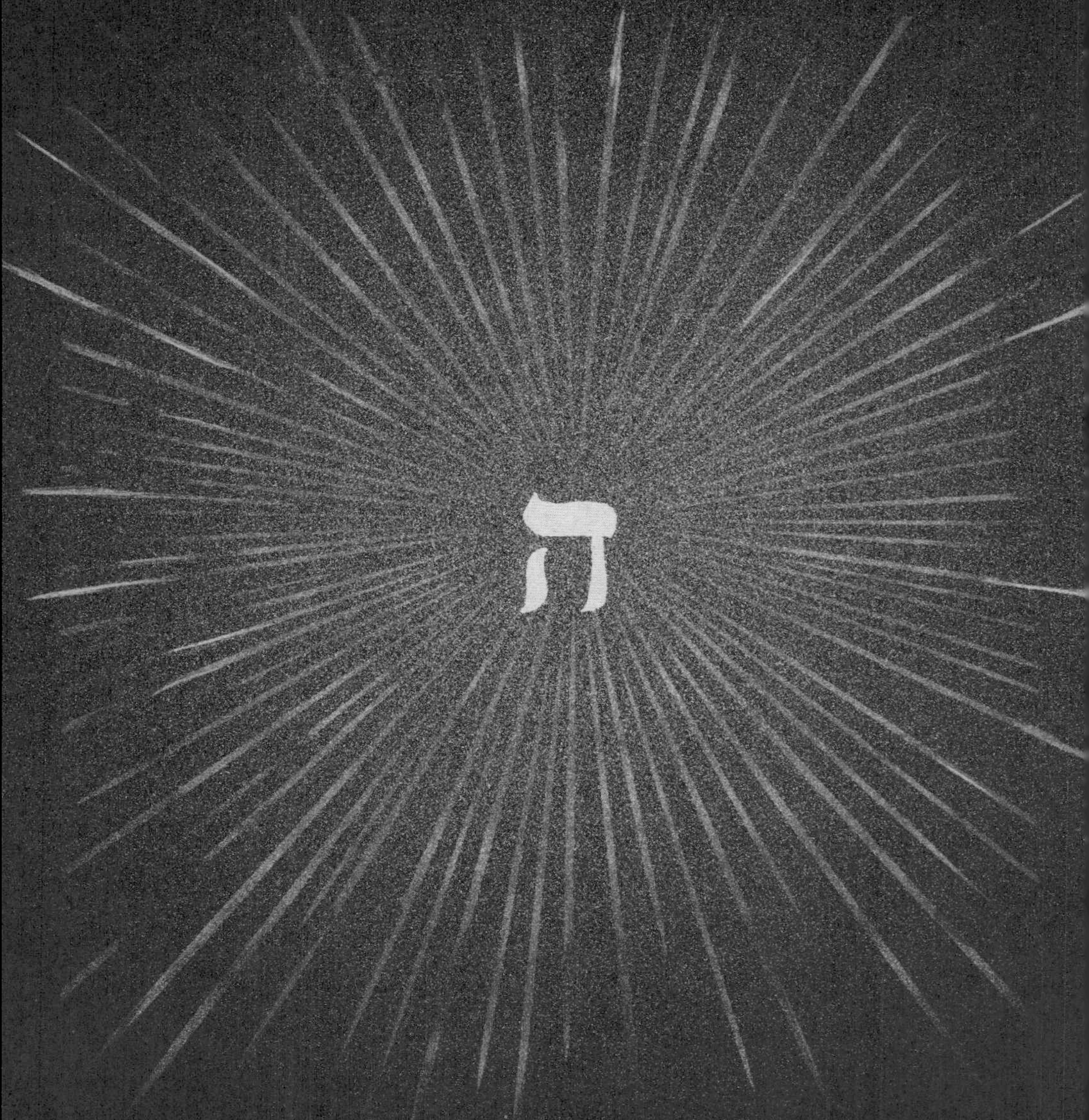
ה

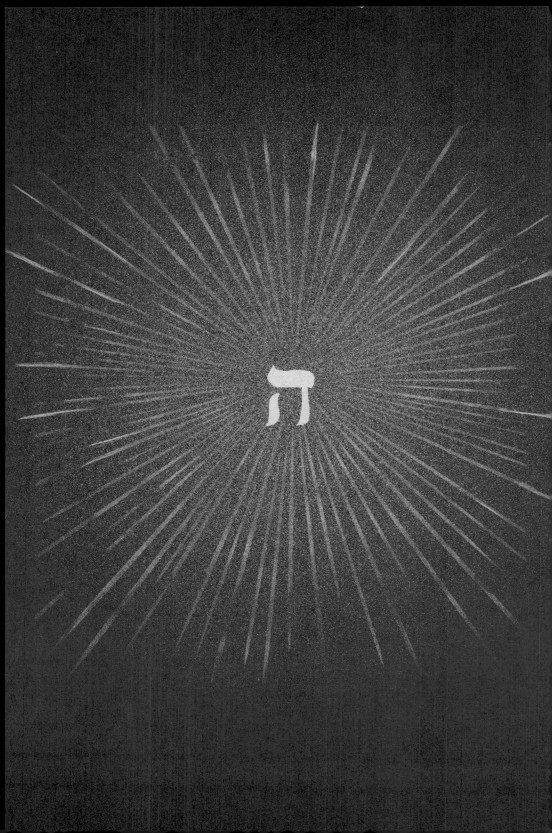

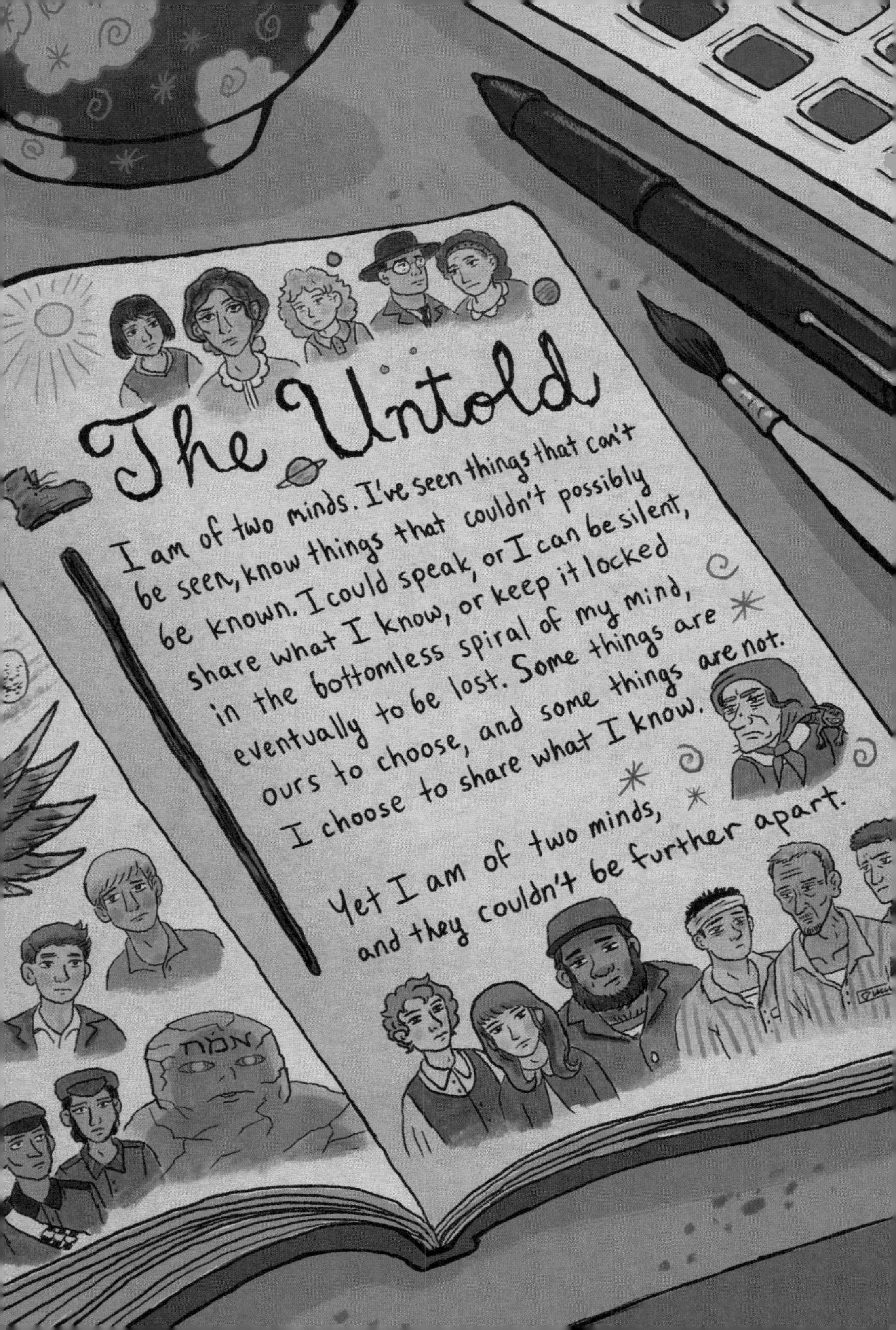
The Untold
I am of two minds. I've seen things that can't be seen, know things that couldn't possibly be known. I could speak, or I can be silent, share what I know, or keep it locked in the bottomless spiral of my mind, eventually to be lost. Some things are ours to choose, and some things are not. I choose to share what I know.
Yet I am of two minds, and they couldn't be further apart.

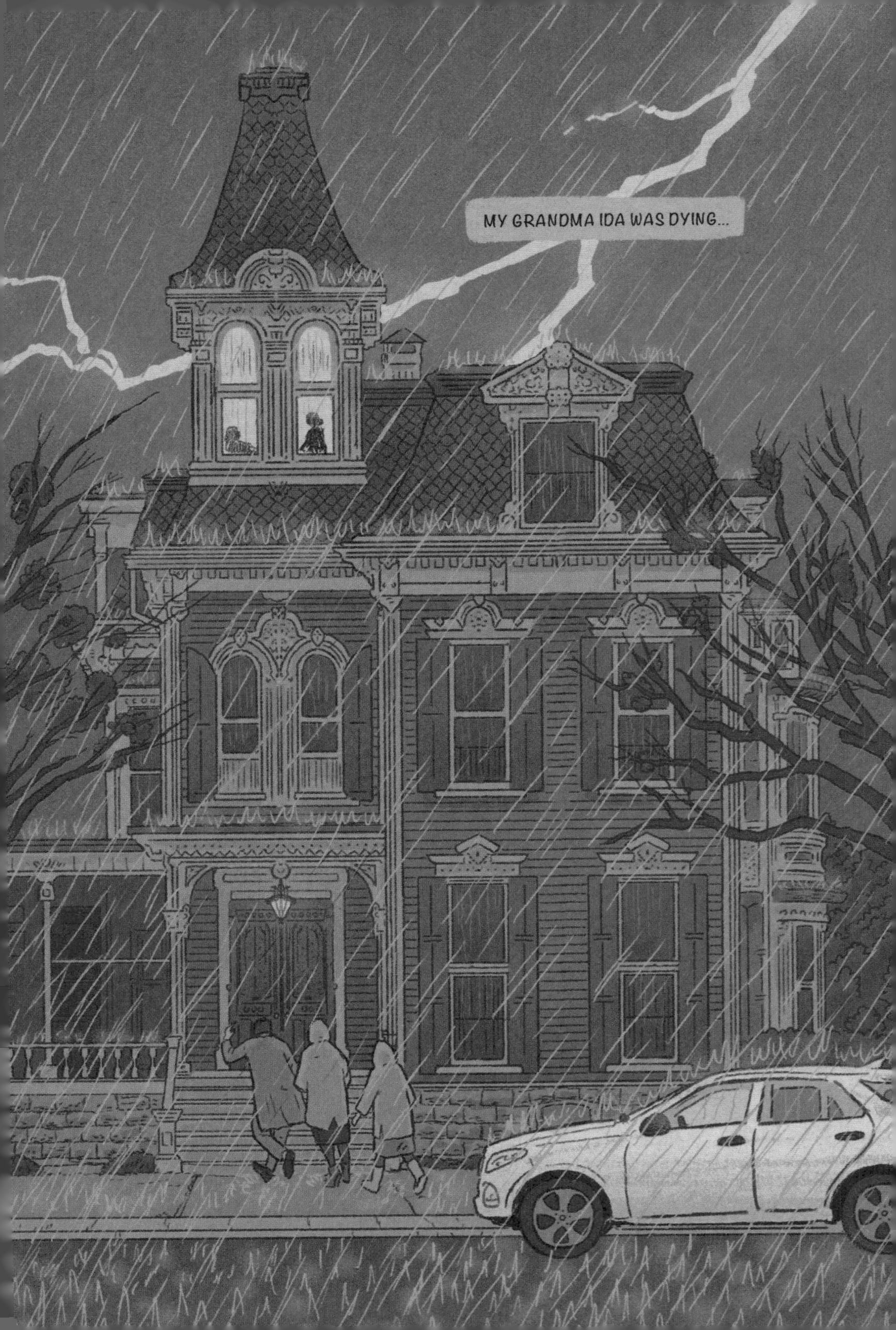
MY GRANDMA IDA WAS DYING...

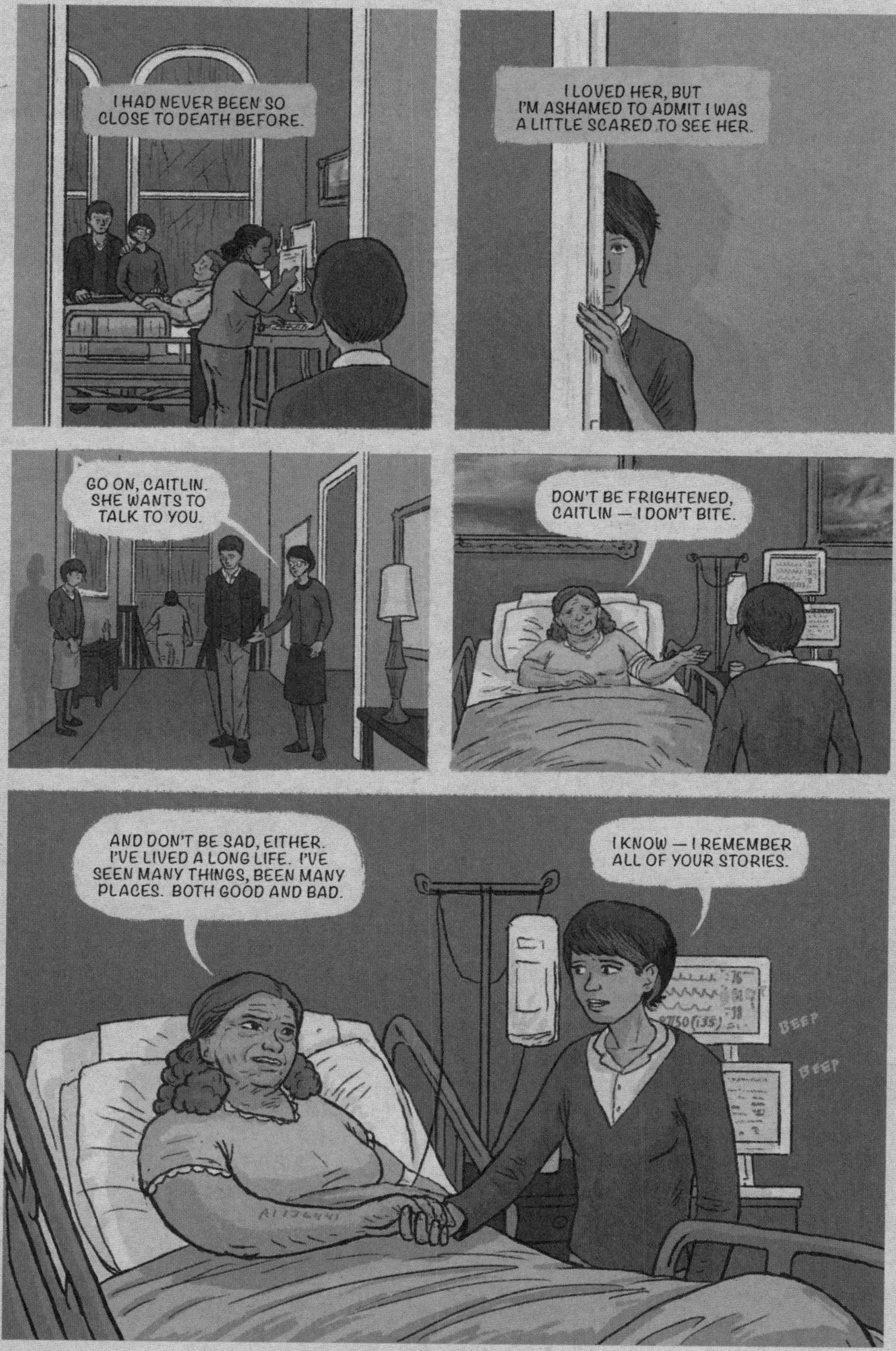
I HAD NEVER BEEN SO CLOSE TO DEATH BEFORE.
I LOVED HER, BUT I'M ASHAMED TO ADMIT I WAS A LITTLE SCARED TO SEE HER.
GO ON, CAITLIN. SHE WANTS TO TALK TO YOU.
DON'T BE FRIGHTENED, CAITLIN — I DON'T BITE.
AND DON'T BE SAD, EITHER. I'VE LIVED A LONG LIFE. I'VE SEEN MANY THINGS, BEEN MANY PLACES. BOTH GOOD AND BAD.
I KNOW — I REMEMBER ALL OF YOUR STORIES.
BEEP
BEEP

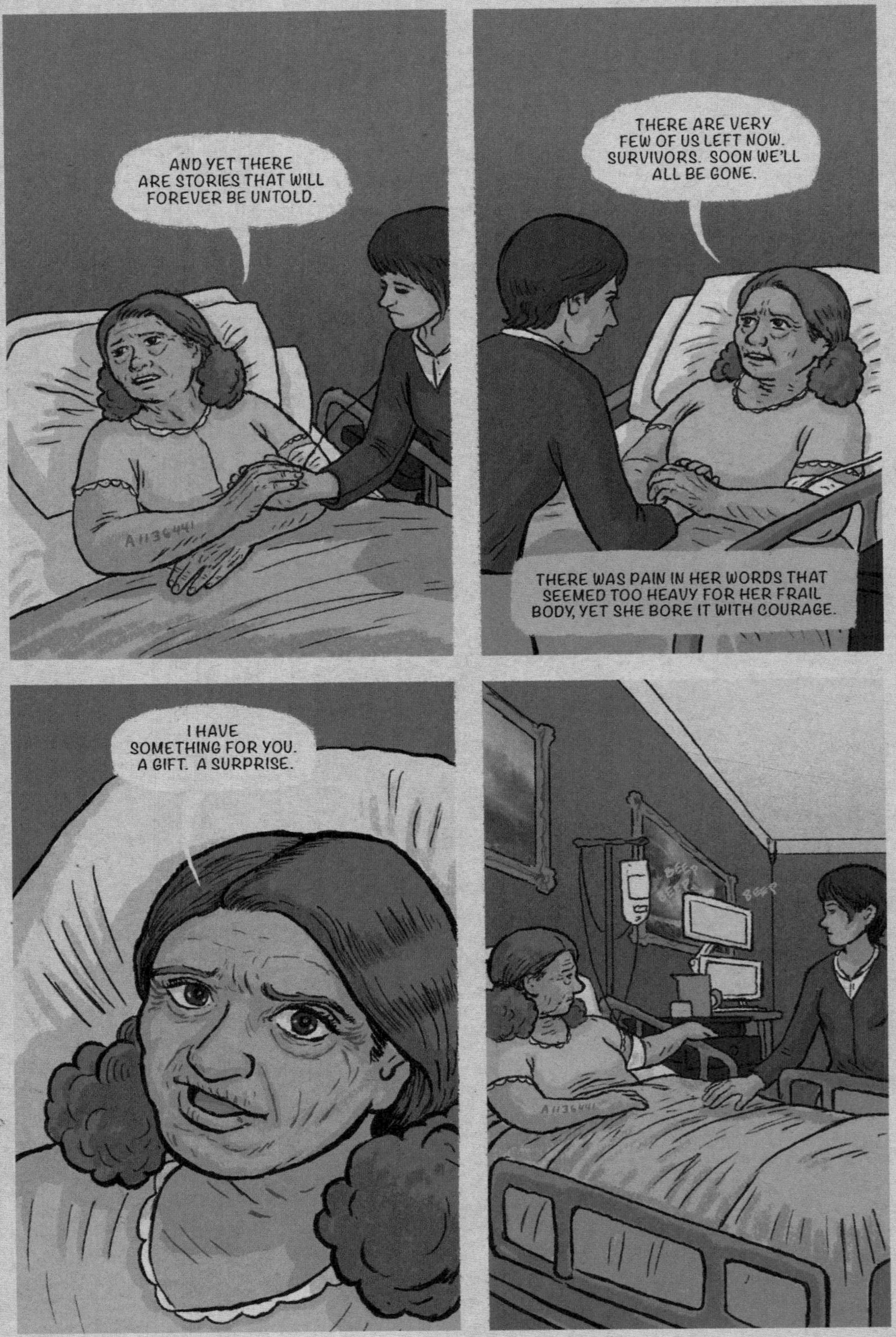
AND YET THERE ARE STORIES THAT WILL FOREVER BE UNTOLD.
THERE ARE VERY FEW OF US LEFT NOW. SURVIVORS. SOON WE'LL ALL BE GONE.
THERE WAS PAIN IN HER WORDS THAT SEEMED TOO HEAVY FOR HER FRAIL BODY, YET SHE BORE IT WITH COURAGE.
I HAVE SOMETHING FOR YOU. A GIFT. A SURPRISE.
BEEP
BEEP
BEEP

BEEP
87/50(135)
WHAT IS IT?
IF I TOLD YOU, THEN IT WOULDN'T BE A SURPRISE.
AND THEN SHE SAID THE STRANGEST THING.
OPEN IT WHEN YOU'RE FEELING STRONG...AND WHEN YOUR HEART IS READY.
A1136441

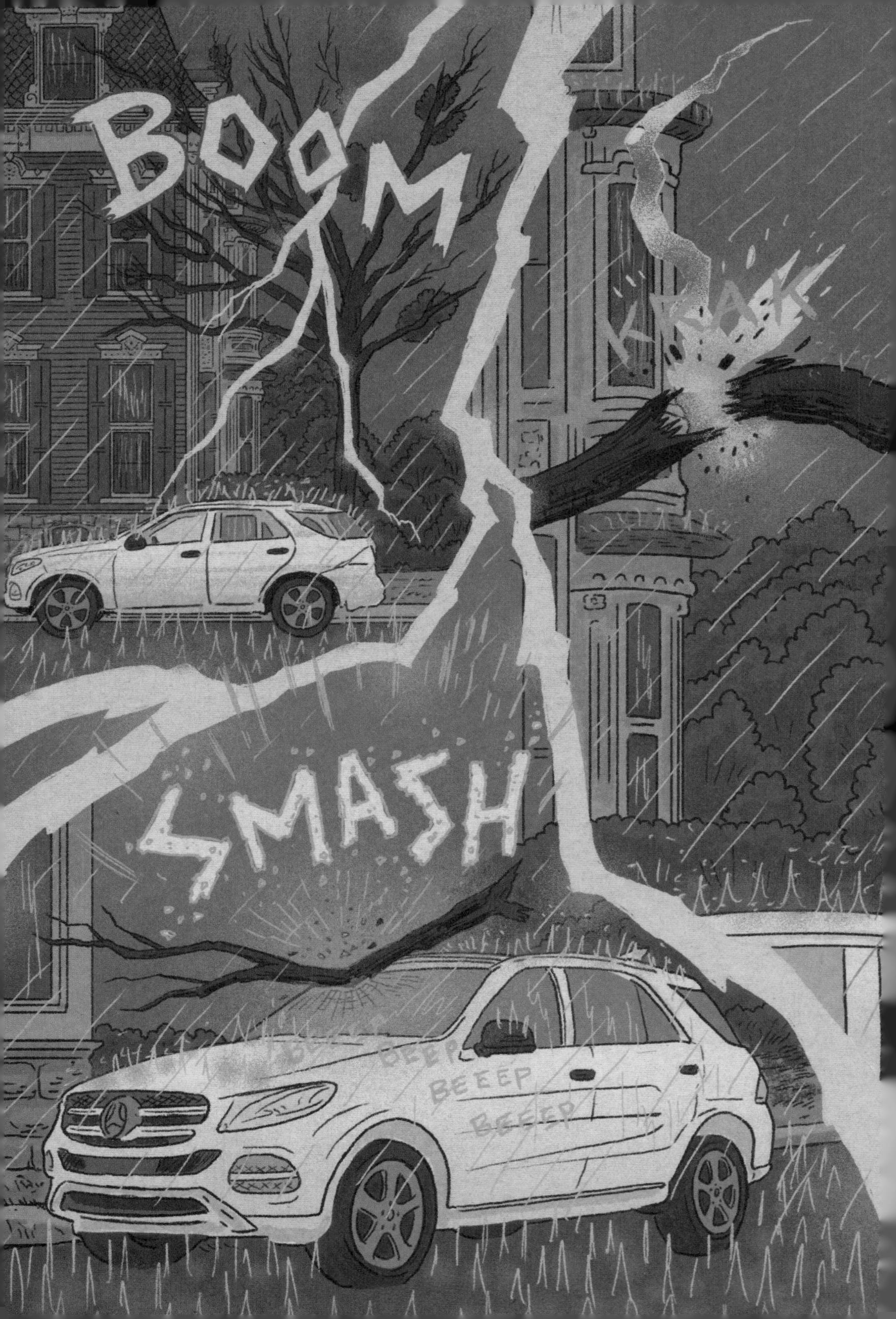
BOOM
KRAK
SMASH
BEEP
BEEEP
BEEEP

OH MY GOD! GRANDMA, DID YOU SEE THAT!
BEEEP
BEEP
BEEP
BEEP
BEEEP
BEEP
BEEP
GRANDMA?
BEEEEEEEEEEEE
EEEEEEEEEEEEE
A1136441

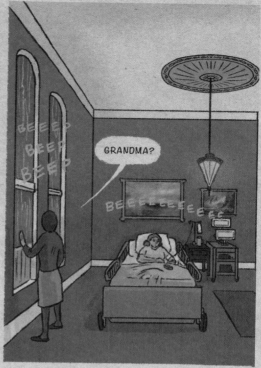

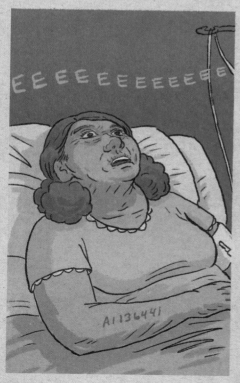

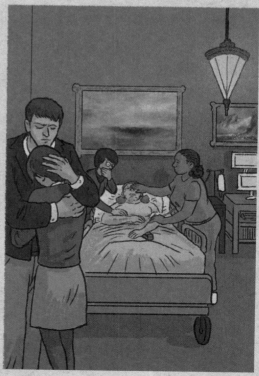

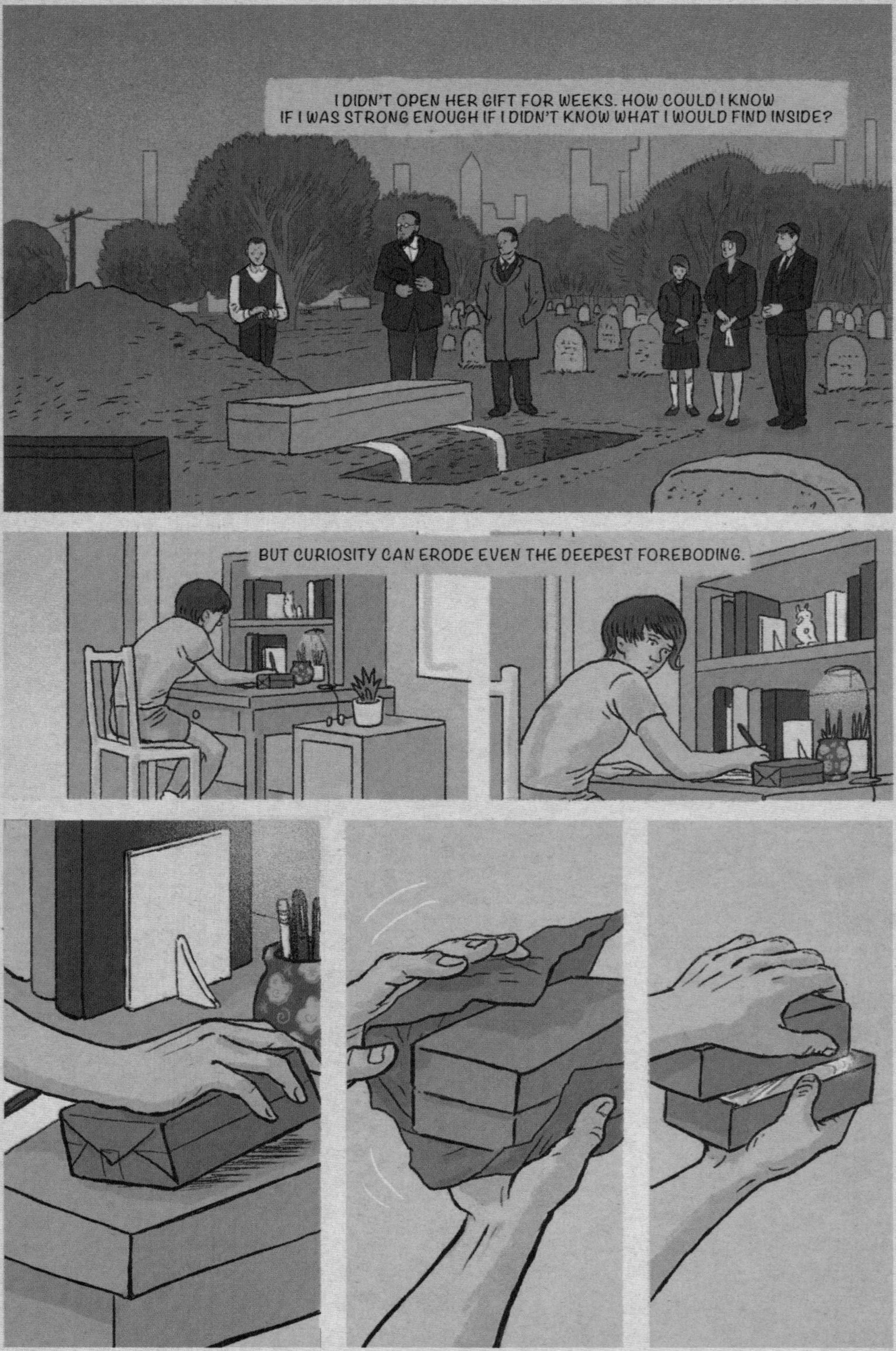
I DIDN'T OPEN HER GIFT FOR WEEKS. HOW COULD I KNOW IF I WAS STRONG ENOUGH IF I DIDN'T KNOW WHAT I WOULD FIND INSIDE?
BUT CURIOSITY CAN ERODE EVEN THE DEEPEST FOREBODING.

WHAT'S THAT?

GRANDMA GAVE IT TO ME.

A SHELL MADE OF GLASS?

CRYSTAL. FUNNY, I'VE NEVER SEEN IT BEFORE.

THE CRYSTALLINE SHELL CAST TINY RAINBOWS OF LIGHT AROUND MY ROOM. THE SLIGHTEST TWIST OF MY WRIST WOULD MAKE THE STREAKS OF COLOR SHIMMER AND DANCE.

IT'S VERY PRETTY.

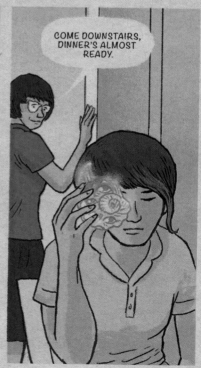

COME DOWNSTAIRS, DINNER'S ALMOST READY.

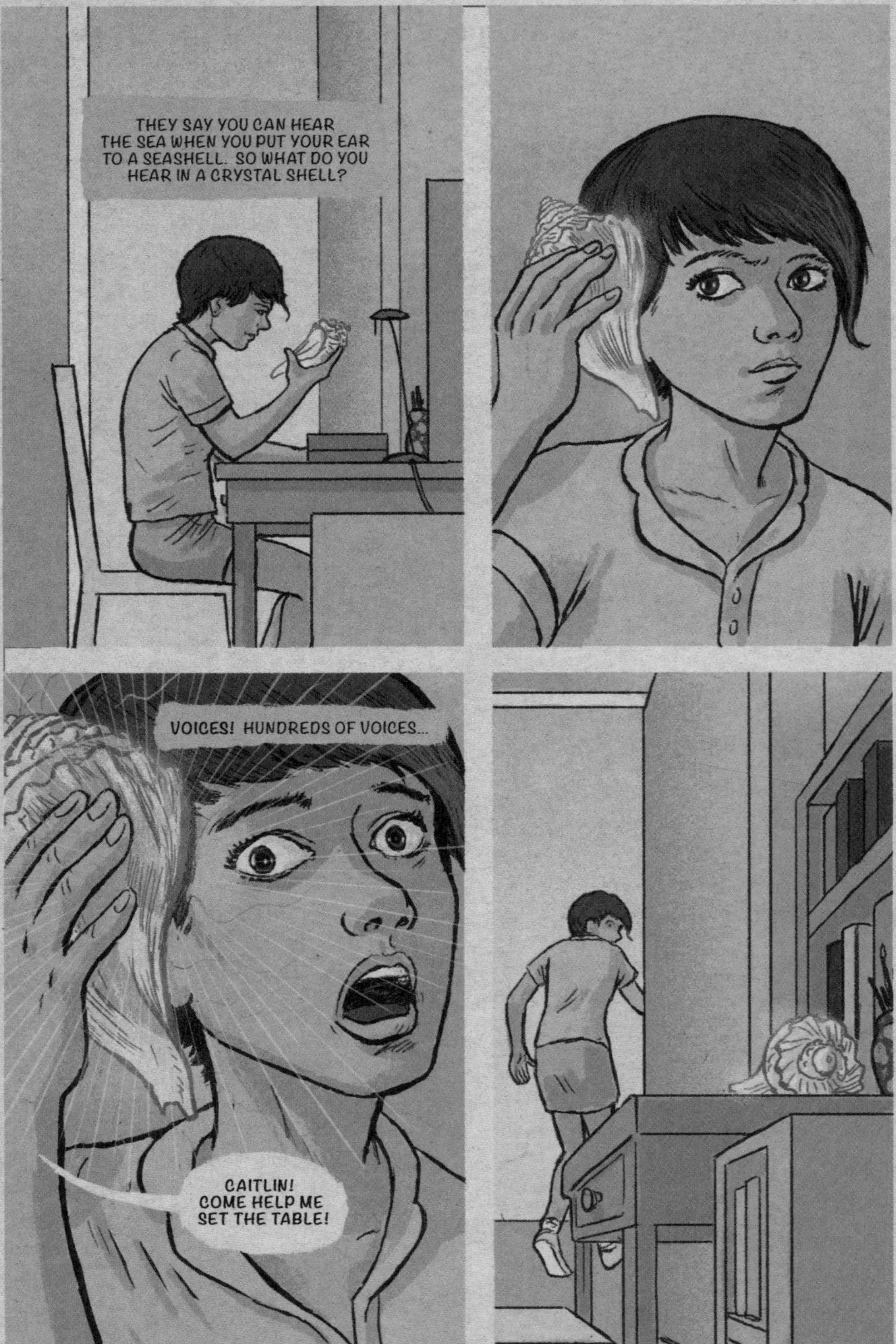
THEY SAY YOU CAN HEAR THE SEA WHEN YOU PUT YOUR EAR TO A SEASHELL. SO WHAT DO YOU HEAR IN A CRYSTAL SHELL?
VOICES! HUNDREDS OF VOICES...
CAITLIN! COME HELP ME SET THE TABLE!

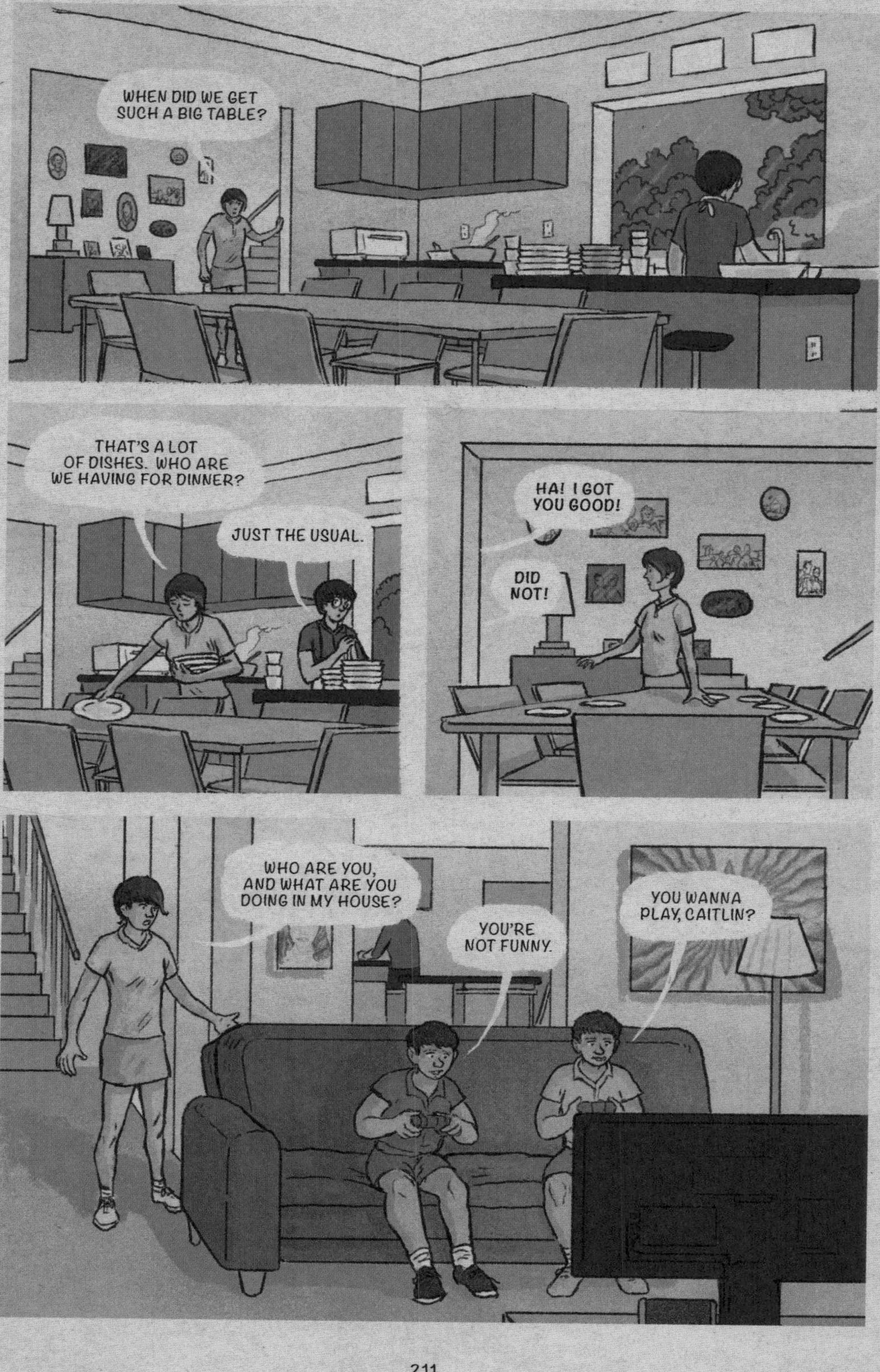
WHEN DID WE GET SUCH A BIG TABLE?
THAT'S A LOT OF DISHES. WHO ARE WE HAVING FOR DINNER?
JUST THE USUAL.
HA! I GOT YOU GOOD!
DID NOT!
WHO ARE YOU, AND WHAT ARE YOU DOING IN MY HOUSE?
YOU'RE NOT FUNNY.
YOU WANNA PLAY, CAITLIN?

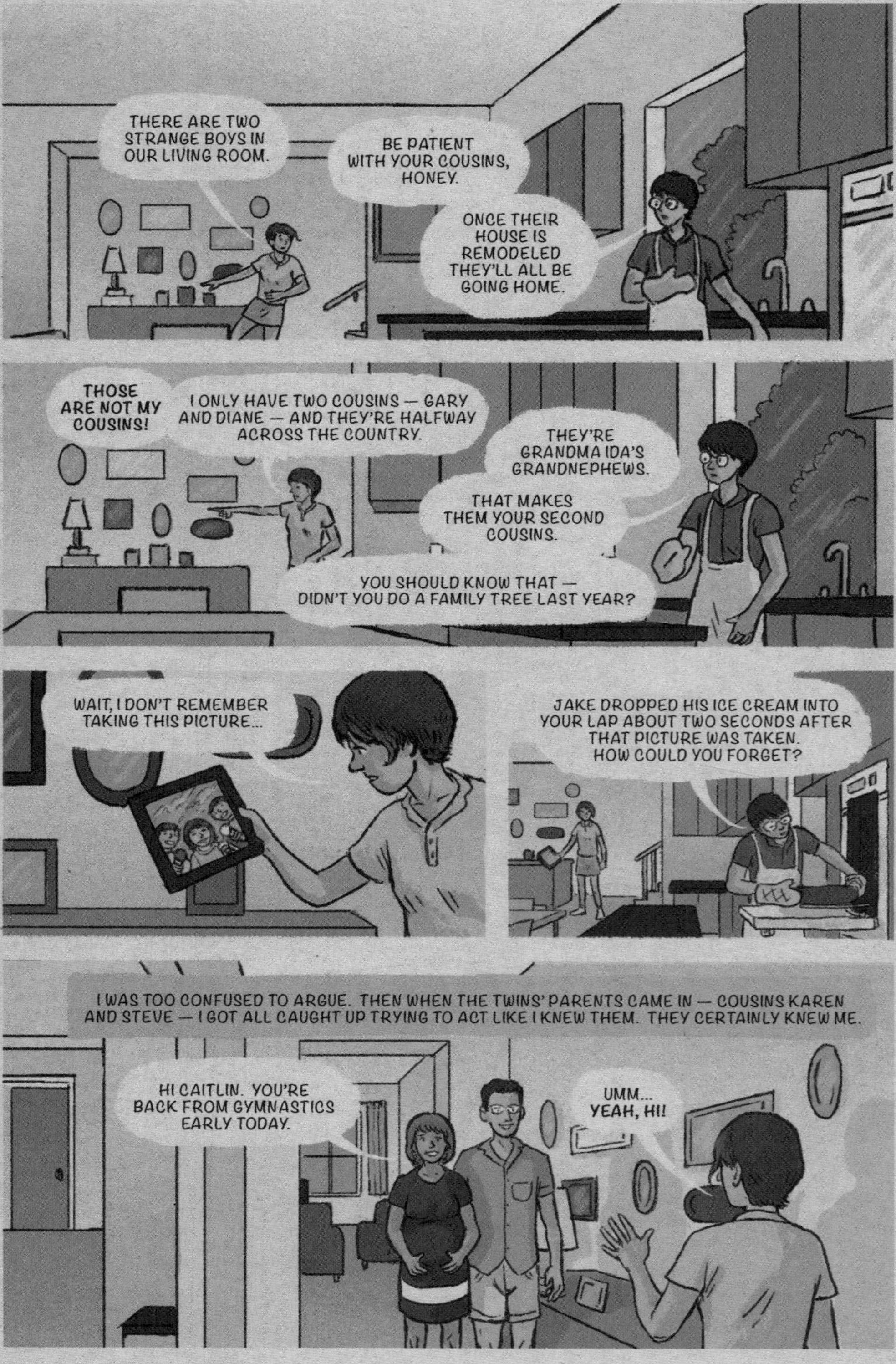
THERE ARE TWO STRANGE BOYS IN OUR LIVING ROOM.
BE PATIENT WITH YOUR COUSINS, HONEY.
ONCE THEIR HOUSE IS REMODELED THEY'LL ALL BE GOING HOME.
THOSE ARE NOT MY COUSINS!
I ONLY HAVE TWO COUSINS — GARY AND DIANE — AND THEY'RE HALFWAY ACROSS THE COUNTRY.
THEY'RE GRANDMA IDA'S GRANDNEPHEWS.
THAT MAKES THEM YOUR SECOND COUSINS.
YOU SHOULD KNOW THAT — DIDN'T YOU DO A FAMILY TREE LAST YEAR?
WAIT, I DON'T REMEMBER TAKING THIS PICTURE...
JAKE DROPPED HIS ICE CREAM INTO YOUR LAP ABOUT TWO SECONDS AFTER THAT PICTURE WAS TAKEN. HOW COULD YOU FORGET?
I WAS TOO CONFUSED TO ARGUE. THEN WHEN THE TWINS' PARENTS CAME IN — COUSINS KAREN AND STEVE — I GOT ALL CAUGHT UP TRYING TO ACT LIKE I KNEW THEM. THEY CERTAINLY KNEW ME.
HI CAITLIN. YOU'RE BACK FROM GYMNASTICS EARLY TODAY.
UMM... YEAH, HI!

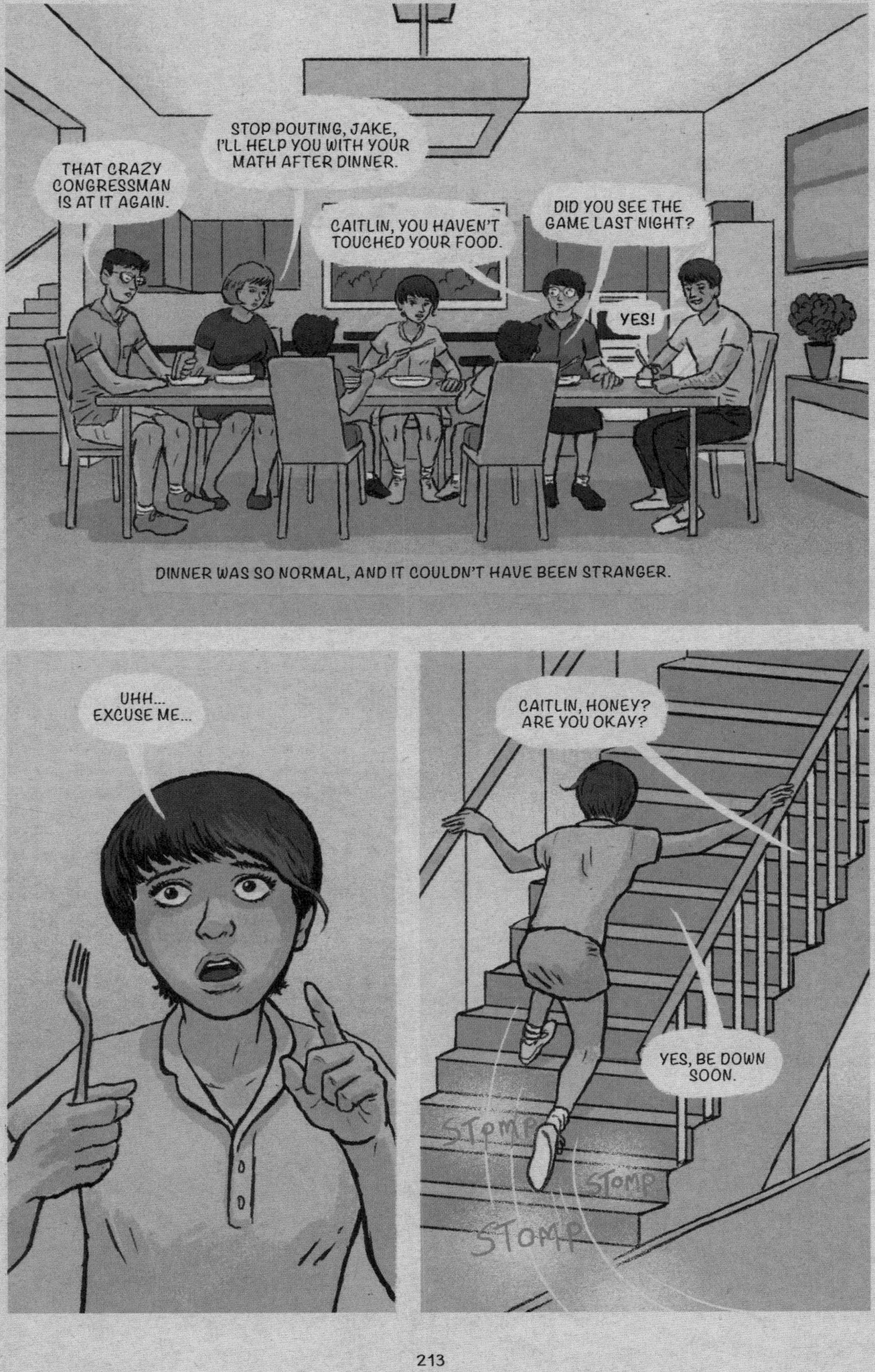
THAT CRAZY CONGRESSMAN IS AT IT AGAIN.
STOP POUTING, JAKE, I'LL HELP YOU WITH YOUR MATH AFTER DINNER.
CAITLIN, YOU HAVEN'T TOUCHED YOUR FOOD.
DID YOU SEE THE GAME LAST NIGHT?
YES!
DINNER WAS SO NORMAL, AND IT COULDN'T HAVE BEEN STRANGER.
UHH... EXCUSE ME...
CAITLIN, HONEY? ARE YOU OKAY?
YES, BE DOWN SOON.
STOMP
STOMP
STOMP

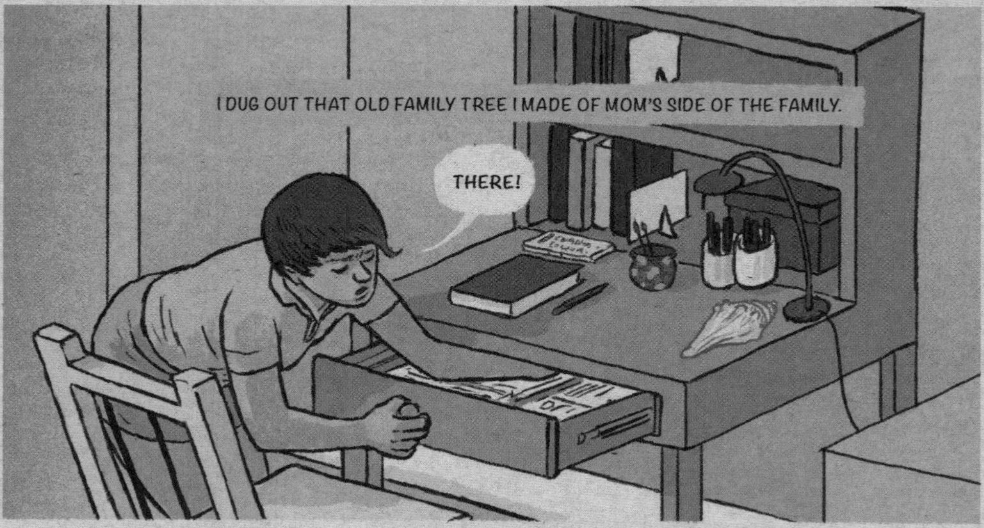
I DUG OUT THAT OLD FAMILY TREE I MADE OF MOM'S SIDE OF THE FAMILY.
THERE!

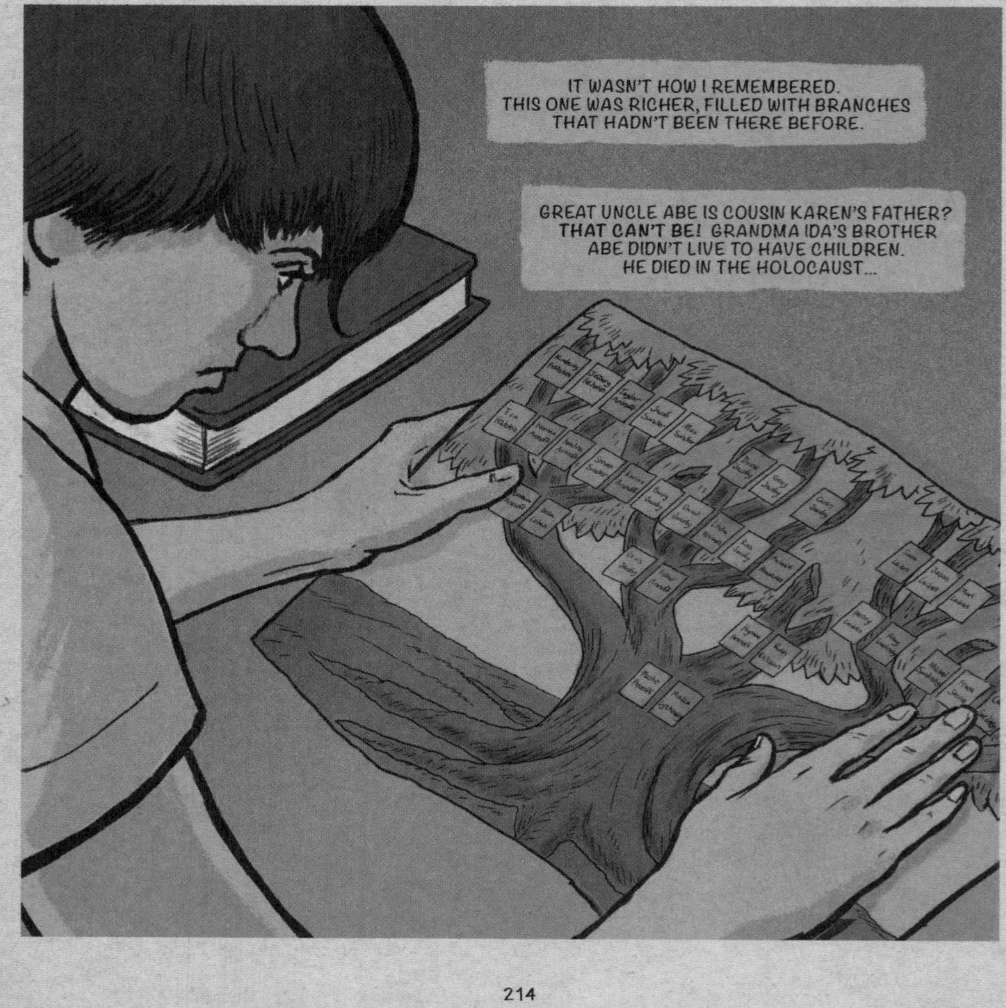
IT WASN'T HOW I REMEMBERED. THIS ONE WAS RICHER, FILLED WITH BRANCHES THAT HADN'T BEEN THERE BEFORE.
GREAT UNCLE ABE IS COUSIN KAREN'S FATHER? THAT CAN'T BE! GRANDMA IDA'S BROTHER ABE DIDN'T LIVE TO HAVE CHILDREN. HE DIED IN THE HOLOCAUST...

IT COULDN'T BE.

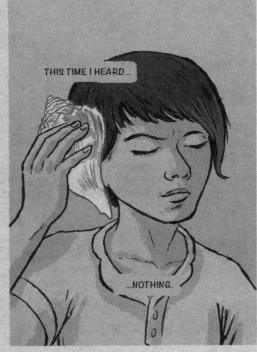

THIS TIME I HEARD...

...NOTHING.

IT WASN'T JUST SILENCE — IT WAS A VOID SO COMPLETE IT MADE ME SHIVER.

CAITLIN, COME BACK DOWN — YOUR DINNER'S GETTING COLD.

OKAY, COMING!

Kraina Golde Aronoff

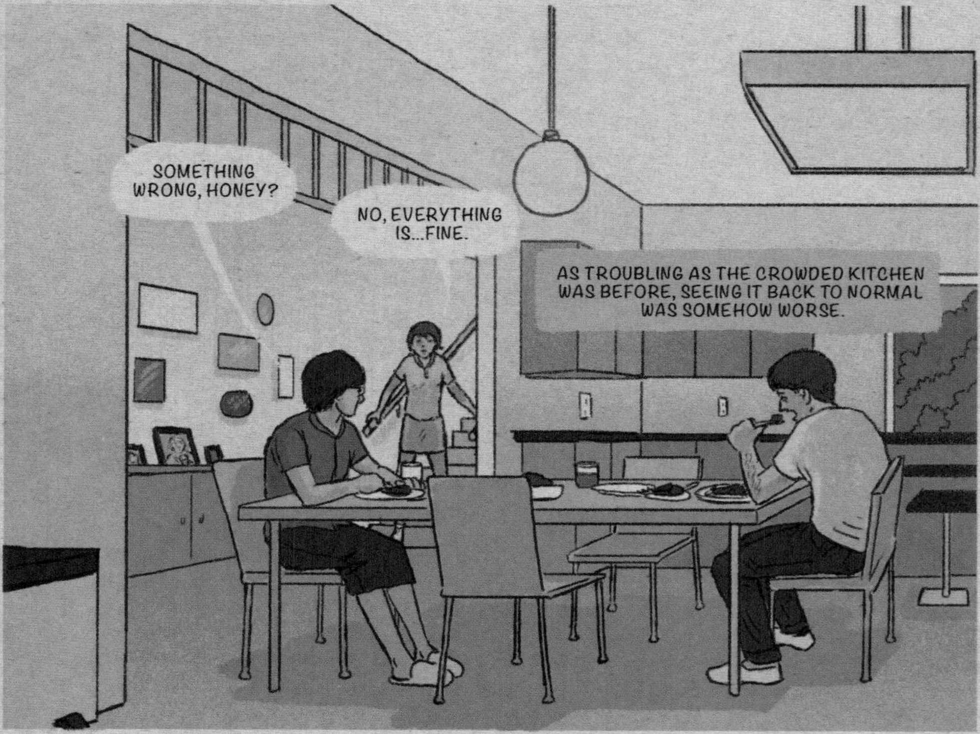
SOMETHING WRONG, HONEY?
NO, EVERYTHING IS...FINE.
AS TROUBLING AS THE CROWDED KITCHEN WAS BEFORE, SEEING IT BACK TO NORMAL WAS SOMEHOW WORSE.

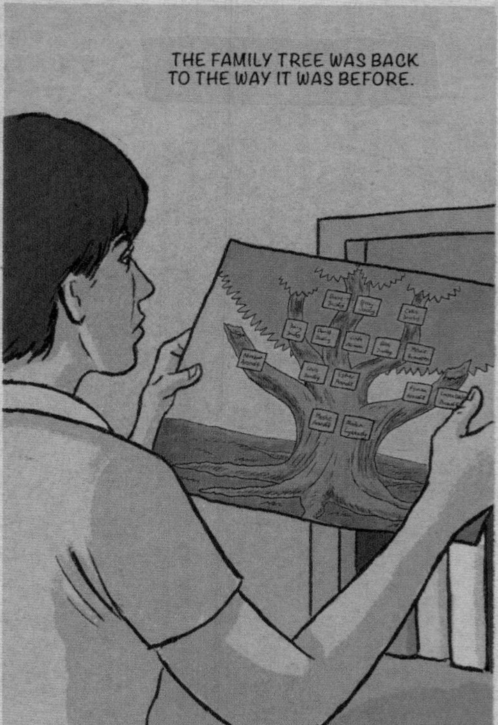
THE FAMILY TREE WAS BACK TO THE WAY IT WAS BEFORE.

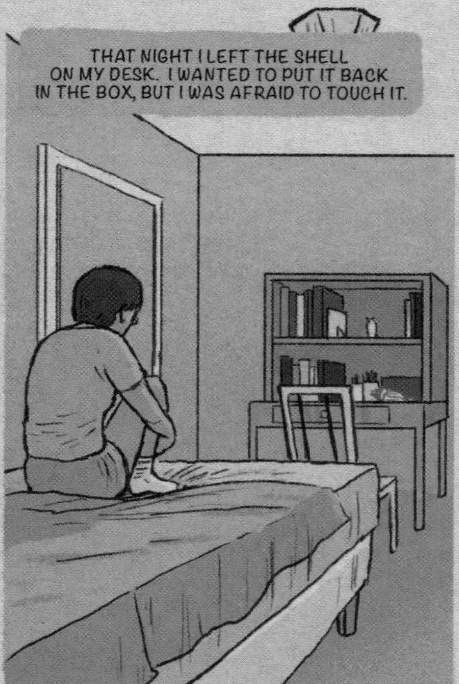
THAT NIGHT I LEFT THE SHELL ON MY DESK. I WANTED TO PUT IT BACK IN THE BOX, BUT I WAS AFRAID TO TOUCH IT.

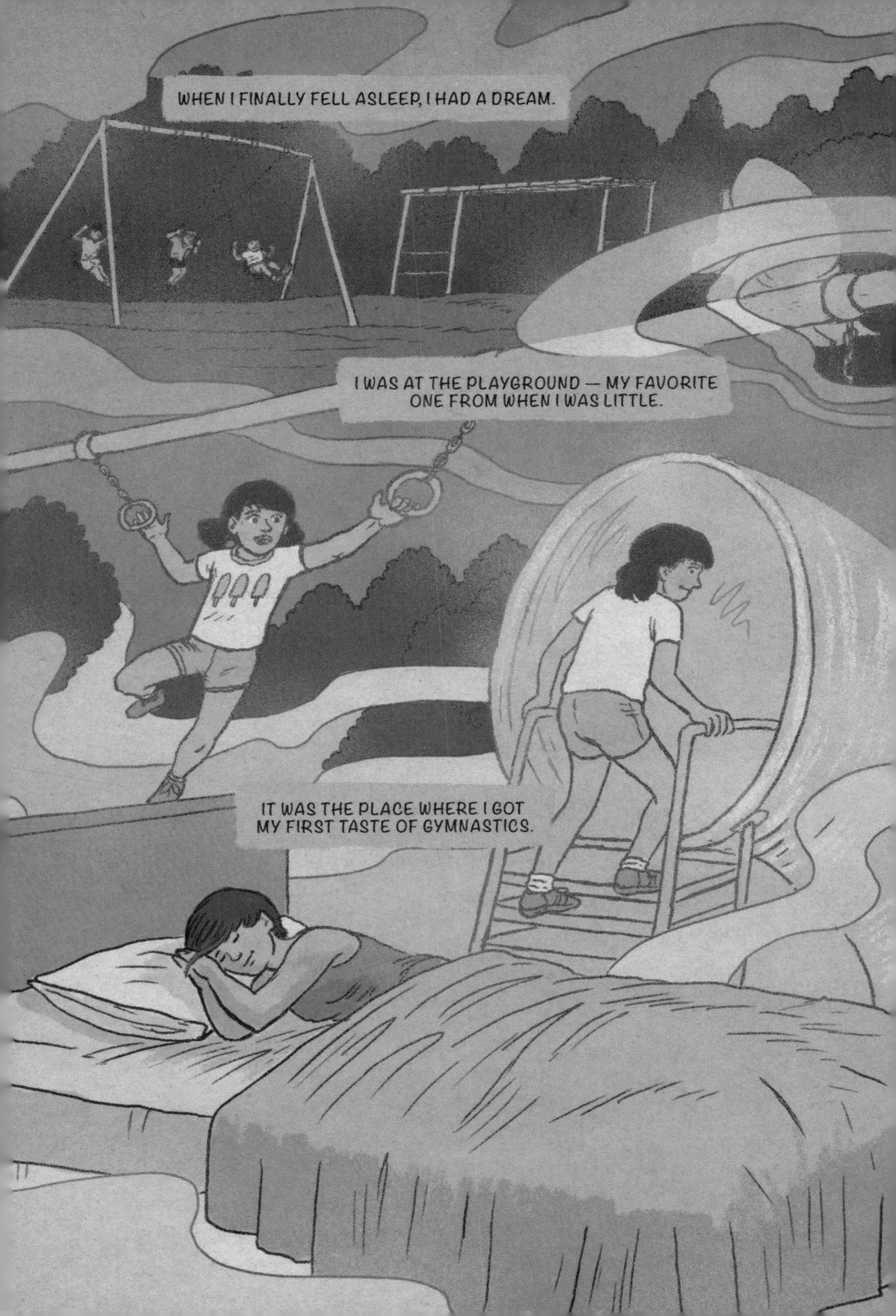
WHEN I FINALLY FELL ASLEEP, I HAD A DREAM.
I WAS AT THE PLAYGROUND — MY FAVORITE ONE FROM WHEN I WAS LITTLE.
IT WAS THE PLACE WHERE I GOT MY FIRST TASTE OF GYMNASTICS.

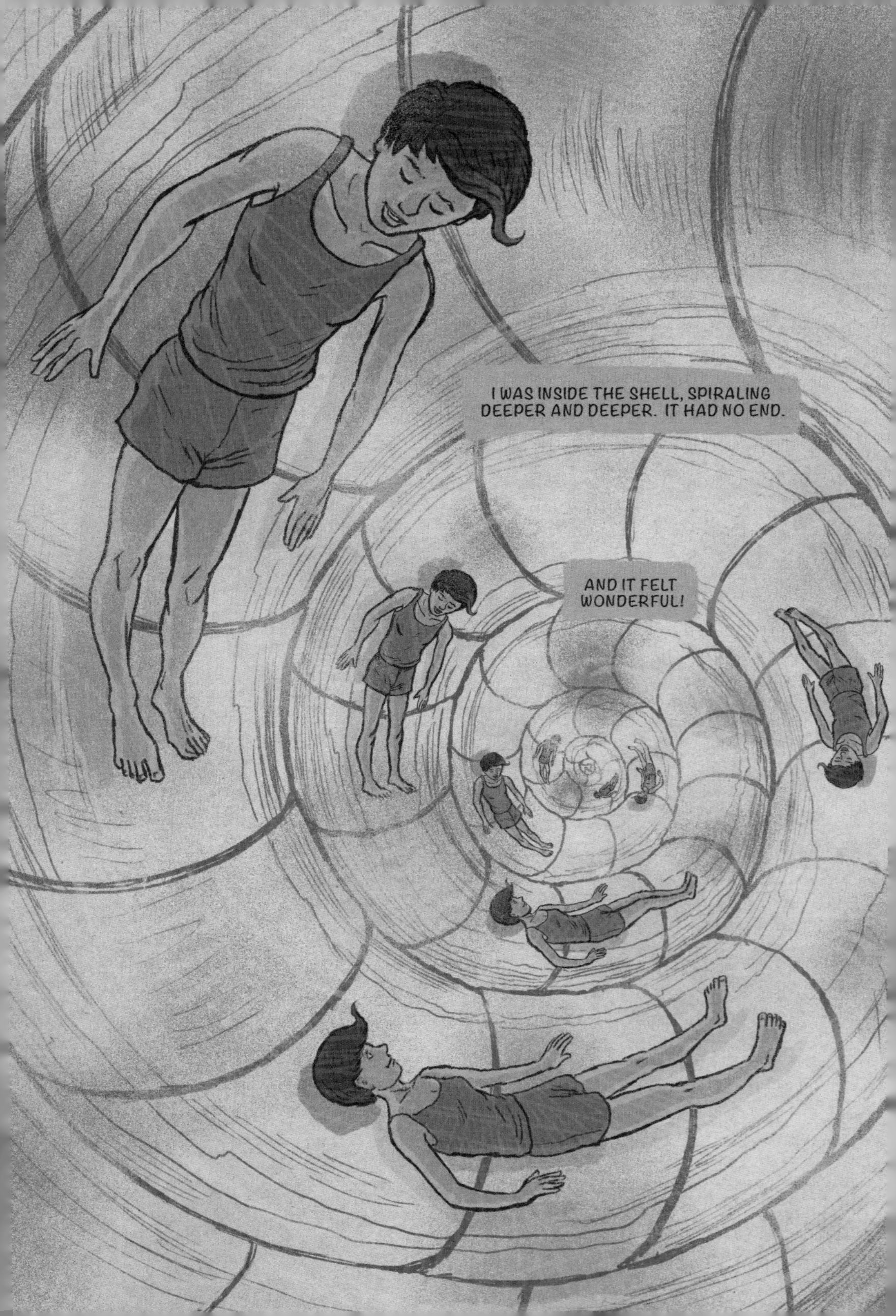
I WAS INSIDE THE SHELL, SPIRALING DEEPER AND DEEPER. IT HAD NO END.
AND IT FELT WONDERFUL!

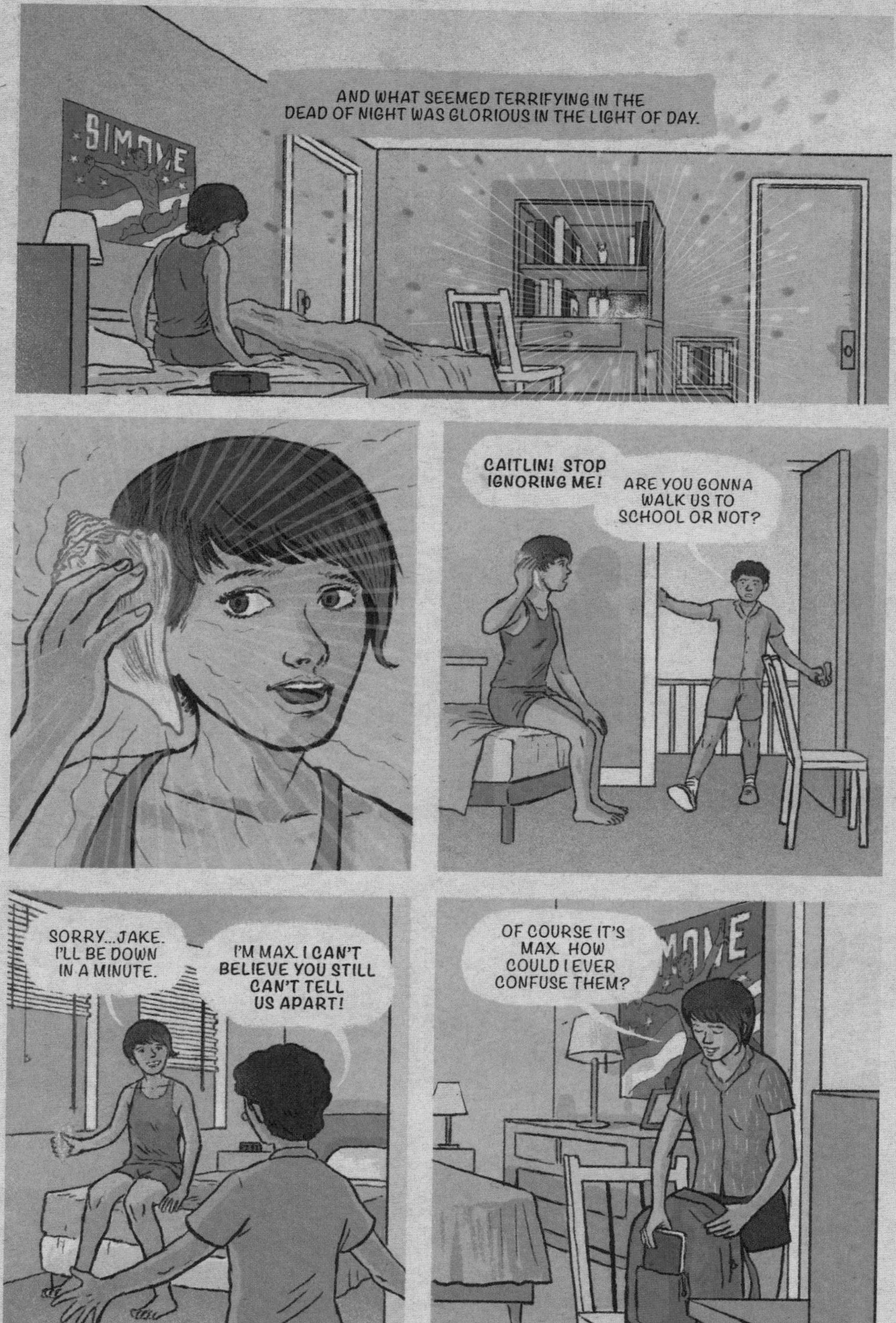
AND WHAT SEEMED TERRIFYING IN THE DEAD OF NIGHT WAS GLORIOUS IN THE LIGHT OF DAY.
SIMONE
CAITLIN! STOP IGNORING ME!
ARE YOU GONNA WALK US TO SCHOOL OR NOT?
SORRY...JAKE. I'LL BE DOWN IN A MINUTE.
I'M MAX. I CAN'T BELIEVE YOU STILL CAN'T TELL US APART!
OF COURSE IT'S MAX. HOW COULD I EVER CONFUSE THEM?

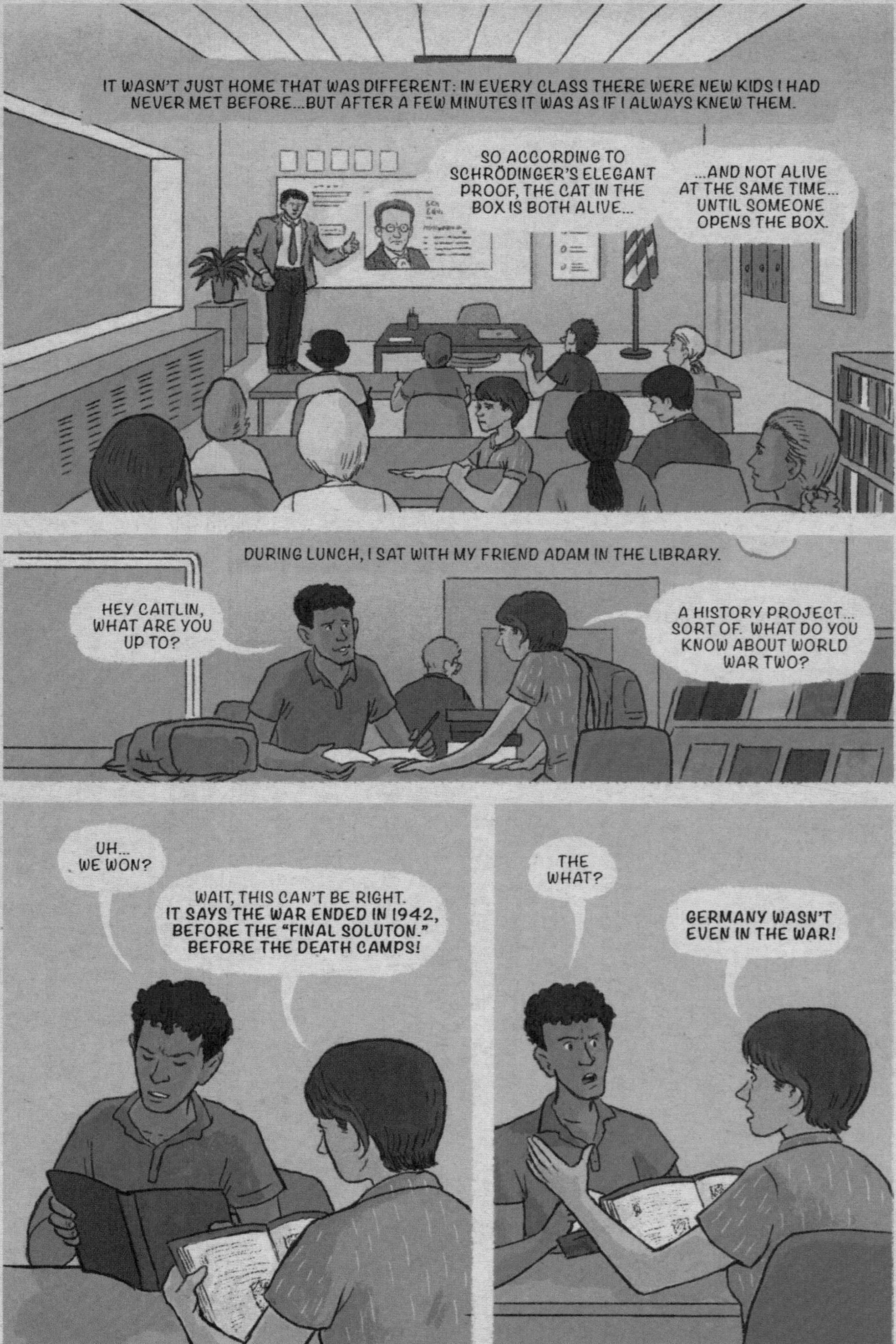

IT WASN'T JUST HOME THAT WAS DIFFERENT: IN EVERY CLASS THERE WERE NEW KIDS I HAD NEVER MET BEFORE...BUT AFTER A FEW MINUTES IT WAS AS IF I ALWAYS KNEW THEM.
SO ACCORDING TO SCHRÖDINGER'S ELEGANT PROOF, THE CAT IN THE BOX IS BOTH ALIVE...
...AND NOT ALIVE AT THE SAME TIME... UNTIL SOMEONE OPENS THE BOX.
DURING LUNCH, I SAT WITH MY FRIEND ADAM IN THE LIBRARY.
HEY CAITLIN, WHAT ARE YOU UP TO?
A HISTORY PROJECT... SORT OF. WHAT DO YOU KNOW ABOUT WORLD WAR TWO?
UH... WE WON?
WAIT, THIS CAN'T BE RIGHT. IT SAYS THE WAR ENDED IN 1942, BEFORE THE "FINAL SOLUTON." BEFORE THE DEATH CAMPS!
THE WHAT?
GERMANY WASN'T EVEN IN THE WAR!

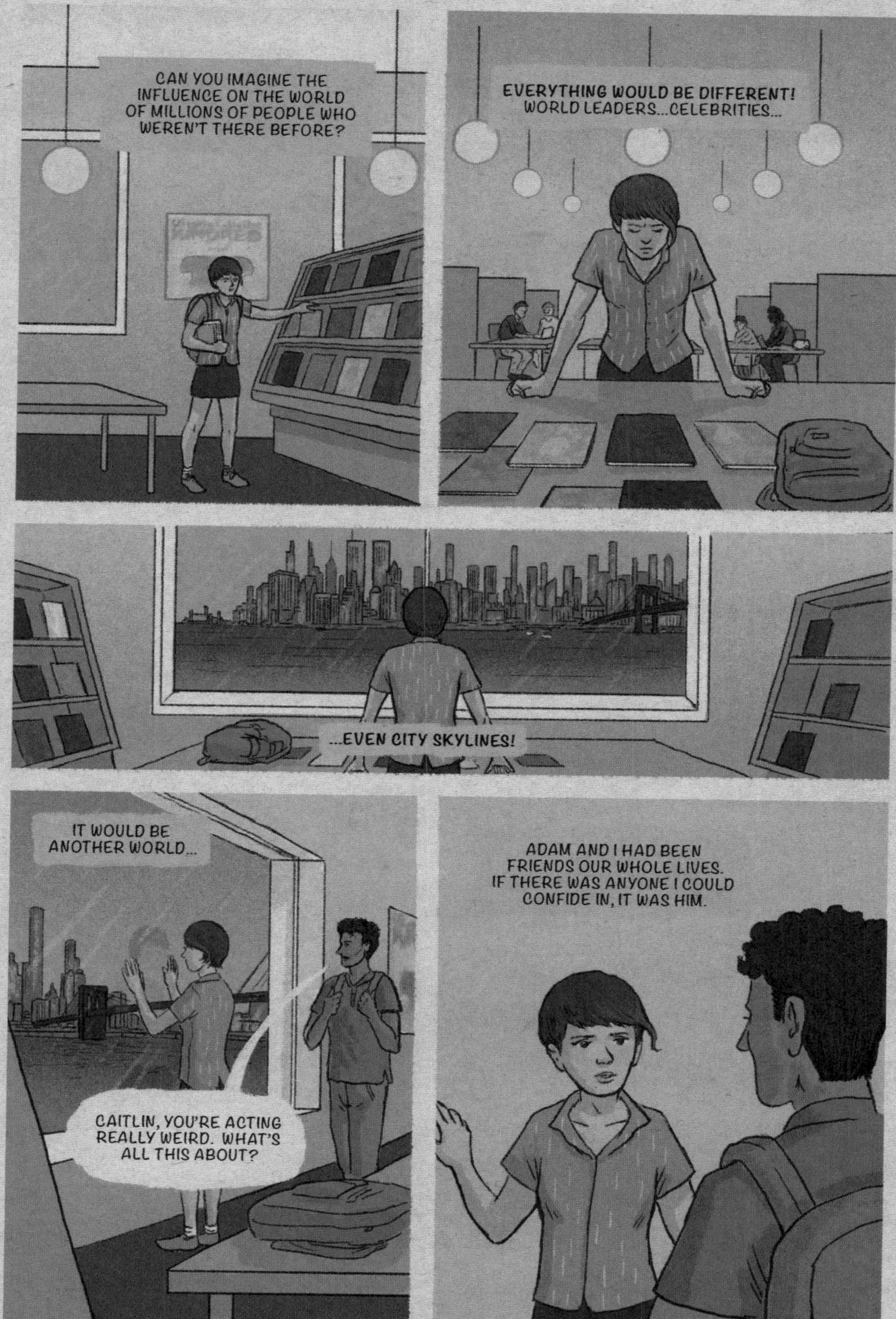

CAN YOU IMAGINE THE INFLUENCE ON THE WORLD OF MILLIONS OF PEOPLE WHO WEREN'T THERE BEFORE?
EVERYTHING WOULD BE DIFFERENT! WORLD LEADERS...CELEBRITIES...
...EVEN CITY SKYLINES!
IT WOULD BE ANOTHER WORLD...
CAITLIN, YOU'RE ACTING REALLY WEIRD. WHAT'S ALL THIS ABOUT?
ADAM AND I HAD BEEN FRIENDS OUR WHOLE LIVES. IF THERE WAS ANYONE I COULD CONFIDE IN, IT WAS HIM.

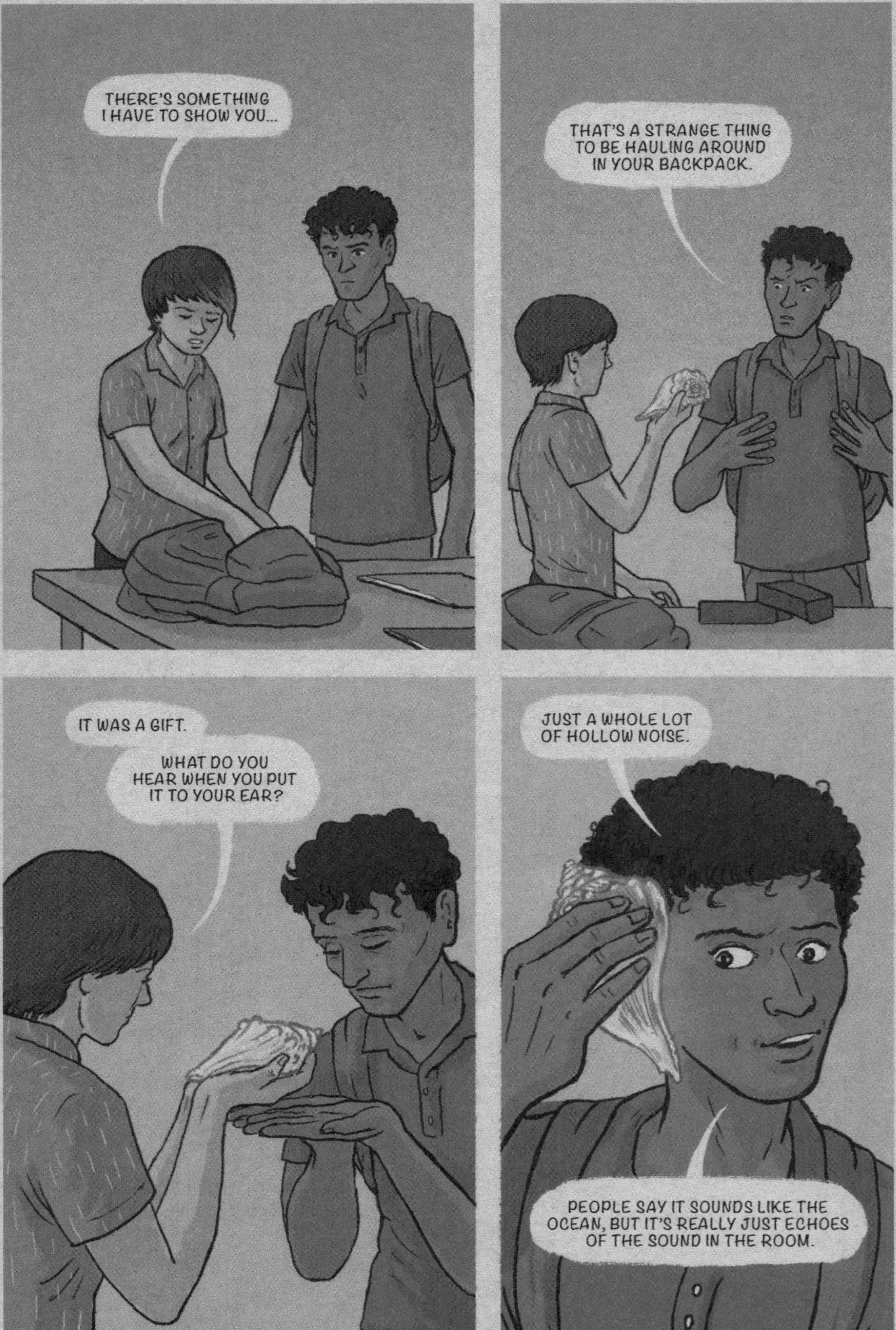
THERE'S SOMETHING I HAVE TO SHOW YOU...
THAT'S A STRANGE THING TO BE HAULING AROUND IN YOUR BACKPACK.
IT WAS A GIFT.
WHAT DO YOU HEAR WHEN YOU PUT IT TO YOUR EAR?
JUST A WHOLE LOT OF HOLLOW NOISE.
PEOPLE SAY IT SOUNDS LIKE THE OCEAN, BUT IT'S REALLY JUST ECHOES OF THE SOUND IN THE ROOM.

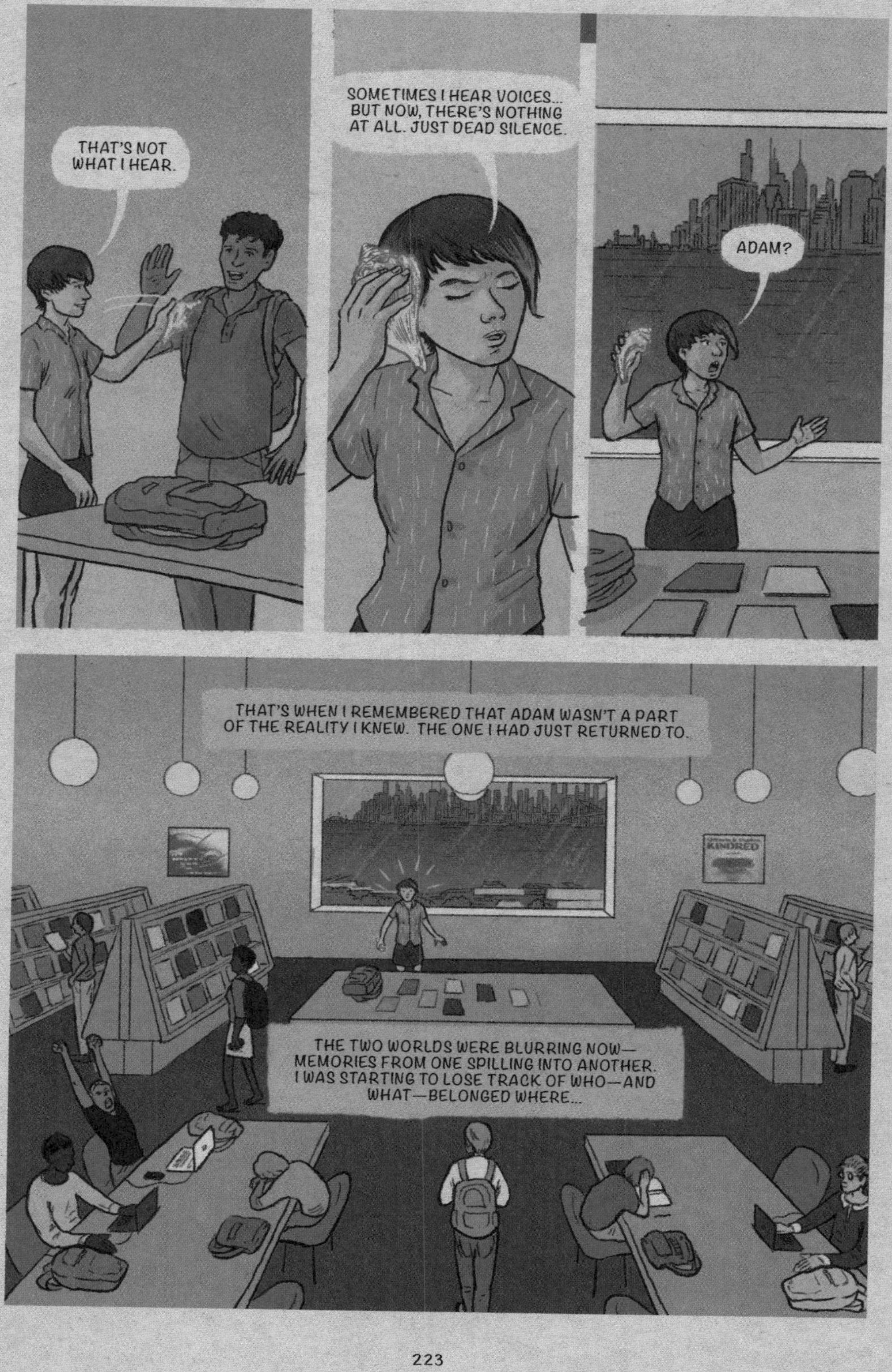
THAT'S NOT WHAT I HEAR.
SOMETIMES I HEAR VOICES... BUT NOW, THERE'S NOTHING AT ALL. JUST DEAD SILENCE.
ADAM?
THAT'S WHEN I REMEMBERED THAT ADAM WASN'T A PART OF THE REALITY I KNEW. THE ONE I HAD JUST RETURNED TO.
KINDRED
THE TWO WORLDS WERE BLURRING NOW— MEMORIES FROM ONE SPILLING INTO ANOTHER. I WAS STARTING TO LOSE TRACK OF WHO—AND WHAT—BELONGED WHERE...

WHEN THE WORLD BEGINS SLIPPING OUT FROM UNDER YOU, YOU TRY TO FIND COMFORT IN THE THINGS THAT ARE FAMILIAR, THE THINGS THAT YOU KNOW.

SO AFTER SCHOOL, I WENT TO GYMNASTICS PRACTICE, JUST LIKE IT WAS ANY OTHER DAY. I TRIED TO LOCK MYSELF INTO THAT REALITY, IF ONLY FOR A LITTLE WHILE.

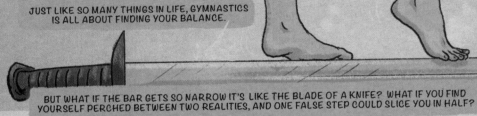

JUST LIKE SO MANY THINGS IN LIFE, GYMNASTICS IS ALL ABOUT FINDING YOUR BALANCE.

BUT WHAT IF THE BAR GETS SO NARROW IT'S LIKE THE BLADE OF A KNIFE? WHAT IF YOU FIND YOURSELF PERCHED BETWEEN TWO REALITIES, AND ONE FALSE STEP COULD SLICE YOU IN HALF?

WE DON'T GET TO CHOOSE BETWEEN WHAT IS AND WHAT MIGHT HAVE BEEN.

BUT WHAT IF WE COULD?

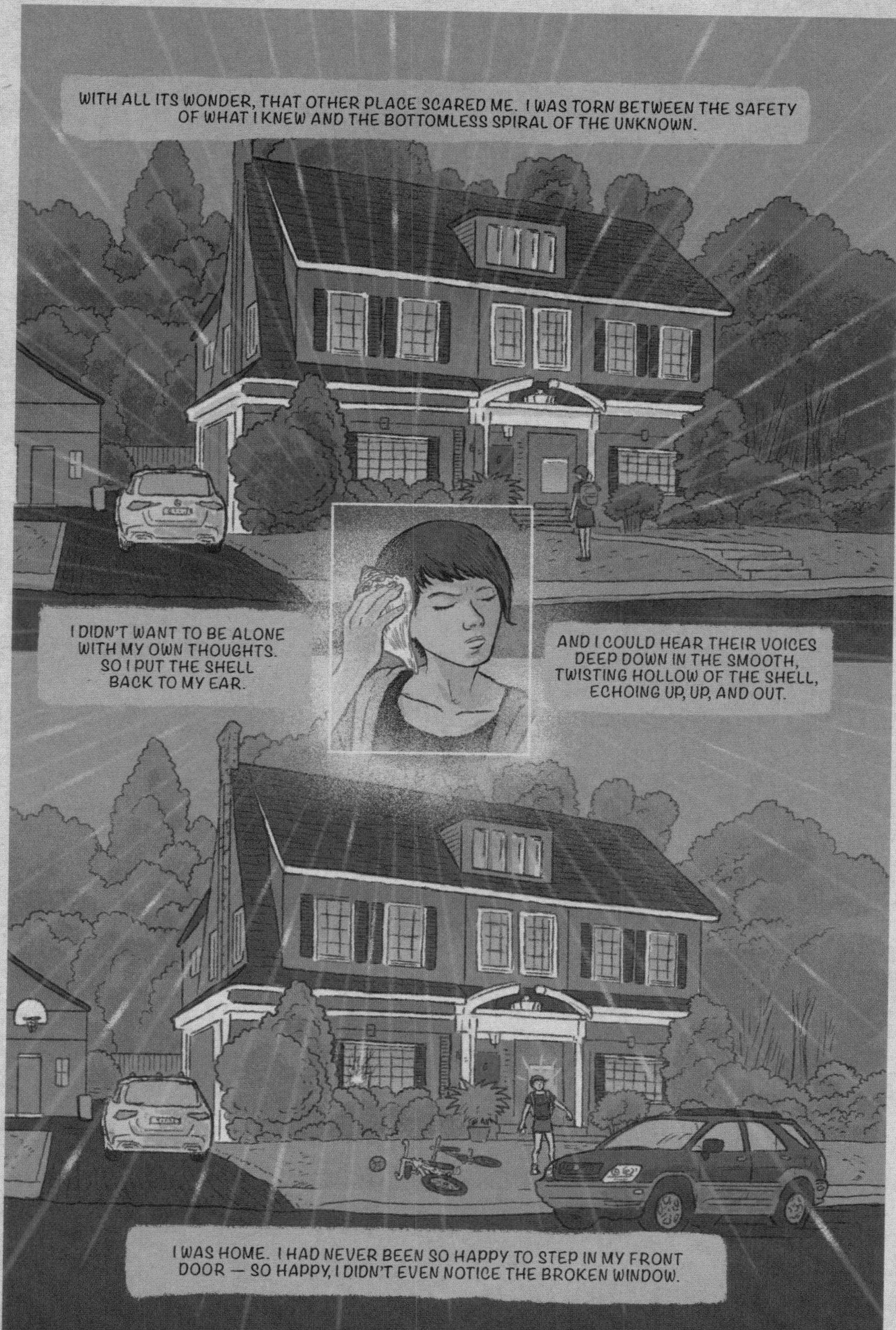
WITH ALL ITS WONDER, THAT OTHER PLACE SCARED ME. I WAS TORN BETWEEN THE SAFETY OF WHAT I KNEW AND THE BOTTOMLESS SPIRAL OF THE UNKNOWN.
I DIDN'T WANT TO BE ALONE WITH MY OWN THOUGHTS. SO I PUT THE SHELL BACK TO MY EAR.
AND I COULD HEAR THEIR VOICES DEEP DOWN IN THE SMOOTH, TWISTING HOLLOW OF THE SHELL, ECHOING UP, UP, AND OUT.
I WAS HOME. I HAD NEVER BEEN SO HAPPY TO STEP IN MY FRONT DOOR — SO HAPPY, I DIDN'T EVEN NOTICE THE BROKEN WINDOW.

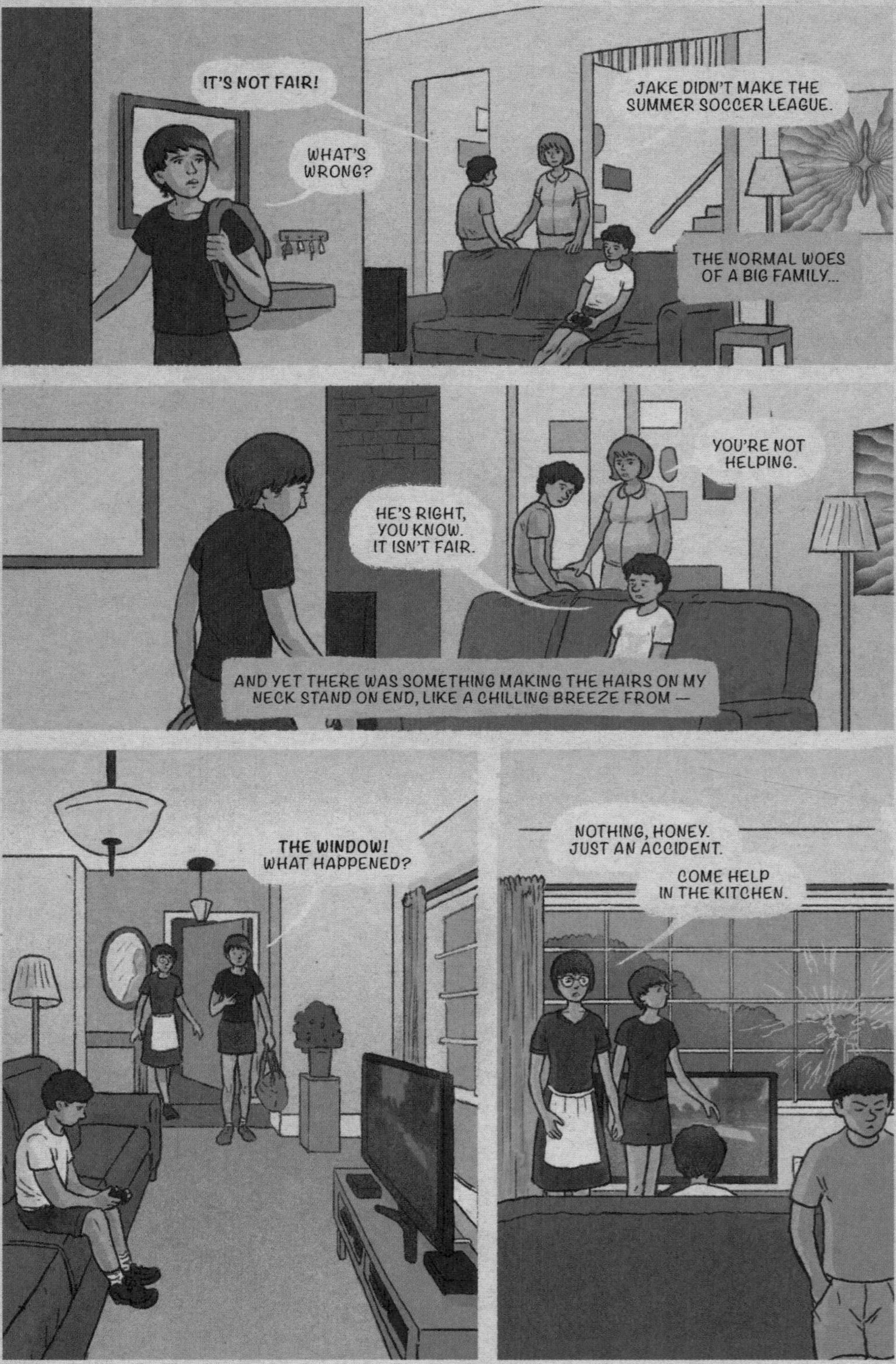
IT'S NOT FAIR!
WHAT'S WRONG?
JAKE DIDN'T MAKE THE SUMMER SOCCER LEAGUE.
THE NORMAL WOES OF A BIG FAMILY...
YOU'RE NOT HELPING.
HE'S RIGHT, YOU KNOW. IT ISN'T FAIR.
AND YET THERE WAS SOMETHING MAKING THE HAIRS ON MY NECK STAND ON END, LIKE A CHILLING BREEZE FROM —
THE WINDOW! WHAT HAPPENED?
NOTHING, HONEY. JUST AN ACCIDENT.
COME HELP IN THE KITCHEN.

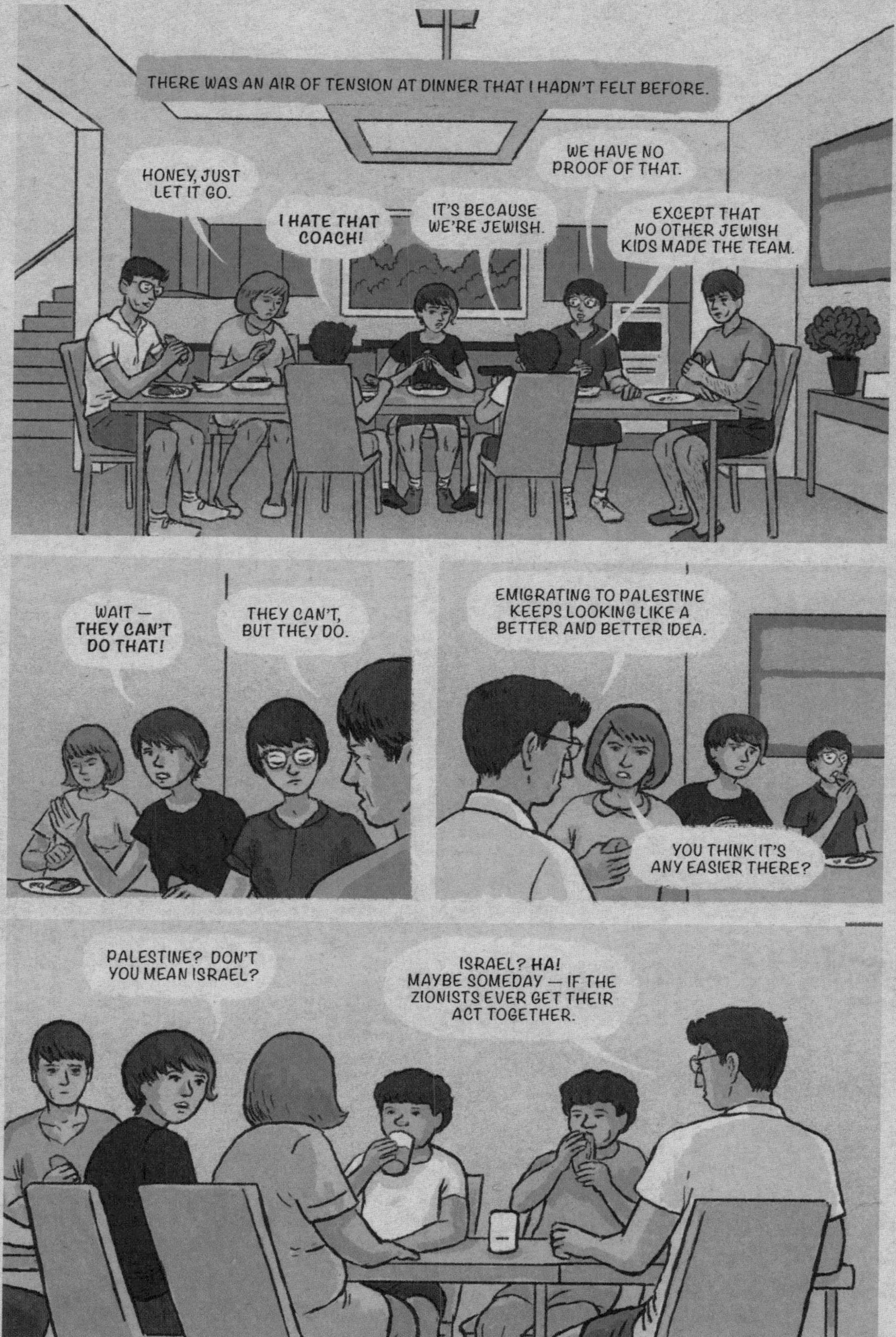
THERE WAS AN AIR OF TENSION AT DINNER THAT I HADN'T FELT BEFORE.
HONEY, JUST LET IT GO.
I HATE THAT COACH!
IT'S BECAUSE WE'RE JEWISH.
WE HAVE NO PROOF OF THAT.
EXCEPT THAT NO OTHER JEWISH KIDS MADE THE TEAM.
WAIT — THEY CAN'T DO THAT!
THEY CAN'T, BUT THEY DO.
EMIGRATING TO PALESTINE KEEPS LOOKING LIKE A BETTER AND BETTER IDEA.
YOU THINK IT'S ANY EASIER THERE?
PALESTINE? DON'T YOU MEAN ISRAEL?
ISRAEL? HA! MAYBE SOMEDAY — IF THE ZIONISTS EVER GET THEIR ACT TOGETHER.

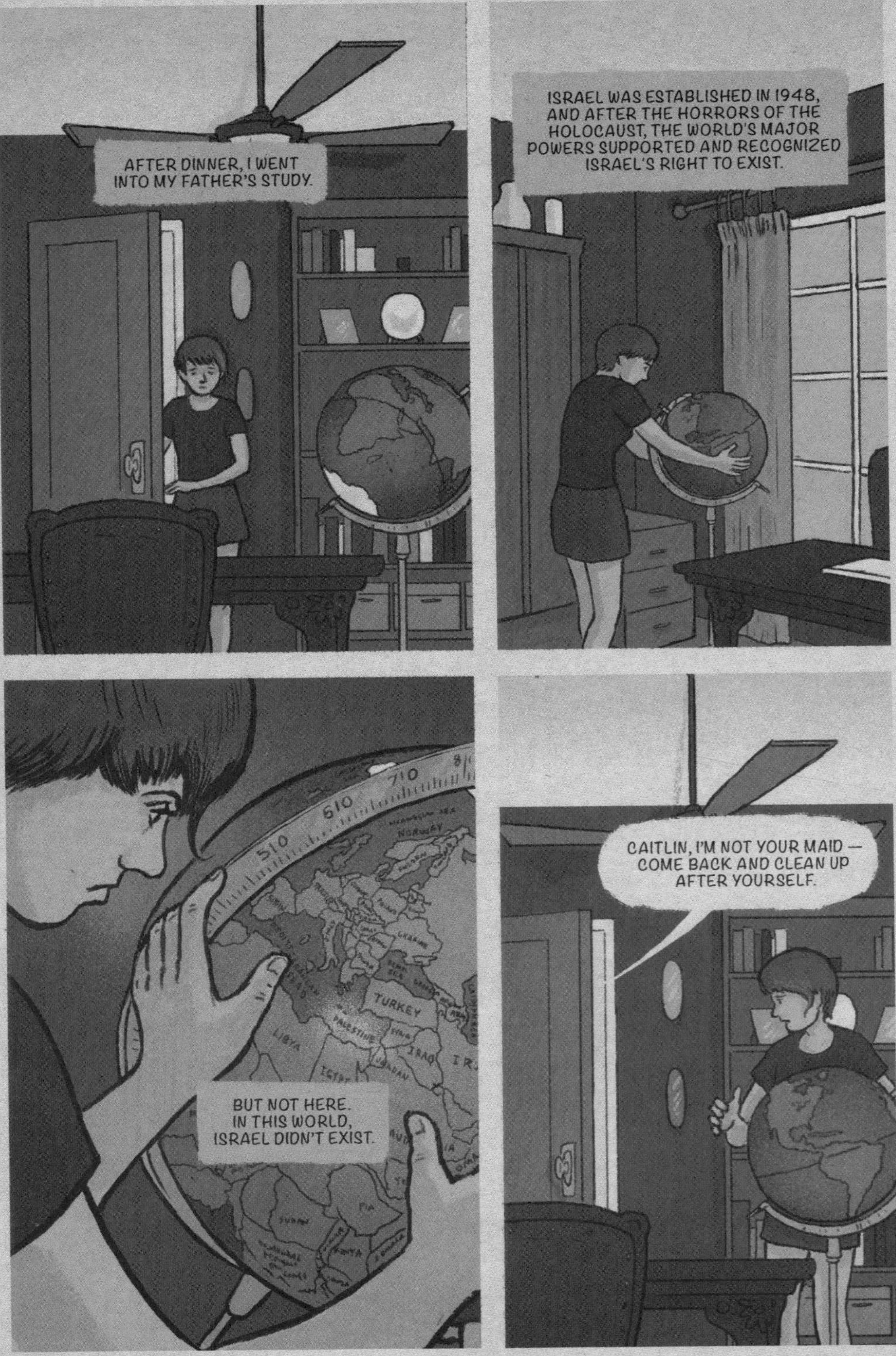
AFTER DINNER, I WENT INTO MY FATHER'S STUDY.
ISRAEL WAS ESTABLISHED IN 1948, AND AFTER THE HORRORS OF THE HOLOCAUST, THE WORLD'S MAJOR POWERS SUPPORTED AND RECOGNIZED ISRAEL'S RIGHT TO EXIST.
TURKEY
PALESTINE
BUT NOT HERE. IN THIS WORLD, ISRAEL DIDN'T EXIST.
CAITLIN, I'M NOT YOUR MAID — COME BACK AND CLEAN UP AFTER YOURSELF.

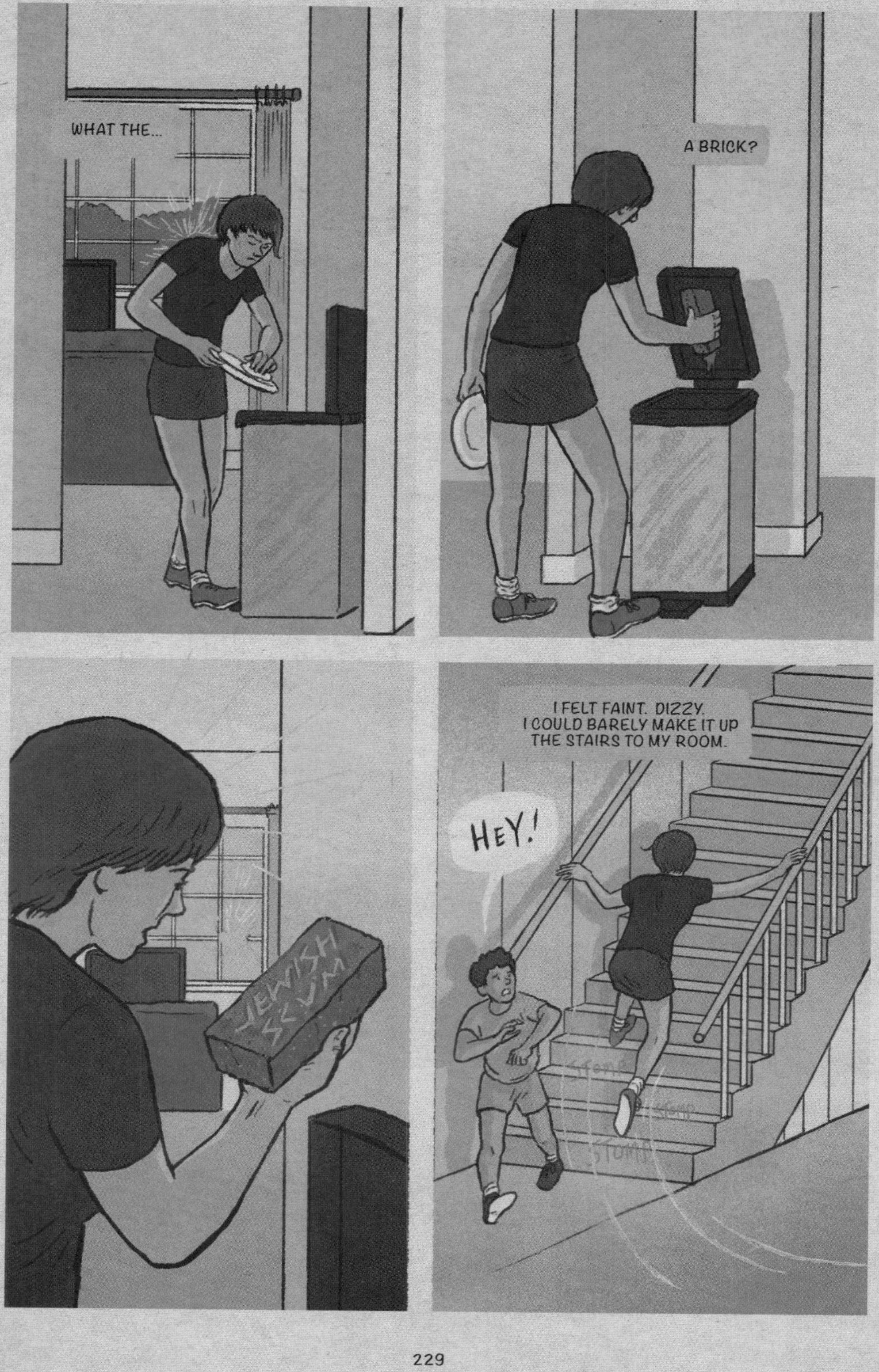
WHAT THE...
A BRICK?
JEWISH SCUM
I FELT FAINT. DIZZY. I COULD BARELY MAKE IT UP THE STAIRS TO MY ROOM.
HEY!
STOMP
STOMP
STOMP

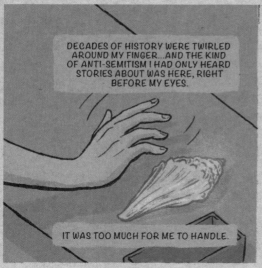

DECADES OF HISTORY WERE TWIRLED AROUND MY FINGER...AND THE KIND OF ANTI-SEMITISM I HAD ONLY HEARD STORIES ABOUT WAS HERE, RIGHT BEFORE MY EYES.
IT WAS TOO MUCH FOR ME TO HANDLE.
THIS TIME, THE SILENCE OF THE SHELL SEEMED TO SUCK THE AIR OUT OF THE ROOM.
I GASPED...AND EVERYTHING WENT BACK TO NORMAL.
610
510
NORWAY
I WAS BACK IN THE WORLD WHERE I STARTED.
TURKEY
ISRAEL
LIBYA
EGYPT
IRAQ
JORDAN
I PROMISED MYSELF I'D LEAVE IT THERE. I'D NEVER LISTEN TO IT AGAIN.
AND I DIDN'T...

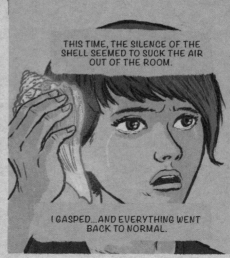

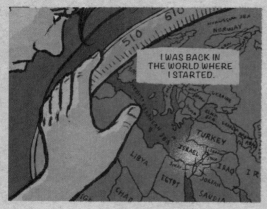

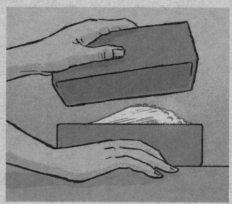

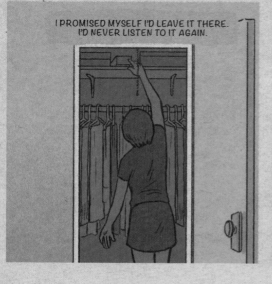

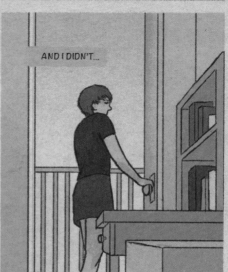

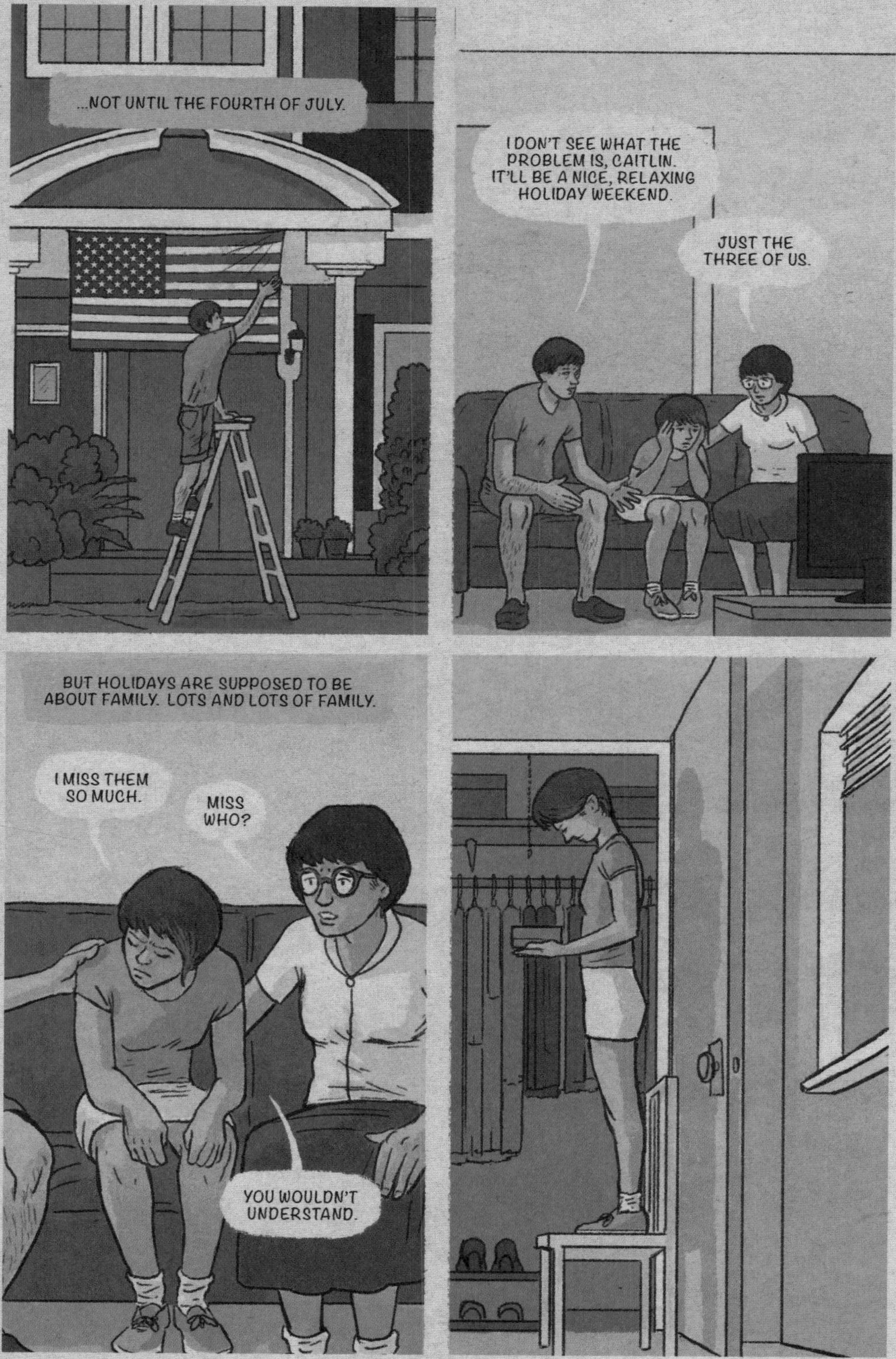
...NOT UNTIL THE FOURTH OF JULY.
I DON'T SEE WHAT THE PROBLEM IS, CAITLIN. IT'LL BE A NICE, RELAXING HOLIDAY WEEKEND.
JUST THE THREE OF US.
BUT HOLIDAYS ARE SUPPOSED TO BE ABOUT FAMILY. LOTS AND LOTS OF FAMILY.
I MISS THEM SO MUCH.
MISS WHO?
YOU WOULDN'T UNDERSTAND.

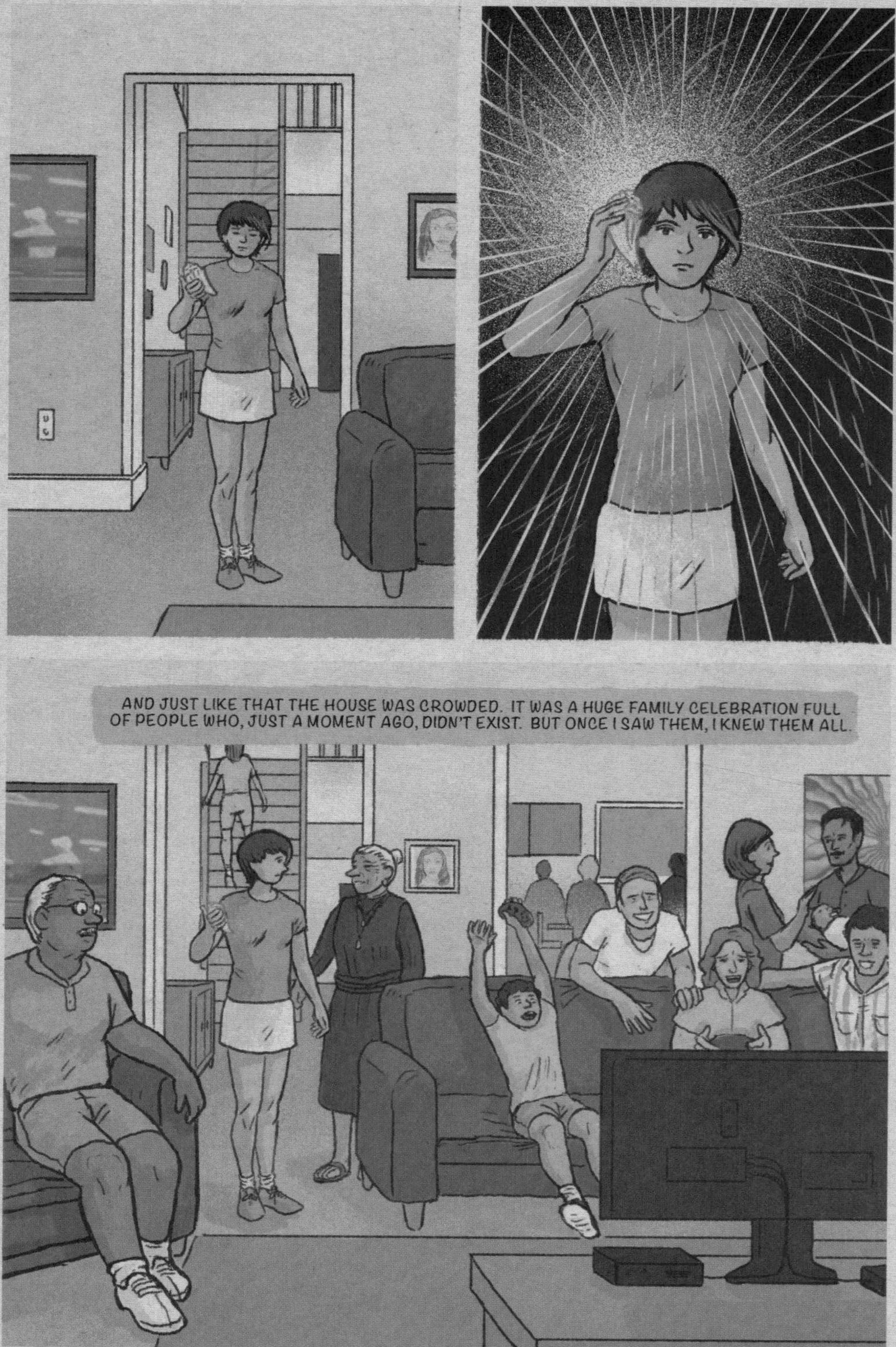
AND JUST LIKE THAT THE HOUSE WAS CROWDED. IT WAS A HUGE FAMILY CELEBRATION FULL OF PEOPLE WHO, JUST A MOMENT AGO, DIDN'T EXIST. BUT ONCE I SAW THEM, I KNEW THEM ALL.

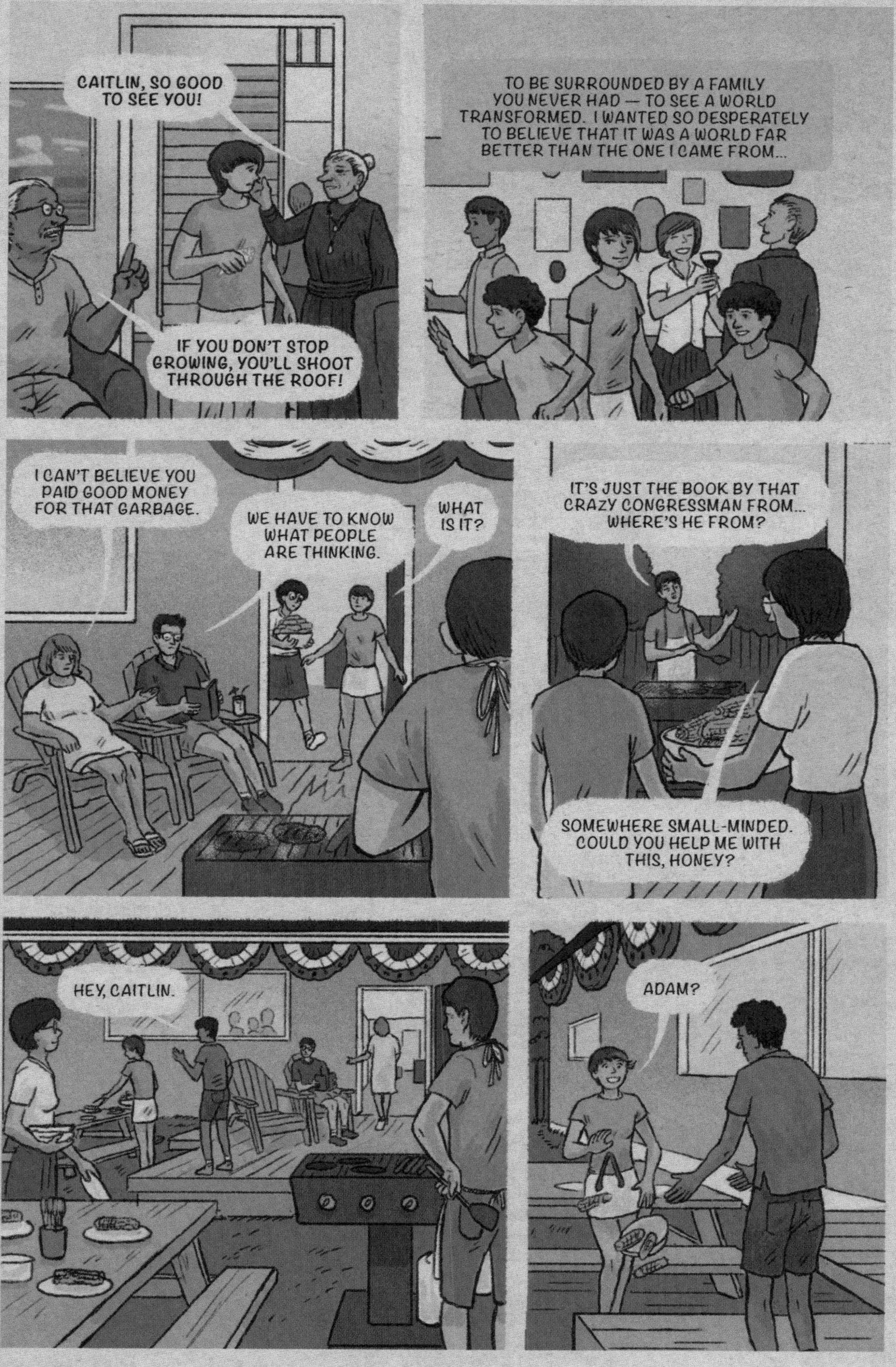
CAITLIN, SO GOOD TO SEE YOU!
IF YOU DON'T STOP GROWING, YOU'LL SHOOT THROUGH THE ROOF!
TO BE SURROUNDED BY A FAMILY YOU NEVER HAD — TO SEE A WORLD TRANSFORMED. I WANTED SO DESPERATELY TO BELIEVE THAT IT WAS A WORLD FAR BETTER THAN THE ONE I CAME FROM...
I CAN'T BELIEVE YOU PAID GOOD MONEY FOR THAT GARBAGE.
WE HAVE TO KNOW WHAT PEOPLE ARE THINKING.
WHAT IS IT?
IT'S JUST THE BOOK BY THAT CRAZY CONGRESSMAN FROM... WHERE'S HE FROM?
SOMEWHERE SMALL-MINDED. COULD YOU HELP ME WITH THIS, HONEY?
HEY, CAITLIN.
ADAM?

ADAM! I'M SO GLAD TO SEE YOU!

YOU JUST SAW ME YESTERDAY.

THE GUY'S A HATE-MONGER. RATIONAL PEOPLE WON'T TAKE HIM SERIOUSLY.

AND YET IT'S A BESTSELLER.

WHY'S THERE A SPIDER ON THE FLAG?

IT'S SOME ANCIENT SYMBOL HE'S USING FOR HIS "MOVEMENT."

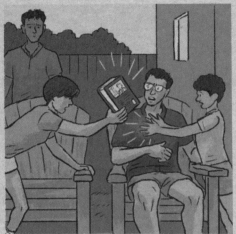

CAITLIN! WHAT'S WRONG?!

NO! IT CAN'T BE...

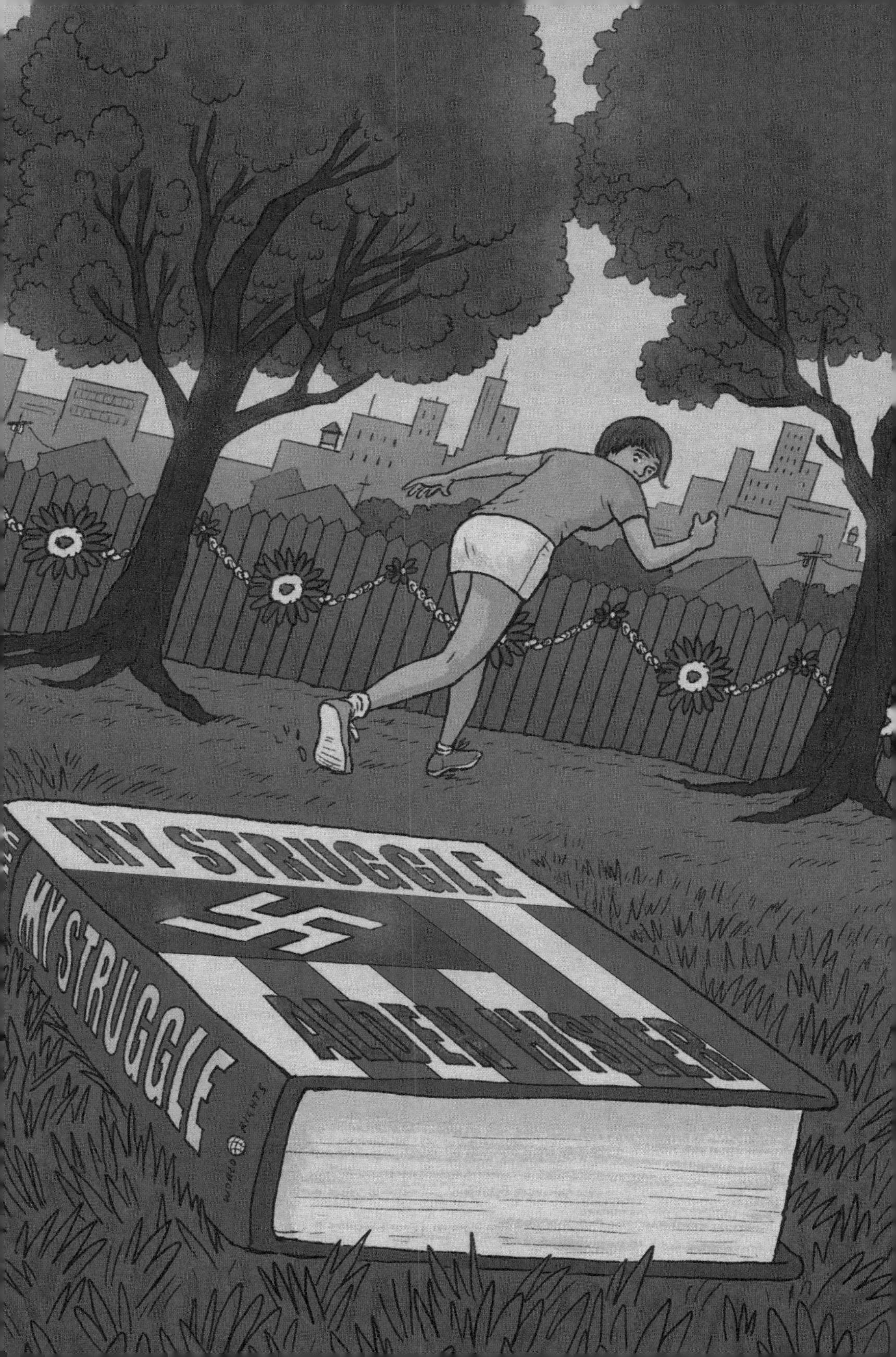
MY STRUGGLE
MY STRUGGLE
WORLD RIGHTS

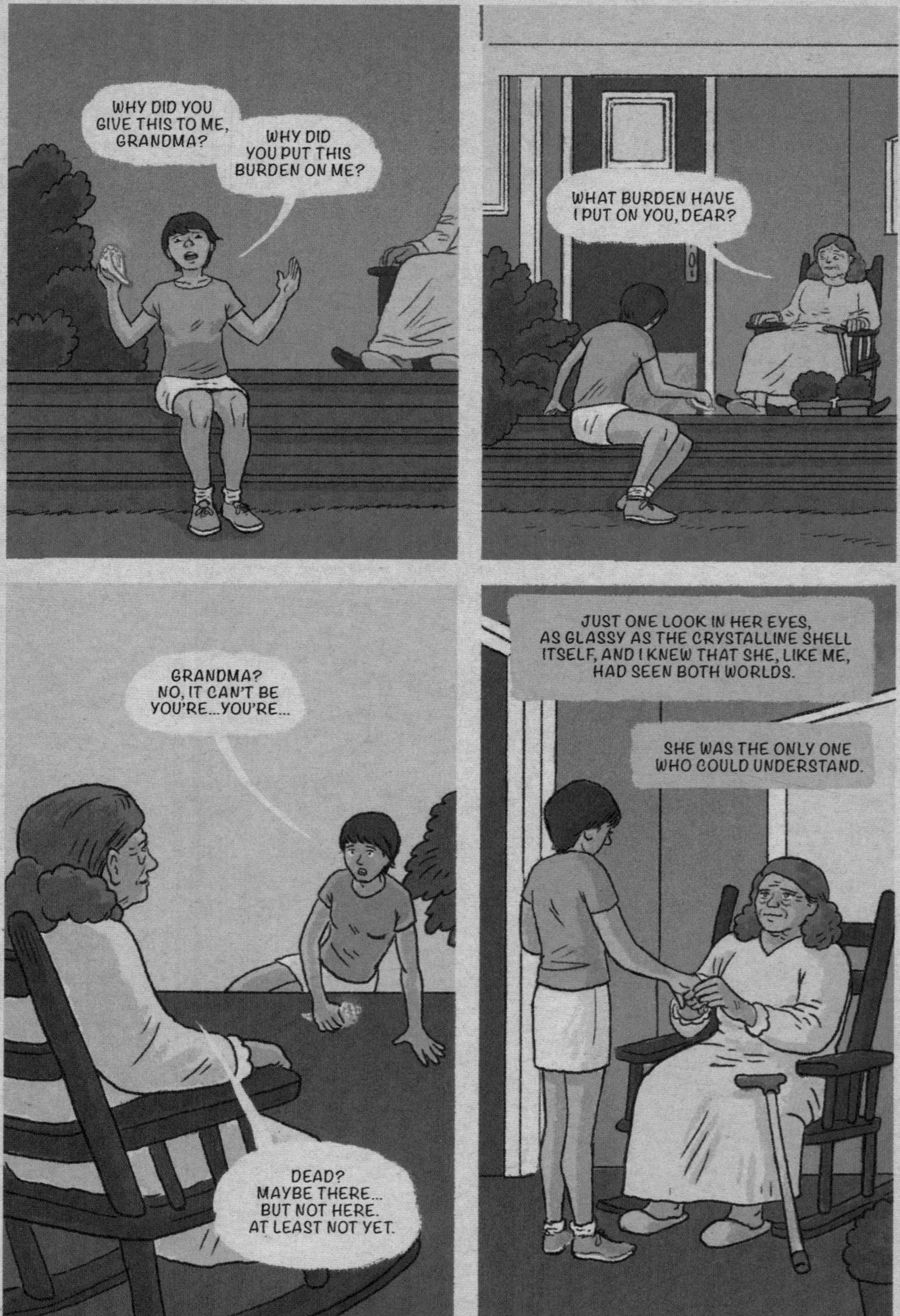
WHY DID YOU GIVE THIS TO ME, GRANDMA?
WHY DID YOU PUT THIS BURDEN ON ME?
WHAT BURDEN HAVE I PUT ON YOU, DEAR?
GRANDMA? NO, IT CAN'T BE YOU'RE...YOU'RE...
DEAD? MAYBE THERE... BUT NOT HERE. AT LEAST NOT YET.
JUST ONE LOOK IN HER EYES, AS GLASSY AS THE CRYSTALLINE SHELL ITSELF, AND I KNEW THAT SHE, LIKE ME, HAD SEEN BOTH WORLDS.
SHE WAS THE ONLY ONE WHO COULD UNDERSTAND.

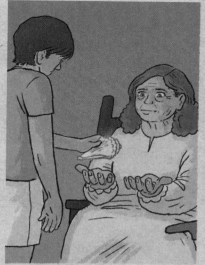

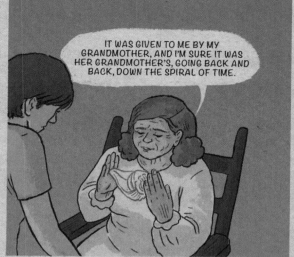

IT WAS GIVEN TO ME BY MY GRANDMOTHER, AND I'M SURE IT WAS HER GRANDMOTHER'S, GOING BACK AND BACK, DOWN THE SPIRAL OF TIME.

SHE TOLD ME SHE PUT IT TO HER EAR DURING THE POGROMS IN THEIR SHTETL, WHEN JEWISH VILLAGES WERE BURNED TO THE GROUND.

SHE TOLD ME SHE SAW A WORLD IN WHICH HER FAMILY STAYED PUT AND FOUGHT FOR THEIR LAND INSTEAD OF COMING TO AMERICA. BUT I'M GLAD SHE CAME. IF SHE DIDN'T, I WOULD NEVER HAVE BEEN BORN!

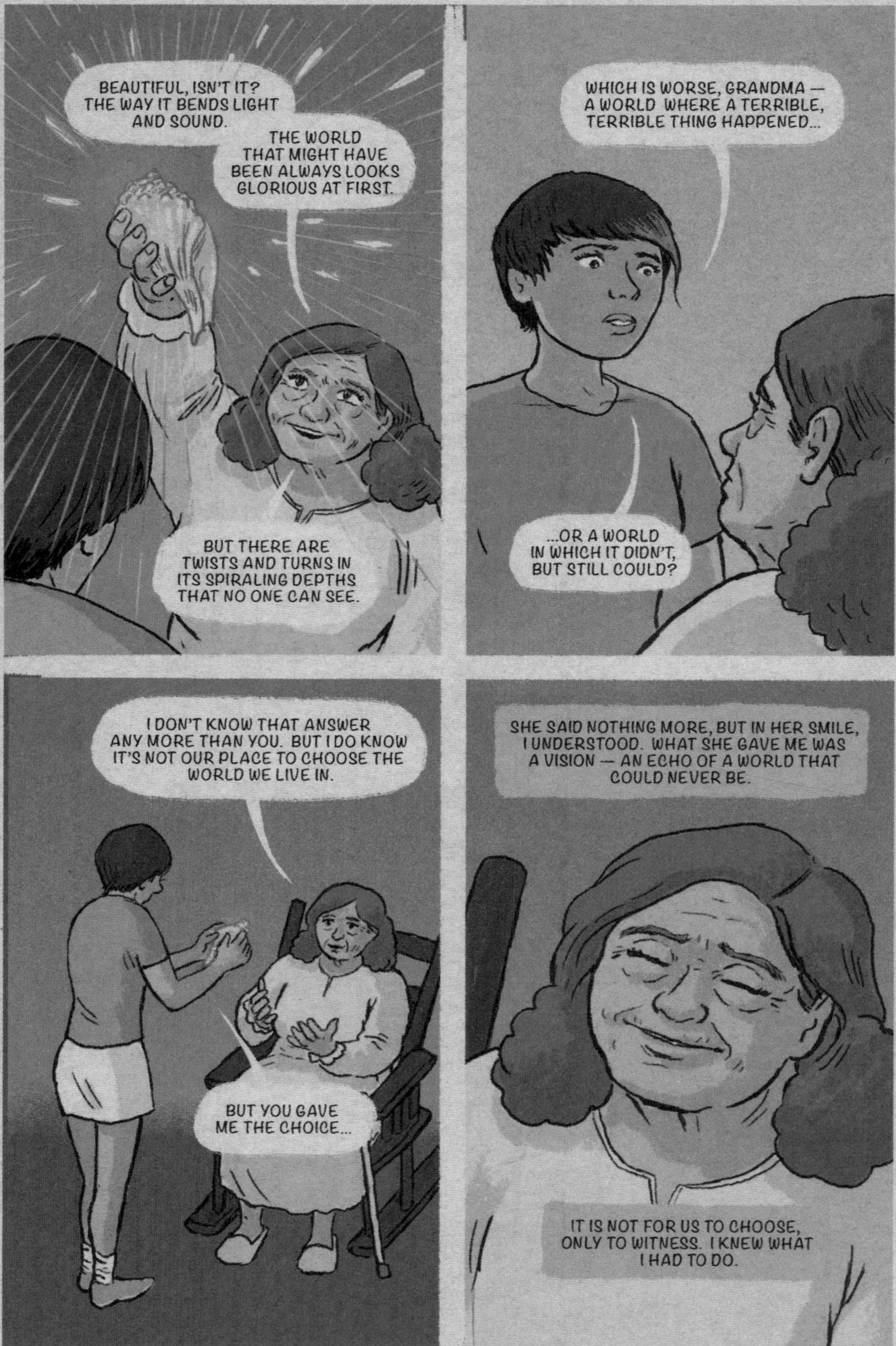
BEAUTIFUL, ISN'T IT? THE WAY IT BENDS LIGHT AND SOUND.
THE WORLD THAT MIGHT HAVE BEEN ALWAYS LOOKS GLORIOUS AT FIRST.
BUT THERE ARE TWISTS AND TURNS IN ITS SPIRALING DEPTHS THAT NO ONE CAN SEE.
WHICH IS WORSE, GRANDMA — A WORLD WHERE A TERRIBLE, TERRIBLE THING HAPPENED...
...OR A WORLD IN WHICH IT DIDN'T, BUT STILL COULD?
I DON'T KNOW THAT ANSWER ANY MORE THAN YOU. BUT I DO KNOW IT'S NOT OUR PLACE TO CHOOSE THE WORLD WE LIVE IN.
BUT YOU GAVE ME THE CHOICE...
SHE SAID NOTHING MORE, BUT IN HER SMILE, I UNDERSTOOD. WHAT SHE GAVE ME WAS A VISION — AN ECHO OF A WORLD THAT COULD NEVER BE.
IT IS NOT FOR US TO CHOOSE, ONLY TO WITNESS. I KNEW WHAT I HAD TO DO.

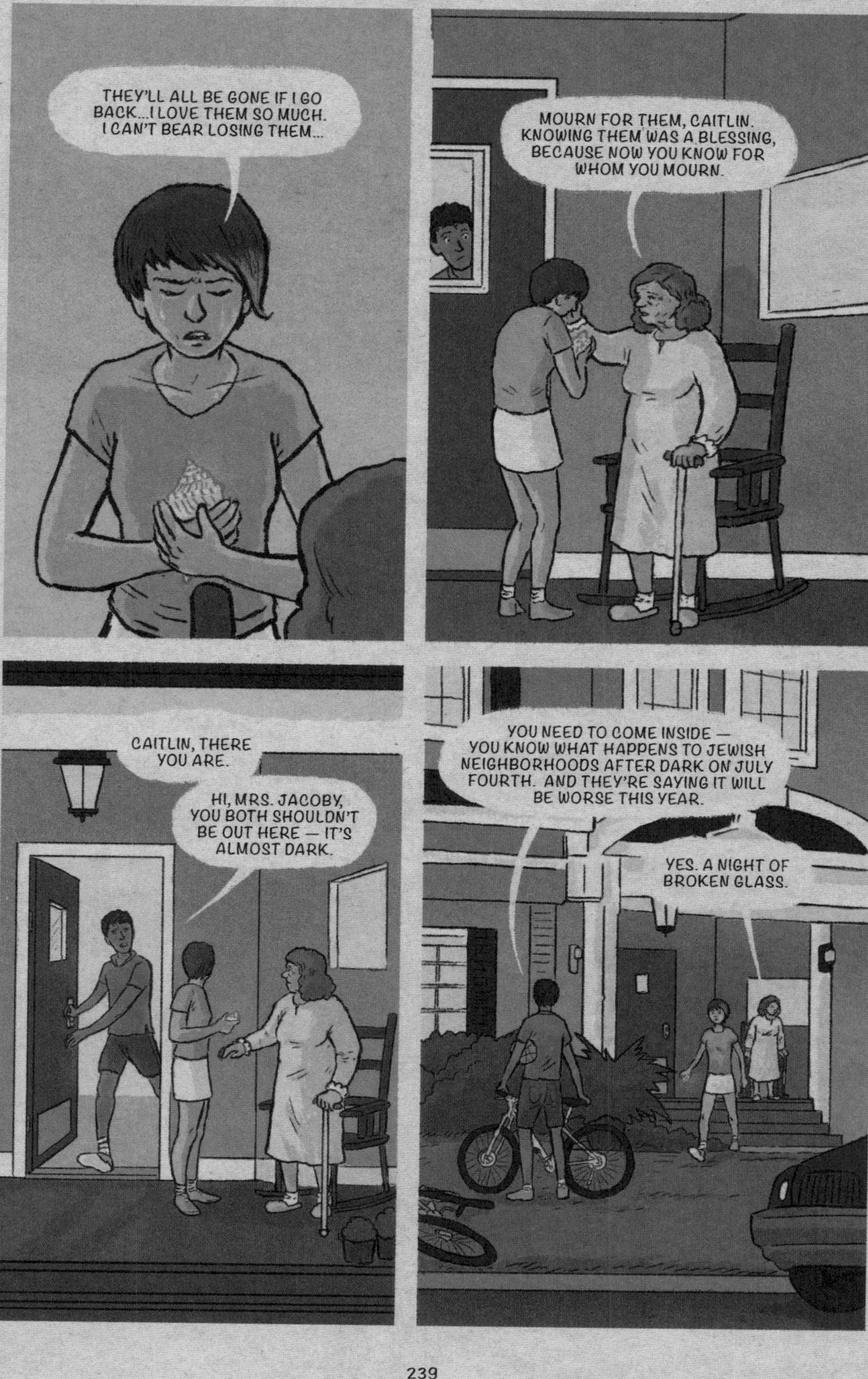
THEY'LL ALL BE GONE IF I GO BACK...I LOVE THEM SO MUCH. I CAN'T BEAR LOSING THEM...
MOURN FOR THEM, CAITLIN. KNOWING THEM WAS A BLESSING, BECAUSE NOW YOU KNOW FOR WHOM YOU MOURN.
CAITLIN, THERE YOU ARE.
HI, MRS. JACOBY, YOU BOTH SHOULDN'T BE OUT HERE — IT'S ALMOST DARK.
YOU NEED TO COME INSIDE — YOU KNOW WHAT HAPPENS TO JEWISH NEIGHBORHOODS AFTER DARK ON JULY FOURTH. AND THEY'RE SAYING IT WILL BE WORSE THIS YEAR.
YES. A NIGHT OF BROKEN GLASS.

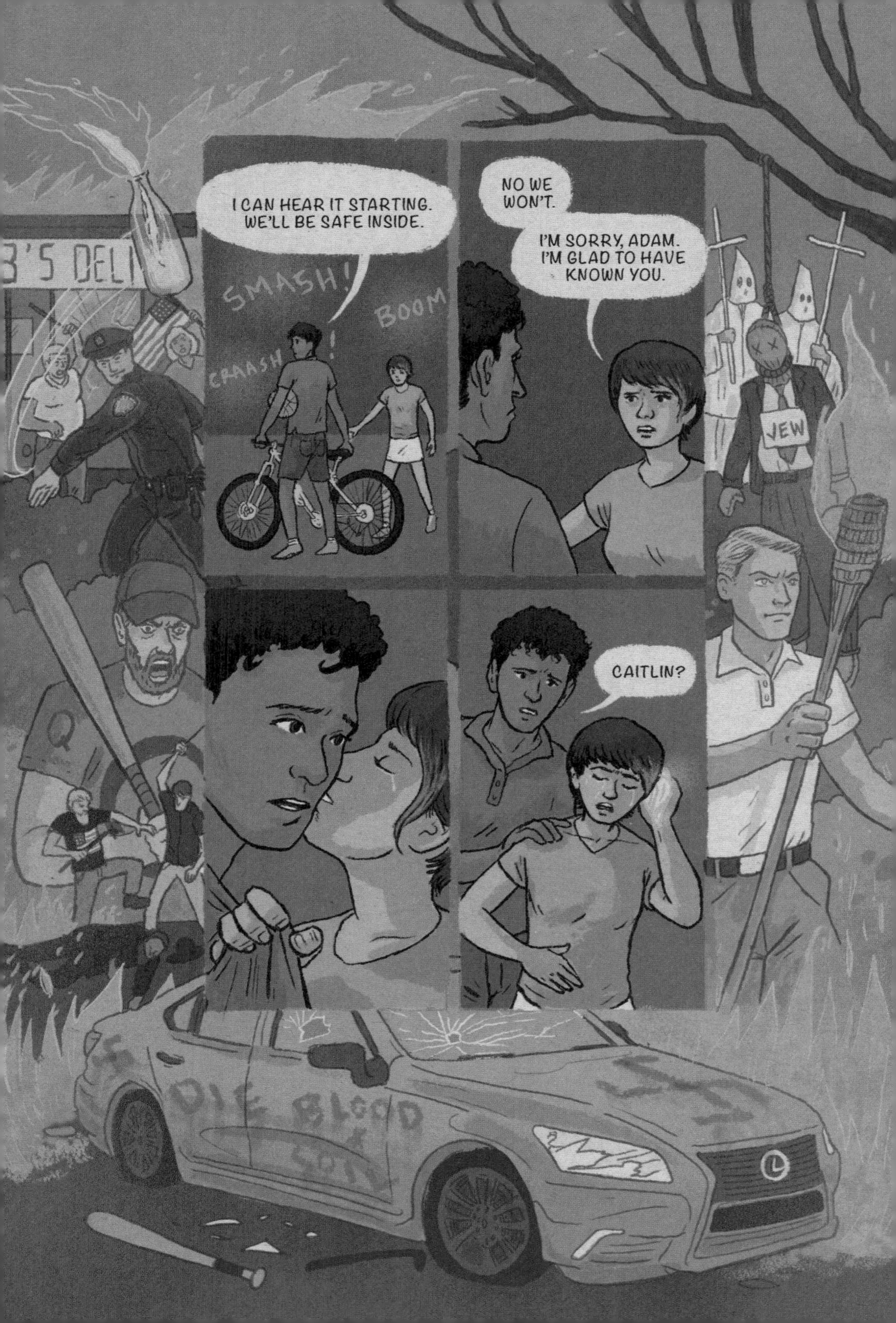

B'S DELI
I CAN HEAR IT STARTING. WE'LL BE SAFE INSIDE.
SMASH!
BOOM
CRAASH
NO WE WON'T.
I'M SORRY, ADAM. I'M GLAD TO HAVE KNOWN YOU.
JEW
CAITLIN?
DIE
BLOOD

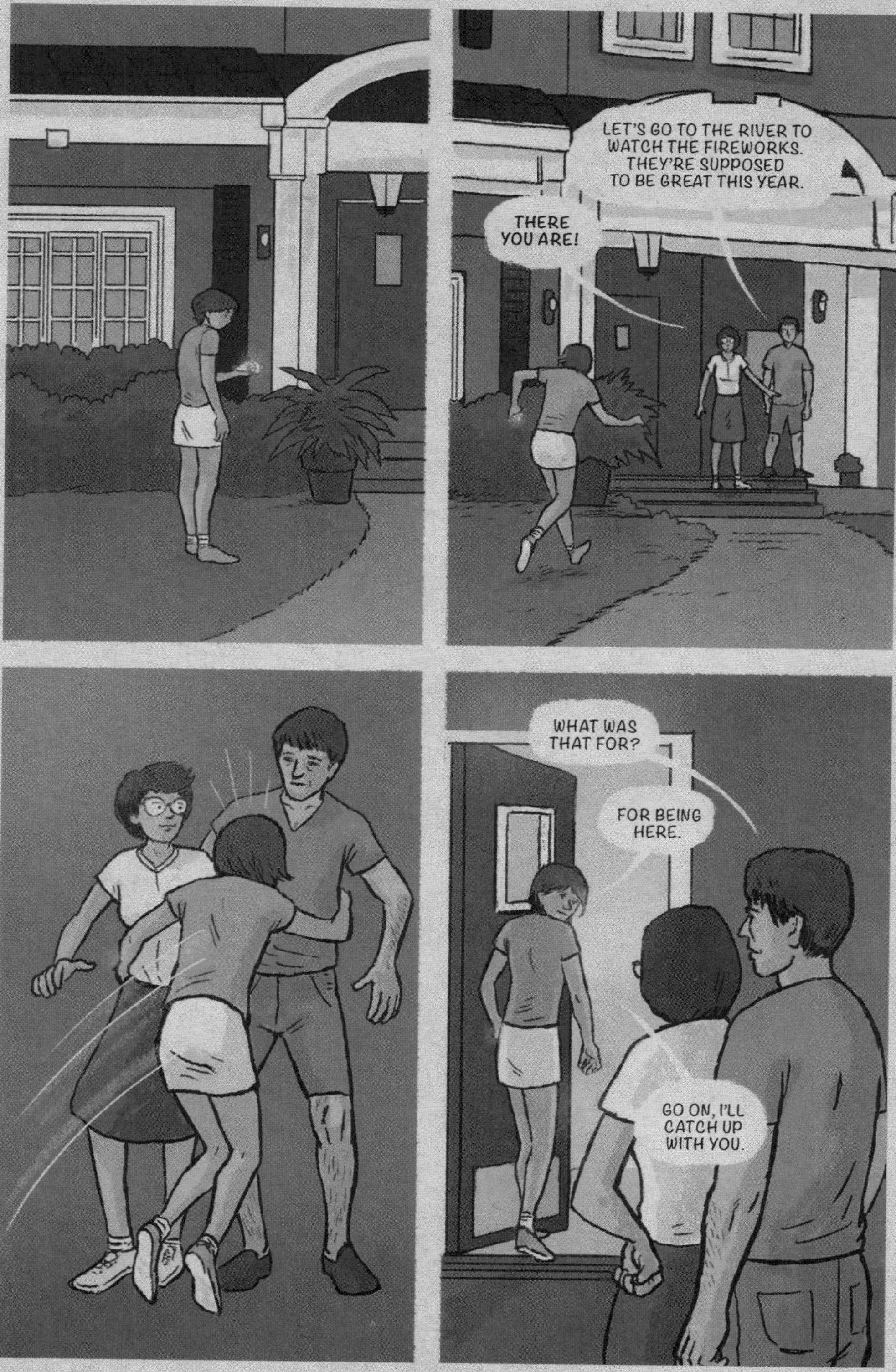
THERE YOU ARE!
LET'S GO TO THE RIVER TO WATCH THE FIREWORKS. THEY'RE SUPPOSED TO BE GREAT THIS YEAR.
WHAT WAS THAT FOR?
FOR BEING HERE.
GO ON, I'LL CATCH UP WITH YOU.

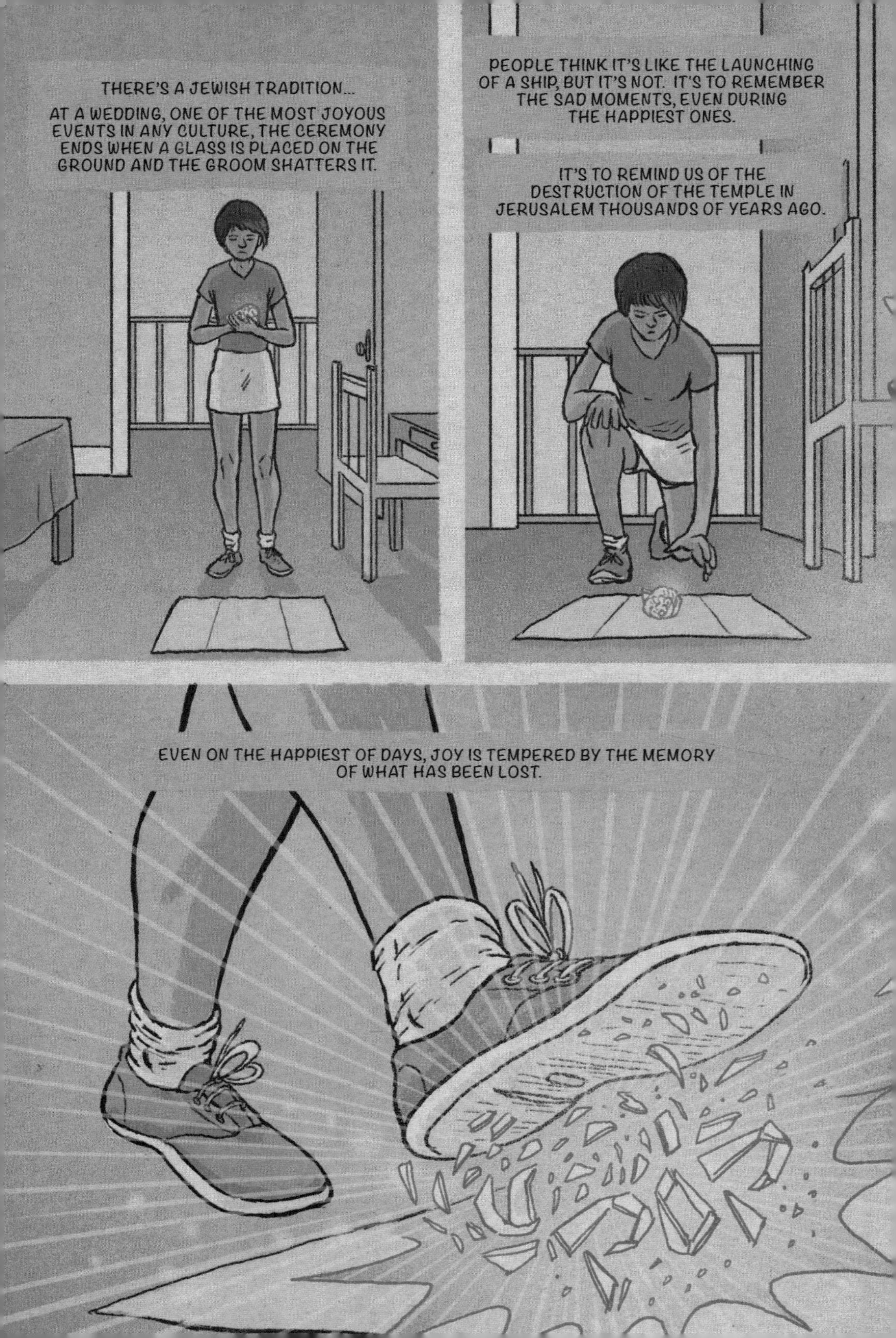
THERE'S A JEWISH TRADITION...
AT A WEDDING, ONE OF THE MOST JOYOUS EVENTS IN ANY CULTURE, THE CEREMONY ENDS WHEN A GLASS IS PLACED ON THE GROUND AND THE GROOM SHATTERS IT.
PEOPLE THINK IT'S LIKE THE LAUNCHING OF A SHIP, BUT IT'S NOT. IT'S TO REMEMBER THE SAD MOMENTS, EVEN DURING THE HAPPIEST ONES.
IT'S TO REMIND US OF THE DESTRUCTION OF THE TEMPLE IN JERUSALEM THOUSANDS OF YEARS AGO.
EVEN ON THE HAPPIEST OF DAYS, JOY IS TEMPERED BY THE MEMORY OF WHAT HAS BEEN LOST.

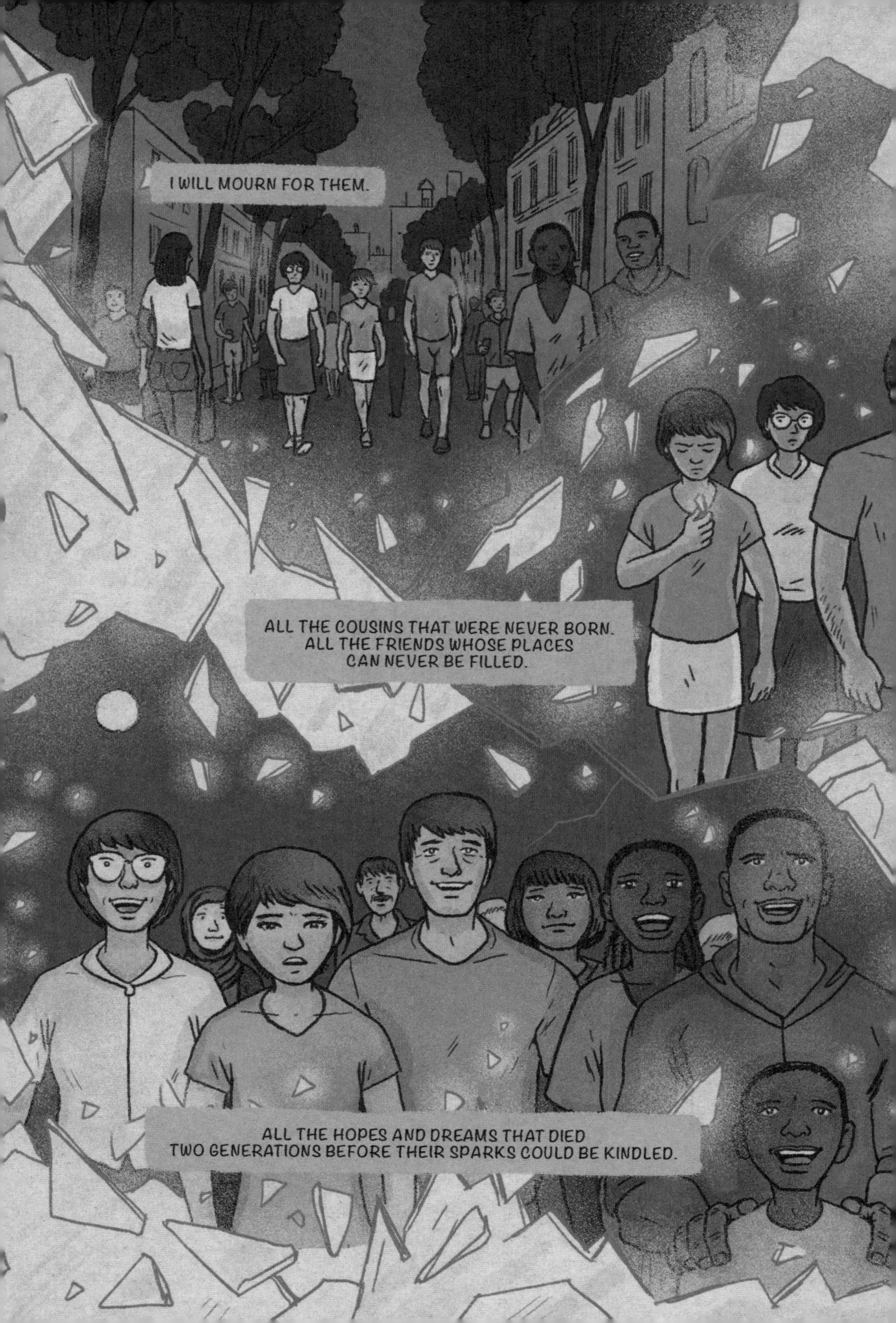
I WILL MOURN FOR THEM.
ALL THE COUSINS THAT WERE NEVER BORN. ALL THE FRIENDS WHOSE PLACES CAN NEVER BE FILLED.
ALL THE HOPES AND DREAMS THAT DIED TWO GENERATIONS BEFORE THEIR SPARKS COULD BE KINDLED.

I WILL REMEMBER WHAT NEVER WAS.
AND IN THAT MEMORY, I WILL FIND STRENGTH...
...AND PURPOSE...
...AND THE COURAGE OF MILLIONS.

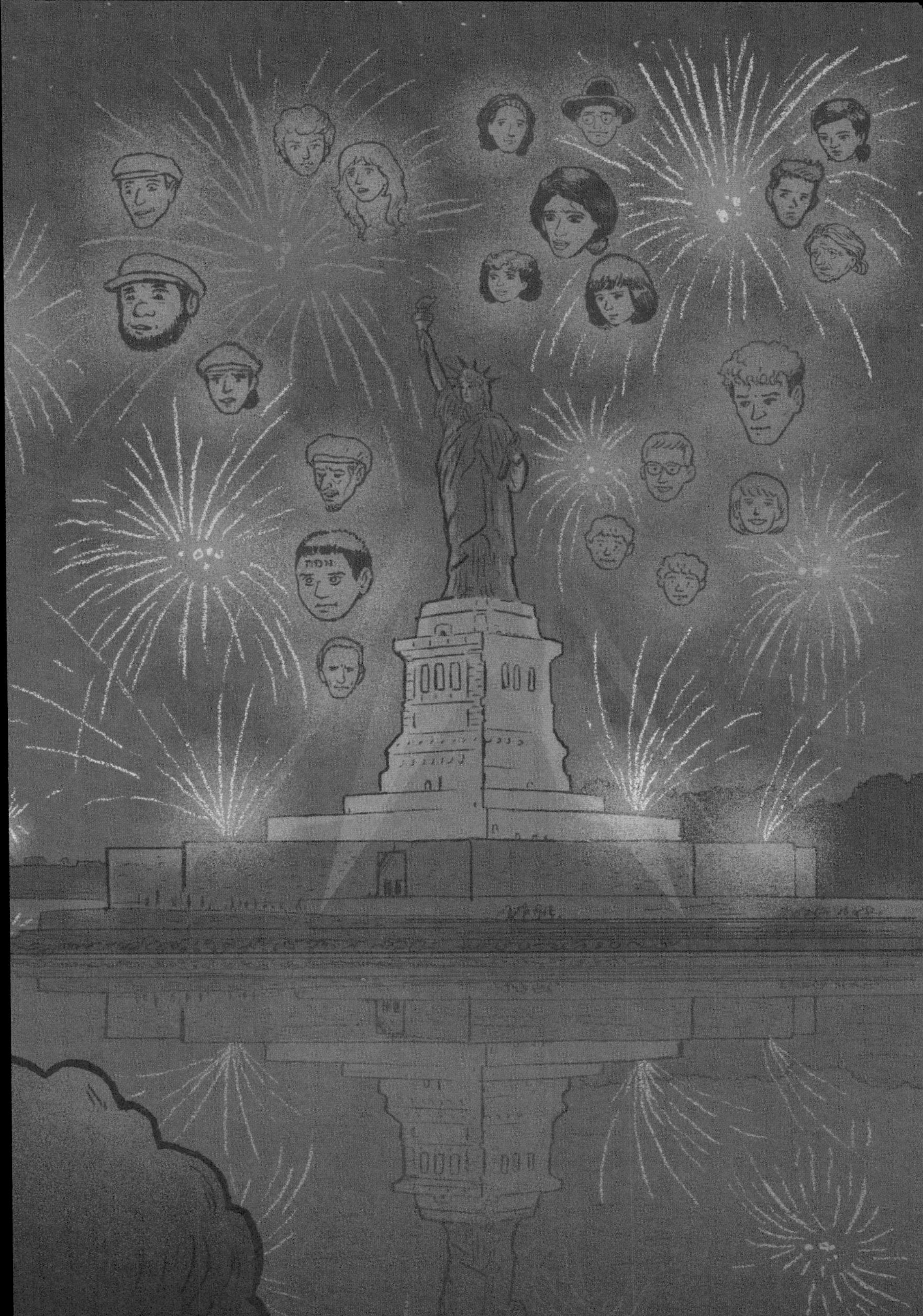

Imagination and the Unimaginable

I've wanted to write a Holocaust-themed book for many years, but the prospect always daunted me. What can I add that has not already been said? What authority do I have, as an American Jew, to tell the stories of the millions lost before I was born . . . and do I have the courage to stare into that dark abyss?

Yet as I've seen the very real specter of hate rise in the world — both abroad and as close as my own backyard — and as I've seen the unmitigated evil of Holocaust denial take root in the fertile soil of willful ignorance, I knew I had to do my part. I had to put something out there to shine some light into dark corners where things fester.

When Andrea Pinkney at Scholastic approached me with the idea of a graphic novel, I realized this was the opportunity I was waiting for. I had a short story — "He Opens a Window" — that I decided to adapt into graphic format, as the cornerstone of an anthology. But what would the other stories be?

The very concept of fantasy stories with a Holocaust theme felt both exciting and uncomfortable to me. Where is the intersection of fantasy and the grim reality of murdered millions? But the more I thought about it, the more I realized there were powerful stories to tell. There are stories of wish fulfillment, where the tragedy lies in the fact that they can never be fulfilled. And there are stories we've told over the ages that bridge the gap between folklore and harsh reality, to help save us — stories with magical beings and mystical objects that stand as metaphors for hope, survival, and collective grief.

As the stories came to me, I realized that this was a unique way of addressing the Holocaust and perhaps engaging readers who might not otherwise go there. Also, I wanted these stories to be a way to not just condemn the perpetrators and honor the victims, but also to acknowledge the thousands of individuals in Germany, Denmark, and the rest of Europe who made a difference. These were the "Righteous among the Nations," who saved Jews and others targeted by the genocidal Third Reich, often at risk to their own lives.

I also felt it was critical to take an unflinching look at a reality where the Holocaust never happened — but in which it still could. How much worse would the horror have been with twenty-first-century technology? In a perfect world, the Holocaust would never have happened and never could . . . but as we all know, we do not live in a perfect world.

The stories had come together, but at that point, it was still just text. Words and ideas are just a blueprint for a graphic novel — it was still a blank canvas aching for poignant and powerful visuals. I was thrilled when Andrés Vera Martínez was brought on to the project! His amazing artwork raises the book to a whole new level with such images as the dream worlds outside of Anna's window, Duvid triumphant even as he dissolves back to ash, and the ships rising in the churning Øresund. Andrés's artwork takes my breath away each time I look at it!

It is our hope that *Courage to Dream* will reach the broadest possible audience and give readers a new and poignant perspective on humanity's greatest crime — as well as provide a warning for what happens when authority gives permission to hate.

Perhaps these surreal stories will encourage readers to dive deeper into the reality of the Holocaust — because it takes knowledge and perspective to exorcise the shadows of hate and ignorance — and if this book can, in its own small way, enlighten . . . that would be wish fulfillment for me.

— **Neal Shusterman**

The Power of Art vs the Wickedness of Hate

When I received the manuscript for *Courage to Dream*, the first thing that struck me was how Neal masterfully entwined Jewish history and folklore into the same stories. I had never read anything like it, and I knew I had to be a part of the project.

Courage to Dream is engaging and deeply necessary. It allows young people and the adults in their lives to have the difficult conversations about our history. We need stories like these, not just for humanity to learn from its mistakes, but to heal and to dream into existence a more just future.

As the cartoonist, I was tasked to create the visual world in which the stories take place, how the characters look and interact, and to bring it all to life. Fantastic elements and harsh realities played a powerful part in Neal's nuanced storytelling. I needed to find an artistic style that mirrored that balance. As part of my research, I collected numerous historical photos to help me accurately depict clothing, architecture, uniforms, and even landscapes of the time. Then, I turned to art history to research the extraordinary aspects of the stories, searching through dozens of ancient paintings, sculptures, and period illustrations to design the magical elements and characters. This intensive research proved to be a very fulfilling part of rendering the world of *Courage to Dream*.

The bigger challenge, given how serious the subject matter is, was finding my own motivation for the work. I found strength in my Tejano family's experience of surviving the violence of white supremacists in my home state of Texas. My people have experienced some 5,000 state-sanctioned lynchings, as well as uninvestigated police shootings, land theft, forced deportations, racially motivated mass shootings, and divisive segregation policies for more than 150 years. Neal's stories are a stark reminder to all of us that if injustice is not openly dealt with and addressed, we, as a society, remain threatened by violence rooted in the hatred of our differences. This is the truth that inspired my artistic vision for the book.

While *Courage to Dream* illuminates one of the darkest periods in human history, I understood that it was necessary to find an artistic style that would engage young readers. My search led me back to the work of Jewish American comic book artists that inspired me as a young person. My introduction to drawing and superheroes was through my Uncle Adam's comic book collection. When I was young, Tío Adam would entertain me by drawing — with great skill — our favorite characters. My lifelong love of art and storytelling was sparked by trying to emulate my uncle's drawing skills and by reading Marvel Comics.

Being a fan of Marvel Comics writers and artists as a boy led me to become a writer and artist. Stanley Martin Lieber and Jacob Kurtzberg, better known as Stan Lee and Jack Kirby, the creators of the Marvel Universe, became my real-life heroes. I studied their early life and careers. Lieber and Kurtzberg had changed their Jewish names to Lee and Kirby. They grew up enduring discrimination in the United States just like me and my family. Jack Kirby and Stan Lee and a long list of talented Jewish American writers and artists formed the backbone of the comic book industry. I continue to admire their careers and how they have shaped popular American culture. Although our backgrounds are different, I found a lot in common with them. As a Native American Spanish artist from Texas, I do my best to channel the superpowers of Stan Lee and Jack Kirby in every project. If you look closely at the main characters in *Courage to Dream*, you will see I try to tell the stories with Marvel's unique blend of relatable humanity alongside powerful punches, blazing energy beams, and magical mystery, fighting for justice on every page. Neal Shusterman's *Courage to Dream* has given me the chance to express this, and I feel very fortunate to be part of this long tradition of making fantastic illustrated stories full of inspiration and hope.

— **Andrés Vera Martínez**

Acknowledgments

What an amazing twelve-year journey this book has been! There are so many people to thank, I don't know where to begin. No, wait, actually I do. Andrés Vera Martínez! Andrés, your spectacular artwork not only brings these stories to life but infuses them with startling imagery that stays with you long after you're done reading. Your artwork still, literally, gives me chills when I look at it! I can't thank you enough!

And just as importantly, Andrea Pinkney, my editor. Andrea, your passion for this project over these years has never waned; you have been a grounding and inspiring force. When I felt overwhelmed and daunted by the magnitude of this undertaking, you were there to champion the book and encourage me. Never before was I so in need of an editor to tell me "you got this," and with a Jedi swipe of the hand, make me believe it. I also thank publisher David Saylor and everyone else at Scholastic who worked behind the scenes to make this book possible — including creative director Phil Falco; production editor Holland Baker; and Ed Masessa, who championed this book from the very beginning!

My heartfelt gratitude to Holocaust historian Peter Black for his expertise in Holocaust history and in making sure the book was as accurate as possible — from the facts, to the authenticity of the fiction, to the details of the characters' uniforms. I'd also like to thank Rabbi Daniel H. Freelander for his many valuable insights.

Thanks to my literary agent, Andrea Brown, not just for being an amazing agent, but for being such a dear friend. Thank you, Taryn Fagerness, for your work selling my books globally — and a special thanks to all the international publishers who have been bringing my books to the rest of the world!

I am forever grateful to my managers, Trevor Engelson and Josh McGuire, my entertainment industry agents Steve Fisher and Debbie Deuble-Hill at APA, and my contract attorneys, Shep Rosenman and Jennifer Justman. Guys, I love you all like the brothers and sisters I never had. Thanks to artist and friend Jeffrey Schrier, whose Judaic artwork truly inspires me. Jeffrey, it is an honor to call you and Jeanne friends, and although we didn't get to work on *Courage to Dream* together, it is my hope that we might still collaborate one day.

Thanks to my two closest friends Eric Elfman, for helping me with research for the nonfiction sections that give context to the stories, and Keith Richardson, who has taken it upon himself to be my (amazing) marketing manager and who worries about me like a Jewish grandmother.

I am grateful to, and for, Rabbi Gersh Zylberman, who has been a guiding light to our family for years, and with whom I shared early drafts of the book. Rabbi Gersh, your thoughts and encouragement have meant so much to me on every level.

Thanks to my assistant, Barb Sobel, who is remarkable at managing a long-distance life, and my research assistant, Symone Powell, who always finds a way to make me laugh and knows my own books better than I do! Thanks to my social media managers emeritus, Matt Lurie and Adam Alonsagay, who have handed the virtual reins over to the capable hands of Mara De Guzman and Bianca Peries.

As I mentioned in the dedication, this book is for and about family — those with us, those we've lost, and those who never were. I am so lucky and so grateful for my own family — my kids who are now grown and finding the courage and convictions of their own dreams: Joelle and Jarrod, as well as their respective partners Nathan and Sofi, who are welcome additions to our family; Erin, who had to give up the dorms and spend over a year with me in quarantine, which made me grateful for the time together; and Brendan, who's in Thailand, but only a Zoom away, and feels as close at heart as ever.

Thank you, each and every one of you, for giving me not only courage, but mountains of love and support enough to dream big!

— N.S.

A big thank you to the Scholastic Graphix team: Andrea, David, and Phil. Thank you for choosing me for this project and for your belief in my skill and talent.

Thanks to my wife, Na, whose continual love and support is everything, and my kids, Meilan and Pablo, who lovingly encourage their dad to keep going during long projects.

A special thank you to my big sister, Valerie Cabrera, who was my first art critic and continues to be the first to see my work.

A much appreciated thank you to Sadie Lappin for the assists on colors and to Meilan Martínez for illustrating "The Untold" chapter title.

Thanks to my agents, Tanya McKinnon, who helped me to the finish line, and Bob Mecoy, who brought me to the project.

— A.V.M.

Bibliography

Aunt Naomi [Gertrude Landa]. *Jewish Fairy Tales and Legends*. New York: Bloch Publishing Co., Inc., "The Jewish Book Concern." 1919. (Scanned at sacred-texts.com, March 2005. Proofed and formatted by John Bruno Hare. This text is in the public domain in the US because it was published prior to 1922. These files may be used for any non-commercial purpose, provided this notice of attribution is left intact in all copies.)

"Baba Yaga." Ancient Worlds. Accessed May 5, 2022. https://ancientworlds.net/aworlds_direct/app_main.php?pageData=Post/1277976.

"Bielski Brothers." Yad Vashem. Accessed May 5, 2022. https://www.yadvashem.org/articles/general/solidarity-bielski-brothers.html.

"The Bielski Partisans." United States Holocaust Memorial Museum. Accessed May 5, 2022. https://encyclopedia.ushmm.org/content/en/article/the-bielski-partisans.

"Documenting Numbers of Victims of the Holocaust and Nazi Persecution. "United States Holocaust Memorial Museum. Accessed May 5, 2022. https://encyclopedia.ushmm.org/content/en/article/documenting-numbers-of-victims-of-the-holocaust-and-nazi-persecution.

"Escapes and Reports." Memorial and Museum Auschwitz-Birkenau. Accessed May 5, 2022. www.auschwitz.org/en/history/resistance/escapes-and-reports.

"The Holocaust." Yad Vashem. Accessed May 5, 2022. www.yadvashem.org/holocaust.html.

"The Holocaust Explained." The Wiener Holocaust Library. Accessed May 5, 2022. www.theholocaustexplained.org.

"Hundreds of Jews Escaped Death Camps by Jumping from Trains, Study Finds." Haaretz. April 9, 2014. Last modified April 10, 2018. Accessed May 5, 2022. https://www.haaretz.com/jewish/jews-jumped-trains-evaded-camps-1.5244501.

Jewish Virtual Library. Accessed May 5, 2022. www.jewishvirtuallibrary.org.

Pelling, Hereward, dir. *Escape from a Nazi Death Camp*. Aired May 20, 2014, on PBS. https:/www.pbs.org/program/escape-nazi-death-camp.

"Rescue and Resistance." United States Holocaust Memorial Museum. Accessed May 5, 2022. https://encyclopedia.ushmm.org/content/en/article/rescue-and-resistance.

"Rescue in Denmark." United States Holocaust Memorial Museum. Accessed May 5, 2022. https://encyclopedia.ushmm.org/content/en/article/rescue-in-denmark.

"Rescue of the Jews of Denmark." United States Holocaust Memorial Museum. Accessed May 5, 2022. www.ushmm.org/information/exhibitions/online-exhibitions/special-focus/rescue-of-the-jews-of-denmark.

"Resistance During the Holocaust." Anti-Defamation League. 2012. Accessed May 5, 2022. www.adl.org/sites/default/files/documents/assets/pdf/education-outreach/Resitance-During-the- Holocaust-NYLM-Guide.pdf.

Rohr, Brian. "Who Is Baba Yaga?" Brian Rohr Storyteller. Accessed May 5, 2022. brianrohr.com/eating-baba-yaga/who-is-baba-yaga.

Shalom Life. www.shalomlife.com (site discontinued).

"Teachers Who Rescued Jews During the Holocaust: Benjamin Blankenstein." Yad Vashem. Accessed May 5, 2022. https://www.yadvashem.org/yv/en/exhibitions/righteous-teachers/blankenstein.asp.

"Teachers Who Rescued Jews During the Holocaust: Gerda Valentiner." Yad Vashem. Accessed May 5, 2022. www.yadvashem.org/yv/en/exhibitions/righteous-teachers/valentiner.asp.

"Treblinka Death Camp Revolt." United States Holocaust Memorial Museum. Accessed May 5, 2022. https://ww2gravestone.com/treblinka-death-camp-revolt.

"Women of Valor: Johanna Eck." Yad Vashem. Accessed May 5, 2022. www.yadvashem.org/yv/en/exhibitions/righteous-women/eck.asp.

"Women of Valor: Klara Baić." Yad Vashem. Accessed May 5, 2022. www.yadvashem.org/yv/en/exhibitions/righteous-women/baic.asp.

A Note about the Hebrew Letters in This Book

Each story in *Courage to Dream* is numbered with, in order, one of the first five letters of the Hebrew alphabet, also known as the alef-bet. In addition to being a letter with a numerical position, each symbol has a spiritual meaning and also a meaning for each of the stories.

Alef — (A, 1) is the first letter of the Hebrew alphabet and indicates oneness and unity. In ancient times, it stood for the oneness of God in the face of polytheistic beliefs. It's worth noting that alef is actually silent and requires an additional symbol to have a vowel sound. So, it also represents the idea of the very beginning of the universe: something from nothing. For "He Opens a Window," I see it as representing not just the silence of those in hiding, but their potential voice.

Bet/Vet — (B/V, 2) is the second letter of the Hebrew alphabet. (A dot added to the center differentiates the "B" from the "V" sound). It is the first letter in the Torah, the first five books of the Hebrew Bible. It represents the beginning of duality. Light and dark, heaven and earth, creator and creation. Its form represents a container, a vessel, a house. In other words, the physical world. It's the perfect letter to represent "The Golem," which is a vessel of spirit created to help those in mortal jeopardy.

Gimel — (G, 3) The third letter is often seen to spiritually represent the balance between two extremes, harmonizing opposites — and, as a touchstone between opposites, it represents giving and receiving, also reward and punishment. The folk characters in "Spirits of Resistance" are certainly arbiters of reward and punishment!

Dalet — (D, 4) Dalet literally means "door," and its form reflects that. It represents structure, but also selflessness and humility, because it resembles a bowing figure — perhaps because one had to bend over and humble oneself to cross through an ancient door. In "Exodus," the idea of moving through a door — transitioning from one place to another — makes dalet the perfect symbol to mark this story.

Hei – (H, 5) Hei is the first Hebrew letter that requires an expulsion of breath. It is seen to represent the breath of life, and even life itself, as well as divinity. It is the first letter in the word *haya*, which means to be, or to exist. In "The Untold," that's exactly what the story is about: those who exist, and those who were denied the chance.

There are twenty-two letters in the Hebrew alphabet, and each one has meaning beyond merely the sounds of language!

GABY GERSTER

Neal Shusterman is the *New York Times*–bestselling author of numerous award-winning books for children, teens, and adults, including the Unwind dystology, the Skinjacker trilogy, *Downsiders*, and *Challenger Deep*, which won the National Book Award. *Scythe*, the first book in his popular series Arc of a Scythe, is a Michael L. Printz Honor Book. Neal also writes screenplays for motion pictures and television shows. He is the father of four, all of whom are talented writers and artists themselves. Visit Neal at Storyman.com, Facebook.com/NealShusterman, and @nealshusterman on twitter and Instagram.

ENID ARVELO

Andrés Vera Martínez is a cartoonist and illustrator. He is the co-author of the acclaimed graphic memoir, *Little White Duck: A Childhood in China* and the co-creator and illustrator of the graphic novel series Monster Locker. Andrés's work has been recognized by the *New York Times*, *School Library Journal*, *The Horn Book*, NPR, the Society of Illustrators, American Illustration, 3x3, Junior Library Guild, and Slate Cartoonist Studio. He currently lives in New England with his family. For more, find Andrés at andresvera.com and @avm_draw on Instagram.